A LONG TIME UNTIL NOW

Baen Books by Michael Z. Williamson

Freehold
The Weapon
Rogue
Contact with Chaos

Better to Beg Forgiveness . . .
Do Unto Others . . .
When Diplomacy Fails . . .

The Hero (with John Ringo)

Tour of Duty

A Long Time Until Now

To purchase these and all Baen Book titles in e-book format,
please go to www.baen.com.

A Long Time Until Now

Michael Z. Williamson

BAEN

A LONG TIME UNTIL NOW

A Baen Books Original

Baen Publishing Enterprises
P.O. Box 1403
Riverdale, NY 10471
www.baen.com

ISBN: 978-1-4767-8033-7

Cover art by Kurt Miller

First Baen printing, May 2015

Distributed by Simon & Schuster
1230 Avenue of the Americas
New York, NY 10020

Library of Congress Cataloging-in-Publication Data

Williamson, Michael Z.
A long time until now / by Michael Z. Williamson.
   pages ; cm
ISBN 978-1-4767-8033-7 (hc)
I. Title.
PS3623.I573L66 2015
813'.6--dc23

                              2015004249

Printed in the United States of America

10 9 8 7 6 5 4 3 2 1

⊹⇒ DEDICATION ⇐⊹

A good editor makes any story better,
without changing the author's voice.
So this is for Toni, Tony, Jim, Jim, Jim, Angel and Bill,
for fifteen years of support.

A LONG TIME UNTIL NOW

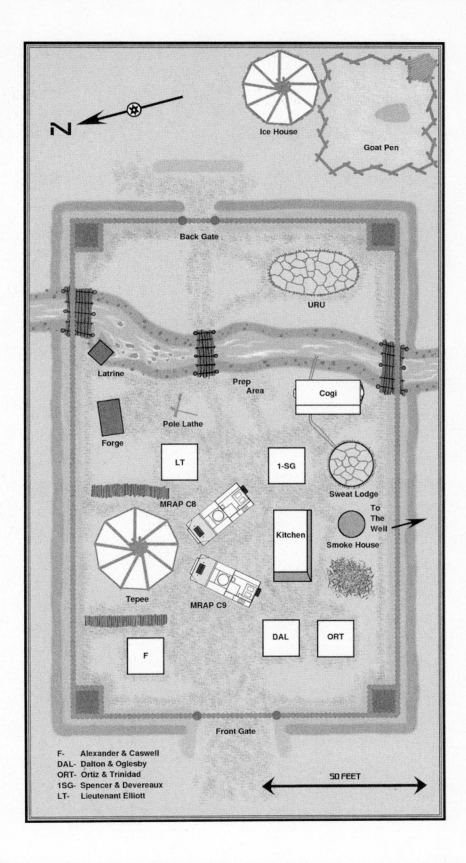

N

Ice House

Goat Pen

Back Gate

URU

Latrine

Prep Area

Cogi

Pole Lathe

Forge

LT

1-SG

Sweat Lodge

MRAP C8

To The Well

Kitchen

Smoke House

Tepee

MRAP C9

DAL

ORT

F

Front Gate

F-   Alexander & Caswell
DAL- Dalton & Oglesby
ORT- Ortiz & Trinidad
1SG- Spencer & Devereaux
LT-   Lieutenant Elliott

50 FEET

CHAPTER 1

First Lieutenant Sean Elliott sat sweating in an MRAP in the ass end of Afghanistan, waiting for the convoy to roll.

He wasn't a new 1LT, though no one here knew him directly. He'd pinned it on a year ago. A month ago he had been on his first convoy, and his first firefight. Neither had been noteworthy. Some RIF had shot at them, they shot back and rolled through. He could honestly say he'd exchanged fire with the enemy, though. Or rather, one of his troops had, and he hadn't ordered them not to.

Hopefully this trip would be easier. He was tagged onto a mixed convoy of Civil Affairs people meeting locals to offer them continued money and infrastructure improvement, to do some obvious and surreptitious checking for hostile development, to relocate stuff between COBs, and to deliver some vehicles.

It was hot and dusty, and sweat beaded behind his Wiley eyepro. Then it steamed. He wrinkled his brow to dislodge them so they'd clear a bit. Sweat pooled in his pits, down his back, and in his crotch. They had AC, but until they rolled, the doors were ajar. He thought about a Red Bull, but decided to wait.

Troops trudged back and forth, some boarding the convoy, some crossing between vehicles on some task or other. Ahead, someone was under the hood of another vehicle. That might mean swapping out or dispersing that load.

One of the trudging troops stepped close to the vehicle and asked, "Sir, do you have room for one more?"

5

He looked her over. The uniform said "ALEXANDER." She carried a camera bag.

"You're our photographer?"

"Yes, sir. Three other vehicles passed me around, then sent me back here."

"Sounds normal. Yes, we have a seat, jump in."

"Thank you, sir." She had a ruck, a duffel, another bag, a weapon, the camera bag, and she wasn't large, though not some skinny waif, either. She looked about thirty and unremarkable. She struggled and grunted to get her gear aboard, but didn't ask for help or play weak. Good.

She climbed in back and set next to Caswell, who had been the token female. Caswell was USAF Security, along for the purpose of searching any local females they might have problems with. You never let a man search a woman in A-stan. It would lead to an instant riot.

A lot of Soldiers didn't like Airmen, and vice versa. It wasn't just interservice rivalry. The two branches operated differently and had some conflicts. When they both did the same mission different ways, it rubbed people. Caswell was dressed for the mission, presented honestly and seemed professional. He'd accept her as that.

The hood slammed on the vehicle farther forward, and with thumbs up, three men jogged to board it.

The radio called "Charlie Eight, confirm status, over."

He keyed his headset mic and replied, "Charlie One, we are ready to roll, over." After releasing the mic, he said, "Still ready as we were ten minutes ago, Major."

At the wheel, Staff Sergeant Bob Barker smiled and almost snickered, as he shook his head a fraction, then leaned back behind his eyewear. He looked like some NASCAR racer, with a 'stache that pushed regs.

Sean took a deep breath, because there was nothing to be gained from stressing out. It would take as long as it took, and they'd roll when it was time, probably two hours late.

Apart from the unregulation mustache, Barker looked crisp. He periodically revved the engine a bit. That wasn't really necessary for diesels, but it didn't hurt anything.

In the back was a mixed bag. Armand Devereaux, medic. Ramon Ortiz, a veterinary NCO who was going to be helping the locals with goats. He would man the M240B on the first leg. They had a cooler full of caffeine, other drinks and candy, and bottled water.

"What rank are you, Alexander?"

"Sergeant, sir."

"Are you getting out anywhere?"

"At the first stop, apparently. Ferderer?"

Caswell said, "That's where I'm debarking. COB Ferderer."

"Good. Battle buddy for the time being?"

"Sure."

Elliott was glad of that. Caswell had been the only female in this end of the convoy, and she seemed a bit high-strung and remote.

Really, everyone for that stop should be on one vehicle. Troops wanted to be with their own elements, though, and some had assigned positions. When the juggling was done, it was always a mess.

He spoke loud enough for everyone and said, "We're stopping there briefly, then continuing on. This vehicle and the one behind are stopping at COB Ferderer. Then we fill into the others and continue."

"That's why we have the extra space," Ortiz said. "Enjoy it while we have it."

He added, "Oh, yeah, we have some boxes of stuff back there. Soap, shampoo, other crap, and some pencils and writing books and colored pencils. May as well help yourself to any of the hygiene items; the Afghans won't care." Civilians sent care packages for both troops and locals. The locals generally didn't have much use for the stuff.

A radio call was punctuated with puffs of exhaust from ahead. Charlie Seven started lumbering.

"And we're rolling!" Barker said.

Barker slammed his door, shifted into gear, and waited. Elliott closed his. When Charlie Seven vehicle reached fifty meters ahead of them, Barker eased forward, as the convoy stretched like a worm.

They drove past the local bazaar, inside the gate, then wove through the Entry Control Point barricades, out onto the road, and were in Afghanistan proper. They followed fence and berm, with stacks of conex boxes just inside, until they hit a T and turned west and downslope from the plateau. There were fields here, with the river just west. It was quite pretty in a way.

Nothing should attack them this close to the base, and hopefully nothing would at all. On the other hand, it got really boring really fast over here. He couldn't decide if this was something like a prison sentence, since he'd never been to prison. He did know he'd be here another nine months.

Someone in a Route Clearance vehicle came on air. "Right side, fifty meters past the outcropping. Burned pickup. Clear."

They'd call for everything accounted for, vehicle, wreck, suspicious bush, though there weren't many of those.

It was almost 0930. The distances weren't great, but the roads weren't very good, and would be full of farmers, flocks and potential IEDs.

It was a day like any other day. Long and crappy, with new stupidity that would be exactly like the old stupidity. Sun burned down, dust rose up.

"What do you think, Sergeant Barker?" he asked.

Barker shrugged. "I try not to, sir. But I can't even do that right."

"Fair enough. What I mean is, have you been on this route before?"

"About half of it. It's mostly pretty casual. Hajji fires off a rifle now and then. One RPG that missed. It's been mostly quiet the last three months."

"Good." That's what his briefing had said, but real world confirmation was nice.

He pulled at his collar to vent some sweat, and loosened his armor slightly to let the AC cool him off. Quiet was good. He'd had a real firefight, this was a real combat tour. He'd much rather be doing engineer stuff, but this would work at promotion time, too.

A massive bang sounded, and the vehicle crashed back to the ground. It jarred his spine. They'd fallen several feet. Then the ride got bumpy because they were off the road.

"Contact! Find contact!" he shouted. What the hell was it? Not an RPG, not an IED. They were still rolling, then they swerved. He shouted into his headset, "Charlie One, we have contact."

"No sign of contact," Ortiz called from above.

"Bullshit, find me contact. We're off road." How did that happen? They were bumping up a long slope.

"No contact," Barker said. "There's nothing around us." He slowed but kept moving.

"Tire blowout?" Sean asked.

"Negative, everything looks good." Barker wiggled the wheel. "We're fine."

"Fucking weird."

Alexander said, "Maybe we hit a local vehicle."

"Possible," he said. "Well, get us back on the road and we'll regroup and assess." He keyed the headset. "Charlie One, contact is nonhostile, possible vehicle accident, over."

Barker said, "I can't see the road."

The radio said, "Charlie Eight, this is Charlie Nine. We hit whatever it was, too."

"Downslope." Where the hell was Charlie One? "Charlie One, say again, contact was not hostiles, possibly a vehicle strike, over. Break. Charlie Nine, what was it, over?"

"Charlie Eight, this is Charlie Nine. I don't see anything, over. Just you, I mean, over."

He looked at Barker. "Okay, then stop. Back up slowly."

"Nothing from Charlie One?"

"No," he replied.

Again Barker said, "I don't see the road. We are on grass. Green stuff."

"Fuck. Stop. Perimeter. Fast." He keyed the mic. "Charlie Nine, this is Charlie Eight, unass and assess, over."

They kicked the doors and the ramp and rolled out, carbines raised and alert. Ortiz and Caswell were on the right, Alexander and Devereaux on the left.

They were on a hilly slope. There was no sign or sound of hostiles, just brush and stubby trees. Those were a bit odd. The growth was knee high and wild. They'd been traveling through cultivated fields before.

He cautiously walked back to Charlie Nine, now only twenty meters or so back. SFC Spencer was that vehicle commander. He and his three troops were kneeling, weapons ready.

"Man, it's chilly here," Spencer commented as he glanced around. "What happened?"

It wasn't chilly, but it was maybe 80°F or so, rather than well over a hundred.

"How's the vehicle?"

Barker came around the back, examining the passenger side. "Nothing. Nothing underneath, nothing on the body. We're fine."

"Okay, we couldn't have gone more than a couple of hundred meters. Is there any sign of any locals, hostile or otherwise?"

"Negative."

"Stand by," he said. Grabbing the tiedowns on the hood, he climbed up, then on top. He grabbed the cupola and took a long, measured look. Then he flushed and chilled at the same time.

"LT?" Spencer asked.

He couldn't think of anything to offer. "I got nothing."

The female SP, Caswell, called up, "What do you see, LT?"

"I do not see the road. I do not see vehicles. I do not see the convoy."

A troop from Charlie Nine said, "Dust. All the way across there." He pointed upslope. Right. They were below the road. It felt as if they'd gone left, but they'd gone right.

"And damage to growth." Spencer pointed at the tears they'd left.

"Raking fire?" the troop asked. His nametape said DALTON.

Spencer said, "No, I think it was an earthquake."

"Shit, I—" *hope the rest of the convoy is alive*, he didn't say.

"Call JSTARS," Elliott said.

He was very afraid they weren't going to get a response. Something was *very* wrong.

Spencer jumped into his cab. "Trumpcard, this is Charlie Nine, over." He rattled off their chalk number and route ID. "Trumpcard, this is Charlie Nine, over . . . Any allied unit, this is Charlie Nine, request confirmation and response, over." He shrugged his hands and stared at Elliott.

What next? "Dalton, Spencer, go uphill two hundred meters. Go west two hundred. Make it a box and return."

"Hooah, LT," Dalton acknowledged for them.

"You, cover them." He pointed at the gunner on Charlie Nine.

"Trinidad, sir. Roger that," the Filipino nodded and jumped up into the cupola.

"Anything on GPS?"

Barker said, "That's not working, either. No signal."

He hoped no one could see him shiver. He clutched his weapon tight against himself, because his hands were half numb and jittery. Shock.

He watched Dalton and Spencer as they moved carefully uphill. He'd wanted them to be cautious, and he wanted them to get done and get back fast. He twitched.

They turned west, which was right, and a few moments later, Spencer tossed a handful of loose dirt and waved.

"Let's drive up there," he said.

Everyone remounted. Barker fired the engine, and drove a careful circle in the right direction, then rolled uphill. It was jolty off road, as expected, and he could see the trail they'd cut on the way down.

Into view came a wide, ragged area of bare dirt and tumbled weeds. Something had plowed the hell out of this area. Then he saw where their tire marks started and went downhill.

He didn't see an origin for them.

The tracks started in the middle of the rough area. There was nothing farther uphill except grass-covered slope.

CHAPTER 2

"Okay, everyone gather round, keep alert, listen up," Elliot said. They clustered within a few meters, but kept enough distance and randomness to avoid being easy mass targets. They were all on the upslope side of the vehicles, in the sun.

He said, "We are lost. We will take steps to get unlost. It may take a while. Got it?"

"Yes, sir." "Roger." "Hooah."

Specialist Dalton asked, "What do you mean by 'lost', sir?"

Yeah, he had to have some kind of answer, and he didn't know. He tensed as much as he could to avoid shivering in fear, while trying not to look stiff. But the commander had to be firm and sure, or the troops would panic.

He said, "We don't know where we are. We don't know where anyone else is. Shit's acting weird. We can receive radio in the immediate area, but have no contact with anyone else. GPS is down. There's some damage to the terrain. I'd almost guess some kind of EMP device."

Dalton made an odd face. "Nuke? Seriously?"

"It doesn't have to be a nuke. The Air Force has conventional EMP weapons. So could anyone else. But it could have been an atmospheric nuke. We all saw that flash."

Caswell asked, "But what about the road, sir? And the convoy?" Her voice shivered a little.

"Yeah, I have no idea about that. For right now, it's quiet, and we see

13

no hostiles, so we'll set watch, eat lunch, and think over some strategies. If you have any ideas, let me know."

He watched while they glanced about, then took turns climbing into the vehicles and digging out MREs.

He swung up into Charlie Eight and grabbed one of his own. At least it was spaghetti.

Spencer sauntered around, had his pocket knife out faster than anyone, and sliced a couple of packages open for people. Then he walked over to the front of Eight, stood for a moment, and around to Elliott.

Alongside, in a quiet mumble, he said, "You don't think we're going to find anyone, do you, sir?"

"No," he admitted. "I don't know what kind of sci fi shit happened, but we're not in A-stan anymore."

He had no idea where they were, and his legs were weak, his pulse hammering, and his head spinning.

"Yes, we are." Spencer pulled off his helmet and ran fingers through his cropped hair.

"How do you figure?"

"Those mountains to the south. They haven't changed."

He looked. "Damn. You're right. Shit."

"Or actually, they have."

"How?" he asked.

"Do you see any roads? Any farms? Any cuts for power lines? Any indication of people at all?"

He stared. He desperately wanted to find something, like that . . . no, that wasn't anything. Spencer was right. There was nothing indicating any human presence.

"We are so fucked," he said, feeling a wash of tears that he blinked back. The nausea didn't show, but he wasn't hungry anymore.

He rambled. "Parallel universe? Everyone magically transported away? Time travel? We missed the Rapture?"

"I'd say every one of those is bullshit, and explain how," Spencer said. "Except I can't."

"When do we tell them?"

"Bit by bit. We don't have a panic yet. I don't want one." Spencer held up a hand and stared at it. He was trembling as if he had Parkinson's. His hands were visibly damp.

The need to stand watch and eat did keep them busy. And yes, it was a lot cooler than it had been. From the 90s or 100s, it was down to high 70s or low 80s. Quite comfortable. Wind blew from the west, very, very fresh. When it dropped he could smell the trucks.

"Police up that trash, Dalton," he ordered. "We don't want to leave a calling card."

"Yes, sir." The kid had been about to stuff all his plastic under a rock. That wasn't a good idea tactically, and this place was so pristine he hated to spoil it.

Alexander turned and said, "Sir, I was going to get some pictures . . ."

"Sure. Go ahead."

"Yes, sir," she said. "But I don't see any landmarks except the mountains."

She'd figured it out.

"Yes, that's our next problem."

She raised her eyebrows. Her lip twitched.

"Understood, sir," she said with a slow nod and a cold face. She didn't look reassured. She grabbed her weapon with one hand, nodded and slowly put the hand back on her camera.

Ten minutes later, the grapevine had it.

Dalton asked, "So where the hell are we, sir? If it's okay to ask. If we know."

"I'm pretty sure we're still on Earth," he said. He was confident of that. Mostly. The gravity, air and sun seemed right. In fact, yes, there was a quarter moon . . . and . . . it had been near full the night before. He wasn't going to say anything yet. And what the fuck had happened to the sun? They rolled at 0923. That was an afternoon sun.

What the fuck had happened?

Had they been knocked out for days? Because if not, then, no, he wasn't going to think about that, because . . .

"Where, then?"

Everyone had gathered around, and this time they were much closer, not wanting to stray from the safety of the vehicle.

"Sergeant Spencer and I were discussing that. Everyone knows we're really lost, right?"

"Yeah. As in, no signs of any people at all. Like we're suddenly in the middle of Siberia."

He sighed. "Well, at this point, we can't rule that out."

"What did it?"

Dalton said, "God is testing us."

Alexander snapped, "Oh, please fucking spare me . . . argh. Dammit."

"No religion, no politics," he ordered. "We have no idea. Divine power is one idea. So is some kind of space warp to a parallel world. Or we may be back in time. Or somewhere remote like Siberia." He wasn't going to mention the familiar skyline to anyone who hadn't caught it. Slowly on the discovery. And anyway, he didn't know what happened.

"Really?" Caswell said. "What is this bullshit?"

"Do you see any sign of people? Powerlines, roads, villages on the hillsides, cleared areas for agriculture, anything?"

"No, but lots of this country is vacant."

"Not around here. Sparse, but not vacant. And not this green."

He was amazed there wasn't more panic. Though Trinidad was reciting the Lord's Prayer. Devereaux and Ortiz went to join him, holding hands.

Dalton asked, "What the fuck do we do?"

"For right now, we stay right here, where we landed." He pointed for emphasis. "We have good visibility downslope, some cover from that outcropping, and working vehicles. We bivouac here."

"That's it?" Dalton sounded irritated.

"What else would you do?"

"You travel downhill until you find a watercourse, and follow it downstream until you find people."

Spencer nodded. "Per the book, that is a guaranteed way to find people. But it assumes there are people to find. Look at that hill," he said.

Dalton argued, "And people around here might stick to the valleys."

"Do you recognize that hill line, Corporal?"

And that was it.

"We're still here," Ortiz said.

"Close enough, yes. Within a few kilometers of where we were when whatever it was happened."

"Shit."

"So we bivouac," he said at once. "And gather intel, and then plot a course of action. We have the ammo, food, water and fuel at hand, and that's it. So we don't use it until we're sure."

Alexander said, "Sir? Latrine break?"

"Yeah, around that rock," he pointed east. "Take a buddy."

"I'd rather take two. Sergeant Spencer, will you cover us?" She indicated herself and Caswell.

"Yes," he agreed.

Elliott nodded. "Yeah, we need to stay in close proximity. We don't know if it will happen again."

Spencer and the two females headed around the rock, but not far. He could see their heads as they squatted. He was glad they were within sight. What would happen if or when they jumped back . . . or elsewhere?

And thank God for sci fi movies. Whatever had happened fit concepts they all knew about. Fifty years previous, he would have had a panic on his hands. As it was, they were too shocked to panic. He'd need to keep them busy.

Oglesby lit a smoke, after a half dozen attempts with trembling hands. Elliott decided to let it slide.

Except he was panicking himself. He didn't know where they were, or what happened. There was the sound of wind soughing through long grass and shrubs, and the occasional chirp of a bird. Otherwise, it was silent. He'd never been anywhere this quiet in his life.

When Spencer and the females returned, he said, "Okay, watch in alphabetical order by last name, one hour each, starting now. Use the cupola. After dark, we'll overlap two hours, with two people up. I don't want anyone falling asleep or panicking. This is some serious shit, but we're U.S. Army Soldiers and will deal with it."

"And tomorrow?" Dalton asked.

"Tomorrow, we'll widen our search and go from there. Also, as of right now, I want everyone to have weapon loaded, chamber empty. It only takes a second to charge a weapon, and we don't need any accidents because of nerves."

There was a rattle of charging handles and magazines, as everyone cycled their chambers empty and reinserted magazines.

Barker asked, "Can't we run the vehicle?"

"That falls under the category of wasting resources, and breaching noise discipline. No."

"Aye, aye, sir."

"Yeah, Barker, you were Navy before you joined the Reserves?"

"Yes, sir."

"The 'aye aye' gave it away."

"Sorry, sir."

"Don't worry about it."

"Well, what do we do until dark, sir?"

"Hasty positions, and I want another patrol farther uphill, tracking back the line we took downhill."

"To find what?"

"Whatever there is to find."

Spencer didn't seem too sure, but he said, "Yes, sir."

Alexander had her camera up, with a big telephoto on. He was about to say something when she said, "S-small herd of animals, sir. Y-you want to see this."

She lowered the camera and stepped over. He reached for it, she pulled it away, looped the sling around his neck, then handed it to him. Yes, he could understand why she'd be protective of her very expensive equipment.

He held it up, looked through the viewfinder, and aimed it where she pointed. Yes, a small herd. They were hairy, brown and tan, and had big heads and long horns on their noses.

They were shaggy rhinos. About a dozen of them.

He took a long, ragged breath and tried not to panic. It was completely impossible. He looked again. One of them galloped a couple of steps, and reached out a long horn toward its mother, who was cropping thick, green grass.

He stared at Alexander. He looked around at the others.

Caswell raised a hand to shield her eyes and squinted. Then she asked, "Are they . . . ?"

"Yes. They are rhinos," he said. There was nothing to be gained by stalling.

"What the fuck are rhinos doing in A-stan?"

Alexander said, "Woolly rhinos. From when it was cold."

Caswell got it, and shouted, "*We're in the fucking Stone Age?*"

He felt it himself. His entire body shook, there were splotches in front of his eyes, and he couldn't talk.

No one else said a word, but they were all obviously shocked. Lips trembled, then whole bodies. "Lost" could be frightening. Knowing they were . . . this . . . was terrifying. Then he felt himself flush and shake.

Devereaux ran for the rock, tugging at his fly. Dalton dithered a moment, then followed.

"We see rhinos," he said. "Presumably we're in the Stone Age. It could be a recreation, some kind of image, or I could be having a drugged-out dream in ICU." He hoped so. Please, let it be a messed-up dream. They'd been hit by an IED and he was hospitalized, recovering. Missing limbs would be better than this.

Barker sounded surprisingly calm.

"How did we get in the fucking Stone Age? That bang we heard?" He was smoking, too. Oglesby was chain lighting another and almost brushed the coal off as his hands shook.

Spencer said, "That had to be it. I have no idea how, but that's when everything went bugnuts." He was crying.

Barker's voice was much softer as he asked, "And how do we get back?"

Elliott saw they were all shaky, and he needed to keep discipline. He started talking, slowly and with measure, as he'd been taught by one of his mentors.

"Listen up. Leak if you need to, then get back over here. I'm going to keep talking.

"First, we're going to deal with the immediate situation. We are a small unit, but we are large enough to support ourselves, and God willing, we'll make this work.

"I don't have an answer on getting back. First we have to find out where and when we are. Then we need to survive and thrive. Then we focus on finding our way back.

"I need fifteen minutes to make some notes. Then I'll dictate our plan of attack."

Hopefully he could silently scream it all out in fifteen minutes. Or maybe he'd throw up.

Martin Spencer was surprised he wasn't more shocky. Woolly rhino, cool weather, lusher growth, no people. Time travel. There wasn't any other explanation. Time travel was impossible, except in sci fi and movies, but it had obviously happened.

His brain suddenly remembered an old joke. *You may get drafted or not. If not, no worries. But if so, there are two possibilities. You may deploy or not. If you don't, no worries* . . . his mind raced through to the ending. *If you get wounded, you may survive or not. If you survive, no worries, if not* . . . *but there are usually two possibilities.*

It was either time travel, or time travel. He was alive. He had people, tools, skills. Either they could get back or not. Always two possibilities if you looked for them.

The LT, though, was sick with shock and fear, and he couldn't think, and he was angry, and he couldn't think.

"Sir, can I offer some suggestions?"

"No," Elliott replied, gripping his rifle, trembling, and staring at the horizon.

"Understood, sir."

That was bad. The man was shaking, wasn't making decisions, and wasn't all there. He needed backup. If the man wasn't in command, the troops would panic all over the landscape.

But a few moments later, Elliott turned around and gave orders.

He said, "It's dry but going to be cool tonight. Dress as you need to for the weather, let's hang some ponchos or tarps around the wheels like lean-tos, and we can sleep under there tonight. We don't have much fuel, but I want a small fire in that crack in the rock. Two people on watch as I said, and keep feeding grass stalks to it if nothing else. The smoke will help with bugs."

The ponchos went up in a few minutes, but no one crawled into the shelter.

Dalton said, "If it's okay with you, sir, I'll be first watch."

"You and me, then," he agreed.

It was pretty clear no one was going to sleep. Elliott could order it, but it wouldn't work.

Still, he was giving orders. That was good. Spencer added, "Keep the fire small. Light, a little heat, a little smoke."

"How about three on watch, sir?" Barker asked. "We can keep an eye out in three arcs at once."

If there were rhinos, there might be mammoths, bears and sabertooths, and he doubted M4 carbines would stop them, but they might have to try.

Elliott said, "Yeah. There should be a good view from the ledge."

There wasn't much talking. Spencer didn't even know who'd lit the fire, and that bothered him. It was dusky. They'd been here for hours, and where had the time gone?

Was time moving at a different rate, too? Or had they just completely zoned out in shock? He checked his watch. No, it had been eight hours. How?

He needed to piss again, badly. He went to the side of the outcropping and let loose. He kept looking over his shoulder to make sure everyone was still there.

The fire was the only warmth he felt. He moved in as close as he thought safe, and felt a nervous itch in his exposed back. He closed his eyes and focused on leading by example, then opened them in fear. He realized he was shaking in stress, and nauseated.

It's like a firefight, he thought. *But it's been going on for eight hours, and there's nothing I can do to take cover or evade, or call for support.*

He heard someone make a deep, shuddering sigh that turned into sobs, and in moments, they were all whimpering and gasping. They'd be panicking until they got through every stage of dealing with trauma, he expected.

He thought about suggesting camp songs, cadences or even jokes, but . . . nothing felt right.

I have to do something, if only to keep a perception of discipline, he thought. *We have to stay together.*

Absolutely nothing came to mind.

Devereaux said, "If you look up, you can see the constellations. We're in late summer, early fall, and we're about the same latitude we left, possibly a bit farther north. So we're not terribly far away."

"Except in time."

Devereaux's camo showed up better in the starlight than his dark skin. His outline was ghostly. He said, "There's a fifteen billion light year universe we could be lost in, and eternity. We're not far. Whatever screwed up is likely to happen again. We just need to watch for it."

He sounded confident. He needed it to be true, and Martin did, too.

Someone asked, "Why? We couldn't see this one."

"We weren't looking."

Caswell said, "No pollution. Look how bright and clear they all are."

She was right. He'd never seen anything that bright in the remotest areas of A-stan, Alaska or even on the side of the Tetons. The stars were icy points, and there were billions of them. Except for the fire, it was completely, utterly black.

That brought everyone silent for about ten seconds.

Then the sobs started again.

They stopped when a wolf howled. A big wolf. Then others.

Everyone fumbled with their weapons.

Barker said, "No shooting. Those are a long way away."

"Can I spotlight something?" Dalton asked.

He was about to say, "Yes," when he remembered something. "We have night vision on the trucks."

Dalton nodded, and took a tentative step toward the hatch, then stopped.

Spencer said, "I'll go with you." He'd rather be in the truck.

Dalton let out a breath and nodded.

Yeah, they were all terrified. It was bad enough being alone in the dark. Any distance from other human beings was unwelcome.

He scanned with the NV and looked at the terrain in monochromatic green. Grass, creepy-looking scrub, and a few herbivores. He breathed a deep sigh and felt cold.

He reported to Elliott, "Goats. Some kind of antelope. Maybe wolves way to the west. And I could swear I see a lion."

Elliott asked, "How far can you see?"

"With moon and no pollution, a long way." It was a little less scary in monochrome.

The LT said, "Okay, I want one on cupola and one on night vision."

"I don't think anyone's going to sleep, sir."

"Yeah. Rotate through just the same."

He was getting cold. It was quite chill, and damp, but he wasn't going to go into the other vehicle for his gear. There were people out here, and there weren't in there.

They couldn't see him shake or tear up again.

There was no coffee unless he used an MRE packet or opened a jar of Folgers instant and heated water. He grabbed a Ripit. He didn't want to sleep.

As dawn grayed in the east, Gina Alexander felt a little better. Her eyes were gritty, her bladder very full, and she wanted some light before she went to drain out. She was uncomfortable to the point of pain. That wasn't enough to overcome the cold, loneliness, and sheer panic. She was damp and sticky all over from sweat and dew. They were lost beyond anything imaginable, anything real, and she was terrified.

It got a bit grayer, and pressure overcame fear.

"Caswell, can you come with me? Latrine break. SFC Spencer, can you be backup again?"

"Sure." "Can do."

She leaned against the rock, rifle across her lap, and it came out in a flood. Caswell took care of business, and Spencer politely kept his back turned. Or maybe he was more afraid of what might be out there.

She buckled fast, and they jogged back to the trucks.

It was a striking sunrise, and she fumbled with her camera, but couldn't recall how to shoot that close to the sun, and she was disoriented from fatigue.

Spencer said, "With your permission, sir, I'm going to suggest we take turns napping in daylight, inside the vehicles. Two hours each, two at a time."

"Yeah. Do it."

"Roger. Alexander, Ortiz, you're first, lie down. You both look rough."

"Thank you, Sergeant," she said.

On the one hand, she didn't want to sleep. There was too much to do, and she wanted nothing more than to be close to everyone else. What if they all transported back and she got left behind alone in the MRAP? But she was delirious, nauseated and hallucinating. She climbed up the metal stairs and into the back in the gray twilight, slumped into a seat, and realized she was passing out as she reached for the collar of her armor.

Bob Barker dug through the piled crap in the back of Charlie Eight, looking for his E-tool. He'd use the shovel if he had to, but the entrenching tool, there it was, was better. He needed to take a dump something fierce, and he didn't want to leave a mess.

When he got back he'd need to say something about cleaning stuff up. The back of the vehicle looked like a trash truck. If they couldn't find their gear, they couldn't react well.

Without a word, Trinidad followed him. He nodded. No one wanted to be out of sight of anyone else, and they knew there were wolves here.

In the movies, something always took people home, or they pulled together into a team and accomplished greatness. He didn't see that happening. They were all scared shitless, or rather, scared into not shitting. He felt like he had a rock inside.

He scooped out a hole fast, dropped trou, and squatted. He could smell various human urines. They'd need a proper field latrine, too. Everyone was freaking out.

Then he was, too. A rush of heat, panicked breathing. He couldn't see the vehicles. He looked up at Trinidad, who looked back briefly, then toward the troops again.

He wiped with a paper napkin, tossed it in the dip, pulled up his pants, and shoveled dirt back over it.

He should probably have some water. He'd been eating the coffee powder, and his throat was raw from a half pack of Marlboros.

He was going to be out of those by tomorrow. Crap.

He noticed Alexander and Oglesby had their phones out. They might be looking at pictures or listening to music, but they needed their attention here on the mission, whatever that mission might be, not moping. He wanted to grab his, too, but he shouldn't.

"You need to put those away," he told them.

"But . . ." Oglesby looked like he was about to argue. Alexander just powered hers down and slid it into a pocket. Oglesby followed suit. He looked annoyed.

Armand Devereaux was surprised to find he'd actually napped, and hard. He woke as Barker kicked his boot. He squinted and twisted. He was too tall for these seats, and his neck ached.

"Yeah, I'm up."

His dream had been messed up, too, but he didn't remember it already.

Using one hand for support, he staggered out the back.

"Drink water," he said. It was almost a conditioned reflex to remind the troops, and right now, they needed it more than most. Where the hell were they? "And brush your goddamned teeth," he added.

He hadn't prayed in years. Sure, he went through the motions, went to Confession and Mass, but that was largely for Mama. It was important, but he'd been a pretty undevout Catholic.

He was praying now. Perhaps Mary could intercede for them. He had no idea which saint would apply. So he picked several.

The troops were going through motions, too. Ortiz and Caswell were atop the guns. Dalton and Oglesby wandered around the perimeter. The CO was swaying.

Spencer met his eyes and flicked them toward the lieutenant. He nodded.

He approached the lieutenant from the side and said, "Sir, you need rest, too. We'll need you alert later."

"Can't sleep."

"I have Benadryl, but I would rather save it."

Spencer said, "He's right, sir. Listen to the medic. I'll cover things; you take a break."

"Goddamnit, okay."

They watched him mutter and stumble his way up into Number Nine. He was literally unconscious in twenty seconds.

"What do you think of this, Sergeant Spencer?" he asked.

"I think it's fucked up, but I don't think we can do anything about it."

"Yeah. And we're definitely a long way off."

"Oh?"

"Did you see the constellations? They shifted slightly."

"I'm well read, but not that much."

"I'm taking some astronomy. The stars have moved a bit. We're either later or earlier."

Spencer said, "Earlier."

"Unless some future Earth is a park and some aliens have brought us here as a zoo exhibit."

The SFC raised his eyebrows and said, "Damn. I hadn't considered that one. But you're right. Could be."

"I always wanted to get out of Queens so I could see more stars." Spencer shrugged.

Armand looked him over. He was haggard.

"You rest next."

Spencer nodded slowly. "Yeah. If I can."

"You will. Right now, can you help me get people to drink?"

"Yeah. Listen up!"

Armand said, "Drink water. That's an order. You should have had a liter each today at least. And no more Ripits or Red Bull. Caffeine withdrawal is ugly."

A couple of them grumbled, but they all complied.

"Hey, I don't want to have to stick you and bag you out here. And someone dig a latrine."

"Already did," Barker said. "Just a squattie, but it'll keep things cleaner."

"Thanks."

Martin Spencer woke in pain. His back ached from trying to sleep in odd positions, and he wasn't twenty anymore. He was sweaty and grimy. His guts burned because hadn't been taking his stomach meds, and had been chewing MRE coffee powder. Stress and lack of sleep wasn't helping. He washed down two of the meds. Then he thought about that.

His paranoia was a good thing. He always carried a year's supply of meds, but had about three months left. If they were stuck here, he'd need to develop workarounds, or he'd start dying slowly and painfully.

Outside, everyone moved around stiffly. They were all fatigued, all scared, and all worn ragged.

The LT stared off to the west at the falling sun. Another day had gone by, of combat naps, panic, and pulling twigs from the grass for firewood.

"Anything you need, sir?"

"No."

He wasn't going to push the issue, but he understood he might have to remove Elliott and take over. That was one of those things they mentioned in BNCOC, but you hoped never happened. That didn't make this any easier.

"I was going to put people on shifts tonight, if they can," he hinted.

"I have it. Thank you."

"Understood, sir."

He backed away cautiously.

He hoped the man did have it. Though if he did assume command, he had no idea what he could do differently.

He noted the available water was depleting.

"Okay, listen up! Save your water bottles, we may need to refill them. Don't crunch them up, and don't throw them away. And get the pop cans, too."

"What's it matter?" Oglesby asked. "Either we get back or we don't."

He'd known that kid was going to be a problem. He was a specialist, and a mouthy one.

"Secure the crap. It matters because we may need water storage, and because leaving trash here is an OPSEC violation."

Then Oglesby was in his face.

"Newsflash, asshole! There aren't any Taliban around here. We're in some fucked up sci fi world, and either we find water or we fucking die! Didn't you—"

He punched the kid.

Oglesby fell backward and sprawled, a welt already showing on his cheek.

"Put your helmet on, too."

The kid came up fast, looking angry, but Barker and Dalton grabbed him.

Dalton said, "Dude, it's cool. Save the bottles, okay?"

They eased him away, as Spencer burned. The young kids always thought they knew better, and for whatever reason, he was frequently ignored, even as an SFC. It had to be his presence. Whatever it was, he couldn't command people properly.

It was obvious to him that tossing bottles off a convoy was different from leaving them in a hasty bivouac. He grabbed two, and a Monster can, and tossed them into the back of Charlie Nine.

He saw the LT, whose jaw was clenched, but said nothing.

He turned back to Oglesby and said, "Are you finished? We do the best we can. Keep track of everything. If you fire a weapon, find the brass. Keep the MRE pouches, we may need them to hold water, or as dressings. Keep cardboard, we can write on it or use it as tinder. Burn cigarette butts and all other small trash. Everything must be kept neat. It may be all we have for a long time."

Devereaux said, "Everyone should have had about six bottles or a full Camelbak by now. And change your socks. Hygiene."

Martin really didn't want to go to the effort of taking his boots off, but he'd just made a stink about keeping cans, so he led by example and took his boots off. Then he put them back on to climb into the truck and dig through the pile of bags until he found his, and dig through that for socks. Under the gore-tex, under the towel, into the other boots, where the clean socks were.

He changed them, noticed his feet were black and lint covered, with creases from the socks and whatever sandy grit had gotten into the boots. He put the dirty ones in his laundry bag, and resecured everything, then tied his boots.

That did feel a bit better. And how did a very simple task become such a labor?

Fatigue, stress, everything.

The others were changing socks, and there were creases and stains on their feet, too.

Then he realized he actually was hungry. He'd have to go get an MRE.

He hadn't mentioned that once the food ran out, they'd either be hunting or eating grubs. There wasn't much else around here.

The chicken fajita MRE was adequately edible. But it made him thirsty. Another bottle of water went down.

The LT was still standing, staring at nothing. But he had changed his socks.

"Sir, water is going to become an issue shortly. We'll need to find some."

The LT replied, "What do you suggest?" without any emotion at all. That was creepy.

"Downhill, sir, north, to where there's likely a watershed."

"Denied. We will wait in this location for recovery."

They could wait a bit longer. He'd give the LT another day before taking action.

"Understood, sir."

The man was completely gone.

Oglesby was violent. Caswell seemed to just sit against a rock ignoring everything around her. He wasn't sure about the others. Both Trinidad and Ortiz sat chattering in Spanish, cursing occasionally and throwing pebbles. Alexander kept looking at things through her camera. He couldn't tell if she was taking photos. Dalton bowed his head and prayed a lot. Barker seemed reasonably together; he'd dug the latrine and neatened his gear. Devereaux kept sorting through his med pack, laying stuff out and putting it back.

"I'm going to suggest everyone neaten your gear up, and find cold- and wet-weather gear. It was a bit cool last night, and we don't want to get rained on."

It took a while, but everyone did comply. He didn't blame them for being slow. He saw that all the time in the field. This was worse than any bivouac he'd ever done.

Alexander had some kind of flat panel laid out. Battery charger. Good. He used rechargeables in his flashlights, so that would help them if this turned out long-term.

He didn't see any way it wasn't long-term, and another mild panic attack rushed through him. They couldn't get home. Whatever sent them here appeared random and unplanned.

He tried thinking about that. No aliens or future people showed up demanding or requesting information or help. They weren't facing any particular threat. There were no real resources. Sticking them here wasn't accomplishing anything for anyone. They were just here.

He could think of no way to get home.

CHAPTER 3

Armand Devereaux watched with trepidation and interest as the sun set and the stars came out. There was the Dipper. He saw Hercules but not Cassiopeia. Damn. He sighed deeply.

Barker had the fire built up again. He'd scavenged a lot of small twigs and sticks in the area, from various scrub. It might be enough to last all night. Otherwise, they were going to be dark and scared. And knowing what he'd seen, the stars weren't friendly at all.

It was bright enough. God, it was clear, with no pollution or city lights at all.

They all gathered around, for the little heat, and the more comfort.

Barker said, "Sure is bright and clear. You know if it gets cloudy, it'll be darker than a bag of coal."

Ortiz asked, "But how long until now? Our now?"

He said, "A long time."

Oglesby asked, "When did wooly rhinos become extinct?"

Spencer said, "I'm guessing about twenty thousand years ago, though other types of rhinos survived later. I may not be exact."

Dalton looked irritated, and muttered a barely heard, "Ten thousand."

Elliott said, "What was that, Dalton?"

Dalton looked around nervously and said, "The Earth is no more than ten thousand years old. All that other stuff was disproven in the nineteen fifties."

Yes, it figured a Creationist would have some specific troubles.

31

Armand had no idea how anyone could take Genesis literally. No one took every verse literally, even the most literal. It just wasn't possible. So why obsess over that part?

Elliott said, "Well, with respect to your faith, I have to use what information fits my training and viewpoint to make the best decisions I can. It's how I think. You're welcome to your opinions for your own calculations."

Dalton shrugged. He looked annoyed, but he wasn't going to fight.

Armand nodded slowly. The LT was a bit tighter now, and obviously had dealt with Creationists before.

Elliott said, "So, ten thousand years or more. But less than a million, because the stars would look very different. Probably less than a hundred thousand. I recognize the Big Dipper at least."

Good. The man was tracking a bit. Armand had been worried he was completely gone.

He spoke up, "I do some astronomy in school, and it's a hobby. The Earth's axis wobbles like a spinning top. Polaris is a bit off, but Vega is still well over there, and Deneb there, bracketing the axis. Precession of the Earth's axis would put Vega as the pole star in about fifty thousand years, so assuming the same is true in reverse, we're looking at fifteen or thirty, more or less."

"Then let's go with twenty to twenty-five."

Alexander broke down in outright weeping at that point. He couldn't think of anything to offer to her, so he didn't.

He said, "It would be one or the other. It doesn't average."

Elliott said, "Yeah. Well, it's not now. Our now."

Trinidad asked, "How do we get home?"

"We wait for whatever brought us here."

"What if it never comes? How do we get home?"

"That's all there is."

Trinidad shouted, "Don't you tell me that!"

Armand ran over fast, was alongside, and suddenly it was a man on man hug with bawling tears.

He saw nothing funny or unmanly about it. He was barely keeping it together himself.

Sean Elliott felt ill. He realized he'd neither eaten nor drunk all day, and forced himself to swallow a few mouthfuls from his Camelbak.

Then he chewed some jerky. He didn't feel better, but his stomach eased off a bit, and his headache faded.

Had he spent all day just staring into space? He was supposed to be in command.

Spencer came over as soon as he moved.

"Sir, can I consult with you?"

"Yes, what is it?" He tried to make eye contact and failed. He masked his shame by glancing around.

Spencer indicated with his thumb and head. They moved away from the group and around the back of Charlie Eight.

Spencer looked rough. He hadn't slept either, and might even be in shock.

"Sir, with respect, you are not handling this well."

"I . . ." he was about to erupt in an ass chewing, because no one could handle this shit well, but he needed help, and Spencer was trying to offer it.

"I'm open to suggestions," he said.

"Sir, it's been almost three days. We haven't secured food, water, shelter. Whatever dropped us here is gone. It may or may not come back, but we have to make the call to take care of ourselves here, now."

"I'm afraid of leaving. We don't know when it will come back." It had to come back. If it happened once, it would happen again.

"We don't know *if* it will come back. And we're running out of resources. Water. Food," Spencer repeated. "Fuel. We have limited ammo. We need to relocate while we have fuel, then settle in. If there's some kind of time portal, and someone is looking for us, they'll do what SAR does and find us. We can leave signals."

"What if they don't know we're here?"

"Then, sir," the man said, with a very deep breath, "they won't be looking for us, will they?"

Every time Elliott was sure he was all adrenalined out, something came along and kicked him again.

"Yes. I agree. But I really don't know what to do. And Spencer . . ."

"Yes, sir?"

"Between you and me, I'm fucking scared."

"Well, that means you're like the rest of us, sir. But we have what we have."

"I'm sorry I weirded out." He burned in embarrassment. He was the officer, and he'd sat here doing nothing.

"It can happen to anyone, sir. Glad to have you back."

"Thanks. You don't mean that, though."

Spencer stuck out a hand and he took it and shook.

"Yes, I do. I'll run things myself if I have to, but you can see the kids don't respect me. They never have. You, they actually listen to."

He nodded. "So you tell me what to do and I'll tell them."

"No, sir. You're the officer, you need to command. I'll implement."

He had a moment of cold clarity.

"There's no way I could resign anyway. Not here," he realized.

"No, there isn't, and I wouldn't let you. They need you."

He noticed the man didn't say "I need you."

He breathed again, and took in the impossibly fresh air. He could smell the truck, and otherwise, the clearest air anywhere. It was refreshing, but frightening.

"Downhill, to the river, and dig in there. They can find us. But what after that?"

Spencer said, "We try to find somewhere we can build long-term camping, like an overhead between the vehicles, and windbreaks. Hooches if we can. If there's saplings—"

"I can advise on building hooches, Sergeant. I'm an engineer."

"Yes, sir. See? You can get us comfortable and healthy. Fresh water, too."

"Yeah. And we have a box of soap, asswipe and toothpaste. That'll last a while."

"Yes, sir."

"We might be better walking down. These bitches are overbalanced even on a road." He pointed at the MRAPs. They were crap off road, but here they were.

Spencer said, "We'll need to be careful. But they're transport, they're shelter, and we can rip parts out of them for survival. Hoses, metal."

"We could come back for parts. It's not like anyone is going to steal them."

"We could. Your call, sir. But I'd like to get them as far as we can before we abandon them. It means less of a march later."

"I'll take that under advisement." Yeah. That would help. If the damned MRAPs didn't roll and injure someone on the way. They weren't meant for military patrol other than convoy or urban. Even dirt roads were problematic.

First, he needed food and hydration. It was late afternoon, too. Actual sleep was called for, if he could. They'd travel in daylight only.

Every young officer wanted a combat command and to show his mettle. Well, the good ones wanted to show it. If they managed, they held onto the title of "good."

This was not what he'd had in mind, but he didn't have a choice. He'd make it work.

Sean Elliott did sleep, restlessly but well enough. The nightmares were probably a good sign, he told himself. His brain was sorting out conflict.

Spencer had kept things running overnight. Whatever the man said, he really didn't need Sean Elliott. But there were few enough of them they needed everyone.

He took another look at the terrain, and the map. The two were close enough generally. Downhill would lead to whatever watercourse there was. Assuming they were when and where they thought they were, and at least approximately in the area.

All the troops were gathered around the protruding rock, and he could tell which side the latrine was, when the wind shifted. That was rank.

Spencer caught his eye. He nodded.

Spencer said, "Listen up. Informal formation. Keep eating, but pay attention. The LT and I have been talking, and he has a plan."

They looked at him. Some seemed curious, others hopeful, some annoyed. Well, that was his own fault. But, they did look to him.

"Okay, what should be the Amu Darya river is twenty miles north. It's rough terrain, but we're going to try for it. It's a major watercourse; that means water, power, transport, whatever resources there are. Whatever there is here is likely in that area."

No one said anything, but there were a couple of nods.

He continued. "The movement will commence at once. We will thoroughly police the area of all trash or identifying material, including filling in the latrine. Do not mark it. We will stow all gear securely. We will leave a blaze in the turf indicating our direction.Charlie Eight will be the lead vehicle, and I will be aboard. Charlie Nine will follow, with

SFC Spencer as vehicle commander. We will have three personnel on the ground as reconnaissance ahead. They will stay within one hundred meters of each other, and of the vehicle. We will follow at a walking pace, because these beasts have shitty balance. This movement may take up to a week, though it is possible we can accomplish it in two days. Exercise light and noise discipline.

"The advance party will look for a clear route, paying attention to near and distant terrain. They must also be alert for dangerous animals, which is anything large or carnivorous or both. We will try to avoid interacting with animals, and retreat to the vehicle if necessary. We'll shoot if we have to. I want both guns manned and alert. Any shooting will be by my order only, but anyone may shoot if there is an imminent threat of being attacked. ACH and armor will be worn.

"We will rest briefly every two hours to swap out advance parties, and for latrines and food.

"With all that covered, anyone with experience in rough terrain or ground guiding in the field should volunteer to be the lead in each shift, and I'll assign two others to support and observe."

There were glances back and forth, then Barker, Spencer and Trinidad raised their hands.

That was a relief. "Okay, Spencer first, Barker second, Trinidad third. That covers six hours, which is likely most of today. We'll rotate again if needed. Caswell and Dalton, you're up first. I'll take second with Alexander. Ortiz and Devereaux third. Oglesby is backup. Police everything, double check with your buddy and someone else, and let's roll. Dalton and Trinidad, do you know how to make a direction blaze?"

"Yes, sir," Dalton replied.

"Please do that while we load."

"Got it.

He decided to drive lead himself. It was effectively combat, and the lives of these nine depended on him doing everything right.

Inside he felt utterly cold and terrified. *What if? What if? What if?* He couldn't answer, so he was trying not to think of the questions. But he felt insecure even starting the vehicle. What if it stalled? Got stuck? What if three minutes after they left the area, whatever had caused the jump came back and they weren't there for it? But they couldn't sit on the side of a hill forever, hoping.

After ten seconds of cranking, the engine responded, and troops started climbing aboard. He should probably double check the cleanup, but he didn't want to get out of the vehicle now. Every bad emotion was hitting him at once—laziness, hopelessness, anger, despair. Nausea hit him again as his guts clenched.

Out front, he saw Spencer, Caswell and Dalton. Alexander and Ortiz were aboard with him. He noted Alexander was up on the gun. He assumed she knew what she was doing. Barker, Trinidad and Devereaux were aboard Charlie Nine. Oglesby gave him a thumbsup and climbed in.

"I'm last, sir. I count ten."

"I counted ten, too, and we'll be moving at a walking pace. Let's roll."

He revved the engine in lieu of a horn. Spencer turned to look at him, and he stuck a thumb out the window. Spencer nodded, waved back, and started walking.

Martin Spencer shivered. It wasn't cold, though even moderate temperatures got chilly if you were out in them all day, and anyway, they'd been in scorching heat until three days ago. But, as much as he liked being alone, he did not like being this far from the rest. He had an ongoing panic that the vehicles were going to disappear and leave him here with two soldiers, neither of whom he thought were that good.

He slogged through tall grass and low scrub, like prairie set on an angle. It dragged at his boots and pants, and he left a very obvious trail. It was tough, slow going, though it would be easy for the trucks, as long as they stayed upright.

The LT wasn't handling things well. What he should do was roll at speed, with a good eye ahead, get to the river fast, and keep them all in close proximity. Their water and food were limited, and if this took a week, they were going to be in sad shape. The fatigue alone was killing him.

He decided that he'd take some melatonin that evening. He needed the sleep. Though he'd rather wake up from a nightmare than be stuck in one.

He should probably stop chugging Ripits, too. Though he probably had to. There didn't seem to be any left. He'd chewed the coffee powder from the MREs. He'd caffeined and adrenalined himself sick.

He kept his head swiveling. No doubt it looked to the LT that he was very earnest in his task. In reality, he wanted to keep a good eye on Caswell to the left, who was edging in closer, and Dalton to the right, who seemed to be keeping position. Dalton was also muttering to himself. The kid was probably praying. Spencer didn't blame him. If it helped, good. He almost wished he could.

He did keep an eye open ahead, but the ground was rolling hillside, with no terrain the vehicles couldn't handle. He pointed at trees as he passed. Ahead was another rock outcropping. He clambered up and stood there to point it out, until the LT gave him a thumb. He took a few moments to view all around. Yes, that low line of trees was likely the river, right where it was supposed to be.

Not reassuring. They really were in the fucking Stone Age. Were there any Paleolithic people around here yet? And were they Cro-Magnon, Neanderthal, or something older? If Devereaux was right, anyone here should be modern humans. That helped. Then he wasn't sure if he'd rather meet other people or not.

There were little herds of goats or such dotting the ridges. He saw something that looked like large, ugly antelope in a small family group. A hare darted through grass ahead of him. Startled, he looked around and up.

Then he realized they'd barely moved a half mile. That was two point five percent of the trip. If that held true, this was only a two-day trip. But even then, he'd be gibbering nuts.

Caswell was getting too close.

"Move back left," he reluctantly ordered.

"Yes, Sergeant." She didn't argue, but looked uncomfortable moving away. He understood that.

Ahead there were more goats. At least they'd have plenty to eat, and those didn't taste too bad. But they had to find salt, and edible vegetables, and he'd need chalk.

His stomach hurt like hell, but he had to ration out the ranitidine as long as he could. Once it was gone, he might manage on chalk added to all his food. Or he might start dying slowly and painfully. Or he might start puking in agony until he put a bullet through his brain.

Fifteen years ago, he'd been a physically textbook Soldier. Now . . .

This dip was likely too deep for the undercarriage.

He called, "Caswell, direct them your way."

"Roger."

He pointed, she waved, the LT stuck a hand out, and the vehicles angled west.

He took the same course, and waved Dalton to do the same.

He made a point of drinking. It wasn't hot, but he could still dehydrate if not careful. The sun was getting high.

A double rev of the engine sounded. He turned and the LT waved him back. Had it been two hours?

The ache in his legs said it had been. He started to stumble back, but the LT drove forward to his position. It made sense.

Barker dug a hasty hole behind Charlie Nine, they took care of draining in turn, and shoveled the dirt back in.

Climbing into Charlie Nine was a relief. It was warm, dry, and sounded like the twenty-first century. And now he was terrified that whatever brought them here would take the ground guides back. He swallowed. It was PTSD, and he'd get over it eventually. They all had it, and there was nothing to be done about it.

The LT, Alexander and Barker moved out front to guide. He took the wheel.

Gina Alexander shook. She could take photos under fire, but this was terrifying. Her head floated above her feet, not feeling anything. Stone Age. Stranded. She had Blake, Dylan and Aislinn at home, and knew she'd never see them again.

She knew it was a panic attack, but they weren't supposed to last three days. She hadn't slept beyond nausea-filled naps, even more than she had trouble sleeping anyway. Medication . . . but when it ran out, she knew what awaited her.

She choked back a sob. Something had to take them home. Please.

She stepped in a dip and her ankle twisted. She winced, but it wasn't crippling. She limped for a bit, but kept on. That, too. She wasn't physically fit enough for this. She was a middle-aged Guardsman, on loan, for publicity photos. She could handle an occasional combat sortie. But this . . . no.

She heard the growl, twisted and fumbled, and fell. Then it jumped on her.

"Gaaah!"

It was a dog, a wolf, several of them. Something was stuck on her boot, and something chewed at her knee pad. She smelled rotten breath and felt it blow wet on her head, as jaws crunched at her helmet. Claws scraped and dragged through her shirt sleeve. Hot, wet drool splashed on her face.

She squealed again, jammed her carbine into something and pulled the trigger. The animal yowled, kicked and rolled away.

Two more shots sounded, another fell and convulsed a few feet away, then Lieutenant Elliott stood over her.

"Alexander, are you alright?"

"I think so, sir. Covered in wolf drool, but no damage. They got my boot and kneepad."

"Stay down for a moment."

"Yes, sir."

She lay back and sighed. Five minutes into her shift, and she was a casualty and liability.

Devereaux arrived at a run, but she already knew she was fine, just freaked. He looked her over.

"I don't see any punctures. Do you have any strains or tears?"

"I don't think so." She flexed each joint carefully. "Just overall soreness like from wrestling or PT."

"Okay, we'll put you on next shift. Oglesby is up."

She wanted to argue, but she needed to curl up in a ball and scream.

"Definitely wolves," Barker said. "Big suckers. Not dire wolves, but big Asian wolves." He toed the one the LT had shot, which still twitched. He pulled a knife off his gear and jabbed it into the beast's throat.

"What about that one she shot?" The lieutenant asked.

Barker said, "It might die eventually. It also might heal. Five five six isn't much of a round for a big animal, but it was point blank into the guts. I'd rather not try to track it down, but if you insist . . ."

"Negative. I was just curious if we have enough guns. And we only have the ammo we have."

"Yeah. We need some spears and bows, as soon as we find a place to hole up."

They were ignoring her, which was good and bad. They weren't worried, but they also didn't need her.

I am not crying! she insisted, and tightened her face.

"Hey, Alexander!" Elliott shouted.

"Yes, sir?"

"They came up fast. No one saw them. You did good."

She wasn't sure he meant it, but she was glad he said it.

"Thank you, sir."

And now she'd be the old lady in the passenger seat.

Bob Barker was stiff. Sleeping three across in the back of the trucks wasn't comfortable, though it was safe, with two people up top on watch. Dalton had elected to sleep up top, and it had been dry. He wasn't sure the LT was sleeping, and that was a problem. The man had wigged out pretty badly already.

Bob also felt cold. It wasn't the temperature. He liked it cool. It was an emotional cold.

On the one hand, he was confident enough, since he knew flintknapping, tanning, firemaking, and how to make several types of tepee and wickiup. It was really cool to have that knowledge and to know how his ancestors lived. On the other hand, doing so didn't really appeal, but he didn't appear to have any choice.

He heard a distant yip.

If those damned wolves were around, they'd need spears or bows. The ones that hit Alexander yesterday had been beautiful animals, and he respected them. They'd also yield a warm fur that frost wouldn't form on.

If they were here forever, he planned to wear a few.

He wanted to change his underwear and his socks again. It was going on two days since the last change, and they were crunchy. Hygiene was important. The field was messier than garrison, but there was no reason to become lice-picking savages.

MRAPs were completely the wrong vehicles for this terrain. It was amazing they hadn't rolled them both. The walking pace helped; had they just driven they'd definitely have spilled. Even like this, though, they constantly pushed twenty degrees of incline, and that was risky.

He had seen the river earlier. They weren't going to die of thirst. That long line of trees was obvious. It was a long way, though, especially detouring so the vehicles could have as flat a run as possible.

There were all kinds of animals here. They'd seen a second herd of rhino. There were goats by the billions. Some large antelope things that might be saiga or a relative. Rabbits, or probably hares, popped up here and there. Wolves. They might have seen a lion. Caswell thought she had.

Devereaux whistled and waved, and pointed. He angled over that way at a fast walk.

The ground in front of Devereaux was rocky and lumpy under the scrub. Spiky stalks of bushes protruded between them. Yeah, that would have stopped the vehicle, permanently. The LT was being cautious, but he'd been right. Spencer would have driven right up on it, possibly into it, before identifying it.

"Good find. It's clearer over my way. They'll have to turn sharp left."

He jogged back through clouds of bugs and windblown grass and gave Spencer that information.

Spencer nodded. "Right. I hope we don't run into any dead ends."

"It's getting better. I can see the trees."

"Yes, I can too. But that means the terrain will get rougher."

"Hopefully the glaciers did their job."

Spencer nodded. "Hopefully."

If Doc was correct about when it was. If they were there.

There was no way home right now, so he tried to put it out of his mind.

Martin Spencer was chagrined. Yes, they really did need to go that slowly, and he should have known that, and he'd have wrecked a vehicle figuring it out. The fatigue and fear were affecting him as much as anyone.

They made slow progress, but it was progress. They were all together, so if anything happened they'd hopefully not wind up with three poor bastards left behind while the trucks went home, but he was afraid of that every moment he was detached to the ground. A mere 100 meters was causing him to freak out.

He scratched at his chin. The growth there was enough to be irritating, even before a helmet chinstrap. They were all looking and smelling like bums. His skin was greasy with sweat, and gritty.

A blast from the horn made him jump, and he turned, expecting more wolves.

Elliott waved him back. The trucks were at a nice flat spot he'd crossed a few minutes before. They throttled off and everyone debarked. The sun was sinking in the west over long hills. They'd been at this fourteen hours. Barker was breaking sticks and starting a small fire in a little hollow.

Elliott said, "Okay, we'll bivouac here tonight. And we need to assess food and water."

Water was getting critical. If they didn't find some tomorrow, they'd be out.

"What do we do for water?" he asked.

Barker said, "We can dig a sump anywhere there's damp rocks or a hollow. But we have to find them. If we find a stream or meadow, we use it."

Spencer said, "We reach the river down there fast. We can see it. We need to get there. Otherwise, we need to sit out a day with a solar still over plants and a latrine and get what water we can, but it's not going to be enough. We have to move."

"It's hilly down there," Dalton said. "Ridges and stuff."

Elliott said, "We seem to have about eight klicks to go. We'll do it tomorrow. We have the fuel. If need be, we'll run along a ridge or valley instead of crossing them."

Barker and Dalton were muttering something and not paying attention.

Spencer looked over, irritated. "Gentlemen, as informal as it is, this is a formation."

Dalton said, "Sorry, sir, and Sergeant. We were discussing something."

"What?"

Dalton looked at Elliott. "Permission to shoot a goat, sir? At least we'll have some fresh food, and it'll mean the MREs last a bit longer."

Good catch. They were down to a day's worth, and most of the pogey bait was gone. He'd stashed a bag of chips. That was all he had left.

Elliott asked, "Can you get one?"

Dalton gestured. "Hell, they're within fifty yards. Headshot, bang."

"But is an M-Four big enough for one?"

Barker nodded. "Oh, hell yes. Not for anything much bigger, but it'll bag a kid."

"Go ahead. Ears, everyone."

Dalton raised his rifle, took a breath, steadied in textbook fashion and squeezed off one round. Fifty-odd yards away, a goat convulsed and dropped. Some of its friends scampered away, while others merely stared in confusion.

Barker took off at a jog. That caused the rest of the flock to disperse.

Elliott nodded at Dalton. "Secure your brass," he said.

Dalton didn't argue, he just scanned the grass until Ortiz pointed out the empty case, then grabbed it.

Spencer said, "We might want to fabricate a brass catcher or two."

Elliott said, "Yeah, we'll get there. First, I want a place to live."

Barker obviously had experience hunting. He drained the goat's blood into two canteen cups and set it by the fire. He gutted, skinned and sectioned the animal in about three minutes flat. With some scrubby, bent sticks poked into the ground, he had a not-quite rotisserie set up in short order. He dunked the goat chunks in the blood and set them over the fire to roast.

"Ortiz, can you take watch?" he asked.

"Sure, Sergeant. Save me some. I like goat."

"Good. Goat. It's what's for dinner."

CHAPTER 4

Sean Elliott's training covered a lot, but despite that, taking a dump in the Stone Age, surrounded by hostile animals, roving flocks, a squad of troops and no privacy, with only an ammo crate as a seat, was not high on the list of fun things to do. That, and the short water had him dehydrated and slightly constipated, and the MREs and stress weren't helping. That had hurt. He wasn't sure how long the paper would last, either. That wasn't going to be fun. Having a guard stand over you with a weapon while you took care of business in the open was that much more unique. He wouldn't wish this on a loudmouthed sergeant major. Well, maybe a certain one.

Oglesby turned and nodded after Elliott pulled his pants up and started fastening them. He nodded back, grabbed the crate, placed it carefully behind Charlie Nine, and headed to the fire. He had bleach wipes but wasn't going to waste them, and would just do the Muslim thing of using one hand to eat and one to clean.

Barker had meat sizzling on sticks. It was fragrant, brown, and bubbling with juice. He took a skewer and sat against a rock. Carefully, he blew to cool the steaming gobbet, and nibbled at it.

"Huh. Not bad," he allowed. It wasn't bad at all. Better than MRE for sure.

"Yeah, the blood provides some needed salt. But the protein is going to make us thirsty."

Sean tried not to blush. He'd wasted three days, and was moving overly cautiously, and he knew it.

"Tomorrow the river," he said.

Barker said, "It'll be good to have a proper bivouac and stretch out a bit, but I think we all napped while in the back of the trucks."

"Badly, but yes."

"I am in pain," Ortiz said, rubbing his shoulders. "I don't know how you big guys manage."

Alexander said, "Try it in body armor not cut for your body shape."

Around a mouthful of goat, Caswell asked, "How much water is there?"

Oglesby said, "One cooler half full of melted ice. One pack of bottled. Aren't you a vegetarian?"

"When circumstances allow, yes. Right now, they don't. So I'm eating meat. Got a problem?" She fixed him with a gaze.

"No problem." He looked a bit taken aback by her tone. He lit another smoke. He had to be getting low.

Barker looked at the cooler. "We should have a bottle each for tonight."

"We're running out."

Spencer said, "Yes, but we can always run out. No need to schedule it. We need to be operating and healthy for tomorrow. There's no advantage to running out early."

Sean said, "I'm not sure I follow what you said, but one bottle, go ahead."

"Neither am I," Spencer said. "I meant, we will run out sooner or later, so let's stay hydrated while we can."

Caswell asked, "What about that care package? Anything useful?"

Alexander said, "It's got ten toothbrushes, five mini-tubes of paste, three rolls of floss, twenty bars of soap, four packages of pencils, one of pens and some envelopes and paper, some crayons, a box of tampons, six used bestseller paperbacks, a box of double A batteries, six pairs of tube socks, a pack of disposable razors, four chapsticks and some lotion. It had two boxes of cookies, but we killed those yesterday."

"At least it's mostly useful stuff," he said.

Spencer said, "It's all useful. Someone did us a favor."

Alexander pointed to the back of the truck where the box was. "If we ever get back, you can write them a thank you letter. They included their address."

"I will," he said.

Far Eye was enjoying the evening. It was a little cool, and he pulled his cape in tighter.

Strangers were here on the Mid Hills. They left a deep trail to the south, up onto the flats, but had a village here, away from any water, flint or good trees.

Their huts were strange. The sides appeared to be slabs of dun rock, and they were open at the bottom. He also wondered how they'd built and settled here without anyone noticing.

They were short. Their robes were of a very strange hide, mottled in colors. It wasn't any animal skin he recognized. It would blend in well if they held still. Two were female, with fine figures, but slender. The strangers wore belts and carried sticks, and their speech was strange. It had few sounds, but they ran the sounds together into a stew of sounds.

The one atop the rock was obviously a watcher. He held his stick in both hands. It might be a magic stick. It was carved into an odd shape with limbs sticking out cut short.

"See?" he asked Scraggle.

"Far away strangers."

"Assume."

"Meet?" Scraggle asked.

"Watch. Meet tomorrow maybe."

"Maybe spirits?"

"Look like small people."

It was strange to have only two females. None of them looked like children. The men should have mates. They acted almost like a hunting party, except they were villaging, not hunting. They had those large huts.

They were not like his people. They were not like the other newcomers.

He would watch. They wouldn't see him from here.

Sean Elliott knew he'd done badly, but he felt better now. Though they were still low on water, they were within sight of the river at least. They'd take care of that tomorrow. There were plenty of meat animals to hunt. They'd have to find vegetables to balance it out.

Trinidad spoke up in his high voice.

"Sir, there are two humans on the lip to our west."

"Stone age?"

"I dunno, man. They seem to be wearing loose fur hides, so I think so. Tall. One has a dreadlock Mohawk. The other has three stripes of hair, like a skunk."

"Are they aware of us?"

"They know the fire is here and are peering. They think they're well outside the light. I guess they don't have night vision."

Devereaux said, "The Afghans don't have night vision."

Elliott almost chuckled. "Yeah, we can make those jokes. But the locals have found us. Should we try to contact them?"

Spencer said, "No, sir, I'd say don't spook them. We'll try for daylight."

Stone Age people. If they were here for a long time, and it seemed like it, local contact was necessary. Trade. Primitive skills. But it was one more crushing responsibility of many.

"Sergeant Spencer, can I talk to you for a minute?"

"Yes, sir."

Once again they went around the back of Charlie Nine, but only there. He wanted to be within quick reach of the others, just in case.

"I'm sorry, I don't know your first name. It was on the manifest, but . . ."

"Martin Spencer, sir."

"Martin. Thanks. I don't want to get too informal, but we need to be friends as much as soldiers until this is over."

"Yes, sir."

"I'm Sean."

"Noted, sir, but I'm going to keep this form of address for now."

"That's fine. And I respect that. How old are you?"

"Thirty-eight, sir."

He hadn't looked that old before, but now, shaggy with bits of gray in his beard and sunken eyes, he did.

"Deployed a few times?"

"Third rotation."

"Good. I can rely on you for advice, then. Okay . . ."

He took a deep breath.

"I have to sleep sometime. Eventually. I'm not, really, and I know others are having problems. We may need to medicate for a few days. But I can't handle everything twenty-four-seven by myself.

"I know you operate differently than I do, but can you give me honest feedback when I'm awake, and keep the general gist of my instructions when I'm not?"

"Since I'm effectively acting first sergeant, yes, sir. I can."

"Thank you. Any immediate advice?"

"I think you're doing okay now. I won't hold the last four days against you. It's insane. None of us handled it well, no one could."

"Thanks, but that's true of combat, too. It's got to be handled."

"Yeah. Well, we're handling it now."

"Do you agree we get to the river first, then find locals?"

"Yes, sir. Water. Food, and the river will have fish as well as watering holes for game. It will have reeds, and I'm pretty sure there are cattails or such, which are edible."

"Really?"

"Yeah, like a mild watercress, sort of. And the tops make tea, or can be used for bandages. It can be pressed into paper. Useful stuff. Anyway, after we have food and water, then we can find locals."

"I figure we need to recon the area, see who's here and if they're friendly, and then find a good place to settle in for a long wait."

Spencer nodded. "Very good, sir. We don't want to be too close to neighbors, but I hope we can work out trades."

"Yeah. I want to talk about this a lot more, but I'm groggy, and we need to reach the river. Long term planning after immediate needs."

"You should lie down, sir. We'll take turns, you, me and Barker, I guess."

"Okay. But wake me at once for anything."

He stretched out in the back between the seats. Ortiz lay on one. Devereaux was on the other, his feet on the floor. Tall, that man was.

It wasn't comfortable, but he'd manage. It was better than the ground. He tucked his helmet at the angle that worked for a pillow, sort of, drew up his feet and crossed his arms. That would work. He closed his eyes and listened to the mumbles outside.

Martin Spencer awoke for the third time at sunrise. He vaguely remembered dawn and the depth of night. He'd slept sitting back against the tire, and leaning forward on his hands. It wasn't good sleep, nor a lot of sleep, but . . . well . . .

"How are we doing?" he asked. Caswell and Barker were on watch. The west was still dark purple fading to a gorgeous blue behind and east. He shivered slightly and was damp from dew.

Barker said, "Our observer slipped away about an hour ago."

"Okay. Well, we assume he's following us. It suggests there's a settlement not far away."

"Hopefully. Do we really want to meet them, though?"

"I don't think we have a choice. We're moving into their territory."

"Yeah. I just don't know what we're supposed to do."

"Is the LT up?"

"Yes, I'm here."

"Any ideas, sir?"

"A bit. I want everyone to eat and drink. Clean uniforms all around. These are getting nasty. We'll wear body armor and take weapons. We'll walk on foot to the river and see if we can find signs of these local people. Anyone any good at that?"

Barker said, "I'm pretty good, but they may be better."

"Yeah, well, we do what we can. Water first. Look around the terrain. If we don't find anything, we come back here before dark. We can move down closer tomorrow, after we're sure we won't get stuck in the mud."

Martin asked, "Body armor and what else, sir? Water of course. Food?"

"Yeah, enough food for today. What's left?"

Barker said, "Some MRE components and a few candy bars and snacks. Running out of that, too."

The CO winced. "Crap. Okay. Take it. Sleeping bags also. Fully armed but light otherwise."

"Okay. Then machetes and knives as well."

Alexander added, "Toilet paper."

Elliott said, "Definitely asswipe. Fair enough on the blades, but everyone keep things sheathed, and empty weapons. I don't want any NDs, any trigger play, any accidents. I'll tell you when to load. Two mags each is plenty."

"Hooah. What about wolves, sir?" Ortiz asked.

"Yeah, if you see an approaching threat, say something and load up. But we're not here to fight, we're exploring and trying to be friendly."

The man definitely sounded more in control today. A little shaky, but that was to be expected. At least he was giving some kind of orders, and they made sense.

Twenty minutes later, Martin had to snap, "Move!" Everyone was reluctant to leave the vehicles. Well, so was he, but they couldn't use them for this.

The LT locked Charlie Nine, Barker locked Charlie Eight. The machine guns were inside, bolts pulled, and should be safe from anyone in the Stone Age.

"Everyone has food, water, weapon with two magazines, knife, armor including eyepro, sanitary supplies, bedroll and clothes."

"Hooah." "Yes, Sergeant." They had quite light rucks, probably under fifty pounds. Even with armor and helmet, that wasn't bad.

"Got this, too," Barker said, holding up the empty drum cooler. "We can get five gallons of water additional." He could carry it easily in one hand. It would be heavy when full, though. They could probably lash it to sticks and sling it, however.

"Good idea. We walk. North to the river, but it's a straighter route down that way, so that's what I suggest."

He waited for the LT, who nodded assent, and started walking.

"Close interval," he said. "We're not worried about gunfire, just wolves and angry men with spears."

He didn't hear anything.

He whipped around, and staggered when the ruck kept going. Everyone was behind him, adjusting their interval.

"Christ, don't be silent, I thought you'd got magicked home. Keep talking."

Barker called, "So these ten soldiers walked into the Stone Age."

Oglesby replied, "And one of them says, 'that's not the stoning I wanted.'"

They kept chattering, and he felt better, but after only a few minutes, he stepped aside, ostensibly to count people, and let Barker take point. He really wanted to be in the crowd, not out front. Shameful, but he couldn't do it.

He moved into third place, behind the LT. He should probably be last, but that was as frightening.

It was ridiculous. Nothing was going to send them home, or it would have already. Or it would know somehow they were out of whack, and send them no matter where they were. Or it would be random in the formation, and anywhere was as likely.

He was panicking; it was unprofessional, and he couldn't stop it.

Or maybe he'd read more sci fi than the others and knew just enough to be scared.

He sipped some water, looked around again, and forced himself to drop back two more slots. Everyone deserved a turn, and he should cover the rear.

It took four hours to reach a ridge overlooking the river valley. A mile and a quarter an hour. Not much faster than they'd done guiding the trucks.

"Stream over there," Ortiz said. "Looks pretty fresh."

Martin said, "Okay, fill up. Expect to have intestinal distress."

Trinidad asked, "Is that the polite name for what you call the screaming shits?"

"That's exactly what it is."

The stream was a trickle with lush growth along both sides, but they found a mostly bare spot of rock, covered in moss, where they could bend over to plunge Camelbak bladders and bottles into the splashing flow.

He risked a taste.

"Tastes clean," he said. "Faintly musty. Good. We'll want to mark this."

"Got it," Dalton said. He had a pocket compass and was writing on a notepad, presumably azimuths. The compass looked to be halfway decent—not a professional one, but it would be good enough for this. And, it was probably all they had. GPS was useless.

From atop the rock, Barker said, "Sir, there are obvious settlements ahead, along the river bank."

"That's good and bad, but it is a complication."

Martin breathed relief, hurried forward, and said, "Sir, as a SERE graduate, may I offer input?"

"Please."

"There are two ways to approach this. We can go on foot, quietly, acting nonthreatening. I doubt they'll recognize any of our gear for anything other than odd pouches and sticks. They have nothing to compare to. We can negotiate, find out a good spot, likely get some food and water in the meantime. The other option is to roll in like gods. We don't need to negotiate, we just benevolently agree that we'll take whatever empty spots they can direct us to.

"I recommend the former. I'm not comfortable playing God, and in the stories where people have, eventually the primitives figured it out and there was trouble. I'd rather say we're explorers from far away and want to be good neighbors."

"I agree," Elliott said. "We'll mark here, walk in, be sociable. What else?"

"Here's where it gets tricky," he said. "If they're hospitable, they'll likely offer food and drink. We have to drink the local water, we don't have a choice, and we can expect those screaming shits to follow. The food may be bugs, fermented meat, whatever. We can refuse citing vows to our gods or such. But it has to be polite. If that doesn't work, try, 'I'll save this for later.' And you may just have to suck up and swallow something disgusting."

Oglesby said, "So, if someone asks if we're gods, we don't say 'yes'?"

"Correct. Amusing as the line is, this is deadly serious. We're asking our new neighbors, who may number in the tens of thousands, if we can have a chunk of land."

"We covered some of that cultural stuff at DLI," Oglesby said. "I never thought I'd need it."

"Same with SERE," he said.

Elliott said, "Okay, magazines in, chambers empty. We need to stick in close proximity, but spread enough to form two fire teams."

Martin said, "One more thing yet: Alexander, can you pretend to be my mate? And Caswell should pair up with one of the younger males."

Caswell said, "What the hell for? You want to start out by placing our position subordinate, based on gender?"

Oh, Christ, not that feminist crap.

"No, that is not what I want to do. It's fine if you're equals. We'll adapt presentation once we see how they handle it. But I'm guessing they'll have some sort of gender division."

She said, "Band societies are usually very egalitarian. There's a division based on personal interest, not on artificial constructs, and . . ."

"And that matters in fifteen thousand years," he said. "We don't know; we have to be prepared for anything."

Elliott saved him.

"Sergeant Caswell, please go along with the presentation for now. Couples can be equals. We're just buddying you up. Rest of the males, buddy up as well. We'll have five pairs, and I'll take pairs Caswell and Dalton, Barker and Devereaux, and Oglesby can be my buddy. That leaves Spencer and Alexander, if you're okay with that, Sergeant Alexander?"

"I'm fine with that," she agreed. Good.

"And Ortiz and Trinidad." They nodded.

"Okay, then we head west, since that seems to be where they are. We need to get close while it's still well-lit, so we have time to back off and bivouac if need be." It was well past noon already.

Barker said, "It looks like it's about three miles, rough terrain. We should assess each mile."

"Okay, then you lead off."

"Yes, sir. Also, I have some training in primitive skills. I know a bit about my Native culture."

"Good. And Caswell, I am interested in your training, too. There's every chance they will act like you say. I just don't want to assume so."

That seemed to mollify her.

"Yes, sir. I'll let you know."

He pulled at his ruck straps, let things adjust, and slid them back into place.

CHAPTER 5

Elliott was nervous. This was a contact mission, with a completely unknown group. He really had no idea how they'd act, and hoped Caswell was correct. People were people, right? They all ate, crapped, reproduced and needed shelter. There was that Hierarchy of Needs by someone.

He led the way, because he was the lieutenant, but he hoped they couldn't see his knees shake. This was worse than anything he'd done.

Alexander had a huge telephoto lens, almost looking like a cannon, and scanned the settlement ahead.

"They seem to use rock bases with logs and thatch above. It's a lot more advanced than I'd have expected. And painted hides. Pretty good artwork."

Spencer said, "I think they found a settlement south of here, above Mazar-e-Sharif, that was built on rock foundations."

Caswell said, "This could be that culture then."

"It was about the time frame we think we have."

Elliott twitched his mouth and sighed. There was less and less likelihood of this being some trick. Everything pointed to the Stone Age. That some of the troops even knew which culture it was scared him, though it was helpful.

Gina Alexander figured they were at the one mile mark from the settlement, more or less, when some natives came to meet them.

They made her uncomfortable. They were tall. She was average height for an American woman, her husband broke six feet, but all of these men were over six, closing on six and a half. They were almond skinned and almond eyed, with long, dark, kinky hair. And yes, several had dreadlocks. She shuddered. That was disgusting.

They held spears, and what looked like atl-atls, spearthrowers. They wore skirted loincloths and robes, of what was probably brain-tanned leather. One had a wolf fur cape. He was probably the head man here.

Barker moved toward him slowly, hands up and forward. She twisted slightly so her rifle was ready at hand, just in case.

The native said something, and it was a birdsong.

Not really, but it was very smooth, lyrical, tonal, full of clicks and nasals.

Barker said, "I don't understand your words, but I greet you." He pointed at himself. "I am Staff Sergeant Robert Barker, United States Army. I call myself 'Bob.'" He pulled his goggles over his helmet lip and rolled them into his hand.

There was more music. They didn't seem hostile, but they were definitely curious. One came toward her. He looked puzzled by the helmet, armor and ruck, then seemed to decide she was female. The lack of a beard might have helped.

He drew a long tube from under his robe. It was a bone, dead but fresh. He extended it toward her.

Next to her, Spencer said, "*Females!* Accept nothing as a gift!"

Right. Some primitive cultures might regard that as an invite to mate. She shuddered again.

The native looked puzzled, and offered it again.

Spencer extended his arm, palm up. She pointed toward it.

There was no way to read the expressions. She couldn't tell if the man was unhappy or not, but he gave the bone over to Spencer.

Spencer took it. "Marrow in it," he said. "I think it's a food offering."

Caswell said, "An offer of food is usually one of hospitality."

"Yeah, and this is full of fat. I think that's positive."

He poked a finger into the broken end, pulled it out oozing blood, and sucked it.

"Thank you," he said with a slight bow, and returned it.

The man took it with a nod that might almost be a bow in return.

"Now I need a drink," Spencer said. He grabbed the hose of his

Camelbak. That likely wasn't something the locals would recognize, and they didn't.

In a few moments, they were all walking toward the village, the five men chattering like birds.

"That seems easy so far," Elliott said.

"I get the impression they're not short of meat, fat or water," she said. "If there's salt around here, they're in fine shape. They wouldn't have a reason to fight."

Caswell said, "Band societies tend to fight only rarely. Sometimes over borders, but rarely in large encounters. Honor challenges."

Oglesby said, "The language. It's very rich in phonemes. There's a theory about that, and this seems to fit with it. Some of the African languages have two hundred phonemes, and by the time you get to South America or the Pacific, you're down to a dozen or two. It's as if language devolved with isolation and distance."

Elliott said, "Well, let's keep our distance. We're not friends yet, just visitors."

Gina felt better. The lieutenant had been worthless for the first couple of days, but now he was acting like a leader, and there were some good skills in this ersatz squad. They might actually survive.

One of the men whipped it out from under his loincloth and urinated, right there. She wondered if it were symbolic, but the others didn't seem to take any particular notice and kept walking. It was just a thing to do.

There were utters of disgust from the troops.

Barker said, "That's common among the Dene cultures, and they may be distantly related. No real modesty."

Dalton said, "Yeah, they've clearly never heard the word of God."

She rolled her eyes and replied, "Private toilets existed before Christianity. And some cultures still have public ones, even with Christian influence. Finns. Japanese."

He didn't have a response to that. Good.

Elliott said, "Well, he's done, so we follow them. If anyone needs a rest break, now would be good."

She felt a little pressure, but she wasn't going to drop pants and squat in front of everyone. She'd find somewhere later.

"Permission to uncover, sir? Since Sergeant Barker did?" she asked.

The LT paused to think for a few moments, then said, "Yeah, I don't see why not. Keep your helmets handy, and armor on."

Arriving at the village was neither the huge production Sean Elliott worried it might be, nor the complete nonissue he hoped. Children came running out, shouting, then some adults. The rest waited.

Led by the hunters, they strode in. The terrain was not very defensible against animals. The huts had doors facing the central fire. There were some midden heaps and obvious workshop arrangements, but no real wall. Wolves could come right in, or bears. They didn't seem afraid of people in this time, but perhaps the fire helped.

The kids were like kids anywhere, dancing around, reaching out hands. *Hey, mister, did you bring us anything?* He wasn't sure what would pass as candy or treats here. He settled for smiling and holding out a hand for them to grasp and rub. Then he had to bat inquisitive fingers away from his weapon and gear. They didn't seem to be trying to take anything, just curious. He felt hands tug at his ruck and had to turn and wave a boy away.

And they reeked of sweat and dead animals. There were flies, too. There hadn't been many up on the ridges. There were here, at least around the guts and other animal processing.

It was apparent that the locals had visitors periodically, and were probably peaceful. They were unafraid of the soldiers, and some of them did no more than look up before returning to work.

The village had perhaps a dozen huts, ranging in size from pup tent to TEMPER tent. Around them, people beat leather on frames, yanked at animal guts, twisted rope, practiced with spears, knit some kind of net, probably for fishing, and lolled about.

It wasn't civilization, but it was human settlement.

A group of four headed their way, shooing people aside. They were presumably some kind of leadership.

They were a good-looking people, tall and straight of stature, almond skin, dark, broad eyes and hair that was tightly curled but not quite afro. At least the men were. The women had plenty of butt, if you went in for that sort of thing, and ponderous breasts. Well, no bras, constantly nursing, that wasn't unreasonable, just unfamiliar. They probably looked like that in modern A-stan, but they wore clothes.

The man in the lead spread his arms in a universal gesture, so

Elliott did the same. They both smiled. The man was a little shorter, grizzled gray and wrinkled, and could be any age, just "old and worn."

Then the man spoke and communication fell apart.

"I don't understand your language."

Looking quizzical, the man spoke again.

"Still don't."

He was patient, but Elliott shook his head and repeated himself until the man shrugged and gestured behind him. A woman had what looked like an animal skin canteen.

"Oglesby, any help?"

"I can't quite repeat the sounds right, but they're saying ak!a, with a click. It sounds a lot like 'aqua.' And they're pointing at what looks like a bag of water."

"Do you think that word is the same?"

"It's a standard word in both PIE and PIA."

"Does that mean yes?"

"Sorry, sir. It means maybe. We're a long fucking time until then, but it's not impossible. A handful of basic words have cognates in a lot of languages. It could also be pure coincidence and a false cognate— sounds similar and similar meaning but from a different origin."

"Anything you can learn helps. We need a pidgin of a hundred words or so, yes?"

"A couple hundred or a thousand is better. Smart people can make it work with a couple of dozen and gestures, but we don't have many gestures in common."

"Do what you can."

"I can point and ask. We'll get nouns first."

Their hosts were starting to look anxious. Bracing himself, Elliott accepted the bag and hefted it. It sloshed. It was the whole skin of some small animal, tied closed and treated into leather. He raised it up, watching his counterpart, who smiled and pantomimed drinking.

It smelled half rotten and tasted earthy, rotten. It wasn't terrible; he'd drunk sulfur and iron laden water that had been as bad, but it wasn't pleasant.

"Good sign," Alexander said. Spencer and Caswell agreed.

Caswell said, "You don't offer hospitality to enemies, and it's a neutral enough gesture. Water isn't something they're likely to consider overly valuable, this close to the river."

"Well, good, because it's almost vile." He handed it back and smiled. "Thank you," he said. Then he pulled a sip from his Camelbak. It was a lot fresher.

They all stood around, and the native examined them. Sean politely but firmly blocked hands from his weapon and pockets. They didn't seem to have pockets, and the idea of a pouch on clothing delighted them. One was in his thigh pockets, and he had to dance around to dissuade them. They were amused.

The chief still looked puzzled, and waved for them to follow. He paired back up with Oglesby, which he realized was a good choice, translator and commander. He checked the others had also paired, nodded, and walked across the village to the southwest side.

Regina Alexander looked around. Their houses were fairly sophisticated. They had a rock wall about two feet high at the base, then arched and lashed limbs covered with hides. Some were almost longhouses, around thirty feet by ten, about the size of an old GP medium tent. Several were close to being tepees. They were painted with geometric and anthropomorphic designs in medium earth tones including an obvious fish and elk. She wanted photos of those, but wasn't sure how they'd react to her pointing a camera. They'd probably have no idea what she was doing, but . . .

Everyone was dirty. Mud, blood, animal guts, tree sap, dust, debris from the leaves and branches covered them in layers. Two of the dirtiest were washing in the river, down an embankment to a stony beach.

The Paleo people looked almost Caucasian, almost East Indian, but had kinked hair, not straight. All the men had scraggly beards, which wouldn't compare to the coarse, full beards the soldiers were getting in a hurry. Most had dreadlocks. Some women did, too, though others had cropped tresses. A few of the men had shorn patterns in their hair. They all wore breechcloths. They didn't have much body hair.

And they were all tall. The women were six foot, the men taller. The twelve-year-olds running around were as tall as she. Or they might be younger than twelve.

They had a lot of kids, and they nursed well into walking age. The women's breasts sagged, and had long, chewed nipples. Most women had stretch marks and hollows or sags. She'd avoided that with plenty of exercise and a considerable amount of technology.

They did have all or most of their teeth, however, and those were generally quite straight. They had large jaws and plenty of room for the teeth. It occurred to her that mutations to the contrary would likely not do well, until agriculture and modern technology came along. In that regard, modern people had devolved.

They were friendly. They were too friendly. They approached her, hands out to touch, and the smell was revolting. They didn't bathe enough, couldn't wash off the animal refuse, and it all turned into a disgusting stench that rolled past her. And those dreadlocks were sickening.

She stepped back and against Spencer, and held out a hand.

That gesture seemed to work. They drew back.

Friendly was good, she reflected, but it was possible to be too friendly. They obviously didn't fight much. They had no sense of a comfort zone.

Trinidad, the Navy intel guy, said, "Okay, those two are in charge. Everyone else looks toward them."

Spencer said, "We need more words."

Oglesby said, "I'll work on it. So far, I have water, hut, ground, I think I have man and woman, spear, baby and fire." He was scribbling in a notebook as he went.

"Good start."

The two leaders came over and waved, an obvious "come on" gesture. She looked at Spencer, who nodded, and they followed, as did the others. Another of the Paleos, a woman stepped in to lead them to a hut.

They were being shown to one of the larger lodges. Ten troops could sleep in a GP small if they had to. This was almost twice that, so there was plenty of room for people and gear.

It was marginally more comfortable than it had first appeared. The floor was dirt, but packed. There were raised beds along the sides, of turfs and moss and tree cuttings. There were three hearths. There were several baskets and other containers.

Their host laid hands on the beds and seemed to describe their comfort. She pointed at the baskets. She pointed at firewood and charcoal left near the hearths, and the smoke holes above. Then she waved them back outside.

They gathered just out front, and Gina was really glad for a buddy. Spencer seemed like a decent guy, very smart, and able to help the lieutenant keep on track. With him and with her rifle, she felt safe enough. But it was close to sunset and would be dark soon. She really wanted company.

Spencer said, "It's a small enough camp. Ortiz, can you and Trinidad stay with grounded gear . . . here?" he pointed at a spot between the central fire and the large hut.

"Hooah."

"Thank you," she said, and gratefully shrugged out of the straps. She pulled her camera bag back onto a shoulder, and popped her armor open at the hips and neck. That helped. Even a light ruck was half her body weight.

Elliott was glad of the hospitality. It wasn't that necessary, but it was a good thing to be on friendly terms with potential neighbors. He'd already decided they wouldn't be staying in this village for long.

The chief and his assistants were joined by two more women. He took the first by the hand, and brought her toward Elliott. There was a stifled giggle behind him. Yes, it was hilarious to see them try to gift him with a concubine or wife, but there were complications.

"Sergeant Spencer, I need help fast." He noticed there was a bit of a crowd gathered at a distance. There were long shadows, too. It was evening.

"Yes, sir, stand by. Follow my lead."

Spencer stood in front of him, waved a disapproving finger, and pointed at the sun.

"The sun god would not approve, sir. As your Holy Man, I must advise against this. Corporal Dalton, you come advise us also, and both women."

Alexander joined the huddle, then the younger two. Alexander asked, "What exactly are we doing?"

Spencer said, "Faking a religion so we don't upset our own people, and using it to justify refusing hospitality. Let's hope it works."

"Please," Elliott said. "I'd rather not get involved with the locals." He didn't want to be party to some treaty sealed with sex. Or any contact if he could avoid it.

Dalton said, "Yeah, you'd want her bathed before being brought to your hovel. And shaved." He smiled slightly at the joke.

Caswell rolled her eyes and muttered.

"So what's your plan?"

Still waving his hands flamboyantly, he said, "Well, the two senior couples and your Holy Man advise against carnal contact. Now we need to explain it to them. Let's see if I can do this."

Spencer turned to face the chief, and started pointing.

"His most Excellency the sun, lord of all lemurs says we must not engage with females. They are most attractive, and you are most magnanimous a host to extend such hospitality. But now I must step back and make distance. I will pour a measure of aqua into my hand and drink, and I will offer you the same."

That was utterly bizarre, but the chief was distracted by the splash of water from the Camelbak straw into Spencer's hand, and extended his own hand when offered. He licked at the water, then drank off his hand and grinned broadly.

"Ak!a arluee."

Spencer stepped back another step, faced the sun, bowed his head and opened his hands. He then crossed them on his shoulders and stepped back.

The chief seemed confused, and went into a huddle with his own advisers. There was some back and forth, and obvious agitation that didn't seem angry. The shrugs were universal.

The women seemed a bit miffed at being rejected. They apparently liked the idea of exotic strangers for bed.

Another woman, a girl, a young man and a teen boy brought over food. The woman had a twig basket of berries with some dried plant pods. The man had most of a smoked kid. The teen had two roasted rabbits, and the girl had a leather skin that held nuts and a pile of what appeared to be fried grubs.

Elliott asked, "Spencer, what do we do?"

"To be polite, try the grubs and decline with a bow or something. We eat the rest. If you want to avoid them entirely, I'll make another petition to the Sun Lemur."

"Yeah, I guess I'm the officer." He reached in and grabbed a couple of the crunchier looking grubs. Making sure his Camelbak straw was ready, he tossed them into his mouth and chewed.

They weren't the worst thing he'd ever tasted. Actually, he could probably eat them if he had to.

He took a swig of water and swished it while bowing, then reached for an apple. It didn't seem to have any resident pests, but it wasn't in great shape, having been pecked and chewed. He found a side that looked reasonably clear, and bit into it.

"Mmm. Nom." He smiled and nodded slightly. That was understood to be affirmative.

Behind him he heard, "Hey, sir . . ."

He turned to see Devereaux flanked by a bevy of women, and Barker looking frazzled. They had hold of Devereaux's hands and were examining his burnt-coffee skin. Barker obviously wasn't going to hit them, and didn't really have any other options, so he just stayed close to his buddy.

Spencer high-stepped over, hands on shoulders, and made another pronouncement to the Sun Lemur. More splashes of water went around to the Paleo women and to Devereaux.

The Paleos were persuaded that the soldiers were not going to be available for whatever trade rituals they had in mind.

"Can you explain to me, Sergeant Spencer?" he asked.

"I think Caswell has the info on that."

He turned to her, and she said, "Sir, it's common to be exogamous. They're a small band. If they understand reproduction, they want outside genes. It's also considered polite in many to offer companionship, especially if it might be cold at night, which winter here is, even if summer isn't. And they seem fascinated by Devereaux's skin and my hair." She'd removed her helmet, too, and her copper hair was a tangled pile. "I don't think either is common, since they all appear to be sort of south Asian with dark hair."

"We don't look like them, either."

"No, but they've probably seen albinos, and may have seen proto-Europeans. And your facial structures aren't that far off."

Devereaux said, "I don't mind the attention, but yeah, they need some better sanitation."

Spencer said, "Well, we have food, we appear to have shelter. Now we need to figure something we can give them in return, and some way to swap information."

Oglesby said, "I'm still working on nouns, making notes as I go."

Trinidad spoke. "For exchange, we have some big knives and a couple of machetes. We could cut some brush for them."

"I'm not sure we should show them modern tools."

Caswell said, "Sir, they'll figure it out soon enough if they watch us, unless we never plan to use them. And we have to have something to offer."

"Yeah. Okay. Well, let's ask about that large pile of limbs over there."

It was like being in some native village in Africa. Except even in remotest Africa they would know about steel, usually about cell phones, and have some way of communicating, even if it was pidgin French or Arabic.

Oglesby was able to get across the point of chopping brush, and got an agreement. Barker, Trinidad and Spencer pulled out machetes and started chopping. The rest gathered by their gear.

The Paleos looked on. They clapped, giggled in amazement, and generally got in the way. They seemed a lot less concerned about cutting safety than anyone in the modern world. Twice Barker had to turn his back and block young men from touching the notches he was chopping.

Trinidad did better. He seemed to almost dance around, and was definitely the go-to guy with a machete. He took long, lazy swings that ended in a wrist snap that would sever right through a branch.

Spencer almost took off someone's finger, then gave up, moved back, and tried to act as warden.

It took only a few minutes to reduce the pile to neatly stacked kindling and fuel. Elliott wasn't sure how the natives did it, other than by breaking off what they needed. Perhaps by scoring with flint tools? Although the sticks in the fire were scorched at both ends, so maybe they just burned big chunks into smaller chunks.

In the meantime, he noticed something else. They were very friendly people.

"Sergeant Caswell, are they . . ." he had no idea how to ask.

"Yes, they're very intimate within the group."

That they were. They touched each other frequently, including intimate areas—buttocks and breasts, but occasionally groins. They kissed in passing. They leaned foreheads against each other. One younger couple in a tight embrace were shooed along with laughs and shouts that clearly meant, "Get a tent!"

No, the soldiers would not be comfortable here. They needed a bit of food, and a guide if possible, and information on where they could settle without disturbing this group or neighbors.

It seemed as if the lodge was theirs to use. The chief wandered off with two of the women. His advisor or deputy went back to wherever he'd come from, and the adults largely dispersed to their chores. They were obviously watching, but not that intently.

Caswell said, "The strangers have food, water, shelter and don't need company. Without a language there's little more to be done."

"Good sign?"

"I'd say so. They've extended hospitality, don't seem offended, and don't regard us as a threat. This doesn't mean that can't change after they talk to some shaman or other, but on the whole it's positive."

"Okay, then let's check into the hotel," he said. He grabbed his ruck and carried it in.

The lodge wasn't bad. The overhead was low; he couldn't get above a crouch. But it seemed to have a good roof of hides over sticks. The walls were hides that could be flapped open for light or breeze, in two layers. That was pretty impressive.

On the other hand, it wasn't symmetrical in either height or base. They'd just sort of thrown it together. But then, without measurements, shape didn't really matter.

Spencer echoed him. "They care a lot less about symmetry than we do."

"I'm wondering what else they do in here. You don't build a lodge unless you expect to use it."

Devereaux said, "Cold winters, maybe? With all three hearths burning low and everyone stuffed in, it would be quite warm."

"That does make sense. People want privacy within the family when they can."

Caswell said, "Some Inuit do something similar. But I wouldn't bet on a lot of privacy. And the attention," she took a deep breath, "is creeping me out. Badly."

"You don't like being an object of worship?" Dalton asked with a smile.

It was the wrong thing to say.

"No, I don't like being an object of 'worship' when the only worship they have in mind is to gangbang me for hours, based on a very shallow characteristic. They've been grabbing and stroking my hair, trying to fondle me through armor, and violating every personal boundary I have. I get that it's a system that works for them. It doesn't work for me. They're filthy, nasty, and very direct, and honestly, most modern men aren't any different, they just have a slightly more refined approach. Don't think I haven't seen your glances."

Spencer cut in with, "What can we do to help you with that?"

She sighed and shook her head. "I don't know. But I hate it." She turned away, trembling.

Elliott was sympathetic. Despite her gruff exterior, she was rather vulnerable, and the culture here was partly familiar, partly alien. The thought of mating with any of these people was revolting, and they had been all over her. Over both women, actually, and over Devereaux.

Being here was an admission they weren't going home. That made it that much tougher. These were the neighbors they had, at least for the moment.

They stacked arms, laid out bedding, and set gear.

Elliott said, "We'll need more water."

"I don't think they'll stop us going to the river."

"Good. Oglesby, you want to talk to them more. Barker, please go with him, fill the cooler."

"Can do."

They had met the natives. The natives were friendly. He really wasn't sure what was next.

Ortiz said, "These beds are pretty simple. Looks like they used turf and moss, and just kept filling in as needed."

Caswell said, "They probably sleep using animal hides, above and below. That will provide some cushion. They seem to have shaped them like a bivvy hole."

He nodded. "Yeah, I see hip and shoulder hollows. I guess they'll work."

Trinidad said, "More comfortable than the truck. Especially for you tall guys."

"No doubt about that," Dalton agreed.

Spencer rubbed his chin. "I really need a shave, and I wonder how long our razors will last."

Elliott said, "Yeah, the locals are scruffy, but not heavily bearded. I have a rotary razor, works on a gyroscope. I'm willing to share as long as it lasts. After that, we have blades until they run out, then we sharpen a small knife, I guess."

Devereaux asked, "We're not going to grow them out like Special Forces?"

Elliott grinned, but said, "I'd rather not. We want to maintain our appearance so we retain our identity. We're not cave men. We're U.S. Army Soldiers."

Trinidad said, "And a Squid and an Airedale."

Elliott said, "Yes, we're a multiservice force, but I'm standardizing. And I appreciate the broad skill sets everyone is bringing. You're all going to be necessary. And tonight, something I should have done already, I need to know everything you all know that might matter."

The entrance flapped open and Barker came through, hefting a full cooler in his hands.

"I took the water off the top, upstream from any disturbance. I skimmed off some surface crud with a handful of cattail leaves. It's as potable as we're going to find around here."

"Good. Thanks much."

"No problem. If it's okay, I'm going to change to PT shoes." He indicated sodden boots and wet pant legs. They were dripping into the packed ground.

"Go for it."

Barker got dry and changed. Dalton asked, "Should we see about lighting fires? Do we need to?"

"It is getting dark fast." He noticed it now. Everything was gray, and the chill was becoming damp.

A call from outside got their attention.

The apparent chief stood near the fire, and it was built higher. Flames offered some illumination. He was waving and obviously saying something along the lines of "Come!" or "Gather!" Elliott motioned for the others to follow.

"Dalton, load and keep an eye on the gear," he ordered.

"Hooah, sir."

There were stones and logs around the fire, and a couple of piles of something covered in hide. It was cool, but the Paleos seemed unbothered. He found a smooth stone, probably pulled from the river, though it might be glacial, and sat. It was uneven and cold under his butt, but it was better than the ground.

With a big grin and broad gestures, the headman told a tale. Even without knowing the language, the presentation was obvious.

Elliott listened intently, knowing he'd never understand a word, but it was a beautiful language. It was tonal, singsong, with clicks and nasals and whistles in among the common vowel and consonant sounds. It didn't seem to have a lot of words, but there was broad variety in their expression.

The audience responded, but it wasn't formal. They talked, pointed, joked. The leader made his way around, eventually reaching the soldiers.

He put out a hand and patted Elliott on the head, then motioned him to come to the center.

Sighing slightly, Elliott stood. He had no idea what this was about, but he'd follow for now.

He was expected to speak. Everyone watched him, intently and patiently, and the leader opened his hands and stepped back.

"Okay, well, I don't speak your language, so I'm going to use mine," he said. "I hope you'll show me the same courtesy I showed you. Because I really can't do anything else."

A couple of his troops chuckled.

"We come from a long way away and a long time away, so far we couldn't describe to you even if we did know your language. We're lost, we're short on resources, and we're very grateful for your hospitality. You don't seem scared, and that's good. You've offered far more than we need, which we declined with gracious thanks.

"I wish we could stay, but we're too different as groups. So I'm hoping we can make our needs known in a short time, for a guide and a place to settle. I hope we'll be good neighbors, because we are few, but so much stronger than you can imagine. So let's be friends.

"And even though we're new here, we will make ourselves comfortable, and hopefully learn a little from you, while teaching you a lot about the future. But either way, we plan to make it work. There are only ten of us, but we have broad knowledge and skills, and we're American Soldiers. We do not accept defeat, even in the harshest of conditions. Thank you."

He bowed slightly and stepped back out of the light.

There were "Hooah!"s, a couple of cheers and a whistle from his troops. He blushed. He hadn't really intended to give a pep talk, just fill some time as his counterpart had. But if it worked, it worked. It was hardly the greatest commander's speech ever, though it might be the best for fifteen thousand years. Or ten, at least.

The dark was less enclosing with the fire. Behind them was a curtain of black. The fire was home. He'd found that in Boy Scouts, and felt it that much more strongly now.

The chief led some odd cheering that was half whistles, half whoops and half laughs. It didn't seem to matter what was said, just that everyone shared the fire and was hospitable.

A woman started singing. It was soft at first, and repetitive. She reached a modest volume, and others joined in. Shortly, it was a long, sonorous unison chant.

The troops sat politely, listening as the Paleos added rhythms with sticks, claps, shuffles and stomps. It had a very simple beat, and Elliott had no idea what it was supposed to express.

People wandered away bit by bit, going to their huts. Elliott waited until about half had left, then said, "Us too, soldiers. Rack out."

They rose and headed for their assigned hall, and Oglesby turned his light on with a dim red filter.

Even that was enough to draw attention, and there were shouts. In a moment they were surrounded by excited, chattering Paleos.

Elliott moved in close to him, and Spencer slipped in along the other side.

"What do I do?" he asked, as jabbering, smelly Stone Agers grabbed at his gear, especially his light.

Spencer asked, "Mini Maglight?"

Oglesby said, "Yeah, the Surefire is too bright. This is my night light." He kept batting hands away.

"Let them have it tonight. They'll run the batteries down and lose interest."

"Can we get it back?" Oglesby sounded worried. Sean didn't blame him.

Spencer said, "Yes. I'll make sure of it."

"I was hoping to use it for a while before they go dead."

"Well, you brought it out, now they've seen it."

"Sorry, I slipped."

Spencer kept his voice moderate, but his tone was urgent. "It's fine. Now give them the goddam light."

Oglesby surrendered it, and someone shouted gleefully, holding it aloft. It did in fact get passed back and forth, shone into people's faces, and then the red lens came off.

"Batteries will last about a day, figure, on that LED bulb."

Spencer waded into the party and emerged with the red lens and rubber cap. He handed them to Oglesby.

"Okay, now we sleep in the dark, unless someone lights a fire."

It was awkward feeling around in the total darkness. Oglesby was near the back, so he made his way by touch to his sleeping bag and kit.

Up front, Spencer said, "I'm here. Alexander was just beyond me. Barker was directly across. Find your buddies and make your way through that way. I think we want a small fire, especially as we'll need a watch anyway."

"I'll build it," Barker said. "Watch needs to stay on the door side of the fire, backs to it, when not tending, so they get illumination of anyone coming in."

Sean checked his sleeping bag wasn't against the side, to avoid condensation. The shaped bed seemed workable, though a bit tall for him. It had hip and shoulder hollows and was lined with a couple of inches of fresh grass. That and the bag should be workable, though he figured he'd be sore in the AM.

Then he realized fatigue was beating on him and he . . .

Bob Barker woke as someone came close. It was Oglesby.

"Your turn on watch, Sergeant."

"Got it. I'm going to roll out to their head."

"Okay."

He wiggled out of his bag, slipped on his boots, and tied them in a hurry, because he *did* need to go.

Outside the lodge was beautiful. It was cool and crisp, the moon was down, and the stars were amazing. With some rest and some nearby people, it was much easier to appreciate them.

But it reinforced that they were fucked and far from home. What in the hell had happened?

There were vague hints of gray in the east, and there was a fire tender watching the camp's fire. Whoever that was looked up, but said nothing, so he ignored them back. Part of him would have liked to socialize, but he was needed on watch, and he couldn't have talked to them anyway.

The locals used just a line of rocks at the west edge to mark the night latrine. He pissed over the line, felt better, and headed back to the hut.

He scratched briefly at the hide on the door, whispered, "Barker," and crawled back in. He made his way cautiously to the fire and around, wished for a jacket, and settled for hunching in close and adding another stick to the coals.

Oglesby said, "Thanks. Nothing happened. See you in two hours." They intended to be up at 0600, but he wasn't sure if the natives would wait that long. He had plans.

He wasn't sure who'd been on with Oglesby, but Caswell was on now.

"Morning," he said, casually.

"Yeah, whatever," she replied, sounding annoyed. Well, it was early in the morning, chilly and they were lost. So he left it at that.

It did feel a lot better to sleep on an actual bed, even if it was field conditions. The truck and the ground had not been pleasant.

There was nothing to do except watch the coals, so he let it become meditation, as the heat shimmers drifted across the broken blocks of scorched sticks. He used a twig to push stray lumps back into the glowing mound. He added occasional fuel, shoved the burned pieces into the middle and marshaled it. There was just enough heat to cut the shiver, and just enough light to show the door.

At 0600, his phone buzzed in his pocket. Others must have, too, because people started stirring.

Caswell said, "I'm hitting the latrine now, before the rest do."

"Go."

The locals were casual about elimination, and Barker figured he'd probably learn to be, too. A lot of civilized rules were luxuries they weren't going to have here. He had some practice. Now it was real.

"Calm all night," he said. "So we're ready for the day."

Spencer said, "Goddam, I do feel rested. Did I snore?"

"Occasionally. Sounded like a damned diesel."

"Yeah, I do that."

Elliott said, "I'm also good. But don't get too comfortable. Actually, hold on, we'll have formation in here when everyone is back."

When everyone had returned, the LT said, "Okay, we don't have much food, we do have a way to refill water, but it's going to be river water. We're going to try to get information from our hosts and observe them for a day or two tops, then find somewhere to settle ourselves. Pack up all your gear, don't leave it for the curious."

Spencer raised his hand for attention and said, "Not only curiosity, they're going to have very slippery concepts of property. If you're holding it, it's yours. Don't let anything go, it's probably considered sharing or gifting. Be polite but be firm."

Elliott nodded. "I want to leave two or three people in camp, right here, watching anything we've grounded. As Spencer says, polite, firm, shout for backup if needed, be creative on religious rituals, that seems to work. Good thinking, Spencer."

"That's SERE training, sir. From when I was a flight engineer."

"Okay, either way, we use it. Whacking sticks if you must. I don't want any weapon fire unless we're being swarmed."

"What is the plan, sir?" Trinidad asked.

Barker liked what he was hearing now. The LT had definitely come around. That was good.

He said, "I'd like to take two others and see if we can join a hunting or scouting party. Dalton, and Ortiz?"

"You want me to save the animal after you spear it?" Ortiz asked with a grin. He was a vet assistant.

"No, but you'll be able to tell me what their butchering method is like."

"Ah, true. Sure, I'm in."

Elliott said, "Oglesby goes around gathering language and helping translate. Spencer is here, acting as our holy man. The rest of you I'm not sure about yet, just be ready for taskings. When you have time, tell me all those useful things I asked about."

Devereaux said, "I can't stress enough for you to wash hands as best you can. We have a little meat they left us, and some marrow bones, but they're not cooked." He pointed at a pile. "They must be a lot more resistant to bacteria than we are."

Spencer said, "I'll try to convince them we need cooked food. And there's fire, so we can cook our own."

There was movement outside. "Well, I hear them getting up themselves."

Spencer said, "So stick close to the hut for now. Inside and right outside. Let's see what we can do."

Outside, there indeed was a hunting party forming. They had spears, skin bags hanging by leather thongs, and fur capes over their kilts.

Bob walked up, and Ortiz and Oglesby came with him. The apparent hunt leader was the same guy as yesterday, very tall, lean, hair in a sort of dreadlock skunk pattern with shorn areas in between.

"Good morning," he said clearly and cheerfully. "Can we come with you?" he indicated the spear and himself.

It seemed clear enough. The leader smiled.

"We need spears," he said, and indicated it again, and his own empty hands.

There was some singsong shouting and someone came out of a hut, looked, made some kind of gesture, then ran inside and back out with a spear. It was presented to him with some formality, and what seemed to be an admonishment to "Take care of it, it is a good spear."

He nodded and said, "Thank you, I will." He held it up, examined it, and put it over his shoulder as they did.

The spear was interesting. It was cut from a thin sapling, barked, then shaved smooth. The skinny end was down, the fat end carved into a tang and imounted with a thin bone that was held on with pine pitch. The bone was cut and ground at an angle, to give it a point like a syringe. It was probably very effective, and balanced for short-range throwing.

They had a chuckle over Ortiz's 5'6" height, then handed him another spear. It looked as if they got it from one of the youths.

"I thank you for this," he said, as he hefted it for feel.

Good. It was important to treat the locals with respect, and it *was* kind of awesome to be among their tribe, with their handmade tools.

Felix Trinidad hung out with Oglesby. The lieutenant seemed to have missed him completely. For an Intelligence Specialist, that was a feature, not a bug.

In his estimation, these people didn't fight much. The wall around the camp was mostly brush, some rock, and appeared to be a result of clearing the area and throwing away non-waste debris. Sewage went into the latrine pile, or the river in daytime, and waste food went into the river or over the wall to the vermin.

So their sanitation was marginal, and they faced no threats that could cross a two-foot wall.

Likely, the wolves and other large predators didn't like the smell. It was pretty ripe. More so than villages in modern A-stan usually were.

The people were friendly and curious. The chief came over and

Oglesby managed to greet him with some word or other. Then the touching began again.

The girl was probably about twelve, pubescent, and wearing little. The boy wore a minimal breech cloth. Most here wore little. They had kilts and capes for the evening, and he wondered what they did in winter. Their technology was crude. They weren't dressed even as well as poor villagers back home.

No, it was "good enough." It kept them warm, fed and dry. That's all they needed.

He kept gently pushing hands away. They seemed to grasp what his pouches were, and they wanted whatever was inside. He took to adding "No!" as he detached groping fingers, just as he'd say to a child.

That got him thinking about Isabel. His sister's class had been sending regular boxes of treats. Now what? And would he ever see her again?

Eventually they understood, and stayed back about three feet, in a circle. Most were children, but one was an adult male, probably twenty or so, and one female, age indeterminate, but probably no more than twenty-five, if she squeezed out babies regularly.

They were all curious, and cheerful, and didn't seem afraid of anything. Of course, sharpened sticks were about the height of their technology. He did see those spear thrower things primitive people used, but no bows.

He was glad of the people they had. Dalton probably wasn't much good technically, but likely a sturdy fighter, and if he could shoot, he could probably use a bow. The Air Force female, Caswell, knew something about sociology. Barker seemed to know several primitive skills. Spencer had some variety of training. They had a medic and a vet mate. It wasn't many people, though. He was the smallest here, and the Paleos were giants. They were a solid foot taller and broader.

As long as the LT could keep his head, with Spencer advising him, he figured they'd survive, but it was going to be an entire life of field exercise, with no going home.

Which was better than being blown up.

Whatever had sent them here was apparently a fluke, or else was intended as a one-way trip by whoever had done it. It made him angry. A few feet to either side and they'd have been safe. A bit ahead or behind. Why right on top of them?

He assumed it was on purpose, aliens or something wanting to study them.

They better learn what they needed faster than he did. If there was a way home, he was going to find it. Revenge might figure in, too. Felix was very good with a knife.

Ramon Ortiz huffed along. Barker was taller, and these Stone Age bastards had legs like ostriches, and about as skinny, but *goddamn* they could run.

This river wasn't the same as the one in their time. It was younger and more defined, cutting its way through the land. It was edged with trees and had bluffs and rocks.

The ten archeos ran through the growth barefoot, Barker behind and him trailing. There weren't any paths, but it didn't seem to bother them.

He was about to call for a break, because they'd done at least four miles at a serious clip, when they piled to a halt.

That thing was some kind of antelope, sheep, something. It was large, had horns, and was definitely a steak to be. It resembled a saiga, and might be some variant.

The natives spread out quickly, so silently it scared him. Barker sidled up to a tree and looked back, finger to lips. He nodded. He got a tree between himself and it, and stepped up to it quietly.

The beast snuffled along, big, and quite alert. It looked like no breed he knew, but was definitely a bovine.

Then in a moment of action, four spears flew in from four directions, striking it in the neck, thorax twice, and belly. Barker turned just as it gurgled and heaved his spear straight into the throat.

Realizing he was late, he took two steps and threw, his spear sticking into the mid-back, above the intestines. He hoped he hadn't nicked them.

The beast snorted, roared and made as if to charge, head down and pawing at the ground, but it kept pawing as its rear legs collapsed, and in a few moments its pained cries quieted to breathy, blood-foamed baying, and unconsciousness with death imminent if not accomplished.

What happened next shocked and revolted him. The natives swarmed in, carefully drew out the bone-tipped spears, and started lapping blood from the wounds. Okay, he'd heard of that, but watching it was disgusting, even if there weren't potential diseases from raw cow blood.

They waved, obviously wanting him to participate. He panicked.

Barker said, "fake it," and bent over. He came up with blood on his lips and cheeks. Well, Ramon had been covered in worse from animals and people, so okay. He could do it.

There was a warm iron aroma to the blood, which mixed with the scents of hide, dung and dirt.

Their literal bloodlust satisfied, they moved in for some butchery. They weren't bad, but he could do better, so he did.

He needed to be cautious. These guys swung those flint knives around like they were trading cards, swapping between two or three different ones as they cut through hide, meat, tendon. They shouted to each other, joking and poking.

Once situated over the left foreleg, he drew out his Ka-Bar and started cutting. They seemed to understand it was a knife, a lot larger than theirs, and sharp, and didn't get in the way.

"Don't let them get hold of it," Barker said.

"Yeah, they'll keep it."

"Or get hurt, or both."

But the hunters seemed reasonably polite. They let him cut flesh. When he pulled out the saw on his Gerber tool to cut the joint, there were obvious ooh and aah sounds, but still no one got in the way. They seemed to recognize he knew his way around a carcass.

It was exciting, bewildering and creepy to be chopping up a feral cow amongst these people. He kept saying "Africa" to himself, but he knew it wasn't Africa. Even the remotest Africans knew about steel knives. This . . .

He cut through ligament and had the leg loose. He held it up for whoever would take it, and someone did, hefting it like a barbell and shouting in triumph.

He went to work on the next leg, as Barker did one of the rear ones. Then he got filthy and covered in blood and grease hacking open the sternum and working up to the throat.

He was bloodied to the elbows by the time he got the cavity well open, and someone snatched the liver almost before he finished cutting it, the blood vessels discharging a gush of undrained fluid, dark and thick. Then he had the guts cut, and someone took those, draping them over and around his shoulders like a steaming gray snake.

He assumed those would get used as lashing or something. This was creepy.

He had to hack at the head and between the vertebrae. He wondered if they ate brains, and they did so right there, raw and steaming, followed by the eyeballs, and he almost vomited. Someone offered him a handful of gooey, dripping brains and he held up his hands for "no" and crossed himself. He hoped they'd see it as a spiritual gesture and *Madre de Dios*, he needed it.

Barker peeled skin back from muscle, and cut off a section of rib and filet. In a half hour, the entire beast was sectioned up and ready to carry back to the village. He took a full rack of ribs, which the natives apparently considered a low cut, and was quite happy. They could have the organs and brains. Ribs suited him fine. He was drenched in blood, goo, ichor and a little bit of shit. He hoped the troops appreciated the food. He'd worked for it.

Ashmi Wise didn't know what to make of the visitors.

They had two women and eight men, so they acted like a hunting party, not settlers. Settlers would be couples with children. But they had no spears. They worked eagerly, but mostly at camp chores, like the old and young. They politely refused comfort. They wore lots of fancy robes and carried many items, so they were wealthy. They had at least two leaders and two shamans. They spoke no words.

"They must be from very far away not to know any words," he said to Kotlra Far Eye, who squatted in front of him at his hut.

Kotlra said, "I think so. Brali!kny's Band is a Moon west, by the Cold Sea, and they speak words. The visitors' speaker shaman says they are from the far west, even farther than that, two hands of that distance."

"That is a long walk. How long have they been walking?"

"I couldn't understand. He does not yet have enough words. They are not like those other people we saw."

"No. They had finely crafted sticks and stones, and small wolves."

"These have no sticks, but very fine items." Kotlra pointed at the ones in sight, wearing lots of nice-nice things.

Ashmi said, "I wonder what the items are. They don't like to touch or share."

"They are strange, but friendly, but also rude." Kotlra stood and stretched.

"But they have items, yet seem poor. No spears. No dried food. Yet they have nice-nice bedding."

Kotlra nodded, "It looked like rolled up hides, of very soft leather."

"Yes. No one has seen anything like it."

"They are short and pale, as if ill. But they are not ill. They all have the same short hair, as if they have no need to style."

Ashmi said, "The women are beautiful. Even if pale. The one has the red hair the ancient ones were said to have. I would like to see her shape under the robes." He gestured with his hands. "I think she is juicy." He would need to ask his longest mate about the new woman.

"She is," Kotlra grinned. The one man has very dark skin, and then two look almost normal, but even smaller than the rest."

"It is as if they are not the same people. They don't even look like people, really." People came in all sizes and shades, but not anything like these. They almost looked ill, but were very healthy and well fed.

"Tell me again about their camp," Ashmi asked. He turned a bit to get the sun out of his eyes.

Kotlra pointed and signed. "It is east, not west, a quarter-morning hike. Their lodges looked like great insects, standing on legs. I could see underneath and through them. The sides opened like wings and they climbed inside. They are taller than our lodges, but about as long and wide. They had two."

"What were they made of?"

"I don't know. They looked like stone. But they were too big to have been moved."

Curious. "Strange. Could you guess when they were built?"

"I don't know. How is the one doing with his words?"

"He learns fast, and makes marks on something like bark with leaves in it." Ashmi had been impressed. The marks were not painting, but meant something.

"What else has he said?"

"I couldn't say the leader's name, it is silly sounding. He is titled Ell Tee. That means a leader of a band."

"What is the speaker shaman's name?"

"He is Dan Who Knows Speaking. But he doesn't know much speaking. He is learning."

Kotlra pointed, "Here he comes, with Ell Tee."

"Greetings, Dan Knows Speaking and Ell Tee."

The visitor replied, "Greetings, Ashmi and Kotlra. We have water."

"Yes. Your water skins are nice clever. You should give us one."

"Our spirit, the Sun Animal, refuse."

"You should pray to him more, or find a better spirit." Why would they pray to a spirit who wouldn't help them?

"We work more? Wood, stone, hide, water?"

Why would they want to work so much? They were not children or old. There were two hunting, that was good.

"No work for now. All is done. Who is the female with fire hair?" He had to point and shrug to be understood.

Dan Who Knows Speaking gave a name that sounded silly, and then said, "She is Jenny Who Leads . . . no word."

"Tell about the word."

"Fix . . . trouble . . . people."

Trouble-fixer was a silly saying. "She is also a shaman?"

"No. People, trouble, hit, stop them." He demonstrated a punch and a grab.

"Why you stop fighting when they have problem must fix?"

The short man shrugged. "Jenny Who Leads Fighting."

"Why she lead fighting if she stop fighting? You make no sense."

"Words behind words . . . broken."

"You make no sense," Ashmi told him.

Dan shrugged again.

"How your people trade mates?" Ashmi made a hugging gesture.

"No, no, Jenny not . . . mate?"

"Why not female mate?"

"Her spirit, no."

"Your spirits very trouble. You want find others. Who is other female?"

"Regina Leads . . ." he made motions of drawing.

"Marking?"

"Yes. Regina Leads Marking."

"How many seasons is she?"

"Seasons? Sun?" he waved his hand along the sun's path.

"Yes, sun turns. Nine seasons."

"Sun turns, she," he held up fingers. Ten and ten and ten and ten and five.

"How many?"

The visitor repeated his hands.

"Four tens and five?" He repeated it back. That was also silly. She was a young woman, her face was smooth, her shape was juicy.

"Yes."

"You mean seasons, not turns."

"No, four tens and five turns."

"She can't be that old. Perhaps two tens five?"

"No, four tens and five."

"She also has no mate?"

"She has mate. Home."

"Home is very far?" he asked.

"Yes."

"She can mate here also."

"No. None mate here."

They were very upsetting. Fit men, unusual women, nice-nice items, but they refused to share anything, only offer simple work.

He couldn't make them trade and swap. That would be rude. But they were rude.

Kotlra asked, "When will you move on?" Good. Yes. If they didn't want to trade they should go away.

"Two-three days. Four?" he waved his hands flat, which seemed to indicate that was the longest.

Well, they could tolerate these strange people for four days.

He said, "Other visitors here four days. Less strange."

Kotlra said, "I will talk to Jenny Who Leads Fighting myself."

Sean Elliott was trying to track everything going on around him. Oglesby said, "Sir, did you get that?"

He said, "I think so. He wants to flirt with Caswell." That had the potential to be bad.

"I think he means more than flirting, but I don't think he will be violent."

"Hopefully. Caswell!" he called. She was in front of their lodge, with children watching her from a distance.

"Sir?" she turned and looked, and saw Kotlra heading her way.

"He wants to proposition you. Please be gentle with him."

"Understood, sir. He doesn't know better."

"Very gentle. We need a couple more days." He wasn't sure how to diplomatically ask her not to clobber the poor savage, when she had a right to by her standards, and was vocal about it.

"I'll try, sir, but there are lines I am not going to cross." She sounded firm, bordering on angry.

"Of course. I don't want you to violate your rules, just don't hurt him if you can avoid it, and keep it minimal."

"Will do, sir."

Kotlra had reached her, and was smiling, hands open. He stepped closer, and she turned slightly, to use her shoulder as a block.

Oglesby said, "Ah, Caswell, they, uh, do it from behind." He sounded embarrassed even mentioning it.

She nodded, and faced back, just as Kotlra reached out and caressed her. All he got was body armor, but she visibly tensed.

He stepped back.

But he resumed, with cooing sounds, and reached out again.

She deflected his hand and said, "Nooo!" as if to a child.

He looked dejected, shrugged, and walked away.

Hopefully that was the end of that. But there were a lot of apparently single men, or mated men with open slots for more women.

Oglesby said, "I told them four days tops, sir."

"Yeah, let's keep that promise."

"He mentioned some other visitors here for four days. It seems to be a good amount of time. Enough to rest, hunt, resupply, and move on."

"Makes sense. We'll stick to that, too."

Alexander had her camera out. It wasn't bothering the natives, probably because they had no idea at all what it was. He agreed with her idea. The more information they had, the better. Another local male approached her.

She was bent in a half squat, and she had a pretty good shape from that side, for an older woman, muscular and rounded. The local saw it, too, and had his hands free for action. And these people liked to touch and grope even in friendship.

Elliot was about to open his mouth, but the hand was already extended.

It never touched her. She shifted aside, turned, caught his wrist, said, "No!" sharply and shoved it aside hard enough he staggered a step. Whatever martial art she knew, she was decent.

Well, at least the locals were picking up that word, which wasn't dissimilar from their "*Ni.*"

Off in the distance were shouts, and the hunting party appeared through the woods. They carried large chunks of something dead.

"Antelope!" Ortiz shouted. "A big one." He fairly staggered under a rack of ribs, and the others carried . . . good God.

Watching them process the chunked animal was impressive, and revolting. They squeezed out the guts, leaving a pile of shit near the water's edge. Then one of them shoved a hand inside, grabbed, pulled, and started turning them inside out.

"Sausage casings and water bags," Barker said behind him. "Possibly gut rope as well."

"It smells like blood and shit, and . . . rotten meat."

"Yeah, that it does. We'll be doing that for sausage casings and bowstrings. They like Ortiz. He sectioned it pretty thoroughly."

"I've seen this animal before," Elliot said. He kept tight control of his stomach and watched only the parts he could handle. It was unnerving to see so many guts laid out.

Barker said, "Saiga, I think."

"How do they taste?"

Barker shrugged. "Like cow or venison, I guess."

Ortiz knew how to help the cooks, who used a chunk of mostly clean rawhide as a prep area. Barker joined them, and Caswell and Alexander showed up with some wild onions.

Caswell said, "We'll need to stay in touch to find edible plants, sir," she said. "But these are good."

They looked like tiny onions with big scallions on top, and likely were, but had a bit of garlic scent.

"Oh, shit, they have salt!" Spencer shouted. "God, yes, we need salt, eating, preparing hides, industrial use. We need that info. And it's possible they'll have coal."

Trinidad asked, "Heating for winter?"

"No, I'm going to build a forge."

"Hah. Do you know how?"

"Yes. I do."

"Oh . . . excellent."

That was good news, Sean thought cheerfully. A forge? Iron tools would make this a lot easier. The trucks only had a few.

The carcass bits got salted and herbed and cooked into an orgy of meat. Some was roasted, some grilled right on the coals, some on hot rocks, some in a depression in a hide, as a stew heated with rocks. That contained the blood, marrow bones and some of the organs. It looked revolting and didn't smell much better. Elliott hoped to avoid that and eat the steaklike bits.

Other parts were completely wrapped in salt-filled leaves, probably for preservation.

Barker brought over a twig skewer of juicy meat, about medium, hot, and handed it over.

"Thank you," Elliott said. He took it, blew on it, and cautiously bit. That did not suck.

It was steak. It was tough and chewy, but it was definitely steak, and a decent cut. The blood, salt, fat and bits of herb made it into something quite enjoyable, even if it was a chore to chew.

Spencer had an MRE package discreetly open. One of the side items, not an entrée.

"Ah, shit," he said.

"Spencer?"

"Yeah." He held up the package.

In the dim light, Elliott could make out, PATRIOTIC SUGAR COOKIES. Yeah, those things, shaped like little Statues of Liberty, flags and other stuff. The last thing anyone needed to see right now.

"Should I share them? I like sugar, but goddamn."

"Uh, is it safe?"

"Small amount of sugar and starch. They'll like it a lot. Shouldn't cause any problems in small quantities."

"Go ahead." He wanted the packet himself, but understood Spencer needed to get rid of it, and this would help with diplomacy.

Spencer said, "Hey!" and motioned the chief. He pantomimed food to mouth and handed one over.

The chief took it, nibbled, and got wide eyed. Then he made "mmm" sounds.

In a few minutes, each of the main hunters, several senior females and the shaman had one each. He broke the rest into pieces and made sure each child got a nibble.

"Now they won't leave me alone," he said. "All gone." He shook the empty package, wadded it up, and stuffed it in a case on his armor.

There was no formal fireside chat this night. The locals weren't hostile, but were cool and uninterested. Apparently, romps with passersby and gifts of stuff were how their culture worked.

"Oh, yuck," Ortiz said.

He looked over. A woman with a toddler looked like she was kissing the child. She was. Open mouthed. He was about to utter something himself when she pulled back.

Caswell said, "Pre-chewed food."

"Uh, I guess that makes sense, but is that common?"

"I don't think I've heard of it in our time, but I've heard of it."

Wow. That was messed up.

Caswell echoed his earlier thoughts. "I mentioned exogamy, and trading gifts is a staple in most cultures that have anything. You notice they don't really seem to have a concept of personal property, beyond which hut they choose and a favorite spear or bag. They share tools, the fire, each other."

"It sounds very socialist."

"It is, but not in a bad way. The problem comes when someone decides to stake out more material for themselves, and justify it."

Spencer said, "As they will. I notice the chief has access to most of the women, even as trade goods."

"They're not property," she argued. "They're willing, because they're not seen as property. It doesn't last, but it needs to."

"Not our problem."

Barker said, "LT, I have an idea on an offering."

"Go ahead?"

"If we can get a bird, I can fletch some darts for them. They have spear throwers, but not bows. Their darts have a bit of fluff at the back for stability, but that also slows them down. Feathered darts won't be much of an advantage, but will be an improvement."

He thought about it. Hospitality, yes. But giving them a new technology seemed risky.

"I'm worried about affects to the timeline that might make our odds of getting back even worse."

"I agree," Spencer said.

Devereaux said, "I worry about staying alive now."

"Yeah, really, how do we hide two MRAPs in the layers?" Alexander asked. "Do we slowly scrape the metal down with rocks?"

Trinidad said, "What about guns? Do we never use them to hunt? Do we take native women? Or spend the next fifty years squatting in a cave like hermits and jacking off?"

Everyone was scared, and so was he, and he understood it.

"Okay, Barker, do it."

The voices continued.

"At Ease!" he snapped. "I said 'At Ease'!"

They quieted down.

"Our hosts are staring at us. Oglesby, say something polite, we're going to bed. You can all sit in the dark and meditate on this."

Spencer said, "Oh, I got the MagLight back. Batteries dead. They're uninterested anymore. I think they're also disappointed. So, Barker, definitely do those darts."

A sudden stabbing pain caught Sean low in the guts, overlaid with a punching sensation.

"And here come the shits," he said, as he ran for the wall, pulling at his belt.

Oh, god, it hurt. He could feel it percolating, boiling in his belly. Sweat burst out as he pulled at his pants and twisted to get his ass over the wall.

The eruption was hot, sulfurous liquid that burned like acid. It splashed off the rocks, onto his pants, shirt, balls and thighs.

He had only a moment to wince at how disgusting it was before round two spewed out. Then he realized he was sitting on a wall used by God knew how many other people, and pissed on, and . . .

Devereaux was standing a few feet away. He didn't need a fucking audience.

The third bout caused his stomach to flop, but he felt mostly empty, wrapped in cool darkness. He gasped, panted, and clutched at his belly. He felt nauseated, pained, dizzy. He wanted it to stop.

Devereaux handed over something white.

"Bleach wipe, sir." He sounded completely calm and professional, and Sean appreciated it.

"Yeah. I need regular paper first. A lot of it."

"Here." The medic handed him a roll. He tried to be frugal, but his hands were smeared with liquid shit in short order, and he used a third of a roll, then the bleach wipe on his balls and hands.

Devereaux asked, "Do you have spare clothes?"

"One uniform. Glad I did." He'd have to wash this one, and clean his hands again, and bathe.

"Okay. Can you walk?"

"Yes. I'll change in the tent."

He eased forward and upright, and waddled toward their lodge.

He did not feel particularly welcome to the Stone Age.

Jenny Caswell was scared.

It wasn't being in the Stone Age, but that was scary enough.

She was suddenly the prize woman in the world. The natives hadn't seen anyone like her, and her hair set them off. To the Americans, she was young, female, and that was enough, even if she wasn't as well developed as Alexander, and she was at risk, too. The local men wanted an exotic mate, her teammates wanted someone clean and familiar. There were eight men, and a lot of men, and only two women with the exotic looks, and Alexander just seemed to disappear into the crowd. Looks had nothing to do with it. Presence was all it took. She was present.

At some point, she expected to be raped, possibly gang raped. Not within a week, but after a month or more, one of these men, or a pair, were going to decide she was their property. The LT might stop them. Spencer wouldn't. She knew that look when she saw it.

She couldn't live alone, and there was no way to partner up with any one of the men; that would just lead to fights and stupid male dominance shit. It was a patriarchy in microcosm.

Alexander would be second, but either way, both of them were going to be sexually assaulted, and spend a lifetime as effective sex slaves.

The only other option was to find some native man and move into this village, or another. And while they were well-built, no way. They stank, they were uninteresting socially or intellectually. She might study them as a thesis. She would not involve with any of them.

And there was no birth control. She'd be pregnant, and delivering Stone Age babies. She hadn't ruled out childbirth, but it was definitely a "later" thing. Now it was a "now" thing.

She sat back to the fire, hunched in on herself. She'd taken first watch because she wasn't able to sleep.

A worse thought was that she might acquiesce to being nothing but a sex toy, rather than fight it, or let the men fight over it. There was no moral persuasion she could use, no chain of command other than a very flaky LT, who was a potential threat, and a senior NCO who was a bigger potential threat.

She was not suicidal, but there was the possibility that her death would prevent a number of social battles that could kill the others. She didn't want to go there. She could imagine that a couple of the men might, if they didn't get what they wanted.

Spencer was on duty next to her. He evidently saw her tension, because he whispered, "Things alright? Anything you need to talk about?"

"No."

"I think you mean, 'yes, but not now,'" he replied. "I'm here if you need. Or let me know if you need someone else."

"No one can help," she said.

"Yeah, I know," he agreed. He probably assumed she meant being lost, and that was true, too. She might discuss this with Alexander. In fact, she needed to. Spencer, though, needed to be kept at whatever emotional distance she could manage.

She noticed something and said, "Huh."

"What?" Spencer asked.

She pointed to an item on the rock ledge of one wall. "Hollowed out stone with moss."

"Oil lamp?" he asked.

"I think so."

In a few moments, they had it on the hearth and lit. It burned with a sputtering, low flame with a lot of blue under the bright, but it easily doubled the available glow to that of a good nightlight.

"It's clay," she said as she saw it better. "Unfired ceramic."

Spencer said, "They're so good at some things, so clueless about others."

She said, "I think they say exactly the same about us."

"You're probably correct."

He probably didn't even understand the risk he posed, from that position of privilege.

She did.

CHAPTER 6

Felix Trinidad couldn't shut his observations off. They were down at the beach on the river to get clean. They'd all had diarrhea, all their clothes were at least sweat-crusted, and they were sticky, slimy messes under their uniforms. They'd changed socks daily, because Doc insisted, and underwear twice. They were still out of clean clothes. There wasn't even any way to air them out in the sun, with grabby native hands all around.

They had a couple of bars of soap, and cold water. It was better than some COBs, much better than some places in the PI, and he felt a lot better after a cold splash, a soaping and a cold rinse. He ignored the naked men around him easily, though some of the urbanites were more tense than he was, and he felt that. The water was too shallow for modesty. It wasn't great for shaving, either, but his face itched terribly. When he was done scraping, it burned and stung.

Farther out the river was deeper, and quite broad. Not as big as the Mississippi, but maybe the Mindanao, but younger and faster. He wondered if the natives crossed it or if it was a hard barrier.

He didn't mind grit and leaf debris as he redressed. He realized how filthy their uniforms were, though. He almost itched, but figured it was in his mind. The other uniform he'd brought had been cleaned with soap, wrung out, and was over a tree branch to dry.

The natives were fascinated by the layers of clothes and armor, the softness of fabric rather than leather, and the Multicam patterning. They had no idea what the weapons and other gear were, but knew they were something special. Caswell was guarding the men's gear as they plunged.

"Hurry up," she said. "It's cold water, not a hot tub, for fuck's sake."

"I'm dressed," he said, as he finished fastening his armor. They didn't bother with helmets, but they still felt safer wearing armor.

"As soon as the guys are done, you and Barker are covering me and Alexander," she said.

"Okay."

That was interesting. The women had used Spencer for several days. Now she wanted Barker and him. Why the change? Possibly he was perceived as less of a threat, and Barker was more familiar with native crafts.

She hadn't liked Spencer's advice to buddy up. Apparently that was personal for her.

So he'd have to be very discreet, getting an eyeful of her naked, and never mention it.

Downstream, there was a web of stakes and sticks, and two men were pulling fish out of it, into baskets. That was a labor saver. Wherever they settled would have to be on a watercourse, and that would be a useful tool to have.

Rank was only one way of sorting people by status. Knowledge was another. Sergeant Barker was probably the best at skills for this environment. Spencer and Caswell seemed useful, too, at least on social matters.

Felix would have to analyze everything he could to help.

Barker came over, also dressed, and checked his weapon.

"Hell, we don't need these in camp," he said. "Fobbit central."

"It is. But we do need to watch the locals. They're after the stuff."

"And our women."

"I noticed." Yes, several of the men were on the bluff looking down at the river. He took a quick, professional glance.

Caswell was lean and fit, but he liked a little more curve. She had a great ass, though, and he shouldn't think about that.

Alexander had curves, almost too many, but worth looking at. *Nice* tits.

They were both pale as ghosts.

Well, he'd file that for later "analysis." Meantime, he did need to keep kids away from gear.

He couldn't do anything about the whistles from above. He didn't think the girls liked them.

Doc yelled, "Before you leave, brush your goddamn teeth. I don't want to pull them with a Gerber plier."

The man was right, but damn, he was annoying.

Bob Barker found his mood improved. They had feathers, and he found something close to willow saplings, straight and even. He cut five, barked them and scraped them, and left them in the hut. Pine sap wasn't hard to find. Some way of cooking it, however, was. He finally settled for rolling it in a chunk of gut. There was so much leather and gut around that no one tracked it. They had more every day.

While that heated near the low daytime fire, he sliced pheasant feathers along the shaft, scraped and trimmed, all with his Leatherman tool. Three elfin kids sat and watched in fascination, jabbering away to each other. There were a lot of sounds in the language, but not a lot of what sounded like words. They had enough sounds and tones for a small vocabulary.

The sap boiled until it oozed out of the tied gut, then burst it, and he worked quickly, using a twig to smear some on the shaft, slap down a feathered vane and stretch it taut, then press along its length with the butt of the twig. He burned himself on the hot pitch on the third one, and swore. He repeated eighteen times, because he flubbed three fletches and had to repeat.

He realized Spencer was watching from his right, and Caswell from his left.

"I need to peel a bit of sinew to tie them with," he said.

Spencer asked, "What about a tight ring of rawhide?"

"Yeah, that would work, but sinew is better."

He'd peeled some from a bone earlier and had it soaking in a hide-lined hollow in the ground.

"And that's how they discovered tanning," he said.

"Mmm?"

He explained as he worked. "The chamber pot in the lodge is a hole lined with a hide. They close up the hide in the morning and dump it out, then rinse it. Hide plus fat plus piss equals tanning. Anything they didn't scrape fully would wind up tanned, and be very supple wet, very hard when dry. Once you know that, you have leather. Then when you use it as a windbreak or cover, the smoke colors and softens it."

"Ah. Makes sense. Isn't that something everyone wondered about?"

"How it developed? Yeah. And now we know."

"And no way to get rich off the idea, even if there were much money in it."

"Well, have Alexander take some photos."

"I am," she said from behind. "If we do get back . . ." she stopped and paused for almost a minute, hiding her wet eyes behind the camera as she pretended to shoot more photos. "I'll have lots of information."

The sinew being soft enough, he peeled off a cordlike strip with his blade. He made a loop, a tuck, pulled, wrapped, poked and pulled again. The front of one fletching was done. He ran a twist around and along the feathers, then made another terminal wrap at the rear. He'd made hundreds of them over the years, for friends. Now he had to make them to work.

"They can add their own points," he said. "Now, how do we want to demonstrate these and gift them?"

"Throw them at a target."

"So I need to tip one of them. Slate will work."

He found a broken piece near one of the walls, and beat it into a very rough point. He wanted weight as much as anything.

That done, he bored into the end of the shaft, melted more pine tar, and set the tip in place, adding a wrap of sinew as supplement.

It was already evening and the sun sinking behind trees when he stepped to the eastern wall, set his finger into the hollow he'd carved there, cocked back and hurled.

The yard long, inch-thick dart flew a good fifty yards.

The kids cheered. They were different kids from earlier, but they knew he'd been making something.

One of them ran out, brought back the dart, and shouted enthusiastically. He pulled the kid's fingers off the fletches, said, "No!" and threw it again.

By the third throw, most of the adults had gathered.

Spencer said, "Start with the chief."

"Yeah. Oglesby?"

Oglesby stepped forward with him, and started chatting.

"I said you are Bob Who Makes Things. The Sun Lemur has

approved of us showing them your spears that fly with feathers like a bird. I think that's what I said."

"Cool. Now tell him this one is a gift. He may wish to replace the tip. It needs to be stone for weight."

The chief brightened immensely on receiving a gift, and held it clumsily, but aloft, and shouted approval.

"Let me show you how," Barker said, and moved in, and damn, the man stunk. He'd sweated into the breechcloth. On the other hand, Bob was pretty ripe again despite his dip in the river.

"Finger here, hold here, lean back, and throw."

The chief managed a good thirty yards, and there were more cheers.

"Now find me the senior male and female hunters."

Barker presented one each to them, and they did even better. He gave a slight bow as he waved the other two darts in a broad arc, then handed them to the chief as well.

At once, the shaman and someone he recognized as a stone knapper were handling the shaft, caressing the feathers and sniffing at the glue. They had the idea. No doubt their first few dozen would suck, but they'd learn soon enough.

Spencer said, "I think that went a long way toward the balance sheet."

Yeah, they were a lot more interested in the soldiers now.

That evening turned into another party. There didn't seem to be any days of the week here, nor any schedule other than hunt, fish, dry some food, eat the rest, chop the bones and hide up for use, and hang about playing games. It was almost an idyllic life, and the meat made the bastards tall. But goddam, he wanted a bushel of apples and a salad. It had been nothing but meat and a few nuts and a handful of berries for the duration.

Tribal rites weren't anything new, but these were unlike any he'd seen, of course.

They gathered around the main fire again, and several conversations went on at once. There wasn't any real order until the headman stepped up and said something, in lyrical tones. He came over, placed a hand on Barker's head, and held aloft his new, cherished dart. He shouted something, and there was a cheer in response.

Unable to think of anything else, Barker stood and said, "Thank you," with a nod and his hands open. He hoped he hadn't been adopted or something, or if so, he didn't suddenly have some obligations.

Around the circle, several somethings were being passed hand to hand, apparently food. People nibbled as they came around.

The first was dried, salted liver. It might have been salted in blood or urine; there was a sharp tang to it.

The second was very dry, very tough, very chewy. He didn't have the jaws these people did, and had to work and twist to tear off a bit. After five chews he was pretty sure it was dried gut. He kept chewing, made a surreptitious pass with his hand and got rid of it. Gah. They ate anything here.

Then the entertainment got interesting.

Regina Alexander used her camera as a shield. Behind it, she could observe anything calmly, even enemy fire or death. The locals had no clue about technology at all, and as long as she didn't use flash or view screen, she could shoot as she pleased. She'd slapped a band-aid over the LED and not had the problems Oglesby had with his flashlight.

This was the cursed work, though, shooting through an IR lens with the fire and a hand held illuminator for light. Her husband had given her the light with the IR filter, and it was far too hot a spot for any photography, but it might be useful for searching or whatever, so she'd brought it. Now she needed it. She'd rather have him.

She blinked tears again. There was nothing to be done about that, and other issues that were critical. Back to photos.

"Caswell, can you hold this for me? Point it where I say."

"Sure, hon," Caswell said, and took the light. She had nothing against Caswell, but they weren't likely to be friends, but she was glad not to be the only woman. "Hon" wasn't really appropriate from a subordinate, but Caswell was an SP and Gina had originally been airborne intel in the USAF. As the only two females, with similar background, she didn't really mind and didn't see a need for formality.

"Getting good shots?" Caswell asked.

"I think so," she replied. "I can't tell until I can look at them."

"Old school."

"Almost."

She wanted to see these photos on the screen, but that would have to wait. She thought that was a good shot of the chief and Barker.

Caswell did okay, following the camera lens and lighting whatever seemed to be the subject.

Then she paused. Two of the women had stepped out, but were starting to dance. They wore wrapped skirts, draped half-ponchos and beaded headbands that looked to be made of shells and bone. "Headdresses," she said, and zoomed in for a shot.

It was an odd dance. It had tempo and beat, with both claps and stomps, and some percussion with sticks and sections of bark.

Then the singing started, and it was a slow chant, not very melodic, but oddly resonant. Then it sounded like a bullroarer.

"Oh, throat singing!" Caswell said.

"Dammit," Gina swore, and fumbled with the camera. She was a still photographer, not a videographer but . . . dammit.

She pulled her coat around and over her head, ducked down, and flicked the screen on. Options, settings, there, video. She closed the screen.

Now the two women were singing, too, holding hands and stamping feet while echoing deep sounds from their throats, almost like didgeridoos.

They moved into an arm-to-arm embrace, and Caswell said, "That's almost like the Inuit. Even to the headbands."

The others were also chanting, softer, somewhat harmonically, and the percussion softened to background, but still palpable.

The Paleo people had much smaller personal spaces than modern people. But even so, these two had to be close friends or relatives.

Or . . .

She kept videoing, and around her, she could almost hear the held breaths.

The two women danced arm in arm, face to face, cheek to cheek. There was a harmonic resonance with their voices that close together that added shimmery sounds to the echoey resonance.

Their eyes were closed and they were in trance, like some club dancers or meditationists.

Then they were supporting each other, one leg raised, wrapped around the other, in a remarkably stable and almost erotic stance. She wished she could get some stills, too. The symmetry was striking.

They hit a harmony and kept the chant going in stereo. They were very close to each others' notes, but there was a faint warble, like tuning an instrument. Phase cancellations? Yes. Ethereal. And they were more than close, they had hands on each other and inside their minimal clothing.

Devereaux muttered, "Goddamn."

She always felt embarrassed watching people make out, but she kept rolling. She could put about twelve minutes on each of these cards, and she had ten cards with her, but she had already filled three. She might be able to load some to her phone.

Caswell said, "That's a new one to me. Sensual touch between close associates or sister-mates is not unusual, but I've never heard of sexual contact. But it seems more for feedback than sex."

Gina wasn't sure. Their breathing turned to panting a couple of times. Their hands writhed all over, not just on erogenous zones, but there was definite masturbation involved.

"Given the casual way they touch here, it's not that shocking." Talking about it clinically was the only way not to be embarrassed.

"No, but I haven't heard of anything like it."

Then the women flowed apart again, the deep singing continuing, but the intensity and volume slackened slightly.

That wasn't all. Someone had a curl of bark stuffed with some kind of leaf. They applied a glowing stick, waved it to flame, blew it to char, and inhaled deeply of the thick, oily smoke emanating from it.

Oglesby said, "Uh, yeah, what do we do, LT?"

The LT hesitated, and Spencer said, "Under the circumstances, have a polite whiff and pass it on. Fake it if you need to."

Oglesby was first, and accepted the scroll gravely. He held it up, drew at it with his mouth, and almost coughed.

"Strong," he said, as he passed it to Devereaux. "I don't know if it's weed or what."

Devereaux did cough, and seeing as how she was allergic to smoking and found it disgusting, Gina made a token show of waving it under her nose, arched so it looked like she expanded her chest, and passed it.

Caswell inhaled a sip through her nose, as Oglesby said, "Oh, shit, whatever it is, I got a buzz."

Caswell sniffed a bit deeper, coughed. Her hands shook as she passed it, and as soon as Barker had hold of it, she sneezed.

"Oh, that was nasty."

Barker took a deep drag and didn't seem at all bothered.

"Not quite pot. I wonder if it's some fungus on a leaf?"

Spencer didn't seem fazed. Ortiz and Trinidad passed it quickly, and Dalton faked it very badly. The LT lingered over it, not inhaling but making a good show, before passing it to the shaman, who took it with a flourish and grin.

There was more chanting and drumming, and two couples wandered away from the fire circle. Then another.

"Looks like they're breaking up, LT," she said.

"Yeah, we'll stick around a bit. Watch out for anyone trying to pair up with us."

Spencer said, "The Sun Lemur would not approve."

Devereaux said, "Sister over there has a nice shape to her. I'd be happy to help with some diplomacy."

Elliott said, "I'm sure you would, but there are a lot of reasons why it's a really bad idea at this point."

"Yeah. Including diseases we have no idea about."

"Did everyone hear that?" Spencer noted.

There was zero chance she was going to involve herself with any of these men. They were aesthetically pleasing, but socially disturbing, and she was married. The idea of strange, Stone Age STIs made them even less appealing.

The barkajoint came round again, and she waved it past her face. Oglesby looked disoriented, and Barker was almost out of focus.

"Yup, I'm betting on some form of ditchweed with some mushroom sprinkles," he said. "Wheee."

It was hilarious to see him stoned.

Caswell said, "Maybe morning glory, too. Mild hallucinogen."

Gina was still recording.

She ducked under her coat, switched back to still, swapped memory cards, placing the one very carefully in a case in a dedicated sealed pouch on her gear. She could swap cards under fire in seconds. Then she got a shot of Barker standing, staring at his hand.

Looking around, she realized all the Paleos had gone to their huts, and it was a bit cool.

Spencer said, "Goodnight, everybody. Alexander, we're on first watch."

"Yes, Sergeant."

Sitting by their dim inside fire, she wished she had a real video camera, and the ability to check all the images here. She had her laptop and the solar charger, but was reluctant to let the Paleos see anything that wasn't just a chunk of material. They were at the truck anyway. It would have to wait.

Spencer said, "We'll have Oglesby and Barker on last, so they have time to sober up."

"Are they in trouble?" she asked.

He shook his head. "No, we needed to be social with our hosts. They had two hits each. But that stuff must be strong. I had one toke and I felt it for about twenty minutes."

"So we're leaving tomorrow?" She was of mixed feelings.

"If we can. We'll see if they can recommend a place for us. And we've learned a bit here."

She said, "We have. I've learned I don't want to live with them. They're very nice neighbors, and good fences make good neighbors."

"Indeed. I'm also worried about the younger males wanting to shack up."

"Only the younger ones?"

He raised an eyebrow. "There's nothing like the personal habits and the physiques of the thirty-year-olds to make me appreciate the simple beauty of my right hand," he said. "They age fast."

"They do, but they don't seem to age past that. From twenty-five on, they all look the same."

"Yeah, but their twenty-five is a well-worn fifty for us."

She raised a hand at a noise, but it was a voice, and sounded as if someone was well impassioned.

Spencer caught it, too.

"People who live in grass houses shouldn't throe moans," he said. "Throe with an E."

She tried not to choke and failed.

"I shouldn't be laughing," she said through a sore throat and leaking eyes. "We can't get home."

"It doesn't seem like it. So we need to deal with it." His eyes were wet, too, much as he was trying to hide it.

"I'll swap bad jokes for a bar of dark chocolate." She missed chocolate, and was going to miss it a lot more. Even Hershey would be welcome now. As for Ghirardelli . . .

"Yeah. Coffee. Oglesby and Barker want smokes, I want coffee. Goddamn I want coffee."

They wanted their families, but weren't going to say that. So . . .

"There is coffee. All you have to do is reach the ocean and paddle five thousand miles."

"I've thought about it. But our home isn't there yet. It would be all raw wilderness and no more familiar than this."

She said, "And I don't know the history of coffee in South America."

"Ethiopia, actually. We could walk there, in theory."

"Oh, right."

Either way, it didn't matter. They were in the middle of Central Asia, with no guidebook for the trip, and no way home.

They stared silently at the skin door.

In the near distance, they could hear dogs or wolves growling and fighting over the offal from the hunt. It had been tossed into the woods.

CHAPTER 7

Sean Elliott felt a lot stronger mentally than he had last week. They were still lost, with almost no resources, but he had an idea on the environment now, and at least a summary plan. That didn't make it easier to pack up and leave the native village. The huts, fire and people made it a home of sorts, and now he was taking his element off to create their own camp. There were over a hundred people in this village. He had ten.

But, those ten had skills. They had a translator, a medic, a vet tech who could be another medic, two people with SERE training, who were both reenactors of different historical eras. Barker knew a bunch of Native American primitive skills. They had someone who knew sociology, and a couple of skilled hunters. Then, Trinidad had grown up in a remote village and knew about wells and animals also. Sean was an engineer. Between them, they had the brains to make it work. He wasn't sure if they had enough muscle.

There was nothing to be gained by remaining, though. This wasn't their culture and hopefully never would be. He needed to jump now before he chickened out.

"Ready, Oglesby?" he asked.

"Ready, sir," the man said, and held up his notebook. He'd done an impressive job with the language in only three days. Hopefully, they could make their point known.

"Caswell?"

"Got it, sir." Caswell had suggested donating some plain wooden pencils. They were biodegradable, would wear out quickly, and were gimmicky. They didn't do anything charcoal wouldn't do for these people, but they'd hopefully be appreciated.

Outside, he sought the chief, hoping the man was up, even though it was early. There wasn't any real schedule here. The natives hunted, trapped fish, played, lazed about, had sex, and ate as they wished.

But the chief was awake, and responded to Oglesby's greeting, along with the shaman. A couple of others loitered nearby, and moved in closer. They weren't quite too close this time.

Caswell stepped forward and held up a pencil. She had a small piece of rawhide and a stick, peeled to clean wood. She took out a sharp rock flake and scraped a point on the pencil, then marked on the stick, then the leather.

There were oohs and ahhs. She gave them the one to play with, and there was much giggling and pointing, waving and excitement.

Then she handed over the rest of the dozen, unsharpened.

This time there were cheers. The visitors had finally given them something neat.

She stood stoically with a panicked look on her face as the chief grabbed her shoulder, tried to cup her through her armor, and patted her ass. She took his shoulder, slapped his buttock lightly, and stepped back.

It took a few moments to get their attention back from the pencils, while Oglesby stepped forward with his notebook.

He used a combination of pantomime and native words. "We (gesture) ugyi (point at hut) build (gesture of piling sticks). Va!se (point at river) runs west (point) from the east (point). Where should we (gesture) go (arms forward and out) to build (gesture) ugyi (shrug)?"

There was a modern sounding exclamation of "Ah!" and a huddle. It sounded like a flock of birds throwing nuts at trees, but in only a few moments, three people stepped forth, one woman and two men. They were from the party that found them, and hunted the antelope.

"Rish," one of the men said, pointing east. He ran to his hooch, emerged with a small wrapped bundle and a spear, and started walking.

"Crap. Folks, grab your gear fast, we're marching!"

Luckily their three guides moved at a leisurely walk, and waited a few yards out for the troops to catch up. They looked bemused. As soon as they saw the last troop out of the lodge—Alexander—they turned and resumed trudging.

Their pace was not brisk, but steady. They stayed above the wood line of the river, along the high steppe. Occasionally, game would leap away, and once a large wildcat.

"Damn," Alexander said, from behind her camera.

"Alexander?"

"Lions, sir. A pride of four females and a male. Up the hill that way."

"I see, barely." Lions. Yet another animal that would eat them.

That rise right there was where the trucks were. He didn't want to try to answer questions about them, even though they'd likely been seen by some party or other. He lagged down toward the trees, and it worked. The hunters didn't stray far up, and kept walking.

It was another two miles across hummocky terrain above the river and the forest that edged it before they came to a wood line running south and uphill. It grew low and rugged, with some straight trees right along the edge.

The lead hunter chattered something, and Oglesby said, "He says, 'good camp here.' It seems pretty good to me, sir, and well away from them."

"It's workable. Thank them, and tell them we'll meet again soon."

Oglesby spoke back, clutching hands with each of them, and they departed.

They were such a simple people, and he meant that in a good way.

Elliott said, "I want to look uphill before we pick a spot, and we may bivouac for a day or so before finalizing."

"Final." That word. They were choosing their homestead in a place that would be Afghanistan in about 12,000 years.

They strung out in patrol formation and worked their way uphill. The slope was gentle. The terrain was prairieish with knotty trees here and there, bushes, clumps of heavier grass.

"Looky there," Elliott said as he crossed a rise.

Ahead was a merging smaller stream and a line of small trees.

"Good?"

"It means there's enough water. We don't want to be on the river because of floods, and we don't want to be too far from it—we need water and sanitation."

They moved up, a bit closer together, but always looking around and feeling that creepy wrongness.

The line of trees was on a watercourse that was more a ditch than a side stream, though it likely held water during wet season. It was spongy and full of moss and small trees, birch or something like it, along with brush and thorns.

Alexander said, "Thorns mean it stays wet."

"Good," Elliott nodded. "So let's move downhill just a bit, a hundred meters or so."

Gina Alexander watched as he led the way, with that zoned expression again, though it wasn't panicked this time. He just looked lost in thought. That was good. He seemed to be taking charge. Even if he wasn't a great leader, he needed to be some kind of leader, or step aside and let Spencer do it.

At almost exactly a hundred meters by her estimate, the LT stopped and stood, then turned slowly around, shifting his weight and gazing. He mumbled to himself and pointed.

Spencer opened his mouth to speak, but Alexander nudged him and shook her head. He gave her a quizzical look. She raised a finger to tell him to wait. She'd seen her husband assess problems like this. And that made her sob again.

After about three minutes Elliott spoke.

"I don't like the slope, but it's what we have. We need to decide between a low spot to minimize wind, and high ground to give us a field of fire. Unless anyone has a good reason not to, I'm choosing that hump there. We'll make that our camp for the duration."

No one objected.

Alexander saw what he was doing. That wasn't a bad choice. They had the stream to the east, what looked like a seasonal ditch uphill to the south, the river less than a half mile to the north, enough exposure for sun, decent position for observation. They had a line of trees along the watercourses, and a copse a bit downhill in what was almost a meadow. It might not be the most comfortable, but it was probably the best combination of resources and tactical location.

"Okay," he said. "I'd like to leave a detachment here while the rest get the vehicles. Five to go, which is a ground guide, and a driver and gunner for each, and swap off. It's only a couple of miles. It should be a one-day thing, starting in the morning. For tonight, I want a low fire, three up at any time on watch. We'll dig hasties and bivouac, unless someone is eager to build a lean-to."

"Looks clear enough for tonight," Dalton said.

She'd rather have some kind of overhead. Much rather. She could work something with her poncho and some sticks, or even with dug earth and the poncho, but they were all in a group, it wasn't likely to rain, and she didn't want to stand out nor go to that much effort.

"Where's the latrine?" she asked.

"The stream. South of that rock there," Spencer said.

The lieutenant nodded. "Yeah, for now. Keep it downstream from there. We'll get water upstream. Everyone done with assplosions?"

She was, but that reminded her that her ass was still burning, itching, oozing. It could have been worse. She could have been stuck in a convoy vehicle. But it wasn't pleasant.

Dalton raised his hand and spoke.

"Sir, may I offer an invocation?"

"I would like that, yes. Please be brief."

Dalton looked around, bowed his head, and said, "Heavenly Father, we thank you for guiding us to our new home. Bless our labor, courage and teamwork through the coming adversity, so we may thrive. Amen."

"Amen," replied most. Devereaux, Trinidad and Ortiz crossed themselves.

Dalton added, "And for some of us, this is in Jesus' name."

Spencer was silent. Alexander felt uncomfortable. Christians always had to make it about their God.

Barker said, "Sir, I'd like to kindle the First Fire this evening. It's a tradition we have."

Yes. If they could pray, she could have a holy fire. Barker was a good guy. She'd ask him about her rituals, too.

"I'd like that, too. When?"

"I need a couple of supplies. Alexander and I can do it. If we're going to cook, I'd say I start by seventeen hundred."

"Let's get hasties dug and some sort of barricade first."

"Roger that, sir."

They dug hasty positions in a circle around where the fire would go, earth ramparted out, and dragged some scrub from the ditch. Barker and Trinidad went to work on some local bushes with their machetes, and they had a kraal of sorts. It did help psychologically define their territory, and it would slow wolves. It might not stop lions. Her hands were sore after her turn with Barker's E-tool, but she felt better.

Rich Dalton threw himself into digging. These were a bit better than hasty positions, because he expected they'd expand them later. If not, they'd work for latrines, storage or trash.

"Dalton," the LT said. "I see a lot of goats. Please shoot us some dinner."

"I'd rather have steak, but we won't do it with these damned things," he said, shaking his M4. Hell, it was barely enough for people even if you did hit. But he took a walk east and leapt the stream at a spot only eight feed wide or so, with Trinidad following. The grass was thigh deep, thick and tangled, and threw up dust and occasional angry bugs as they trod. The dust coated his uniform in short order.

He looked over at Trinidad's machete, held out in the man's right hand.

"Are you going to chop it up on the spot with that sword?"

"That's right, man. You shoot, I chop. They can have leftovers." The short man grinned a big white grin in his brown face.

"Cool. Well, I see some right over there, but eventually they're going to get scared of us." He choose one fat one that was nearer than the rest.

"Maybe we can pen some in and farm them."

He thought that was a good idea. "Yeah, a small farm would be good, but I think we have to build a bunch of stuff first." He lived in Louisville, but there were enough farms around he'd seen plenty. They wouldn't be ranching this year. Next year, though, if they were still here, definitely.

He aimed, breathed, squeezed the trigger, and the goat thrashed and fell. He thought he'd scored a headshot, but it might have been neck.

Then he realized the goat wasn't fat, it was nursing. Some little kid came braying out, squealing about his momma. Crap.

Hating himself, he lined up and shot, and Junior became hors d'oeuvres.

Trinidad clapped him on the shoulder. "Eh, they're small. We'll chop them up there. Here's one of your brass." The Filipino dug a bit more, and found the other.

At least God provided plenty of food for now, though he wished for a salad. And a soda.

He grabbed the goat, Trinidad shouldered the kid, and they trotted back. The smell of dead goat didn't help his feelings, except it also meant food, so that was okay.

Barker, Spencer and Alexander waited right across the stream.

"Double, eh?" Barker asked.

"Yeah, I got the mother first and wasn't going to let the little critter starve. Not cool, but it is what it is."

"Yeah, well lay them down here and we'll get them ready and start the fire. Ortiz wants to chop up more animals."

There was already a circle of rocks, dragged from the stream and still wet, to mark the fire circle. He slapped the mother goat down just outside of it.

Alexander bent over and . . .

"Did you just suck goat milk from a dead udder?" He was fascinated and revolted at the same time.

"Yes."

"What the . . ."

"It's the only milk we're going to get around here," she said, wiping her lips.

Spencer knelt down in the grass and did the same thing.

Caswell said, "I want to pen a few; we can get milk, butter and cheese," echoing what Trinidad had said. At a gesture from Spencer, she added, "No thank you." Yeah, he wasn't about to go for milk *that* fresh either. He hoped.

"Oh, hell yes," Ortiz said. Dalton stared at him. "I mean the butter and stuff."

If the animal handler wasn't interested in goat milk from an udder, he wasn't either. Thanks.

Elliott said, "Barker, please proceed with your fire, and dinner, and we much appreciate your services in this."

"Yes, sir." Barker spoke firmly, but there was a faint crack under his baritone voice.

He opened his pack and started pulling out gathered sticks, then bark, twigs and some leaves.

It was still full light, but afternoon, and they'd want time to dig in more. Anyway, they were hungry. It made sense to eat now.

Dalton was respectful. In a perfect world, everyone would hold to Christ's teachings, but it wasn't a perfect world, and while "diversity" was used as an excuse by many, it was important. They had their paths, and he'd Witness to them if they asked, support his fellow soldiers regardless.

Barker was actually making fire by friction, with a firebow made of a bent limb from some scrub tree, twisted bark as the the cord, and some bits and pieces. He tied and twisted and pulled until he had a loose bow, whittled at a stick, used his knife to drill at a broken slab of some other wood, and piled leaves around something else. He seemed to know what he was doing.

Alexander squatted near him, with some kind of grass, some dirt, and something clutched in her hand.

Everyone gathered at a respectful distance, but close enough to watch. Barker wrapped the stick in the bowstring, placed it on the chunk under his foot, and started sawing back and forth.

Rich sent a prayer out that God would bless the proceedings, and the camp. He then focused on the fire circle again.

In only a couple of minutes, a faint curl of smoke rose from the board. Dalton raised his eyebrows. He knew this could be done, and probably the Stone Age people could, but to see it in person by someone modern was fascinating.

The twisted bark parted suddenly, falling away. There were sighs and groans, but Barker grabbed another length, twisted, pulled, wrapped it around the bow, inserted the stick and resumed.

Alexander muttered something. She placed a hand on Barker's shoulder and kissed the bundle she held, then moved it back down to the board, where smoke was curling again already.

In another couple of minutes, Barker bore down on the stick, bowed furiously, and the smoke thickened. Then he dropped the bow to the side, scooped up the board, tapped it and blew.

The fuzz and grass puffed out white smoke that turned filthy yellow, then dark, then there was as faint glow that turned angry red, and a small flame crackled through straw.

Everyone sighed out held breath and let out soft whoops and cheers. Next to him, Trinidad said, "Fuckin' a, man."

The burning tinder went under the fire lay, and in a few seconds there were obvious flames, a fire.

They had a camp. They'd built it, would improve it, and they had a fire they'd started. He felt it. It was a charge. They hadn't needed a lighter or fuel, just native materials and patience. They controlled the elements.

Alexander caught an ember on the bundle she held and waved it to white smoke, which she carried carefully out to the circle of soldiers, and around them before going over to the creek. She muttered something as she went.

She strolled back to the fire, and ground the smudge out on one of the rocks, then tossed the dead bundle into the flames.

Barker said, "Okay, it's lit. Make sure we keep it fed. We need a good bed of coals at night, so we can blow flames up in a hurry if we need to. And we'll want some kind of cover—a movable lean-to—against rain. But tonight looks clear."

Dalton hadn't had any objection to the ceremony, but now he was in favor of it. This was their fire, dammit. Not just *a* fire.

As Barker gathered up the fire sticks, Dalton moved in and shook his hand.

"That was inspiring, Sergeant."

"Thanks." Barker nodded but did little else. He was very stoic overall.

"I'm guessing you've got Native American heritage?"

"One-eighth Sioux. My grandmother." Barker stowed the fire-starting stuff in his ruck, and started scavenging sticks for fuel from the grass. There was already a small pile, but they'd obviously need more.

Rich said, "Well, it's awesome you've got those skills. Thanks, and well done."

"No problem. I just wish they weren't quite so useful."

"Yeah. And you, Alexander?"

"An eighth Cherokee," she replied.

"Really? I mean, you're a very pale blonde." Then he wished he hadn't said it. That was pretty insensitive.

She said, "Some were."

"Okay. So your traditions were close enough you could do that fire ceremony?"

Alexander shrugged said, "I have no idea, actually. I don't know anything about that side of my family."

"Oh. I gathered from the herbs and your ritual it was something of yours."

"It is, just not Indian."

"Oh?"

"I'm Wiccan."

"Huh?" He heard it but—

"I'm a witch. That was a spell to secure against spirits and bring good luck to the hearth." She pulled her dog tags and held them out to him. Religious preference, Wiccan.

"Okay," he said, trying to be noncommittal.

She smiled, but looked pretty put out underneath it.

"I don't do spells against people, they're not really magic, any more than any other form of prayer, and we don't worship Satan."

"Yeah, I've heard that," he said. He wasn't going to have a debate on how the Adversary might work through the gullible.

He'd thought she was an atheist. Caswell was obviously a hardcore feminist, but was Lutheran, and the realistic woman was a practicing Witch. It just seemed ass backwards.

He'd need to watch his manners. He got along with most Christians, though most were too casual for his taste. Jews were okay. He liked the Hindus and Sikhs he'd met. He wasn't real comfortable with Muslims. He didn't know anything about Native or other primitive beliefs. And he really wasn't sure how to respond to a woman who professed to be a Witch.

Obviously, God wanted him to learn more about people. Whatever else happened here, he had a sign to do that.

And if Native American rituals were similar enough to witchcraft he couldn't tell them apart . . .

For now, he was going to enjoy the fire. Whether or not he'd enjoy another round of barbecued goat remained to be seen.

Gina Alexander didn't mind dark at all. Dark in the literal middle of nowhere with predators around, she hated. There was also still that fear that there might be another bang, and everyone sent home, except her. It wrecked her sleep and her calm.

She really wanted some kind of tent. A bivvy bag on the ground felt so exposed. Then there was the matter of dew. She did the best she could, dossing down between Barker and Caswell. Dalton was down past her feet at an angle. That left her head toward the fire.

She dragged her carbine inside with her, ensured by touch that the chamber was empty, a magazine inserted, and safety on. It made her feel a lot better. That, and her Ontario tanto alongside. She hated mummy bags, so she'd brought her own mountain bag, but even in there, it was cramped, with uniform, the weapons, her other knives.

The stars were cold, bright points in swaths overhead. That was most definitely the Milky Way and she could even see individual Pleiades. She dozed fitfully in and out, startling awake to animal noises, the sound of wood being added to the fire, the clatter of a rifle against rock, and occasional mutters.

She wanted to look at the clock on her phone, but there was no reason to. It wouldn't make things come any faster, and the ability to recharge was limited. They'd set approximate time based on finding noon with a stick and shadow. They'd have to correct that again soon, but at least it gave an approximation.

It was chilly, but clean and brisk. Camping trips like this would sell for a lot of money.

Sighing, she pulled up her phone. The ghostly glow said it was 0037.

She lay back, breathed deeply and tried to relax.

There were almost no insect noises, but she heard occasional howls of wolves and grunts from herbivores. It was shocking how far sound traveled here.

She woke again, and the stars had moved, possibly an hour's worth. The moon was down, but it was in early phase anyway.

Silently screaming in frustration, she wiggled out of her bag and grabbed her boots, which she'd set upside down on stakes to keep them dry and free of bugs. She shook them out anyway. Those donned, she pulled on her gore-tex, trying to keep the noise down, grabbed her rifle, and moved over to the fire.

Caswell, Barker and Trinidad were on watch.

"Hey."

"Hey," she replied.

"Can't sleep?" Caswell asked.

"Not well."

They sat, staring at the very low fire, nothing but a bed of embers. Too much light would be a bad thing, she knew.

Combat Survival School had been useful to her, but wasn't entirely applicable here. At least she knew she could eat, no matter what happened. Bugs and slugs weren't tasty, but get hungry enough and they were protein. In fact, she'd almost be willing to cook some slugs in lieu of more goat.

Trinidad said, "Time to wake Devereaux to replace me."

Barker said, "I'll do it," and leaned back. He thumped the medic's bag.

"Yeah, I'm up."

Shift change took five minutes, including time for both men to leak in the stream. They didn't have to drop trou and either splash their boots or lean back against a rock.

In five minutes, it was quiet again. Devereaux poked at the fire with a twig.

"I'll grab some more sticks," Caswell said.

"Hold on," he said, looking up. "Dayum."

"What?"

"Unfuckingreal."

"What is it?" she asked.

"Do you see the faint glow to the west?"

"Yes. It's not predawn flashes."

"No, that's Gegenschein."

"Geggen shine?" Barker asked.

"German. Gegenschein. Interplanetary dust reflecting sunlight."

"Ah."

Caswell said, "Neat."

It was mildly interesting, in that she'd never seen it before, but not interesting enough.

He continued, "Yeah, but that's not the neat part. Look up to the west, south, about where I'm pointing."

She saw, "Something . . ."

Caswell said, "Very faint red tinge."

"Yeah, that's a Kordylewski cloud, I think."

"What's that?"

"The L Five point of the Earth-Moon system can accumulate dust."

She knew what that was.

Barker said, "Spot where the gravity balances between them, right?"

"That's L One. L Four is leading the Moon sixty degrees. L Five is trailing. L Two is behind the Moon, centrifugal force balances gravity. L Three is the same thing behind the Earth. Four and Five are reasonably stable."

"Ah," Barker said. "I'm guessing we can't see them in our time."

"Very rarely, nowhere near a city."

"Well, it's cool and all, but I'd rather see a city."

"Yeah. Me too. Crap. Anyway, there has to be complete darkness, no moon, clear sky and dust concentrations."

Regina rummaged for her camera bag, found the night vision attachment by touch, set it, pointed up, and got some shots of that and the Guggenheim or whatever.

Suddenly she did feel tired, whether it was due to adrenaline running out, or depression, or something.

"I'm crashing again," she said.

Caswell asked, "When are you on shift?"

Barker said, "She's on in an hour."

"Damn, sucks."

"Yeah, wake me."

She crawled into her cold sleeping bag and tried not to cry.

She did sleep, until Devereaux nudged her.

"You're on," he said.

"Right." She blinked and was half-nauseated.

He was a medic. Good enough.

"Devereaux, can you cover me while I take a leak?"

"Yeah," he said, sounding a little embarrassed. Well, she didn't like it either, but she wasn't walking down there alone.

There was just enough glow to carefully pick her way, and two cold, damp rocks made an uneven but workable seat. He stood about ten feet away, facing the other way, which she appreciated for discretion, and scared her because he wasn't watching behind her. Gods, she hated this place.

That done, she staggered back to the fire.

It was graying in the east now. She was up for the day anyway.

Two hours later, after gnawing on some stale, roasted goat, she fell into rough patrol formation with Barker, Ortiz, Oglesby and Dalton. The trucks should be only a couple of miles west, slightly south, and over a slight ridge. They should be easy to see. Dalton had a compass, with notes for azimuths to landmarks, because it would still be possible to miss them in all this rolling terrain.

They walked about five meters apart, and she looked around

constantly. The goats were endemic. There were also family herds of some ugly antelope, occasional large cows, and the yip of dogs, well, wolves, off up the hill.

In between that, they muttered to each other, because talking about anything meant human beings were nearby. They all kept looking behind them, including her, irrationally afraid of being followed.

They wore armor and carried rifles, because they just might need them. The ammo wouldn't last forever, especially with them hunting an animal every couple of days.

It still seemed unreal. Ten of them, here, with nothing they didn't carry. She knew how to weave, how to spin, how to sew, how to dye, and none of that would matter if they didn't pen some goats for wool, or find plants that could be retted into fiber. Even so, that was a full-time job, and they had to build their own village first.

The so-called "simpler" times were nothing of the kind.

Up ahead, Barker called, "Good news and bad news."

Oh, shit, what now?

She jogged forward, following Dalton, and drew up with the others at the top of a hummock.

The trucks were there, unhurt, just as they'd left them. However, the shadows next to them were occupied by a pride of lions.

Dalton asked, "Can we scare them off with gunfire?"

Barker said, "Nah, large animals usually think gunfire is thunder. And these critters have never heard gunfire, so it would be less than useless."

"What then?"

"Looks like we can reach the rear of Number Nine, if we're careful. Let's hack down those two bushes," he said, indicating two scrubby trees. "We'll use them as shields, and shoot the shit out of one if we have to. Once we're inside, we can drive around until they get scared."

"Yeah," Dalton said.

She didn't have a better idea. It was sound on the surface, except it meant approaching lions who had no reason to fear humans.

She and Dalton kept an eye on the lions while Barker and Ortiz chopped through the bases of the two shrubs.

"Glad I have gloves," Barker said. "Okay, I'll take this one, Oglesby, can you handle that one?"

"I'd be better," Dalton said.

"Yeah, but you're rated expert. I want you clear to shoot if you have to."

"Hooah. What's the ROE?"

"If they approach, safety off. If they start batting at the tree, start shooting, and you, too," he pointed at Regina and Ortiz.

"Roger that," she agreed. A small-bore rifle against a lion? Yeah, that was smart. But it was all they had. She started jittering.

They advanced down the slope, obliqued over to keep the vehicles between them and the lions, and made quiet, steady progress.

Not quiet enough. One of the lionesses woke up and came around to investigate, padding slowly and confidently.

She seemed confused by the trees and the camouflaged forms behind them, but she closed her eyes and sniffed.

Uttering a growl, she moved to the side, trying to get a better view.

"Swing the trees!" Barker said, and shifted his around in a strong grip, feet spread, as if wielding a chainsaw or machine gun.

Gina kept her rifle ready, and already had the safety off, orders be damned. The Army had this paranoia that troops couldn't manage a point-and-click interface, and if so, why did they issue the damned things in the first place?

The lioness backed up, growling.

"I'm going to watch this side," she said, and moved to the right. If another animal came past there . . .

Then they were to the rear of Number Nine, and easing around the side. Barker handed the tree off to Dalton to guard the front with as he fumbled with the padlock on the passenger side. That done, he scrambled up and they retreated back to the rear as he thumped through the inside, and dropped the ramp.

She stepped against the grate and worked her way in, then put the safety back on her rifle. Ortiz slid past her, then Dalton, waving his tree as he backed up the ramp.

Dalton hit the lever and the ramp rose and locked.

It was tight, musty and metallic smelling. It took a week of fresh air to remind one how stinky these things were.

"Okay, fire the bitch up," Dalton said.

"Working on it," Barker replied.

The diesel needed a few seconds preheat on the glowplugs, then turned over and caught easily.

The lions took off at a trot, then slowed to a walk, but they kept going.

That done, Ortiz hopped over to Number Eight.

With Barker and Ortiz driving in column, the others walked ahead. The vehicles were unsteady going across the terrain rather than with it. Several times, Barker backed up and eased around an obstacle.

This time, no animals bothered them, but they were walking in much closer proximity. She chose the middle and no one made an issue of it. Dalton took left, Oglesby right.

By midday she was hungry, but the thought of more goat didn't appeal. They needed to find something green, or something crunchy. She sipped water and kept walking, picking a route that seemed clear and flat as the terrain allowed. She pulled her eyepro down to cut the glare.

Eventually the camp came into view, and there was a shelter of some kind, and piled brush marking the perimeter. She realized she'd been staggering in exhaustion, and suddenly felt lighter. How could a mere couple of miles be such a drain?

The others stood waiting as they rolled in, and she walked past and shook hands with Caswell.

"I'm taking a nap. Please tell anyone who cares."

She lowered her weapon, popped her armor and helmet, and sprawled on her bag.

Far Eye flattened and became rock. The huts weren't huts, they were beasts. They growled and rumbled. Were those wings that opened? And the travelers got under them.

They were powerful wizards if they could control such huge beasts, and hide in the bellies.

Yet these wizards didn't know words and had poor manners. Their robes were strange. They shaved their beards.

The great big beasts started moving, with smoke coming from the rear. Their legs moved like rolling pebbles.

It was probably a good thing they were going, but they were only a half morning's hike away. He regretted not leading them farther. They seemed harmless, but they rode in animals and had magic stars contained in sticks, and those strange water skins, and the big waterskin.

The other newcomers had wolves that walked with them, and the little spears that flew fast. What was the name of the one? Yes, Bob Who Makes Things. Bob had made those small spears with feathers. They were almost like the little spears.

It might be good to visit and see if these wizards became more polite. Some of their nice-nice things would be very helpful. Perhaps one of the long knives that didn't chip?

He must tell Ashmi what he'd seen. They would smoke to the spirits. There was a lot to smoke about.

Martin Spencer was glad to see the vehicles. The damned things were terrible off road, and he'd been afraid one would roll, once he remembered it was a very real possibility. In fact, he'd almost done that himself. Having both gave them a few more clubs, containers, and potentially an alternator to use for electrical power, either hand cranked or on a windmill. Maybe not soon, but he was damned well going to have the best gear possible, including power tools as long as they lasted. He might scavenge some metal for tools as well, from the strapping inside, the springs and such. He'd have to carburize it for tools. They needed that forge.

Elliott stood next to him, looking satisfied. Then he resumed talking.

The LT asked, "What's the best way to chop small trees? The axes? Or should we just burn them at the base?"

"You're thinking of a palisade, sir?"

"Yes."

"Burning might be better. We can do a bunch of them at once and just keep the fires fed, and the ash and charring might help them resist decay." Besides, the pioneer tools were all they had for heavy equipment, unless he could get a forge up and reduce ore to make others.

Elliott squinted around. "Okay, we can use the tools for trimming, and for shoveling a rampart, then."

"Yeah, we need something defensible, even if it's only against animals or stampeding herds."

"Right. And as much as our neighbors seem friendly, I'd like to be able to button up."

They talked for another couple of hours, some of it random BS, some of it repeats. They knew what they needed, but not how to do it. The others wandered in and out. For now, that was fine. They needed a bit of down time.

Martin said, "What we need is a full platoon. I'd even consider borrowing some natives."

Elliott nodded. "Yeah, I thought about it. But we'd have to teach them how to do everything."

Oglesby said, "Worse than Afghans."

Elliott said, "Much worse. The Afghans function adequately at the iron-age level at least, wouldn't you say?"

Martin said, "That's a good summary, sir. The rural ones."

"Yeah. The locals have no idea as to anything."

Oglesby said, "And they'd want to share everything."

Elliott kicked the ground. "We're alone. One short squad. That's my biggest concern."

"Agreed. Give me three strong backs and I can set up a forge and start beating tools tomorrow. But we need the palisade, shelter, food, water, plumbing of some kind—"

Elliott raised a hand and said, "One at a time. I have a rough plan for the palisade."

"So what's the plan?"

Elliott held up a note pad with a sketch. "About a two- to three-foot ditch with a two- to three-foot packed earth mound. Peak of the mound will have the palisade, and I want the saplings set down a couple of feet deeper. We'll dig and fill as we work around. If we can bore holes through them at the top, we can drive twigs in to pin them in place, or we can set backbraces and lash them on if we can find a stringy bark."

Barker said, "Do both, and use rawhide from animal skins to lash with."

"Excellent, good," he said. "We'll buttress every ten feet or so. Then we'll build shooting platforms. We'll use the vehicles as high point for now, but we'll want to build a central tower when we can. Eventually, we'll want an actual moat and then start working on stone walls, but we may do that on the other side of the stream and a bit down the hill."

Oglesby asked, "How long is this going to take?"

"Does it matter at this point?" Elliott replied.

Martin hated hearing it like that, but there it was.

Elliott continued. "We're here for the duration. We need the best defense and best comfort we can get. We also need some latrines with seats, and then see about running water for washing, cooking and showering."

Alexander came over, looking a bit better. She'd been ragged. Sleeping problems? He had those, too, and this environment made it worse.

He said, "Understood, sir, and I agree. So, how high do we want the palisade?"

"Well, if they're two to three feet down, and two to three feet up, call that five feet. Another five feet of timber gives a good height, but I'd rather it wasn't reachable by hand from the outside. Ten feet would be better. But that means fifteen to twenty feet of log, which gets heavy and is limiting. So we may be replacing this as we go. For now, we want to start between us and the neighbors, so we at least have engagement cover."

Alexander said, "Shrubs, sir."

"Shrubs?"

"Outside engagement range, say two hundred yards, we should plant long rows of shrubs close together. Let them tangle up, and it creates something else to slow them down. We can make gates so they're channeled. And since they don't have firearms, it means they're outside both spear range, and the range they can throw anything flammable."

It was working. They had a project, they were interested, and they were busy. Elliott was turning out to be alright.

He asked, "Do you know what shrubs will work?"

"I can find something useful, and transplant a few."

Elliott said, "Do it. Now, what about shelter? Lean-tos?"

Alexander said, "I can stitch leather using sinew or cut thongs. A-frame tents with goat or antelope hide will keep us dry." She wrinkled her face. "I'd like something a little classier than the squats our neighbors are in."

"Good. Hold on. Formation!" Elliott called.

Everyone came over and gathered, but not in formation. They faced to cover a broad arc, and all had slung weapons. Good.

"Okay, first things first. There's no way to correct deficiencies in gear, but be honest. Does everyone have at least five uniforms, undies, socks? Two boots and athletic shoes? Cold weather parka or gore-tex or something, and gloves? Hats or helmet liners? What about work gloves?"

Four people had work gloves.

"Okay, I'm glad of this so far. Everyone has a poncho or wet weather coat, I hope?"

There were assents.

"You all have rucks and weapons. Okay, then we have the basics. We also have a solar charger for phones and laptops. How many of those?"

Everyone had a laptop. Everyone except Spencer and Barker had smart phones. The two old guys were holdouts. Martin nodded to Barker with a slight smile.

Elliott kept talking. "We need to conserve vehicle fuel, but it's not impossible we can distill some kind of oil from hemp or vegetables to make diesel. That will have to wait, though. In the meantime, we have a means to compute and record, and possible communication or at least traveling notes that don't waste paper."

He wanted to start work, not kick things around endlessly, but the LT needed reassurance, and needed to have his formations and discussions. To be fair, it might mean better planning, less labor and not overlooking something. So he'd deal with it.

Martin Spencer, along with Barker, backed and filled the MRAPs, while Elliott waved and directed them. They pulled up on the west side, with Charlie Nine angled slightly to create an arc. They were circling the wagons, as best they could.

The four precious coils of razor wire and piles of brush had to suffice to close the circle for now. The brush would turn into firewood once not needed.

They idled down and Martin unbuckled and got out. Even if it didn't matter, he was going to let the engine cool before he shut it down, possibly for the last time.

As dusk grew long and dark, the damned wolves howled.

Martin wasn't much of a dog person, and those wolves were large, mean, unafraid of humans generally, and likely hungry.

It was tragically beautiful here, with streaked purple twilight, and chill, and terrifyingly raw and wild. And he'd never get home. Allison was lost to him.

No one could see him blink back tears in the dim light, and no one would say anything if they did. Everyone had some kind of family or friends.

He was glad to be in the arc between the trucks. That was good planning on the LT's part. One person was on the floor of each vehicle, the rest in that arc. Next to him, Oglesby had headphones on, listening to something techno or club mix or whatever. It was just loud enough for Martin to hear, and it sounded like a grinding engine.

He wasn't listening to anything at night, though he really did want music tomorrow. At night, it was just too creepy to not hear every sound, and hearing them creeped him out even more.

Barker and Dalton seemed to enjoy sitting up top on the guns, so that helped. But he really wanted to see that palisade up in a hurry. To his thinking, they could burn logs down and chop others with the axes as fast as they could make it work. They were going to need about a thousand of them for the perimeter, then more for reinforcement. They were going to have to drag them, too. That copse to the east was going to disappear before they were done. It would take weeks to build that.

"We need some flat rocks by the fire," Barker called down.

"This fire?"

"Wherever we put our cooking fire."

"Ah, I get you," he agreed. They'd fry stuff on those rocks.

He said, "Yeah, and I need a spot to put a forge, near the creek. A large granite rock will work as an anvil until I can do something better."

An en masse howl of wolves interrupted their thoughts. After it died down, Ortiz said, "And some land mines."

"I thought you liked wolves."

"I do. That doesn't mean I want to get eaten by them."

Indeed. He'd always found wolves to be handsome creatures. Not now.

He took a long time getting to sleep.

The next morning he woke up stiff. He winced, jerked in pain, and tried not to let it show. When younger, he could sleep on a pallet of gear or a pile of rocks. Not anymore. He was going to spend the rest of his life waking up in contorted agony, then when his stomach meds ran out, he'd spend the days in pain, too. He wasn't a fan of suicide, but he expected there were limits to his tolerance for a life of torture. At some point he'd probably find nothing worth existing for.

For now, he was going to do what he could to create a comfortable camp, because he'd run out of interest that much faster if he didn't.

Nearby, Elliott rolled out of his bag, then went to the creek to drain. Already there was a path worn through the grass to their preferred rock to piss from.

As the LT came back, he said, "Morning, sir. Ready to start building?"

"Mostly. I sketched out a layout. Can you double check me?"

"Sure."

He took the notebook and looked at the improved sketch.

The proposed site was roughly pentagonal, so in an attack they would have a troop at each point and one at each base for crossing fire. That drove home how small their element was. They could just barely defend their position. It was centered around the trucks, which would serve as a redoubt.

"The design's good, sir, but it's not big enough."

"I want to keep it as compact as possible. What more do we need?"

"To be honest, sir, quite a bit."

Elliott chewed his lip.

"Well, I'm glad I asked, but goddammit, I'm frustrated at getting everything wrong."

"It's not wrong, sir. It's just based on being here a month, not forever."

"Yeah, that wasn't exactly covered in my training."

"Nor mine. This comes from reenactments."

"Okay, go ahead."

"You have the perimeter, two lodges, the vehicles, a latrine, a shower area, a kitchen area, and an arms room. We have space to work out and an undefined 'work space.' Those are all good. But long-term, we're going to need a few more things. Some will need to be outside for safety, or because they stink. But ideally speaking . . ."

As Martin spoke, he listed those things on the bottom of the page. "We'll need at least two more lodges. People need privacy. We need a sauna we can put a hot tub or bath in for the winter. I'll want somewhere to put a smithy, near the stream also. We'll need a place above the latrine, down from the smithy, to work leather and other animal products. We'll need a smokehouse for meat and leather. And it would be a good idea to have some space for some other industry—a loom or such."

"That means more perimeter and more buildings." Elliott looked disappointed.

"Yeah, it's going to take a while. And pentagonal would work with say, fifteen. But as few as we are, a square is just easier. We can build corner towers later, possibly. This means lots of cutting and hauling. Oh, we might be able to produce fertilizer, and even possibly gunpowder, in addition to the oil you mentioned."

"I'd thought of that, and yes, that's messy. As far as all the cutting, do you think they'll do it?"

"What the hell else we got to do, sir?" It was going to be a life of manual labor.

"Yes, I had thought to keep people busy."

"Well, let me take the four strongest other than you, and we'll clear up by the ditch. That gives us firewood, a brush barricade in the interim, a potential location for a well or an aqueduct—we can dig it deeper so it fills from the stream—and we'll see what we can put up."

Elliott said, "And I stay here and manage. Yes, good for today. I'll need some field time, too, though, for both familiarity and leadership."

Martin extended a hand.

"Let's build a future in the past, sir."

God, that sounded corny.

"Good. First, I'm going to loan out my gyroscopic shaver to anyone who wants to use it. By which I mean they don't have to use it, but have to shave somehow."

"Understood, sir. And thanks." Martin rubbed his bristly cheeks. As long as possible, they needed to look like soldiers and act like them.

"I wish we had a flag to fly," he said.

"We do."

"Oh?"

Elliott said, "It's one of those 'been on a combat patrol' things. I was given it before we boarded. It's behind the seat."

"Yeah, we should definitely commandeer that."

"I agree. We'll run that up an antenna for now."

They officially had American territory.

CHAPTER 8

Armand Devereaux was feeling twitchy. He wanted to be useful, but that wouldn't happen unless people got hurt, which he didn't want. He was constantly worrying about hygiene at the moment. He scratched three days of beard and could smell his sweat-soaked uniform again. They just didn't have the immunity for most of the local bacteria, and they had field conditions at best. It would get cruder before it got better.

He waited while Barker trimmed his beard off, leaving a Fu Manchu mustache, then took the shaver.

He yanked the cord, felt it spin up like a gyroscope and buzz, and started applying it to his chin.

It wasn't great, and left him with bristles, but that was safer for his skin than being smooth, since he was prone to pseudofolliculitis, and it was more comfortable than spiky curls.

He was still sweaty, but felt fresher trimmed. He'd need a haircut soon, too.

At least they were all done with diarrhea for now. But he had to stay on everyone to cook meat well done. Dalton and Oglesby liked it rare, and that wasn't safe here.

Food had other issues. They needed variety, and salt. Then, some of the squad would have medication. He'd heard Spencer mention GERD. There wasn't much he could do on a field expedient basis for that.

And the women would need sanitary supplies. How did you

improvise that in the field? He had a couple of boxes of tampons to plug into bullet wounds in an emergency. Those wouldn't last long. Then what?

He'd determined what day of the year it was, approximately, by timing dawn to dusk and calculating against the latitude. He'd set clocks at local noon. On the one hand, he was glad to help. On the other hand, knowing the day with no idea what century had pissed most of the troops off.

There really wasn't anything he could do except identify problems. He'd need to talk to Spencer and Alexander, since they had some experience in primitive skills, and Barker did. Otherwise, he and Oglesby would have to ask the locals to explain their superstitions. They probably had some herbal remedies that were better than nothing.

His worrying was interrupted when Spencer shouted, "Dalton, Devereaux, Barker, Ortiz, come with me. We're going to clear some brush."

He climbed to his feet and dusted off. That would at least keep him busy.

Spencer talked as they walked.

"Weapons loaded, no goddamn discharges, okay? Everyone keep an eye out for wolves. We have two axes, two machetes. So that's two people chopping, two trimming. Though we may drag some back and trim in camp, since it's only fifty meters or so. Stay in buddy pairs, and make sure you don't leave me alone."

The terrain was all hummocks and dips with stalks and weeds. The ditch was a shallow contour with an occasional deep eroded section in the bottom, and cattails and grass sprouting lush from those.

Spencer continued, "The fifth person is going to be starting a fire around the base of a tree and knocking it down that way. That's how we'll rest from chopping. Eventually, we're going to need about eight hundred small trees for the palisade, a hundred more for reinforcements, and another few hundred for lodging and other buildings. I plan to rotate the smaller troops through, but I want a good start today so I can gauge the probable time involved. Got gloves?"

"I do," Barker said.

"Yeah, and me," Ortiz said.

Devereaux said, "Sergeant Spencer, I volunteer to start with the fire."

"Ah, pyro, are you?"

"Yes, sir, Sergeant. I am a huge pyro." He grinned. Burning a tree sounded like fun.

"Why haven't I seen you at the club meetings, then? Sounds good. Burn the base of that one."

"Sure. Sergeant Barker, can I borrow your lighter?"

"Damn, what kind of second rate pyro doesn't have his own lighter?" Barker grinned and tossed over his Zippo.

"We may as well use that one first," Barker said. "Since the fuel evaporates. And we can always bring something from the fire in camp."

Spencer said, "Also, Devereaux, is there anything like poison ivy here we need to know about?"

He thought for a second. "Assuming it's like modern A-stan, some nuts, like pistachio. I'd say if it's a fuzzy vine, don't touch it. Watch for berries. Stick to actual wood or woody vines."

"Okay. Why don't you have a fire going yet?"

"Working on it."

"And the commander suggested we use using personal names. I'm not sure about that. I like being friendly, but we need discipline. So I'm likely to stick to using formal address, but I don't mind if we're a bit casual and laid back about it."

Dalton said, "What about this one, Sergeant?" He was next to a straight tree about six inches in diameter.

"Yup, good size. Get to chopping. Keep an eye out for drop angle." Spencer chose one himself and started swinging.

Armand stuffed a pile of dead leaves and twigs around the base of the tree in question. It was about six inches diameter at the base, reasonably straight, and looked like a tree. That was good enough for now.

The Zippo was hot before he had reliable flames, but once lit, the piled burned smoothly enough. He walked back and forth, clenching handfuls of small twigs and leaves, then stuffing them into the embers at the base. The flames licked up a bit, scorching the bark. Filthy yellow smoke rose. It stung his eyes when the wind shifted, and made him sneeze. He backed away, in case that was something toxic.

The growth here wasn't like anything he'd seen back home. This was a mad nest of everything growing, tangled around itself and the trees. Ortiz and Barker slashed away with their machetes, clearing paths while waiting for a tree.

It was slightly cooler under the trees, but damper, and the fire quickly made him hot again. Behind him, he heard the hollow chunk of axes hitting bark.

He found some deadwood nearby, snapped it into chunks and piled it in close. He suspected it would take several hours to burn a tree down. In the meantime, he could do others. There were four other trees of similar size. He stuffed them with a mess of leaves and debris, added twigs, and dragged fire over to get them lit.

The ditch was probably seasonally wet. Some of the debris looked to have washed along with water. There was a lot of low scrub. He wondered if they were going to leave that or chop it out. It also might not fare well after the trees were down.

"I lit four more, Sergeant Spencer," he said as the NCO came back from the chopping.

"Yes, however many you can get going, then I'll have you swap out with Ortiz."

"Roger that."

Setting fires was fun, but it was work to keep them where they should be. He moved around, kicking embers and fuel in close, making sure he didn't actually burn the tree, just the base.

He had to slow down. It was tempting to build bigger fires. That wouldn't work. Slow and steady was the key. That, and not getting acrid smoke in his eyes.

"Timber!" Dalton had one down. Three minutes later, so did Spencer. Then Ortiz had one down from machete chops, without an axe.

Spencer said, "Okay, Devereaux, Armand, right? Cool. Swap with Ortiz. Ramon. Just realized the two of you are our medical element."

"Such as it is, yes." He took the axe from Ortiz, who was sweating and panting.

He paused a moment, doffed his shirt and redonned his Camelbak. He made sure his medical kit was nearby.

With a nod to Ortiz, he found a tree and started chopping.

He didn't have much experience chopping. He realized that in a hurry, and everyone else did, too.

Barker came over and said, "Here, slide your hand up, then down, bend so you come into the tree like that. You're going to notch it. Don't worry how neat it is, just take this half of it out—on the side it leans toward. Then you come around back and you're going to chop there until it falls."

"Thanks. Not many trees to chop in Queens."

"Come to Missouri. We got a crapton."

He was glad for the borrowed gloves. He could tell from the exertion and movement he'd have blisters without. It took five minutes to erupt enough sweat to soak his shirt.

They stayed busy. In twenty minutes, he had the tree cracking, and shouted, "Timber!" It seemed silly, but it was a fair warning. It crashed down through the limbs of other trees, and bounced onto the ground.

He swapped off with Ortiz for a machete and trimmed branches, starting with the smallest. They'd have a lot of decent sized firewood when this was done. He tossed the limbs into a pile, which Alexander retrieved an armful at a time, and stacked closer to camp as a fence.

Spencer said, "We'll drag all the trimmings down to make a barricade. It's better than nothing, will at least slow animals and potential intruders."

"And then we burn it." He found an angle that worked, and chips flew as he hacked into the limb.

"Yes, but slowly. That's cooking fuel, and we're going to need heat in winter."

"How does an engineer unit do this in the field?"

Spencer said, "With several aircraft loads of gear. We're going to be busting ass every day."

He kept at it for a bit, then Ortiz said, "Swap off, go to the fire."

He nodded, and drank more water. Damn, he was thirsty. He gulped several swallows and felt it pool in his stomach. He wiped sweat from his eyebrows.

Spencer called "Chow break," and he realized it was near noon.

They had a dozen trees down, each about a foot diameter, and a dozen smaller ones. Barker leaned into the first one he'd lit the fire under, and it cracked, threw sparks at the base, and fell.

That became a game, with Dalton doing a flying kick that knocked down a tree, and had him drop to the base and roll through the embers. He skittered out of the sparking coals.

"Son of a bitch!" he shouted.

Armand said, "Yeah, don't do that."

The man lay down, and Armand took a quick look. He probably had some soft tissue abrasion even through his pants, and the impact likely hurt, but there was no sign of major trauma.

Spencer said, "So don't do that again, anyone."

Dalton limped toward camp, chagrined. Armand sighed in concern, then grabbed one of the downed trees by a lower limb and started dragging. The others each took a section or the end, and hauled it across the landscape.

He was glad it was only fifty yards or so. And he was glad he'd be able to sit down and eat.

Martin Spencer looked at the down timber and considered. Twenty-five small trees in a morning. If they could do that twice every day, it would take two weeks to chop the trees, then a month or so to trim and align them, and another month to set them. It wasn't going to be fast. But some of the bigger trees would make main supports, and their top halves were still enough for a palisade spike as well.

All that chopping would denude the ditch, and take quite a few of the trees along the stream, too. On the other hand, that gave a clearer field of fire.

Elliott said, "I agree the loose stuff can be piled around the perimeter. It means moving it twice, but we need some sort of delineation. And damn, I wish I had a full company of engineers. Or a full company of anything."

"It'll take longer as we clear the area, sir," he reminded.

"I know. And we'll need to start planning on firewood, too, for both cooking and later for warmth." ʹ

"What about interim shelter?"

Elliott said, "Barker suggested a tepee. We can use ponchos and tarps to cover it." And dammit, he wanted a tent fast, but they did need some kind of screening.

"Yeah, that's likely quickest. We'll want one really serious log cabin as HQ and redoubt. Shake or slate roof, not thatch."

"Yes, that was my plan. The vehicles work meantime. Nothing animal or native can get into them. What about other log cabins? They're warm."

He said, "I like them, but they do take a lot of work. I'd call that a long-term project. We can make hooches from saplings lashed together and covered with hides."

"Do you really think we need one each?"

He'd expected that question. Young officers for some reason often didn't grasp why. Did he have no idea why young men would want privacy? Hell, he wanted some himself.

"Sir, buddying up is great for a few weeks, or even a couple of months. After that, people are going to go bugnuts. And you can expect the younger guys to want native women after a while."

Elliott scowled. "Yeah. I'd say no way in hell would I ever find them interesting, but I don't think that's a realistic assumption."

"We're going to need to brief everyone regularly, have staff meetings, and disseminate info. Can you believe it? Lost in the goddamn Stone Age and we're going to have everything but PowerPoint."

Elliott actually smiled. "Our own personal hell."

The LT worked on site layout. As the bivouac resolved, Spencer was impressed. Elliott wasn't doing badly, now that he had his head on, and to be fair, they'd all been pretty fucked up the first couple of days.

Elliott was an engineer officer. He'd laid out a camp with sticks stuck in the ground. Alexander and Trinidad were standing as markers while he walked a line back from them and placed another stake.

Then it was back to chopping trees. The ditch was running out of timber fast. There might be another twenty good trees if they were lucky, though the slimmer ones would work for Barker's tepee. Then there were some smaller straight ones they could stack up for hooch construction or such. They might as well take them all.

"Hey, Sergeant Spencer," he heard Dalton call from atop Charlie 9, and turned.

South and uphill, a lioness stared at them from the dappled shadows of the ditch.

"Okay, no one move fast, keep your eyes open, and have rifles ready. If she attacks, it might take a dozen shots to put her down even with the machine gun. Which means you have to hit. Is everyone out of everyone else's line of fire?"

"Hooah," "Yes," "Yup."

"Do we have any rocks we can throw also?"

Barker said, "No, and I'm going to cut some saplings for spears as soon as she's gone."

Shortly, the graceful beast turned and padded away.

"She may come back. Might have smelled lunch. But *we* smell like a dead goat, which means we're a predator. Keep eyes open, whoever's watching the fire."

The palisade was a joke to start with. They really didn't know how to do it. It sounded good—wood ash for an alkali base to protect the wood, dig a hole, set a pole, pile up dirt. Then you realized you had to put them side by side in a trench, and keep them upright, not sagging. They had to be lashed to each other and to cross pieces. Logs weren't machine cut, so there were gaps, and each one took twisting until it fit right. The ditch in front had to be evenly deep and wide. They had to dig around rocks, and dig some of those out then refill. They had two shovels and an E-tool, and some buckets for hauling. Barker tried to lash a shovel together from split wood and a sapling, but it might only be good for shoveling snow. It wasn't usable for digging.

The logs piled up faster than they could set them. Three days in they had a dozen uprights buttressed in place, looking pathetic.

The tepee was easier. Barker and Trinidad did it with machetes in an afternoon. They chopped and set a tripod of sapling poles, more poles around that, some tarps and ponchos, all lashed with parachute cord, and they had a mostly dry place to sleep. That was easy. It gave them something to point to as an accomplishment. The covering flapped in the wind gusts. It was crowded and dank, but it was overhead cover. Between it and the trucks, everyone could sleep flat.

Spencer was glad they had Barker along. He was the go-to guy at this stage. Higher tech would be Spencer's, but the burly old sailor knew his primitive craft. His spears were straight saplings, peeled and scraped, with large nails embedded in the tips for now.

"I'll knap flint later, or we can saw some metal bar from the seats to use."

Dalton asked, "Won't it need to be tempered?"

Spencer said, "It doesn't for what we're doing, and it would have to be carburized first. Stone will work just fine, or those hypodermic-looking bone points the natives use."

Five spears, a rack to hold them, a tepee, a fire place with hot rocks to cook on. It was the barest bones Army camp he'd ever seen, but it was something. Then a lot more sticks got stuck into the ground to serve as clothes hangers and boot trees, and a couple of logs got rolled over by the fire as seats.

Midmorning on the third day on site, September 6 by their calendar, late into the local summer, Barker showed them a crude screen.

"The latrine has a wall. It's on this side only so far, but we can piss in peace, and not be ogled." He grabbed the structure. It was two saplings set into the bank, wedged and buttressed, then woven with boughs. It would also be a windbreak.

"Here's the seat."

He'd peeled three thick limbs and lashed them in a triangle. They were set on posts that ran to the rocks. Underneath it was flowing water.

"Ortiz and I diverted a channel. It's rock lined. That slab is safe to stand on," he pointed at a flat chunk of limestone. "It may dry up in summer, and ice may be a problem, but for now, we have a place to sit, and it'll wash downstream."

It wasn't even as good as a porta-potty, with no roof. They also didn't have a paper substitute yet. Wiping with rocks, Afghan style, wasn't appealing.

Devereaux said, "Everyone needs to designate a cloth or an old T-shirt as a wiping rag, and wash it after use. You can hang it on a stick to dry. Eventually we'll make soap or vinegar for sterilizing."

That wasn't really any better than rocks.

In the morning, Sean Elliott awoke to the rising orange sun to find Barker frying something on the fireplace rocks. It was goat.

"Thanks," he said, as he took a skewer. "Though I'm hoping we can get something else soon."

"Should be able to, sir. We can get fish in a day or two. Likely some big trout and some kind of sturgeon analog, and it's spawning season soon. There are antelopes, but those will take a brain shot. There's some kind of big cow, Spencer called it an aurochs. We'll need nets or blunt arrows for pheasant and such. We'll have variety, it's just going to take a while."

"Good. I'm also thinking about some kind of vegetable for the nutrition, though."

Caswell came back from gathering green stuff. He'd never missed vegetables until he didn't have any.

Between the two NCOs, they'd put together a fairly effective kitchen. One ammo can had been scoured clean and was kept full of water, which was boiled and dumped into the cooler, to reduce future infections. Another was used for each day's leftover bits, which were simmered with bone, blood and fat into a broth. It was greasy to the palate and fairly bland, but it was probably nutritious. He could manage a bite a meal, no more. They had skewers for roasting, flat rocks for frying and baking, and a couple of thin knives, close enough to kitchen knives to work. One had been Spencer's, one Alexander's. They used leftover drink cans for steaming and roasting small vegetables. Those would burn out eventually, and he wasn't sure about ingesting aluminum vapors. It probably didn't matter long-term. The cans were well blackened already.

Oglesby looked hungover as he rolled out. Spencer groaned and creaked, but seemed alert once up. Dalton looked fresh from the get go.

Caswell came over and said, "I found a few things, sir. Besides cattails, there's dandelions, wild plantain, garlic, mustard, various sunflower type things, and some pine nuts or needles maybe."

"Do any of those make a nice biscuit?"

She shrugged. "Maybe the cattails, if we can find a way to grind them."

"Damn. Not much variety."

She shook her head. "No, sir. Most of what's edible here is animals. That's why I gave up being a vegetarian for the duration."

"I'm glad for your knowledge." Yeah. Not having to move in with the stinking locals was worth the work, and all the knowledge helped.

She said, "Also, everyone needs to be careful with nuts. There are probably almonds here, and they're probably toxic."

"Toxic?"

"Cyanide."

"Then how did we make them edible?"

Dalton muttered something about God, and she said, "I don't know exactly. Early agriculture was just encouraging plants that were edible. Cultivation came later."

Barker said, "I'm hoping there's wild rice in the river. We can see about pudding at least."

Something would be nice. "Please. But how long is all this going to take?"

Barker shrugged as he poked meat with a stick. "Yeah, we have ten people, sir. I don't know what we can do."

Spencer said, "I'd love to trade for some stuff with the Paleos, but I don't know what we have."

Trinidad said, "Sir, I can trade some stuff from them."

"Without a common language?"

"I managed with Chinese, Indonesians and Koreans without a language in common."

"Okay. What are you thinking?"

"Trinkets. We have tools to make them."

Barker said, "We can make some nice wooden beads using sticks chucked in the drill."

Trinidad said, "You can, but not even that. Metal blades and files make carving much easier. Wooden spoons are better than those spatulas they use. We can also eventually make alcohol in better quality and quantity."

Barker said, "Hah, I get to feed firewater to the natives. Awesome."

"I expect the salted meat would prove popular."

"You think that's enough?"

"They have hides from every animal, and an existing industry to tan them."

Barker said, "I'll teach them bark tanning. That'll give us more variety of leather, too."

It was so frustrating. They had more than enough skill and knowledge. They had too few tools and not nearly enough people. With a company, or at least a couple of platoons, they'd easily build everything they needed in a year or two, and be at least at colonial levels of technology. As it was . . .

"What about bows?"

"What about them?"

"We're going to be using them. They'll figure it out soon enough. We swap an apprenticeship for more goods."

Trinidad twisted his face up. He said, "I may need Oglesby for abstract concepts. Though I think I can pantomime that."

Spencer said, "Next problem is that winter is coming. It seems to be September here."

Devereaux said, "I said it was. Once equinox hits, I'll know exactly."

"Awesome. But I'm worried about having dried food on hand, and firewood. The food will need to have a lot of fat. We'll need to dry berries."

Barker said, "Pemmican, jerky, and smoking. We'll need a smokehouse. It can be a small tepee."

"It never ends," Elliott said with a sigh.

Alexander said, "My charger can keep the truck batteries up, while we have light, and we can feed off the inverter there. Anyone else got solar?"

"Small one for my phone," Caswell said. "If you bring me your phones, I'll keep them charged for you. I have the universal jack kit. I won't loan it out."

Barker said, "Got one in the tool box. It's good enough for phones, not laptops."

"So we'll be using phones as nightlights, notepads, entertainment."

"But not GPS," Oglesby said.

Dalton held his up. "I have compass and a weather setup with a small probe. And the compass I used to get to the trucks."

Spencer yelled, "Yes!" then "Sorry, sir. All I have is this." He held up a basic phone, and a pocket compass that was second rate at best. It would find north, but wasn't going to work for actual navigation. "But my flashlights are both rechargeable. One USB, one via charger, which I have here."

Damn. That was good.

Elliott said, "I'm reluctant to commandeer personal possessions."

Spencer grinned. "I'm reluctant to let you, but since you're letting me borrow your shaver, I'm okay with letting you use one of the flashlights."

"Thanks. And yes, I want to keep the truck batteries charged so we have night vision. Also, I don't mind if you listen to music while sleeping, but keep the volume down in case you have to react, Hooah?"

"Hooah, sir," people replied.

Sean Elliott had a schedule, but the troops kept varying it. Usually, they had good ideas, but it did slow down the wall.

By the eighth day, Alexander and Caswell had lashed together a hut with a slant roof. There'd been some amusement, because the saplings were cumbersome, but he'd made the guys heel. He asked if they wanted help, only to be brushed off with a curtly polite, "We have it, thanks."

It wasn't bad. They'd used twisted bark instead of paracord, thatched the roof and reinforced it with MRE packets and cardboard from water flats with the plastic still wrapped around. It should keep them mostly dry. It also reduced crowding in the tepee and gave them some privacy.

By the tenth, the site had forty feet of palisade along the west.

He observed, "Well, that's half of one side, then we need to do two more sides, then figure out what the hell we're going to do on the stream side."

Spencer said, "It makes a good block to anyone on foot."

"Sure. But it won't stop arrows."

"Our armor and the range help with that. We can fix that later."

"Agreed. But eventually I want us buttoned up." He was much less sanguine than the older NCO.

Caswell said, "We can make a wattle fence over there and use it to pen goats. That means a steady supply of meat. It also slows any attacker a bit, and they'll make noise coming in."

"I like it."

"I'd really like a roof and more windbreak on the latrine. Can we use some goat hides? They'll cure in the sun." They already had ten hides drying and getting stiff. Barker and Caswell assured him they could make softer leather, too.

"For now use the hides," he said. "Eventually I want to split some shakes."

The Army loved formations, but Sean Elliott didn't want to get in the way of work. They met around the fire in the morning, and at night, and stuck to field conditions. There was no reason to stand around in groups. They did calisthenics to warm up, and a response exercise to potential threats.

After breakfast, he walked up above the kitchen area, down the path they'd already worn through the brush and between two trees. At the stream, he opened the lid on his Camelbak, and plunged it into the cool, clean water. Once they had gotten past the "intestinal distress," the water here was pretty good. It was tasty, though occasionally earthy, clear and clean enough, and ran right through the camp. That made it easy to stay hydrated. He wondered why this area wasn't occupied by locals already.

That done, he went back to Charlie Nine to go through plans.

He seemed to always be looking at plans. At least he could have them on a laptop, and Alexander even had Photoshop, PowerPoint and AutoCAD. That and the solar charger meant saving paper, and the ability to create substantial maps and documentation. Which meant he was stuck here, not out digging in poles. They had little enough manpower, and it wasn't kind, but true, that the females just weren't up to the heavy lifting the males were.

Onscreen, he adjusted a vertical for one of the lodges they planned to build, letting the worries run on their own mental channel. The weather was decent enough that he was quite comfortable in the back of the vehicle. He wondered how long that could continue. They'd need firewood soon, and that meant fireplaces in each hut. Crap. There was some way of doing them in wattle and daub, he recalled. Maybe Spencer knew. Oh, right. Caswell had mentioned that. But he'd feel a lot better with stone or sod. There were enough rocks here. They kept finding them while digging the ditch.

Dalton came up to the rear, knocked on the side and said, "Sir, do you have a moment?"

"Yes," he replied. It would be good to take a break. He stretched. There was just no way to be comfortable in the back of these things.

Dalton climbed up and sat across from him.

"Tomorrow is Sunday. Do we have any plans for worship service?"

"I hadn't planned on any, sorry." Yeah, they needed at least a little down time, and a chance to talk to the Lord. No one else was going to get them out of this.

"Would it be okay if I hosted something?"

"Please do. Keep in mind the Catholic members may want to do their own thing, and I suspect Alexander and Spencer will not want to participate."

Dalton said, "Yes, sir. I don't want to be pushy, but I do want to hold a service."

"I'll put the word out tonight."

"Thank you, sir."

"No problem."

That evening, they had goat for dinner again, but it was a little different.

"Mushrooms?" he asked.

Caswell said, "There was some tree fungus in the ditch. I made sure to do a spore test. And I've eaten some."

Barker said, "I sautéed them in suet on the rock." He pointed at a flat chunk of slate set on four stones. There was a bed of coals underneath. They'd gone from a rock next to the fire, to a griddle over it. "There's a little bit of kidney mixed in for salt. I rinsed it well. Unrinsed kidney is nasty."

It didn't sound that appetizing. He lined up gamely, though.

Instead of skewers, they had more flat rocks to eat off. The slate worked well enough, as long as you didn't have too much liquid. One dribble of grease ran off and over his wrist and cuff.

He wondered how long MRE spoons would last. Otherwise, it was pocket knives. He assumed they could whittle spoons from wood, or at least chopsticks.

The mushrooms weren't bad. A bit mild, but it was good to eat something other than meat. They were a little salty tasting. There were some kind of grassy herbs mixed in. They tasted surprisingly good. The goat was just goat. It had been interesting for a couple of days. Now it was just food.

Barker said, "We've got some cattail we can turn into flour. We'll see how that goes. We also need to start looking for eggs, and birds we can clip and keep as layers and roasters. I'm sure there's some kind of wild rice down there."

"No wheat, I assume?"

Caswell said, "Any grass seed is edible. It's just not really worth the effort, and it won't taste like much. That's a Neolithic Revolution development, sometime in the next five to ten thousand years."

She kept her eyes down on her platter, but he could see her tearing up. She didn't have close family, that he was aware of, but that didn't make it easier.

They were here forever. It was a life sentence at hard labor, and there was no appeal.

"Okay, we're going to have nightly formations, and they're going to be informal, but mandatory, unless you're detached or sick. Specialist Dalton has something."

Dalton stood up and said, "Tomorrow is Sunday, so I'm going to set up between the trucks at about oh nine hundred. I'll be spending some time with the Bible and anyone is welcome to join me. We may build a church eventually, but for now, we're the church."

Elliott said, "I'll be there. Medic Devereaux, your turn."

Devereaux stepped forward, and took a good, authoritative stance.

"Health is critical. My supplies are limited, facilities nonexistent. So, first, sanitation. We have water. Use it. Creek water is better than not cleaning. Clean when you use the latrine, before meals, bed, whenever you can. You know we have that box of soap, shampoo and other stuff the civilians sent for the Afghans. It's ours now. We'll use that until it runs out. Save the shampoo to use as soap, too. It's for hand washing, not laundry or hair.

"We'll have a laundry detail using water and possibly homemade soap. The latrine is designated, no pissing or crapping around the camp. I know some of you use drink bottles to urinate in at night. That's fine, but keep them well-separated and save them. We can't spare any. And I haven't seen nearly enough tooth brushing. I talked to Lieutenant Elliott. You will all brush your teeth for two minutes at formation." There were giggles and chuckles, but he kept on. "We will time this. You will brush your teeth for two minutes after each meal and thirty seconds after each snack. I have almost no facilities to fix teeth, and dental caries can kill you. It is not a joking matter.

"I've treated two of you for blisters and one for splinters. We have gloves. Use them until they wear out and your hands toughen, and we'll need to try to make more. We need your hands. Wear your gloves, the sex life you save may be your own." Devereaux smiled and pointed as if it was a commercial.

Sean chuckled, and hoped no one got offended, but who the hell were they going to complain to?

A moment later, the rest laughed, too. Good.

The medic continued, "If you get injured, see me as soon as you can. Every blister, splinter, hangnail, I need to put eyes on, just in case.

Don't wake me for minor stuff, but do see me at sick call in the morning. It won't be formal, but I'll be here. And we will have PT."

There were some groans as he said that.

Sean said, "Yeah, I feel it, too. We don't know when or if we can get home. We're just hoping whatever happened sorts itself out. Depression is possible, anxiety, whatever. No, not whatever, I mean other issues, I don't want to minimize them. And we'll have more as we go. Talk to each other if you need to. And talk to me." He took a deep breath. "UCMJ remains in effect, but any problems we can resolve here will stay here, and I will keep the communication privileged. Assuming we get back, I'll be reporting on events, not thoughts or comments. Consider me the chaplain in that regard. There has to be one. I'm not very religious, but I take your welfare seriously. I'll say again—anything that doesn't need to be shared, I'll keep as privileged. We can't have a lot of secrets here, and the environment means our ROE has to change."

He pointed through the purple dusk. "Charlie Eight vehicle is designated a private area for now. Each of us gets one day or night to use it for sleeping, meditation, music, whatever, undisturbed. We're a small group. We all need privacy and escape. The only reason anyone should knock and go in is if there's a life or death emergency. We need the safety valve."

That had been Spencer's idea, and it made sense, once he thought about it.

"And with that, Sergeant Devereaux is going to lead us in brushing our teeth."

It took a couple of minutes for everyone to dig their kits out. He was about to make a snarky comment about Caswell having an electric brush, very Air Force, when Doc pulled one out, too, saving him from making an ass of himself. No one had expected to be here, and he'd heard they cleaned better. He'd make do with his old reliable. He had a well-worn spare, and there were a dozen or so in the care box, so they could manage a few years.

There was something ridiculous about standing in a circle, brushing. It was almost childish. But, he knew it was easy for troops in the field to neglect it, and it was critical. He brushed vigorously and well.

Half a minute in, he realized Barker was humming the Jeopardy theme. Within seconds, they all were, and stifling giggles.

"That's two minutes," Devereaux said. "Honor system for other meals, but don't neglect it. All I can do for bad teeth is pull them."

Spencer said, "Well, you might manage a temporary filling with hot pine pitch. It'll need replaced every month or so."

That was creepy, and didn't cause anyone to laugh.

Every time Elliott thought things were as primitive as they could get, something like that came about and shocked him again.

Armand felt better with a morning sick call instituted. It let him do his job. Most of the stuff was minor, but fixing minor stuff prevented major issues.

This morning, Alexander had a tick on her ass, rather close to the perineum. Easy enough to guess it jumped aboard while she was relieving herself.

She was bent over the seats in the back of Charlie Eight, facing the ramp to offer what privacy there was, though most of them had relaxed about body modesty. And this was not a bad view, but he was working.

"Semi-professional question," he asked.

"Laser hair removal. Worked very well," she replied, anticipating the question.

"Okay. Well, that will help prevent sweat rash and make parasites easier to locate." The tick was middling fat. He pulled her skin taut, grabbed a lighter and said, "Heat coming, hold still."

A flare of flame and it twitched, crackled and popped. He swapped lighter for tweezers and started gently working the mandibles loose.

"That was part of my thinking, not just social," she said. "I've also had tubal ligation and endometrial ablation, so I won't be having any issues with pregnancy or periods."

"Understood," he said. He wasn't going to say "Lucky you" because he didn't know the background. He made a tiny incision over the bite and applied a suction cup for a few seconds. She hissed and said, "Ouch."

"Not safe for me to have more kids," she said. "And my hormones are bad enough with my thyroid issues."

"How are you doing with those?" he asked as he swabbed the site with a precious drop of alcohol. Spencer and Barker insisted they could have a still going in a few months, but . . .

She hissed in pain and flexed her ass, and damn, that looked pretty good.

She said, "Running out of medication, then I'll start having problems with mental acuity, sleep, memory, and weight."

"I'll see what I can come up with," he said reassuringly, but he had no idea what to do about that.

"All I have would be eating the thyroids of animals, and trying to find stuff with zinc in it. It might help. I read something about it somewhere, but I have no idea how reliable it was."

"Yeah. I don't know, really. We'll do what we can. It's clean. It might itch. Try not to scratch it."

"Roger. Thanks."

She straightened her uniform while standing.

From Charlie Nine's gun turret, Caswell called, "Approaching party!"

They both scrambled for weapons and down the ramp.

It was a local hunting party, coming up from the north, waving and calling. They carried meat, and one of them limped painfully between two friends.

Elliott shouted, "Oglesby!" uphill toward the stream, where more trees were being cut.

Caswell stayed up top, covering them with her rifle. Everyone else had gotten armed, and the tree party had a good crossing fire zone.

As they got closer, Armand could see the injured man had been gored by something with a horn.

"Tell them to bring him in. Get a poncho down for me to work on." He ran back inside to grab his pack.

Barker had a poncho from the tepee fast. At Oglesby's direction, they laid the casualty on it. Armand moved in and started assessment. It was cramped between the seats, but he preferred overhead cover to open sky.

The man was a tall, lanky bastard. Armand was 6'2", and this guy was almost a foot taller, with long, lean muscles and little fat. He was mostly tall in the limbs, but his torso wasn't short, either.

He had thoracic damage, probable pneumothorax from the weezing and gurgling sounds. Seeping, wet wound. Probable broken ribs. Cuts and abrasions all over, including a nasty hematoma and a superficial scalp wound.

Elliott was alongside, and said, "I'm a combat lifesaver, can I assist?"

"Yes, keep him calm, look at the minor stuff and get it clean. Oglesby, tell him this will hurt, but I can heal him."

"I'll try."

Spencer said, "If the spirits favor him."

"Oh, right," Oglesby said and continued in Paleo.

He took vitals, and listened to the chest. Yes, traumatic pneumothorax, and possible lung damage. Not good.

Elliott asked, "Not to be a dick, but how much of our resources will this take?"

"Not much."

"Good. It's neighborly and I want to help, but there are limits."

"I know." Yeah, he knew. Once he ran out of stuff here, that was it. Cleaning, bandaging and suturing would be all that was left.

The locals jabbered to each other, and to the patient. They brought out some weed that they lit from the fire and made pronouncements to the sky, and anointed what he presumed was the man's spear with animal blood.

"If you can, please explain to them I need some distance."

Spencer said, "Tell them the healing spirits need room to approach."

Oglesby said something. They backed off, but started moaning and crying in sequence, to appeal to the spirits, he supposed.

"Somebody hold him down. This is going to hurt."

"Anesthetic?" Elliott asked.

"I'd rather save it for us. He's already getting antiseptics I can't replace, and I figure he's more used to pain than we are."

"True."

"And barely conscious as is. The ribs broke clean, but in two directions." He pulled on gloves. He had fewer than five hundred pairs, but he didn't know what germs this guy had, and there was no need to spread any of his. Hopefully they'd not need them that often.

He manipulated the ribs into rough position. They'd heal, and be ugly, but shouldn't get in the way of the pleural sac.

He wiped down the wound area and applied a Hyfin Chest Seal. Then he wrapped the chest with Ace bandages, moving them carefully under the man to minimize movement.

"He will need to stay here a couple of days, and not be moved a lot. I'll need to use a magic needle to treat the lung every few minutes."

They seemed to accept that, after lots of back and forth, and gestures.

Spencer asked, "Can we haul him into the tepee?"

"If we're careful, yes. How many caretakers can they leave, LT?"

Elliott's face moved as he thought, and replied, "One."

"Sounds good. I'll need to stay with him and monitor."

"Okay. We can handle one up and one injured."

Oglesby said, "Sir, they're offering to bring us food or help in some other way. I took the liberty of explaining the treatment a bit."

Elliott asked, "What did you say?"

"That the horn had damaged his lung, and it was necessary to get the lung back to shape so it could heal."

"They got that?"

Oglesby said, "Sure. They've killed enough animals to know what lungs are. They just aren't clear on how they work exactly, or what to do when damaged."

"Ah. Well, tell them we'd welcome food. Do they need help with the kill?"

"Yes, they'd like to leave meat here, and go for the rest. Then they'll send a runner to their village."

Spencer said, "Alright. Everyone remain armed in Condition Two, and keep control of your stuff. Oglesby, stress to them the tepee is a spirit place, and no possessions can be removed or borrowed inside."

The bleeding was controlled; it looked as if the man's breathing would recover, and he'd live, though he was moaning in pain as he regained full consciousness. There was no feeling like that of saving another man's life. Armand smiled.

"Okay," he said. "Four people, roll the poncho as an emergency stretcher, and carefully take him inside."

The next morning Oglan, the hunter, was much improved. He nibbled on some meat and drank a little broth. He coughed a few times and writhed in pain when he did, but smiled afterward.

The Paleos looked very confused as the soldiers brushed teeth. They understood there were so many gadgets, but really had no clue what most were, nor even about their bases. They didn't recognize the vehicles as anything other than odd huts, but kept staring at them.

Spencer wondered if they could keep the natives around a bit longer. They were happy to haul logs, raise them up and help set them. They figured out a shovel in short order, and understood axes, as a much larger version of their own clubs and hand axes. In an afternoon, another fifteen feet of palisade went up.

"This thing keeps lions and wolves out?" one had asked through Oglesby.

"Yes." It would also keep people away, but he wasn't going to say that.

"You should give us the stick that chops trees."

"I'm afraid we can't. We need both of them."

"Will Arman Healer heal others?"

"Yes. But not everyone can be helped. It also takes the support of the spirits."

"You should know the best spirits, with all the fine things you have developed."

Dalton said, "We do. Our God can do all, but He does what is best for all, which isn't always best for one."

Oglesby had translated it automatically before Martin could say anything. He felt a buzz of worry.

He said, "Careful, son. The no proselytizing rule applies here, too."

"Hey, they asked, Sergeant. I can only witness what I know."

"Yeah, and if the Oglan guy dies, you've just told them that our super spirits don't care about them. Not an auspicious start to the church you want to build." The man meant well, but there were political and diplomatic things to consider, and he was too damned eager to talk about his god.

Dalton twisted his mouth. "Okay, I'll wait until he's better."

"At least."

A man named Isria, asked, "Will this stop !Katchathaynu?"

Oglesby looked as confused as Spencer.

"What is that?" Oglesby asked for them.

The man held a hand in front of his nose, another in front of his forehead, with first finger extended.

"Woolly rhinos," Martin said. "Yes, it should stop Kachat-hainew. They will think it's a cliff and go around."

He hoped Oglesby was learning from this. Lots of talking was going on.

A five minute attempt at chopping brush into firewood ended when one of the natives gashed himself with a machete. The man wrapped a leather strip around it, and Martin helped him limp into the tepee, so Devereaux could stitch him up.

"Yeah, a couple of sutures to hold it and I'll wash it clean with water." Spencer sent Dalton to get water boiled from the fire, though the water in the mountain brook was surprisingly clear and clean.

"How's the other guy?"

"Lucky. The horn was blunt and didn't pierce his lung. Though the pneumothorax would likely have killed him, or at least crippled him."

"Glad he's going to make it."

"Yeah, well, I expect they'll want sick call now."

"As long as they exchange labor, I think we can work out a deal."

"We should teach them how to make soap."

"They know that ash and fat cleans the crud off their hands, and they wash in the river in summer."

"I'd like them to use more of it."

Martin figured where that was going.

"Especially the women?"

"PREEcisely." Devereaux grinned.

Martin said, "That's probably coming eventually."

"Yeah. Life with two chicks you can't touch is not much of a life." Devereaux rolled his eyes.

"Seeing as I'm missing my wife, my sons and my daughter, I'm all sympathy, dude."

"Yeah. Sorry about that, Sergeant." Doc did look genuinely sad on his behalf.

He leaned out the door, grabbed a stick and heaved it at the horizon, watched it spin, tumble and drop.

"Hell, it's not your fault. But . . . I mean, they're not missing me, because they haven't been born yet. Except I'm not going home. So they'll think I'm dead in a blast, or worse, MIA. I'll never know what happens to them, except it hasn't happened yet. And I promised Andrew I'd teach him to drive next year. So much for that."

Then he was tense and flushed again. It had been a month, and that wasn't long enough to come to terms with something that was worse than death in many ways.

"Well, I miss Mama. My father and I were never close, and he left after they split. We talk now and then, but he's not significant. I guess that makes me the lucky one here. But my mother's going to need a caretaker eventually, and it won't be me."

His patient winced and hissed as he pulled a suture tight.

"Sorry. Okay, let me clean it and we'll be done."

The native man certainly didn't understand the words, but the tone and the washing carried the message. He smiled as Devereaux bound the leather strip back around his leg.

"Tell Oglesby I'll need to pull those sutures in a week. And could someone bring me a bite? Even goat?"

"Can do. And you're in luck. They had chunks of cow. So we're having steak. They also brought some salt."

"Who's cooking?"

"Barker and Caswell."

"I think I love them. In a fraternal fashion."

They were both thinking a lot more than fraternally about Caswell, and she was a problem.

Martin helped the man out the doorway, and he walked gingerly but steadily. It wasn't a crippling gash, but fairly deep, and he'd better keep it clean. He reeked of sweat, but seemed fairly kempt otherwise. His hair was tied back in a ponytail and had obviously been brushed.

Devereaux said, "Oglesby, tell him we need to take the sutures out in a week, and to change the bandage for a clean one twice a day. Stress it has to be well rinsed and dried between uses. The bandage, I mean."

"Got it."

He wandered to the outside fire, where, judging by the smell, Barker and Caswell had herbs and salt and something else and meat.

"Hey, Devereaux would like a snack."

"Of course," Barker said, and peeled off a thin piece of tough but juicy looking steak. "But you keep your hands off until dinner."

"Yeah, I know."

Caswell was lashing together two quite comfortable-looking chairs, or at least the frames. They'd need leather or woven seat sections. She was working on another, using straight sections of branch, leather thong and a knife.

"Those look good."

"They'll look better with footstools and woven seats. And I may be able to make a rocker."

"Oh, hell yes."

They were doing it. They were building stuff from the 1800s. They'd never get home, but they would manage to survive comfortably.

"How goes the garden?"

She waved at the tilled spot she'd scraped out with the E-tool.

"Well, I've planted everything I can identify, and it's real late in the season. It's mostly to get practice. I'll plant more rows of each next year. The LT and Sergeant Barker think we can put in field tile and irrigation on the other side. So each year we'll have tenderer, sweeter fruit and veggies, and eventually a few nut and apple trees. But, sir, understand that's a project that will take decades or centuries. We'll never see it."

She'd said, "sir." She'd slipped into Air Force lingo.

He said, "It's a start for us. The next generation will carry on."

"Which next generation is that?"

"Yeah, I realize it's not going to be ours. Probably adopted."

She said, "That's an entirely different level of diplomacy, sir. It may not work."

"Well, we're going to try. It's all we can do."

He watched her lashing a T joint, which seemed to be socketed as well. It was likely she could bore a hole afterward and set in a pin. It was amazing how fast that skill had gone from an historical hypothetical to something they did easily. Bore a hole, hammer in a twig as a dowel.

"I do wonder," he said, "if we've affected some timeline and the vehicles will get excavated at some point in the future. Or if they'll remain hidden somewhere for a long time. Or destroyed. Or maybe we're in an alternate timeline."

Between yanks on the leather thong, she shrugged.

"No way to know, sir. It's all possible, I guess."

She was a problem. She was skilled, yes. She was a useful shot, yes. Practical enough. Her vegetarianism got dumped in a moment once they were in trouble. But she had an abrasive personality, and that very strong liberal arts streak that was at odds with both her practicality and often with reality. She didn't like reality, and wanted it not to be.

She was quite good looking, which meant pretty damned hot by deployment standards, which meant the hottest piece of ass in this particular universe. It was obvious to Martin she wasn't interested, and he didn't blame her, but damn, she looked good bent over in the stream. Gina Alexander was nice enough, and looked a lot younger than she actually was, but Caswell, damn. And if he felt it, then the young bucks felt it. If she hinted at availability, they'd fight. Then there were the Paleos . . .

They really did need some liaison with the native women, except that required another layer of diplomacy, safety, birth control, and delicate negotiations. And then they'd likely expect kids. In fact, they'd been begging for them.

Not this year. That needed to be understood.

"Important formation tonight, spread the word."

"Roger. And make sure no one shows anything modern around the Paleos."

"Oh, crap, you're right."

Yeah. Nonfunctional stuff was just stuff. A lit iPod or flashlight was magic.

The word got spread and the balance of the hunting party came back with more meat. They jabbered and groped at each other, then most of them left, leaving three caretakers for whatever the injured guy's name was. Elliott had conceded on that when they worked so industriously.

The steak was very chewy, but it was steak, Regina decided. Now she knew what aurochs tasted like. It tasted like chewy, stringy, under-aged steak. Still, it wasn't goat.

She was glad she and Caswell had their own hut. The tepee was going to be snug with four extra bodies. She'd also need to tell the watch to make sure the Paleos didn't go exploring. She was not interested in being seduced.

Home was gone, this was home now, like a permanent military barracks crossed with a college dorm, until the kids grew up.

Caswell was not a great hoochmate. She had all these theories, some of which Gina agreed with. But she took everything to a logical conclusion that came down to blaming white males, or white people in general, without regard to the fact that she herself was about the whitest person here.

Elliott stood, stepped into the firelight and said, "Keep eating, but I'm going to cover a few things. This is for us, Oglesby, so don't translate."

"Got it. They've started to grasp a handful of words. Nouns, affirmatives, negatives."

"Roger that. Okay, the palisade is coming along, and we'll thank our friends for that in a bit. We're getting more variety of food. We're working on individual shelters though I'm leery of spreading out too much, or of concentrating in one tent. There really isn't a good answer. Sergeant Caswell has made two really nice chairs this week, and I'm hoping she'll make more. Then we can use leather for some stools. It's nice not to sit on the ground or rocks.

"Wear whatever is appropriate for the weather and work. There's no Uniform of the Day. If PTs work for you, wear them, just keep in mind they're not as durable. Part of me would prefer you not mix uniforms, but if it's necessary, I won't complain.

"We have enough power for devices at present, but only two flashlights can be recharged, so the rest of you will have to rely on phones to get around at night, and not in front of our neighbors, yet. We do have rechargeable batteries we can use in another light.

"We have a lot of work ahead of us, but be proud of what we've done so far. We're making good progress on everything, and it'll get easier as we continue to acclimate, and learn as we go.

"The important thing for tonight is a social issue. I know some of you are interested in closer relations with the locals, for both extra labor, and social interaction, including the women."

There were chuckles and a hoot, and she said, "I'm not interested in the women."

That got laughs and a "Boo!"

"I'm glad you can joke about it," Elliott said. "I'm sure eventually we're going to have closer involvement. But Sergeant Spencer and I have decided we're postponing that for a year." He paused to let that sink in.

That made sense. Though it would keep stress on them here. She didn't see any better option, though. The men were going to be rutting idiots.

"After we have our own village, tools, and know what we can do, and what we need, then we'll see about allowing others in, slowly, and making sure they acclimate to us and don't try to displace us. We have a huge tech advantage, but we're only ten. They're hundreds, thousands, tens of thousands. The best way to avoid trouble is just to avoid them, at least until we feel each other out and learn how to interact without offense. They apparently thought us rather rude at first for not swapping partners and not giving enough of our stuff. Keep that in mind."

Dalton said, "To be clear, we'll reconsider this in a year, not that all bets are off, right, sir?"

"Exactly. Don't ask me about it until next year. Then we'll discuss the issue. You all get input, but I'm the CO, just as if we were POWs. We're soldiers in a lost, detached element, until we get things organized. Then and only then will we consider how to adapt things. I'm not saying this is how we'll do it, but we might go by expiration time of service, adjusted to the current calendar. Or by age. Or some other way. But you're still under orders until we have that discussion. Hooah?"

"Hooah." The men generally did not look pleased. Caswell was hard to judge. She seemed to be weighing the matter.

"Okay, make sure you take care of hygiene including teeth. No lights while we have guests. Now we'll thank them. Oglesby, bring them up."

Oglesby grabbed a small package of hide from Barker. He unwrapped it and held something glittery up in the light.

"These are small arrowheads that Bob Barker chipped out of a beer bottle someone left in Number Eight. They're really shiny, and sharp." He carefully handed a pair of them to each of the three hunters, and two more to the lead man. "Give these to Oglan."

The locals ooed and aahed appropriately, seeming delighted with these acquisitions.

Spencer said, "I'm not worried about the bottle glass. It's just glass, and if someone does a detailed analysis in fifteen thousand years, they're less unlikely than two MRAPs."

There were nervous laughs.

The locals cheered, and kept scraping the arrowheads against their nails. They were impressed, and that was positive. Dalton and Barker kept them penned on that side of the fire, so they couldn't mingle.

It would be a long time, though, before she'd consider living with them, or anything more. A long time. The men were quite attractive, well built, and friendly, but the culture was too foreign, and she still liked soap and shampoo. And her toothbrush. That box of sundries was worth more than its weight in gold. If only it had toilet paper and beer.

She found her way to the latrine in near pitch black, shivered in nervousness astride the seat, then made her way back past the fire to her hooch. It was definitely fall, and she was glad of warmth of the bag, as much as she hated the enclosing shape. Caswell's presence next to her was reassuring, even if they'd never be close friends. She laid her rifle on the platform next to her, and zipped up to sleep.

"Night," she said.

"Night," Caswell replied. "I really wish the LT had told them to fuck themselves raw with the locals."

"I know," she said. "The Army's the Army. It is what it is."

"Until we get all the manliness to deal with."

"It'll be fine for a year," she said.

"I doubt it."

Gina wasn't sure. There were reasons that was a complex matter for her, and she wasn't going to discuss them here.

She lay there listening to the frame creak and walls shift in the breeze. It wasn't much of a hooch at all, but at least she didn't have to bed down with all the men. That was okay if there was lots of discipline, but here, different story.

Shortly, there was a spattering sound of raindrops, then more. It turned into a steady splash, and then she felt large drops falling onto her bag from a leak in the roof.

That was going to suck.

There wasn't any way to avoid it, she doubted the tepee was any drier, and Doc and Oglesby were sleeping in the trucks. She could run for a cab and sleep sitting up, or she could stay here and wake up in a puddle.

It was just too damned much effort to get up. She felt the water leak through and start soaking her.

Her phone was charged, she had headphones, and Evanescence at least kept her brain warm as she itched to sleep in the wet. At least her ass had stopped burning.

CHAPTER 9

The next morning, Bob Barker unbanked the fire. There were still coals despite the rain, and he used his Ka-Bar to peel shavings from a stick to get smoky flames going, then added bigger fuel. Breakfast was going to be late. His hands were raw, dirty and numb by the time he was done, and he warmed them over the growing flames. His eyes were used to the acrid smoke by now. It would blow, he'd squint, and that was it. He could even smell it in his moustache.

It was overcast, with deep, heavy clouds that predicted more rain. He really wanted to put up another overhead to protect the food and fire. For now, there was a spare fire in the tepee, but they'd have to build up a platform for it. It was half puddle. That fire still burned too, but barely.

It had been cramped in the tent, with the four Paleos. They slept quietly, but took up a lot of room, and smelled. They probably didn't smell worse than the soldiers, although Bob was still using deodorant every two to three days. But they did smell different. It was noticeable. They were musky, earthy, sharp and pungent.

Devereaux examined Oglan and pronounced him fit to travel. He gave instructions to walk steadily, not flex his right arm, and not hunt for a month. He should do light exercise in the meantime, and he demonstrated some isotonic techniques.

"And tell him to rest and eat well. He could use some fat and starch, as much as they have."

Bob was sorry to see them go. He'd learned quite a bit about their skillsets and tools. But if they liked his archaic points made from a beer bottle, they'd be back. Of course, his supply of glass was very limited. Though he could do the same with good quality chert or flint, and teach them archery.

The others gathered around the fire one by one. They didn't really bother with reveille. Everyone was up shortly after the sun anyway. Most of them wore gore-tex and sat on the rocks and logs. Elliott stayed standing.

"So how much information do we want to give them, sir?" he asked while chewing on some steak cooked until it was almost jerky, that tasted almost like leather. It would have to do.

Elliott said, "Well, they can't understand where we came from. I don't want to show them anything modern in use, meaning weapons, electronics or vehicles. Axes and knives are okay. They don't need to know about night vision. As far as primitive skills, I really don't see how upgrading their weapons is a problem, done slowly. They can't do much to us. When did bows come about?"

Spencer had joined them, and the two men swapped glances.

Spencer said, "If I recall, there is some possible indication of fletched arrows thirty K years before our time. But we're not seeing that here."

The LT nodded. "Right. Make bows for us, so we can save ammo. Keep them out of sight as long as possible, then teach that, too. A little bit at a time will minimize the shock to them, and give us trade advantage. They'll want to be friendly to see what we do next."

"I would like permission to use a roll of the dental floss for bowstrings. Dacron is a lot stronger than sinew or rawhide, and a lot easier than gut."

Elliott screwed up his face. "I hate to waste it."

"It really is better. Once we can replace it, it's still usable as floss, barring a little fraying."

"Okay," Elliott agreed. "Do it."

"Roger." Yeah. He had no idea how gut string would work. Only theory. As in, he knew it could be done.

"You really are good with that stuff, Bob," Spencer said. "You knock out points faster than they do. I'm glad you're here. Well, actually, I wish you were home, but if *you* are here . . ."

He said, "I gotcha. Thanks."

"Do you have a native name?"

He grinned. He loved this part.

"My Indian name is Bob."

There were laughs all around.

Spencer said, "Bob is our man. As to the bows, sounds good, sir. And now it's time to chop more trees."

Chopping was hell on his back, but Spencer was right. The ditch was almost denuded, having only scrub left. Even all the deadwood and crud had been removed and stacked as fuel, doubling as a low wall along the north. The east had the creek, gradually losing trees along this bank along the frontage. The palisade was about long enough on the west, and they'd hopefully start along the south today. But until they had a solid wall, he wouldn't be entirely relaxed.

It was also bath day. Hopefully it would get into the low 70s midday, and he could splash in the creek and get clean. Trying to sponge bathe with a washcloth and an ammo can of water was not as effective, though it was much more comfortable.

Sean Elliott felt better. Good relations with the neighbors and some diplomacy meant potential resources for them. They'd already agreed to bring more salt, and knew a place to get it. Eventually, they'd want to seek out other groups, too. As soon as they had a solid camp. And better food sources and enough fuel.

He understood why even in the nineteenth century some people never made it outside their own county.

He was going to do some chopping today, and he felt guilty about not doing it earlier when it had been hotter. It was quite mild today, with a soft breeze and just enough haze to cut the glare.

He was pondering that when Alexander came up.

"Sir, are you busy?"

"Always, but I need a break and I'm here for you. What do you need?"

"Operations proposal, sir."

"Go ahead."

"I'm not as physical as the others, but I hope to do a bit more with the solar power, and with the laptops."

"Long-term, yes. Is everyone keeping their phones charged?"

She said, "Now they are. I had to institute a schedule."

"Okay. Well, I do want lots of photos for documentation. If we ever do get back, that proves our legitimacy, and I'm sure the scientists will be all over it."

She lifted her camera bag. "Twenty-four, seven, sir. But I'm talking about regular old Forty-Two Alpha administration, orderly room style."

"I've got enough of that already. It's burying me." God. PowerPoint in the Stone Age. He still couldn't get over that.

She was trying to sound confident but not managing, as she said, "But that's why you need me, sir. You need to know what we have, a charging schedule for phones, maps, lists of edible foods, a calendar and almanac, journals of what we find and learn to manufacture. We need reliable, regular schedules for duty, long term, because the seasons are going to matter. Farming will definitely require documentation."

He hadn't really thought of it, and it still sounded secondary. But she was right, they did need records of weather and farming at least.

"I can have everyone write a log in the evening," he said. "It's a good idea."

"Yes, sir, but then it needs collated so you can find it. No, the search function isn't enough. You remember college texts. They have a bibliography and index. That's my civilian job. Companies call me in on contract to sort their files, define their positions and create databases and SOPs."

"Well, what do you think we need?"

"All the things I said, and whatever else I can come up with. I have to see what people log and build the database as I go."

That made sense. Admin was necessary to run a unit, though it was hard to think of something the size of a squad needing that much support. And they did need muscle power. But . . .

"You do have a training in this, I assume?" Her job description suggested it.

"Three degrees."

". . . three?"

"Bachelor's in IT and financial management, and a master's in forensic accounting." Before he could ask, she explained, "I go into their files and find the missing figures. IRS auditors hate me."

And she held three MOSes, or two and an Air Force AFSC.

Regardless of her physical condition, she sounded like a formidable mental asset.

"Then go ahead, define what we need and do it."

"Thank you, sir." She gave a professional nod.

"May I ask a personal question?"

"You can always ask."

"Why aren't you an officer?"

She said, "I was too old when I came back in."

"Understood. Though you should be a senior NCO at least."

She looked mildy annoyed as she said, "Well, that depends on a Guard unit having its shit together. If they lose files enough, no one's promotion paperwork gets to Brigade. I can't find what hasn't been entered into GFEBS, iPERMS or AKO."

"I see. Well, have at it, though I'll still call you if we need backup labor, and your other technical knowledge."

"Yes, sir. I'd like to brief everyone this evening."

"Agreed."

"And I can still do physical stuff, including guard duty and hauling or chopping. This just makes me more useful in ways I can be, rather than pretending I'm as strong as Dalton or Ortiz."

She climbed up into Number Nine and started moving stuff around.

"Is that going to be the Orderly Room?" he asked.

"Yes, sir."

It would have been nice of her to ask, he thought.

On construction, Spencer was a decent manager. The logs came over steadily, carried by troops and locals. When a few feet worth were ready, the ditch and rampart were dug, the bases burned, ash dumped in, and the logs erected. The fill was tamped down with the shovel and a ball bat from the Hajji-Be-Good box in Number Nine. The brush pile grew. Visibility got better as the trees came down.

It was muddy in the morning, but better by afternoon, though cooler, probably 60s.

He took a turn chopping, enjoying the feel of his biceps and core flexing and straining. He panted for breath, sweated and felt invigorated, as his hands went numb from the impacts, and chips flew past his legs. He took down three uprights and pruned them smooth.

"You're pretty good with an axe, sir," Dalton said.

"Thanks," he replied as he swung and sheared a limb, twisting as the axe descended to throw its velocity at an angle. That was a physics trick, though he'd learned it long before at his uncle's cabin. Uncle Walt was long dead, but he missed him even more now.

"How do you do that twist?"

"Like this," he said, raised the axe, lowered his body, twisted and raised his elbow as if batting. He did it slowly and just nicked the next limb. "Let gravity bring it down, twist it like batting, and follow through the same way." He took another swing and severed the limb.

"Damn. Good stuff, sir. Let me try."

He let the axe drop, bit down, and passed it over handle first.

Dalton got it within a couple of swings, and turned his brawny shoulders into it. He fairly walked along the down timber, cutting limbs every couple of steps.

"Damn, I came out here to help," Elliott said. "Not to be outclassed."

"Ah, hell, sorry, sir." Dalton seemed embarrassed.

"No problem. Use it tomorrow," he replied. It wasn't as if they were going to run out of wood to cut.

He went back to pruning.

Food was improving. Barker and Caswell really knew this stuff. That evening, there were several edible grasses chopped up in the small cooler lid, and more greens. It was a sort-of salad. The stalky things were probably cattails. He bit into one. It tasted a bit like cress. At least it was juicy and not meat. The variety helped.

"What's this?" he asked about something green and leafy.

"Sorrel," she said. "The long stalk is wild plantain, and is a bit like asparagus."

Barker said, "The meat is deer of some kind, roasted in herbs with wild onions. But I really need to find a salt lick, sir."

Yes, that would help. "We'll need to make a recon patrol."

Spencer said, "I'm going to need ground bone meal. My stomach meds are running out, and that's the closest I'm going to find, unless I eat actual chalk daily."

Barker said, "Damn, that sucks, dude." Others made comments of support.

Spencer shrugged. "I can last a couple more months. I always knew it was an issue. Are we going to tan the deer hide?"

Barker said, "Yeah, hair on. It'll make a nice rug or wall hanging, but that's going to take some work. You can chew the bones for calcium."

"I was thinking of the bones for tool handles and eating utensils. We may be able to trade for a few, too. It's not like the Paleos lack them."

"Good."

Oglesby said, "They're called the Urushu. Singular and collective both."

"Got it," Spencer said. "Urushu."

If there was anything Elliott was going to thank God for every day, it was that he had troops with these skills. Without them, they'd be reduced to living with the Paleos and depending on charity. This world was so alien to him it might as well be another planet, but Alexander, Spencer, Caswell and Barker knew how to make it work.

"Okay, formation for the evening. Everyone listening?" He looked up to Caswell and Ortiz on watch. They thumbed up. "Good. Sergeant Alexander is going to be our admin, logistics, armorer and readiness NCO. Go ahead, Alexander."

She looked around, stepped slightly forward, and spoke.

"Just as the lieutenant says, we must account for everything. I'll be using Number Nine as the HQ, office, armory, whatever. Everything will be stashed in there. If you need something, see me first. If I'm not around, neatly take what you need and log it. There will be an open notepad on the laptop. Don't try to update the spreadsheets. I'll do that. Just write it and sign it so I can look you up if I need to."

She stepped back. There was muttered assent and hooahs. Everyone seemed to understand.

"Let me reiterate," he said. "I know a lot of you don't think of admin as serious. It is. The Romans became the world power they were because of documentation. Otherwise, everyone else was barely above our neighbors here." Emotionally, he wasn't convinced, but mentally, he knew she was right, and that he'd appreciate it in future.

That got quiet but attentive nods.

She added, "I can log enough information we can find a growing season. That means better food. I can map out salt, rock, timber, edibles. I'll have walking times to reach them. Everything. It means you won't have to scratch your head and think, or try to find someone else. I'll have the info. You just have to give it to me."

They seemed to understand.

She said, "Look, let me give you background. Some of you know this, but I don't want to tell the whole story ten times. I was active duty Air Force in the early nineties. Airborne Intel equipment operator aboard an AWACS. I came back in the Army Guard after September Eleventh. I've been in Iraq, Kosovo and here. I'm a photographer and an admin, and I have college degrees in management. But I've got bad ankles, bad knees, bad wrists and thyroid problems. My medication will last about three months. After that," she sighed. "After that, my memory will get fucked up badly, my attention will slip, I'll have trouble sleeping, my blood sugar will get chaotic, and I'll probably gain weight, too."

She sounded tired just from sharing that.

Next to him, Dalton muttered, "Can Caswell make a wooden wheelchair?"

She heard him.

"Corporal, when you've survived a forced landing in an E Three, a car wreck, two kids, surgeries on your joints and are forty-three years old, you get back to me."

Elliott cut in fast. "Yeah, easy on the jokes. We're all going to get old and worn out," he said, with a firm glance at Dalton.

"Sorry," he said. "Bad attempt at humor."

She said, "Accepted. And I'm sorry to be sensitive about it. For now, I can keep up, and there may be some dietary workarounds. I can use an axe. I can haul wood."

"Good." Was there any way to work around that medication? Probably not. And yes, he was assuming they were here for life, because he didn't think there was anything they could do about getting back. He had no idea how they got here, so getting back was the second problem, and he didn't think they had any control over it. And there was something else, but he couldn't remember it.

Armand Devereaux was on watch at sunrise two days later, ready to grab a bite. They had fifteen feet of the north wall done, the corner reinforced with a mound of earth and two buttresses. He felt a bit more secure.

Off to the closed side, he saw movement, and called, "Natives approaching from the west. Five people, three with spears." They didn't seem troubled, but they weren't really enough for a hunting party.

Caswell and Dalton went out to meet them through what would eventually be the front gate, but for now was a framed opening with a sill. He kept them covered from the hatch.

Caswell was good. She graciously offered to carry their spears, and then they were disarmed. She came in and stowed them in Number Nine, along the floor.

"I think you're needed," she said. "I get the impression one of them is sick."

"Okay, want to cover me?"

Barker clattered up and said, "I will." He climbed up the outside as Armand wiggled down inside.

Caswell was back and talking to the woman, with Oglesby translating. He was getting pretty good at their language, and maybe they should all learn some. Something might happen to him.

"What's up?" he asked.

Oglesby said, "This is Ai!ee. She's been cursed with illness in her genitals. They stay inflamed and leak poop smell, I gather." He blushed.

Caswell said, "Oh, goddammit. Ulceration of the vaginal canal. Happens in Africa. The women tend to work until they pop. Strain can cause abrasion, and then add in delivery. The tear is from the vaginal canal to the rectum."

That wasn't something he was trained for.

"So she's leaking feces through a fistula."

"Basically, yes."

He thought about it. He wanted a reference book, but that sounded straightforward enough. "I can do minor surgery. My concern is sterility, anesthetic, and I've never done a procedure like that. Sort of a high-end episiotomy repair."

Caswell said, "I'll help."

"First you've got to explain it to her."

Oglesby was clearly embarrassed and uncomfortable.

"Okay, what do I need to say?"

"First I need a look. Caswell, do you know what we're looking for?"

"Sort of."

They led Ai!ee into the back of Number Eight, and he grabbed a flashlight.

"I don't have anything resembling a speculum," he said, as Ai!ee pulled her skirt aside and leaned back.

"Spoons," Caswell said, and ran to grab two MRE spoons.

Using those to spread her hair, her labia, and the vaginal canal, he could see a discolored area, and got a definite whiff of bowel.

"That's it, yes?"

Caswell bent over and took a look.

"Yes," she said.

"Okay, we'll do surgery. We can fix it with knives and sutures. She has to purify herself for two days with only water. Then she must purify herself afterward with a special diet. This is in accordance with the spirits."

Oglesby spoke slowly to Ailee and her friend. It took a good fifteen minutes back and forth, between him and them, and then between each other, to come to an agreement.

"She asks if you can actually fix an inside tear. They seem to know what the problem is."

"Tell her yes, we can do it. It will be sore, and it will have to heal, but it's doable."

After a few more minutes, Oglesby said, "She asks about fever spirits."

"We should be able to keep fever and infection controlled. We can't guarantee it, but we'll work hard on it, and the spirits often listen to us."

"She says she will bring two speakers with her, to talk to the spirits. They will also guard her to make sure she stays pure. She asked about her family. I said they should pray at home, that separation increased the odds."

Caswell said, "Good, we don't need spectators. We will also wash her with special soap against the spirits, when she returns."

There were some pleasantries which he took in with half his mind, while trying to remember more about this type of thing. If he opened the edges of the tear and sutured it closed, it should heal. He didn't know much about plastic surgery.

Caswell seemed to have some idea. He'd need to talk to her.

The natives had brought some sausage, stuffed into cleaned animal intestines, and a decorated hide that obviously was significant to them. He smiled and thanked them, and did look at it for a few moments. It held geometric designs and images of stick figures.

Caswell retrieved their spears and sent them on their way.

He said, "I need to figure out how to do this."

She said, "We need to make it ritualistic."

"Well, we have clean clothes, gloves, masks, hats. That's pretty ritualistic. But I meant the surgical process."

Oglesby said, "Sorry I'm twitchy about it. I really don't like stuff that personal."

"You did fine."

"Thanks. And they said there's salt north and east of here, toward that rise."

Barker overheard and came over. "Really?"

"'Blood rock,' they call it. Salt."

"Goddamn, we're in business."

"Yeah, that'll be a nice plus."

"It's not just a plus. Cooking. Food preservation. Curing leather. Several other processes. We need salt. I'd even think about taking a vehicle, but we probably can't risk it. We'll need a sizeable party or several trips, though."

"Okay. Well, I'm glad the information helped." He still sounded embarrassed.

Spencer arrived and said, "Yeah, I need that, too, and it's just possible there's coal around. Otherwise, we have to do a charcoal burn. And by that, I mean several tons of wood."

"One thing at a time, dude."

"Yeah, I know. And bone meal. Nice, tasty bone meal to settle my stomach."

Armand asked, "Having trouble?"

"Not yet. I have enough Zantac to last another three months. But once it's gone, it's gone. I thought we discussed this."

"Ah, you want to test the idea first. Very wise, old man."

"Thanks. And I'm not an old man, boy."

"Heh. Sergeant, I'm trying to figure out how to do OB-GYN surgery on an injured woman. My brain isn't all there."

"No problem. You work on that, I'll find something to chop."

Regina had Number Nine full in short order, with the solar panel up top and the laptop up near the turret. She brought the panel in at night and during rain, religiously. Once that was gone, they had no power unless they burned fuel. Her charger could handle batteries for Spencer's two flashlights and night vision, her own flashlight and camera powerpacks, her laptop, and it could trickle charge the truck batteries. It would also handle AAs, as would the small 110v charger Caswell had, with six batteries that worked in two more flashlights. With her USB kit she could charge all the phones and tablets.

She set up a schedule to keep the phones going, since those served as entertainment, note-taking devices, clocks, alarms and nightlights. The night vision in the trucks and on Spencer's rifle had to be kept up for security. The lights would only need periodic charging. The other lights would all be useless once their batteries were exhausted. She had a bin for them, and spreadsheeted them by brand in case any spare parts could be scavenged. Otherwise, they were sturdy, waterproof containers.

Pens, pencils and paper were precious, but as long as their devices worked, they could use those.

There was probably some way to rig a wireless network. She'd covered that briefly in school, and tried to recall if she had enough equipment here to create a wireless router. It wouldn't have much range, but photos from the perimeter, and text messages, could be useful during any kind of attack.

The biggest page, though, was a list of projects, chores and tasks. It was huge. They all pulled sentry duty every day and a half. They might decide that wasn't necessary, but for now, they were still scared of animals. The wolves patrolled regularly, the lions stayed in the area, and there'd been leopards sighted.

She had CAD software, and Elliott had been using that for design. She cracked it and ripped a copy for his computer. Then she cracked and ripped every program she had, copyright being no longer an issue, and backups being desirable. Then she decided to do everyone's systems. When she announced at evening formation, there were some astute nods. Yes, sharing all the software possible increased their resources and their recreation. But how long would the systems last? It was unlikely any of them would still work in a decade.

The laptop sat at on an ammo crate at a slight angle due to the lean of the truck, and she propped it with a stick she shaved flat on two sides. She kept her weapon next to her, and there was the box of cricket and ball bats, clubs and irons known as Hajji-Be-Good. Melee weapons were still useful. There were also a glove and a ball, but no one wanted to risk losing them in the rough terrain. Maybe someday they'd clear a field.

The third day of her glamorous duty, she came in to find an ugly, flashing malware banner demanding she pay for "viruschek" or "stay infected."

"Hey, LT!" she called.

He stuck his head around from the side a moment later and asked, "Yeah?"

"The laptop has a virus. How did that happen?"

"You're sure?"

"It's pretty obvious." She pointed to the screen.

"Oglesby was in here last night, right?"

"Yes. Thanks, sir. Hey, Oglesby! Come here!"

He trotted over.

"Yes, Sergeant?"

"Did you have a geekstick plugged in here last night?"

"Uh . . . yes." He flushed red.

She held out her palm and made the gesture for him to hand it over. Then she looked at the gawkers.

"Shoo!" she said.

The problem was she needed a boot disk to fix it, and didn't have one. But she had her own flash drives, and she used the LT's laptop to make a clean boot file.

Once she had it up in boot mode, banishing the malware still took two passes. She had to remove the root, then it changed names to "Save" her from itself. And without any online references, she was cracking from scratch. But it worked. Then she had to remote scan his drive.

Five minutes later, she knew was right on both suspicions. Oglesby's flash contained porn, and some of it had been swapped for in theater, and was corrupted. As soon as he'd opened that file, the system was toast.

She scanned through the porn. It was pretty typical, nothing that made her twitch. Lesbians, blowjobs, fucking. She found the dirty file, killed it, checked it was gone entirely, and scanned again.

Once done, with the files back and not corrupted, she said, "Oglesby, here! You lost one corrupted file."

He came over at a jog and took his precious personal information back.

"I only removed that one, though a few of the others may be

damaged," she said without a smile.

He blushed again.

"Thanks, Sergeant."

"It's safe with me."

While she was at it, she might as well scrub everyone's files.

Rich Dalton was chopping a log, of course. He heard his name, finished the swing, let the axe bite wood, and looked up.

From Number Nine, Alexander shouted, "Dalton, you're next, bring me your phone, your tablet and your drives."

She leaned around the hatch, wearing pants, a T-shirt and sneakers. She was pretty well shaped for a woman, and that was starting to look way hot. The running joke was that a four back home was a ten after two months in the field, and she'd been a six or maybe a seven to start with, given her age. She looked a lot younger even with her laundry list of damage.

Most troops had dogtags and flash drives around their necks. Some had religious symbols or jewelry. He'd thought she had a drive or a large religious doohickey, possibly some Thor's hammer type of thing. He saw now it was a small push dagger, hanging just underside and between her domed breasts.

She had a folding knife clipped in her pocket, that huge tanto on her thigh, and a small sheath knife on her hip as well.

He wiped sweat on his T-shirt as he walked over to the tepee, panting for breath.

Inside was hot, dank and nasty, so he grabbed the stuff quick and got back into daylight and breeze. He walked around the trucks to where she was waiting.

"How come you two b—females have so many damn knives?"

She almost rolled her eyes.

"Think," she said.

"I have. I don't get it," he said.

"Well, I suppose I should be glad of that. Just take it as a fact that you won't see either of us 'b . . . females' without a knife, even when asleep or taking a crap."

"Oh," he said, suddenly getting it. That was an uncomfortable subject. But he needed more information and there was no way Caswell would talk to him.

"I didn't realize the risk was that bad," he said. He didn't want to believe it. Most guys were decent. The constant harping . . .

She said, "It depends. Really bad among some of our eastern European allies. Or among the natives. Modern natives. And there are always some dangerous males even in our Army."

"Sorry."

She shrugged. "Not your fault. The Army doesn't want anyone to drink, look at porn, jerk off, tell rude jokes, then expects us to kill people, go back to the FOB and become monks. And then there's that five percent of men who are just abusive assholes. It's a bad combination. And we're the only two here, and the natives find us just exotic."

He wasn't sure what to say. He nodded. He wasn't going to admit he'd considered her a few times late at night.

"And that's why we're bitches with knives," she said.

"I don't blame you," he said. "I'll let you work."

"This won't take long," she said. "Have a seat."

He sat on the ramp steps and watched her. She might not be a warrior, but she knew computers, and apparently cameras and night vision. His first thought had been that insisting on admin was an excuse for her to slack off, but she had two laptops up, cables from the solar panel running all over, and his files on screen.

Yeah, those files that . . .

His porn scrolled by too fast to see, but slow enough to identify. But she didn't say anything, or give any indication she was upset. He still shifted uncomfortably. This was very personal.

"You were airborne intel?" he asked, hoping to distract her slightly. He was blushing.

Without looking from the screen, with folder "redheads" up, she said, "Sort of. I maintained the equipment for battle management. And that stuff was archaic. Built in the seventies."

"Crashed?"

"Yes, North Carolina. A couple of planes have been lost entirely to bird strikes. We got lucky. Ingested geese into two engines on takeoff. Made it over the trees to the field beyond. Landed hard, all survived, but beat to hell, and the plane was a total loss."

"No way to avoid the birds?"

"Not really. They fire guns and air cannons, shoot a few, bait them away, try to schedule around their cycle and watch for mass flocks, but eventually, there's a lot of birds and someone's going to eat one."

She moused, keyed, closed the file and handed the stick back.

"Phone next," she said.

He had all kinds of stuff on his phone, including his journal notes, religious thoughts, shopping list and bank info. But she scanned by eye and by software, nodded and handed it over.

"So why the Army Guard, not Air Guard?"

"Air Guard won't take me with the bad ankles. Army Guard will take almost anyone. I keep up most of the time. I can't run much, but I can walk as far as I need to."

Yeah, she had.

"I noticed. I'm sorry for my comment the other day."

Without looking from the screen, she said, "Well, you're young. Apology accepted. Keep in mind you'll be Spencer's or my age eventually."

She was old enough to be his mother, and she had a great rack, and had just scanned through his porn files.

"Yeah, I'm going to be old here."

"Please don't remind me. Here's your laptop," she said as she powered it down. "I defragged and did some routine maintenance while I was at it. It should be a bit faster."

"Thanks. Facebook will be much easier now."

She ignored the joke.

"Actually, we might be able to set up a local network," she said, "I need to think about that. It wouldn't work for more than a couple of hundred meters, but we could swap images from the perimeter."

He didn't really see how that would be useful, but Oglesby had been wrong about the Ripit cans being trash. Those were being used to steam meat and roast roots.

"Cool. Good luck with it."

"Thanks. Politely tell that red-headed bitch I'll look at hers next."

Interesting. So she didn't like Caswell either.

"Roger."

"Politely," she reiterated.

He slid the laptop under his arm and carried it, since he was going to drop it back in the tepee after relaying that last message.

Caswell was over past the kitchen area, lashing limbs together.

"What's that?" he asked.

"Another wall for the latrine. Eventually double walls for insulation and a roof."

"Cool. That'll be nice in winter. Alexander says she'll look at your stuff now."

"Stuff?"

"Computer, phone, memory sticks."

"Eh. Mine are fine. I check them regularly."

"I get the impression she's insisting on checking everyone's."

"Oh, goddamn her," Caswell replied. She didn't move, though.

Polite. "I've delivered the message. You'll have to argue the point with her, or with the LT or Spencer."

"Yeah, yeah."

He left. He didn't want to argue with her, and yes, she was a bitch. She didn't have age or injury as an excuse. And it wasn't being non-Army. Trinidad was Navy. Barker was Reserve and had been Navy. Alexander had been Air Force also. So it was just her.

Possibly because of her looks? Did she play them for advantage and it wasn't working here? But she hadn't done that at all when the convoy started. Was she afraid of her looks? The natives had definitely homed in on her. She was at least an eight, maybe a nine, and the nicest looking thing around. He wouldn't mind some attention, but even if it wasn't a bad idea, there was no way to approach her.

If God wanted to test a young man, this environment was the way to do it.

He walked back to the tepee. Maybe chopping another half dozen trees would burn off some of the tension. Or at least give him blisters.

The next day, the Paleos returned to see Armand.

"Natives inbound, party of five," Spencer called from the turret.

Armand was nervous. He had a vague idea what to do, and hoped it would work. He had fears of either making the problem worse, or causing infection and death. This wasn't life-saving field surgery. It was a complicated OB-GYN reconstruction. Well, complicated from his experience. He was a second-year student, not a surgeon.

"Are you guys ready?"

"Yes," Barker said.

"I am," Dalton agreed. He looked uncomfortable.

"Yes," Alexander said.

"This is damned near an all-hands operation," Barker added. "Like overhauling a ship."

The approaching Paleos were Ai!ee, two women escorts, and two warriors with spears. They also each carried four javelins like the ones Barker had made. They'd learned that quickly.

"They caught on fast, I see," he said. "I'll teach them other stuff, but we need to remind them how useful we are."

"Sure. In case she doesn't make it," Armand said.

Caswell said, "You'll do fine."

"Okay, ask her when she last ate. It should be two days ago. She shouldn't have drunk since last night. But make them answer, don't lead them."

Oglesby said, "Got it," and turned.

"She says two days, no food, praying to her mother and grandmother and the nature spirits. She's very hungry but at peace and had a good vision last night."

"Good. Bowel movements?"

"Yesterday. And she's thirsty now."

"Okay, wet a rag in the boiled water and she can suck on that."

He led the party into the tepee, and then Caswell chased the men out. On the one hand, he appreciated it. On the other, if she was going to push this equality thing, she shouldn't exclude them.

Not his problem.

They had ponchos on the ground, swept and clean. He figured they could be washed in the creek afterward.

"The spearchuckers are out," he said. "I always wanted to call someone a spearchucker."

"Well, they are," Barker said with a laugh.

Caswell rolled her eyes, but said nothing. She didn't seem to have a sense of humor, though she was interested in science. He'd keep it serious around her.

"Are you ready to assist?" he asked her.

"Ready, Doc." She sounded sure.

"Gina?"

Alexander had instruments laid out in an ammo can lid.

"Is that the correct order?" she asked.

"Yes. You know the names of everything?"

"Well enough."

"Good batteries in the light?"

"Full charge."

He turned to Oglesby.

"I need her naked and on the poncho. We'll need to hold her legs. Her head will be on a pillow, and she can talk with her friends and the spirits. This is going to be as painful as childbirth."

Oglesby explained, and there were nods. She stripped easily from her skirt, and lay down as directed. Her belly was striated with stretch markes, her breasts flat and pendulous. Once they started squeezing out babies here, they aged fast.

Barker and Dalton each sat cross-legged and took one of her calves across their laps. They then pulled masks on.

"Okay, Oglesby, tell them to keep her company and soothed. And there is going to be bright, magic light." He pulled on the magic gloves and masks, and just maybe that idea would catch on and save a few lives.

Her friends cradled her head and caressed her forehead and cheeks. They spoke reassuringly, and even smiled.

So here he was, operating by flashlight, in a hide-covered tepee, scrubbing a Stone Age woman's vagina with soap while Caswell dilated her with two spoons. The squirt bottle made a handy douche for rinsing.

He peered in by flashlight, as Caswell straddled her belly and reached down with the dilator spoons.

"It's not as smooth as I'd hoped," he said, feeling a bit embarrassed even on duty. "I can't localize the tear. Suggestions?"

Caswell said, "You may have to illuminate from behind."

He thought about that.

". . . yeah. Okay, I need my backpack," he said as he pointed.

Alexander ran to get it.

"What's in there?"

"More gloves. And a microlight."

It worked. With some lube and effort, he inserted the wrapped glowing light into her rectum, and found the perforation where the light was brightest.

Two careful nicks with the scalpel sliced the membrane and exposed tissue. Ai!ee tensed and hissed, but didn't move.

The tough part was suturing. There wasn't much room, and he had only an improvised speculum.

"Wider, carefully," he told Caswell.

The patient actually didn't move much. There were involuntary muscle tremors of her wall muscles, and her ass puckered a bit, but no significant reactions to pain. And it had to hurt. Her friends chanted in a steady rhythm that was hypnotic and annoying. He glanced around Caswell. Ai!ee's face was screwed up tight, but she didn't twitch as he stabbed a suture needle through tender flesh.

Dalton mumbled something, he looked over, and realized it was the Lord's Prayer. Well enough. Armand would do his part, the rest was up to the Almighty.

In fifteen minutes he was done, nodded, leaned back and then shifted so his foot wouldn't cramp.

He never wanted to be that close to a native woman again.

He removed the light as Caswell removed the spoons.

"Okay, we need her to rest here. She is not to get out of bed until tomorrow, and no lifting anything for the rest of the week. Oh, and no food until tomorrow, and no sex for a month. She needs to drink lots of water and have help while urinating. I doubt they have bed pans, but they'll need to hold her so she's not straining muscles."

Oglesby translated at length, and said, "I told them she should also pray twice a day."

"Good."

Barker said, "She really didn't fight much."

Dalton concurred. "Yeah, No real trouble. Tough constitution. But that was not a pleasant view."

Caswell said, "It's medicine." She sounded cross.

Alexander said, "They're male. It's instinctive."

"Okay, these gloves are now industrial, as long as they last. Any goat guts to process?"

"Yeah, I'll take them," Barker said.

He took a deep breath. That had gone okay, as near as he could tell. He wanted to know she had survived without infection. Because it sure as hell wasn't the last surgery he'd be doing.

He wished they had booze. This called for a drink.

Caswell said, "There's one other matter, and I'd like privacy."

"You and her?"

"And Oglesby and you and the two women. Rest of you, get the fuck out, please."

Damn, she was blunt. Barker and Dalton rose and left without comment. Gina shrugged and followed.

After they were out the flap in the door, she looked around, then said, "Oglesby, I need to ask them what to use in lieu of tampons."

That was a damned good question Armand had wondered about himself.

Oglesby turned beet red, nodded quickly, and turned to the women. He pointed at Ai!ee, gestured with hands, looked words up in his notes, and repeated.

"They say you should ask the spirits for a baby. Get pregnant and nurse, and you'll stop having moon sickness. I told them that wasn't possible. Hold on."

He looked very uncomfortable. He talked and pointed more.

"They say it doesn't happen often. Only to women who are really well fed and not with men. They seem to use rawhide and cattail fluff."

"Fuck," she said. "I guess I wad up a T-shirt in my panties and waddle around. Goddammit. Well, thank them for helping. Are we done?"

Armand said, "You can go if you need to. I have it."

"Thanks."

After she left, he told Oglesby, "She meant to thank you, too."

He replied, "No she didn't. But I guess I can't blame her. That's pretty damned personal."

"We're all going to know too much about each other after a while."

"'Going to'?"

CHAPTER 10

"Formation," Spencer called. It was already a tradition, and important. Though he was calling it before dinner.

Barker and Ortiz were up in the turret, the rest around the fire.

"Smells good. What is it?"

Caswell said, "One of the Urushu knocked over a pheasant with a thrown stick. Pheasant, mushrooms, ground cattail tortilla and a little salt from the locals. I've got some evergreen needles chopped in with some wild onion."

"Almost a stew."

"Well it's stewed, but I wouldn't call it a stew. But I like how it smells. Should I serve?"

"Yes, please do," Elliot said. "I'm doing formation early, because I had an idea. And being a wise lieutenant and all . . ."

He let them chuckle, and stepped aside for the commander.

Elliott said, "Alexander gave us her background. I really think everyone should do that. We need to know who we are, since at this point we're basically brothers and sisters as well as a close unit. We need to know about each other.

"So I'll go first. I've been a One LT for four months now. I was ROTC out of Purdue. I'm a mechanical engineer, but I don't know what good that will do me here. I'm out of Fort Sam. I'm single, and I guess it's lucky my girlfriend left me a couple months before I deployed. But I miss my parents and my brother. They're going to miss me. As to stuff to share, I have my computer and phone, I have some extra ammo stashed, and plenty of socks and undies if you're my size. I don't mind sharing movies, in fact, we should have Sergeant Alexander swap everyone's movies so we have backups, and have entertainment."

"I can cross-load all your porn, too," she said with a faint smile. "You'll know all about each other then."

There were shouts of "Woah!" that turned into laughs, even from Caswell.

Spencer laughed himself. He was glad they could make jokes. Morale was important.

"Yeah, that may be a bit too much sharing," he said.

Elliott said, "I've got that gyroscopic shaver that doesn't need batteries."

Spencer said, "I love you for that in a chaste, manly way."

"Yes, and we've been sharing it. I don't expect anyone to maintain full grooming standards, but do your best to keep the beards trimmed and close. I have scissors, too, and as long as we have power, I have a pair of plug-in clippers. I have a lot of note paper, but I expect to use it all eventually."

"Spencer, you're next."

"Right," Spencer said. How much did he want to say? He decided to keep it short. "I'm a fair mechanic, Ninety-One Bravo out of Knox, but I'm lacking tools here. I can do blacksmithing and have, but building a forge and finding a rock to sub for an anvil is going to take time, then we have to find a source of ore. I know how to reduce it, but I've never done so. I've done a variety of other low tech skills, including wood carving and such. I have a dumb phone, laptop, no tablet, a few movies, lots of music, headphones and spares. The LT has one of my lights, I have the other. They're rechargeable as long as we have the solar panel. I may be able to convert a vehicle alternator to wind power, and I may be able to work out a vegetable or animal oil for fuel. It won't be much, though. We'll be able to use them for power, not for travel. I have a box of a dozen small sheath knives we can use. I brought them to trade with Afghans. They're all ours now.

"Oh, and as mentioned I have reflux, and my medication runs out in about three months. Then I either try to compensate with chalk or bone meal, or I die slowly and painfully. There's not much Doc can do for me without drugs or modern surgery." He sat back and poked at the fire with a stick.

"We heard from Alexander, who drills where?" Elliott prompted.

She said, "Springfield, Illinois. I live in Rockford."

"Okay. Ortiz."

Ortiz actually stood up.

"Ramon Ortiz. My parents moved from Mexico when I was three. They worked ag in south Texas, then started their own farm, then moved up to distribution. So I know a bit more about veterinary stuff than the Army taught me. I'm a vet tech. I've been in five years, was going to get out after this and take college. My girlfriend was dumping me anyway. I do miss my brother and sister, but at least we're all grown. I've got assorted stuff for animals in my kit. I can butcher them, castrate, birth them. I can do rough electricity and carpentry, but don't have much experience chopping wood, or didn't until now." He held up calloused hands. "So I can probably castrate food animals and do some basic care. If they get sick, I guess we eat them or get rid of them. I don't know much about butchering, but I know enough to section them. I've been letting Sergeant Barker do the fine work. I know enough about suturing and setting bones and such to help Doc. I'm also pretty good at masonry. It's in my blood," he said, holding up his brown arms. There were chuckles. "I'm out of First Cav at Hood. I live near Houston, we've been ranchers for three generations. Will be. Whatever. Fuck it. Not going to talk about that. If we can capture some I can pen them and raise them.

"I've got all the usual crap, and I do have a couple of spare knives. I don't mind sharing music and movies. I have some scissors, so we can trim our beards. iPhone, tablet, laptop and binoculars because I wanted to look around."

Elliott interrupted, "Binoculars. Can we borrow them? Say yes."

He flushed and said, "Sorry, sir. I wasn't trying to hold back. I just forgot. Yes, they're mine, but you can use them for patrol."

The man was embarrassed, but picked back up. "I know something about leather and gut and such. I've been helping with that. If we do pen any animals, I can do everything from milking to birthing. Otherwise I'm good for manual labor."

"Once we have domestic animals, we should be able to have milk, butter and cheese. I know a bit about processing hides, and so does Bob. We've been stripping guts and sinew for bowstrings and such. You're also going to see it as sausage casings. We're stacking the horns and bones for now, letting the ants clean them for us, but those make tools, material for small utensils. I'll be helping with food preservation and helping Doc with minor stuff·that doesn't require his expertise, just patching."

Martin said, "We *will* be ranching," to reassure the young man, and himself. He wanted real food again. Meat should be aged, and yeah, castration made it a lot better. Not nice, but true.

And damn, the body parts stunk. They were piled to the Southeast, inside of gun range, outside of fly range, but still putrid and nasty. He hoped they could process stuff soon.

"Okay, Caswell, your turn to tell us about you."

She fidgeted for a few moments, zipped her coat up more, and rocked as she talked. She stood and tried to look firm, but she really only came across as an awkward combination of timid and pushy.

"Jennifer Caswell. I'm female and Air Force and hate getting shit about it, but you folks have done okay so far, mostly. Yes, I identify as vegetarian, even if I can't be one here. I'll work on that. I grew up in Wisconsin; I guess my mother's a hippie. I can find wild stuff to eat or smoke. But a lot of the stuff here is different. Agriculture contaminated even wild plants. Anyway, I enlisted, I'm stationed at McChord, Washington. They grabbed me because I was on base and female, and I was along to deal with female locals for a couple of weeks, and I still sort of am. I'll advise you what I think I see, and I'd rather you didn't mansplain to me how I'm wrong. I actually have a background in this. I studied cultural anthropology as a minor while I take criminal justice. I was planning on being a cop. I wanted to work in poor neighborhoods and do resolution rather than just rack up arrests."

She paused, and let that line drop, and picked up again.

"I've been identifying edible fruits, vegetables, seeds, fungus. Even if it looks and smells sweet, don't touch it. Report it to me, I'll check it out, and we'll go from there. Everyone can expect gathering parties in the future. We'll be drying some for winter, or in case we hit a dry spell or something—"

Or never get home, Martin thought quietly.

"—and we'll need to look for certain industrial plants, for storing food, cooking, preserving it, tanning leather, other things. Then we'll try to find things we can cultivate here to save all that walking. I'm rated expert with rifle and pistol. I'm decent with electronics. I did AV in college."

She took a breath. "I've been cooking, but I expect to teach the rest of you. We need cross skills. I need to learn how to sharpen knives properly. Besides the two we use in the kitchen, I have three others."

"Oh, and once you know how food is found, I'd appreciate getting out more. Not just hunting trips. I don't like killing animals. I can haul stuff, too. Don't baby me because I'm female."

She stopped. Clearly, she didn't want to say more.

Martin said, "I'm very glad to have you. Edible plants are making a big difference. I'd hate to be stuck on all meat."

"The Paleo people could help," she said with a shrug.

"Yeah, but you're here and speak English."

"Thanks, then," she said, looking flustered. Obviously, she was not a social person.

Elliott pointed and said, "Corporal Dalton, your call."

"Uh . . . Corporal Dalton. I enlisted out of high school. I'm Infantry, play a lot of online games and Xbox. I was good at shop and electronics in school. I did some cabinetry for my uncle. I shot expert, I've done some hunting up through bear and deer. With fishing and spears or bows as well, the ammo should last the rest of our lives, as long as we're careful. I'm the only Expert here, so I figure I'll be taking most of the shots. I'll be working on bows with Barker's help. We can also work on spear throwers. We want to hunt from a distance, not up close. Then we'll work on traps. I know how to build fish traps, and Barker knows some others."

Caswell had her hand up. Elliott recognized her. "Go ahead."

"As I said, I'm also rated Expert," she said.

"Really?" Dalton let out.

"Do you think women are unable to shoot?" she replied. Goddamn, was it impossible for her to be anything other than snide or sarcastic?

"Army or Air Force expert?"

"Both, since I had to shoot the Army course to come over. It was easy."

Arrogant bitch. But it was hard to call her on it if she'd done it. If. The only record was her say-so, and he'd known women to lie about credentials just as much as men did. Given she had an axe to grind, he was skeptical. She'd have to prove it.

Elliott said, "We'll believe her, and use her where we can."

Dalton continued, "I'll keep holding services. You can talk to me, though I know a couple of you aren't comfortable. Hey, it's a learning experience for me, too, to learn about other faiths. That could be why God put me here, at least. Otherwise, I've put on some muscle from all this fresh air and hard work. It's a small thing, but it's a positive. I feel good about that."

Martin couldn't decide between rolling eyes or snarling. The man didn't have a wife and kids. Sure, it was good he was adapting. Martin didn't want to adapt. The nightmare could be over any time and he could go home.

Elliott said, "We'll cover more tomorrow night. Work is going well, and we've got better relations with our neighbors, sitting there patiently. So let's eat and not scare them."

The palisade was coming along. Bob Barker looked at it in satisfaction, as he straightened up to prevent a backache. He was pouring sweat. Nothing like exercise and no dessert to run fat off and muscle on. He had a better physique than he'd had in a decade.

Elliott came alongside, with Caswell.

"What do you think?" the LT asked.

"I think it's going to bust our balls, sir. But it's going to be strong when done." He wiped his eyebrows and hair. He should probably get a haircut. He was approaching 70s porn star style.

Dalton, Devereaux and Ortiz were raising a pole, along with two Urushu, whose names were something like "Fen" and "Ka'la." He couldn't make those clicks and had trouble with the nasals.

"Down back there, and up there," he said, pointing and indicating. "Set it. Good. Okay, Dalton, drive it home."

Dalton walked the log upright and it shifted and dropped. Fen pushed it from the side, and Ortiz ran up with a hide thong to hold it in place while pins could be set.

They had it down to a smooth process, but it was body-bruising labor.

Elliott said, "Going well. I hope we can have it done before winter."

Bob said, "I'd say we could go with something lighter to fill in the gaps if we don't. Brush, thorns, firewood."

"Possibly. But I'd rather do it right first if we can, rather than do it twice."

"Yeah. Just time is an issue."

"Well, this is going to make time worse." He indicated Caswell.

They must want to borrow some labor.

"Ah, hell, go ahead, sir, Jenny."

Elliott nodded at Caswell, who said, "I want to save ammo by building a goat pen. It might work for small antelope, too."

"You figure to bait them in and bar the gate?"

"Yes, just that."

"Posts set in stone, filled with earth, and rails with woven mesh?"

She actually smiled.

"Exactly. I take it you've done one before?"

"Nope."

"Crap." She frowned.

He clasped his hands in mock excitement and said, "But I always wanted to learn."

After a few snarky comments between them, Elliott said, "I'm going to survey and stake out with five-fifty cord on the other side of the stream. We'll use the straight limbs we've trimmed. After they're rocked into holes, we'll pour mud in until it settles."

"Ash would help."

"If we have enough."

"How big?"

Caswell said, "I figure twenty foot square to start with. We can add a second one later. We may have to rope some goats if we can't bait them."

"Ortiz may know something about that." He turned and shouted to the ditch, "Hey, Ortiz! Break."

Ortiz was ripped. He'd been muscular to start with. He was a pocket sized monster now.

"Yeah, what's up?"

They explained the idea. Barker asked, "Can you rope goats?"

"So we're going to have a genuine goat rope?" he asked. "Possibly, or tangle trap them. I'm sure I can do something, but why so much work on the pen?"

"We want it to last."

"Why not just zigzag the timbers, and run buttresses at the joints?" He interwove his fingers to demonstrate.

"Will that work without the goats climbing?"

"It does on our ranch."

"Well, shit. Why didn't we do this before?"

"I figured we'd do that next year," he said. "But we can do it now. If you don't mind losing that potential firewood, although we can always recover it later, we just carry it and stack it. We need a hundred and twenty-eight of them."

Elliott said, "That's pretty much everything I see in that pile." He indicated the pile of limbs and large saplings waiting to be pins, stakes, buttresses and firewood.

"Well, if it's a bit short, we can do some tricks with staked brush, or wait to cut another dozen trees."

Elliott shrugged. "Yeah. It's wood. We're not going to run out."

Caswell said, "I think it's awesome that you just said that, sir. Gives me hope."

"What's that?"

"That's what the early American settlers said. Have you seen Long Island lately?"

He grinned. "Noted. I want to leave Doc out of it. We need his hands in good shape."

Bob noticed she wasn't grinning. It was sarcasm, but not humor.

"I agree on Doc," he said. "There's plenty of stuff for him to do." There'd be plenty of splinters after this, even with gloves. No need to injure the medic, but that reduced labor even more.

Caswell walked back and forth on the timber pile, pointing out the thicker and straighter ones for the bottom of the fence, slimmer ones for the top rails, crooked ones for buttressing. By dinner, they had a pen about thirty feet square.

As they sat down to leftover meat with no veggies, they continued the discussion.

Ortiz said, "It's easy to expand, too. Just open one side, move the rails, stick more in. It doesn't even have to be very symmetrical, and it follows the lay of the land."

Elliott said, "I definitely overthought this."

"You, sir?" Bob said. "I was all ready to dig the river a foot deeper to get the rocks."

"Well, the environment is happy a while longer."

"Not really," he said. "I'll need rocks for the sweat lodge, and I've thought about damming the stream so we create a plunge pool. That takes rocks and logs."

"Hmm. Possibly next year. Now, how do we get goats?"

Ortiz said, "Either we bait them with grain and a salt lick, or we rope and carry them."

"Can you do that?"

"I can probably rope some. Easier would be to lay out the cord in a crisscross, wait for goats, yank it tight, wrestle goats, and toss them over the fence."

"Is that fence tall enough?"

"Yes for goats. Maybe for some antelope."

Bob asked, "Are we wrestling tomorrow, then?"

Ortiz wiggled and leered. "Grease me up, big boy."

"It sounds like fun, actually," he said.

Ortiz stared at him in mock horror.

"Not greasing you up, you sick fuck. Wrestling the . . . oh, shit, there's no way I win this one, is there?"

Everyone lost it completely.

Spencer said, "Daaaaddy!"

Elliott said, "Okay, let's eat, and Bob can tell us his background wrestling goats."

"I've actually never wrestled a goat."

Ortiz said, "It's okay, no one will judge you here."

Bob said, "I was Navy. I wrestled Marines."

"How does that work?"

"I worked in the radio shop. If they wanted it fixed, they had to do as I said. And we did have a wrestling league aboard ship."

"When was that?" Elliott asked.

"Ten years ago. But that doesn't help here. What does help is I know what a salt lick looks like, but we're going to need a source of water to refine it. The raw stuff is just gray mineral dirt. We'll need to filter it. I've gutted animals and done some curing, but I think we need to pool knowledge. It's likely Ortiz knows the science better than I do. I'm working on buckskin and rawhide, and the bows. Gut strings are gonna be messy."

Caswell asked, "How long do bows take?"

"A quick one is just a stick, but doesn't last long. A good one is split from wood and shaved, not carved, drying as you go. Better ones take specific sections of specific trees, or glue, but that's later. As to the Navy, I actually got out, and into wholesale industrial equipment sales. Then went into the Reserve as an equipment operator. I wanted to be on land. So here I am."

Spencer said, "I dub thee, Landsquid."

"Talk to Trinidad," he said. "He's been on land the whole time."

"Yeah, pretty much," Trinidad agreed. "Funny how a kid from a Bataan village winds up in San Diego, then A-stan, then the Stone Age. Honestly, there isn't a lot of difference."

"You've supported the Army the entire time?"

"No, did a lot of Naval work the first three years. Aboard ship, even. The *Peleliu*."

"Well, glad to have you," Elliott said. "Tell us about you."

Trinidad shrugged. "My sister and parents are in the PI. I always wanted to join the Navy, so I made sure to learn good English. Intel sounded neat. It was a bitch to get my TS clearance. I had citizenship paperwork filled out and pending. I guess that doesn't matter now. I've been watching how the locals move, and I can actually apply the same skills to animal routes. Then there's their resources and stuff. Otherwise, I'm really good at cutting brush and you could have asked me about the fence as well. We don't have a lot of fasteners back home."

Bob said, "Well, let's eat, drink and be merry. Tomorrow we wrestle goats."

Alexander said, "Get me the cord. I'll show you how to crochet a net."

"Really?"

"Really."

She walked over to the kindling pile, dug through for a straight stick. She pulled out her small sheath knife and carved a notch near one end, grabbed the parachute cord and started hooking it.

Between bites of meat and root, she made large loops in squares about 6" across. It went surprisingly fast. Bob started on another one, following what she did.

"You're too fast," he said.

"Sorry. Let's try again. Loop here, pull, twist, pull again. You missed a pull there."

"Yeah, got it."

By the time they were down to firelight he had to quit, but had a piece a couple of feet square. Hers was about five foot.

She said, "Hey, we'll take all the goat or small antelope hides the Urushu can get us. That tepee cover isn't coming together fast enough." She pointed to where a third of it was now dressed in stitched raw hides, stiffening in the sun. Actually, with that, it was becoming structurally more like a yurt.

"She's right," he said. "Heavier cover for winter, stitched to be weatherproof."

Oglesby said, "I'll ask them. I guess they owe us, *if* they have that concept, which I'm not sure they do."

Gina Alexander woke up and stretched. She hurriedly pulled on boots and lumbered for the privy in the gray, foggy dawn. She was glad the men just stood on the bank to pee. She much preferred sitting to squatting, and the one ersatz seat was a bottleneck. Caswell was right behind her.

No one paid attention to it anymore. If you needed to go, you went, much like in survival school, or the how the Urushu did, though the soldiers still preferred a little discretion, and they needed to keep that. It would be so easy to lose their civilized veneer.

She wiped off with the old T-shirt she'd designated for the purpose, and made note to rinse it out today. That done, she walked back to the hooch to get the rest of her stuff, and a coat. It was cool, definitely early fall, even if the trees weren't starting to tinge. Her ass had chilled on the dew-damp toilet seat.

This was a PT day, and she walked around the perimeter as the others ran, lapping her. Twenty-six laps was two miles, and they were done completely before she got three quarters of the way. She tried not to be self conscious about it. Her ankles didn't work anymore. Inside, she still felt old and under par.

No one said anything as she came to the fire to eat. They never did.

Barker called, "Firewood detail, Oglesby, Dalton. Hunting and goat detail, Caswell, Alexander, Ortiz. Camp detail, Trinidad, Devereaux when not handling sick call. Sergeant Spencer and the LT are working on setting stakes."

He had leftover meat, warmed on the rocks, and handed her a strip as she walked by. It was edible, but really getting boring fast, and tiring to chew. She had a sore tooth and suspected meat fiber was stuck in the gum.

"Hooah," she replied in acknowledgment.

"Scrambled eggs?" Dalton asked, seeing something.

"Of a sort," Barker said. "Want some?"

"Yeah!"

She wasn't going to have any. They were in no risk of starving to death, and she knew—

Dalton said, "Hey, this tastes like there's chicken in it."

Trinidad muttered, "Balut."

Dalton apparently understood the word, and stopped in mid bite. "You fuckers."

"What?" Barker asked. "They are duck eggs."

"With bits of baby duck?"

"Fetal duck, but yes."

Dalton looked ready to heave. Trinidad laughed and kept eating. Dalton didn't eat any more, and stuck to the warmed goat. She didn't blame him. Proper eggs could wait.

Done eating, she grabbed her gore-tex and gloves.

"Caswell, should I bring helmet and armor for hunting?"

"Good idea. Just in case of wolves." Caswell was grabbing hers, and her carbine.

"Yes. Though they're getting scarcer."

From the front of the tepee, Ortiz said, "We smell like predators." He had a bow, and the pouch he used to field dress game, which now held a folding saw, a large knife, some pliers and thong, among other things.

She needed to distract Caswell from the bow.

"Indeed we do." She asked Caswell, "How are you managing on all this meat?"

Caswell shrugged. "It's not possible to keep vegetarian here. If it ever becomes so, I'll see what I can do. But part of my rationale was resources, which aren't short here. And we look the animals in the face as we kill them, which is more honest."

That made sense. "Fair enough. I love meat myself, but damn, I want bread. I wasn't supposed to eat much back home anyway, with my thyroid, and I didn't, but here . . . it's all I want. A whole damned loaf."

Caswell said, "I know. I want a fresh salad with oil and spices, not just weeds. They're nutritious but not tasty. And little beyond minerals and vitamin C."

"We need to gather rosehips for that, if we find any." They hopped over the stream, which now had four stepping stones. Then they went up the bank, which had been muddy but was now covered in pebbles, and headed into the eastern meadow. Bit by bit they terraformed their property.

"And replant some here." Caswell indicated the area she'd roughly cleared, using an E-tool as a hoe, attached to a pole. They tromped past it through tall growth.

It had surprised the men for Caswell to be a rifle Expert, partly because she was female, and a lot because she was Air Force. That was a good lesson for them not to underestimate either. She could headshot an animal with ease, and had.

None of them had commented much on her ability to recognize edibles, except to be grateful. She was an arrogant young bitch, but she did have useful skills.

The bows, though, had pissed her off immensely. Bob Barker had shaved them down to eighty pounds. He said he wanted that weight for larger antelope. He could draw it. Dalton could. The other men except Trinidad could mostly manage. But neither woman could. It was an upper body weapon, and they didn't have the strength.

Caswell had bitched long and loud as if it was a personal affront to her. Gina understood the practicality behind it. Heavier bows meant heavier kills. Something smaller just wasn't lethal, and it took strength to draw one, that few women would ever have.

It was bound to come up, though. Gina said, "Well, I'd like to avoid goat for a few more days. Small antelope?"

Caswell said, "If I can get a head shot." Ammo was finite, and an M4 was not a large game rifle. Dalton had said nothing over two hundred pounds was a safe target, except for a few with thin enough skulls for a brain scramble shot. Yes, she was going to use the rifle as often as she could, since a bow was not an option. Gina understood it, but it was still annoying.

Ortiz said, "Or pheasant, if we find any nesting."

Gina said, "I'm glad we have you along to chop them up. I can do it, but they just turn into a mess of pieces if I try. My husband does the butchering in hunting season. I just do the veggies and manage the camp."

Ortiz said, "It's not what I trained for, but I'm glad to do it. Barker can gut or fine cut, but nothing in between."

"I wonder about standardized tasks. But I also wonder about flexibility."

"We can't all do everything," he said. "I'd need half a magazine to take one down."

"What's that?" she asked, pointing ahead.

Caswell had much better eyes, too, which of course helped. "Small. Furry. Not entirely sure. It's not moving."

"There it goes."

Something darted through the grass.

"Cat!" Gina exclaimed. "That's a cerval or caracal!"

It was definitely feline, probably a caracal, and it limped.

Ortiz said, "Injured leg. Wish we could put it down humanely."

Caswell followed the movement. "He can recover. There's a lot of small pests around here."

"Not limping like that."

The poor creature was exhausted, and limped to a stop, gasping. He rolled into some broad-bladed grass that flopped over him, wet and concealing.

Gina loved cats.

She took the lead and walked toward it, Caswell and Ortiz behind her.

It snarled as they approached, and raised clawed paws in threat.

"Gloves then. And glad we have the body armor." Gina pulled on her gloves, slung her rifle, and crept up, making soft noises.

"Hey, fella. It's okay. We're hunters, too."

It lashed at her and tried to run, but stumbled on its injured paw. He. Definitely he. He was gray with ticked fur and big tufts on his ears. His fangs were long, and he growled, matted hair spiking all over.

He was beautiful.

"Come on, big guy."

She reached in, and his claws struck gore-tex and clung but didn't pierce. She shifted him around, got hold of both pairs of legs, being careful of the front right.

Ortiz looked in.

"Lacerated," he said. "Probably a fight with something bigger."

"Fixable?"

"I can suture, but he's not going to like it."

"Cats are smart. He'll figure it out." He was a big, handsome fellow, about twenty-five pounds. And he was a cat. If she couldn't have family, she could damned well have a pet.

"Yeah, we can feed him something, too."

The cat growled, but seemed to realize he wasn't going to escape. He also probably understood that, if they hadn't killed him yet, they weren't going to.

Caswell reached over and gave him a slight skritch behind the ears. He tensed and stiffened.

"Detour back?"

"Yes."

They trudged back, keeping a tight hand on the feisty fellow. Even injured, he was a lot of muscle. He would tense under her arm and try for purchase, then tuck up under her armpit. She'd pull him back down, and he'd growl. His voice would suit something twice his size.

As they crossed the creek, Trinidad said, "We eat dogs in the PI, cats are for the Chinese."

"Good, then he's safe," she said.

"Injured?"

As they reached the kitchen area, Ortiz said, "Paw. I'm going to try to suture him."

The man knew what he was doing with animals. In under a minute, he reached behind her and lashed the rear legs with thong from his kit, then lowered the animal carefully to the ground, with Caswell holding the rear quarters over a stick.

The cat was not happy. He snarled and hissed, as she gripped the left foreleg in her fist and the right paw firmly with thumb and finger. He tried to sink fangs through the glove. She felt pressure, but they were tough shells and he couldn't puncture them.

Ortiz ran for the tent, and returned with a basic sewing repair kit and a water bottle.

He washed off the cut, which was a good two inches long, and pulled out tweezers and a needle.

"He's not going to like this," he said.

"Holding," she agreed, and squeezed while trying not to injure.

"Wait," he said, rising. He grabbed a stick from one of the piles, pulled out more cord, and splinted the leg to it.

The cat really didn't like it, howling. He tried to bite again. She wrapped a gloved hand over his jaw.

"I need a stick," she said.

Spencer slid one in and caught the creature's fangs around it.

By now everyone had gathered around.

"Are we making bagpipes?" Spencer asked.

"Sounds like it, doesn't it?" she said.

Oglesby said, "Aw, hell, break its neck cleanly and be done with it."

"Fuck you," she snapped. "Just . . . go away."

She wanted this creature to survive. She needed it. Oglesby probably didn't understand, but she was going to put some effort in.

"He's fine," Ortiz said. "He's going to be in pain, but he's going to survive and heal."

Someone muttered, "Eh, who cares? Stupid cat." They mumbled something else that she figured was about her.

Caswell put a hand on her arm, and she shook it off. She didn't want anyone touching her right now.

She clutched the splint, Ortiz grabbed the needle, ran it through his lighter flame and wiped it off.

They all tensed.

Possibly the wound had gone numb, or hurt too much for the needle to matter, but the animal didn't protest much. He wiggled now and then, but was fully immobilized with sticks and cord.

Then he tried to kick his rear legs up, arched and snarled again.

Ortiz waited for him to stop, and continued.

It took ten minutes that seemed like an hour. He appeared to do something to the muscle tissue, he washed the wound again, and sutured up the skin in several spots. Then he pulled out a scalpel and sliced off a bit of crusted flesh.

Again the animal screamed outrage and pain, but soon collapsed, panting.

"Okay, done," Ortiz said as he cut a thread and pulled his tools back.

Caswell said, "We need a bowl of water and a bit of food. Something fatty and rich."

"Nothing fatty, but we do have a bit of scorched goat liver."

"Perfect. And water."

Carefully, they twisted the long animal onto his side.

"I've got it," Spencer said, and reached down with a crumbled bit of dark liver. He put it right in front of the cat's nose.

The cat sniffed it, then again, took a lick, then devoured it in big snaps of his jaw and tongue.

Spencer said, "Yeah, I'll bet you're hungry. Here." He put down a scraped out piece of bark with water, and another piece of liver.

The cat stared at him while gulping it, growled at Gina, took a lick of water at an odd angle, and twisted again, then whimpered as his leg pained him.

Ortiz said, "Okay, unlash the prisoner. We'll take him down to those bushes and leave the liver and water with him. He'll know where it is."

"Do you think he'll be around to remove the sutures?" Gina asked.

He shrugged. "If he lives. If he's tractable. Who knows?"

"Well, we tried, and I feel better."

He was a very handsome animal. Muscular, long body, those tufted ears. Definitely a caracal, probably young, and a fine specimen. Gina had always wanted an exotic cat.

As the thongs came off, the animal struggled more and more, then sprinted away at a limp, to stop behind the tepee and stare at them.

Elliott said, "Everyone back to work and go around. Leave the beast some room and he can have my share of liver."

Yeah. She knew they needed the nutrients, but liver was never tasty, no matter how fresh, what animal or how cooked. It was medicine, not food. She ate it for the Vitamin D for her thyroid, and hated every swallow.

Caswell said, "Okay, having saved an injured animal, let's go blow the brains out of a healthy one."

Ortiz said, "The circle of life!"

CHAPTER 11

The next day, Bob Barker found the goat wrestle was almost anticlimactic. As Ortiz said, they laid out crisscross parachute cord over the brush on the slope, waited for three goats to step into it, and started pulling. The goats jumped nimbly up, straight into the crocheted nets thrown by Ortiz and Caswell.

Bob waded in and untangled one, bit by bit, with Ortiz helping. The scruff of the neck worked a bit to slow their thrashing.

Then he was picking up a smelly, squirming goat and carrying it across the field. He stopped after fifty yards, squatted down to hold the thing in place, and gasped for breath. While he did that, Caswell reached under his ass and tied the creature's legs. That felt weird. There were so many jokes. She'd definitely be pissed if he said anything, so he didn't.

"Go on," she prompted, and went to tie the one Ortiz carried.

He made another fifty yards, another pause, smelling stinking goat, feeling it breathe in panic. He'd much rather wrestle the injured cat.

It took a good twenty minutes to reach the corral. He chose an inward point of the fence, reached the corner, heaved the goat up, waited while Caswell untied its feet, and dropped it in.

Ortiz rolled his over the side, and they went back for the last. Caswell had it pinned, and clutched the net to keep it down. The two men grabbed it front and rear, and carried it like a casualty. He had an arm under its chin to stop its biting, with it in a half chokehold. He was sweating heavily in his jacket, despite the cool air.

At the fence, Ortiz lowered the legs and he shifted. He got arms

195

under the bristly hair, hooked the legs firmly, and heaved. It struggled and kicked him in the thigh, the balls and the guts. He grunted, clamped down on it, and hefted it like a kid with a puppy. Its gyrations did little, then.

He kicked something as he walked, and realized the damned thing had dropped a deuce on his boot. Of course, the old slick boats would have shed it better than the sueded finish on these.

"Crap," he said, and realized the irony.

He fairly tossed that one over. It rolled, stood, and brayed at him.

"Yeah, fuck you, too, pal. You'll be over coals in a week, if I have anything to say about it." He couldn't blame the animal, but he didn't want to be friends with dinner, either. Much better to hate them.

"How many are we going to get?" he asked Ortiz.

"Eventually we need breeding stock, and we'll eat the kids to keep the milk coming."

"Yeah. Cheese. Someone here said they know how to make it."

"I do," Caswell said. "Spencer says he does, but I expect like a lot of his skills, it's stuff he's read about and not actually done."

"Well, we've all got some of that. Like Oglesby and sex."

Caswell gave him that stare.

Bob said, "Look, I'm sorry. I joke about stuff so I don't get pissed off. I've got goat crap on my boot, bruises on my groin and thigh, goat smell all over me, and no cigarettes."

Ortiz saved him. "I figure a half dozen for now, and we'll expand the pen, but we'll need to make sure they're fed and watered. Someone has to come dig a pond in that low spot and start bringing water in, until we can run a pipe."

"Good point. Don't want them to bind up their guts and die."

"Just toss all the food waste here, and all the trimmings off the trees. We'll recover some sticks we can burn."

"I'll do it. Hey, the two of you are going to get me my breakfast cereal. You are my heroes."

They got three more goats into the pen, and even though it seemed they could climb out, the animals ran around, then butted the fence, then settled down to munch grass.

"Not the sharpest spoons in the drawer, are they?" he said.

Ortiz said, "They're not. But we'll need other animals eventually. Still, this will make it easier to get a few things."

That done, he looked across the stream at the site. The north wall was half done to the stream. Progress. They needed to find some way to trade with the Urushu for something other than medical care.

He walked down to the rocks to wash the stink off. Cold water was better than warm goat. He did wish the course was deeper, though.

Felix Trinidad was glad Alexander had found the cat. She seemed to be taking it harder than the others, and given her age and family, and her fitness, something to help her relax was probably a good thing. Chopping wood took a lot of stress off, but she really didn't seem fit enough for much of it. She dragged branches, but that wasn't the same as hacking bits off.

Or maybe he was just atavistic. It worked for him, but possibly not the others. Also, he needed to pay less attention to the females. They weren't available, though he'd love to jump Caswell, but she didn't seem like the type to go for men at all. A very angry, closeted lesbian, if he had his guess. Even if she did anything with men, it wouldn't be with him, and it wouldn't be very good. She was a large bundle of negative emotions.

Alexander was just depressed, and it wasn't all separation. She had a fairly tough façade, but was not at all happy. The combination of being the oldest, and female, and with health problems meant she'd never fit with the rest, either.

Though she had that faintly mousy presentation, she was probably a firecracker in bed. But it would be up to her to make the call.

She seemed to get along best with Spencer, who was closest to her age. She didn't notice Felix, found Oglesby annoying, didn't like Dalton's religious presence, and definitely didn't care for Devereaux. She might consider the LT, but kept a very professional shell.

Which was a long-winded way of wondering when he was going to get laid. These women were off limits, so the interaction with the natives needed to continue until they could bring some in for socializing. And those women were tall, which was just fantastic. If only he could persuade them to be interested in a shorty like himself.

Back to the wall. They had one side, half of another, two natural obstacles—the creek and ditch—and several piles of brush. The more they got built, the better he felt. Spencer was correct about that. They needed their own territory, their own secure area, and they'd have both less labor and more comfort.

They had some fittings to install, that he'd helped carve. If the LT's design worked, this would be a hinged gate.

Spencer said, "Trinidad, you're the little guy, you're voted."

"Of course," he said. "It's always Felix up the pole."

He grabbed the post, braced his feet, and shimmied. He reached up for the pin and thong holding it to its neighbor, and hoisted himself to the top of the wall. He was breathing a bit as he wedged a foot between poles. Barker tossed up the headpiece to him, a tumbling, rough-hewn block. He caught it and he wiggled it down the gatepost. It had been preshaped by drilling with the power drill from the toolbox, filing, chiseling, and finally just spinning it around and around the post until it fit. It had two holes cut for dowels.

The three men below shoved and pushed the gate section into place. He slid the headstock down, twisted until the dowel holes lined up with the recesses in the gatepost.

"Hammer," he called, and Barker lobbed it underhand to him. He tapped the dowels in until they started to mush on the ends.

"Try it," he said.

The pivot worked smoothly enough. They opened the gate both ways. The inside would be reinforced with a crossbar and logs set into the ground. Nothing the natives had should be able to open it, and most animals would detour around. A stampede might be a problem, but even then, after a few bumps, most animals would go past, not blindly into a wall of logs.

Barker walked the gate in and out, and it was surprisingly smooth. The rough spots had been well worn. Socketed top and bottom, it was a functional hinge.

"Good job, Bob," he said.

"That was Sergeant Spencer's work."

"Still a good job. Can I get down now?"

"Sure."

"Thanks." The poles were biting into his ankles. He dislodged himself carefully, stepped back and dropped.

"We'll put the second door up tomorrow."

"Good. Once we do some more trenching it will be awesome."

Spencer came over. "There's going to be braces that prevent the doors swinging back, top and bottom. Then a crosslet bar in case we need extra reinforcement. And a sill."

He asked, "Punji spikes in the trenches?"

"I am considering that, yes."

Hah. He'd been joking.

So he added, "Also vines and twine to tangle whoever it is."

Spencer said, "Right, but we also need to start on stone walls. Constant improvement."

That . . . sounded odd.

"Who are we trying to defend against?"

"Anyone or anything. There's thousands of them, ten of us. Enough bodies can climb over, or ram through, or maybe they'll learn to control rhinos. I don't know. Since we can't get back home, we want a castle, fields full of serfs, a noble class of us and kids, who are well-educated, and then we'll see about windmills for electricity, teaching people to mine metal for us. As far as we can go. Unless you want to eat grubs and baluts and chase native chicks."

"The native chicks are starting to look pretty good. But yeah, we might as well work on being tops."

"Visitors to the north!" Oglesby called. "Large group, a dozen or more."

Elliott ordered, "Be ready, stay in camp. I want someone covering the gap." The south wall was twenty feet shy of the stream while they figured out what to do about that.

"I have it," he said, and grabbed his rifle from the log he'd leaned it on.

"What loading?"

"Magazines in, chambers empty," Spencer said.

He climbed up the ladder on the back of Number Eight and got a good view downslope. Barker came up next to him. Oglesby was in the turret of Number Nine. He did a quick scan by eye. Spencer came up, and Elliott too, and settled next to him. Caswell and Dalton had the east covered from behind logs. Ortiz and Alexander were watching the north from the brush pile.

"More than a dozen," he said. "Sixteen? And those are some other group, not the Urushu." It was less than a kilometer, but there were trees down there and assorted terrain features covered in scrub. Visibility was about twenty percent.

Barker said, "They're significantly more advanced."

"How do you figure?"

"I'm looking at the bindings on their spears, and the cut of their clothing. And they have bows. And tamed dogs."

Yes, and he should have caught that. "Yeah . . . think they're going to move in?"

"I expect so. Likely some advance or scouting party."

He said, "Well, this is a major river valley. There's bound to be both transients and settlers."

Spencer said, "Be glad we got as good a spot as we did."

He turned and said, "I was joking earlier, Sergeant, but I agree. We need to work on some stone, and mortar."

Elliott said, "Slaked lime we can do. Water and sand we can do. I'm trying to remember the rest."

Spencer said, "And it would be much better to get flat stone, or find some way to cut it. I can crack it and burn it, but it takes so damned long."

Barker was still watching the travelers. He said, "Those dogs bother me. They're not wolves. They're dogs. Domesticated."

Elliott looked quizzical. "Okay?"

"So how do they have domesticated dogs? We haven't seen any others."

"They may be first in the area."

Ortiz called up, "I don't think so. Breeding dogs took centuries. They'd be all over. What do they look like?"

Barker said, "Wolfhounds or large malamute types, but definitely dogs."

Ortiz was standing, but stayed in position. "I might be able to tell if I could examine one."

Felix was intel. He wanted to talk to them.

Elliott had the binox and was studying them.

He asked, "Can I take a look, sir?"

"Yes, here," the lieutenant said and handed them over.

"I'm next," said Barker.

"Then me, goddammit," said Spencer.

"I'm behind you," Alexander said. She held her camera with telephoto. "Strap around your neck first, and for gods' sake, be careful."

"Got it," Spencer said, taking it and carefully looping the strap over his head.

Felix zoomed in on the visitors. "They're less Asian looking, more European looking. Shorter. Less robust."

Barker said, "Agreed."

Spencer said, "I hate to jump to conclusions, but if they've got bows, dogs and small stature, it suggests they're post-agricultural revolution. We know bows existed nine thousand years ago. Before us, I mean. Before that it gets sketchy. We know dogs started about now, but took a while. We know people got smaller after agriculture from eating more grain and less meat. And of course, all that is entirely speculative now that we're on the spot."

Felix said, "All I know is they're more advanced. I see bows, lighter throwing spears, shoulder bundles, the dogs, and the clothing is more sophisticated. It has actual sleeves and leggings."

Elliott asked, "Do they see us?"

"I would assume so. We're hard to miss. Though possibly they think we're just some odd landscape formation. No, wait, they're looking this way. Huddling, passing messages back and forth as they move. So they're aware of us, but want us not to be aware of them."

Elliott said, "Then let's keep quiet, and goddamnit, I wish I had enough troops for patrols."

Spencer said, "After we finish the walls, maybe. Another month."

"It'll be almost winter then," Elliott said, "I want two on watch. I am not trusting them. One up here during the day. Two at night."

"Still think I'm crazy about the palisade and ditch, Trinidad?" Spencer asked.

"I didn't think you were crazy," he said, a bit defensively. "I thought your schedule was a bit rushed."

"Fair enough."

"They're moving on," Felix said. "But I assume they'll be back."

"Definitely," Spencer said. "Sometime."

Something occurred to him. "Are these the other visitors the Urushu mentioned?"

Spencer flared his eyebrows. "Possibly. They said they were wizards who talked to animals."

Dalton said, "If they're lost in time, how many others are?"

✢ ✢ ✢

That was something to consider, Sean Elliott thought. There might be other groups displaced. Some of them could be from forward in time.

Well, so far, no one wanted a fight. God nor aliens had come down to tell them how to live. Either they were being left alone, or it was a bizarre natural occurrence. But had some kind of breach caused a bunch of stuff to come through in the same place? No, they'd have seen others. So not the same place, but within a few hundred miles?

He asked Spencer, then realized he should also ask Trinidad, who was intel. The man was so quiet, and Navy, and, yeah, he'd been defaulting to the old white guy. Or was it just that Spencer was older and knew this stuff? No, Devereaux was studying astronomy, and calculating the calendar. He should be talking to him, too.

He'd been inadvertently racist. Just a bit, but there really wasn't room for it here. They were all one people for this.

"Okay, everybody, formation around dinner. And it smells good. Stew?"

"Antelope," Caswell said. "With wild onions, some kind of pine bark and needle, some chopped cattail, plantains and a bit of what I think is burdock. It's safe, I ate some."

"Excellent. Bob Barker said he would be looking for fish and wild rice in the river."

Barker said, "And I still will. I want to get the wall finished even more now, though. Sergeant Spencer wants more firewood."

"How's that going?"

Spencer said, "We have the brush piles and we can chop more logs. They need to season. I figure the dead of winter we drag a log or two into the tepee and just feed them in toward the middle."

"How much do we need?"

"I read a story somewhere about a guy in a cabin in the Canadian Northwest. He had eight cords."

Eight? "That's a crapton of wood."

"It is. But if it's too much, we have it next year. If it's not enough, it sucks at least, kills us at worst."

As if to emphasize it, Dalton put another split piece of wood on the fire.

Ortiz asked, "Can we ask the Urushu?"

Oglesby said, "They all gather in that large lodge and have a half sleeping, half orgy winter. I already asked."

"We'll skip that," he said.

"Please," Alexander said. She turned and tossed a bit of food down by the bank of the stream.

Dalton asked, "Are you trying for a pet?"

"If you must know, yes. We need something furry to hug."

Dalton looked as if he were about saying something, but she was right. They didn't have partners or spouses. They needed something for companionship. It was either adopt Urushu children, or pets.

The cat limped slowly out of cover under a bush, crawled low, and snatched the food. He squirmed back into a hollow.

"Sergeant Devereaux has the date fixed."

"Sort of," Devereaux said. "I may be off by up to a week. I think I'm within two days. We'll know on Twenty-One December. For now, I'm calling it October Third."

"What year?" Dalton asked.

Devereaux said, "Thirteen thousand, two hundred ninety-six BC."

Dalton about dropped his food. He stopped in mid chew.

"You're shitting me."

"Of course I am. There's no way to tell. But you believed me."

That had to be a poke at Dalton's Creationism.

Dalton took a moment to swallow, looked half amused and half disgusted, and said, "Bastard."

Devereaux said, "So we've got a month before it starts getting cold, not just cool."

Trinidad asked, "How cold will it get at night?"

Devereaux and Spencer exchanged glances.

Spencer said, "This should be a small climate optimum between the Older and Younger Dryas. The temperature in those dropped back to Ice Age levels within three generations. This should be a bit warmer, more moderate, and lusher, and so far, it is, compared to what we had back in A-stan. This assumes we have the time frame right, that the research I read is right, and I remember it right. Winter will still be down into the sub-freezing range at least, though."

That was a lot of maybes, but winter was winter.

"I endorse the plan for a lot of firewood," Elliott said, to make sure people knew. "It's always useful as a barricade and windbreak, and fuel for next year. Stack it deep."

Spencer said, "We need to finish that smokehouse ASAP and get to smoking meat, salting meat and drying meat. We can use it as a sauna, too. Eventually it'll be a hot water spa, with a tub."

Ortiz said, "Goddamn, we could rent excursions here to rich Manhattan bitches for a grand a day."

"Yeah, if we could." Dammit.

He spit out a bit of gristle, and tossed it over where the cat was. Hell, they might as well have a pet. They planned to domesticate food animals, after all.

"So what about domestic animals?" he asked.

Ortiz said, "We need to clip bird wings, and build some cages out of willow sticks or something else skinny and straight. We move those around where we plan to plant crops and the guano will prep the ground. Goats are easy, we have the fence, and toss enough stuff for them to eat. Rabbits can go in cages framed in wood and meshed with the Kevlar RPG mesh off the vehicles. Bigger stuff we should just let graze. There's enough of them hunting isn't a big problem."

Elliott said, "Okay, moving on, Doc's been doing great work with everyone. So give us your background."

Devereaux leaned back on the log he sat on, hands behind his head, and stretched.

"Armand Devereaux, Sergeant, New York National Guard. Second year med student. I took a break from school to raise more money and look after my mama. I'm a combat medic. This was my first deployment. I was supposed to be doing some local charity stuff for a month, then going home. I'm fucking pissed about that.

"Anyway, I'm from Queens, joined up to get the college, get out of the city, and looks like I did."

He paused a moment and took a drink from his Camelbak. He was almost never without it.

"I've got a good basic kit and few extras, but it won't last forever. I know I've said that. I'm glad I can help our neighbors, and all of you, but you've got to stay hydrated, keep clean, be careful. I sound like your mom, don't I?

"Goddamn, I miss home," he said, and stopped talking.

Elliott quickly said, "Thanks. And thanks for helping with the calendar. Knowing what time of year it is is going to save us. Oglesby, you're next."

Oglesby said, "I'm a Specialist, I enlisted early and finished AIT right after high school. I'm an Urdu translator but I'm pretty good with Arabic as well, and some Hindi. I've always liked languages and I'm familiar with roots and development. That's called ethnology. I'm out of Campbell, and I was supposed to rotate home in three months. Guess I missed that.

"I'm drawing up glossaries and dictionaries so you can speak without me, just in case something bad happens."

"I guess that's about it. I have a younger sister and parents, and I really don't want to talk about them."

Elliott said, "Hey, translation is critical. You made our entrance a thousand times easier. Don't sell yourself short."

To all, he said, "You all hear how we have all these skills, right? It turns out we know a lot more than we thought we did. We're constructing a camp, we're fed, we're getting more variety of food. Doc's doing a great job with us and the locals. We're making progress on developing relations with them without letting them too close too fast. It's working. It will get better from here.

"I'm going to say again that I'm both leader and chaplain. Anything you tell me in confidence stays with me. If you can't talk to me, talk to Martin Spencer. If not him, find someone else. Cover for each other. Let's not split into factions and let's not squabble like siblings."

"If I may, sir," Spencer put in.

"Go ahead."

"Shaving and haircuts are obviously already nonreg. That's fine. Keep them neat for now. I've been shaving about twice a week, and it works well enough. I'm kempt without being too strack. I can cut hair reasonably well, male and female. Let me know and I can help you trim down. A couple of us have scissors and I may be able to sharpen them, and I have knives and sharpening tools."

Sean ran a hand through his own hair, which was civilian thick, though he kept it whitewalled around the ears and blocked in back. His beard he kept trimmed short, but scraggly, between growth and uneven clipping. It didn't feel professional. He'd ask about a monthly haircut or even head shaving.

"We should keep using the soap and such from that care package as long as it lasts. I don't care if you only bathe once a week, but wash your damned hands after taking a dump and before eating. And I know a lot of you aren't brushing your teeth enough. Doc has pliers, or we can drill it out with a hot wire and jam it full of pine tar, and repeat monthly. You don't want that. Back to you, sir."

"Anyone else?"

Caswell said, "I made a roof panel for the latrine, of grass and leaves. That gives us three sides and a roof. I'll need help with a door."

"I can do that," Spencer said.

Barker said, "As soon as we can split a couple of logs, we'll make a proper one with planked walls and roof. It'll add some insulation, too."

"Good," Elliott said. It would be nice to take a crap in private.

Alexander said, "If I did it right, I got wireless working on the laptop, as a hotspot. It means we can use our phones for a couple of hundred meters as long as we're in line of sight."

Dalton snorked. "Two hundred meters? What good is that?"

She smiled in the faint firelight as she said, "More useful than shouting, and infinitely farther than zero. Also, you can text me updates on materials, inventory, or AARs."

Elliott said, "I see it for watch. We can relay photos, too. Or give orders quietly. Thank you very much, Sergeant Alexander." The range was pathetic, but hell, it was progress. They had the vehicles and parts of them, the gear and their personal stuff, and their skills. It was a lot better than it could be.

"You're welcome, sir." It sounded as if she were emphasizing just to drive it in.

"We can test that tomorrow. I'll also do a periodic inspection of what we've got so far. So with that said, I guess it's free time. Keep the watch schedule. Spencer."

Everyone wandered off, but only a few feet. The glow of tablets and phones indicated movies and music. That helped a lot. It would get repetitive eventually, but for now, they weren't entirely cut off from civilization. He'd wondered at first if a full break was better, much like Basic Training from civilian world. But they needed some connection.

"Sir," Spencer said.

"So, we were right on the walls." He started walking the perimeter. Spencer followed.

"Hell, I knew that, sir. Animals, natives. Someone is going to be hostile."

"Yes. Can we speed up the north wall?" He walked along the laid-out line and the huge gap.

Spencer said, "It's getting faster as we go, except we're dragging logs farther. The straight ones are getting scarce. We're carrying them five hundred meters, now. We'll be taking them from downstream and dragging them uphill."

The drag marks were quite visible, where logs had ripped grass and brush from the hillside in furrows. In the dusk they were creepy, like giant worm tracks. The trimmed limbs and branches lay in a long pile that would at least hinder attackers.

"Do what you can. What's our strategy if we are attacked? Fire the brush?"

"I'd rather not. We need the fuel. It won't flare up that fast. It won't burn very long. We've got a pretty good break at the moment," Spencer said, pointing. "It spans most of the gap and is about ten feet wide, five feet tall. It's a lot of brush, and no one is crossing it quickly. We just dive into the trucks and button up. We have the turrets."

"What if we have to shoot?" He'd really prefer to avoid violence with the natives.

"Then we shoot. They don't know how much ammo we have. But that later group bothers me."

"Yes, but why?" He had his own theories.

Spencer said, "I suspect they have more belief in gods than spirits. Some modern tribesmen think they're immune to bullets through various magic. It never works, which just means they need more magic. Casualties don't dissuade them."

If so, that was concerning. "Then it depends on if that's a small group of time travelers, or a regional takeover by contemporaries." Certainly there was local internecine conflict of some kind.

Spencer said, "And what other groups are out there? If we're suspecting two, there could be more."

Spencer had the same thoughts he did.

With a slow nod, Sean said, "Yeah. Get the north done. I'll figure something out for the river side."

"Earthworks in several rings, fences, brush, the river. But we need some type of crossing."

"I'll design something."

"I mean the fence crossing the stream. Then we'll want a bridge, too."

"Yeah, I got that," he repeated with some exasperation.

"Sorry, sir, just making sure."

"Should we store stuff in the trucks?"

"It's very inconvenient, we don't have a definite threat yet, and we have at least half a perimeter and modern weapons. I think we're okay. But we do need to keep the watch up."

Spencer pointed up where Oglesby and Dalton sat. Dalton was on watch, Oglesby was just shooting the shit, but as long as it kept the watchstander awake, that was fine. Dalton kept scanning the distance.

He said, "I'm tempted to suggest a night vision scan every half hour."

Spencer replied, "I think that's a good idea. Possibly not all the time, but definitely the next few days."

"As long as we have rechargeables, I'm going to make it a regular thing."

"I'll spread the word, sir."

CHAPTER 12

The next day, the two latrine sides went up, and the roof went on. It wasn't perfect, nor was it a private bathroom, but Martin Spencer felt relieved. He didn't like shitting in public, and he was sure the women liked it less. Everyone had been discreet and polite on the matter, but the more civilized they could remain, the better. He felt creepy when he caught a glimpse of the women squatting.

They'd need a door and plank walls next. Though Barker was working on that sweat lodge and it would be done in a few days. That would be welcome, too. It had been two months since he'd felt hot water. For now the lodge was just a lashed frame of withes. Alexander was supposed to stitch pieces of goatskin to cover it when she wasn't busy with administration, helping gather herbs, or chopping firewood. Despite snarky comments from Dalton and Oglesby, she did her share of work. They also liked sleeping in the tepee she stitched the cover for. Well, was still stitching. Some of it was still draped, but that was coming along. They got goat hides with every kill, and tendons and rawhide for stitching them together.

He knew of tepees from books. Barker had built them. With the inside liner and cover over the living area, reflected heat was keeping it quite warm for now. It was also very dark, and darker as the ponchos and plastic got replaced with stitched hide. Eventually, they'd need to scrape some lighter ones, or weave something. But he suspected they'd appreciate the heaviness in a few weeks.

Dalton and Trinidad were chopping trees. Caswell was hunting with Ortiz. Barker was cooking. Oglesby was down and in Number

209

Eight to enjoy privacy. Elliott, Doc, Alexander and himself were doing camp labor—dragging brush, cutting it into firewood, stretching leather, and shortly they'd be macheteing grass. Eventually he'd have to make a scythe. Forge first.

He dragged a pruned bough over to the woodpile and started sectioning it into sticks and small loglets.

Right then, Doc said, "Chilly this morning."

"Yeah. Winter is coming," Spencer agreed. They'd had frost. The leaves had started to turn yellow, except for some kind of ivy around the trees that was turning an absolutely brilliant crimson red.

"That breeze is stiff. I almost want to take cover behind the woodpile."

He burst out laughing.

Devereaux stared at him. "Eh?"

"Old, very racist slang."

Doc stared at the sky and thought for a moment, then said, "Oh. Ooooh. Hehehe. Good thing we're not where I can file an EEO complaint, Sergeant."

"Yeah, good thing my only familiarity is historical. Seriously, Armand, I'm very glad we have you. I expect to get old first. You're going to be my savior."

"Hopefully. I've got limited facilities." Devereaux pointed at him. "How's your guts?"

"Bone meal seems to help, as does the low carb diet." He seemed to be okay taking a pill every other day, and had a little irritation but no pain. Still, he might be dissolving his esophagus from that, and eventually it would kill him. He or Alexander would be first from their medical issues, unless rampaging animals trod Caswell or Dalton into the mud.

"Good. I wish I had some way to scope you, but there isn't."

"I'm more concerned about the palisade at the moment." His stomach would kill him slowly. The predators or intruders might be a lot quicker. They'd had a bear walk through the previous night, and crap behind Number Eight, less than twenty feet from Ortiz on watch, thirty from the tepee.

"At least we're getting buff and fit," Devereaux said, and flexed a bicep. He'd been wiry and lean before. He had bulked up and ripped down from the diet and exercise.

"We are. Pity there's no one we can use it on."

"Native women. Eventually. They're very nice to look at, when they're young and healthy."

Martin said, "Yeah, but they don't stay that way long, and you'd need to teach one hygiene, I have no idea what we do about age restrictions, and they have families who want gifts."

"I know." There was a long pause. "Martin, since we're using first names for now, what do we do about the regs? How long do we try to remain U.S. Army?"

He'd thought about that often.

"I'd say as long as we can. It's frustrating, but we need the framework for discipline. In a way, this is worse than death. It's a lot like being a POW."

"It is. It's depressing. I'm worried about a couple of our people."

"Which ones?"

Doc checked his fingers. "Well . . . Alexander is depressed, partly environmental, partly endocrinal. Caswell seems constantly hyperalert and ready to break. And the LT. He's prone to zone out."

There was a hollow thumping sound. Was someone fitting another pole? He thought today was chopping day.

Martin said, "I think Elliott will be okay. Alexander is a medical case, but she responds when you prod her. Caswell . . . she seems to have a lot of issues. Some of it's being Air Force among us. Some is being female. Some is that unrealistic view she's had of the egalitarianism of primitive societies. A lot of feminists have that, even though nothing I've read supports the idea. They want it really badly, but it doesn't have much evidence on its side."

"I wondered about that."

The thumping came again, and he said, "Stop wondering and start running, it's a stampede." He turned and shouted, "Dalton! Trinidad! Stampede! Head for the stockade."

They had plenty of time. It wasn't quite a stampede, but it was a large movement of animals. To the west, the large, ugly antelope ran in streams among the wooly rhino, who stirred up dust and plant debris with their gallops.

Spencer shouted, "Open the gate!" as he climbed up onto Number Eight, and without looking down called, "Oglesby, we have stampede," as he climbed up into the turret.

"Uh? Oh." The man had been sleeping.

Trinidad called back, "Why the gate?"

"*Open the fucking gate!*" Why couldn't he just do as he was fucking told?

The kid did it.

"I don't get it, either," Elliott said as he climbed up the back.

"Half a gate. They'll bump it and might break it. Better they run right through."

"Logical," Elliott agreed, then said, "Everyone aboard the vehicles."

"Ramps up?"

"I don't think that's a problem, but keep a spear handy."

The rhino weren't numerous, but they were huge. One of them lumbered through the gate, snorting, and drove straight through the fire circle without damaging anything. He appeared to move a lot lighter than his bulk suggested, but the ground shook. He charged over the tree stumps and brush by the creek and kept going, splashing mud as he scrambled up the far bank.

Several gazelles followed, and one of the ugly saiga type beasts.

That was it. A few others had gone around the ditch, and some south of the wall. All in all, a nice livestock show.

"I wonder what set them off?" Alexander asked below him.

"Could be anything. Something disturbed one, he jogged, bumped another, pretty soon they're charging. Everything else around them either takes it as a hint, or tries to get out of the way."

From the roof of Number Nine, Ortiz said, "That was a small one. There's lots of room. They don't seem to form huge herds, just family groups."

"Yeah. Not like zebra or buffalo."

Barker said, "I saw a couple of those aurochs, and some wild boar. We need steak and ham."

"Oh, yes. But I don't think you can take them down with a rifle?"

"Brain shot will, or we build a trap. I'm not interested in being sporting. I'm interested in eating."

The excitement over, they dispersed.

"We need that other gate ASAP," Spencer said.

Trinidad said, "Let's grind the pivot and get it moving."

"I need a damned hatchet. The axes are too big, and the machetes are suboptimal."

Dalton said, "So forge one." He was being half derisive. Yes, it was going to take a while to get to that stage, and the kid would be less smartass then.

"I will, eventually. Several." He hoped. First they had to find ore. He could definitely reduce it, eventually. He even knew how to carburize, which put him above anyone before the year 1000 or so.

In the meantime, the rushing animals proved they needed the barricade.

Shaping the pivots took a lot of chiseling and carving. Trinidad was murder with a machete. He used a combination of slicing chops, hacking chops, scrapes and cuts with wrist twists to turn the top point of the log into a quite smooth cone. It wasn't as smooth as a lathe would make it, but impressive.

"We should have done this sooner," Martin said as he watched.

The socket was a beast. It wouldn't be done today. They hammered, chiseled, gouged with knives, filed and scraped.

Trinidad said, "I need a lump from the fire and a reed," he said. "Just burn it deeper."

"Not a bad idea, hold on."

Actually . . . yes. It should work.

Trinidad ran that way, and Spencer noted the increase in the man's muscle mass. They were all getting bigger from manual labor.

Caswell and Ortiz returned with something small and meaty looking. It might be a yearling deer. They hung it in the kitchen area.

"We got a stampede," she said.

"Yeah, it came through here."

"Luckily, they didn't seem crowded. I thought a rhino was going to stomp me into the ground, but he shifted at the last minute."

"Good. I'm not sure what we can do about that while hunting. It doesn't seem to happen often, though."

"Approaching party!" Barker called from the lookout.

"Oh, goddammit. Paleos?"

"Negative. Large party, numbering about three zero. Armed with bows, with dogs."

A chill ran down him.

"Body armor, weapons. Magazines in, chambers empty for now, but be ready. I'll do the meet and greet, the LT has the trucks."

"I'll meet them," Elliott said. "You keep the trucks."

"Understood, sir," he said, and felt disgusted with himself for feeling relief. He really wanted to avoid fights.

So why had he started snapping orders and assuming command?

Because he didn't trust anyone to do the right thing, and he could avoid his fears by giving orders to others. Not good.

The troops were running in and out of the tepee, quite briskly, and wearing armor and helmets. If someone wanted to get stupid with a bow . . .

"Two-forty mounted," Barker called. "Belt in the box, top cover open."

"Good, keep it like that for now."

Yeah. If they got stupid . . .

Please, don't get stupid.

Sean Elliott shrugged into his ITV and tossed on his ACH. It felt comforting, but almost unfamiliar. It had been weeks since he'd bothered.

"Oglesby with me. Dalton. Caswell. Ortiz . . . no, Trinidad."

He was risking Trinidad, the intel expert, over the vet, and their edible plant expert, but dammit, he couldn't leave everyone safe, and he only had nine people.

Alexander ran up with his Bluetooth. He shrugged and stuck it in.

Barker called, "Five hundred meters. I count three-two adults. I'm calling it a war party."

That was not what he wanted to hear.

"Roger that. We'll head out so we're in view." He wanted that gun covering him. Was Barker good enough to miss him if he fired?

"Go ahead and load," he ordered. "Fingers off triggers, muzzles safe. We're not going to start anything."

Dalton said, "But if they do, we'll finish it."

He said, "Be frugal with ammo. Start with two warning shots."

Caswell said, "Sir, they have no context for a warning shot. It's just a loud noise. If nothing happens, it won't have a good effect, and it means if we do shoot one later, they'll decide the noise isn't always deadly."

"Okay." That was logical. It limited his options though. "Then I guess you shoot to disable or kill. Once they're down, stop, and Doc will try to save them."

"Just like Hajjis," Dalton said. "Has A-stan ever changed?"

"Here we go. Oglesby, let me know if you have anything."

The man nodded. "Hooah, sir. It's possible there will be some PIE. It's even vaguely possible I'll recognize it if they talk slow. That would be awesome."

"I'll take your word on it." He'd meant to ask what PIE was last time, and hadn't. Obviously something linguistically common. Presomething?

The approaching element was visible, and not trying too hard to stay hidden. It could be a friendly meeting, then.

"What is PIE?" he asked.

"Oh. Proto-Indo-European. The root language for all modern Indo-European languages. Everything from Sanskrit to Greek to German and English."

"Babel," Dalton muttered.

He felt sorry for Dalton. His worldview had to be taking a beating. Sean was religious, believed there was a God directing everything, who didn't interact with people very much. But the Bible had been written by people who had no grasp of modern science. How much could God explain to them in terms they could understand? Babel did seem a good metaphor for this PIE. It didn't need to be literal to be true.

His Bluetooth said, "Can you still hear us, sir?" It was Barker.

He replied, "I can. What can you see?" as the others looked at him. Yeah, he'd want to watch that with the visitors. They might find it as heavenly or demonic, or just not grasp it at all.

Barker said, "They're smaller than you. Five six or so. Robust looking fellas. Bearded. Spears seem optimized for throwing. So far, they're clumped up. I'll let you know if they try for envelopment."

"Please do." There wasn't much range on the Bluetooth, but he had outside eyes. That mattered.

He could easily see them now. Despite the hummocky ground, they were perhaps a hundred meters back. They ambled over the lumpy terrain, and there were two large wolflike dogs with them.

"We'll wait here," he decided. The dogs were a complication. "Barker, can you shoot around us if necessary?"

"I can."

"Are you good enough with that thing?"

"I've shot and hit from a moving vehicle. I can bracket you easily." The man sounded confident.

"Excellent. Don't unless I say so, or I go down with a spear. That includes being wounded. Once I'm down, let them have it."

"Roger that, sir."

The advancing group were mostly dark haired, but there were a couple of blonds. They had shaggy but kempt beards, some of them trimmed, and their hair was obviously combed and dressed, either cut at the neck or braided. They wore goat hide in various shades, with leggings and moccasins.

The leader stepped out, raised a hand and said, "Haylaa!"

"Hello . . . to you, too," he said slowly.

Oglesby said, "Well, that's one, but an easy one."

Caswell said, "Clear syllables that are easy to say and hear. It may be widespread."

"Shut up," he said.

They mumbled "Hooah."

The Stone Ager went into some lengthy introduction of himself, shaking his spear and waving, with emphatic shouts.

When he was done, Elliott asked, "Comment?"

Oglesby said, "I didn't get anything at that pacing, though there's probably a handful of referents I could get if he slowed down. He's telling us how awesome he is."

Caswell said, "How awesome he is. He's not awesome enough to have someone do it for him. That's likely a later concept. This is still a band society, not a kingship. But he's the current leader, probably through prowess."

Apparently, the discussion took too long. The group moved forward.

Elliott raised a hand. "STOP!"

The man paused for a moment then lumbered on through the hummocky weeds.

Then he realized the chief or whatever he was planned to knock him down. They weren't going for kills, they wanted slaves.

The easiest way to end this would be to draw an M9 and shoot the chief through the face. Dead, done, behold our magic weapons. Except that might provoke mass violence, and he didn't want to wipe out a village. Also, the Paleos were useful, the Neolithics probably would be, and would be more so with trade. And fuck it, they needed to help them develop. It would be better all around, there really wasn't any other choice, and his duty was to keep his people alive now.

Well, the arrogant prick was burly and muscular, and probably knew how to roughhouse, but did he know Jiu Jitsu and Kung Fu?

He knew aggression. The man was short, but had knotty muscles, and wanted to prove his dominance. He came in fast. Elliott dodged and tried for an arm bar.

Tried. He got the wrist and elbow and shoved, but the bastard was strong enough it didn't work. The man actually lifted him clear of the ground as he swung his arm, trying to dislodge Elliott. They were bounding across the ground, trying to keep their feet as the sky whirled. He was suddenly glad for the wrestling practice they'd had.

The other Neos fanned out into a semicircle. He saw the soldiers draw back and aim rifles. But if they could do this without shooting, it would be better. For one thing, their ammo was finite.

He let go with his left arm and tried to kidney punch the big man. That didn't work. Then a strong slap caught him upside the right ear, under the helmet, and his vision blurred as his ears rang. He gripped as tight as he could, and a moment later became aware he was in a strong bear hug from behind, his arms at painful angles and feet dangling. The guy had reached right around the armor.

He strained for breath and took two kicks. Those were knees or shins behind him, and he drove his booted heels back in a one-two. He was rewarded with a roaring scream.

However, the chief then collapsed forward, pinning him against the ground in a heap and bending his wrist back so he convulsed in agony. He had about two inches free with which to batter his helmet back against the man's nose, then got an arm free and added some jabs. His knuckles stung, but he was hitting cheek or eye socket, and got some groans, and stinking breath past his face.

The man shoved and stood, and Elliott rolled forward fast, catching a glimpse of a foot trying to stomp him. The other one came at him, and he grabbed, twisted and shoved back. That brought the guy down with a heavy thump, and Elliott got to his feet fast.

In a moment Elliott had a boot on the character's neck, the man's throat pressed into his other boot, and his right arm twisted far back with the wrist bent. He leaned on it just enough to ensure the guy couldn't struggle. He couldn't decide between waiting for submission, breaking the arm or giving a firm boot to the face. Instead, he kept pressure on his throat until the straining roars turned to groans, moans and the man went limp.

At this point he wasn't sure if he was supposed to kill the man, humiliate him, take over as chief, or roar and thump his chest. Hell, if he remembered right, the Zulus and a few others might have raped him.

Instead, he looked for the two largest, closest men, pointed at them, pointed at the limp form, and turned away, which had to be a sign of contempt among hunters. Hopefully, it wouldn't trigger a thrown spear. Though Dalton and Caswell still had rifles raised and were ready to fire. He wondered if any of the primitives had figured out M4s were weapons of some kind.

Jenny Caswell was impressed. The Neolith was built like a wrestler or quarterback, and the LT had ground him into the dirt. Though the armor had no doubt helped a little.

Two of them dragged their chief's limp form back to their huddle, and they all gathered around. One of them hesitantly stepped forward, a little closer to her, and she threw on her command face, shook her head once, pointed at him, pointed at the group, and took a half step toward him.

He skipped back to the group without argument.

Dalton said, "Nice job, sir."

"Thanks," Elliott replied through heaving breath and a pulse throbbing in his neck. "Let's keep it quiet for now and assume we all know I'm a badass. Nice save, Caswell, thanks." His helmet was askew. He straightened it. It appeared he was trying to moderate his breath, too.

Dalton said, "Hooah."

"Thank you, sir. Does he need treatment?" she asked. "The chief?"

"Maybe. I hope I didn't kill him." Elliott turned to face them. He seemed a bit disturbed. "I'd rather he was alive."

She thought about proto-pastoral cultures and hoped they were similar. "That depends on their culture. It's possible the loss is a shame that requires death. He'll be more dangerous. But probably he will lose status. He'll have to make amends and gifts to the men, sacrifices to the gods, and try to recover grace with a successful hunt."

"I hope that's the case."

"Without seeing their culture, I can't say," she admitted. "And we don't even know when they really came from nor where. Sergeant Spencer may have a bit more information about early cultures, if we can find out. Though I find him to have a bit of a bias."

"Everyone has a bit of a bias," Dalton said.

"This is true," she said, and decided to drop it. The Neos seemed unsure what to do. The soldiers didn't have spears, but had easily bested their leader, and didn't appear afraid.

She was actually quite afraid, but at this point, she knew her eventual fate with whatever group wound up dominant. She just had to make sure she got the best status possible. Concubines rated higher than war trophies.

Elliott said, "It concerns me they came from the west. The Urushu are that way. This is a big, well-equipped group that passed us by the river at least once."

"I can recon, with two people for backup," Dalton offered.

On the one hand, she'd love to have the information herself. On the other hand, that was a risk.

"Not right now," Elliott said.

There was a whistle from the gate. She looked back to see Alexander pointing at her ear.

She looked at the LT. Crap.

"Sir, your Bluetooth."

"Oh, shit," he said. "I forgot it completely. Fell out in the scuffle."

"We'll sweep for it after they leave."

Oglesby said, "It wasn't lost in the first go round. I saw it."

"That helps. Caswell, you're female, do they perceive you as lower status?"

"This group? Almost certainly, sir." At least he'd asked.

"Would you shooing them off help or hinder?"

"I honestly have no idea, but I'd be delighted to perform the experiment." It might work on spectators, too.

"You saw him fight. Can you take one?"

"Knowing they're coming in fast and testosteroned up, I think so." They charged like teenage boys. Smart and strong, but not wise and not forward thinking.

"Please do."

"Right away." She turned, feeling more pleasure than she should in the task.

"You. Shoo. Go away!" She waggled her hands and took a step toward them.

One of them stepped toward her.

She took another step.

He hesitated a moment, then advanced a bit more.

She swung her head momentarily, said, "Do not interfere. I have to handle this. Take my rifle," and turned back. She leaned her rifle back behind her and let it fall. Taking a step, she pointed. "Go!"

Nope. He wanted a fight. His chest was puffed out, his arms slightly spread, and he leaned slightly forward. It might be he didn't recognize her as female, or didn't care. Though this group was all male, which suggested solidified gender roles.

He probably wanted to wrestle. That was his strong suit. He was her height, about 5'5", but had about 40 pounds on her, with similar reach. She would rather not wrestle.

Well, she had kneepads, boots and armor. It was three paces, he likely expected some challenge, so she strode in, let him thrust his chest at her SAPI plate, and kneed him in the balls. He blocked that, and completely missed the fist she'd brought in from the side into his ribs.

He winced, bent, whuffed, and she took his shoulder, pried it up, and kicked down on the side of his knee. He squealed faintly, dropped to the weeds, and sipped for air. She raised a foot as if to kick him in the face, lowered it deliberately, pointed at him, and laughed loudly.

He almost appeared to cry.

Then she turned and walked back to the others, sighing in relief and shaking slightly.

Elliott whispered, "They may regard that as an attack on his manhood."

Yes, they very well might, and she enjoyed it. A lot.

"Good. Either they want to fight or they don't. Either they'll spread the word that women can kick their asses, or they'll keep zipped and just not come back. As it stands they're oh for two, and either have to admit we're tough, or make a point of ignoring us as unworthy."

"I hope you're right."

"So do I, sir."

For now, at least, the Neos decided they'd had enough. They helped their two injured tribesmen limp a few feet, until those shook off their supporters, growled and walked freely but in shame.

On the whole, she felt pretty good.

It actually felt like a good day for a steak.

Atavism was starting to have an appeal.

"Let's find that Bluetooth," Elliott said. "No, wait . . ."

He reached under the collar of his armor.

"Well. That's lucky. Carry on."

They all laughed.

She'd boosted her status slightly, and her threat level. For now, being the baddest bitch around was a useful tactic.

Martin Spencer considered the event. For an awkward Air Force chick, that had been a pretty good fight. He'd had no questions about Caswell's technical competence with the food, and she was definitely an asset, despite her rather annoying personality, but that she could keep her cool and put up a good fight was a big plus.

"Nicely delivered," he said, as she walked in the gate, offering a high five.

She looked him up and down, up again, and made a token slap.

Well, he'd work on it. He might never like her, but he could probably learn to deal with her.

"Well done, sir," he offered, as the man headed for the trucks.

Elliott said, "Thanks. Almost lost this," and pointed at his Bluetooth.

"Yeah, we figured the rumble did that."

"So it helped marginally, but almost got lost. We'll need to refigure that."

"Still useful from OP to any towers and down here."

"True. Every time we have any kind of problem, I wish we had more people and more gear. But we never will."

"We can make some," he said. "Gear, not people."

"Eventually, yes."

Conversation resumed around the fire. For now, everyone stayed in camp, especially as it was late in the day, the lowering sun burning streamers through high clouds.

Martin said, "Barker promises we'll have the sweat lodge within the week. Then we need to see about a hot tub."

Dalton said, "I remember you talking about that and I can't recall the problem. What's wrong with a leather tub? Even if it seeps a bit, it should work for getting clean."

"Leather shrinks and stiffens with heat. It would be a one time use, no bigger than a bathtub. For a proper hot tub, we need shaped lumber. We'll need to split boards for a base, split coops, or whatever barrelmakers call the longitudinal pieces, then either carve a wooden frame or bind well with lots of rawhide."

"Understood. So that part might be next year."

"Very likely. But steam by itself sounds wonderful."

Elliott said, "Good. On with dinner, then."

"Yeah, it's about that time."

Barker had skewer-roasted some kind of antelope steak Caswell and Ortiz brought in, and there were a few skinny tubers, roasted and salted. He craved a beer, or a dinner roll, or some goddamned ice cream. Or a cup of cheap-ass coffee. He missed coffee. He had no idea how Barker and Oglesby handled the lack of smokes.

The meat was chewy but it was tasty. Venisony, rich and it had salt and some other seasoning. A green that gave it a sharp taste. "Mustard greens?" he asked.

Caswell said, "Something in the carrot family. Coriander, fennel, cumin, carrot, Queen Anne's Lace are all related. The roots are edible when young. The greens and flowers are crude herbs. They're completely undomesticated, but there's some kind of flavor to them. The tarter ones are turnip and mustard family."

She tossed a piece of chewed meat down where the cat hung out. They might domesticate him yet. He was still hanging around, came out at night to lurk near the circle without approaching closely, and would accept food. He still limped slightly, but seemed to be fit enough.

Looking back to his food, he said, "It's weird, but it's good." Actually, he wasn't sure he liked the combo, but it was better than dry meat. He'd deal. She was the best they had at finding stuff other than meat, and he wanted her to be enthusiastic in her task.

Elliott said, "After action review. The apparent Neolithic people have decided we put up too much of a fight. Can you hear me up there, Ortiz?"

"Yes, sir," was the reply.

"I can, too," said Doc.

"Good. I expect they'll be back, so night shift stay alert and use

NVG from time to time. We'll keep working on the wall. We're past halfway, but the last quarter is going to be a pain, with the stream.

"Oglesby recognized a word or two. We may eventually be able to communicate with these people, after they decide we're not someone to conquer. Until then, we'll sic Jenny Caswell on them. Well done on her fight."

"And on yours, sir," she said.

After chow Martin was really ready to sleep. It had been a long day, with intrusions by people and animals, and lots of manipulation and labor. He wanted sleep. Or at least alone, away from people. Even if all he had was a sleeping bag.

He made eye contact with the LT, got a nod of assent, then headed for the tepee. The round door had seemed awkward when first built, but now he could roll right through it.

His section was marked off with his poncho on one side and Ortiz' on the other. With a towel and a coat toward the middle of the pie section, it was quiet, dark and he could pretend he was alone.

At that, being comfortable alone meant he was adapting to this place, and accepting they weren't going back. That pissed him off.

But there was really nothing he could do.

"Fuck, it's cold out there," he said, suddenly realizing that with the tent around him and fire in the middle it was still cool. He pulled off his boots and started opening his bag.

"Hey, uh, Sergeant Spencer, did you brush your teeth?"

He sighed in irritation and . . . but no, Doc was right.

"I'll do it now, Doc." Then he very consciously said, "Thanks for the reminder."

He slipped on his boots, stepped outside, and brushed his teeth carefully for a full two minutes, while shivering and counting. He rinsed with water from a small bottle, spat, and went back inside.

The others were still talking.

Doc said, "We need some women to snuggle with."

Ortiz said, "Caswell would let us freeze even if it was a medical necessity."

"No problem. Alexander has better tits." Doc indicated shape with his hands.

She did indeed. He even had a clandestine photo he was never going to admit to.

He said, "I honestly have no idea how she'd respond. In an emergency. For now, I expect she'd tell you to fuck yourself."

Doc grinned. "If only I had that much meat. Or could bend that far."

Ortiz cracked, "Going to invent Yoga?"

The difference between the women was striking. Alexander could handle banter as long as it wasn't directed at her, occasionally rolling eyes or snapping a comment. Caswell locked up tight and sought privacy. In that regard among others, segregated quarters helped.

For Martin, though, porn was one thing. Fantasies about other troops he served with were unprofessional, dangerous, and cheating. Except Allison didn't exist in this universe and never would.

He cried himself to sleep.

CHAPTER 13

Bob Barker woke up, and it was chilly. Fall was definitely here. Hell, it was a nice, mild fall, since they were well into October. But the trees were yellower, orange and with some tips tinging red. Though the trees now started a good hundred feet from where he stood.

He blew up the fire, and put some leftover goat meat on the slabs to heat for breakfast. After that he approached the LT.

"Sir, I'd like to borrow more help today, and get the sweat lodge finished."

Elliott fidgeted.

"With hostiles moving in, I really want the wall done. And I haven't done that inspection."

"So do I, sir. But we need the sweat lodge. Eventually it'll have a hot tub. For now, it means we can sponge off warm."

He could see that tempted Elliott.

He continued, "Hot fire, hot rocks, warm water. And a warm lodge, not just hot water in cold air."

Elliott grinned. "Yeah, yeah, you make a compelling case. What do you need?"

"Anyone who can sew. We're going to finish putting goat hides over it and stitch them down. We'll need a few more goats. Also, we can smoke meat and fish in this thing."

"Okay, can you do it in a day?"

Maybe.

"I can damned well try, sir."

Barker turned to the group under the ramada. "Alexander, Spencer, Doc, Ortiz, I figure all of you can sew in some fashion."

They responded in the affirmative.

"Good. Let's get this thing done."

What he had was a rough but workable dome of lashed withes. It was taller than traditional, and wider. Eventually they'd dig a pit, line it with concrete or fitted wood, and make a hot tub. If they could figure out concrete and make or fake enough tools.

As the dew burned off, they laid out the skins they had, over the lumpy grass and worn muddy spots.

Alexander was good. She asked him, "Height and diameter?"

"Six feet and fifteen feet."

"It looks like a chord of a sphere."

"Approximately, yes."

She ran to Number Nine, came back with a stick and some 550 cord.

She stuck the stick in the ground, measured off a length of cord by hand, said, "Hold this on the stick," and started scratching arcs into the grassy dirt, like a compass. There were still a few stalky weeds here, but most had been cut, plucked, chopped in passing by machete-wielding troops, or stomped down during construction. The camp was pretty mucky in the low spots.

That done, she pointed and said, "We stitch until we fill that shape. Trim to the lines. Stitch down the sides. It'll be a dome. But let me do the trimming. We need to have enough overlap to stitch."

"Awesome, woman. I was going to hammer holes with a nail and then stitch with sinew."

Doc Devereaux said, "I can do that. Running stitch or just loops?"

He hadn't thought of that, and they jawed about it while Alexander started laying out hides.

She said, "You know, the LT is an engineer. He probably could have laid this out, too."

Bob was embarrassed. "Crap. I didn't even think of this as engineering."

She made a face at him and he laughed.

Doc said, "Okay, let's do it."

It went faster than he'd expected. By lunchtime, they had large chunks of hide ready to trim and assemble. He was also covered in goat hair, some of the slime from inside them, sweat and dirt. Yeah, he planned on being among the first inside, if he could.

They ran into another problem when they started trying to lay it over the frame. It acted as a sail, just like a little igloo tent. The twigs hadn't needed any stakes, but it would now. He cut some scrap hide into ropes and used his machete to cut some stakes. Five whacks per stake—tip, end, notch, done. He'd gotten good with it.

Ortiz hammered holes about two inches apart in the hide sections.

"Crap, you need to start over," he said.

"Why?"

"You need to overlap them and hammer through both edges at once so it lies without wrinkles."

"Ah. Shit. Okay."

They resumed. Ortiz pounded holes, Doc and Alexander ran rawhide and tied, and piles of stiff hide shifted over them.

It was near dinner when they got the hides rolled into a bundle.

"Okay, are we ready?" he asked.

"Let's do it!" Ortiz enthused.

They placed it on the north side, with the door in place, and tied it down. Then they rolled it up the frame.

Creaking warned him not to lean against it. He and Doc had the middle, Ortiz and Alexander the bottom. The flesh side rolled against the frame, and they worked it up.

"Okay, I need a push stick," he said, and Ortiz ran to grab him a limb.

Carefully, making sure not to punch holes in light goat skin, he lifted and unrolled the cover as the others rolled by hand.

Then it was over the top and easily worked into place. They punched holes at the bottom and tied it to the frame. It had a few inches of slack in it, which would tighten up as the leather aged and dried.

He realized they'd missed lunch entirely. But it was done.

He stood back, stood up, and wiped a greasy arm across his greasy face and crusty beard.

"The first fire goes inside, to smoke the leather. Later it'll be outside and we'll use hot rocks inside. Bring me the boiling pan, and we'll have a hot sponge bath." He grabbed a handful of twigs and went in to get it started.

He'd wanted it for cleanliness, but the ritual importance was still very present. He had a sweat lodge for meditation.

Sean Elliott was interested in the sweat lodge proceedings. The thought of a hot wash was fantastic. Though the second stage, a tub, would have to wait until they finished defensive works. He wanted to follow up on Alexander's idea of protective brush, and possibly a second ditchwork. They could button up tightly enough in the vehicles, but that wouldn't protect their few, valuable possessions unless they were all aboard, and it would be possible to start a fire under the vehicles and cook them.

He wanted the north side finished ASAP. The stream side would take some work. It honestly might be easier to put a solid rampart there and a gate for the latrine and water. Having those inside was very advantageous, but meant gaping holes in the defenses, which they seemed they were going to need.

Well, north wall first. They'd go from there.

Since the troops were so engaged, he took a chunk of yesterday's meat, dredged it in blood, sprinkled it with a little precious salt, and tossed it onto the grilling rock. He'd been chopping wood, and went back to it, with Spencer watching overhead.

Uphill, he saw Trinidad, Caswell and Oglesby hurrying back.

"Apples!" Caswell called. "We found apples!"

They had armfuls of them, he realized as they approached. Caswell tossed one to him.

"This looks like a real apple," he said.

"Yes, these haven't changed much." Their pockets were full, and they had more in a ruck.

It was small, sap-green fading to orange-red, and mostly round. It had a pockmark from something or other, but the skin was intact.

She prompted him, and he took a careful bite.

It was sour, a little bitter, not very sweet, but refreshingly delicious.

"Damn, that's good!" he said. It was only about two bites, and he nibbled down the core.

"They also make starch for stew. They'll fill it up like potato. Then they can be baked or roasted."

"You are fantastic," he said, and held out a hand for more apples.

"Thank you, sir."

Apples had never tasted so good.

"We also found beehives."

Trinidad said, "I know a bit about building them. You have to space the slats right in a hive or they won't use it. I don't recall the exact spacing, and we don't know if these bees act like the ones I know. But we can try several spaces using split wood."

"That sounds like a job for Barker or Spencer. Have one of them help you."

"Yes, sir."

"Okay, you've distracted me enough. Show me the kitchen."

Caswell nodded, walked over, and explained.

"The fire has a deep pit for roasting, or placing cans. It's got a slate bed here for coals. The rocks are for frying, and the mounded oven is for baking. This is the stew and soup pot," she indicated an ammo can, without its top. "This one is for boiling water. The wooden dippers are for serving, and are sterilized with the fire and boiling water. We have three knives from Alexander, Barker and Spencer that we use for prep work, and Ortiz provided a skinner. Sergeant Barker's machete serves as a cleaver. We have dry storage here under the lean-to."

The oven was a mound of rocks with mud over the outside. He'd seen it used. It worked. The rest he'd seen in books as well, but here it was real.

"Good. What is next?"

"Wooden walls and a proper hearth, is what Sergeant Barker mentioned," she said.

"Thank you. Sergeant Barker, can you show me the tepee, even though I've slept in it recently."

"Sure, sir," Barker said as he led the way and pointed. "Goat hide cover, that's shrinking as it ages. We'll need to replace with scraped and cured hides. Slate hearth there, too, and we're graveling a walkway in, and keep rushes on the ground but I'd like to make planks at some point."

He toured the camp and looked at everything. The rack of bows, arrows and spears next to the rifle rack, in Number Nine. The leather processing area, the knapping corner of the ramada they ate under, but it was getting too cold for that. The latrine was improving, but he wanted it dug deeper underneath, with better water flow, and more windbreak. He inspected it by using it and paying attention to the drafts and creaks.

The walls were getting there, and he wanted those done fast, except he wanted other stuff done, too. They needed more leather, more wood, more tools, eating utensils, they needed more salt trips. That was another thing for the schedule, or for trade.

"Looking good," he said at dinner time. It was stewed mystery meat with unknown vegetables, but had enough something in it to be thick and hearty. Apples and something salty. Maybe kidney. He didn't ask.

"I'll make at least monthly walk-throughs so I stay up-to-date," he said. "Always be aware of the next improvement or upgrade. Eventually we'll have a stone castle with running water and electric lights."

"Hooah," came the reply. Everyone was busy eating. It was chill, crisp, and they'd all been busting ass.

"How's the sweat lodge, Sergeant Barker?"

"It seems to be up, sir. I want to try it after dinner. Just a quick steam to check it."

"Go ahead. Do you mind spectators?"

"Not particularly, but I will be naked."

At his sweat lodge, Barker felt the heat from the decayed fire inside through the open door. He checked the outer skins, and they felt well-cooked, and warm to the touch.

He said, "I'm going to risk it. Bring me the hearth rocks. Use the lid to carry them and don't get burned."

"Please?" Alexander chided.

"Please," he agreed.

She and Ortiz carried rocks from the cooking fire as he looked the dome over. The fire he'd kindled inside had burned down, but there was still an acrid haze. The leather was quite stiff.

He still hadn't eaten, which was fine. A sweat lodge was a spirit meeting. It was appropriate for the first use to be like that. Afterward it could be a physical cleansing for everyone, but he wanted the spiritual cleansing first.

With the rocks placed inside, and a pan of water, he stripped down in the cool evening, heedless of spectators. He breathed deeply, and ducked inside.

It was hot, dark, meaty-smelling and musty from the hides. There was the aroma of steaming wood. His lungs constricted, but he felt the wash of heat and steam.

He realized there was nothing to sit on, so he'd have to stand. He turned slowly, feeling the heat in shimmering waves, inhaling the fumes, getting almost dizzy.

He stood still for a moment. It wouldn't do to fall on the scalding rocks.

He was sweating, with a cold draft around his feet. Beads rose on his eyebrows, beard and chest hair. He felt the heat of the rocks, of the world, and connected through his feet.

But it was cooling fast. There wasn't enough heat in here. He'd sweated off some muck, but it wasn't what it should be.

But it worked.

He stepped out and felt the chill suck the heat from him.

"It works," he said. "Steam baths tomorrow."

"Want a towel?" Doc asked, handing him his beach towel.

"Oh, yeah. Thanks."

He suddenly felt silly standing there naked. "We have sweat lodge," he said as he toweled himself.

Clean sweat felt much better than grimy muck.

CHAPTER 14

Sean Elliott looked around in a mix of satisfaction and frustration.

The north wall was finished. It stood under the cloudy sky, a pointed barrier to the Paleolithic world outside. Inside, the technology was at least Iron Age.

That gave three sides. The south, uphill, had the ditch, now denuded of trees and brush, but still a bit of an obstacle for any attackers. They had clear fields of fire west and south. To the east, they had the stream and its banks, but visibility was still not great. Though the rest of the trees there would be down before this was over, either as construction timbers or firewood. Then, of course, they'd have to find ways to get firewood. Five hundred meters down to the river wasn't far, and there were trees much closer than that, but they still had to be dragged. They used it for cooking, and increasingly for heat.

The Stone Age peoples likely weren't going to be a problem. They weren't trained in unit tactics as far as he knew, and could be bottlenecked. If they had to kill a few, that would likely scare the rest away. After all, no one yet knew they had guns, unless someone had been watching the hunting. Rifle fire would be terrifying to them. If it escalated to machine guns or grenades, the troops would likely be elevated to demonhood and avoided permanently. Which had some negative side effects, but might be unavoidable. On the other hand, the strong structure of the wall might cause any contenders to try diplomacy, and shared technology would let both parties benefit.

So he was still going to finish that wall.

He had to think long term. If they got below seven people, they wouldn't have enough for tasks and sentry. Also, the men were going to want women, one way or another. Goddamn, he wanted some sex himself. He couldn't sleep some nights from loneliness and frustration.

They only had two women, which wasn't enough. He didn't want their women degrading themselves as whores, they wouldn't do so, it would lead to fights anyway, and there wasn't any way to have a discussion about it. So once the anniversary hit, he'd need a plan on securing relations with locals. Possibly, local women brought in would feel themselves to be of status and beholden to their mates. If so, they could continue, with grown children on watch, and the weapons in reserve for the soldiers. Until what? They all aged and died? The ammo ran out from hunting? Without knowledge of ammo, the weapons might still be credible threats, and they had a few grenades.

Once the ammo was gone, the weapons were useless except as raw material. Spencer said he could forge things. The aluminum might be ground up for thermite. The plastic would have to be burned. The vehicle springs might be useful for something. Alternately, bits of metal might work as barter goods, and a rifle barrel was still a solid club, or possibly could be converted to an air gun.

As far as the machine guns, they weren't much use here. Then how to get rid of the trucks? How did time travel work with those? Was this an alternate timeline where that wouldn't matter? Did they somehow figure out how to hide them, say in the river, and they wouldn't be found until after they disappeared in the twenty-first century? Was the discovery of the vehicles a key to getting back, or would it screw things up? Would not hiding them help or hinder?

He'd read some science fiction. Spencer read a lot of it, as did Devereaux. They'd discussed this. They were no closer to an answer.

For now, he figured those banks were tall enough he could place the east wall about thirty feet on the other side. The bridging of the stream he'd figure out afterward, and possibly after any spring floods, since winter was upon them.

They also had apples. He'd have another one. It was a nice day for an apple.

Oglesby up top, called, "Incoming party! It's the Neolithics."

"Goddamn it, didn't they learn?" he muttered around a mouthful of apple.

"They may have, sir. I only count ten, and a dog."

"Okay. Who are the best two unarmed fighters?"

"Uh, probably Dalton and Trinidad."

"They're with me. Oglesby, you too. Caswell, take over for him."

"Hooah, sir."

He dove into the tepee and grabbed helmet and armor, shades, weapon and Bluetooth. This was getting tiresome.

Bluetooth in place, he said, "Watch, this is Elliott."

"Receiving you, sir," Caswell said. "I can advise based on what I see and hear, if that's what you want."

"Yes, and keep the gun handy. Also, watch in case this is a distraction. Spencer's in charge if that happens, if I can't respond."

"Roger that."

"Do we still have a count of ten?"

"One zero, sir, correct, with two dogs, not one. No others in sight in any direction, but there are aurochs and antelope east and north. Skilled trackers could use them for concealment."

"You're aware of that, so watch it for me. Have the others standing by." He'd want to get the corner ramparts done soon, too. Packed earth and timbers would reinforce the corners, and give firing positions. Then the same thing next to the gate.

Dalton, Trinidad and Oglesby met him at the gate. He nodded, and Barker opened it just enough to let them walk out. Wind eddied through as it was opened, then turned into shifting gusts. He led the way out, Oglesby to his left, Dalton and Trinidad fanning right.

"What do we have?" he asked Caswell.

"They stopped as soon as I waved. They waved back. About one zero zero meters."

"Understood."

Even if it was short range, being able to chat rather than shout helped.

Smaller group. They wanted to parley, he hoped.

Three of the party detached and came forward. They didn't have spears. He watched them approach, loping over the ground. They'd obviously lived their lives on wild terrain.

They slowed at about twenty-five feet. He let them get to twenty and held up a hand.

"That's close enough," he said.

"Haylaa."

"Hello," he said slowly.

His opposite number was bearded and long-haired, but clean enough. As before, he wore a breechcloth, leggings, moccasins and a small capote that looked like a tunic, belted in with a leather strap. The pouches at the belt held what looked like a knife hilt and some other stuff.

The man could see Sean was bearded, and not heavily. He couldn't see eyes. Sean was also dressed and armored and an enigma who was six inches taller. For bargaining, that helped.

The man started to talk, indicating himself as he did so.

Oglesby said, "I recognize this from last time. It's his title and name."

"What is his name?"

"It seems to be 'Rogga.'"

Rogga nodded, so apparently that was. He rattled off his intro again.

"Well, Rogga, I am"—he pointed to himself—"Sean Randall Elliott, First Lieutenant, U.S. Army Corps of Engineers, Chalk Leader of Charlie Eight and Nine, and Commander of Contingency Operating Base Bedrock." He indicated the palisade behind him, which did look pretty sturdy and intimidating.

Caswell spoke in his ear, "Good, sir. Long titles indicate status, but I figure you guessed that."

"Hooah," he said, wanting to acknowledge without confusing their visitors.

Rogga pointed at himself and his cohorts, pointed at the camp, and opened his arms in an understandable gesture.

"What do we think?" he asked quietly to his troops. "Let him in?"

Caswell said, "Spencer recommends three only. I agree. Your call from there, sir."

Trinidad said, "I can take one any time. Say the word, I can either immobilize or cut his throat before he can respond."

"You're that sure?"

"Oh, hell yes, sir. I'll swarm him." Trinidad almost sounded eager to do so.

Dalton said, "I'm pretty sure I can throw the other. He's bulked, but I'm better trained."

"Okay, then please don't. We'll invite them in for now. Caswell, have someone get the gate."

He gestured for Rogga to come with them, held up three fingers and pointed at him. The man nodded, pointed to two others back in the group, who followed, their spears shouldered with points back. His two unarmed assistants rejoined the others.

Sean led, Dalton and Trinidad filled in the back, with Oglesby to the left again.

At the gate, he let them precede him in. They looked nervous, but walked in upright and proudly.

He assumed they'd spied from the other side at some point, but he wasn't sure. They stared at the vehicles. Assuming they were still pre-wheel, they'd have no way to identify them other than as huts of some kind, elevated off the ground. They eyed the tepee for a few moments, and the smoke hut/sauna and the women's lodge.

Spencer came over, made a show of coming to attention and saluting. It looked out of place with his beard and hair to his ears.

"Welcome, sir. I want our guests to see you are held in respect and treated with deference. With your permission, I'll take them over to the fire."

He returned the salute.

"Please proceed."

"Yes, sir." Spencer saluted again, then turned and gestured to the Neolithics. "Come with me, gentlemen."

At the fire, they were seated on logs.

"Bring water and food. We want to show we're hospitable to friends."

Barker said, "You're in luck. I have salted, smoked trout and a haunch of kid in here." He indicated the smokehouse.

"Perfect."

Given water in wooden bowls, and smoked meat on a platter, the men relaxed slightly. They accepted graciously if a bit messily, but made their approval known with "Mmm!" sounds and nods. Those also seemed universal.

Oglesby went over to sit with them, and with Spencer, and started poking at the dirt with a stick.

Caswell asked, "Sir, permission to swap out and visit with them, too?"

"Yes, but since they're all male, keep that in mind. Ortiz, take over up there."

She said, "Yes, sir, I'll try not to hurt their fragile egos."

He started to comment and she said, "I understand what you mean, sir. I've got it covered."

He decided to sit back and observe.

Oglesby made notes in his book, and seemed to develop a few words. It was also amazing what he could express with those few words and gestures. Each one of these troops was turning out to be a boon. He'd like to introduce anyone who thought soldiers were mindless drones to this element.

Especially since that would mean getting home.

He overheard Spencer.

"Ask him about the seas around the swampy land. It's important."

Caswell followed up with, "What about grain? Do they plant?"

He went back to the vehicles, where Alexander had her helmet and weapon grounded next to her desk.

She looked down and said, "Anything I can help with, sir?"

"No, carry on."

"Whee. Documentation." He gathered she'd rather be watching the guests.

He called up to Ortiz standing in the turret.

"What are they doing out there?"

"Shooting the shit and flicking sticks."

"Good. Do they need food or water?"

"That might be an idea, sir."

"Okay. Dalton can take it out to them, if he's willing. I figure they won't touch him while we have three of theirs." He turned and got assent. "And Trinidad, join Ortiz up top and please keep them covered from here."

"Understood, sir."

"Continue with chores in camp."

He wanted to do something useful, but he also needed to be nearby to be the officer. He let the others handle the wood and crafts.

Dalton took out a pile of meat and fruit on a slab of wood, came back promptly and unhurt.

He reported, "They appreciated the food, sir. We may be making friends."

"Glad to hear it." Yeah, that was the ideal outcome.

Alexander said, "Sir, it's getting near dinner time. Are we hosting them inside, outside, or sending them away?"

"We're sending them away," he said. "You catch that, Oglesby?"

"Hooah, sir. I'll find a way to break it to them gently."

With some shooing from Spencer and Caswell, the men were escorted slowly out the gate. Alexander stood on the steps of Number Nine, holding her tanto. The damned thing had a blade more than a foot long. They seemed to understand what it was, and the implication that the hospitality was backed up by more force.

Once they were out, Sean climbed up alongside Ortiz to ensure they did head out of sight, over the ridge and away. He watched them retreat into the sunset, which was vivid in orange and violet.

He ordered, "Keep a close eye tonight. There's always a chance they'll come back."

"Hooah."

Back on the ground, he went to the fire and joined the others.

Spencer said, "Okay, sir, I'm guessing they're from about six thousand BC, in what we call Doggerland."

"Where's that?"

"It's now the North Sea. Back then, it was above water."

Okay. "How sure are you?"

Spencer said, "That it was above water? They find fossilized and even rotten plant and animal residue, and occasional human tools. It's only about forty feet deep in some places."

"Okay. So it flooded after that?"

"About then. These guys report rising water and swamps, and flooding of low areas. And they have high ground west and south. The Baltic was a lake. The Irish Sea was already flooded, long since. So Doggerland it is. They were farther north than here."

"How do they know that?"

"They don't, I do. Longer summer days. Very short winter days. Lakes to the east, sea to the north."

"Roger. So they're from halfway between now and our time, from the far side of the continent."

"Yup."

"They could even walk back and be just in time to meet themselves," he commented.

Spencer snickered. "Yeah, we made that joke amongst ourselves. Us, not them."

"What else?"

Caswell said, "They arrived about a month before we did, and spent time building a village to the west. They've actually lamed a few aurochs to keep them nearby, and use the dogs to herd the goats. They've been harvesting fruit and know of some other tubers."

She looked really angry as she said, "They conquered the Urushu. There's about two hundred of them. They moved in, killed a few, enslaved the rest. Especially the women, the fuckers. They see it as a divine right. The gods removed them from bad land to better land and gave them superior tools."

That was not good.

"That's unfortunately logical. How do they view our tools?"

Oglesby said, "They don't know what we have, but they seem astute enough to recognize the fabrication. We all have the same helmets and gear. We have the trucks, which they think of as huts. I said we can move them by touch. They didn't seem convinced, but didn't argue. I think we want to do something to impress them."

"Hunting?"

"Or more chores. They saw us chopping brush. They recognized the machete as a cutting tool, and something they can't make."

"Yeah, we'll want to make sure they know we can take them."

Oglesby asked, "Can we? Two hundred of them?"

Spencer said, "Figure half of those are adult males, and yes, we can. Easily. As long as we know they're coming."

Caswell said, "They don't have domestic crops, but they do weed around their preferred fruit trees, including apple. They trap fish and animals, and are proto-herders. They follow the herds around and use dogs to move them, and protect them from other predators. But if the time frame is correct, there was agriculture starting in the Middle East about the time they exist, and possibly in China. Actually, there may already be rice agriculture in China and Korea now. It would be interesting to know, but we can't."

It was all so fascinating, and he wished he knew more about it. "Okay. We'll work on further relations with them. We're going to build the east wall beyond the stream, and start on inside corner towers and a gate house. Well done, everyone. Let's eat."

Tonight's smoked fish was a bit dry, but good. It made a change from red meat every day. The wild onions and salt had seasoned it nicely and added a fresh taste. The apple and pine smoke gave it a bite.

Around a hot mouthful, he mumbled, "You know, I think Caswell and Barker deserve a medal for emotionally supporting their soldiers and maintaining our nutrition. I miss a lot of things, but this food is delicious. It's like being in a foreign country. Different, but great."

"Thank you, sir." "Thanks."

He tossed a bit of skin with meat still attached to the bank. The cat wasn't visible, but definitely lurking around. The creature understood that people offered food. He knew where to hang out to get it. He'd even come into camp a few times at night or early morning and picked around the woodpile for rodents and bugs. Sean wasn't sure where he hid anymore. The leaves were getting sparse from fall, and the weeds along the bank were getting thin from being walked on.

They needed more fat, though. The marrow pot tasted good now, and he was seriously considering animal brains. Fauna around here was quite lean. They'd had rabbit, and rabbit could kill you from lack of fat, eventually. The birds were wiry and tough. They needed fatty fish, or something with a hump, like a yak or camel. Both passed through occasionally.

Sean said, "Tomorrow we're back on the wall. Far side of the stream, about thirty feet out. We'll work on closing it after, and on towers as we go. Any excavated dirt or rock goes into the corners," he pointed. "And keep an eye out for any infiltrators. How are batteries holding up?"

Alexander said, "Double As are fine, sir, we just have to keep swapping them around."

"Okay. As to response against intruders, we probably want to start with spotlighting them. What's that big light you brought, Spencer?"

"Nitecore TM Thirty-Six. Eighteen hundred lumens on a four-inch reflector, sir. I could signal satellites in orbit. They'll think they're seeing a sunrise."

Spencer jogged to the truck and came back with the light. He offered it for inspection.

Sean looked at it. It was machined black aluminum.

"Are those cooling vanes?"

"Yes, not decoration. The circuitry gets hot. It'll throw a Broadway spotlight over them at a kilometer."

That was hilarious. "Yeah, that first. And if you decide you need to shoot, don't, unless you decide again. If you do shoot, shoot to kill. Not to try to scare. We're not thunder and lightning. We're death. Hooah?"

Several "Hooah" came back.

"Put me on watch at oh two hundred to oh four hundred. If they do try anything, that's when it'll be. I'll take that shift the next three nights."

Alexander said, "Got it, sir. I'll adjust accordingly."

"Cool. Thanks again for the great food and support, and the hot sponge bath. I'm for rack ops, as Sergeant Spencer calls it."

Ramon Ortiz liked evening watch. It was dark, but not yet midnight. The air was still, crisp and clean. Having one other person was just enough company to make it tolerable, without feeling human presence. It was as alone as he cared for, and he found it refreshing.

It was even more so after a hot wash. A bitch bath with an ammo can of hot water wasn't the same as a shower, but it was a fuck of a lot better than splashing in the stream. Every third day was enough to keep the stink and grime off, and it meant staying relatively warm while dressing afterward.

And God, he needed to bathe regularly. Milking goats. Brushing goats. Butchering animals. Then the meat had to be hung and aged, and the milk aged for butter. It was a lot of work, but damn, it was good to have butter and milk. Hopefully they'd have cheese next year. Caswell had ideas.

Caswell was in the other turret, and still inscrutable. She was educated, but didn't want to talk. Some of it was political, except she talked to Dalton on occasion. Dalton was insanely religious in his opinion, but she was Lutheran, though not particularly observant, but she did pray. A vegetarian feminist Lutheran in a military police field. It took all types. Ortiz was Catholic, and he saw her on Sundays when he stood together with the others for prayer.

He wasn't going to force her to talk. She wasn't evasive or insubordinate. She just didn't talk much. He was probably glad for that. She had made comments about "machismo" that she probably thought were egalitarian, but had a distinctly negative snark about Hispanic culture. She'd probably accuse him of "patriarchy" or some other crap, then criticize the same Lutheran church she claimed to belong to, and the Catholic Church, for supporting traditional values. So he enjoyed the silence, and figured it was mutual.

There were cicadas here, different from the U.S., and some sort of grasshopper buzzing away. The night was disrupted by winds soughing in rustling leaf and stem, cracking from tree limbs, chuckles from the stream, and occasional herbivore sounds punctuated by even rarer wolves or lions. He'd seen a bear once, too.

The stars were beautiful but cold. He'd once dreamed of being an astronaut. He was further from that than he'd ever been in his life. He'd be lucky to ever get fifty feet above the surface now. Or unlucky, rather.

Sometimes he wished they were closer to the river. Fish, plants and more timber were just down the slope. But the trees were dark enough to be creepy, and they didn't know what the spring floods brought. Field of fire and high ground were good. Besides, they could always move again. They had nothing but time.

"What do you think, Caswell?" He spoke softly because they didn't need much to be heard.

"I took a look through night vision. There's a few antelope east. No predators tonight, probably because it's waning quarter moon and cloudy."

"Makes sense. Do you hear the wind?"

"Yes. Probably seasonal. I don't see anything that would indicate a storm."

"Getting chilly, though."

"Maybe. I'm fine."

"I'm a lizard. I actually liked Iraq."

"What about A-stan?"

"I'll never find out now, will I? I'd been in country about a month. Not as hot as Iraq, but good enough."

She whispered, "Wait, I have movement."

"Where?"

"Uphill, quiet."

She turned very cautiously in the turret, and leaned up look over the side plate. He did, too.

She whispered, "Middle of the wall. The two scrub trees in the ditch. People."

"Yeah, I see them. Those are Urushu." He saw vague outlines. He could grab NVG, but she already had them, so he kept quiet and let her do it.

She said, "Or want us to think they are, but yes, robes and kilts with half leggings, not tunics."

"Are they standing?"

She said, "I think they can hear us, and want to be seen."

"Let me try something. I'll flip my phone open for a bit of glow, outboard on this side."

"Go ahead."

He dug under his armor into his pants pocket, eased out the phone and flipped it. It wasn't much light, but here, it had nothing to compete with.

"They see you," she said.

"Response?"

"Arms out. They're hoping we see them."

"Am I justified in lighting them? As in, illumination?"

"I don't know. They may have enemies."

"Are there only three?"

She said, "Yes. Spears, small rolls. Hunting party at best. And none of the Urushu groups have offered anything but hospitality."

"Try to wave them to the open side," he advised. Ordered, he guessed, since he outranked her.

"Are we waking the rest?"

"Not yet. Gun is live, though," he said, reaching to check by feel, with a careful unlatching of the top cover, then reclosing. That ammo would rip those bodies to bloody bits if he did fire.

She said, "Okay, they're coming carefully around the wall. Moving quietly but hands visible and not hiding."

"I see them."

"They're heading for the cooking fire."

"Yup." The embers were low, but gave enough light to see by with the almost complete darkness elsewhere. The three of them moved into the log circle, flipped open their hide rolls, and lay down.

"I think they want rest and shelter," he said.

"Could be they're being chased. The LT can decide what to do later."

"Yeah. They're down and quiet."

He made sure to watch them regularly, and keep an eye out for movement. They didn't seem to be fully asleep. Nervous about something, obviously, but was it the troops or the Neoliths? He also watched for any other elements outside the palisade, or animals. He found himself tracing patterns in the condensing dew atop the vehicle roof.

These did make a handy central redoubt and watch tower. He was fourteen feet up, and could look right over the wall in every direction, except where the tepee blocked it. He constantly imagined what it would have been like to be on foot patrol when the shift happened, or to be separated from others. What if it took a bunk room with four people? Or just a field shower with him alone?

There was constant shuffling in the tent, and from the hooch where the women slept. Only Alexander was down there now. She had been in okay shape when they arrived. She was hot now, and it wasn't just the isolation. She had a wicked ass.

Caswell was muy hot, but she just wouldn't do anything. He wasn't sure if she was a lesbian, sexless, or just had some psychological thing going. She was distant. She had a terrible, pushy personality and all that crap with it. Despite that, he'd nail her, given the chance. Alexander was flaky, but would at least talk.

Goddam, he wanted some pussy. The year limit made sense. It was a deployment length. But after that, they needed some native chicas.

The shuffling sound changed. LT was coming out, and Oglesby.

LT came up underneath, and he ducked down.

"Sir, three of the Urushu appeared a while ago, south in the ditch. We used signs to direct them in to the fire circle. They're sleeping there. We think they may be seeking refuge."

Elliott sprung awake and ran his hand over his eyes.

"Damn. Okay. No trouble? And only three?"

"Three only, no sign of anyone else. Do you want to wake anyone?"

"No, we'll talk in the morning, if they want to sleep."

CHAPTER 15

Martin Spencer crawled out into the rising sun. He hoped they could eventually weave a lighter tent. It was warm, if dank and bitter smelling. But it was dark. He blinked and slitted his eyes, letting them adjust. It was like coming out of a cave.

Alexander was on the steps of the HQ truck, leaning forward with her PT jacket unzipped enough to show cleavage. She'd just raised the flag.

There were three Paleos in camp, and Oglesby and the LT were talking to them.

Alexander saw his expression, and said, "They arrived late, we invited them in, they bedded down out here. They're from the village we started with. It's trashed, converted to Neolithic. Many of the men were killed, most of the rest driven off. The chief is dead. The women are captives of the Neo men. I gather they were short of their own women."

"Or just wanted extras."

She shook her head. "I never understood that. Most men can't handle one woman."

I'd enjoy handling you, he thought. They weren't going home, she was a good match for him, and from her comments he gathered she wasn't very inhibited in bed. And fixed, so no more kids. She was a bit older, but still firm.

Goddammit, he wanted his off day to hurry up and get here.

"So what are we doing?" he asked. He recognized one of the Urushu from the hunting trip he'd been on, those weeks past. It seemed forever.

247

"Screw it, I gotta drain out first." He ran for the latrine area. It was foggy and chill, and the grass on either side of the trod trail was thick with crystalline dew verging on hoarfrost.

Then he went back for his toothbrush. Doc was right.

By then, everyone had gathered around for breakfast and to hear the story. Barker was up top on Number Nine. Caswell was cooking alone, and had a cooler full of apples and other fruit, and some roasted something or other. He took an apple and a piece of meat and approached slowly.

Oglesby had extensive notes and had gotten pretty good with their language. His head swiveled back and forth between Elliott and the Paleos.

Elliott said, "I don't want to throw them out. Do they have relatives in another village they can live with?"

Oglesby said, "They do. But they want to rescue their families."

"That's a much tougher question I can't answer right now. Tell them I'll have to consult with our spirits and my shaman."

There was animated, serious talking in reply.

Oglesby said, "I'm not quite getting their response. In the past, they've said we should find new spirits. This time, they're saying they've talked to our spirits. I think they mean that no worthy spirits would refuse."

"That's possible, but I have to discuss it first. If they have someone they can be safe with, they should. If not, they can stay near here, but they'll need to camp across the stream, and I'll need them to work."

The translation came back, "They offer to work their entire lives for you, as a great chief, if you will bring their families."

Spencer realized this was serious. He looked at Elliott, who took a deep breath.

"It's very flattering, but I have to talk to the spirits first. If they'd like to hunt something for us, we'll make sure they stay fed. But it won't affect the spirits. Only clean thoughts and prayers will help with that. Anything you want to add, Sergeant Spencer?"

He crossed his arms and stepped forward in the same manner he had in their village. Then he pointed up.

"The Sun Lemur will need to hear as much as possible from us. Then, if we decide to help, he will need details from them. I don't know if they grasp maps and large numbers."

"Understood." He turned back to Oglesby. "We hope to let them know something tonight."

The Urushu were up and hunting within minutes. They didn't seem to have much of a schedule, and these three men likely had little else to do at the moment.

Elliott asked him, "So, what do we do?"

"I don't think we can do any fighting, sir."

"I agree, but what are your reasons?"

He held up fingers to count. "We don't know what happens if we kill a bunch of people. It's not our fight. Stuff like this happens all the time, and we can't police everyone. We didn't cause the problem, so it's not ours to fix. There might be a time we need to defend ourselves, and ammo is limited. Since we're in diplomatic talks with both, perhaps we can help them come to some accord. If not, we tried."

"Yeah. I don't want to be the local gods, the local lords, or the local police."

Dalton was nearby and said, "Sir, may I?"

"Go ahead."

"If there is going to be violence, a little now may be better than a lot later. Both groups know we have neat stuff. They don't know how neat, or how powerful. I'm not suggesting we start violence. But if there's going to be some, we might want an object lesson."

That was pretty astute. Dalton was not stupid, even if he did hold to archaic religious nuttery.

Elliott said, "Yup, that's the other side of it. I think first we should try diplomacy. Then if we need to we can use nonviolent force to try to shake things up. Caswell, do you think the women are in any danger?"

"Other than being raped daily?" she asked. "I guess if that's not considered danger, then no." She looked pissed.

Martin opened his mouth, and closed it. It wasn't his place to say anything. Yes, she was correct, but that was not the way to phrase it.

But what was?

Elliott paused himself, then said, "Yes, they are being held prisoner and presumably forced into being mates. What I'm asking is, will punitive action be taken against them if we try to rescue some?"

He speculated while talking. "Given that they seem to be chattel and the Urushu men were killed, but the women weren't, they probably won't be murdered. They'll be considered subordinate. A lot like Afghan women."

Dalton muttered, "Man, it hasn't changed. And they still want the U.S. Army to fix things."

Martin twitched an eyebrow and said, "And we'll still screw it up, the Army way, no matter what course we follow."

Elliott said, "I think we need to send our own embassy to see them. I'll go, with Oglesby and Dalton."

Caswell said, "I can do cultural assessment as well as tactical, sir, and I know how to deal delicately with the women. That's what I was on this convoy for anyway."

"Yeah, but I really want Dalton along for backup."

"I can shoot expert. You've seen me take one of them hand to hand. Why do you need backup to be a man?"

Dalton muttered, "Well, thank you."

"Yeah, I'm sorry if I hurt your feelings," she said. "You can't do what I can. I can do most of what you can. If one of us is staying and one going, then it's not a problem to swap, is it?"

Martin wanted to rage. He forced calm, and was going to point out her very nondiplomatic approach, when Elliott spoke.

"While we're trying to be a family group here, this constitutes a military action. I will make the decision on who goes."

Alexander came up and said, "You'll need photos."

"Good. I'll take your camera."

"Pardon me, sir, but no, you won't. Do you know how to use it in IR? Switch to video? Disable flash?"

"No, but I'll just take daytime shots. Or use my phone."

"At what f-stop and shutter speed? What will you do as establishment? Can you annotate in a meaningful fashion?"

Elliott finally reached overload. "Okay, everyone back the goddamn fuck up and stop."

He sat and stared at the fire for several moments, while plucking at a few stubborn blades of grass under the log that hadn't been beaten down yet.

"Get working. Put debris into the corners so we can stomp it down. I need to think."

Martin decided it was a good time to pull out his hatchet and reduce some of the trimmings to cut fuel. It worked off some energy.

He had nothing against women in the military, but Caswell needed to grasp how this culture worked, not just all those civilian cultures. Alexander needed to remember she wasn't in fit condition for combat. And he needed to work on his temper. They were being people, and NCOs were supposed to deal with people.

He had a stack of tinder and inch-thick fuel trimmed when Elliott said, "Okay, listen up."

He slid the axe into his belt sheath and walked over to the fire.

Elliott said, "I can't send everyone. Oglesby has to go to translate. I want a female along, and Alexander is right about intel photos. She's going. Dalton's going to assess combat capabilities and tell Alexander what to get photos of. It may not be perfect, but it will work, and we'll repeat if we have to. It's a four-mile trip or so. Gear up with armor. Take rifles with one magazine each. Plan on bivvying if they don't have space, and stay safe. Look at everything, touch nothing without permission. Don't make any deals that hold us to anything, but if they offer, take it."

"Hooah, sir."

"Caswell, you're here because I need your shooting and your other skills. I'll try to send you on any followup with your background."

"Very good, sir." She sounded mollified.

Alexander asked, "Who's in charge? I'm ranking person."

"Yeah, that's complicated. You're in charge, but I would really like you to take advice from Dalton, being that he's combat arms. Hooah?"

"Hooah, sir."

Martin wasn't sure that was a good setup, but he couldn't think of one a lot better, so he didn't offer anything.

He stuck to camp chores. They need more timbers, more woods, weeds trimmed, trees cut. There was plenty to do. Something else was there, though. He couldn't make it surface.

They needed some way to preserve all that fruit, too. It could be dried with fire. They couldn't pickle or can it. Without enough sugar, it would rot, or at least ferment . . .

"Barker," he called. "Is the round cooler in use for anything?"

From the turret, Barker called, "Fresh water."

"Can we use something else for fresh water?"

"Possibly, why?"

"I have need of it."

⁜ ⁜ ⁜

Gina Alexander was elated at finally getting to do her real job. Tempering that was the long walk on her damaged legs, the separation, knowing they were going to be dealing with injured refugees, and Caswell trying to cram her full of feminist dialectic and anthropology.

She finally shut that off with, "I may have studied some of this myself, and I understand the mechanism of sexual assault. Thank you." Yes, she understood it very well, and didn't need a twenty-something to explain it to her. Bad, old memory.

Dalton took point, she took the middle, Oglesby brought up the rear. They kept spacing at ten meters, so they were close enough to offer support, far enough not to get mauled. Those lions might still be around. In fact, since they were walking on the slope above the river, they were about where she'd seen them before.

Her ankles always hurt. This didn't help, though she was surprised they didn't worsen. Her knees, however, did. Add in the usual ache of backpack straps on the shoulders and it wasn't a comfortable walk. And how did she keep winding up on these? Oh, yes. She'd asked for this one.

It was sweaty, dusty, with bugs flying around and one in her teeth. She spat, rinsed and drank. Her head ached numbly from the helmet.

Rough terrain and heavy brush meant it was midafternoon, sun ahead of them, before they sighted the Urushu camp, now the Neolithic camp. It had several more huts, like low tepees or wigwams. The wall was banked and lightly staked, almost like their own palisade but smaller.

Dalton said, "Let's close up. We stay together inside."

She said, "You'll need to follow me to the latrine."

"I'll politely turn my back, but yes, I will. I don't trust these savages. They're proof that monotheism is a positive thing."

"I disagree with that, and it's not the time to argue," she said. And yes, she wanted someone standing guard when she had to squat.

A party came to meet them. It was five men, all armed. They were only her height, but they were muscled.

Dalton said, "Alexander, I want you to chamber a round, please. Don't shoot unless we're attacked."

"Hooah." She cycled her rifle with a push while gripping the charging handle. That aftermarket Gunfighter handle was tough, and easier to use that way, with a bigger latch than the issue one. She was surprised at how few of the element had any accessories for their weapons. She wasn't the gun nut—her husband was—but this was an easy upgrade and made it a lot easier to load.

The armed party didn't start trouble, just escorted them in. She did notice their spears were held across, not up, though. No doubt the plates would stop spears. Would the soft armor? And her arms and legs were certainly unprotected.

"I need to use my camera. Have Oglesby charge his weapon."

"Noted. Oglesby."

There was a metallic sliding and clack behind her.

"Ready," Oglesby said.

She started pointing and shooting. The gateway was just that. There was flat ground into the camp, with a wall on each side creating a channel. There were piles of bush they could throw up as a gate. There was an open common area, with their huts around it. They'd saved the long lodges of the Urushu, which in her opinion were better. She took photos to both sides.

A spit over a bed of coals held a haunch of something, and they had broad leather bowls of spices and herbs. They were obviously well organized to have this much stuff built this quickly, unless their village had come through with all contents. That fire setup was sophisticated and interesting, however. Click. Though on silent mode there *was* no click.

This is why they needed her, not some amateur with a phone cam who wouldn't know what he was shooting, nor what it was afterward, nor how to describe it. She raised her phone and whispered into the record mode, "Fifteen hundred local approximate, gateway, village placement shots north and south. Fire hearth with complex tools and foodstuffs." She'd caption it in print once she was back to her laptop.

"They've come a long way," she said.

Dalton said, "Lots of labor and no time wasters. Much more labor than we have."

There was a sort-of paddock to the south. It had a low mound and wall and a rude rail fence. It contained antelope and goats, and they all limped.

She said, "Interesting. It looks as if they lamed a bunch of females. I gather the males show up freelance to reproduce."

Dalton said, "That also means they're bait for hunting."

"Disturbingly clever."

"Yeah. Effective, though."

"As a female, I'm not thrilled." She was half sarcastic, but some cultures placed women on par with animals.

"Oh. I can see that. But I'm not going to let anyone touch you."

I wasn't just thinking of them, she thought. She grabbed a few images of that.

Some of the Urushu women recognized them, or at least their Multicam uniforms. They came over and seemed cheerful enough, not significantly different from before.

One of them shouted and smiled. It was Ai!ee moving well and seeming fit. Was there an undercurrent of something? She couldn't tell.

Dalton said, "Oglesby, you talk, I'll reply. Let me know if anything comes out to you. And Alexander, let me know whatever you see. These are some building mofos. That wall's actually useful."

"Will do," she said. It was a halfway decent defensive work. She got photos of that.

Oglesby said, "Haylaa!" and went into noises that almost sounded like words, just with more throaty sounds.

She didn't like the crowd gathering around them. They all had spears, and looked interested, but not the casual interest in a traveler. They wanted loot. They had no idea about the weapons, or her camera, but they knew the soldiers thought they were valuable.

"They're getting too close to suit me," she said. "And I think they want another dominance game."

Oglesby said, "I don't see the guy we dealt with. Either he wasn't the chief, or he's off doing something else."

"Well, who's *this* guy?" Dalton asked, pointing at their opposite.

"His name is Qalaka, close enough."

Qalaka pointed and said something. It sounded like an order or demand.

"They're getting closer," she said, quite scared now. She dropped the camera on its sling and hefted her rifle.

One of them grabbed at her. She raised her leg and kicked, shoving him back hard against his buddies, then she backed up against Oglesby.

"Yeah, they're on this side, too," he said.

Dalton shouted, "Back off!" and jabbed one with his muzzle. He said, "Wish I'd fixed bayonet."

"I've got my knives," she said. "Are we avoiding shooting?"

"If we can."

She caught movement and turned. One of them had brought up a short spear, about the size of a Zulu stabbing spear, and jammed it into Dalton, or tried to. It skittered off his SAPI plate and the tip shattered.

Dalton said, "Motherfucker, you did not just" BANG!

At that range, Dalton caught him right through center mass, and hit someone else behind. The man screamed loudly, rattled and collapsed, dead. The one behind him howled and clutched his arm, then thrashed and rolled in agony.

Firefight.

The others retreated in a hurry, but they gave Dalton more room, because that's where the noise had been. The ones on her side were within ten feet.

One of them cocked his arm back, with a large, sharp rock. She saw him hop to adjust his point of aim, and as his arm started to move, she raised her rifle, placed the dot and snapped the trigger. His face hollowed like a kicked ball and the back of his head erupted. She'd shot him just under the eye.

Oglesby fired at something or someone, but the rest were in full flight. They sprinted to the wall where the latrine was, hopped over and cowered down.

"That's *not* what I wanted to happen," Dalton said. "LT is gonna be pissed."

Gina's head rushed, and her eyes got fuzzy. She'd just blown a man's brains out. She could see them splashed on the ground around his shattered head. He writhed and kicked like a dead cat she'd run over once.

Dalton shook his head and said, "Well, fuck it, we've come this far. Let's take any of the women we recognize."

"If they want to," she said. She sounded very distant to herself.

"Why wouldn't they?"

"We don't know what they want or like."

"We don't have time for that."

"Ask them if they want to," she insisted. "Oglesby?"

"Yeah, I can do that," he said. "Give me a moment."

He twisted his brow, moved his lips, then called out something musical and syncopated.

Several women poked heads out of huts, or from behind cover.

He repeated it.

Three stood out and hesitantly stepped forward.

Several men behind the wall stood and shouted.

She started walking that way, very slowly, very deliberately, weapon raised. If they wanted a fight, she'd give it to them.

They looked at the three bleeding, broken bodies on the ground near the troops, and the two others screaming and clutching at wounds.

They didn't want a fight.

Oglesby repeated himself in a more moderate voice.

"What are you telling them?"

"'Females, we will take you to your mates,' as best I can manage. The grammar is slippery. I'll try another variation."

He said something similar, and more came out. Shortly, about forty women gathered in a huddle.

"Hold my helmet," she said, and handed it back to Dalton. Without it, her face looked more feminine, and she had long enough hair to make it obvious she was a woman. It worked with Afghans. It might work here.

She slung her rifle but left the safety off, and spoke with a calm voice, feeling very exposed.

"Come with me," she said, making slow "come here" gestures.

Dalton said, "Great, you lead, I'll back out with them in sight."

She coaxed until they did follow her, in a group.

"Oglesby, take the north," she said.

"Okay. Any particular reason?"

"I dunno. Animals maybe. I want you somewhere."

"Got it."

She was fully in charge now, she realized. It made sense. The women were more willing to listen to her, even if she didn't know their language.

Another round cracked off. Dalton shouted, "winged one. They've decided not to follow."

"Pity," she muttered, and "Good!" she shouted. Respect for other cultures be damned, these Neolithics were brutal savages.

There were probably all kinds of complications from this. She'd worry about that when they got back, which needed to be soon. The sun was well behind them, dipping toward the trees and hills far to the west.

Just like that, her vision came back in color. She realized she'd seen everything since it started in black and white, and missed most of the details after the shot.

She thought about a mind cleansing ritual. It was that or booze, and there was no booze.

Through Oglesby, she reassured the women once again that they were going to see the other Urushu. Though she wasn't sure how many survived beyond the three who'd come to camp.

The women walked without protest or bother. What was four miles to them? But even here, she'd been largely sedentary in comparison. Her feet stabbed in pain before another mile.

It was near dark when they trudged into view of COB Bedrock. The name was amusing, and it was good to have a specific referent, but it would be nice to have more than one. Maybe that was possible, if they wound up adopting some of the Urushu. Ironic that the Urushu's offer to adopt them would have ended very badly.

Caswell and Spencer came out in gear, while Elliott watched and Ortiz manned the gun.

Spencer called, "Talk to me."

"The Neos started a fight. We won. These are the Urushu who wanted to come with us."

"Where the hell are we going to put them?"

Caswell said, "We need more brush anyway. We'll put them on the far side of the creek and they can build some lean-tos for now."

"Fair enough. Guide them around the outside."

"Can you, please, Sergeant?" she asked. "My legs are killing me."

He thumbed over his shoulder at the gate.

"Go."

She staggered forward with a nod.

Rich Dalton wasn't sure how the LT was going to react. Still, he couldn't actually be court-martialed, and he hadn't started the fight.

It felt good to be inside the gate, and not have a platoon of civilian women to worry about.

He went straight toward the LT, who was standing behind Number Nine.

"Sir, I need to give you the debrief."

"Yeah. I hear fighting was involved?" Elliott came over at a walk.

"Gunfire was involved."

"Dude . . . shit." Elliott didn't look pissed, but he did look bothered.

He'd rehearsed the story the whole way back, but forgot all that and said, "They got close. Whoever it was we spoke to wasn't there. They didn't respond well, got pushy, and someone tried to stab me with a spear." He indicated the rip on his ITV, and the scratch on the plate under it. "He was that close. I reacted and shot him."

Elliott tilted his head and said, "Better than dying and losing both you, and some of our stuff."

"They didn't take the hint. My round peppered the guy behind him. Oglesby shot one in the guts. Died quick. Alexander blew the brains out of one. She may be a bit shook up. I don't think she's been up close before."

"Have you?"

"Yes, sir, I've done house to house." And it was a rush, like this. He tingled all over, and felt good, which was perfectly normal, and scared civilians.

"Okay. I'll check on her. Thanks. You're sure you didn't provoke it?"

"There wasn't any way to. They didn't communicate much. They gathered around, demanded stuff, then pulled out spears."

"So either gross miscommunication, or bad signals, or they're just violent SOBs."

"Yes, sir. I am sorry. I was trying hard to avoid violence." He really had been.

"I believe you. We'll need to be prepared for them to try to counterattack. That sucks."

"Sir, I'd expected you'd be more upset." He wasn't sure if that was the right thing to say.

Elliott half shrugged.

"There's nothing I can do about it, and I'm surprised it's been this long before we had any violence. That group started off by attacking me. It was predictable they might try something stupid."

"Well, now they know what guns are. Or at least that guns can kill."

"They probably can't figure one out easily, but let's make sure they don't. Avoid cycling rifles in front of them."

"That means having them loaded when we approach."

The LT said, "It does. We know they're a credible threat. So plan accordingly."

"Got it, sir."

Elliott nodded, and he turned and left. Rich sighed. That had gone better than he feared it might.

The women were on the far side of the stream, and Caswell was among them, looking very determined. She almost buzzed. Why did the hot ones always have to be crazy? She was even religious, but had that new-age feminist stuff going on.

She'd fought decently though, and so had Alexander. Caswell had kicked that one clown to the ground, and Alexander had dropped that guy with the rock like he was an empty pop can. They weren't hefty enough to haul logs, but they could fight well enough, and weren't the type to get into girly crap like makeup. He hated that in a soldier. These two were okay.

He also knew he shouldn't be tallying up the native chicks for his own drives, but at some point he was going to need a wife, and this is where they were.

The three Urushu men were thrilled. They'd found their mates, and possibly one or two more, with the way they didn't actually have defined spouses. They typically had one at a time, but drifted back and forth between partners. Serial monogamy.

But those Neolithic types would probably be here in force. Or skulking. It might be an idea to set up some booby traps or signals. He'd talk to the LT about that.

He sat down alone in the dark on the woodpile west of the tepee and thought about things.

The time frame bothered him. The Bible said the Earth was about 6000 years old. Ussher had calculated 4004 BC for Creation. He could be wrong by a few years, but it was hard to place where these groups might be. Assuming it wasn't long after the Deluge, the Old Stone Age and New Stone Age had to be within a few generations. Could people look that different in that short of time? Obviously, if God dictated so. Bows were not that big a development. As to dogs, that Russian experiment had taken only a few generations to domesticate foxes.

But Devereaux knew his Scripture very well, quoted it a length, and insisted they were fifteen thousand years back. That was nine thousand earlier than Ussher's dating. Could Usher have been off by that much?

If the year had changed in length, which was one of the theories for the Deluge, then sure. That would be a really neat bit of information. The irony was he couldn't take it back home.

Of course, all the researchers he might discuss this with were in the future, too, and everyone here thought he was crazy.

Then he decided they were all crazy in their own way. Alexander had her new age goddess worship. Caswell had feminism. Spencer thought he believed in nothing, which was obviously false. They each had their thing.

He'd killed a man today, who'd not been baptized in Christ, but probably didn't know of Christ, so his soul should be safe. He'd pray God for forgiveness, and let Him know he respected the man's soul. He too was lost in time and in the world, unable to understand what was happening, and didn't have a Christian moral code. He deserved compassion, not hatred for his fear and anger.

After that, it was in God's hands, and God would do what was best.

This exile had brought him closer to a true feeling of the Holy Spirit than he'd ever felt. Perhaps that was why he was here. It was even possible God would send them home, once they had learned what they must. He'd pray for that, too.

They needed to avoid firefights as much as possible. That was something else to think on. There was nothing wrong with violence when necessary, but these poor bastards were so outclassed it wasn't fair, even with the numerical differences.

Feeling calmer, he stood and walked back to the kitchen. He realized he was still in full battle rattle with a loaded weapon. He cleared and safed it against the woodpile, then opened his armor for ventilation.

There was something smoked for dinner, and more roots and greens. But dang, he'd love some potatoes, or peanut butter, or both.

Crap, that sounded like something a pregnant woman would crave.

He grabbed a wooden plate of grub from Barker, thanked him, and found a seat under the windbreak. He was the first one with food. Caswell and Oglesby were busy, and Ortiz took food to them.

Alexander was in the truck. Doc was out with the guests, too, and the LT, leaving Trinidad on watch, Barker serving.

"How are you doing, Dalton?" SFC Spencer asked, sitting second.

"Good enough, I guess," he said. "I don't feel real great about killing some poor dumbass who had no way to know about body armor and rifles."

"They don't know about NVG either. Which may be useful. But yeah, it's not a fair fight. From what the LT says, they attacked first and you didn't provoke them."

"I tried not to. I guess we could have set off some signal we don't know about."

"Can't help that. You kept our people alive and rescued those women. It wasn't what we intended, but it's a good outcome. Well done," Spencer said with a firm tone.

Rich said, "Thanks. Though I figure the men will try to come get them." The savages could learn, but didn't seem to do so very quickly.

Spencer said, "Well, then we may have to teach them a bit more." He chewed while staring into space.

"It almost sounds like you like the idea."

Spencer said, "Not really. But if we need to do it, bring it on."

"How's that wine of yours coming?" He indicated the tent, where Spencer had the five gallon cooler.

"Do you know anything about fermentation?"

"Not a lot. It ferments, it makes alcohol."

"Yup, and it's making alcohol. But it's still full of must—ground up fruit, and yeast and residue, which is bitter. It needs a few more weeks to finish, then we'll have to filter it. I try a whiff and a taste every few days."

"Is it going to be any good?"

"I've used wild fruit before. It'll be dry and musty, but should be drinkable and alcoholic."

"Awesome." He didn't drink much, but damn, that sounded good about now. "If only we could have bread and cheese with the wine."

"Cheese we can do, with the penned goats. Good cheese from goats."

"Roger that. And bread?"

Spencer shrugged. "I think Caswell said all grass seeds are edible, but we'll have to harvest a lot of them, roast and grind them, then make dough. And these are going to be smaller grains and have thicker husks than anything in our era. The last century, back home I mean, grain was bred and modified a lot."

"I'll take it. If we can do cheese, can we do butter?"

"Yes, eventually. Me, Alexander, Barker and Caswell all know something about bread, cheese and butter."

He said, "I know what I want for Christmas."

Spencer said, "Likely next fall. We just don't have the manpower."

"Yeah." He paused a moment. "I find beliefs here interesting."

"The natives?"

"Them too. The Urushu sort of pick and choose their spirits. Animism, and not much of it."

"Right."

He chewed a piece of meat, then crunched up a root. Not bad. Not as chewy as before. The smokehouse helped age stuff, too.

He said, "It doesn't seem very useful. They can't really pray for anything, or try for anything."

Spencer said, "That's typical. They have no basis for understanding the world. And organized religion with a pantheon or a head deity has to have rules, which you can learn."

"Right. That's the key to Western Civilization. It wouldn't exist without Judeo-Christian ethos."

Spencer shrugged. "Eh. The Hindus and Buddhists might argue. And Islam as an offshoot of Judaism. But you're not wrong, no."

"I really don't know anything about Hindus or Buddhists or Shintos? Yeah, Shintos. What I'm getting at is, if you can pick and choose and change your beliefs easily, you don't develop. It's like a kid's game with no rules." He hadn't thought about this before. He hadn't had to.

Spencer stared into the dark east. "Yeah, that's a good way of looking at it."

"I have no idea what these Neo people think. But it's probably not a monotheism. The word of God wasn't out here then."

"I don't think the word of your God was anywhere at this time, but I know we disagree on that."

"So that brings us to us. Most of us are Christian, about half Catholic, half Protestant. Similar enough in the basics. We have a belief, a faith, the Trinity, God's Scripture, and His rules for the universe. Physics, chemistry, whatever. And right and wrong, which are codified in law."

"Yes?"

"Well, you've got your beliefs and Alexander has her new age stuff, if I can call it that. You talk to her a bit."

"I do talk to her. I find her beliefs as . . . well, I really don't see any difference."

"You don't see any difference? Between that . . . stuff and Christianity?"

Spencer shrugged. "Not enough to matter."

"But . . . all her stuff came about in the last half century."

"Yes, and? It's based on older stuff, some reconstructed, some inferred, just as yours is based on the Councils of Nicea and other assemblies and conferences."

"Well, sure, but we have documentation."

"So does she. And beliefs."

"I haven't talked to her much, but other pagans I've met are flaky."

Spencer licked the wooden plate. The juices had been pretty good. After they finished, they'd rinse and smoke the plates to sterilize, and scour them with rocks every couple of days.

Looking up in the dim flickers, Spencer said, "Yeah, she calls them fluffy bunnies. The same criticism you have of the Urushu. They pick and choose and don't actually get anywhere."

That was ironic. And interesting.

"Okay."

"As I said, not much difference between you."

He said, "But that last ritual she did. I watched because I was curious. It was damned near a ripoff of a Christian service."

"Well, sure. The Celtic, Greek and Roman paganisms influenced Christianity. And now Christianity influences their reconstructions. I'm sure any pagans in Japan have some Shinto roots. Read Tom Sawyer?"

"Yeah?"

"Tom had all these occult and superstitious things he did, but was in a strong Christian environment. Beliefs create, and beliefs also follow."

Spencer bit into an apple. The crunch sounded a bit mushy. It was end of the season for those, and Rich was going to miss them until next fall.

He *did* remember that from Tom Sawyer. The Doodlebug, the deathwatch, the oaths in blood.

"That's so obvious I don't know how I missed it."

"Because you're inside and I'm outside."

"Okay, can I ask you about that?"

Spencer said, "Sure, go for it."

"So what are your beliefs based on?"

"Nothing." The man sounded completely calm.

"Oh, come on. You have to believe something."

It was dusk and hard to see, but in the faint glow of the fire, Spencer shook his head.

"Nope. The universe exists. I know that, because I'm here. Other than that, I have no idea and won't guess. I can guess what the Aral Sea, northwest of here five hundred miles, might look like. I have some information on it. What people are there, I have less of a guess. I know there's glaciers north, but not how far north. I don't know what year it is. I don't know how we got here. So I don't guess."

"You don't guess why we're here?"

"It could be anything. Some natural phenomena. A side effect. Deliberate, but by whom?"

"The 'whom' is what I'm interested in. That's the why."

"And I have no information, so I can't guess."

"But everyone believes in some sort of higher power."

Spencer shook his head, rather firmly. "No, they don't."

"You don't believe that."

Spencer sighed and said, "I get that *you* do. I get that most people do. That's fine. If you need something to reference, I support it. Life's tough. But I don't believe in any higher power that we could communicate with, or would be concerned with individuals. I suppose some agency may have created the universe, but without any evidence, I'm not going to guess at the nature of it."

"But evidence is all around you."

"The world is all around me. Some parts I understand, some I don't. Some the scientists do, some they don't. It exists. That only proves it exists."

"I don't understand how you can look at the world and say there's no God."

"And I don't know how you can look at the world and pretend you know there's a God and what he wants. So we're even."

"Nothing? You never once felt the Presence in combat, or in an accident, or when sick?"

"Nope."

He wanted to feel sorry for the man, but he seemed perfectly comfortable and cheerful.

"So what drives your moral compass?"

Spencer leaned back, largely shadow in the increasing dark. "Ah, that question. Well, the largest part is enlightened self-interest. If we all help each other, eventually it comes back to us."

"But you could get ahead by taking."

"And if everyone did, society would fall apart. Witness communism."

"They lacked God."

"They lacked concern in their culture, because it was imposed. There's a couple of books about this I don't recall the titles of . . . and we wouldn't have them anyway, but citizen armies do better than slave armies. Why did you enlist?"

"To serve my country."

"Exactly. *Your* country. We own our country. It doesn't belong to some petty king who thinks he's God. And your God asks you to help others, which is a practical and smart thing to do. Religions bent on theft and brutality don't lead to stable cultures. If there are any. People seem to be pretty social."

"But you don't have, or claim you don't, have any power to stop you from doing that."

"Sure I do. That power is me."

"That's pretty arrogant."

"Maybe. But I know *I* exist. And I have to answer to *me*. And consider this: I'm not expecting any punishment or reward. I take my actions free of any eternal consequence."

"You'll face them."

"Possibly. But I don't know the nature of them and don't believe them, so they don't matter, any more than Gina's Triple Goddess matters to you. I take my actions because I decide I must."

"That doesn't seem stable."

"What percentage of Death Row inmates are atheists? What percentage are Christian?"

That one. "Yeah, I've heard that before. Those aren't good Christians."

"Fine. Where are the bad atheists? They should be about five percent of the total. They're under a quarter percent."

"So you believe your system is better, then?"

"No, because it's not a system and I don't believe. I observe that atheists commit fewer crimes."

"But without a moral compass—"

Spencer cut in, "Without *your* moral compass. But clearly, we have one."

He sat and stared for a moment.

"Sergeant Spencer, this has been a very productive and educational conversation."

Spencer asked, "Something wrong?" He sounded concerned.

"Nothing at all. I still don't understand you. But I guess I grasp that *you* understand you."

"As well as a man can, I try to understand myself."

"I have a lot to think about."

"Sure. It's watch time for me." Spencer rose and headed out.

Rich often said in public that any faith was good that led to a peaceful world, but he didn't really mean it. But here, an atheist and a pagan did as well as he did. With viewpoints he couldn't grasp. How could one not believe in some kind of God? But the man wasn't lying and didn't sound confused. And he didn't seem to believe anything. All the other atheists he'd met had some sort of belief system and were in denial.

Maybe he was closer to Buddhism, and could clear his mind?

A world without God made no sense.

There was a lot more to think about.

CHAPTER 16

Dan Oglesby sat down late to dinner. Half of the team were dealing with night chores or asleep. He hoped his façade worked. He'd never been in combat until today, and he'd shot a man. The poor fucker didn't have a chance, stick against bullet.

He wasn't hungry, but he needed to eat.

Elliott joined him. The fireside was himself, Caswell, Barker and the LT.

"What is this?" he asked about the round little pod.

Barker said, "I'm not sure what it is now, but I'm pretty sure in ten thousand years it will be a very juicy melon."

He must have looked disappointed.

Barker said, "Yeah, I know. There is nothing that looks like what we're used to eating, except animals. Even the wild fruit back home has been adapted from thousands of years of agriculture."

That wasn't it, but if they thought that, it would help cover his thoughts.

"What are the Urushu eating?"

Caswell pointed into the near dark where a couple of fires glowed, "The men hunted an antelope. They've got windbreaks and a fire. The women have been plucking grass and building bed platforms."

"So what's the plan for them, sir?" he asked Elliott.

The LT almost grinned. "Plan? There ain't no plan. They've got relatives upriver. They're all grateful to us. They asked if we could go back for more, but I'm reluctant to try another face to face unless they come here."

Dan said, "The Neoliths didn't really want to talk."

"The ones there didn't. Here they did."

Caswell said, "It may be they have different factions or that they came from two groups. It's possible two villages had a joint hunting party. Or their attitude may vary on the strength they can present."

Elliott said, "So we're going to finish the wall. We may have to adapt to a goat pen inside, with hunting and gathering to supplement. But that would give us dairy, eventually, and hair for spinning into yarn. I'd like to thank Jenny and Gina for their input on that."

"You're welcome, sir," Caswell said. Alexander was either in the vehicle or asleep. He wondered how she felt, having splashed that guy's brains.

He didn't want to remember that visual in the chill dark.

He ate in silence. The man had been about to stab a spear into him. Except his armor would have stopped it. Except the others would have joined in, too. Except they should have planned for that. Goddammit.

The melon didn't taste like much. It was vaguely fruitlike. It might almost be cucumber or squash, but faintly sweet.

He finished, and climbed into the tepee to straighten his gear. He had privacy screens in his wedge, between poncho, a sheet and a towel. Barker's space was on one side, and Ortiz' on the other. The cloth worked okay to create walls, and they worked for visual seclusion, but you still knew others were there, and could hear them snore. Trinidad and Devereaux were halfway around the circle watching a movie on tablet.

He wanted to be actually alone, so he went back outside.

The sun was down, the sky beautiful, but he didn't feel it. The Milky Way arched from north to south across the west, clear enough to show colors. They had an amazing wilderness.

He didn't care.

Across the stream he heard chattering and calls. That was what the fight had been about. Getting those women free, and hopefully back to their families and friends. He walked past the fire.

"I'm going across the stream for a few, Sergeant Spencer."

"Got it. You're unarmed?"

"I have a knife. Is there a problem?"

"No, I don't want to risk a rifle or a fight. It's late, don't be long."

"I won't." He walked in close and muttered up to the hatch, "I don't feel real good about killing a man, and I want to know they're okay in the bargain."

Spencer whispered down, "Okay at being recovered? They came along freely, but I understand."

He crossed on the stepping stones, dull gray against black water in the starlit night. The creek bubbled under them. He took the short trail twisting up the bank and through the brush, and came out onto the rolling ground on the east bank. South was the goat pen, and he could smell it. Caswell, Ortiz and Dalton hunted east of here, but there was no game tonight. There were a couple of lean-tos, two small fires and several clusters of women. The three men walked around with spears. As he approached, they smiled and greeted him.

"Aa!" *Hi.*

"Aa."

"Woo !xe?" *You good?*

"Hm !xe, oo." *I'm good, thanks.*

He walked around the perimeter. They really didn't take much space. No wonder those lodges could fit so many. Though this was a bivouac, and sleeping touching would help them stay warm since they had at most a hide wrap each. All their other possessions fit into a small pouch. The gear he had seemed like a trove by comparison.

On the third trip around, a young woman came up alongside.

"Aa," she said with a smile, and a touch of his forearm. It sent a shiver through him. She had long fingers and met him at eye level.

"Aa."

Her hair was braided around her head, she was his height and as lean as they all were, with firm breasts and a slim but curved ass. He still couldn't define that skin tone. It was olive, café and tan all at once.

"Xi!e, kizh ae oong." She smiled even more widely and laid a hand on his arm.

He didn't know those words, but it came across as "My hero," as lame as that was. Her smile was cheerful and inviting, and that tilt of the head said she was interested.

On the one hand, he was horny as all hell, and lonely, and goddamn he wanted a human being to touch.

She was stroking his arm now.

On the other hand, he wasn't supposed to, and who knew what diseases there were, and she had a strong body odor, and there was a crowd. Not to mention the likelihood of someone walking in on them, or seeing them in NVG.

Maybe if they sat down in this dip for a bit. He could at least cuddle with her.

He had a strong odor, too. There was some deodorant left, but why bother? Every day was filthy and sweaty.

She found his clothes fascinating, and almost broke buttons yanking at his shirt.

"Ni," he said softly. "Hm !ka woo." *I show you.* Context mattered more than word order, as did tone. He undid a button slowly and she reached over to trace the hole in the fabric with her fingertips.

Well, from there, she figured out his pants readily enough. The belt gave her fits.

He glanced nervously around to see if anyone could see them. The moon wasn't up yet, but night vision would work fine.

There was a gaggle of women between them and the COB. Probably not by accident. Then there were still a few trees and shrubs, so he had some additional screening.

He had no idea what they considered romantic, or what she expected from him, but once his belt was released, she slipped hands inside his pants and around him. She seemed a bit confused, and her fingers traced around his circumcision scar. Of course, they didn't do that. She looked up quizzically, then back down, then followed her fingers with her mouth. But even her warm shoulder against his hand was a sensual rush. Human touch was precious. In contrast to the cold air and long deprivation, it was a tumbling rush in his nerves.

Her lips were full, warm, wet . . .

He'd been afraid he'd be done in seconds, but the sensation made him shiver and almost cry. He let his hands follow the contours of her shoulders, her sides, her breasts and back to the warm skin of her neck, and shivered again. Between pre-Mob, deployment, and here, he hadn't even hugged another human being in nine months.

Soon enough, his eyes pinpointed, his brain shut down, and waves of heat rolled over him. He realized he was clutching at her arms and straining.

He had no idea what she wanted in return, or what their culture expected. She sat up, smiled and leaned in to hug him, her lips brushing his neck.

He felt physically calm and sated, while mentally in an intense overload from the sensation of touching someone. But emotionally, he felt worse than before. No one else had this, and he felt as if he'd exploited the poor girl. Then, he wasn't sure how old she was. It was unlikely she was eighteen, despite her amazing technique, but her people didn't care about that; his did. *He* did.

He kept hugging her because it was cold now and she was warm and smooth and felt so good, while he got his pants fastened with one hand. There was quite a bit of grass in them, drawn up the back as he wiggled in.

He said, "Hm wi. Oo." *I go (imperative tone). Thank you.* He clutched hands with her, and she hugged him again. It didn't seem he owed her anything, and that fit what he'd seen in their camp. Sex was just something fun to do, and even their couples shifted around from time to time.

He walked past the screening group, who made a few comments that seemed friendly enough. The stepping stones weren't very visible, but he found them and made it across.

Ortiz was on watch now, and Ortiz wouldn't rat him out even if he'd seen anything. But Alexander was next to him.

"How are they doing?" she asked.

"Mostly calm, healthy."

"Good," she said. Her face was impassive, but as he passed by, she cracked a hint of smile and turned away.

Fuck. Busted.

From inside Number Nine, he heard her voice. She'd ducked down inside the turret.

"Oglesby."

"Uh, yeah?"

"Don't tell anyone. You'll just make them jealous."

"Wasn't planning on it."

Her voice was musical as she said, "Boy, your expression is a billboard. Take a few minutes by the fire until fatigue kicks in."

"Uh, roger that." Thank God she was cool. He stepped up two steps, and whispered, "Er, what did you guys see?"

"I figured you got a blowjob, but I wasn't shooting a porno, if that's what you're asking."

"Right. NVG on your camera?"

"You don't think the LT trusts them this close to camp, do you? And then there's the Neos, who may come back in force."

"I didn't ask her and I wasn't trying."

"Yeah. Well, as they say, don't do it again unless you bring enough for everyone."

"I didn't think you swung that way," he joked. She'd been married for years, right?

She said, "At this point, I swing modern human."

"Right. That's what got me. I just wanted held." He giggled. It was hilarious.

She strangled on a laugh. "So go chill out. Well done."

"Thanks. Uh . . . part of it was in response to the firefight."

"More like an execution. Yeah. I'm not comfortable myself. That's why I'm up here. I probably won't sleep tonight."

"Shot anyone before?"

"No. And I don't regret it, but I regret that I don't. It's going to take some meditation and ritual to get the stain off."

"I might join you."

"For?"

"Meditation and ritual. I prayed a bit earlier, but I'm not very religious. It didn't help."

"Then mine probably won't either, but I don't mind if you try."

"Thanks. And . . . thanks."

"You're welcome. Now piss off." But she said it with a smile.

His face glowed now. He had all kinds of emotions rushing through him. As exciting as that had been, he'd avoid doing that again soon.

And who was he kidding? He was a healthy male. If he got a chance, he'd take it.

CHAPTER 17

Sean Elliott crawled out to see the Urushu breaking camp in the chill dawn. How they managed without sleeping bags or tents in this near-freezing weather amazed him. He was wearing gore-tex, gloves and watch cap.

They were scavenging greens in the field and filling skins with water in the creek. That first part was going to hinder the soldiers' food gathering. Still, they'd managed to rescue forty-three women and girls. He looked around and found who he needed around the fire.

"Oglesby," he said.

"Uh, yes, sir?" Oglesby replied. He looked jittery and nervous.

"We're going to go interrogate them before they go. Caswell, can you come too, please?"

"Of course, sir."

"Good. I don't want to step on anyone or make them uncomfortable, but I need information."

"Roger that." Oglesby nodded eagerly.

They stepped across the river, Oglesby deferring to him, Caswell leading. The grass and growth were well-trodden. One of the penned goats was missing, and there were chunks of a goat roasting over a fire.

"There are more men now," he said. They must have arrived overnight.

Caswell said, "Yes, I count eight."

"Interesting. Well, let's find someone to talk to. Who do you suggest?"

273

She pointed. "Let's try the older lady there."

"Okay. Get us introduced."

Oglesby stepped forward and spoke slowly but apparently clearly in their language. The woman spoke back.

"She's an elder, sir. She says they are very grateful for our hospitality, and regret they have no gifts."

"Assure her that's fine, and we were glad we could help. Did we get everyone?"

The translation was, "She says we got everyone at that camp, but some were taken downriver to a new village. I gather it's a mile or two. She asks if our spirits will allow us to smite them dead, too."

"Tell her we can't now, but will ask our spirits in a few weeks."

Caswell said, "I want to carefully ask, how were they treated?"

The woman clicked, trilled and sang while gesturing, and Oglesby translated.

"She says they were taken in and made mates to the new men. Their spirits demanded a new way of living. Some of the men and boys were killed. The rest were chased off. Some women, especially the hunters, went with them. The elders weren't harmed, nor girls, but several young boys were killed. Some managed to run away but no one knows where they are. Some women ran away at night. Some of them are safe in the village east of here, upriver. The new men started posting guards, I think she said, and forcing them to stay. Since the spirits were with the new men, they agreed."

"Damn. Caswell?"

"I'm conflicted, sir. What's described is classic kill the men and rape the women. It probably starts about the time of agriculture and pastoral herding, with the concept of property. That includes women. Patriarchal societies don't want to raise gene lines they don't control, and commodities became scarce as population increased. At the same time, death and injury are just part of life here, to both groups. They're very fatalistic, so probably don't have a concept of rape."

"Good God, you don't mean they enjoy it?" Was that even *possible?*

She turned dark red. "No, sir. No I do not. But whatever happens is because the spirits require it. Even more than the Muslims with 'Insh Allah.' One adapts to whatever happens and moves on."

"So that village is gone."

Oglesby said, "Alexander has the photos, sir. It's been rebuilt, there's some proto-herding and proto-planting."

He breathed in a draft of cold air. "Goddamnit. Much as I'd like to invite them to live near us, we've got to establish ourselves before we start a feudal town."

Just then, a young woman wove through the crowd, came up to Oglesby and hugged him vigorously, her hands on his neck and chest. He carefully eased her away, but she persisted, confused.

"Someone you saved personally?" Sean asked.

"I think so, sir."

"Well, be polite, but don't get entangled."

"Yes, sir."

Caswell said, "They should be safe enough in their other village, though it depends on potential raiding for slaves. I gather the new group are mostly male."

"I think so," Oglesby said. That chick definitely liked him.

Sean said, "If we see them trying to pass us, we'll have a polite conversation. They know what rifles can do. I'm reluctant to shoot, but much like keeping the peace back home, we're going to keep it here when we can do so."

Caswell asked, "Can we send a security detail with them, sir? I volunteer."

"I'd like to, but I'll have to think about it. When do they plan to leave?"

Oglesby said, "They plan to leave about midday, of course. I asked why. They said the lions sleep then, and they have only eight spears." The girl was on him again.

"Does that give them enough time?"

"Yes."

"Okay. Don't tell them about an escort, but if we can, I'll send one."

"Hooah."

Caswell said, "Roger and thanks, sir."

There was more talking. Oglesby said, "They want to know if Doc can look at a couple of them. One has a lame foot. One has some sores."

"That seems doable. I wonder if my phone works at this range." He flipped it on. "Gina, can you hear me?"

"Yes, sir. A bit fuzzy."

"Send Doc over to look at some people."

After a moment's pause, she said, "He's on the way, sir."

Oglesby said, "They want to know why our spirits can give us thunder, but won't let us take their village back."

"Thunder has a lot of power. It must only be used when talking and arguing won't work, and even then only if lives are threatened."

"They accept that, sir, but say our spirits may be wise, but are . . . detached, I guess."

"Detachment avoids anger."

Devereaux arrived.

"Morning, sir. Do I get to examine the women?" he asked with a big grin.

Caswell rolled her eyes and muttered, "Fucking typical."

Devereaux said, "I wasn't trying to put anyone down, just some field humor."

"Yeah, well, I don't find it funny."

"I apologize."

"Just don't do it again."

"I'll try." He looked embarrassed, flushing purple under his dark skin.

"I need to head back," Sean said. "Caswell, do you want to keep an eye on things here?"

"Please, sir."

"Do it. Oglesby, you need to explain to that girl that she can't stay here with you."

"Understood, sir."

It almost looked like she was romantically interested, but there hadn't been any time or place, had there? Alexander had been along. He wouldn't have done anything in front of her, and they went straight into a fight. He'd been out of camp last night, but only a few minutes, and within sight of the guard post. Right?

Right?

The first woman did have a rough looking foot. It seemed to have some infection. Caswell sat with her as Devereaux went to work.

Sean said, "Oglesby, come here a moment."

"Yes, sir?"

Quietly he asked, "Did you avoid any risk of pregnancy and disease?"

The kid shrunk and turned Day-Glo pink.

"Yes, and I think so, sir. It wasn't anything I planned. More her idea. Is it that obvious?"

"Maybe. Devereaux probably won't get it. I'm pretty sure Caswell figured it out. I can tell. So keep your mouth shut and I'll find a way to tell her."

"Uh. I'm sorry, sir."

"As soon as we decided to interact with them, this was all inevitable. Violence. Sex. Distractions. That's why I was trying to avoid it and will continue to do so."

"Yes, sir. I don't want to just dump her, but it was a one-time thing and they're not staying. So I'm being nice until they leave."

"The problem comes if I send an escort. You have to go."

"Ah, hell, I'm sorry, sir." The kid looked professionally embarrassed.

Kid? He was maybe three years younger than Sean, but those three years mattered.

"Just keep it under control. Invoke our spirits if you need to."

"Yes, sir."

He did want to send that escort. Getting in good with more natives meant potential labor later, and both trade and knowledge of anything else edible.

"Take over there for a bit," he said. "Caswell, can I see you?"

Caswell patted the woman's hand, rose and came over.

He asked, "What's wrong with her foot?"

"A fractured toe. Apparently she kicked something hard. I'm hoping it was an accident and not abuse."

"I figure abuse is likely?"

"It doesn't seem to be, but one of them has some beating that looks like fists. There's always a few men like that. I gather the rest think of them as valuable property."

"Sorry to hear that."

She shrugged. "It's one more disappointment of many."

"I want to send that escort. You, Oglesby, and Dalton. Oglesby because he's the translator. Dalton because he has combat experience. You because you have the sociological knowledge. You'll be in charge."

She didn't smile, but did seem to brighten.

"Yes, sir. Should we prep now?"

"Tell Dalton. If he can't go, we'll find someone else."

"Roger."

"What do you think of Oglesby?"

She said, "He's very good at translating. He may not handle being around the natives well without help."

"I already talked to him about that."

"I understand, sir." She gave a sideways glance that he read.

"So it's dealt with, and not for sharing."

"Of course. It was inevitable, really." That was exactly what he'd said. He'd expected her to be more bothered, but she almost seemed relieved. Perhaps she'd been getting attention or too many stares from Oglesby?

"Yes, but I'd like to limit it. I may be overly hopeful."

"You're doing alright, sir. We're limited on resources."

"Especially people."

"Especially people, yes."

"So take a day, two at most, make nice, come back all in one piece, and don't shoot anything you don't absolutely have to."

"Got it. What information do you want?"

"Anything they have on the Neolithics. Agreements to talk more about food and local materials and cures. Coal, salt, plants, iron ore, anything."

"Will do."

Sean went back to camp, and had Alexander take over making sure they had ammo, water, some food, batteries and lights, sleeping gear and sundries. Yes, there was a reason units had a headquarters section. She was suited for it, and it freed him up to focus on the wall.

"I have it," he told Barker and Spencer.

["What, sir?" Spencer asked.

"We'll drop two really big logs at each side of the wall, and dig them in about six inches over the water. No one can easily get under that. We'll reinforce, as Bob suggested, with rock and timber, make our own little box culverts, with reinforcement around the log ends. The palisade goes over it, and we may even be able to socket it in, if we burn and bore holes. A little gapping won't hurt, because we can't stand on that anyway. It'll keep out their weapons, but a good marksman can still shoot through. We'll buttress at angles."

Spencer said, "That sounds like a lot of grunt lifting, but very sturdy."

"Yeah, it'll take lifting. I'm going to get the Urushu to help in exchange for Bob's knowledge of bows."

"In the meantime?"

"I'd like running water to us and the goats, but that not being feasible, another ten feet of wall will make me happy."

Barker said, "Sure, but I need to find something to cook about fourteen hundred."

"Noted."

Oglesby. He knew Barker had a pool going on who'd get laid first. The bets had been on Doc first due to his exotic looks, or Sean as chief. Oglesby had been second to last before Caswell.

It was going to get a lot more complicated.

There was a momentary interruption as two of the Urushu hunters came over. They'd been uphill along the stream in the scrub, and were carrying a small, coarse, stringy looking pig. This they laid down in front of Sean, and made the arms open gesture.

He did the same in return.

"Oglesby, thank them very much for me."

It was a wiry, tough pig, but it might roast tender given enough time in the oven.

"Hey, Bob!" he called.

Jenny Caswell led the two men alongside the Urushu pilgrimage. The contrast was interesting. The Urushu were barefoot, wore skirts and capes without shoes. A few had leggings. Several had animal skins with water, but they seemed comfortable this close to the river to not worry about logistics.

It was in the 50s, leaves down, and they were barefoot. That was fascinating, and frightening. There were several issues that could cause circulation problems and lead to dead toes at this and below. She hoped they'd have footwear of some kind once they reached their other village.

Each of them had a small leather pouch tied at neck or waist, that contained a handful of shiny stuff. The one she'd seen open had quartz, lapis, ochre and a fossil shell. Most of them had a short flint knife scarfed and bound to a stick. The eight men had spears and two had Bob's style throwing darts they'd presumably made themselves.

The girls among them scooped up the occasional bug and ate it. Now and again they'd grab a plaintain or onion stalk. Dandelions and other growth disappeared as they went, too. Several of the women should have had children, but only a half dozen did. They clung to the kids and used strips of hide above the breasts for the larger ones to hang onto. The smaller ones, under six months, were slung in carriers made of hide. The kids were quiet, either suckling or clutching and staring over mothers' shoulders. When someone needed to relieve themselves, they stepped out of line and did so, then caught back up.

It wasn't just people who did that. She stepped around a pile of deer droppings, and previously had just avoided a plop of aurochs crap.

The march was angling up a valley again, whatever one called those little side valleys. It was tiring, and hurt her ankles.

"Doing okay, Caswell?" Dalton asked.

No, but she wasn't going to say so to him.

"It's unusual terrain. I'll be fine."

"Hooah."

She let her feet trudge, made sure to lift them, and let her thoughts roll back.

In comparison to the Urushu, the troops had Multicam, body armor, helmets, NVG, eyepro, rifles, knives, spears, tablets to use as recording media, plus Oglesby's written notes, dried meat and fruit, full Camelbaks, bivvy bags, spare socks and APECS. Well, she had APECS, the soldiers had gore-tex cold-weather whatever they were called. Actually, she couldn't remember what APECS stood for at the moment.

The difference in definitions of "roughing it" was profound, even when they were cut off from their time.

Eventually, she'd be wearing leather and homespun, though better designed. They'd never be down to the Paleolithic level. But, they had modern tools to work back from. Working forward from this . . . no wonder it took fifteen thousand years.

"I guess they don't take breaks," Oglesby said.

"They seem to do that pacing thing," Dalton replied. "Move fast, slow down, repeat."

"It works. Of course, they're not carrying all this crap, either."

"You'll be glad for that crap when we get there."

"Or meet a bear," she said. Adrenaline rippled. That was a huge fucking bear, in a clump of trees just north.

Oglesby shouted to one of the spearmen and pointed. The man

nodded, and pointed. Two others moved over to that side of the trail. The women bunched up closer.

Either the numbers or the spears convinced the bear she wasn't interested. She padded around but made no aggressive moves. She was huge, brown ticked, and rolly.

"I wonder if rifles are better than spears against those."

"What, M Fours?" Dalton asked. "You're just gonna piss a bear off unless you get it through the eyes. I'm not even sure this would punch through the skull. I think it would reach the vitals, but it's about like someone sticking a needle into you. It won't be fast."

"The spears have to get close."

"Yeah. Bows actually work better for this."

"Than spears?"

"Yes. You don't have to get that close, and a good, sharp hunting point causes hemorrhage. You just have to hope they bleed out before eating you."

As beautiful as the bear was, she shivered. "I see why the LT wants that wall finished." She remembered they'd had bears and lions pad through camp already.

Dalton said, "Oh, yeah. It may be a bit overbuilt, but that's better than the alternative."

Five miles could be done on good terrain in an hour, ninety minutes tops. On this scrubby, undulating mess, it took four hours, and she was panting by the end of it. Ahead, though, was a riverside village in the woods. It had tents and huts but also an overhanging cliff-cave with brush all around.

Messengers had obviously been ahead, and this village and the one downstream were certainly related. Other women and few men swarmed out to greet them, hugging and touching. Some of the young women would clasp each other's breasts.

Oglesby muttered, "Nothin' wrong with that." He probably thought she couldn't hear.

Dalton replied, "Amen, brother."

Neither of them would get it. It was almost certainly a nonsexual compliment to one's breeding or suckling potential. Or possibly had been and evolved into a social gesture.

The older women's breasts hung low and flat from suckling child after child. Primitive life put a beating on people.

Shortly they were in the camp, which had a low piled stone wall. The rocks had come from the bluff and the river, it seemed.

She knew what was coming next, but goddammit, it was hot. She unsnapped her helmet and rolled it off her head, shook her hair to get air through the sweat.

At once, five men headed her way, bearing whatever gifts they had, and cooing what was obviously, "Hey, pretty lady." It got tiresome.

"Dalton, could you—"

"Ayup," he said, and came alongside. He put a hand on her shoulder, and held the other palm up about forty-five degrees. They took that as a bar, without it being a challenge.

"Thank you," she said.

"They don't mean any harm," he said.

"I'm well aware of that," she said. "Different countries, different customs." It still was tiresome.

She recognized several of the Urushu men here. Either they'd come here directly, or by a roundabout way. The soldiers had no information on whatever tribal networks existed.

"It's a bit galling they took off and left the women."

"I thought you were about equality."

"That's bullshit. A woman with a child isn't able to run. The whole point of society is to protect them."

"We agree," he said. "I dunno. Maybe it was a tactical decision? Leave, come back to get them? Maybe it was panic because they're not really violent and didn't understand it? Or maybe they're just pussies."

Sigh, that. "My genitalia should not be an epithet."

He said, "Well, in our culture, the military, that term or one like it has been in use for centuries. So you should get used to it."

She wasn't going to respond to that. She just turned and got busy with . . . children. They found her fascinating. They found her clothes fascinating. She detached hands, and got them to move back a bit.

The youngest responded to peekaboo, and the older ones joined in. One girl about ten reached out to stroke her hair.

"Yes, it's red," she said. "Like an autumn leaf or some mineral or other. I guess it doesn't matter what I say because you don't understand me."

The children weren't judgmental.

Then she heard, "Oh, holy crap!"

She rose smoothly to avoid scaring the kids, turned with her finger near the trigger and thumb near the safety.

Dalton was munching something that looked like a cookie.

"What's that?" she asked.

"I think it's a rice and acorn cake."

"Rice?" She jogged over, gear clattering and swinging, and took one he held toward her.

She bit down. It was crisp but flexible, hot off a rock griddle, and yes, rice, acorn, possibly some salt and onion, and a bit of some kind of antelope suet.

"Oh, my God, that's good," she murfled. It was almost orgasmic. Bread, starch. She felt it convert to sugar from salivary amylase, and if she recalled, studies said these people had less of that gene, and why was she thinking about biology while eating the first bread in three months?

"Oglesby, get the recipe," she said. "That is an order, one of few I plan to issue."

"Yes, ma'am," he said with a joking salute. But it seemed respectful. Who cared?

"Okay, we'll stay overnight definitely. Maybe two. I wonder what they have for breakfast?"

CHAPTER 18

Martin Spencer looked over in satisfaction. It was afternoon. The wall on the east was well started. Eventually they'd want a goat pen inside. That, and running water.

One step at a time. Fortification this year, water and private lodging next year. Or not so private, if Alexander would consider pairing up.

After that . . . cattle or antelope ranch? Work on growing some kind of crop and an orchard? He'd never had any interest in farming. He wanted to be a machinist and build race cars. That, however, wasn't going to happen.

"Break for a bit, regular chores next," he told Doc and Trinidad.

He walked over to Number Nine.

"Time to run up the engine," he said.

Alexander glanced up from spreadsheets. "It's only been three weeks."

He brushed past her, trying hard not to make a point of touching her, the back of his hand just brushing her butt. Damn. Human touch.

He said, "As it gets colder, we need to shorten it slightly. And if we can find some kind of vegetable oil, or render down some animal fat, we can keep them running for years."

"To haul salt?"

"That would be one thing, yes. Or coal. Or we fab a tiller and rip up some ground to farm." He squeezed into the driver's seat and fired it up.

It took about ten seconds, but it did start. The solar trickle charger was a godsend.

"Did you come through the back just to squeeze past me?" she asked.

"Yeah, I guess I'd rather squeeze past you than the LT, if that's okay."

"I'm flattered," she said with obvious sarcasm.

They bantered like that more and more, and he knew there was reciprocal interest. So eventually he'd ask her. It was going to be a long year.

Lacking a road test, he wanted to give it thirty minutes of idle with intermittent revs and some gear shifting to keep the fluid moving. He settled for five minutes. He ran through the gear range with the wheels chocked and brakes engaged, then let it idle down, and killed it.

"Okay, enough goofing off. I have more wood to chop."

"I'm actually done for the day," she said. "I'll help Barker with food, and I'll haul firewood."

Above them, Ortiz shouted, "Approaching party! Big one!"

He ran out the back, turned to Number Eight, jumped on step, ladder and up onto the roof. He squinted into the setting sun.

That wasn't a diplomatic mission.

"War band!" he said. "Hostiles! Gear up and fall back here."

Ortiz and Alexander looked at him and didn't move. They were frozen and confused.

"Attacking hostiles, lock the gate!" he called.

They moved.

Barker and Trinidad had the gate closed, and were shoving timbers in to block it.

Elliott scrambled up next to him. He was carrying Spencer's helmet, armor and rifle.

"Do you have it, sir?" he asked, taking the gear and shoving the brain bucket on first.

"Yes, but watch out for me, I'm late. What do we have?" Elliott took the offered binox, raised them, shielded them from the sun with his left hand, and looked.

"Looks like about seventy men with spears, some with bows, a dozen dogs. They're obviously not happy."

"And we have seven." The LT scanned around.

The LT said, "Close up the backs of the trucks. Lock the doors.

Alexander, watch the gate. Barker and Trinidad, watch the west corners. The rest of us are covering the east and the north-south."

He pointed as he spoke, and sounded firm. Good. A commander who was decisive under fire was much better than the alternative.

How could they have missed . . .

"It occurs to me, sir, that wall makes dandy cover and concealment for them to sneak around." He fastened the armor, feeling it snug and not quite familiar, but becoming so fast.

"Yeah. I wonder why they didn't already, or why they didn't swing along the river and up."

"Probably a tribal challenge. They may have some tactics, but it's probably scream and throw spears."

Without looking over, Elliott asked, "You think so?"

"It's still common some places in our time, and they can't have a lengthy military history to work from." He kept his eyes peeled, too. There was definite movement all around the outside.

"Let's hope so."

The group started shouting, waving spears and making gestures that were probably supposed to be rude, if they had a common language.

"And our translator's gone," he said.

"Yeah. Other than the fact there's apparently a few dozen words that are close if you know the subject, we got nothing."

Everyone was armored up.

"Gloves and shades," he said. "Flint is hard but brittle." He kept his glasses with him, and gloves were in his pants left cargo pocket.

Alexander tightened her helmet strap and shrugged her hands, no gloves with her. She had eyepro. Doc was fully covered. The others mostly were, but Trinidad didn't have glasses.

Elliott said, "Don't fire unless I order it, but if you get attacked directly, you can engage in self-defense. Hooah?"

"Hooah, sir." "Hooah." "Roger that."

Devereaux came up the ladder fast.

He said, "Doc, hop over to Nine and help Alexander. Ortiz, can you dismount the gun and remount on Number Nine? You'll have better coverage of the gap."

"Easier if I have a hand," Ortiz said, as he opened the cover and yanked the charging handle. "Gun is disarmed, someone grab it."

Martin said, "I got it." It wasn't hard to move, but stepping over the three-foot gap between the truck tops took care. As he straddled it, he looked down at the weeds. Those were ugly. It might be an idea to either move the vehicles, or throw some coals back there to kill that crap.

The shouting increased as the men worked themselves into a battle frenzy and got closer. They were passing out of sight as they neared the gate.

"I wonder if they scouted us out and realized how few we are," Elliott asked.

Martin said, "Possible, if they did it in daytime. Would we catch them at night?"

Elliott looked around.

"Maybe. Depends on when we were looking and where they were."

"Should we try not to fight?"

Shaking his head, Elliott said, "Given that they've already been hostile twice, I say we need to fight. It's all that's going to work. We already killed three, yes?"

Martin said, "Yes, and they may think that was magic, or some god thing, and having sacrificed properly, their gods are stronger now." Savages anywhere tended not to be rational.

"Noted."

From the southwest corner up near the ditch, Trinidad shouted, "They're passing around here!"

Something rose up over the palisade.

"Look out, rock!" Martin shouted back.

Trinidad dodged and the rock bounced off his helmet. He staggered and recovered.

Ortiz said, "They're coming around the south corner."

Very calmly, Elliott said, "Open fire."

Martin hated shooting people, especially when they had no idea they were outclassed. He raised his weapon, put the optic over some dude at a dead sprint toward them, and shot. The man piled up and dropped forward. Cracks on either side beat his ears, and two more fell.

Good shooting, he thought. Then an arrow arced toward him and he flinched. It missed.

He shot again, got another, he thought. The guy was wearing hide pants and tunic with a pointy hat, carrying three javelins. Those scattered across the ground.

Elliott shouted, "If they come round more than two at a time, M Two Forty."

Ortiz said, "Hooah," and charged the gun with a loud clack.

Uphill and south, Trinidad was firing through chinks between the logs, while dodging other thrown rocks.

The M240B opened up with its cacophonous clatter, and bodies burst.

He glanced back to see Barker in the northwest corner near them, kneeling and shooting along the north wall toward the stream. Yes, there were some coming in there, too.

"Giant ball of suck," he said.

They'd spread out and were all over the place.

That little bastard in the wolf fur was trying to light the tepee on fire. Martin took aim, fired, and shot him through the neck. He fell thrashing, did the Curly Shuffle, and stopped.

Trinidad obviously didn't like his position, and came out running, with a bayonet mounted on his rifle and a machete in the other hand. He swung at someone and scored blood. Escrima? Kali? Some fighting form.

Alexander stamped her foot at the edge of Number Nine's roof, shouted, "Motherfucker," and fired straight down at someone, then stabbed down with that tanto bayonet of hers. Then she screamed, "OW!", staggered back against the turret and said, "Ow!" again as she bent over it and flailed. Devereaux got in front of her, heedless of her blade and the loaded weapon, and shot down the side.

The rest had had enough. They ran whooping and hollering, leaving the dead and wounded.

Elliott said, "Everyone stay here and keep alert."

Martin surveyed the area. Across the river, the fence was down and the goats were gone. No problem. That was fixable. The sweat lodge had a huge dent in the side. Fixable. The fire was out. No biggie, but likely socially significant to the Neoliths.

The survivors moaned and cried. A couple limped or crawled around, looking shocked. What had happened was beyond any comprehension to them.

Alexander had a gash through the sole of her boot.

All the soldiers were alive.

Ortiz asked, "Do we want to pursue, or should I fire after them? They're within range."

"Negative, conserve ammo," Elliott said. "Keep them under observation. Doc, start with Alexander, then the others. Probably Spencer next."

"Huh?" he said stupidly. Elliott pointed at his right arm.

That arrow had ripped his shirt and the skin underneath. It wasn't deep, but would need cleaning and dressing at least.

"Now it hurts," he said.

"You're welcome."

Heedless of that, he hopped across to Number Eight, and carefully took Alexander's weapon. That bayonet was a tanto almost a foot long. Custom and ugly. It had blood and hair on it. She'd stabbed someone in the skull.

Her boot had a hole about two inches long and an inch wide. Someone had jabbed something big up there.

"How did that happen?" he asked, helping her take off her helmet. He wanted something to go under her head, but there wasn't anything.

A tap on his shoulder was Elliott with a patrol pack. That would work. He eased her head up and slid it under.

She said, "They were poking up at me and nnngggh!" as Devereaux worked her boot off. "Tried to stomp on it. Poking at my kneeeees."

"Must have been a long spear," he said.

"He was taller than most."

As the boot came off, blood flowed freely. Doc cut and ripped her sock off, sacrificing it to get to her quickly.

Doc said, "It's not too deep, and I think I got all the rock out. I need to flush it with alcohol. It smells like they shit on their spear tips."

Martin put his hands down for her to grip, and she braced her head back. Devereaux took a large syringe and started squirting and swabbing.

"That means those are dedicated weapons, then, not for hunting. Unless they really don't understand hygiene even that much."

"Filthy fuckers," Trinidad opined.

She had adequate hand strength, he thought, as she clutched down and he felt bones grind in his hands. Teeth gritted, she panted then growled, tendons standing out on her neck and turning red with white streaks. Not pretty.

Doc said, "Done. No bone damage I can tell. Expect a lot of oozing, bruising and swelling. We need to keep her off her feet. Carve some crutches fast."

Barker, leaning up over the edge, said, "Yeah, we can do that."

She collapsed limp, barely conscious, sweat exploding from her pores and her head lolling.

Doc looked at Martin. "You're next."

He was concerned about Gina, but she wasn't going to fall off the vehicle and wasn't in danger of bleeding out. So he forced himself to worry about other things.

He rolled up his sleeve, wincing as he brushed the wound. It had bled profusely, but was all superficial. No veins that he could see.

"This is gonna hurt," Devereaux said, as he folded some gauze.

"Yeah, go for it." He turned his head.

Wet heat rushed through his arm to his head. Fuck. Doc was scrubbing and it felt like sandpaper. *My turn to growl*, he thought.

Then the scrubbing stopped, and the pain turned to a long, slow burn.

"It feels so good when you stop, Doc," he said.

"Good. Wrapping it now."

It ached and throbbed, but he figured it was nothing on a spear into the foot.

"That boot's no good anymore, is it?" he asked.

Barker was up top now, too.

"Maybe," he said. "We can try pine resin to seal it. Possibly a plug out of some of the leftover plastic."

"I have another pair," Alexander slurred groggily.

Barker said, "Only one pair. And now a spare left boot."

Martin said, "Ah. And you all mocked me for insisting we keep everyfuckingthing."

Barker shook his head. "I didn't. You were right. If that doesn't work, maybe we can melt it closed."

He hoped one of those would work. Likely, though, that boot was shot. He knew how to make leather moccasins in theory. He'd never done it without a kit. Or a needle.

Ortiz said, "Sir, we have a lot of wounded down there."

"Yeah, we'll need to deal with that. What about the dead?"

Martin brought his brain back online.

"Burial practice is common, sir. We'd be insulting to just toss them out, which may be what you want to do. Or we wait and try to communicate that they can take them back. Or we toss them downstream and let scavengers take care of it."

"Pile them outside for right now," Elliott ordered. "I want a count of how much ammo we used, as much brass as we can recover, and a body count."

"You heard the LT," he said.

Barker dropped back down and got to work. Good man.

"I want to know why they didn't stop. Hopped up on drugs?"

He replied, "Or religion, sir. Especially in Africa, some groups believe being naked, or dressed a certain way, or drinking certain things, makes you immune to death. If someone dies anyway, obviously he didn't do it right."

"They figure it out when enough die?"

"They figure they were doing it wrong. Then they try something else."

"Christ. How many do we have to kill?"

Martin followed his gaze around the wreckage and wafting smoke from the stomped fire, at the squirming bodies. They were bleeding into the grass and looked macabre.

He said, "Until they figure nothing works, or believe we're superior, or they get pissed off and hang their own boss man."

"What a fucking waste." Elliott looked angry, and a bit ill. He trembled.

"First major engagement, sir?" he guessed.

"Yeah. I wish I could say it'd feel different with modern insurgents, but I don't guess it would."

"No, sir. Everyone dies the same, and anyone behind the tech curve has no idea what they're facing."

Yeah, I'm an expert, Martin thought. *Two previous firefights. Yay, me.* But it was likely half of them here hadn't actually exchanged fire before.

Elliott asked, "Doc, how do you want to triage them?"

"How much of my stuff are you willing to use, sir?"

"Not much." Elliott shook his head and looked sad.

Doc shrugged and frowned. "Then anyone with a solid torso shot is likely to die. We can cauterize and hope it works. We can leave them to moan and scream. We can take care of them while they moan and scream. Or we can put them out of their misery."

Martin had heard of people going ashen, but had never seen it until now. Elliott was that pale, that fast.

"Good Christ, I can't kill them now they're down."

Devereaux said, "They'll be in worse pain if you don't, sir."

"Sort them first."

"Will do. Soap or just water for washing?"

Elliott clenched his jaw and sighed.

"Goddammit. Use soap. Do the best you can without using actual medical supplies."

"Hooah, sir. I'll need to rip their leather clothes into bandages."

"Oh, keep weapons live, in case any are feeling heroically suicidal."

Devereaux said, "If you can't find a pulse, I can't do anything here. Drag them and lay them out down by the latrine. Let me know on the rest."

Since Barker was taking care of bodies near the base of the vehicles, Martin dropped down and started by the fire. The men there had been hit by 7.62mm from the M240B.

"These two are alive," he said. Their eyes were open, and they were in absolute shock. One next to them, though . . . dead to the touch. And another had his torso ripped open. Dead.

The ones around the truck had fared better. One had a shattered shoulder and wasn't likely to regain any use. One had been hit through the foot and would likely recover. Overall, there were twelve dead, four expectant, eight seriously wounded who Doc might be able to save, and thirteen limping and fixable but infection was always a possibility.

The attack had been fast, and they'd had no idea what the weapons could do, or at what range. The return fire had devastated them.

Devereaux looked over the three with gaping gut wounds and one lungshot.

"There is nothing I can do for them," he said, looking frustrated. With modern gear and evac, most of them would survive. Here, nothing. "Gently as you can, place them on the flat ground over there."

It was hard to be gentle with a man with ribs blown away. Barker took the legs, Martin folded the man's arms across his chest and took the shoulders. With Barker leading, he just made sure the guy didn't drag. A ruck or sleeping bag would make this easier, or a spare hide. They'd been converting hides to shelter as fast as they could scrape and smoke them. There weren't any spares.

Devereaux said, "On the minor ones, start with washing and debriding. Two people per in case they struggle."

Martin said, "Walking wounded first. We need to corral them, and make sure they understand it's medicine."

"Yeah."

They found one guy with a crease through his arm, and washed and bound it. He was surprisingly lightly hurt, but clutched at his head. Inspection showed a contusion where he'd run into something.

Ortiz took care of most of the minor wounds, treating them apparently like livestock. That made sense. He scrubbed, washed, pulled, and wasn't any too gentle, but didn't seem to be trying to hurt them.

The one with the perforated foot seemed to grasp he was being treated, and clutched at himself as they rinsed the outside. His foot had already swollen and bruised. He wouldn't be walking for days. The bullet might have broken bones, but had passed through. The whole instep was an angry purple mass and soft to the touch.

"Hey, Alexander, you got payback."

She called back, "I'm thrilled. I'd rather have a working foot."

"What about this shattered shoulder?" The bullet had destroyed the clavicle and the whole thing was a blood-drenched pile of hamburger.

Doc said, "I could attempt surgery, but I'd have to open it up a lot and he'd get infected. I'm going to jam the bones as close together as possible, and we strap him down. Maybe it'll heal. Maybe he'll be gimp. Maybe he gets infected and dies."

It was scary. This could happen to any of them, with spears, hooves or a falling log. Doc's resources were limited.

With two buddies gripping his patient's other hand and legs, Devereaux ran fingers along the bones around the bullet wound, then massaged and pushed until they appeared mostly straight to Martin's eye, though it was hard to tell with skin in the way. Then he slipped a do-rag under the arm and tied a figure eight, followed by strapping the arm down to the chest with gut. Shrugging, he held up the alcohol bottle.

"Will hurt, ow, ow." He poured a splash into the wound and was rewarded with a pained, "NNarrrgh!"

That done, with Ortiz guarding the ones who were mostly functional, they turned to the tough part.

"Okay. Now those four expectant. We've got to do something."

Elliott asked, "What 'something' can we do?"

Scratching his bushy hair, Devereaux said, "Either I use some of our painkiller, we cover them with blankets and wait for them to die, or we euthanize them. That's all I can come up with."

"How long do they have?"

He shrugged. "Minutes. Hours. Possibly days. If we give them water, they might last a week before infection and hunger do them in."

They all stared uncomfortably at each other. Alexander was limp and on the truck. She was probably exempt.

"Draw straws?" Martin offered, feeling ill.

Ortiz said, "I can do it, I think. I'll just have to close my eyes and think of cows."

Elliott took a very deep breath.

"No. No one under my command is doing something that could be considered a war crime." His voice was cold.

That sucked for the casualties, but he understood the logic. "Yes, sir."

Still without emotion, Elliott said, "Give me the sharpest knife we have. Where do I cut?"

Devereaux said, "From here to here, sir," and indicated on his throat.

Martin fumbled out his bowie. It was big, sharp, and perfectly balanced. He shook as he handed it over, hilt first.

Elliott took it, hefted it, turned and walked toward the four men.

They didn't fight. They might have been in too much pain, or just accepting. One at a time, he pulled their heads up, placed the knife, and sliced. One of them twitched, one gurgled, the other two were probably close to death anyway. Pools of sticky blood soaked into the ground under their necks, and kept dripping from the deep cuts. It was almost black in the twilight.

The man came back looking completely stoned. He held the knife out at arm's length, and Martin had to move around him to take it from the side.

Then Elliott slumped to his knees and burst out bawling.

Martin Spencer felt like crap, but with the LT down, and he wasn't blaming the man, he took over.

"Okay, keep eyes on them. I need three volunteers, you with the light wounds there, there, there. Yes, you. Come with me." He indicated with gestures.

He grabbed a shovel and took it along.

"Your dead friends. What do you want to do?" He pointed and shrugged.

He showed how to dig with it. Then offered it to them.

"Or the fire," he said and pointed. "Oh. Crap. Barker, light a fire fast. Show them what we can do."

"Hooah."

Barker jogged to the truck, came back with a propane torch, and had flames in ten seconds.

"Burn?"

They looked back and forth, and one of them pantomimed piling stuff up.

"Ah. Mound burial. Makes sense in that terrain. Here? There?" he pointed at the ground and in the direction of their camp, then shrugged.

Hesitantly, one of them pointed back toward their camp.

"You can do that," he nodded and indicated, or tried to. Point at body, wave arms toward camp.

They didn't seem to grasp that they were free to go. They huddled together, obviously afraid of these superbeings who could call lightning down to rip holes and kill.

They weren't going anywhere at present, it seemed, even if they had all been fit.

Did they wait for the Neolithics to go, send an envoy, bury them here, or drag them downstream for the wolves and scavengers? He hated to do the latter, but he didn't want to put the effort into digging or mounding. They weren't really up to it. Envoys would probably be poorly received. That left dragging the bodies farther downstream.

"Ortiz, Barker, I hate to ask, but we need those bodies away from camp unless and until the dweebs decide to do anything. Can you drag them down over the next lip?" He pointed into the shadowy dusk. Shit, it had been hours now.

Ortiz said, "I'm not keen to, but yes, that makes sense."

"Thanks. Use a flashlight, too. My Fenix is three hundred lumens. Alexander, do you still have them covered?"

"The survivors aren't giving me any hassle," she said, sounding pained. "My foot, however, is killing me. I'll be awake for hours." She sat atop the turret with her foot out, and waved the M240B around from time to time.

This was a hell of a thing.

"Ortiz, after that, shoot them a goat. What they do with it is up to them. If they can't get a fire started themselves, we'll show them how awesome we are again."

"Hooah."

He was angry at the Neolithics for this. They'd been offered peace and rejected it, insisted on violence, and generally showed little restraint or forethought. Then they kept attacking even after they started dying from what were effectively magical weapons. The stupid tendency of humans to delude themselves into denying reality really pissed him off.

He hoped Caswell and company were doing better with the Urushu.

CHAPTER 19

Jenny Caswell was not enjoying the visit. The hosts were very hospitable, offering endless food, some of it palatable, and a comfortable hooch near the rock overhang. Their host was Ai!ee's family, and she was overwhelmingly gracious since the surgery that gave her back her dignity and sex life. That was wonderful to see. Helping someone's life was the greatest thing one could do for another human being.

Jenny had turned down three offers from men before they accepted, with Oglesby's help, that her spirits didn't allow mating.

"Your name and rank translates as 'Jenny Leads Fighting,'" Oglesby said. "I told them your spirits require you to be celibate while you're a sworn warrior. Though warrior isn't a term they seem to have, either. If two people have a dispute, they sort of slap it out and move on. I think I've translated you as part shaman, part hunter, and part protector against predators."

"Thank you. They're so delightfully ignorant of some matters. It's a shame they're losing that."

He said, "They are very friendly on the whole."

"So how are you going to explain to your teenage girlfriend that you're not available?"

He flushed.

On the one hand, she was glad he had sexual company that wasn't her. All the men should be encouraged to do that. On another, she was near furious he'd exploited a recent rape survivor. Regardless of any approach, the girl had been vulnerable and seeking support, and he'd taken sex from it. The Urushu didn't know different. He did.

Oglesby replied, "I said our spirits had not been unhappy, but told us it was a bad idea to become involved. I thanked her gratefully. She seemed a bit disappointed, but not badly hurt."

"Good." Actually, bad. But there wasn't a good here. That would have to do.

The cave seemed to be where the elderly lived. She'd first thought the children should be there, for safety, but then realized it was a rocky climb, and while not that high up—maybe ten feet—it was very steep. It provided good shelter and they'd built hooches in it as well. It was perhaps fifteen feet deep, and ten feet tall at the open end. Lengthwise, it was fifty feet or so.

"Is Dalton behaving?" She pointed in his direction, over by one of the fire hearths under the cave lip. There were several younger women and a couple of men around him. The smoke rose, stained the rock and tumbled out. That seemed to help with bats and bugs as well. They were scarce.

"With my help, yes. He's not been hitting on them, even though they're interested in him."

"Good." She did another look around and headcount. If you knew how one group acted, you could usually spot the newcomers and outsiders.

"It looks like about three quarters of the men survived and are here or arriving, if I'm counting them right and your info is correct. So they lost about ten."

"Yes. Some of the families and women managed to escape anyway. Both downstream and this way. The leader, Ashmi Wise, was killed."

That first was a relief. It had been bad, but not destructive of the clan group.

"That's sad. He was nice to us, hospitable. Can we do something in memorial for him?"

"They say we can smoke with them tonight."

Ugh. That stuff. "We'll try. Then we'll leave in the morning, after assuring them they can visit. Now let's talk to the elders again. Those late term pregnant women need to stop hauling things, or Doc will have more work."

"Hooah."

"Where's their latrine?" she asked. She'd been holding it for hours, and . . . other issues.

He grimaced. "Yeah, about that. They go upstream, in the river. They get their drinking water down here. I have no idea why they think that's a good idea."

Ah. "I've heard of that."

"Yeah?"

She explained, "It means a constant low-level of infection, which helps with immunity when other stuff comes downstream. It'll be pretty dilute."

"So we're going to follow them?"

"No, we'll fill a few meters upstream from the latrine area. Do they just squat in the water?" God, she wanted a real toilet.

"They seem to."

This was not going to work well with her period. She would wrap the tampon in leaves and toss it in the fire just like in camp. A floater wouldn't be a good thing.

And starting next month she'd be using cotton pads stitched out of T-shirts, stuffed with fluff and washed in cold water. It was the best she and Alexander had been able to devise, and Alexander was hand sewing them, or was supposed to. She should follow up. The older woman had memory issues with her thyroid problems.

Sanitation taken care of, with Dalton standing discreet guard as she squatted on rocks, she walked back into the village, rifle slung high across her chest where it was hard to mess with. The grabbiness never stopped, just varied between inquisitiveness and lust.

The place smelled of food, smoke, growth, river and sweaty people. They washed in the river, but only intimate areas. They seemed to occasionally wash hair or body if they got animal residue on themselves—they had a substantial processing industry set up. There were whole guts and cut strips smoking over a low fire. Hides were being tanned in a pit in a ground, and it stank fiercely when the breeze shifted. They scraped and carved wood and bone, and had lots of food being prepared for winter.

She found out what they did for diapers, or didn't. Infants were in leather wraps with moss and grass. Once they were large enough to hold their heads up, the mothers seemed to know from minor sounds and motion when a baby was about to unload, and just carried them to the nearest bush or patch of grass. By the time they could walk, they knew what to do by themselves.

Dalton said, "If they just understood better hand washing and had an actual latrine, or even the river, they'd be pretty modern."

"I suspect the smell helps deter animals. This place smells like rot, sweat and predator waste."

"True."

Ai!ee and her family had relocated here without harm, and were very gracious hosts. They had a late dinner ready, or a continuation of earlier dinner. They were around a fire in front of a new hooch, with more boughs and hides as an awning, with more food. It was roasted fish, and there were several seasonings. Besides salt, there were several oniony things and something almost like sage.

"What is this?" she asked through Oglesby, and they showed her leaves that did look a lot like sage.

"Where?"

All over, apparently. She'd need to look for that. While grain wasn't yet possible, she might manage an herb and tuber garden. But she wished for some real carrots. These fibrous white things weren't carrots, weren't parsnips and weren't much of anything, except filler. They even came out the other end about the same texture.

The family ate from skewers over the fire and stuff grilled on rocks, just as the troops did, with a carved wooden bowl for serving small bits they scooped out by hand. Right hand only.

After dinner, everyone gathered under the rock overhang, around a fire that was large enough for light and radiance. This was important to them.

She sniffed lightly as the weed bundle came by, but Oglesby took a huge, sucking puff. Dalton was fairly reserved, too.

There was drumming and singing and then the local matriarch gestured for her to stand.

"Oglesby, can you translate?" she asked.

"Mostly, if you keep it simple," he said slowly. Yeah, he was stoned.

"No more weed for you."

"Hooah."

She stood and looked around.

"Thank you for your hospitality. You are all very gracious. We appreciate learning about your foods and ways, which we can use ourselves. We're very glad the spirits could guide us to reunite your families. We hope there will be peace between all the groups soon."

She left it at that, not wanting to overdo it, and sat down.

The matriarch threw the weed into the fire, then spat after it.

Oglesby said, "This is apparently a prayer to the spirits, and an appeal that they know these people. We're supposed to spit, too."

"Easy enough," she said, worked up some saliva, and spit.

The drumming resumed. It was a simple beat, and the dancers tranced the way a lot of aboriginal peoples did. After the third couple excused themselves to find a corner, she tapped Oglesby on the shoulder. He was half nodding off from the smoking stuff. Hell, call it "drugs," that's what it was.

"Back down," she said. They needed rest and they needed to find a secure place.

Down below, Ai!ee's mate, Ktral, tried to insist they take the inside of the wickiup, while he, his mate, another woman and four kids moved out.

"Tell them they're very gracious, but we thank them very much for hosting us. We will be very comfortable outside, and want them to enjoy their beds."

Oglesby said, "I think I got across comfort. 'Enjoy bed' means something else."

"Well, they can do that, too. Thanks for transliterating."

"No problem."

The troops split into three-hour watches, and she took first rotation. It sounded as if Ktral was enjoying the bed, with at least one of the women. Other tents and bricked rooms in the cave had similar sounds. It was like the first village. People's hearths were private, and you didn't mention it.

It was cold, but they were well dressed. When Dalton relieved her, she doffed boots, loosened them enough for night trips, and shimmied into her sleeping bag with the bivvy cover. That and the woven awning was enough shelter, now that they were used to the environment, and were in a village. They were adapting to this place, though sometimes things were still awkward.

No music or video. All their devices were powered down unless needed in an emergency. They were just three people with odd clothes.

The soldiers were left alone under the awning, and it was an uneventful night.

Which meant they'd done their job right. So why was she unhappy?

Dan Oglesby woke. Three hours and three hours rest, with three hours on watch in between, was rough.

Breakfast was some berries and parched acorn cake, and utterly delicious, crisp and sweet, hot off a rock. After that, they stuffed their bivvy bags, and started rucking.

A shout from the locals caught his attention.

Five hunters and two others planned to come with them.

Caswell asked, "What are they about?"

The lead man was named Ak!tash, and pointed into his mouth. Oglesby caught, "pain" and "broken." Another raised a foot. "Stuck skin" was the explanation.

"One has a rotten tooth. One seems to have one of those warts on the sole."

"Plantar wart."

"Yes. They're going to see Doc. The rest are escort, honor guard, sightseers, and general friends."

She shrugged. "Okay, I guess we take them. Dalton, point for now. I'll take rear. We'll swap out at rest breaks."

"Hooah. Onward."

The seven Urushu took the middle, but milled around, covering the flanks and chattering away.

Ak!tash was tall, possibly over seven feet, with a lumpy head and jaw and big joints. Wasn't that a symptom of giantism?

"Dan Who Speaks, do your spirits say we be friends now?"

"The spirits talk to the chief and Martin shaman. They decide. I hope we can be friends even if we don't visit."

"You are only ten," he held up fingers. "You should come our camp. You would be very good to stay."

"There is good and bad for staying, but your words are nice-nice and clever. Thank you."

Those cakes were awesome. Acorn flour and rice. Not as good as real bread, but damn, they needed to make those in the meantime. He did have the recipe.

"You show how your thunderspears work."

"Only the spirits and some shamans know that, Ak!tash." It was true to a point. He had no idea about alloys, chemistry or mechanics. Barker and Spencer would talk about those, and lock time, pressure curves, and other stuff. All he gathered was they might make flintlocks in this life, but not modern rifles.

Five hours later he was on point and they were in sight of the COB. He wasn't sure what to report to the LT over a couple of issues. He first wanted some modern food, as modern as their resources allowed, and a soak in the sweat lodge.

The east wall was started, covering about twenty feet. There were visibly fewer trees along the stream banks. That was reassuring.

"What's happened?" he asked. "Look at the COB."

The goat pen had changed. The sweat lodge looked different. There were a bunch of Neo men limping around, helping with the palisade.

"Hello!" he called.

"We see you," Alexander shouted back. Was that a bandage on her foot?

Dan led the patrol across the stepping stones and into camp.

They passed by where Spencer, Ortiz and Trinidad were digging and setting another fresh-trimmed trunk. The Neo men dragged logs and yes, several were bandaged. Had there been an attack?

Spencer turned and said, "Yeah, they tried to swarm us. We're okay, barring some flesh wounds. They took a beating. Go easy on the LT. He had it rough."

"Too much for him?"

Spencer tensed for a moment.

"No," he said with a wide-eyed stare. "It was not too rough for him. Seriously, just don't talk about it, okay?"

Okay, that was obviously taboo. Got it.

"Hooah. Where should the Urushu guests stay?"

Spencer pointed. "They can set up next to the wall and create a lean-to."

He translated briefly, and Ak!tash chose the wall next to the sweat lodge/smoke hut. They had their hides, and they piled some poles from the wood pile. It took them a few minutes.

"Are we feeding them or are they on their own?"

"They've fed us before and will be working. We have enough, I think. Barker? Can we feed the Urushu?"

"How many? Yes. I'll grab another haunch."

He explained that, and the rules of the camp, for Ak!tash. "You will eat with us, guests. Dump there. Wash there. It is our way. The others fought us but we defeated them."

He put off further questions and indicated the fire circle.

The wall was coming along fast. Those Neos were a useful addition. Also, with both groups here, possibly some issues could be worked out. Maybe.

As they entered the camp proper, Dalton said, "I must be insane. I smell bacon."

Barker said, "You do smell bacon. Also ham, smoked turkey, and smoked pork butt."

"How . . . ?"

"I chopped up a young wild pig from a few days ago, salted it, rubbed with honey, smoked in the smoke hut. I'm going to smoke some until it dries, as a test. We'll have something to last the winter."

"Honey?"

"Yeah, I found a hive and got a few stings even with Spencer's bug netting." He held up an arm with red spots on it. "But they weren't bad, and we're figuring out how to make them a new hive with some of the board and crap from Number Eight, and some stuff we split."

Dan asked, "Are we just in time?"

"You are just in time. Crisping up perfectly."

Everyone else piled in.

Atop the turret, Alexander said, "There better be some for me. Oglesby can pass it up."

Yes, he could. Was that an implied threat? He didn't think so. He was just closest. He handed up a board, being careful not to spill the sizzling slab of meat.

"Why are you first?" he asked.

"Because I've been waiting all day, and can't move."

Yeah, if her foot was bandaged like that, it was serious.

He accepted a piece for himself.

"What are the bits on it?"

Barker said, "I glazed it in more honey and butternuts, and fried it on the rock."

Dan took a bite. It was crunchy-sweet, salty, juicy, and exploded in his mouth.

"Oh, fuck me, that's good." Sweet, smoky, nutty and bacon, fucking bacon! It was too lean, and tough and chewy, but it was bacon.

The LT looked as if he were having sex. So did the others. Yeah, it was that good. The Urushu were wide-eyed and chattered excitedly.

He didn't need to hear all the words to know what they were saying.

"If we teach them how to make bacon, we'll gain a lot of brownie points."

Elliott said, "Barker, if we get back, I'm putting you in for a medal."

There were mumbling sounds all around, as everyone chewed and crunched, scarfing down the bacon.

Spencer said, "This is awesome, but a bit depressing."

Barker said, "Yeah, everything is. Reminds us of home."

"Not that. Well, yes, sort of. We know coffee and chocolate exist. All we have to do is walk to Africa, or get to the damned ocean and sail five thousand miles. Hot peppers, too. But we can't possibly develop proper grains in our lifetime. We'll never see bread, sugar, modern fruit."

Dan said, "We have bacon. Your argument is invalid."

Spencer shrugged. "And it's good bacon. But dammit, we need the lettuce, tomato and bread."

Barker said, "I'll settle for buttered mushrooms. Which we can do."

"Yeah, that's a good project."

"I guess that's mine," Caswell said. "We had rice cakes at their village, though. Now bacon. We may attain civilization yet."

"Rice cakes?"

"Rice and acorn flour, with salt and animal fat."

"That sounds . . . good."

Dan said, "We'll work on it. They agreed to help. I got the recipe, as you ordered."

Ortiz moved up to the top watch. Alexander came down gingerly.

"What happened?"

"Stabbed in the foot with a stone spear. My boot is probably trash for anything other than dry weather."

"Crap." There was obviously a story there. He hoped to hear it soon.

Spencer asked, "How are the prisoners looking, Ramon?"

"Eating their meat and not causing trouble. They're afraid of the big gun."

He wondered why Ortiz and Trinidad had tied them to logs. They could certainly untie the knots, or even cut the thongs with rocks, but it would take time. This was obviously to slow down any attack.

"Good. We need to remind them we have even bigger guns inside, if need be."

Dan said, "Once I work out some more lexicon, I can do that." Their language was a lot more complicated than the Urushu, who seemed to have only a couple of thousand total words.

"Where are they sleeping?" he asked.

Barker said, "They have the smoke hut, and we made it clear they don't come out except for the latrine, one at a time only."

The bacon was suddenly a little less tasty.

After dinner, Alexander showed off her new toy. She'd made what she called a drop spindle. It wasn't fast, but how it worked was pretty obvious. It did spin yarn. It was going to take a lot of such yarn to make any clothing. That, and they'd all have to take turns.

"Draw out the fibers, let them spin through your fingers at a steady rate until it's near the ground, but don't let it touch. Pick it up, wrap the yarn, set it here, and do another drop."

"How efficient is this?" he asked.

"We can expect it to be a full time job for someone eventually, shearing, retting plant fibers, washing, spinning. We have a loom in progress." She pointed at a rough frame. "Then the fabric has to be washed in strong urine, dyed if we wish, and washed and dried. Then we have to sew it."

"But you know how to do all that, yes?"

"So do I," Spencer said. "It's not that hard for the basics. But I have no idea how to weave twills and such. I always wanted to learn. I guess we have time."

She said, "You can do it slowly while on watch. It'll keep your hands busy and help you stay awake."

Trinidad asked, "So does our diplomatic party know how the Urushu are doing?"

Caswell said, "Largely intact. Few actually died. The women and surviving children are glad to be reunited. We're held in high regard."

"Do they want more from our spirits or magic?" he asked.

Dalton took lead. "They aren't really interested in our weapons or gear, actually. They want gifts, but they don't want to learn how to use them."

"How do you know that?"

"This time they weren't interested in our devices at all. It was sort of 'oh, neat, gotta go.' It's our magic and unless our spirits agree, they're not interested."

Dan said, "They put it that obviously our spirits were strong and should be abided. They asked about them. They did ask about a rifle, though."

Spencer said, "What did you tell them?"

"That the workings of our thunderspears are magic that only our wizards know. Which is true. I'm no chemist."

"What were the subjects of conversation, then?"

"Uh . . ."

Dalton said, "Since they asked, I told them about the scripture. I showed them my New Testament and explained the marks were drawings."

Spencer said, "Dude, not cool. At all."

Elliott said, "Anything like that should be avoided. We can't share that."

"Hell, Caswell was trying to teach them feminism. I figure they're smart enough to listen and decide what they need to know."

And here it came.

Caswell said, "I was teaching them that division of labor is useful, but doesn't have to be along gender lines."

"Oh, dammit," Spencer said.

Elliott held up a hand.

"Okay, we need diplomacy and calm thoughts, Sergeant Spencer." He turned. "Now, yes, if they ask, you can answer questions, vaguely, in context, in reference to yourself, and not as absolutes. I'm going to recommend against any specific scripture."

"Sir, from an ecclesiastical point of view, they're ignorant of the word of God. Their souls will be better with knowledge."

"I knew that's where you were going. I've been a lay aide for my church. But if you give them partial knowledge, you run the risk of them creating a creole religion, and expose them to potential punishment, since they are aware of the Word."

"I don't think God would hold that against them, sir."

"Probably not. In which case, their ignorance is fine, too. If God wanted them to know, he'd have arranged for it."

"Well, maybe he has."

"Maybe. But now is not the time." Dalton looked to protest, and Elliott raised a hand again. "No, that's an order. Caswell, what did you say?"

"Sir, I only said they should continue as they are, with people fitting the roles they do best in. I suggested one young man had fantastic visual color separation and would be great with berries and roots, among other things. In exchange, they showed me some more plants, including wild rice in the river."

"That sounds less dangerous, but we have no idea what effect any of this could have on our future."

Devereaux spoke up, "I think we're pretty well fucked on that, sir, pardon me, because of the damned trucks. But minimizing the rest is probably good."

Dalton said, "Respectfully, sir, we have to spend the rest of our lives here. I've accepted this."

"It seems probable, but we have nothing to base that on."

Dalton said, "I know when prayer is working, sir. It's working for this. We're here."

Spencer stood up and hurried away, and Dan didn't think it was to whiz.

Elliott said, "Until the year is up, we're calling that we're lost on deployment. You will please abide by SOP."

"Yes, sir." Dalton didn't sound happy, and he wasn't arguing, but yeah, the man talked about religion constantly. Dan had gotten an earful himself.

Elliott said, "Oglesby, how much did you translate for him?"

And here it came, round two.

Not looking at Dalton, he very carefully said, "Sir, with regard to your instructions, I told them we had numerous spirits, each of us picked our own, but once we had picked them we were bound to them, and couldn't change without a lot of meditation and purification. I said that the three of us had similar spirits that we saw in different lights, and that two of us here had completely different spirits altogether. But, that our spirits all commanded us to get along when we could. We are allowed to defend ourselves and others, and help the weak, but we should resolve things through strength and thought first."

Dalton said, "That's exactly what I said."

Dan said, "I did not translate any mention of God or Jesus, or any of the books. The conversation took most of an afternoon."

"But they asked questions back about Christ," Dalton said, looking confused.

"Yeah, I made those up. Sorry." He was sorry, a little. And embarrassed. But dammit, he'd been on the spot, and they'd all been briefed on this predeployment, and he'd had reminders of it at DLI.

"Bu—"

Alexander snickered up above.

Elliott said, "And I should have had the debrief in private. I'm sorry to everyone. So let's stick to what we worked out between us."

Caswell said, "They know other seasonal plants and are willing to help us find them. They can smoke meat for winter, and hunt fresh as well. They spoke about a few roots, but I gather they get mostly meat and a few gathered nuts. The rice is seasonal and takes a lot of wading. They put on fat in fall from fruit, because that's the best starch they get. I'm deducing that, of course, since they don't grasp biology."

"Good."

Barker said, "Indians used canoes and a beating stick to gather rice. We need a canoe."

"Beech bark?" Elliott asked. "I don't see much birch."

"Or pitch-soaked reeds, or hides."

Dan said, "They're willing to swap Doc's attention and more knowledge on building and tools for them doing labor here. I said we'd ask you. They also feel a debt over saving the women. Their greetings were . . . public and enthusiastic." Hell, three others had tried to molest him in the open.

Elliott said, "The labor is definitely useful. We can discuss that on our next swap."

Caswell said, "Sir, I took the liberty of saying they could bring up to three ill people in a day or so, and ten people to work."

The LT said, "Okay. We'll do it by ear, depending on what the spirits say. I think the spirits will be flighty and not allow it every day."

"They want to learn how to suture. They have a vague knowledge, but Doc's stitching is neater."

Devereaux said, "I'm not sure what they can do with bone slivers and sinew. But we can teach them to boil water."

Ortiz said, "Isn't modern procedure beyond them?"

Spencer said, "Boiled medical tools go back at least as far as Philip of Macedon."

"Interesting. I didn't see much of it in Africa."

"Yeah, and I don't know why that is. But it's not new."

"Well," Ortiz added, "It might help if I showed them animal techniques. Those are a little cruder than Doc's, but should work."

"Do both. That's fair enough."

Dan found himself licking his fingers and the tray. Damn. Bacon. Now where was the apple pie? But if there was rice, they might manage those awesome cakes, or pudding. Something.

There were apples for dessert, but no pie. Dammit, bacon deserved ice cream. But if they had milk, honey and ice, it was possible for next year.

That done, the Urushu went to relieve themselves in the stream, then retreated to their embassy.

"One more thing," Doc said as they left. "I hate to bring it up, but it won't get better."

Elliott asked, "Uh oh, what?"

Doc held up a flat Crest tube.

"This is the last of the toothpaste. I'm going to slice it open and I figure we get one good brushing each out of what's left."

Damn. One more link cut.

Everyone sighed, and got their brushes, which weren't going to last forever, but hopefully a few years.

Doc sliced the tube open, and yeah, there was just enough to dip into to make for one refreshing brushing.

He took two minutes, then more, going over his teeth again and again. He'd had minor tartar buildup already, that Doc had scraped off for him. This wasn't a good omen.

Then they were done. No one said anything, they just dispersed.

He didn't feel like hanging out with anyone else, so he sat by the fire. Bit by bit, they were becoming part of this time.

He stared at the embers for a while, until he saw movement. It was the Urushu returning.

"Dan," Ak!tash said in greeting, as he held up a leather-wrapped bundle. "You have not prepared bitter drink. I offer ours."

"What is 'bitter drink'?" he asked.

"From bitter leaves. Roasted, stewed, cooked, stewed again."

Whatever it was, the flakes smelled pungent. They weren't tea. They were sharp against the nose. Could they be proto-tea?

"Caswell," he called. "They have a plant drink. I need help."

"Hooah," she called, and arrived in a few moments.

As he asked questions, she sketched.

"The leaves look like this?" she asked, holding up a piece of bark with charcoal rubbed on it.

"Yes," Ak!tash agreed. "Those leaves."

"It's something like holly," she said. "I think some of the southern bands of Cherokee did that."

"Is it psychoactive?"

"No," she said. Then she called, "Sergeant Spencer, they have caffeine!"

"Fuck me, what?" he fairly bellowed. That was almost hilarious.

"They have a caffeine drink."

Ak!tash said, "If we drink now, we will wake until sun."

Spencer must have heard that as he arrived.

"Don't care, brew pot." He ran under the kitchen and started grasping for pots.

"Caswell, is there a metal pot here or do we use a canteen cup?"

"Use that."

"Will do."

In ten minutes, they had boiling water with a dark cloud of leaves in it. Ak!tash squatted while Spencer reclined in a seat, and used a finger to check temperature and quality of the mix.

"It is good," he said. "Please drink, for the behcawn."

"I will definitely drink to bacon," Spencer said. "Tell him thanks." He raised the cup carefully, spit on his fingers and wiped the rim to cool it slightly, and sipped.

A moment later he grimaced.

"Oh, shit, that's disgusting."

"Not good?"

"Bitter, sour, earthy tasting, charcoal, rope, nasty."

He sipped again anyway, and passed the cup to Ak!tash, who took a drink as a long, careful sip.

Two minutes later, Spencer said, "Oh, yeah, that's caffeine. I can add honey and berries and make it drinkable."

"So, you have coffee," Caswell said.

"I do *not* have coffee," Spencer insisted. "But I do have caffeine."

"Isn't there tea south of here, too?"

"Possibly. Trade goods or road trip." Spencer shook his head and said, "Goddamn, that's strong. Really strong. They weren't lying about seeing the sunrise."

Caswell said, "Hmm. That's interesting. I bet if they only use it scarcely it's almost a drug. Likely that makes it holier and more magical."

He said, "It is magical. I shall call it black magic."

"Hah!"

Spencer said, "Hey, Dan, are you up to helping Ramon for a bit? I'd like two on watch, especially since our guests don't like each other."

"Yeah, I can handle a couple of hours."

He wondered if that was to keep him away from the guest female.

"Good. I'm likely to be up all night as is. I'll wander when I can."

And even if it served other purposes, that definitely was part of the reason for the order.

CHAPTER 20

Felix Trinidad sat on guard, spinning wool and watching the barren landscape, along with ten Urushu moving logs under Spencer's direction. He felt much better as the remaining wall came along. That still left gaping holes along the stream bed, but with more wall and fewer trees, and the leaves off the ones remaining, they had better field of fire and visibility. The stream was uneven, and would slow intruders a bit.

It wasn't just the possible Neolithic response. It was that stampede, and the bear that had wandered through, and the lions who'd drunk from the stream right at the upper corner near the kitchen and sweat lodge.

The LT said he had a plan for bridging the stream. Though he still thought it would have been easier to put the wall on this side with a small people gate. But the fresh water and waste removal was a very good feature.

Looking to the future, they'd have better housing with shake roofs. He'd stayed in wood huts back home. He'd be comfortable enough here. Then he'd really want someone to be with. Losing your family was worse when you didn't acquire new relations.

But convincing the mates to live with them was one problem, then raising the kids to be more modern was another. Unless they organized a school, most of the modern knowledge would be lost, and make only a minor ripple in the development. They could make themselves reasonably comfortable for their life sentences. They couldn't change this world.

And he'd screwed up and made the yarn too thick again. He sighed, unspooled a section, rolled it between his fingers, re-wrapped, and continued.

If they ever did get back, he thought, he'd hunt down some of those "The simpler life was better" types in America and smash them in the face. They'd not last ten minutes in Bataan, and this was notably more backward.

Overhead, the flag snapped in the wind. He pulled up his gore-tex. It was getting much chillier. It wasn't bad here overall, but he was tropical, despite some time at Fort Lewis. They figured it was early December. It wasn't terrible, with daytime temperatures in the 50s, but that was cold when you were in them all day. Then at night it froze.

Had it been less than three months? They'd done a lot of work, undistracted by internet and TV. He wasn't sure it felt like home, but it did feel like a base.

He wasn't sure he *wanted* it to feel like home.

However, he could do without wolves and badgers ripping apart the bodies of the abandoned Neolithics. That was creepy and ugly. That they did it in daytime a couple of hundred meters from the camp was disturbing.

Spencer and Barker changed back to setting poles again, with Dalton and Ortiz and a bunch of natives.

He yelled down, "Hey, next time we need to drag the dead a bit farther away, hooah?"

Barker climbed up the rise at the bottom wall and looked.

"Holy fuck, yes."

"Want me to shoot or scare them off?"

Spencer also took a look, then the LT climbed up the ladder.

Elliott said, "No, not for now, they're . . . mostly done. Definitely next time, though. Then there's the ravens and buzzards."

"And ants," he said.

Martin Spencer was twitchy with the mixed camp. He expected the Neoliths to come back in supplication or force. They and the Urushu might fight each other, or the Neoliths might attack someone in rage or desperation.

Or if he was lucky, they might just run away.

But the burly little bastards were good at setting poles, and a couple of them had learned shovel and axe. They really liked the tools.

With Oglesby translating, they asked about the magic material.

"Heh. Simple steel. Tell them it's special ochre treated with magical fire and lots of prayer."

"That's actually pretty close, isn't it?"

"As close as I can get to explaining to a primitive with no modern terms. It almost feels like I'm giving scripture."

Oglesby said, "Well, I don't have many of their words myself. Their language is more structured than the Urushu, and that actually makes it harder. I'm using babytalk as it is."

"Hooah."

One of the badly wounded Neoliths died that night. His shoulder was too damaged, and he'd kept bleeding and possibly gotten infected.

Oglesby translated, "They want to carry him home, but aren't strong enough. They would like to grant us safe passage."

"Can they guarantee it?"

"No."

"Then no. But any who are fit to travel can do so, and either drag him on a hide or bring back five to help."

After some back and forth, two of them decided to limp their way home.

Trinidad said, "I'll overwatch them for about a mile. Just to make sure they're safe from predators."

"Are you sure?"

"Yes. Keep me covered from on top. I can run fast if I have to."

Martin knew he'd never have the courage to volunteer for that. He liked staying near the rest, still dreading a reversal that would leave him stranded.

"Stout man. Half a mile. It may help; it's a good gesture."

"Hooah."

That evening, a party of ten came back, and removed the body, as well as three well-eaten ones. Oglesby expressed that the spirits allowed and encouraged the fair treatment of brave warriors, and that exposure was considered honorable in these conditions. He didn't sell it well, but the Neoliths seemed scared of their magic weapons and weren't disposed to trouble. That was apparently why they hadn't come back yet.

The walking prisoners all went with them. Two with bad legs stayed, and two fit ones stayed with them. They worked as requested and didn't cause trouble. They built their own wickiup, very similar to the Urushu one built near it, just outside the east wall. Hell, it was similar to the Lapp tents, the tepee, and a dozen other cultures. Pile up sticks, wrap in hide.

By the end of the week, the wall was done.

Elliott seemed much stronger. He'd been quiet and alone for a couple of days, but apparently the challenge of bridging the stream got his brain moving. As to the mercy killings, he'd never mention it to anyone. Even the three who came back didn't have details, though he suspected Caswell and Dalton had guessed. Oglesby he wasn't sure about.

"What I want to do," Elliott said, pointing at his laptop screen, "is drag two good-sized logs across, touching. We'll dig them in and set them with a box of rocks. That might need more timber as reinforcement. I want it about eighteen inches above the water. We'll bevel the bottom of the pickets and set them through. If it looks like we'll get flooding, we'll cut a hole above the cross timbers, too. But in both cases, small enough it's hard for someone or some beast to crawl under."

"A box culvert."

"Exactly."

"You could have just said that, sir," he grinned. "But the explanation does help. What about a bridge right behind it, as a firing platform?"

"Yes, that's on the blueprint, too," Elliott said, pointing at his screen.

"Hooah, sir. I'll get the peasants working."

The Urushu changed every couple of days. They built a second hide-covered wickiup inside the wall but across the stream, and it became a de facto embassy. Alexander and Caswell moved into the tepee with the men. It made sense with the chill anyway. That freed up their hooch as a recovery room for anyone Doc worked on.

Devereaux fixed a couple of broken bones, occasional animal tramplings, infected cuts, torn nails. The Urushu took a beating even with thrown spears. But they appreciated the help, and brought hides, edibles and game.

Martin and Barker moved more into supervision, with Dalton, Oglesby and Ortiz handling labor with the locals. He'd select trees and rocks, they'd work, he'd help. Up above, Alexander covered everyone as her foot healed, switching off with Trinidad.

"This amuses me, man," Felix said. "And ought to piss me off."

"What?"

"I went back fifteen thousand years to become a TCN Escort."

"Yeah. That you did. Better than being a corpse."

Martin Spencer stood and stretched his spine. The work never stopped. Nor was it easier in gore-tex and liner.

There was regular frost on the ground before the wall was finished, but it was ready for winter. The digging was a little harder, but the post holes were neater from the chill. Another small gate was installed, big enough for a person with a bundle of stuff, or an animal.

It was 12 December when the last pile dropped into a gap, then had to be hammered and shoved and pried into place.

"Watch fingers!" he shouted, as Trinidad stood atop the scaffolding and stamped it in place. It slid inch by inch until flush.

Then Trinidad tied it in place with bark, and hammered a peg in to set it, as Barker did the same near the ground. Dalton had two of the Neoliths shovel dirt into the hole and stamp it down.

They stood back.

The wooden culvert spanned the stream. The wall followed it, and now connected to the far side, at uphill and downhill. They had a solid defense on four sides. They were done.

Elliott said, "We'll want to build a diversion in front of the main gate so no one can charge through. Just a few feet. Zigzag."

Done, until the next stage. Then the next . . .

"Can it wait until springtime, sir? We need a shit ton of firewood and smoked food before it really gets cold." Snow was blowing from a gray sky.

"Yeah, I agree. Is that secret juice of yours good for a toast tonight?"

"It's consumable, sir, but it's sour. If you're used to muddy French wines, it's drinkable. For most people, it's rough. But I don't mind decanting some."

"What proof?"

"Probably like any strong wine. Fifteen to twenty."

"Let's do it."

"Hooah, sir. And we have ribs for dinner. It calls for beer, but we'll see what we can do."

He raised his voice, "Dog off, motherfuckers, it's chow time. We're done."

Everyone stretched, cheered, smiled, shook hands and wiped brows. You could overheat even in winter.

The cooler was in the back of the smoke hut, out of sight, though Barker knew it existed. As everyone gathered around the fire, he went to get it.

"You're pulling it?" Barker asked.

"I am. Celebration."

"Awesome."

He carried the cooler out on his shoulder, and set it down carefully to avoid disturbing sediment.

"This is something I've been working on," he said.

Alexander said, "Oh, my gods, is that beer?"

"Wine."

Ortiz said, "Wine?"

Then everyone was talking about it. So much for a dramatic presentation.

"Well, it's a mixed fruit wine. The local fruit is quite tart, and so is this. But it's safe to drink and it's alcoholic."

"Are we serving the Urushu?" There were three in camp. One lightly injured, two escorts.

"If they wish. They can share a cup, or do they have their own?"

"Carved wooden bowls."

"Bring them out."

Caswell had taken it on herself to learn a few words, and went to get them. The one limped slightly, supported by the others, and joined them at the fire.

Martin unscrewed the lid carefully, and Barker handed him a canteen cup. He lowered it, let it fill, and started pouring as everyone ran up to shove cups at him.

One cup each shouldn't be too debilitating, and he wasn't going to serve Oglesby, up top, until his shift was done.

Everyone else being served, he raised his canteen cup and said, "To Lieutenant Elliott for his design. To Barker, and, I guess, me for heading up the operation. To the rest of us for laboring on it. And to our guests, for invaluable help." He tilted his cup in toast to them, made eye contact, and sipped.

It was tart, sour, cool in temperature but warm in sensation, and full of sediment. He wasn't a heavy drinker but no lightweight. Two swallows in, though, he could feel the buzz.

Dalton said, "Dude . . . Sergeant . . . hot damn, this is good."

"It's passable."

"Given you had nothing to work with, it's good."

"Thanks. Well, if anyone wants to consecrate a little in a bottle, you can use it for Communion."

Ortiz said, "Thank you. That's very decent of you."

"Not a problem. Alexander, do you need a little for ritual?"

"A little. Yes. And a little more." She held out her cup. She was smiling and a bit loopy.

The Urushu seemed to know it was an intoxicant, and grinned and cheered. He knew they smoked a couple of things, and used mushrooms. There was some kind of plant fungus they used as well, but mostly the shaman types. He had no idea if they had beer or wine, but they were willing to join in the ritual and seemed appreciative of being included. And they had caffeine.

Elliott said, "We'll still need sentries. Animals are mostly excluded, though wolves could get in under the culverts or gates. We have hostiles, and even if we work things out I don't trust them."

There were "Hooah"s of agreement.

"But this is a hell of a lot more secure. You all did well. Thank you."

Spencer took that opportunity to say, "Now we need smoked meat, dried fruit and lots of firewood to last the winter. Looks like we'll be stuck in the tepee. In spring we can work on cabins."

He served a second cup each. They were big cups, and everyone was well-tipsy or fuzzy by the time it was done. That would leave enough for Christmas, and he'd top the batch off with whatever they had to stretch it.

It would be nice to make some barrels and work on bigger batches of both wine and beer. Eventually. For now he was going to sleep.

He'd just ignore the pain in his guts that the acidic beverage exacerbated.

And take a hot wash.

Bob Barker was glad to be along to help this group. He'd rather not be here, but since he was, at least everyone pitched in. What they didn't know about food, though, would kill them. If it weren't for Caswell, he'd be doing nothing but food prep.

Some of what he wanted would have to wait until next year. He'd not had time to look for rice, for example. He did have some cattail flour, made from both heads and stalks. Now he heard there was, in fact, rice here. He wanted to work out a trade deal on that.

While warming up sidemeat for breakfast, he heard Alexander behind the tepee.

"*Good* Cal!"

"What?" he asked.

The cat came trotting into camp, head high, holding a kid in his jaws, its neck snapped. This he delivered to the front of the women's hut.

"I think he likes you," Ortiz said.

"He can hunt!" she exclaimed. "He's healed. Well, get it gutted. I'd say drag the liver through salt, wave it over the hot fire, and let him have it as his share."

Ortiz cut the throat over the pudding pot, zipped the abdomen, pinched and pulled the guts and tossed them into the waste basket, and started pulling out organs. He was pretty good with animals, Bob reminded himself. The group wasn't entirely reliant on him and Caswell.

Cal came over and nosed around, inspecting the proceedings. Alexander pulled the scorched, crumbly liver off the rock and held it out for him to sniff.

It took only a moment for him to decide it was some kind of feline candy, and bat the chunk from her fingers. He dove on it and guzzled it down, then came back for more.

He purred in a loud rumble, and seemed to be comfortable with people nearby, as long as they didn't touch him.

That was awesome. They had a mascot, and he was a hunting little beast. Hopefully he'd get tame enough to pet. It would be nice to have something warm to cuddle occasionally.

Spencer dragged kid tenderloin through salt and spice, let it sizzle on the rock, then picked it up and started chewing.

"We should keep this cat," he said.

"That'll taste better after it ages. We should save it for dinner."

"Okay. I wish it was fat enough for gyros."

"Next year. Which brings up what I was thinking. I want to trade with the Urushu. Give them some bacon and if you don't mind, some wine. Get some rice for the winter. What do you think, LT?"

"God knows I could use a slice of toast," he said. "If we can spare it, go ahead. But cut a good deal. It's bacon, man!"

"Yeah. Oglesby, can you help?"

"Sure. Those rice cakes were good. Do you want the recipe, too?"

That would give them two recipes for cakes. A good start.

"Eventually. Tell them we want to gift them a joint of bacon, and would like to get some rice."

Oglesby jabbered to the Urushu, who pointed and gestured and made enveloping motions. It had something to do with quantities.

He noticed they had loose moccasins on their feet, fur wrappings on their lower legs, longer breechcloth/kilts, and longer shoulder wraps. One of them pulled on a conical fur hat. The clothing was very crude, but certainly warm. They were gearing up for winter, too.

They agreed on a backpack full of rice, which seemed a decent deal. They'd need a couple more. He wanted to lay in supplies fast. It was sprinkling snow again.

"I want to get some birds, since they seem to have traps. Wish we could have traded earlier, but first we had to have something we could trade."

"They're curious about the cat," Oglesby said.

Alexander said, "If it won't freak them out, tell them I'm a witch and can sometimes—stress the *sometimes*—make animals respond."

Dalton said, "So, I can't talk about Christ, but she can talk about being a witch. Got it."

"I'm not offering to teach them anything or conduct any rituals," she said. "It just explains the cat."

Caswell was there, too.

"There's a difference between saying you have a belief, and trying to bring others to yours. She's not offering to teach them how to domesticate anything."

"She might as well call herself the shaman. But I'm not allowed to discuss salvation."

"With good reason. As soon as men decided fighting was the way to settle problems, and went all brute strength, patriarchy started and equality took a bite it's still recovering from."

Dalton said, "That's women's fault."

"What?"

Yeah, what? This needed popcorn. Damn, he missed popcorn.

"Women do the agriculture. That meant more food, more people, but then they had to fight over the prime land as numbers grew. It's even referenced in Genesis. Adam and Eve had no problems in the Garden. It was when they left and had to work agriculture that things were tough. Look at who attacked us."

Spencer arrived at a run.

"Aaaand this conversation is over. Go to your corners," he ordered.

"But—"

"Go. Chop wood. Stand guard. Kill something edible. Move."

The parties wandered away, leaving the cat to crawl into the shadow of the women's hooch with a chunk of roasted kill. He seemed uninterested in politics. Smart cat.

The Urushu knew some argument had happened, but not what.

Oglesby said, "I told them it was a debate over what foods we should prepare for winter. They recommend smoked antelope. That ugly one that may be a saiga. They say liver and brains are very good together."

Ack.

Spencer said, "Yeah, I know that's ideal nutrition, but oh, my fucking God, no. I'll need to be starving before I do that. Actually, if we get to fat starvation, we'll gladly do that, and hate ourselves while we do it."

Bob said, "I've eaten stuff like that. It won't kill you. It isn't very interesting, though." At least as far as they knew, mad antelope disease wouldn't be a problem for them. He hoped.

"I can eat anything," Spencer said. "Doesn't mean I want to. I'm almost tempted to ask them for some of that weed they were smoking."

"Why don't you?"

"Drug use? Unknown drug use? And that would be the day we get back, and they'd drug test us to find out why we're telling such a bizarre story."

"Is it worth losing your pension to get home?"

With a shrug and thoughtful look, and a hand through his half-shaggy beard, Spencer said, "Well . . . yes. But I'd like to *not* become an addict. Cigarettes were bad enough."

"Yeah. How long had you smoked?"

"Age fifteen to twenty-three. I'm glad to be done with it."

"I'd like to carve a good peace pipe. But I think they've only got diluted pot and whatever that other stuff was. Anyhow, what do you have for today?"

Spencer said, "Firewood. I want to stack the wood a few feet out from the tent, all around. It'll act as wind break and as cover. Dalton, Trinidad, you start, with the Urushu. Everyone else fill in as duties allow."

"Hooah, Sergeant."

"Don't cut it too short. We can always feed logs in. Four feet is probably good. We'll stack it in tepees."

"Got it."

Alexander said, "I need some strips of goat hide. The cover is shrinking and drawing up at the base. I need to add a foot the entire way around, and patch some areas that split as they shrank. Can I get help?"

Spencer said, "Doc, Ortiz, can you do that?"

Bob said, "I can, too. There's a serious gap on my side. I want us to be warm. Then we need to stitch more ozan."

Spencer said, "Goddamn, it never ends. We'll have the locals help drag firewood and we'll cut."

Elliott asked, "You said eight cords, based on some event?"

"Yes, sir. It should be more than enough, since we're already six weeks into heating season. We have a cord or more at present, but we've been burning it as fast as we stack it."

"That's a lot of goddamned wood."

"Yup. Saw the thinner sections, break what we can, chop the rest. We'll have the Urushu help."

Bob said, "I need to start smoking more bacon, then smoking and drying every damned thing we can kill. Get me hardwood I can make chips from."

"Will do."

"Goddamnit!" Ortiz shouted.

"What?" Spencer asked, reaching for his carbine.

"The Urushu who left yesterday killed another goat and dragged it off. We really need to teach them about property rights."

Bob snickered. "You're going to need at least five thousand years for that. They really don't get it. From their point of view, these goats are close and easy, there are plenty of others, and of course good neighbors would share anyway."

Alexander said, "The first livestock raids."

Spencer said, "Yup. And in twelve thousand years, the Irish will turn it into a saga."

Bob turned back to the kitchen. He had cooking to do if they wanted dinner, and apparently, a crapton of firewood to chop.

He was going to have awesome pecs and shoulders before long.

CHAPTER 21

Winter had come up fast. The frost turned to snow the next morning. It blew and eddied around the kitchen, and they huddled on their chairs and benches.

Sean Elliott wished he knew more about the climate here. Everyone had cold weather gear, but would the weather be cold or arctic? How wet? What would they have to do? How would they stay busy?

"I know everyone wants to crawl back into the tent, but we've got to keep working. Gina's got the project list. We're managing."

Alexander had a spreadsheet of food, consumption, fuel, and date estimates. She kept the solar panels charging, though they were less effective this time of year.

Ortiz had organized the gathering of heaps of hay and greenery as fodder for the goats, and a windbreak for them that would protect two sides plus offer a bit of overhead. It was woven twigs, as they'd eat any actual thatch or green. The Urushu didn't seem to grasp the concept of keeping or shielding goats, so they just said it was some of Alexander's animal magic and they accepted that.

"I hope you don't mind us crediting her," he told Ortiz.

Ortiz shrugged. "As long as they goats are warm and we're eating, I'm cool with it. By the way, I think we can make pancakes, when we milk a goat. I don't know what to use for syrup or jam, though."

"Just a straight pancake sounds great." Who knew you could miss bread so much, and have too much meat for comfort? But they did. Bread was taken for granted in the modern world. When someone

327

said, "The greatest thing since sliced bread," they had no idea what a compliment they were offering.

One idea occurred to him. "I have a small but useful project," he said.

Dalton was first to reply, "Yes, LT?"

"I want a bunch of small rocks and gravel from the stream. We've already done inside and outside the tepee door. I want a walkway starting at the outhouse, working this way."

"When do you want it done?"

"I realize it won't happen all at once. I'd say get a good five feet done, and the rest can be a handful every time someone goes. And I know it's getting cold, but I don't want any stinking piss behind the tent. Everyone goes to the stream, hooah?"

"Hooah. Then let's get all hands on it for a half hour or so."

With shovels and boots they got a good pad laid out. Eventually he'd like to add slaked lime and sand and let it concretize.

"When we run out of gravel, we'll have to sift more from the stream, or crack slate and other rocks to use. That needs to go on the task list."

"Got it, sir," Alexander said.

It was sobering how much their productivity had increased with Urushu help. A few more bodies made that much difference. They'd make even more now, he realized, clutching his stinging hands. The wind was cold.

He really wanted a recon of the Neolithics, to keep an eye on them, but that posed a danger. So did not doing so, though. He thought back to the fight and having to slice the poor fuckers' throats. He didn't want to do that again.

"I'm detailing Oglesby and Trinidad to take a discreet look at the Neolithics. I want an intel assessment, and Oglesby's in case of any contact. I need one more experienced sneak to go along."

"Me," Spencer said.

Alexander said, "Photos, sir."

"You're sick list, Gina. I'd love to send you as well, but I want someone who's fit for backup or running."

"Yes, sir. I understand." She scowled in disappointment. Her foot was mostly healed, but she still limped. It was building up scar tissue, too.

"Why you, Spencer?"

"I can shoot, I can run, I can fight, and I'm one hell of a sneak. And I know what I'm looking at as far as their development. It should be me or Barker. We need his knowledge here."

That made sense. "Good case. Do it. Get any phone photos you can. Tell me what they're up to and what they're planning. Try to avoid contact. Can you overnight?"

"It'll be cold, but yes. We should be able to get in closer, and we have NVG."

Alexander said, "Take too many photos. I'll sort them later, and organize them for Trinidad. Make sure they're timestamped. Any notes you can record help."

"Hooah. So let's grab some goat jerky. Can we take one magazine each, sir?"

"Yes, with ten rounds each."

"Roger. We better not need more than that."

"Disengage if it's not safe. There's nothing I need to know about them worth sacrificing anyone, or more than a couple of rounds of ammo. And I'd rather be on good terms if we can, or at least neutral, not actively hostile."

"Roger that."

Felix was glad to finally be doing his job. He'd wanted to look at the various native settlements the whole time. That first visit to the Urushu had been a blast, watching their lifestyles, gestures, movements.

This was even a combat-related function now, with the hostile Neolithics.

They walked west, wrapped in gore-tex and hats. He wished for long underwear. It was frigid with the wind blasting through the cloth of his uniform.

The ground and grass crunched underfoot, and they had to avoid occasional frozen puddles. There hadn't been a lot of rain, but it had settled in low spots.

"I wonder if this would have been easier down by the river on the game paths," he said.

Spencer stopped in mid-step.

"Shit, son, you're right. It would have been, and that's pretty mu how everyone approaches us. We should have the gate on the down side, too. That way they're attacking uphill against it."

"Yeah."

"Hell, we can fix that next year or the year after. Gah."

Oglesby said, "It's all work, all the time. Forever."

Spencer said, "Interspersed with movies, music and masturbation."

"No shit," Oglesby said as he threw a chunk of stick. "We need women."

"Yeah, but some of us are still missing our families. They're not dead, just not born yet. Somewhere they exist. I . . . dunno."

They were silent for a while, moving over the terrain, stopping to whiz, then continuing. It was cold and was going to be a short day.

Spencer said, "I want to head uphill and possibly around. It's unlikely they'll expect us from the far side."

That was a longer hike, but made sense.

"Probably. Are we going to look first?"

"First, last and always. Have you done any infiltration exercises, or hunting?"

He shrugged and grinned. "PI, man. You learn to be quiet around some of the toughs."

Spencer nodded. "Roger. Oglesby?"

"Not really. I went hunting once and didn't spook anything."

"What were you hunting?"

"Rabbits."

"That's pretty good. Do you mind hanging back and covering us if need be?"

"Sure."

"We want to get Trinidad in close."

Felix said, "Actually, I can do a lot of it from photos. Close visuals a nice plus for context and possible HUMINT."

Spencer actually seemed to listen to him, which was cool.

"we want to get them in daylight, or wait for night?"

id, "People will be around in daylight. At night we can get look at resources."

ut remember they have dogs."

int. "Yeah, we'll need to avoid spooking them.

n the open side, or else we stay uphill."

I'm more concerned about lions in daytime and

He shrugged. It wasn't going to be easy.

Spencer eased into a crouch, then down behind scrub, without disturbing it much. Felix followed, Oglesby was just behind, moving slightly aside to avoid bunching up too much. They were about two meters apart each.

"See something?"

Spencer said, "No, I just want to make sure we don't get seen. We're within two miles. It gets slower from here." He raised his rifle and sighted through a large optic that probably wasn't issue.

"Hooah."

After scanning with the glass, Spencer said, "Okay, let me know if you see anything, and when you want to take over. Let's move cautiously, avoid making silhouettes or bunching up, and head for that rock crop over there."

From brush to rock to brush again, they moved in closer. At each hide they waited several minutes and looked around for possible hunting parties.

"Didn't the Urushu mostly hunt in the woods?"

He replied, "Yes, that's probably easier with spears."

"I won't ask how you know that. What about with the bows?"

"They could do open ground, too, but it's easier to hide and corral something in woods."

Spencer nodded. "I only ever used mine on targets."

They got within a half mile, and Spencer said, "I want to chicken out and stay here for a while."

"Okay. Makes sense."

Spencer was tall, but slid easily under the bush and disappeared in shadow. He reclined, looked quite comfortable, and raised his rifle again.

Lowering it, he said, "Looks good. The hunters seem to be sticking to the woods. A couple of our casualties are still limping."

"Am I correct they're all wearing pants and coats?"

"They seem to have leather leggings belted on, and tunics. Leather hats. They're wearing a lot of leather. Want a SALUTE report?"

"It wouldn't hurt if you want to log one."

"My phone doesn't record. Does yours?"

"Sure, here."

Spencer fumbled with it, snapped a photo, and started recording. "Neolith camp. Estimate three five adult males, two five adult females.

Most of the females are taller, suggesting Urushu. Common daytime activity including preparing meals and scraping hides. Visible weapons include spears and light bows, probably under four zero pounds draw." He ended the report and handed the phone back.

"How did I do?"

"You didn't mention the pen of six dogs, the animal pens with goats, antelope and birds with cropped wings. They've cleared an area for farming. They have different fish traps from the Urushu. They're working much more together and under direction. They're more industrious overall. I see a large pit that might contain fruit. They've built quite a bit more than Gina saw in her photos two weeks ago."

"And that's why you're the expert. Anything, Oglesby?"

"It's definitely expanded. I think they've added more huts, too. Those are cruder than the Urushu, actually."

"They probably had seasonal migrations back home. Huts in a couple of locations. I think it may be supposed to get colder again in their time, and smaller huts hold heat better. Or it could be that more work on herding and farming means less time building."

Felix said, "They've built up that wall, and they have all those drying frames for food. They're smoking a lot of fish very fast."

Spencer asked, "Those small mounds, are those burials for the dead they dragged back?"

"I think so."

Oglesby said, "Can't blame them for preparing for winter."

Felix said, "They seem to have food covered, and a source for hides. Fuel isn't a problem. They're short of women. Either they have to double up, bunk with men, or they'll be aggressively looking for more. They want at least one female each, ideally. These don't seem to be the same tribe as was here. I think they found others."

"They've done that once already. This doesn't makes sense. They seem to have been a hunting party. Few women. But they act like they have proto-herding and proto-agriculture."

"They didn't have those?"

Spencer said, "That area's now under ocean. We don't know. Farming had started in the Fertile Crescent, but it took quite some time to reach up there."

Oglesby asked, "Is it farming supplemented with hunting like the Native Americans?"

"Must be. They could have been after something big. Buffalo or mammoth. Oglesby, what time of year was it for them?"

"When they came through? I gather it was a similar season. They didn't say, but didn't mention it. Would they have mammoths if they're later than us?"

"Farther north, there are mammoths right now. I think they might still exist then. If not, a large, all-male group would be hunting something else large. Aurochs at least, and planning to carry them back in chunks. Buffalo. Something."

Spencer asked, "Do you see any signs of baskets?"

Felix scanned with the scope. "I see a couple, and a fishing net, if that is similar." The baskets were being used to carry fish from the drying fire to a storage hut.

"That's crochet rather than weaving. We guess that women did work like that while men were hunting, but we don't know. It could have been more egalitarian."

Oglesby said, "Well, that will make Sergeant Caswell happy."

"Actually it would make me happy. It means they won't be desperate for women to fill in positions."

Felix said, "If they want women, they aren't much of a threat to us." Although they seemed to really like blondes and redheads.

"No, but they may like our location. It's not ideal for gathering, but it's pretty good for ranching or farming. We also have that awesome wall."

He nodded. "I'm also concerned that they haven't been back in violence or peace. Ignoring us is not what I'd expect."

"Yeah. They'll be back at some point."

Felix said, "I think that's all I need. Are we leaving now, or overnighting?"

Spencer said, "It's cold. We can overnight, but we can't have a fire. But we could get closer with night vision. Will getting closer help?"

"Not especially. They've got a lightly walled village, plenty of resources except women, which they're developing fast, and we know they can be aggressive."

He summarized out loud for their benefit, and to help him remember as he took photos. "Two meter separation between huts. Probably very flammable, since they're grass-lined and supported with sticks. They seem to have two adults per dwelling and few children. I think I've counted ten, maybe twelve. That means they only captured women, or killed children. I'd bet the first. The camp is mostly soft targets. The wall is close cover only. They don't seem to keep a regular watch, but do remain armed with bows and spears nearby. I don't see any temple or centerpiece, but I do see a probable head man, in that hut to the north. They all seem reasonably well fed."

Something struck him.

"Oh . . . I don't see any older people. No one infirm needing support. The Urushu do that. So either none came with them or they got rid of any locals, or both. They're staying close to the camp as it gets dark, and the terrain wear doesn't suggest a lot of travel outside the penned areas."

Spencer said, "And I saw all that, except the old people, but didn't note most of it. Thanks very much."

Oglesby asked, "Will they be herding on our plains next year?"

"Likely. We'll need some diplomacy come spring."

Spencer said, "Then if you're done, let's slide out and head back. We can move to a run once we're over that ridge."

Oglesby said, "We have lions."

Felix looked over his shoulder.

"Oh, *tangina*," he swore.

It was a lioness with two half-grown cubs. It was weird to see them in a cold climate, but they did have fur coats.

Spencer said, "Okay, carefully, get guns on them. If you have to shoot, make sure you hit the goddamn face. A lot."

"They're awful close to a settlement."

"Well out of spear range, and the female prey attract male prey. They're not going to be afraid."

"I am," he said. He was shaking and wanted to piss badly.

"Okay, we're going to walk out slowly, stand up and be as big as possible. Watch your thighs. Armor helps with the torso, but our legs are exposed. We're going to spread up as wide as we can, move toward them and spread out slightly so we have a good field of fire. They should decide we're too many and too big to mess with. Otherwise, we shoot if they charge."

Felix said, "They may squat down like a cat about to pounce."

"Yeah, that," agreed Spencer.

The lioness didn't seem sure how to respond. The men stood, stood tall, stepped apart, and following Spencer's lead, raised an arm up high. She hesitated, stepping back and forth, darting but not pouncing.

Then one of the cubs ducked down low.

Spencer hopped forward over a hummock and kicked it hard in the head, just under the ear.

It snarled, half-roared, batted and knocked his foot so he danced to stay upright, but he'd kicked it a good one. Shaking its head, it backed away.

Mother let the cubs precede her, gave one last snarl over her shoulder, and departed.

"That was close. I was afraid if we shot the kitten, mama would freak out."

Distant shouts came from below.

"Well, shit, man, what do we do now?"

Spencer said, "Smile and wave, boys, and start walking."

The Neolithic men did send a small war band of a half dozen. They jogged rather than ran, and were slowly catching up.

"One hundred yards?" he asked.

Spencer said, "Yeah. Easy shooting range. We'll drop one if they do."

"*Tanga.*"

"Eh?"

"Fools. They should have learned by now."

"Conditioned response. Protect the territory."

"Should we jog, too?"

"No, we're not fighting, we're walking. It's up to them if they want a fight. We're not being chased off, because we're not hostile."

Oglesby said, "Ookay."

"Can you tell what they're saying?"

"Not really. I'm sure it's 'Stop, you fuckers,' given tone and context."

"Keep listening."

Felix said, "They're close to a hundred meters."

"Spears cocked?"

"No, over their shoulders."

"We're almost a mile out. Anything, Oglesby?"

"I think I hear 'magic' or 'shaman.'"

"Hostile or demanding or requesting?"

"I don't think they're about to attack."

"Okay, let's talk. Turning."

The three faced the incoming Neolithics.

The men carried their spears carefully, butt-first over their shoulders. That was easier to deploy than the other way. Three had clubs as well. The other three had bows.

Oglesby said, "They want to know why we're here."

"Give them a polite greeting, tell them we were looking for lions and bears. We plan to keep them like dogs."

Felix smiled carefully.

"That's inspired," he said.

"Thank you."

Oglesby translated.

"They say they don't want us around here. It's phrased as a request. It doesn't feel neutral. But I can't tell which of us is supposed to be subordinate."

"Ask them if . . . wait, say we don't want to intrude. Would they like us to bring them a lion for their camp?"

Felix said, "What if they say yes?"

"We fake it."

The animated back and forth suggested they did not want a pet lion.

Oglesby confirmed it. "They're being polite now. They don't need a lion. It's a kind offer."

"Then tell them we're moving on."

"They offered what I think are some diplomatic courtesies."

"Keep an eye out as we leave. And I'm glad we're wearing armor, but it won't protect your thighs from them, either."

"Hooah."

The Neoliths watched coolly as they strode away.

Trinidad kept pace. He faked looking at some gear to get a peripheral glance back.

"They're outside a hundred meters. We should be safe."

"Good," he heard Spencer reply. The man visibly deflated.

"Worried?"

"Yes. I don't seem to have a problem during an incident. I shake like hell afterward."

Oglesby said, "It's almost dark."

"Yeah. Watch for wolves, and watch for obstacles."

It was quite dark as they reached recognizable landmarks.

"Okay, do we call in, flash a light, or wait for them to ID us?"

"I say call. We don't want to give any intel away, if they're following us."

Spencer shouted, "Ho, Bedrock!"

Shortly, Alexander replied, "Who are you calling 'ho'?"

"Can you see us?"

"Yes. Gate will be waiting. Antelope stew for dinner, if there's any left."

"Hooah!"

Ten minutes later they were inside and near the fire. It felt good to not be in the wind, and to have radiant heat.

He debriefed the lieutenant quickly but completely. "So, not a likely threat to us, but probably to the Urushu or other Paleo people. They'll want women, possibly slaves. They are seriously preparing for cold, though."

Spencer said, "Eight Point Two Kiloyear Event. But I can't recall if that's BP or BC. Nor how long it lasted. It's possible they were close enough to that to feel it."

Elliott asked, "What was it?"

"Temperature crash, happened in a couple of generations. Lasted hundreds of years if not a couple of thousand."

The LT looked confused. "I thought it was called something else?"

Spencer explained at length. "No, first we get the Younger Dryas, then it gets warmer again, then we get the Eight Point Two Kiloyear Event, then it gets warmer still, then another freeze around the Roman times, then warmer, then the Little Ice Age, then our time. There are lots of these cycles."

Elliott said, "Wow. Well, we know we need to be ready for winter. We'll keep at it."

"Hooah."

CHAPTER 22

Martin Spencer wrapped up tighter in his parka, and rubbed his itching ankles. It was goddamned cold.

Three days straight they'd been in the tepee, with occasional brave forays for firewood. They had meat in the tent, but they'd need more soon.

Winter moved fast. Temperature had gone from a freezing-to-50 rang, to a 15-to-40 range in a couple of weeks. Now here they were at subzero.

Eight cords had sounded like a lot of wood. He'd been prepared to be the butt of jokes for overprepping. Now he wasn't sure eight cords would be enough. It was midwinter, close enough, and they'd gone through a cord in the last week. It might get chilly. Any warm days were going to be devoted to getting more wood.

He looked up at a shuffling noise, then looked away. By the dim, flickering light of fire, iPod screens, and LEDs, he saw Caswell relieving herself in a bottle. He'd discreetly watched once, just because the mechanics were interesting. He felt rather embarrassed at having done so, and now, it was just background. It was easy to see why the Urushu had no real body modesty. Deep winter wasn't conducive to it.

Cabin fever had set in, then gone. Everyone lay about, listening to iPods or watching tablets and doing not much of anything. He'd watched every Clint Eastwood movie twice, including *Bridges of Madison County* and *In the Line of Fire*, though Rene Russo was hot.

Actually, he'd watched so many movies in the last three months he couldn't stand to look at a screen. He hated reading off screens and hadn't brought any e-books, and his half-dozen paperbacks were completely read and falling apart.

They'd bullshitted all the bull they could shit, and lay about in "hurry up and wait" mode. Snow helped insulate the west side of the tepee, and the howling wind was poor company. There was no established sleep cycle and no PT.

Even the cat had crawled inside somehow, and huddled at the foot of Gina's bedding. He really liked the thick fabric, and settled down on it, probably with fleas, but hey, he was a mascot. He would almost let people touch him, as long as they held out food. He might get domesticated yet, since everyone was trying to coax him. Except he'd pissed on several poles to mark them, and even after they'd been rubbed with brains and ash, the smell lingered.

Worse than the malaise was guard duty, and he was on in an hour. They were on in pairs around the clock now, because no one was out otherwise. Given the neighbors and who knew else might show up, it was reasonable, just effing cold. They'd agreed on buddies doing ten minutes up, ten minutes inside the vehicle, which was still colder than hell, but not windy. It kept them awake and alert.

There was no coffee. They had the black magic drink with honey and some dried fruit in it, that wasn't a tea and wasn't that interesting, except that it was hot and caffeinated. It helped.

He might have thirty more years in him, though fifteen was a better guess in this environment and lacking his medication. He almost hoped for less. Their other option was to relocate south into India, on foot, and see if they could find somewhere warmer.

Maybe next year they'd have solid wooden cabins. For now, they had a shared tent and lots of layers of clothes. Inside the tepee he wore full uniform and kept mostly in his sleeping bag, with bivvy cover, on his geek pad, that on a bed of turf and moss. Their beds ringed the central fire under a secondary ceiling that helped hold the heat. The tepee really was an effective tent.

Getting dressed for duty took a solid half hour. He wore two T-shirts, Multicam blouse, PT jacket, gore-tex with liner and a spare liner, his head wrap and an extra hat, all to go under his helmet with the jacket hood pulled over. He actually did have long johns, though only one pair. Some of the troops had to make do with PT pants under their uniform. He used two pairs of socks and wore the rain boots he'd never planned on needing, over PT shoes. He checked on his gloves and goggles. Their guess on temperature was -15F. Thank God Alexander had stitched those goathides into a tepee cover and done that late repair. Otherwise, all their wet weather and cold weather gear would still be covering it.

With all that he was ready to battle anyone or anything crazy enough to attack in this weather. It had happened in history. The younger troops bitched, and he hated it, but he agreed it was a necessary precaution.

Once done, he realized he needed to piss. The ozan, the tepee's liner, only allowed him to kneel, so he sighed, knelt down facing away from everyone, opened all those layers of clothing, and took a leak in a sport drink bottle. He was glad again he'd insisted they save everything. Later, he'd have to dump it outside without splashing anything.

Thirty more years like this. Or maybe fifteen if he was lucky. He felt sorry for the young kids. And what would they do when they were down to three of them, aging alone among scattered primitives? What about the last one?

"Out the door," he announced as a courtesy, before unbuttoning the inside flap and wiggling past the outside one. There would still be a draft.

It was black outside, too. Nighttime with cloud cover was black, even if it was snowing and the ground pale with accumulation.

The short track to the MRAPs was worn down to ice, given enough traction by blowing snow, and hard packed. It would be a slushy mess come spring, but it worked for now. He grabbed a handful of gravel from the pile near the latrine walk, and tossed it onto the path. Eventually that would build up. He'd created some of that with a hammer and a boulder. The labor never stopped.

This cold snap had lasted three days. Winter was likely to last another three months, and it would be late April or May before it got comfortable, he expected. Then it would likely be too hot again.

He clambered into the back of Number Nine, past the cloth set up as a windbreak, and nodded to Trinidad.

The Filipino said, "Nothing happened."

"Figures. Go rest. Take firewood in with you."

"Will do. Thanks."

"Ready to warm up, Ortiz?" he asked, as Trinidad wiggled through and out.

Ortiz squirmed down from the gun mount. "Yeah, man. This is bullshit, Sergeant."

"I largely agree," he said, as he knelt and climbed cautiously. He couldn't feel anything between the layers and cold. "But there are historical cases of people being attacked, and we know we have a potentially hostile group. So we need to."

"Yeah, they're all jerking off around the fire like we are."

"Most likely," he called down.

The wind bit his face even through the face wrap and goggles. He couldn't see more than the faintest of shadows.

"Have you done a visual?" he asked Ortiz.

"Just did. Panoscan. Nada, hermano."

"Shukran."

"Wilkommen, and screw you. Sergeant."

"Yeah, it sucks. But it's what it is. I feel sorry for you. I'll be dead in a couple of decades, but you've got fifty years ahead."

"I keep hoping we might get home. But we can't build a time machine."

"Nope."

"What was it? Some experiment? God? Side effect of an alien starship? Some asshole fucking around?"

"We'll never know." They had this discussion every couple of days. It was painful. They had no idea how, or why, or who. All they knew is they were here. And it was frigid.

Jenny Caswell didn't find Doc to be too much of a problem. The man largely kept to himself, and was busy treating everything from splinters to chest wounds all the time. He wasn't her type; he was a good guy on the whole, but even he had to make comments. It was ingrained into the culture.

He used something on his phone to crunch numbers and said, "Yes, definitely Solstice today. I'm calling it December twenty-first."

That afternoon, Alexander held a short ritual. She would have been alone, but that didn't seem fair, so Jenny stayed with her for it. Spencer was along, too. He wasn't religious, and he made a point of not showing up for the Christian services, so it was obvious his interest was in Alexander.

The ritual involved the fire, some salt, a sprig of evergreen on a log in the kitchen fire, a couple of prayers and then staring at the flames for a few minutes.

Finally, she said, "That's enough. Let's go back inside."

"Did you do everything you needed to?"

"Yes, my rituals are pretty short. Honestly, it was never really was that important to me. I did some stuff at Fort Meade, some during AT, but I generally didn't bother, and I could never get any Christian chaplains interested in supporting the idea. There were other pagans and Wiccans around, but it was almost impossible to get anything organized.

"But if we actually have reached our first Midwinter here, I wanted to do something for it."

"Yeah, that's important."

There was so much they could lose here, just from lethargy. They needed to keep their sanitation, manners, writing . . . but for what? They weren't going back, obviously.

Her adjusted rotation date was in May. What was it going to feel like when May came and went, and she was still in uniform, still in the Stone Age, and still outnumbered?

She might just want to move in with the Urushu and adapt to their lifestyle. She could be an elder for her knowledge, and arrange to be mostly left alone. With a good knife and martial arts training, she'd be well above them tactically, and could be an ambassador. With better knowledge of their language and customs, the soldiers might do better.

It was definitely something to consider.

Three days later was Christmas Eve. It was still cold. Jenny went with Barker as he plodded out to the kitchen, waving to Alexander and Ortiz on watch. The cold didn't bother her a lot, but it was cold all the time. The kitchen lean-to didn't stop much wind, though ice and snow had sealed the walls somewhat. The open end did little to stop anything. The snowy ground glowed brilliant white under partially clouded skies.

Bob had stashed several smoked goat carcasses here, once the temperature was reliably below freezing. They were in a cage off the ground, to protect from small pests. Large pests hopefully couldn't get into the camp at present.

Inside the structure, he pulled off his gloves and started untying the cage door.

"I'm going numb already," he said through his hood.

"I have it," she said. She unballed her hands, slid them into the glove fingers, pulled them out of her pockets and took over pulling at the knots.

Even attenuated by the frame the wind was cold right through to her ass. This was like McChord, without any modern conveniences. She put her hands back in her pockets to warm slightly.

"I wonder if we can do a straw bale house for next winter," she said, lips rubbery and stinging.

"Maybe, or a solid log cabin would be nice. We could even break it into small bunkies around the fire."

"Something," she said.

"I want to build a proper brick oven, too. If I have to eat the clay and crap the bricks myself."

They were mostly a good bunch of guys, she thought. If this had been an infantry patrol . . . she shuddered. Or some of the "allied" forces . . .

"Yes, a proper oven would make a difference. And build the cabin around it."

"Well, we have fire in the tepee for now. One frozen goat to thaw and roast." He lowered the stiff, gutted carcass to the ground and refastened the cage. "We're running out of salt, too."

"I wonder if the LT would consider sending a vehicle on a supply run."

"Maybe. Spencer still wants to take one apart for making a still and generator."

"The still is all his. I know more about electrical systems than he does."

"Yeah, he said so."

"I appreciate it. Despite being a misogynistic asshole, he's at least honest."

Bob didn't meet her eyes as he asked, "Jen, why do you think he's misogynistic?"

She didn't want to talk about it, but . . . she wanted to talk about it. "Oh, he can't help it. It's cultural for his generation. But he constantly assigns the men to one set of tasks and the women to others."

"He assigns the young men." Barker took his machete and lopped off the haunches of the goat. It was bled and frozen, but the bare white bone and gristle shining through the cuts made her wince. It was necessary to eat animals here. She still found it revolting to kill them and chop them up.

"But not the young women."

Barker said, "You are one of the two tech geeks we have. You and Alexander both. She's not in great shape. You're in good shape, but Dalton and Oglesby are a hell of a lot stronger. You know all these edible plants we need. And you're good at crafting useful furniture. That's as important as chopping logs."

"You're doing it, too. I'm strong enough."

"To haul logs?"

"As part of a team? Sure. I don't see any of you hauling one alone."

They didn't get it. It was all about physique. Prod a male soldier and the argument frequently degraded to "I can do more pushups."

"No, but the young bucks like it, they need to burn off the testosterone, and until we need the grunt, vet or translator, your skills are useful and theirs are best suited to hewing wood."

She shrugged. "It's entirely a cultural artifact. Like pairing us up with dominant males on meeting the natives. Then we find they're more flexible in their roles. Go back another hundred thousand years and there weren't any."

"And they squatted in caves or under brush, picking fleas and half starving."

"Until women developed agriculture. Brains over the brawn of hunting." She shivered in cold. It was cold enough for breath to frost, not mist.

"Yes, that was a good thing, so what's your complaint?"

"Because all of you look at me, longingly." She shivered again and kept her voice from cracking.

He sighed.

"Yes, you're the most attractive woman here. No, we know we can't have you unless you make the offer. Yes, you feature in people's fantasies. It's a very human thing."

"It's a male thing, and it's cultural. Here, the Urushu were a lot more neutral on the matter."

"Casual, yes. Not sure on neutral. And I'm not positive they've linked sex to children yet." He piled up the chopped pieces and rolled them in a hide kept for the purpose.

She really didn't have anyone to talk to about the subject. Few men could see it, fewer in the military, and Alexander was somewhat agreeable, but they didn't get along as friends.

"Look, the locals grab at everyone. They saw me as genetic material, if they saw anything. I'm not the only redhead you've seen."

"No, but you're the only one here. And those same urges still exist."

"I'd hope we'd develop past that."

Bob said, "That's going to take a long time. Another fifteen thousand years, maybe. And we'll have scorched goat in blood sauce. Let's wrap it up and get it inside."

"It had better warm up at least a bit next week. Only two more corpses left, and I didn't like goat even before I was a vegetarian. This is getting boring fast."

"Well, these should help." He reached into a wicker box and pulled out two birds. Pheasants.

"Yes. Thank you. A wing and a drumstick will be much better than haunch of goat, and I hate eating animals, and I hate this utterly nontechnological lifestyle, and I hate my hormones, and I hate being in the tent, and," she felt herself growl into a shriek. She choked back the sobs, because she wasn't going to have anyone playing the "There, there" game.

"It is what it is," he said. "It will get better as we can build more."

"We need a platoon, a company or squadron, an entire battalion. Ten people isn't enough, even with borrowed labor. And you know, I'd like to get laid myself, but it can't be you guys, and it sure as hell isn't going to be any of the others." Why was she telling him this? But she had to talk to someone. Alexander wasn't very social, and was a mean bitch. But they were all her brothers and sisters at this point, regardless.

She'd never been much of a drinker, but now she wished for a bottle of booze she could climb into and at least feel warm, until she felt nothing.

CHAPTER 23

Christmas, Rich Dalton thought. It was cold and white enough outside, and they had a fire. The ambience was good, and Jesus was Lord. It was good to remember that, no matter what happened. Trust in God, live life the best it could be, work hard, and in the end, it would be worth it.

Barker had the bird mostly cooked. There was a brief break in the watch, so everyone was inside. The tent was lit with an LED light hanging from a cord just off-center to avoid heat from the fire. It rotated a bit now and then, setting odd shadows in motion.

He looked around and saw the LT was awake, who nodded to him. He scanned the tent and saw everyone was at least mostly conscious.

"Attention, please," he said.

Everyone turned to face him, though it took Ortiz a few moments to look up from his tablet. Trinidad had to whack him. Apparently his headset volume was pretty high.

"It's Christmas morning. I plan to have a brief devotional over here, and some carols. Sergeant Barker has cooked up something different that smells very tasty. So let's do it."

There was shuffling of sleeping bags next to him, and most of the rest walked around the fire circle. Spencer and Alexander conspicuously remained on the far side.

"Not going to join us?" he asked, and knew he probably shouldn't have.

Spencer said, "I'm good," and Alexander said, "I would strongly prefer not," with an expression that wasn't a snarl, but was negative.

347

Barker said, "I'm here," but sat closest to the fire and the meat.

"No problem," he said.

There was also some light from the small smoke hole above, some dim glow through scraped areas of the goat hide cover, and Spencer turned on one of his lights and dialed up the brightness, then down, so they were well-lit but not too bright.

He opened his Bible, but he needed no page for this. He looked around at the others.

"Thank you for joining me. It's great to be here, fed and warm, no matter what is happening outside. God has provided, and in exchange we work for our bread. Which I hope someday will actually be bread." There were chuckles.

"I guess I've learned to appreciate that no matter where on Earth one is, or when, God has provided. One has to look for it, think and determine how to get it, and work, but it's there. We have fuel, food, shelter and protection, but most of all, we have each other, and no matter what disagreements we have, we're family now. We've met other travelers, and their ways aren't ours, and we know we have to cooperate to make things work. Hopefully we can bring the others on board, by example. Some seem to know of God under a different aspect, and the rest we've tried to bring to Him, though perhaps that approach wasn't as well planned as it could be. And that was a lesson for me." There were a few more laughs and a bit of muttering. Yes, he'd screwed up.

"So with that out of the way," he said, and took a breath, then recited from memory:

"And there were in the same country shepherds abiding in the field, keeping watch over their flock by night.

"And, lo, the angel of the Lord came upon them, and the glory of the Lord shone round about them: and they were sore afraid.

"And the angel said unto them, 'Fear not: for, behold, I bring you good tidings of great joy, which shall be to all people. For unto you is born this day, in the city of David, a Savior, which is Christ the Lord . . .'"

Most knew some of the words, and Ortiz kept pace with him in Spanish. Caswell's voice was clear and in perfect unison with his own.

It didn't matter where they were. He felt a rush, a thrill, and it might be the Spirit itself, but whatever it was, he was full of joy and confidence.

". . . Glory to God in the highest, and on earth, peace, good will toward men."

They all felt it, and the LT had damp eyes, too.

"I see we all feel it. Thank you. Let us all take a moment in silence to pray as we choose."

He bowed his head and thought to himself. It didn't matter if they got home. This was home. It did matter that they lived the best lives they could. That was all. He did ask God to take care of his parents and James. He wished everyone here could be at peace and joyful. There really wasn't much else they needed, when it came down to it. All the trappings of civilization didn't make one a better person. Nor worse, but they weren't necessary.

"Okay, would anyone like to choose a carol to start with?"

A voice started loudly, and in reasonable tune, "Hark! The herald angels sing, glory to the newborn king. Peace on earth and mercy mild . . ."

And everyone joined in "God and sinners reconciled."

Sergeant Spencer, the proclaimed atheist, had led the hymn. Right with him in a very sweet voice was Alexander.

The song was powerful, moving, and it felt as if the tent shook.

"God Rest Ye, Merry Gentlemen," "O, Holy Night" and "Joy to the World" followed, with everyone in chorus, and if it was a little shaky on key, who cared? Dalton wasn't a great singer himself. Devereaux was pretty good, though.

As they finished, Barker said, "Okay, it's crispy field buzzard, in salt, with ground herbs."

Trinidad said, "It is pheasant, right?"

"Yeah, I'm being sarcastic. Here you go." He sliced off a crisp chunk of breast.

Dalton didn't care if it was hot. He wanted that wing. He grabbed it and pulled, and started chewing.

Tough. Very tough. Also too hot. The meat was stringy. But it wasn't goat or buffalo, and it was delicious, with salt and some of the green herbs rubbed on it before cooking. There was a faint pine scent, too.

Cooking on the rocks around the fire was an entire coil of pudding sausages. The cold made those welcome, and the seasoning wasn't bad, though he still didn't care much for the mustard taste. The spices were so limited. No pepper, not hot peppers, no curries. He no longer cared they were cooked in inside out goat intestines.

They all munched in silence for a few minutes, then resumed talking.

"The singing sounded great," Oglesby said. To Spencer he added, "I thought you were an atheist."

"I am," Spencer agreed. "Which doesn't change the fact that some Christmas carols are incredible compositions, moving, and fun to sing."

"Fair enough."

The old NCO smiled. "I need to keep saying it. Just because I don't believe in religion, doesn't mean I object. If it helps you deal with the world, then please, worship as you wish."

Alexander looked bothered and added, "I also like the music, but I actively dislike Christianity. But it's not my place to tell you what to believe, as long as you grant me the same courtesy. Just understand I'll be uncomfortable around it."

Dalton said, "I accept that, I just don't understand it. I mean, God is . . . sorry." He really didn't know how to respond.

Then he recalled a Muslim trying to explain Mohammed to him. He'd not only not appreciated it, he didn't understand why anyone would. He'd been polite and left as soon as he could.

It was like that.

Alexander said, "By the way, catch!" and tossed something. It snaked through the air and he caught it.

It was a long braided cord of goat hair in two colors, with beads knotted in.

She threw one at each of them.

"Thank you very much. What is it exactly?"

"It's a cord for retaining your knife or tool so you don't drop it in the snow."

Oglesby said, "I'll take six," and there were laughs.

Caswell slid a paper in front of him. It was a pencil sketch of him atop the MRAP on guard duty, and quite well done.

"Thank you also," he said. "That's a striking image." It was stark and simple, but had depth and shade. It did look like him, and captured the boredom and intensity of endlessly watching. She'd even caught the clouds and light from the setting sun.

"You're welcome," she said. "It was a great pose. And thanks for the service."

Barker had prepared the food, and also had a leather pouch for everyone, of soft goat hide.

"Medicine bag," he said. "For anything small and meaningful. They're good for rings, coins or such, and it'll go on your dogtags or belt."

Devereaux gave everyone a wristband braided of grass. Perhaps not useful, but intricately made and thoughtful. Ortiz had carved sticks into gnarled faces. Trinidad had peeled and shaped swagger sticks for the LT and Spencer. "If the British had them, you should, too." He'd chosen some beautifully grained wood. The rest each received a wooden monogram.

Oglesby had very neatly written out a sheet with primary words in Urushu and Neolithic, in phonetics. There was a copy for each of them, each in one of the plastic sleeves from the vehicles' logbooks.

Spencer held up a file and stone.

"I'll put a razor edge on anything you bring me. Within reason." He stared at his swagger stick and looked confused. Dalton laughed.

"And we have about two more gallons of hooch."

That was welcome.

The LT said, "I didn't have time to make anything. But I will be adding an extra pass day in for each of you this coming week and a half. I'll cover the supplemental time."

Dalton held up his package.

"I guess I hope you'll all be okay with this. I wrote out a brief Scripture for each of you, that I think applies. I hope no one will be offended." He'd thought long and hard on what verse would be best for each. He couldn't hope to do Medieval illumination, but he'd done his best to dress them up. Each was on a small slip they could easily put in that medicine bag, or toss in the fire when no one was looking.

Alexander accepted hers cautiously, and read it aloud.

"And if a stranger sojourn with thee in your land, ye shall not vex him. But the stranger that dwelleth with you shall be unto you as one born among you, and thou shalt love him as thyself; for ye were strangers in the land of Egypt: I am the LORD your God."

He was very nervous about it. While that seemed to be a sentiment to work between them, other parts of that chapter might offend her.

"Thank you," she said and smiled. "I think of you as the younger brother I never wanted."

Okay, that was funny, even if it was still sarcastic.

She added, "And I'd be happy to illuminate stuff for you. Though this linear style is very elegant."

"Glad you like it," he said.

The rest had been easy.

The LT said, "I hate to break up the party, but two people need to be on watch. I'll be one of them, so Barker can stay warm today. I'm afraid it's your turn, Dalton."

"Roger that, sir. I'll clothe up."

It was a day the Lord had made, and he would rejoice and be thankful in it, no matter the task.

Martin Spencer crawled back to his pallet. No doubt Dalton meant well, but being reminded that his real family wasn't here had not helped his mood.

He hoped the weather would clear soon. Snow wasn't bad, though it wet clothes eventually. Regular freezing temps were okay. This wind and frigid weather sucked.

And he had five pills left. In ten days, he was down to local treatment only. Bone meal or chalk, hope the calcium didn't trigger a heart attack, and hope it was enough to settle his guts.

People settled back in. Doc and Caswell were talking about something. Doc was Catholic, he recalled, as were Ortiz and Trinidad; Caswell Luteran. The LT was mildly religious. He wasn't. Alexander didn't seem to bother with much service. But what holy days did she have and would they translate? Oglesby was hard to define. Barker wasn't very observant.

He'd gone through all this before, he realized. He'd also been zoning on other thoughts, because an hour had passed. He spent a lot of time, too much, staring up at the goathide above him.

He could just see Alexander through a gap between walls. She was lying on her bag, reading something on her phone. Now was a good time.

In the bottom of his duffel, he'd found a package of MRE cocoa powder. He would enjoy it himself, but he knew she liked chocolate the way he liked coffee. He slid it slowly under the hanging poncho.

A moment later she twitched, shifted, and raised the fabric.

In a whisper, she asked, "Where did you get this?"

"It slipped to the bottom of my gear. Merry Christmas or Solstice or whatever."

She held it in both hands and stared at it. Her eyes were wet.

"I don't think I can take it."

"It's mine. I want you to have it."

"I feel like I should share it with everyone."

"You can. But it's yours. If you want to enjoy it, I won't say anything. Just kill the wrapper properly."

"Thank you," she said, her voice husky. "Do you want some?"

"No. Please." He wanted to mix it to a paste and lick it off her body. And he wasn't going to say that.

It was the last chocolate in their world, and it was out of an MRE pack. That was depressing all by itself. He turned away and hoped no one saw his face.

He sat up with the sleeping bag around his legs, picked up a knife and started sharpening it. It looked like Dalton's, though he and Trinidad each had the same Cold Steel SRK that showed up in the PX every couple of months. He'd just place it near the fire when done. People knew their own knives from the wear and feel.

A half hour later, he looked over to see Gina lying prone with her face over the pouch, very carefully spooning out a few grains at a time, desperate not to spill any. She ate it bit by bit, and spent most of an hour over something he remembered downing in under a minute, including time to mix it.

She laid the mostly empty package down, fumbled around until she pulled out a knife, and sliced the package very carefully. Then she licked the residue, with a melancholy expression. She used that tongue well, too. Dammit. He turned away again.

When done, she cut the package into several strips. They went into the little pouch she used for trash, to eventually be burned in the fire.

He was glad he could do that for her. He wished he could do something for all of them.

Hell, he wished he could wish them home.

It wasn't all bad. There were light and positive moments every day. But every day was a reminder that they had too few people and a complete severance from their world.

Dalton came over to retrieve his sharpened knife. By then, Martin had four of them honed and was working on a fifth. Gina's Ontario tanto was damned near a machete, and she had the Spyderco and her SOG Tool out as well. That left the small non-brand knife on her hip, the push dagger around her neck, the dagger in her boot and the RAT-7 on her body armor, off to the side, and that huge custom bayonet. She had good taste in knives, too.

Dalton said, "Thanks, Sergeant." He balanced the knife and checked the edge the wrong way—with his fingers. Most people did that.

"Mm." He decided not to lecture on blade safety.

Dalton stared at him and said, "You don't seem happy."

"Being reminded that my family won't be born for fifteen thousand years, so I can't even really mourn them being dead, because they don't actually exist? No, not really happy."

He hadn't meant to let that out, but there it was.

"Sorry," he said.

"No, I am," Dalton replied. "I'm still learning that everyone's different."

"Yeah. It was okay. I just wish it wasn't necessary, you know?"

"Right." Dalton let it hang, seeming embarrassed. But he'd apologized, so there wasn't really anything else to do.

"Thanks for sharpening it."

Martin said, "Not at all."

Dalton crouch-walked back to his slice of the tent.

"Gina," he asked, and she pulled the poncho aside again.

"Yes?"

"Want me to reshape the grip on this RAT Seven? It's a bit square. I can round the grip some with a file."

"Yes. Please." She seemed enthusiastic, then after swapping glances, went back to her movie. It looked like *Pirates of the Caribbean*.

He decided he'd have three mugs of sour, bitter, sedimenty wine and hope it numbed his brain.

CHAPTER 24

Gina Alexander was glad when it warmed up slightly around New Year's. It was still in the 20-40 Fahrenheit range, but that meant she could work the chargers in daylight, update calendars and sheets, charge batteries, chart wood consumption and food. It was also nice to be out of the tent. She stood in the truck and spun some more yarn between tapping keys, and that was warmer than sitting as well. In between each, she put gloves on or warmed her hands on the kitchen fire.

She had several balls of yarn at this point, enough to start crocheting blankets, which they'd need next year if not as soon as she got them done. Winter should be over by March, and actually seemed to be fairly short. Spencer recalled the era being "warmer and moister." Hopefully he was correct.

They were using ammo faster than they anticipated. Granted, some of that was to stock food for winter, but they really needed to get more animal pens and herding built up. Could they get on good enough terms with the Neoliths to buy some dogs in a couple of years? Then train them for herding?

They'd shot ninety-seven rounds hunting, eighty-two in the firefights, and a sixteen-round burst of 7.62mm. It wasn't much for a convoy, but there was no resupply. Continuing like this would run them out of ammo in under ten years.

Food was okay, they had a couple of weeks' worth handy, and would certainly hunt more in the meantime, or they could make an emergency march to the Urushu for help. It was great to have one set of nice neighbors. Firewood was lower than they should have. There wasn't much margin.

She sighed. It would be easy to sit here spinning all day, but they needed help with firewood. She stepped out, pulled up her hood, and headed for the bridge. *Over the stream and through the gate, to the decimated woods we go*, she thought.

Cal appeared from behind the tent. He'd killed something small and furry, and delivered it to the usual spot. She'd have to move that before it stunk or got squashed into the dirt.

It was reassuring to have wall all the way around. She'd spent too much time on COBs to be comfortable in open terrain. She'd joked about putting Hesco around her house when she got home. This was close.

What would her kids do when she didn't come home? Would they be reported dead or MIA? Would she be a heroic figure for them? Would Blake manage without her? How long would it take for her to be replaced? What would they do when they grew up? Did Aislinn still want to be a chemist? What would Dylan choose to do? The thoughts were cold and bitter.

Spencer and Trinidad were chopping up mid-sized limbs and brush with a hatchet and machete.

"Put me to work," she said.

"Okay. Haul while we cut?"

"Sure. But I need to chop something."

"Go ahead, then," he said, and handed her the hatchet.

She started swinging at the base of a branch on a limb. It shifted, the hatchet slipped off. She grabbed it and chopped again, changing her grip until it stopped bouncing, pinned to the ground under her boot. Chips started flying and bounced into her clothes, her hair, off her cheeks. She chopped until she realized her wrist was aching from gripping too tight. She'd made a mess, sending chips in cascades all around. She'd hacked through three limbs and felt her lungs rasping.

"Feeling better?" Trinidad asked.

"No."

"Yeah." It wasn't hard for him to figure out her distress.

She flayed the limb to splinters and chunks, then gathered up an armful and carried it to the arc around the tent.

Crossing the bridge, she remembered she needed the latrine.

The water underneath had frozen solid, and there was a pile of turds on it, oozing and freezing and looking disgusting. If it didn't melt soon, Barker said he was going to start a fire upstream to sink the ice and flush it. She took care of business without looking down, and wiped with her hygiene rag. That would have to be washed as soon as they had running cold water. It stank as well, of sweat and residue and urine.

She was cold now. SOP was to go inside and warm up, so she did. Inside was dark, dank but several degrees warmer. Ortiz, Oglesby and Barker were inside. It made sense for Barker to stay here when not hauling fuel and food.

She realized how numb her toes were, and her fingers even with gloves. She'd need to remove them and her boots and warm extremities near the fire.

As she did, a waft of stink hit her nostrils.

"What the hell are you burning?" she asked.

Snickers turned to outright howls of laughter.

"Fine, but whatever it is, it smells like burning shit."

That set them off into paroxysms.

Really?

"Are you fucking kidding me?"

"Hey, it was cold," Oglesby said. "I was much more comfortable in here."

"Grow up."

What if that caught on? Nevermind the smell, it was a sanitation issue, and heated germs in the atmosphere weren't a good idea.

"Seriously. Do that again and I'll give you something to regret for the next five years."

"What's that?"

"Permanent tower watch."

"Yeah? How? You're not in charge."

"I draw the schedule and the LT approves it. You understand HHC? The LT and I are HHC. I'll make it happen and he'll agree with me."

"You're . . ."

Whether Oglesby was going to call her a liar or a loon, or a bitch, he thought better of it.

Bored young troops cramped in a tent.

And Martin Spencer snored. Like a B52 on takeoff.

Winter just needed to be over.

CHAPTER 25

Spring was a tease, Martin Spencer thought. January warmed toward the end. February was a plateau that plunged them back into the tent for two days, The ground was mucky and soft, but with Urushu help, they finished graveling from the tent to the latrine, and started on a road to the bridge. That had to wait until after the thaw sent torrents of water down the small stream. It didn't undercut the banks; Elliott had done a good job with the design. They did wind up with a lake all the way to the latrine, and a whirlpool under the culvert. They all took turns watching it in trepidation, fearing the wall would fail at any moment. Three times for a couple of days each the water swirled and gurgled, brown and nasty looking with floating debris and scum, but the wall held. The stream seemed to have dug itself a bit deeper, which meant it would flow easier, but was also a wider gap for intruders. Once through the culvert, it shot like a hose and ate away the banks lower down, too. They'd have another shallow spot there.

Then they took the sledgehammers and chunks of slate, large cobbles and various limestone pieces and beat on them. Swing, crack against the side of the rock Martin wanted as an anvil.

"Just the side," he said.

"This is like golf. So, are we gonna gravel the whole COB, just like back home?" Dalton asked.

"It's not a bad idea. We need to keep the weeds down," Spencer told him, pointing at some hardy stalks sprouting tall already. "However, once we have all the paths, I think we'll be fine. And there's no rush. As long as you don't mind walking in muck, we can wait."

"Funny."

"Ain't I?"

Swing, crack. They had more aches and blisters before it was done.

But by March, daytime temperatures were in the 50s and 60s, nights not much below freezing, and things started to green up. Dandelions came out.

Caswell said, "Good, those are edible, and don't taste too bad."

He noted that she and he had different definitions of "Don't taste too bad." To him, everything green here tasted like some variation of grass. None of them were interesting, and he ate them because they contained nutrients. The end. That and bone meal, which did seem to keep his stomach to a dull ache. It was perpetually irritated, but not in stabbing pain as it had been when he first developed GERD.

The Urushu were back, a few at a time. It seemed they had about four rotations, and the hunters who ran escort were mostly high status. The injuries were everything from children with broken fingers or ripped nails, to more female problems among the mothers, to hunting wounds. Though one case of frostbite required a toe amputation that had been loud and ugly.

They resumed formation around the fire every evening, though rain sometimes forced them into the tent. It would drive right through the bough covers. They'd need to shingle or skin the roofs there, too.

The night right after the graveling was finished, they had skewered roast yearling venison. That was dark, rich, but very lean. Martin was starting to dream of ribeye with lots of marbling. Still, he licked the skewer twig until all he tasted was wood. Their Urushu embassy had brought the deer, and kept the rear haunches and liver for themselves. He was fine with that.

From his chair at the front, Elliott said, "We made a good start in the fall. We made it through winter fed, warm, and only slightly pissed off at each other."

Alexander said, "Slightly."

"I want to work on a bunch of projects for the spring. If we can split wood, I want a better outhouse with a shingled roof. I want to roof the lean-tos to keep us dry. I think it's beneficial to be outside."

Martin sighed. A lieutenant would think that. He'd rather build a cabin.

Elliott continued, "I want to build a log cabin right next to the trucks. We may have to move them, then move them back. It'll give us a three-sided inner defense if necessary, and we can put a door in the back to get to them. Stone fireplace and chimney, which may take some learning on how to do."

Trinidad said, "I've helped build one. I remember a bit about it."

"Oh. Excellent. Then I'd like to upgrade the females' lodging with hard sides and a shingle roof, too. Then if we can, some way to split and hollow logs, and have running water down into the camp so we don't have to keep dipping in the stream. It can splash into a pit near the kitchen, and run out. We'll tile that with stones and let moss seal it. Comments?"

Martin figured he'd offer support.

"If we cook some lime in the fire, we can possibly make a crude cement. It won't be as good as modern concrete, but it should toughen up the runoff, and it'll help seal chinks in the cabin."

Trinidad said, "Filipino, not chink. And you're not sealing me in."

They all laughed.

Ortiz said, "We need to get more goats for the pen. Water and feed them, too, then work on a proper tannery, unless we can trade for smoked hides with our neighbors. Though the tepee hides are pretty set at this point."

They all glanced to look. It really was odd, in a mishmash of tans, browns and creams. But the smooth sides had gotten well smoked over the winter and had dried up tight. They'd added spare hides at the bottom, and those were starting to rot at ground level.

Barker said, "If it's going to be hide, I really want to recover it with better tanned skin. If it's going to be fabric . . . I dunno, how fast can Gina spin that much yarn?"

"Alone?" she said. "Years. If everyone works at it, a few weeks. But we still need a loom to do weaving."

Ortiz said, "It'll have to be hides for a while. I can help tan them."

"So can I," Caswell put in. "It stinks, a lot. We'll want to do that outside the wall."

Barker said, "I also want to work on getting a tub built in the sweat lodge. A hot bath every couple of weeks would be awesome."

Elliott said, "I know something of fitting lumber. That's a pretty tall job."

"Yeah, we'll need planks, notch them as a half barrel, strap them with taut hide rope, and need either a drain plug or some way to bail."

Elliott said, "Right. Let's save that until summer. We don't need it until winter."

Martin wasn't sure of that. Hot water would help the aches he felt every morning. Not everyone found the stream refreshing. He found it barely tolerable.

Devereaux said, "We need an ongoing search for more edible, nutritious and useful plants. Stuff we can felt into absorbent bandages."

"We'll talk to the Urushu, but yes. Technical skills are as important as material goods. What about your bows, Barker?"

Barker said, "I've got the bows. I can shave more. I'm going to gut string them this year and recover the dental floss. Eventually I'd like to use hemp or flax. Arrows are easy, take me about thirty minutes each with bone or horn points. Dalton and I have experience. But what are the Neo people going to think if they see us hunting with the same stuff they have, not our magic weapons? Or the Urushu, for that matter. Can we believably blame it on the rules of our gods? We don't want them thinking we might run out of ammo."

Oglesby said, "I can convince the Urushu. Spirits are very real to them, and change at whim. That's how they explain weather. I don't know about the Neoliths."

Elliott asked, "By the way, do we have a name for them?"

"No demonym as yet, no."

Spencer thought, and said, "I don't think they were able to attach the significant of the magic brass pieces to the rifles. Worst case, we make a show of sticking some into a magazine. They won't have any idea about combustion. Black powder might give it away, but smokeless won't."

Barker said, "Reasonable."

"Okay," Elliott concluded. "Plan on working every day except Sunday, and one person on watch, two at night remains. I don't want our Urushu guests in the vehicles, but if they'd like to do perimeter patrol, that's fine with me."

All in all, it wasn't far from what Martin had planned. And he wasn't the officer. He trusted Elliott and had to keep trusting him, so he'd go along with the program as laid out. He needed to remember to keep his own ego under control.

Alexander said, "Quiet," in a loud whisper. He swung that way, ready to react to something.

The cat was on her lap, and she had her arms wrapped around him. He purred in a loud buzz, and looked unsure about the attention, but writhed against her and didn't try to break free. Her lips trembled and he could see she was crying as she scratched his chest and behind his ears.

Their mascot was now a pet.

CHAPTER 26

Armand Devereaux liked night watch when the sky was clear. He could use the binox to view things he'd never see from a civilized location. With careful juggling of night vision, some quite distant nebulae were visible, though monochrome. Cool nights like this, with still air, were best. The dew had condensed and there was no fog.

He had the turret. Alexander sat on the roof near the back ladder.

"Excuse me a moment," she said, and climbed down, probably to use the can.

Shortly she came back with a bag. She watched him for a while, then said, "You know, the big telephoto on my camera is pretty good for that."

Yes, it might be. He turned and asked, "Could I . . ."

She raised a hand with the camera, its large lens in place.

"Strap around your neck first," she said, as she draped it over him. "Always use the strap."

"Will do, thanks. I'll treat it like a fourteen-inch Celestron." He hefted it like a rifle. It was a big piece of hardware.

"I think I know what that is."

"A Schmidt-Cassegrain reflecting telescope."

"Okay, I know about Schmidt cameras."

"Yup. Same guy." He turned the camera to the sky and . . . damn.

"Wish I'd had this before," he said. "This is awesome."

"Good stuff?"

"Yeah, do you know where the nebula in Orion's belt is?"

"I think so."

"Take a look." Reluctantly, he handed the camera back to her.

She looked, pointed the camera, adjusted it only slightly, and said, "Oh, my."

"Yeah. We have that."

"Hold on," she said, and there was a click, then a few more.

"Cool," he said.

"I looked up a few times back home, but it never looked like this." Then she was sobbing.

"Sorry," he said.

"I miss my kids, and my cats, and my husband. I even think they'd be willing to join me so we could be together, but not even that is possible." She wept, camera in her lap, face in her hands.

"And I'm out of meds," she said. "You said eating sweetbreads might help?"

"It might."

"Then I need to do that."

There was nothing he could do. Instead he made a scan. A couple of wolves were way up on the ridge to south. Otherwise there were the goats, the three visiting Urushu in their hooch, and miles of pristine nothing.

He'd never see Mama again, either. Hell, she wasn't even born yet. That was still hard to grasp.

"I'm okay," she said. "It just hits me now and then."

"Me, too. All of us, I think."

Something about crying made her vulnerable, and he knew what she looked like naked. That was annoying.

"It's getting close to shift change," he said to change thoughts. "Dalton will be up."

"Roger. Wish I could stick to early evening watch. This split sleep wears me out."

"Take care," he said, wanting to say a bit more and not sure how.

"And you," she agreed.

Ramon Ortiz liked having the additional labor. He was good at skinning game, quite expert by now, but the Urushu had a lifetime of practice. They could peel a carcass in minutes. They knew how to salvage blood, drain and clean guts, pull out the prime organs, and even choose some of the finer cuts. After that, he did some general steak cutting before letting them peel the rest, save the sinew and crack the marrow. More importantly, he stayed cleaner.

The alliance was beneficial. The Urushu got better medical care and some useful tools, plus occasional religious bacon. The soldiers got grunt labor and some useful low tech skills, but that didn't mean the natives weren't sophisticated.

They knew exactly which wood was best for fire by friction, how to turn a particular fungus into tinder by putting it in a pit and urinating on it until the crystallized nitrates turned it into what was almost flash paper. They could find edible bark or grubs anywhere, though he hoped to avoid the latter; the bark did bad enough things to his colon. They had several smoking weed mixtures, from mild to stoned out of your brain. They purposed the peeled hides for various different functions. Once Barker had taught them how to fletch shafts, they'd adopted it at once. And all of them could turn a rock into a functional blade with another. None were as pretty as the ones Barker did, but they were as functional. Then there was that trick of gutting a small animal through the neck, tying it off with its own intestines, and hanging it by the fire to stew in its own skin.

He knew he was a productive member here, with his knowledge of animals and ranching, and would be more so in the future. But without Barker and the Urushu, they'd be nowhere. Add in Oglesby's translating and Spencer's knowledge of geography. Oh, and Caswell's ability to find stuff other than meat, and cook it.

Still, the beehive seemed to be occupied, so starting next spring they could have honey now and then. That and berries meant more wine, and some desserts. That was progress.

Yeah, it was a team effort. He wasn't sure about Alexander, but she'd cleaned up his phone as well, and did keep track of a lot of things. She also gathered and split wood, and had no problem lending a hand. Though she wasn't in great shape. She'd firmed up for a while, now was getting soft again, and it wasn't just being a desk potato. She had serious health issues.

He'd wondered why a recruiter had accepted her back in, but then, they were short of bodies and she'd had prior service. He felt it proper to let her get her twenty and retire. Which of course wasn't happening now.

She was the only approachable female locally. Damned sure Caswell wasn't having any, and the Urushu didn't appeal to him yet. Though if he got an offer, he might.

He got to build a ranch from the ground up. A fascinating project. But a rancher needed a wife.

"Approaching party!" Alexander called from up top. "to the east! Large party, in metal armor. Formation is four by six or so. I think they're Romans."

He looked up. She had her camera with the big lens mounted. She could probably read their bloodshot eyes with that thing.

Spencer was fast for an older guy. He was up the ramp, foot on step and bounded onto the roof. He shielded his eyes and squinted.

"I will be dipped in shit, they're Romans."

Alexander said, "I do know what Romans look like, thank you." She looked pissed at being doubted.

"Sorry. I'd put them at five hundred meters and closing."

The lieutenant said, "That's a bit close. Everyone arm up and be ready. Oglesby, tell the Urushu to stand fast in their hooch."

"Hooah, sir."

Ramon ran to the tepee, pulled on his body armor and ACH, and grabbed his weapon. Magazine in, unchambered.

Next to him, Dalton said, "I wonder if they want to fight."

"I hope they want Confession," he said.

Spencer dove through the door and threw gear on fast.

"Heh. They can confess to this." Dalton slapped the grenade launcher under his M4.

"Sure, if the LT lets you load it."

"Nah, don't need it. But you know."

Spencer asked, "Ready?" with an amused but pointed glance, and led them outside. He went straight back up top.

Elliott was ready, and shaking his head.

"Things are really fucked up," he said. "Those are really—"

Spencer called down, "Roman legionaries, yes. And those other guys are Moghuls? I think. Indians with muskets."

Alexander said, "Likely."

Moghuls? East Indians?

He climbed up the ladder, rifle banging his legs, and took a look.

"There are people from all over time here."

Elliott squinted. "Can you figure out a pattern?"

Spencer said, "Fifteen K years, eight K years, two K years, fifteen hundred AD, our present. It vaguely fits some weird asymptote."

Yeah, Spencer was right. He said, "I wonder if someone from the future will show up—a hundred years or so would fit that."

Elliott shrugged. "Well, let's see what the Romans want. My Latin sucks. Spanish may help a little. How many do we want to send out?"

"Five? Loaded?" He suggested.

"Yes. Me. Dalton. Spencer. Oglesby. And one female. Caswell. Barker's in charge here. Everyone got full mags and body armor? Good. Move."

Ramon sunk. He'd really wanted to see this. Still, he could stay up top for a better view.

Martin Spencer assumed the selection was to have the commander present, a reenactor, some extra muscle and a translator. That made sense. Part of him was very eager to see the Roman gear up close, part wanted to hide behind the palisade. He also hated having both him and the CO exposed together.

They slipped out a small arc of the gate, and Barker shoved it closed behind them. Timber on timber sounded, and they were locked out. He swallowed hard. He wanted to adjust his helmet a bit more, but decided it would look clumsy. Romans respected precision.

He wasn't sure if he felt romantic or fraternal toward Alexander, but was glad she wasn't out here. But, she did have useful knowledge, when her brain was working right.

The Romans had gotten close, and her mind had been slipping on occasion. Has she nodded off or zoned out? If so, she'd have to come off watch. That would suck.

There were twenty-three Romans. They were easy to count because they stayed in formation, and were about a hundred meters out. With them, to the rear, were six Indians. They were definitely modern South Asians. The armor and garb was vaguely familiar; that wasn't his era of study. The muskets were very nicely dressed matchlocks. One of those would be amazing in his collection . . . which he was never going to see again. There was the PTSD, over something totally stupid. He was suddenly depressed, angry, hopeless.

It was Caswell who said, "Sir, we could march, but they probably do it better."

"Agreed. And I'd rather they underestimated us for right now. We'll escalate as needed to make our point."

The Romans stood in a very good formation, even better considering the uneven terrain. They didn't look at all bothered. They seemed rather bored, in fact. So they were probably well-drilled veterans.

They wore a mix of squamata and hamata armor, so they were Republic or early Empire. They were all buttoned and tied tight, ready to fight, clutching pilum and rectangular scutae.

"Probably second century, sir, but not much later, and can't be much earlier. One hundred BC to one hundred AD. I can tell from their armor."

"Thanks. Let me step slightly forward. Take a knee and be ready."

Martin said, "Sir, I believe he's a centurion, which was a senior NCO, junior officer sort of thing, in charge of a platoon. You want to be a tribune. An officer."

"Hooah."

The rest stopped, went to knees and prepared to back their commander. He clicked the safety off, and checked a round was in battery. He could shoot easily from the knee, right past Elliott if he had to.

The Roman officer had a transverse crest on his helmet. He stepped forward.

Elliott spoke slowly and clearly. "Bono dia. We are duo millennia tempus futura post Roma. I am Tribunus Sean Elliott, milites United States."

Oglesby asked, "Did you say your Latin sucks, sir?"

"Yeah, because I never took any."

"Just checking. But I think you're getting the point across."

The lead Roman rattled off something in Latin. Spencer could tell it was Latin. He got nothing else.

Elliott said, "*Tardia. Voce tardia.*"

The Roman did speak more slowly, but it was still hard to define. "*Latinam loquisne, nothe? Non loquisne?*"

Oglesby said, "Sir, I think it comes down to, 'Latin, motherfucker, do you speak it?'"

They all smiled slightly.

"Okay, they don't sound particularly friendly."

Martin said, "Yeah, the Romans had a definite superiority complex, and this guy is definitely in charge of this other element from fifteen hundred years later."

The Roman centurion pointed at their palisade, then at himself.

Elliott asked, "Does he want entry or command?"

Spencer said, "Both. And I expect he'll try to burn his way in if we refuse. Folks, if they start hurling javelins or draw swords, just start shooting, from our front left. Same formations we use, that's where the leaders are."

"Hooah."

Elliott said, "There won't be time for any orders, so follow Sergeant Spencer's lead. But I was hoping for a peaceful meeting of minds."

"Yeah, I doubt this guy's met anyone he couldn't intimidate or kill."

The Roman seemed to recognize armor for what it was, but kept squinting. He knew there was cloth outside, and he couldn't know what was inside. Did he suspect leather? Metal? Horn or hide?

After a bit more gesturing, with Elliott making an honest attempt to communicate, the Roman gave an almost Gallic shrug, turned and said something.

The Romans shifted formation, and there was some kind of order given. Three of the Indian musketeers stood to. There was obvious tinder and lighting of matches, waving for embers, charging pans on long, beautifully wrought and stocked matchlocks.

Martin muttered, "Fucking seriously?"

Caswell giggled, then the others found the mirth. It was entirely amusing to watch those men work so hard at impressing their neighbors.

Within a couple of minutes, the three stood abreast, chose a goat fifty yards to the south as a target, and fired.

The volley sounded with a dull boom, and smoke spurted into blowing clouds. The goat fell over and thrashed, squealing.

Martin said, "Challenge accepted."

Everyone stifled laughs.

Elliot spoke softly.

"Caswell," he said.

"Yes, sir?"

"I want you to respond because you're female. Put that poor beast out of its misery, pick two others and give them your best. Double their range at least. Then give us a burst."

"Yes, sir. Three rounds?"

"That's a burst, isn't it?"

"Air Force weapon, sir," she said, jiggling it. "We have a happy switch."

"Oh. Then by all means make it six."

"Got it. You're not worried about them finding bullets?"

Elliott said, "No. Cases yes, bullets no."

"Roger that, sir. Stand by." She slid the leather brass catcher into place.

Martin softly said, "Challenge engaged."

She raised her carbine, pointed and shot. *Her* weapon cracked loudly, as did the supersonic bullet. That smashed through the head of the mostly-dead goat, giving it a humane finish.

Her second bullet was two seconds later. It took another goat at a hundred yards, headshot. It simply dropped where it stood. The third shot rang out, and at about two hundred yards, another animal erupted blood from its skull, then thrashed around in convulsions for a moment.

Then she picked an outcropping and fired a burst. He counted eight rounds. Fair enough. They chipped the stone and ricocheted.

She lowered the weapon, and stared over it at the Roman officer.

The Roman looked thoroughly shocked. His ace had just been trumped. That it was a female who'd done it seemed just to add to the effect.

There was an immediate huddle with him and two Indians who appeared to be officers. They had flashier dress and fancier swords. *Tulwar* if he recalled correctly.

Martin said, "Challenge concluded."

Now the Roman was willing to negotiate. He smiled and spread arms.

"I'm not trusting his sword, sir."

"Yeah," Elliott agreed. He pointed, "Gladius remove."

The centurion chewed his lip, but nodded, drew his sword and handed it to a subordinate.

Elliott stepped back and handed his carbine to Spencer.

"If he tries to kill me or capture me, shoot him dead and we'll deal with the second in command."

"Yes, sir. Caswell, Dalton, keep the LT under watch."

"Hooah, Sergeant." "Got you covered, sir."

"Oglesby, can you assist?"

"Possibly. I know some grammatical and tense stuff. Ortiz would have been better, I think."

Spencer said, "Sir, I'll listen in. I may have some input, if that's okay."

"Yes, thank you."

The Roman really did slow his words down, and Martin could overhear quite a bit. "*Loci*," "*Tempus*," "*Deites*," and other words. So, the Romans had some idea how they'd wound up among "*ferus saeva barbare*."

Elliott had good body language. He was a commander dealing with a foreign element who was less well equipped, and smaller by several inches. He looked down at the Roman and spoke.

"As I said, *Roma futura duo millennia*." He indicated himself and the others. "*Roma conquista* . . . Spencer, who did they conquer?"

Martin spoke clearly. "*Roma conquista Galli, Belgi, Germani, Allemani, Helveti, Brittania, Caledonia, Hibernia, Drurotriges, Iceni, et terra trans mare Atlantia*."

Elliott nodded, and indicated himself. "*Futura Roma trans mare Atlantia. Milites Tribunus*. Sean Elliott."

The Centurion appeared to be a mix of surprised, pleased, and disgruntled. He'd been in charge. Now he was back to being an NCO, though for a greater Rome than he'd left.

Elliott did a good job, Martin thought. The Roman got told, not asked, what Elliott expected. He expected the Romans to depart, they could send a team of quinto to negotiate, arms would be checked at the gate, and he expected them to behave among all the groups. He was a tribune and the centurion would do well to abide by him. The Rome Elliott came from was much more advanced, and respected the great contributions of its earlier men, but had new and improved ways of doing things.

Phrased like that, the centurion nodded in acquiescence, saluted with an open hand, turned and gave orders to his men.

They watched the Romans tromp away, then walked back to the gate and through, and goddamn did it feel good to have a palisade.

"You heard that?" Elliott asked, sagging from restrained stress.

"Well done, sir," he said.

"Yeah. But I'd really like to trail those bastards and find out where they're living. I assume they have camp followers, likely slaves, and I assume they've been tracking us. But I'd need two volunteers, unarmed, nothing we care about losing, and even if I had volunteers," he looked at Dalton's half-raised hand, "I don't think it's a good idea. We'll gather intel other ways."

"And they think we're Romans?" Dalton asked. "I can see it."

Spencer said, "There are historians who argue that we are, by way of Britain, since that was the last stronghold of the Empire, and we still use Latin for science, medicine and law."

Elliott said, "I want to find out where all these groups are coming from. We know *when*. *Where* might help with *why* or *how*."

Caswell asked, "Did Rome ever get this far east? I know the Macedonians did."

Martin said, "I don't think Rome made it past the Red Sea. Possibly into Persia. Definitely not here."

"And those were Indians, correct?" she asked.

"Dot not feather. Yes. Matchlocks place them before seventeen hundred, after fifteen hundred, as best I recall."

Oglesby said, "They speak Hindi. I know a few phrases."

"Good. We're going to need to have discussions on all this."

Doc asked, "They came from the west. What did they do to the Neoliths?"

"Probably already claimed their town and slaughtered anyone who gave them lip."

Devereaux flared his eyes and said, "The Neoliths needed taking down a peg, but that's not cool."

"No, it isn't. And any women are probably Roman slave girls now."

He realized he was hyperventilating and choked down on it. Was it PTSD again? Or fear? He really didn't want to die here, much as he didn't like living here. The Romans were creative about it.

His eyes blurred and sweat burst out, then he got it under control, mostly, but started shaking. He wondered about some medicinal wine. Or some of the weed. That wouldn't upset his stomach the way wine would.

It shouldn't be affecting him this hard. He hoped no one would look at him for the next few minutes.

❖ ❖ ❖

Sean Elliott tried to calm his nerves. He'd just told a Roman military unit he was their superior officer, and made it stick. He breathed a deep sigh, and felt a hell of a rush.

He motioned Spencer to follow him behind the trucks. They needed to crop weeds under and around the trucks again. The stuff had grown fast. Ortiz had said something about tethering goats and letting them crop areas down.

The weeds were fine for now. He stood among some flowering things that looked like flowering things anywhere.

He said, "At this point, if there are four groups displaced, there could be dozens or more."

"Yes, sir. No reason not."

Spencer was flushed and twitchy. Fear? Could be. The man kept his feelings down, mostly, but obviously had them.

"But you said there was a documentable gap."

Spencer breathed deep and said, "Possibly. Five hundred years, two thousand years, eight thousand years. Each four times the previous."

"I think I see distance, too."

"Yeah, distance seems to be about the same. But that makes no sense."

"Why not?"

Spencer said, "Because we didn't all use the same measurements. Our mile isn't a Roman mile."

"That doesn't affect the ratio of the distance."

"Oh. True." Spencer shook his head as if clearing it.

"I think we really need to send a recon element out."

Spencer said, "I agree we need to. I'm still not sure we can risk it."

He was a really dedicated worker and craftsman, but very timid when it came to doing military patrols.

"I'm going to say we do. I'll need you to lead it."

Spencer said, "Yes, sir," and nothing else. He stood very still.

"You really don't like the idea, do you?"

"Sir, it's a valid idea, but honestly, I'm afraid. I don't like leaving the group."

"I figured you liked getting away."

"Personally away, behind a barrier, yes. Not leaving the presence of other people. I've been twitchy since we got here."

He suspected Spencer was a lot more than twitchy. He was probably shaking in fear, which Elliott understood.

"I feel that, too," he admitted. He did, though he thought he could handle the trip. "If you prefer, I'll go, you stay here."

Spencer bit his lip.

"Sir, they respond much better to you than me, especially the younger ones. You're the leader. It should be me."

"Can you do it? I'm not going to force you." Who could he send if not? Trinidad?

"I'm interested, and I know what to look for, but I am scared. I'll try. Who else?"

"Oglesby, and someone for backup. Dalton or Caswell."

"Dalton, definitely."

"You don't have to leave right now."

"Yeah, but it better be within a day or two."

"I'll write up a frag order. Can you manage ten miles west along the river? And visit anywhere else that presents itself?"

"Romans, Neoliths, Urushu if they're still around. Yes. Any message I'm sending?"

"I hadn't thought about that." That was a good point.

"I guess that we're here. We're not going away. We're peaceful. We have no interest in repressing others and want good relations, but refuse to be subjects. Try not to waste ammo, but if dropping an animal provides food from the gods and makes them respectful, do it."

"Okay," Spencer nodded. "Give me a while to get used to the idea. A couple of days."

Dinner was river trout with a cream sauce made from goat milk and herbs. It was . . . okay. Something about it didn't quite work, but at least it wasn't goat.

He brought up his proposal for general discussion.

"I'm planning to send Sergeant Spencer on a recon patrol. I'd like to send Oglesby and Dalton along, too."

"Hooah." "Yes, sir!"

"I want to know what the other groups think, where they are, how they're equipped. We can't keep waiting for them to come to us. The problem we face is this: We have desirable equipment, and few people."

Ortiz said, "But they'd find it easier to fight each other."

Spencer said, "Sure, but why? The Indians and Romans both have iron weapons and armor. Different in style, but not significantly enough to steal. The Indians have muskets, but they load slowly. Their advantage is psychological, and everyone now knows how long they need to load. They aren't even that impressive to the Urushu now, since they've seen ours. They can't make muskets easily, but they can make more powder. The Roman smiths can probably make their own iron and go from there."

He waved around. "We have stuff we can't duplicate, obviously valuable, and I guarantee the Indians can figure out a rifle from their muskets. Getting these," he wiggled his carbine, "equals power and control."

"We have ten people. If two are on watch at any time, we stay on guard around the clock, making sure they do our bidding, or don't try to rob us, enslave us and steal the women. And we won't even really be able to inspect their work, which will have exploitable holes in it.

"We just cannot trust them. If we had a platoon, maybe. But our technological edge is both a blessing and a curse. All we can do is enforce our neutrality."

"However, we can trade resources and information."

Caswell asked, "If they're set in primitive skills, what can we offer? They won't be as impressed as the Urushu."

Spencer said, "More medicine. Some agriculture to the Urushu and Neoliths. I know how to make actual steel, once they have a smelter set up. Just as with the Urushu, we have tools they can use. So we become useful elders. We're not a threat, just reserved."

Devereaux said, "I'm not eager to patch up someone who gets hit with a rusty, crap-encrusted javelin. Even minor wounds can be fatal."

Barker said, "We know beekeeping, so honey and alcohol follow. We may even be able to set up a still and produce liquor for fuel, industrial use, and drinking."

"Keep them drunk and they won't have the energy to attack us?"

Barker grinned while rubbing his beard. "That's part of it too, s We need them to see the benefit of us being alive and unbothered, i dead, not slaves."

Oglesby said, "I'm not sure if it's good or bad we're not fraterni with the locals. They seem a bit insulted, and we're not gaining for work or war. But it shows distance."

Alexander asked, "Would it make sense to take some Urushu, too? Additional eyes?"

"Yeah, I wonder about that. Spencer?"

Spencer said, "On the one hand, yes, more bodies, more eyes. On the other hand, they'd be in the way in a fight, not knowing how our weapons work, and we'd be responsible for any injuries."

"What do we know from the village?" he asked. "Caswell, have they had any meetings?"

She looked at Oglesby, who said, "They knew where the Neolithics were, and said so. Apparently, they arrived before we did, and were camping south on the hillside near a small pond. The Urushu thought that was the end of it. They just figured they were newcomers moving in."

Spencer asked, "Despite the different clothing, technology and trained dogs?"

"Yes. They noted that and figured it was something to do with the spirits."

Spencer said, "Yeah, that's a bit too friendly and trusting. I don't think they'd be a good choice."

Ortiz said, "Sir, since I speak Spanish, I'd be a good choice to go. 'here's some similarities to Latin that might help."

"Hmm . . . If you're up for it."

'I think so."

)kay. I'll have a frag order in the morning. Sergeant Spencer, let
ow when you think you can leave."

'l do, sir. Everyone will need to shave. Remember the word
' is Latin."

shaver was turning into an essential piece of military

ir.
ot

.ing
llies

CHAPTER 27

Of course, it had to be raining when they left.

Ramon wasn't bothered by rain, though there was a lot more here than in South Texas, except during hurricane season. But they'd be hiking through wet grass and mud, then trying to bivouac in it.

The wet grass soaked their pants, and the water ran down into boots. Within a mile, he squelched with every step. He hoped the poncho over the trash bag kept his sleeping bag dry.

"We're actually stopping with the Neolithics?" he asked.

Spencer said, "If we can. We'll walk up, see what kind of reception we get, and go from there."

They took a direct route, angling downhill and diverting around some of the terrain features.

"At least the rain keeps the bugs and the animals down."

"I wouldn't bet on that," he said. "Rain is great cover for a stalk. Watch for the wolves especially."

It was going to be an uncomfortable trip. He hadn't worn a ruck since they got here, and all the hard work they'd been doing was not the same as rucking. It was cold and wet, water now trickling down his back. Nor was that good for the armor, he recalled. The only food they had was several pounds of jerky, though they were all reasonably adept at digging up edible roots and stalks now. Dandelions and wild garlic didn't have much taste, but they did make meat a bit less boring.

By midafternoon they were getting close to the Paleoliths' village. He wanted to see how that had changed.

They were seen by wandering workers, and he got to look at their herding attempts.

"Gimped females," he commented. "I heard you say it, but it's different in person. There's a lot of them."

"Yeah," Oglesby said. "More than last time."

"I expect they're planning to raise a generation in captivity. Many of those are very pregnant."

Spencer asked, "Are those fields uphill?"

"Sort of," he squinted. "They're not quite prepared fields, but they're weeding around what they like, and seem to have increased the seeding. Oh, and they're using the fruit and nut trees as latrine area."

"How . . . special."

He shrugged. "It works. I don't know if they're seasonal about it, just don't pick up any fallen fruit, or figure rinsing any stink will fix it. There's a reason Eurasians are immune to almost everything."

Spencer said, "Yeah, remind me to tell you about Vikings keeping cattle in their houses in winter, and saving all the shit and piss for leather processing."

Oglesby grimaced and said, "Charming."

Spencer said, "In any case, they've seen us." He waved, so Ramon did, too.

"Romans." The group was part Neolith, part Roman.

Yes, that was a hunting party. Five men and a dog. The dog was largely wolf, reminiscent of a malamute or husky. Three of the men were Romans.

"They don't seem to trust us," he said.

Spencer said, "I don't blame them for that. This is going to be tense."

Spencer was shaking a bit. Oglesby flat out trembled like a Chihuahua. Right, they'd had a shootout last time.

The hunters approached slowly. The Neoliths seemed more afraid than the moderns. The Romans were cautious, but seemed arrogant.

"Should I?" Ramon asked.

"Go ahead."

"*Estamos en nuestro camino por el río. Traemos saludos de nuestro Tribunus.*"

One of the Romans replied with a string that included words like, "*hospitia,*" "*habitate,*" and "*noctem.*"

"Do we want to stay over?"

"Sure. Thank them."

"*Assentior. Gracias, Milites.*"

As they preceded the party into the village, he felt his back crawl.

Spencer turned his head and said, "I'm talking to you just so I can turn my head and keep an eye to the rear, using Germanic words instead of those other tongue roots."

"Hooah, Sergeant." Oglesby seemed impressed and enthusiastic. Ramon caught on. He'd just be as non-spic as possible and that should do it.

The three talked back and forth about nothing at all, just to keep an eye on the Romans, who were keeping an eye on them.

Once at the village, it was obvious the Romans were in control. About twenty of them milled about, in armor, buttoned up and carrying javelins. They had leather capes to keep the rain off. The wall was now reinforced with those square piles the Romans used, and a ditch and mound not unlike their own, but not as tall. It looked like it went up fast, though. There was a lodge with water puddling under sticks, probably a bathhouse, and a couple of designated latrines.

Oglesby said, "Well, that explains the improvements in even Neolithic technology since last time. Also, I don't recognize most of these guys. Different group."

"Yeah. I wonder how many Romans there are, total." Spencer kept looking about.

"Enough to split forces. I see they're putting in log cabins."

Ramon said, "Wish we could."

"They've got a lot of labor."

Ramon found himself translating to the Roman NCO on site, a Centurion Laurentius Flavius Brutus.

He had a hard time following even slow Latin, but got an impression from pointing. "He doesn't trust our rifles."

"Well, too bad."

Ramon shrugged, and clutched the M4 to his chest. The Romans could order them to leave, or deal with it. Shrugging back, Brutus pointed at a small cabin. It was just big enough for the three of them to roll out bags.

"*Gracias*, Centurion," he acknowledged.

"You first," Spencer said. "I'll watch them."

The inside had a dirt floor, well-packed. The logs were loosely notched and chinked with mud and river clay. The roof was thatch over sticks, about five feet high. It was an oversized doghouse, but adequate by Army standards, and quite comfy by their local ratings.

He kept guard while the other two laid out their bags, then his, with rucks stacked in a corner.

"We have a servant girl, I think," he said. "Urushu."

Spencer and Oglesby strained their necks around the door frame.

Oglesby said, "Huh. A second change of leadership. I feel sorry for them."

She was Urushu, tall, dark, lean but with broad hips. She carried an armful of wood for a small firepit near their door, which she built into an efficient fire lay.

Oglesby greeted her, and she looked up in surprise. She muttered something, and hurried off.

"She's coming back with food," he said.

When she returned, she had a stick with a coal to light the fire. She put down a leather-wrapped bundle of food, set the coal and blew up the small fire. They had a great view of her ass while she did so, and it had nice curves, but needed some pimples popped and a bath. Every encounter buried the noble savage crap deeper.

That done, she unwrapped the skin to reveal baked meat and roots with some kind of flatbread. It smelled like rice and nuts again.

She spoke, Oglesby replied, then they talked. That language was full of clicks, nasals, tones. It was a beautiful language to listen to.

Spencer slowly reached out and took a cake from the leather sheet, tried it, nodded, and indicated. Ramon gladly grabbed one, and some baked meat that smell then taste proved to be salted beef. It was chewy, but not bad. The cake was rice cake. That was good. *Dios*, they needed more starch.

"Damn. Good stuff," he said quietly.

Oglesby took a couple of bites, but kept talking. Some of the girl's gestures were universal—shrugs and headshakes. Others were unusual hand movements that accentuated something she said. Overall, she seemed sad.

After a few minutes, she stood, almost-bowed with her hands out, and walked away.

"What was that?" Spencer asked.

Oglesby said, "The Shiny Spirits, their name for the Romans, probably due to metal, moved in and displaced the Neoliths, who seem to be called the 'Gadorth.' The Romans killed some of the Gadorth, gave orders, and everyone accepts they speak for the spirits. The Romans put them to work, built a shrine to the spirits, and started building stuff, as well as bringing more animals using their magic. Her job is to provide domestic service and sex."

Spencer half-frowned and said, "Yeah, that's the Romans."

"Her name is Uk!isa. She offered sex for us. I tried to thank her generously for the offer, but stated our spirits required us to abstain while traveling. I didn't want to turn her down."

Ramon asked, "She wants us to use her?"

"It's a combination of them thinking of sex as hospitality and a way to spread genes, and the Romans raising that as a useful skill. She thinks that's her duty."

Ramon grimaced. "Fuck. I want pussy as much as the next man, but not like that."

Oglesby said, "Yeah, and I'm not ready to bang her in front of you guys."

Spencer replied, "Besides, I'm senior, so you'd be getting thirds."

It took Ramon a moment to catch it as a joke, and Oglesby even longer.

"Anyway," he continued, "She doesn't seem terrorized by the Romans, just sort of accepts it as something the spirits have sent, like winter, bad storms or a drought."

"Where is the Roman camp?"

"They took over another Urushu village. It's farther downstream."

"Okay. I guess we need to go there." He frowned. "I hope there aren't too many of them."

Ramon shifted.

"Next problem," he said. "I gotta piss."

"Yeah, we'll cover you. Leave your weapon here. Looks like they're using that tree for urine."

"Hooah."

He felt very exposed, unarmed without backup, walking across the dusky, drizzly compound and approaching the tree. A couple of people's eyes followed him, but no one tried to hinder him. He took care of business, buttoned up and headed back, and what were they going to do in the morning when they needed to dump?

The dogs were surprisingly well trained, and didn't bark at him, now that he was inside the perimeter. Smart dogs. Very handsome. He wondered if they could trade for a couple of those. They'd help with hunting and might make good herders.

After dinner, the centurion came back over with the serving girl. She made introduction, then bowed out. They stepped outside, nodded all around, and managed through some pidgin Latin/Spanish/English.

The conversation went approximately:

"What brings you here?"

"Exploring the area to learn where other groups are."

"For conquest?"

Spencer said, "Tell him 'No, just trade. Our tools are sufficient we don't need to conquer.' Make it sound boring and uninteresting."

"The optio said your banduka are even better than the Indians'?"

"They are. We are from about five centuries past them, and our alchemy and metalwork are much more advanced."

"What do you offer to trade?"

Spencer said, "Tell them we can help improve their iron and medicine, as well as making much stronger wine."

The Roman grinned. "Stronger wine will be what the pilus prior is interested in."

"Noted. Though we can make much stronger iron."

"We have enough to rule these barbarians." He waved dismissively. "It's Roman iron that does that." Ramon added, "Sergeant, I think he means their mettle and discipline in that context."

Oglesby said, "Yeah, I think so, too."

"Tell him I believe him. Our discipline is a direct line from his Rome's."

He came back with, "You don't like the woman?"

"She's fine, but that's not what we're here for. We do appreciate your hospitality, and she was very agreeable in spirit."

"Good, then. She was the most . . . pliable. Some of the others took persuading." Ramon translated that back and added, "I think that's what he said."

Spencer said, "I hope he drops this thread soon. God, I need a coffee and a beer to calm me down. Or some of that native pot."

Ramon asked, "*Podemos imponer por un poco de vino? y habra yerba para fumar?*" He pantomimed what he meant.

The centurion seemed to grasp it. "Heh. Sure, I'll send some over. Make sure the guard sees you if you need to piss in the middle of the night."

"Will do. Thanks for your hospitality."

"We'll be watching you, too."

"Of course."

After the man left, Ortiz sighed, stretched, and realized how tense he was.

"Well, I don't think he's a threat, but I do expect he's going to report back."

"Or ahead," Spencer said. "He may have a message en route now."

The girl brought a skin of wine. It was raw and rough, but drinkable. She had a bundle of leaves that were whatever hemp analog they'd had before.

"I'm skipping the weed," Spencer said. "I need to keep my wits."

"Hooah."

Oglesby looked at it longingly. "Goddamn, I want a smoke. Can we save it?"

"For now, yes."

Ramon took first watch, and slept well enough after, though the damp persisted. His sleeping bag clung and twisted, and he woke several times. It was dead black, creepy, and he expected incoming at any moment. Oglesby stood near the door during his watch. He thought to tell him to stand back a bit, but drifted right back to sleep.

Spencer had the early call, and stood shifting on his feet, against the back wall, a large shadow, moving little.

The Roman guards made a regular circle inside the fence. He could hear them walk past every few minutes. They were left alone. Whether from orders or practicality, the centurion wasn't interested in fighting. He offered basic hospitality to fellow travelers, and left it like that.

In the morning, the girl brought some ground nuts cooked in fat. It was a bit greasy, but a little took care of hunger.

It was damp outside, but misty, not raining. It would burn off and be clear.

Spencer said, "Let's move. I want to get out of here before they start running around. We go through the forest?"

"Yeah, I remember hunting here last year, with the Urushu."

Oglesby said, "They said it was about six miles through the woods, onto a flat plain."

They walked out the marked gate, escorted by the centurion and several legionnaires, who then turned and went back in.

The woods were lush and damp, the soil humus over clay. They made decent time along what was obviously a well-used path.

Spencer said, "I'm surprised the Romans haven't started building a road yet. Expect they'll do so. They'll probably draft the Neos and Urushu as 'auxiliaries' for it."

Ramon asked, "How do the Neolithics seem to be doing?"

"Looks like the Romans have them completely under control. Either they killed a bunch, or split them up and took some to their place. Either's possible. By breaking the tribute nations into small groups, they'll be easier to control. Very Roman."

Oglesby said, "Didn't the Soviets do something similar?"

"Yes."

Dan Oglesby felt a bit jealous of Ortiz. Spanish was obviously useful in trying to reverse engineer Latin, and Ortiz had done so at least as easily as he'd figured out the Urushu limited vocabulary. The phrase book he'd developed would do for most mundane matters.

So now he was along basically as muscle. Ortiz was the translator, Spencer knew the culture. He was backup.

The woods were dank and creepy. There weren't nearly as many animal sounds as in America; they were complete strangers here, and there were animal and human threats. He jumped as some snuffling boar moved ahead of them, disturbed into trotting farther west. Vines and long ivy hung from the trees. Moss covered the ground and some of the bark. There were big chunks of tree fungus on down logs. Some paths were worn by animals or people, and there were marks to indicate it here and there. He was sure he missed most.

A bird rose up in front of them and he flailed for a second.

"How far west does this go?" he asked. "The river, I mean."

Spencer said, "Yeah, it'd be fascinating to take a raft down. Eventually, this hits the Aral Sea, or what will be the Aral Sea. At this time, it probably fills most of the Depression, and may even join the Caspian."

"How far?"

"Five hundred miles or so. But there's no advantage to being there. It probably isn't even a salt lake yet."

"Things changed that fast?"

"Yes. Seas rose a hundred and twenty meters. Doggerland, where the Neoliths are from, becomes the North Sea. The Baltic turns from lake to inundated estuary to sea. The inland lakes here dry up, refill, dry again several times. Agriculture develops. The megafauna finish dying off."

"Heh. Global warming."

"Right. But at some point ahead of us, it suddenly gets cold again for a couple of thousand years. Very cold."

"That won't affect us, though, right?" Ortiz asked.

Spencer shoved a bough aside and said, "I dunno. Depends on what year this is, and how much effect there is here. But when it happens, it happens within a couple of generations."

"Uh?" Spencer sounded knowledgeable but . . .

"Yeah. Climate change can be fast."

He'd figured they'd settle in to what they have and eventually take native wives and build a village. That it might suddenly all freeze . . .

"Ice Age type freeze?"

"The Younger Dryas is pretty close to a mini ice age, yes."

"Crap."

"It's probably not for a couple of thousand years. But we could be off."

Ortiz asked, "So we need more firewood?"

"Hah. And you thought I was nuts. Yeah, given smaller shelters for us each, too, we'll need more. Unless we want to all hooch together over the winter again."

Ortiz said, "I don't want to, but we may have to."

He said, "Hey, if I get to watch the chicks rub off again," then wished he hadn't.

"Oh?" Spencer asked, too casually.

"Well, I don't know. I think Caswell was. I made a point to not watch, and I guess it might be wishful thinking."

"Yeah, we all wish that, but it ain't gonna happen, and if it does, do not ever mention it to her. Or anyone. Even us."

"Right. She wouldn't see the humor."

"No, she would not."

Ortiz said, "Doc's pretty jealous that you got blown. He's learned to like the Urushu chicks."

This was getting uncomfortably personal.

"Look, I'm sorry. Can we change subjects?"

"Good idea," Spencer said. "We're running out of forest ahead."

"Romans?" he asked.

"Not yet, but . . . um, yes. I see someone way ahead. Ramon?"

Ortiz shouted, and something moved. It was a Roman in armor. He wore the lamellar stuff, not chain or leather. It shone.

The woods tapered off, and they were in rolling ground with a high meadow ahead. The sun was high, and warm. The temperature rose ten degrees as they came out from shadow. The brush was shoulder high, then waist high, then knee high.

There was definitely construction ahead.

"Goddamn," he muttered.

Spencer said, "Yeah, welcome to what the legions can do with grunt labor."

The Romans had a palisade at least as good as theirs. It wasn't quite as tall, but it was pointed and sturdy. It ringed the camp and led away from a gate, to channel any approach.

"Well, ain't this just the shit?"

Ortiz said, "I've read about them, but this is impressive."

The ditch and rampart wasn't as deep as their own. The palisade was square-chopped pillars with inset sections lashed together, pointed at each end. One end stuck in the ground, the other straight up. In front of it all were three-spike lashings that looked like jacks. There was no way to charge the position.

One of the sentries—there were three—walked down toward them, hand held palm out.

Ortiz spoke in Spanish, clearly, using what sounded like simple, uncased words. Dan didn't speak Spanish, but knew enough Romance orthography to make out a summary. He was saying they were a mission from their tribune, the future Romans the legionnaire had no doubt heard of. They were making a courtesy visit to establish communication with their counterparts and discuss future trade and work.

One of the other sentries called back to the gate. Another ran out to replace him; he ran inside, armor clattering, and spoke to someone in a small log cabin. Someone shouted an order, and two others pulled aside the barricades at the gate. The runner returned, spoke to his superior, then waved them forward.

Spencer carefully spoke, "Try to use mostly German based words and limit which of theirs we say."

"Hooah."

"I don't trust them not to pick things up fast."

"Roger that, Sergeant."

Once inside, an obvious firing squad of six guys with javelins kept them in view. They stood to one side as the Americans approached the leader, who was accompanied by the centurion who'd visited them the week before.

Ortiz did most of the talking, Spencer did some, too.

"*Buona Dia. Reunion? Embajador?*"

"*Dignum,*" the Roman said, making clear eye contact.

"*Sic, Dignum. Para Tribunus Sean Elliott, Roma futura duo millennia.*"

"*Tibi nomen est?*"

"*Repetus?*"

"*Nomen?*" The man's expression indicated he thought Martin was an idiot.

"Ah, name. Centurio Martin Spencer. Ah, Tesserari Daniel Oglesby et Ramon Ortiz," he indicated them. "I made you corporals. I think that's the closest. I'm a sergeant major."

"You may as well be, here."

The Roman nodded, and replied, "*Et ego recipiam vos.*"

Spencer said, "*Repetus, petitius?*"

The Roman rolled his eyes. "*Ego accept.*"

"Ah, *gratias.* Our lingua evolva hence . . . mutatay?"

"*Mutata,*" Ortiz provided.

"*Sic.*"

The Roman indicated himself. "*Pilus Prior Gnaius Martius Negro.*"

Yes, the man had jet black hair and dark skin. That would fit. If his cognomen was personal or a family reference.

Gnaius consulted with the centurion and two others nearby.

Spencer said, "Look around carefully. See their troops."

Oglesby had been. There were about a hundred of them, doing

construction, guard duty and regular camp chores. They were getting things done a lot faster with ten times as many people. He felt jealous.

A small patrol returned with Urushu hunters. That made sense. The Romans escorted them in and out and let them do the work, and in exchange gave them some food and shelter. Though they likely weren't asked, just told.

One of the troops turned and gestured to the trio. They followed.

The Roman led them farther into camp to a hut with a thatched roof, a bit larger than the night before. It had lashed cots with leather platforms, very reminiscent of modern army cots. He then pointed to other facilities.

There were obvious urinals set into the western wall, and what appeared to be outhouses with buckets to dump—"*Latrinum*." There were several cooking fires and a smoke house. The NCOs had semi-private cabins, the men had some tents and a long, thatched cabin. Another was under construction.

Oglesby stopped in his steps when the Roman pointed. "*Balnea*."

"Bath house," Spencer said. "Of course the Romans have a fucking bath house."

Fires indicated hot water, and it appeared they had a tub of some kind inside.

"Oh, hell, yes, if they'll let us," he said. "Hell, this is better than some Marine Corps COBs."

"We'll get there," Spencer assured him.

The legionnaire left them with a nod and a comment that probably meant, "I'll be over here." He pointed at the barracks cabin as he did so.

They set their rucks down and looked about.

"Keep your weapons handy, and we stay together," Spencer said. "I'm not opposed to blinding someone with a light if I have to. I'd prefer not to shoot, but they know what guns can do. Now, where are those Indians?"

"Up there," Ortiz said. "They seem to be working at technical tasks. Carpentry."

Their outfits were getting worn and replaced with leather, or perhaps those were protective chaps. He'd love to talk to them, if it could be arranged. There were about twenty of them here, but five times as many Romans.

"Yeah, I see them. I don't see their weapons. That means the Romans are running the show."

"So they're high status draftees."

"Right. Not slaves, but not free. Still, it means they have community."

Oglesby said, "It is a bit tempting."

"Yeah, on the surface," Spencer said. "Dude, you have no idea what Roman discipline is like. Take the worst war stories of Vietnam-era boot camp, add in occasional outright torture like the worst of the Foreign Legion, and expedient executions as needed. If we join here, we'll do whatever they say, all day, every day. And the chicks will be the commander's sex slaves under penalty of flogging into submission. If you try to argue on their behalf, they'll split your tongue or possibly crucify you."

"I heard they were pretty rough."

"Most movies exaggerate violence and brutality. I've never seen anything about the Romans that did it enough justice. They're fucking *mean*. Though they were still better than most of their contemporaries."

"So we're keeping them at a distance?"

"Yeah, I'm scoping out their capabilities. There will be no allegiance. There may be alliance. We hope for at least mutual nonaggression. But we're not teaming up. They have numbers."

Ortiz said, "I don't think those women want to be here."

"Maybe. It's entirely possible they're here for the baths and glitter."

"Or those were the bait and they're not happy now." It was a sophisticated camp.

Spencer said, "Well, buying wives and occasional rape on campaign was very Roman. I don't think we can do anything about it."

"Yeah. I agree with you, though. They're in charge."

"Rome doesn't treat. Rome conquers. It's only that we have linear ties, some language, and good knowledge that we can make them buy us as their betters, for now. You realize there's no officers here?"

"Not that guy back there?" he asked.

"Pilus Prior is some sort of senior centurion. He's a regimental sergeant major. They didn't really have officers who weren't nobility. Us telling him Elliott is a tribune probably saved us. That, and they don't really need ten more bodies. Since we have better weapons, they'll leave us alone, for a while. But at some point I expect them to show up and demand tribute. They might want to tax us and have us put the Urushu to work. They won't care how, as long as we deliver."

"What, food?" There wasn't much else they might have. He was certain Elliott wouldn't cough up any materials for the Romans.

"Salt, leather, labor, most likely. And this is important: There aren't enough women here, and ours are in good shape. That Pilus Priapus has a slave girl, I guarantee. He's going to want the hottest slave girl around."

"Caswell."

"If he can get her, yes. He'll try to buy her, steal her, trade or cheat for her. That she's military makes it even more important that he degrade her from being like a man."

Ortiz said, "She is the wrong woman to play that with."

"Right. She'll wind up dead, after being brutally raped, possibly gang raped, and tortured. Then he'll go for Alexander."

"You think it's that bad?" Dan asked. Spencer sounded deadly serious, but he was always high strung.

"They can't think of women as soldiers. He's assuming we're taking turns with them as whores. He'll first show up offering to borrow her for money. Then he'll plan to make the lending permanent."

"Is there a diplomatic way around it?"

"Either enough salt, hides, iron ore or whatever else, or fear that we'll kill him. Not his men; him." Spencer pointed for emphasis.

Dan nodded. "Yeah. Well, I'm glad they fear that."

"For now, one of them does."

"Are we sleeping at all?"

"Sure, but whoever is on watch is upright and walking around inside here. Not outside. You saw how they covered us with a half dozen goons."

Ortiz said, "I doubt I'd die fast enough to avoid screaming, but I'd rather not die."

"Exactly."

Dan asked, "No bath, then?"

"I'm afraid not."

He'd known that. Dammit, it would have been great.

The legionnaire returned, and indicated they should follow him back to the leader's cabin.

"Weapons off safe, no one sit with a back to a door or window, or any of them."

"Hooah."

It was dinner. The pilus prior bade them sit. He wasn't smiling, but didn't seem put upon. It was just standard manners for visiting dignitaries.

There were hewn benches around a plank table, and one chair built of square rods for the pilus prior.

On the table was bread with oil. It wasn't quite bread. It was probably rice cakes, but it was baked and seasoned.

"*Sedite*," their host said, and pointed at the benches.

There wasn't quite enough room for the three of them at the back, and the two Romans had the end seats.

"Ah, Oglesby, stand and act like a . . . helper, please. It keeps you facing and looks cool."

"Hooah. Do I get to eat?"

"Yes. Ramon will pass you stuff."

The pleasantries weren't really, but the food was good. Two women wearing very little brought it in, though it had been cooked by a Roman. Dinner was roast, salted boar. There were roasted tubers with some kind of oil and mint sauce, and some salad greens, again with oil and vinegar with salt and herbs.

It was mostly pre-cut, but they each took out their pocket knives to eat with.

The Roman noticed that with fascination. Gerber and Benchmade were obviously beyond his understanding, but he recognized the technical advance.

He wanted knives. Whatever he'd wanted before, he wanted knives. "*Cultella*," he called them.

Spencer agreed it was possible, if the Roman were to come to their camp and petition the tribune, there might be a couple of spares.

Did the future Romans know why the Gods had chosen everyone for this?

No. The Gods did their own thing. Future Romans knew more about the world, and the Christian and Jewish gods were popular, too, but no one knew why the Gods did what they did. Sacrifices didn't seem to have any effect.

Sour wine, thick with sediment, was used to toast the Gods, and accept their decisions. Perhaps it was Pan or Bacchus having a laugh, or Zeus demanding excellence.

Dan managed to stay fed, though his right hand was even stickier and greasier than usual after it all. He held his wine cup, carved from wood, and put in a few words here and there as Spencer suggested.

The Roman wanted to trade for a rifle.

No. The banduka were valuable personal property, like a man's sword. No man would go without one. The spares were needed for upkeep. There were bigger guns, but those were used like catapults, only with ranges up to three miles. That brought the man up short. Three miles? Yes.

They couldn't spare a woman's weapon?

No, the future women were as soldierly as men, so great was future Rome. Women not only owned property, but voted and served as officers and governors. The redhead was an experienced leader, aquilifer, and trained in medical herbs and wrestling. Her weapon was as much hers as any man's.

If Oglesby gauged expressions right, that was probably the wrong thing to say.

"Spencer, I think you made her sound even hotter to him."

"Yeah. Crap."

He hadn't even seen her, only had his subordinate's reports. Spencer had been right about the value of women. Hell, he'd like one himself, or at least a bit more privacy with his porn.

Their language skills improved a bit, but it was communication, not conversation. As it got dark, Martius bid them goodnight and had them escorted back to their bunkhouse.

"Well, that wasn't terrible," Dan offered.

Spencer said, "No, but we're in a position where we either have to play our hand, or knuckle under. We can't not show them technology, or they won't respect us. That means we have to overawe them something fierce."

"Shooting demo tomorrow?"

"Probably. Knives won't impress them, even if ours are a lot better. And did you see their forge?"

"Is that what that was?"

"Yeah. Looks like they use it for repairs for now. When they find ore, they'll make iron. I wonder if we can make a wheeled cart so we can haul stuff back and forth."

"That would help."

"Iron ore and charcoal. Unless they find actual coal."

"Can you forge with charcoal? I didn't think it was hot enough."

"Sure. It's cleaner, but generates more ash. Not quite as hot, but more bellows help. It worked for the Vikings and Japs."

"Well, you want one of us awake at all times. Should we use a light?"

"No. Dark, and keep an ear out."

"Okay. I'll go first." *Because that is going to suck, standing for three hours in the dark, doing nothing.* "What about phone?"

"Just keep it dim, and no audio."

"Hooah." Yeah, he could watch something or read a bit.

They all went and pissed together, which wasn't an issue anymore, and felt safer than going alone. Then he pulled on another shirt under his gore-tex, because it was chilly already, and it was going to be a long night.

Spencer said, "One more thing. In case they try anything, no sleeping bags. Use a coat on top, and sleep on the cot, boots on."

A very long night.

"Spencer."

He snapped awake to the whisper, to see Oglesby holding a finger to his lips. He had his phone out for faint illumination.

With his fingers, Oglesby indicated walking feet and pointed around the wall.

Spencer nodded, flipped on his NV reticle, and took a glance.

Through cracks in the walls he could see armed men outside, more than just a couple of guards. Crap. He'd hoped they'd be smarter than that.

He tapped Ortiz and they repeated the pantomime.

He waved them in close enough to be kinky and whispered in their ears.

"Optics on. If they open the door with raised weapons, I'll shoot them. You two fire a few rounds back and sides. If they start poking in through the walls, shout and shoot."

They both nodded back and gripped hands.

This was it. The Romans wanted a fight. He'd hoped the

demonstration had been enough. Evidently, they thought they had enough bodies . . . and they might.

"Keep shooting until they retreat or surrender."

Oglesby whispered back, "Are we going to have to kill them all?"

Given what he knew of Roman discipline, it was possible.

"Dunno. Do it."

The legionaries seemed to respect guns enough to not risk a dynamic entry. The door inched open bit by agonizing bit. The leather hinges had been well-greased, and the reason was now apparent.

He realized it was pretty damned cold. His hands were near numb, as were his toes inside his boots. His guts were not liking the Roman food.

The Romans were entering a dark room, and the soldiers had night vision. Spencer could very readily see the lead man backlit by faint illumination from the fire in the courtyard. He wore no armor, but did have his sword drawn and held in close. He had a day's worth of beard and close cut hair. He was boyish, about twenty perhaps. Two others stood right behind him, very visible in the glow. There was mist out there, too.

Then the leader stepped over the threshold and raised his sword. Spencer took that as the initiation of hostilities.

At this range, the 5.56mm round blew through the first two Romans. The muzzle flash momentarily lit the expression of shock and pain on the man's face, and the barking report ruined everyone's hearing. He heard several more shots behind him, though the flashes were somewhat muted.

He fired twice more to make sure, the second a head shot, then nailed the two behind the leader before they could do more than flinch.

He shouted, "Charge, Oglesby go left!" and headed for the door. He felt them stack behind him, then he was through spiderwebs, spinning right and shooting, shooting, shooting. Ortiz covered the exposed area forward, they had the building as hard cover, and Oglesby was behind him, shooting.

The Romans fell back, fast. At least a dozen were down. Modern rifles made gaping holes and impressively sharp bangs.

"Back inside!" he shouted, and switched to burst. He snapped the trigger toward the guys with the javelins cocked. Two went down. He figured he was at about half a magazine. Good for now.

"Covering!" Ortiz shouted.

He backed in himself, jumping to the side and feeling something smash into him.

A javelin had hit his boot, but hadn't penetrated, with the combination of range and his foot being a flexible target.

Oglesby said, "What now? Are they going to set it on fire?"

"Yeah, I expect so. Where the fuck is that commander?"

"I think that's him pointing and waving." He pointed out the open door. They still had shadows as cover, and shock and awe. The Romans shouted, screamed, yelled. Several sounded badly wounded.

"Alright, I have him." If that asshole went away, the rest might be a bit more reasonable. He rolled into prone supported in the moldy straw with his feet at the back of the hut, took careful aim, ignored the arms and head for center of mass, and squeezed.

The shot took the Roman right in the heart, through his armor. It splashed bright blood in the image intensifier. Someone behind him took some of the bullet in the shoulder. The primus priapus dropped, clutched at himself, and died.

There was a pause and confusion.

Trying to still his heart and breathing, he called loudly and clearly, "Parlay. Negotiare. Intercesse. Communicado." He hoped one of those was close to the Latin.

There was some huddling, and then the other centurion, the optio? came forward slowly. He stopped about twenty feet from the hut. He looked terrified, his knees shaking.

"*Loce.*" Speak.

He thought for words and said, "*Ego desidera egress emigro sine violenta.*"

"*Migre.*"

"*Castrum non vexi.*"

The man nodded assent.

"*Vale.*" Then he muttered, "And adios, motherfucker." Louder he said, "Okay, men, fingers on triggers, walk out proudly. If you hear anything that sounds like an attack, be proactive. Hand me my ruck."

He took it one arm at a time, keeping his weapon handy. The

Romans did nothing aggressive as they left. He figured a couple of the wounded might survive. Or they might take several days to die from lung or gut shots. He felt sympathy for the poor bastards, but he wasn't about to stick around and try to help. The Romans had dealt the hand, they got to pay the house.

They couldn't hear much after the firefight. Using their optics, they walked out the open camp gate, past sentries who stood to sharp attention and made no eye contact. They scanned around themselves as they went. The Romans shied back from the cyclopean figures, and he expected they'd figure out those things were for night use.

"This is going to be a sucky walk back," he said. It was cloudy. That meant it was blacker than the inside of a hole. It was chilly.

They weren't any closer to diplomatic ties with their neighbors.

And they were probably down another fifty rounds of irreplaceable ammo.

It had been lonely and creepy to march out here. Marching back at night had him panting, his pulse hammering, dumping more adrenaline than in the firefight. But they couldn't stop near the Romans, and they had no way to shelter, really. It was a few kilometers, but that seemed so much farther in the thick darkness.

The woods were terrifying. He hesitated going in, but knew they had to. Once in, he didn't want to stop. There was one section where the birds rioted overhead, chirping, singing, making a racket, and he dropped down hugging himself, dammit.

There were few insect sounds, but occasional growls and snorts. Their passage disturbed animals that skittered through the brush. Branches cracked as they shifted.

"Gotta piss," he said. "Bad. Wish we could use light." NVG made things eerier and flat.

"We have to go past their other village," Ortiz said.

"Yeah, but I don't think they can send a message before we get there."

He drained into the trees, as did the others in turn, steam rising from the splashes. They took a couple of minutes to reorganize their gear and adjust straps. He hated having his back to the woods, but didn't want to face it, either, and whichever way he turned he did both. He took point because he had to, and because he felt things behind them. Not Romans. Imaginary things. He knew it was stupid, and he knew he was freaking out, and he knew there were wolves and such.

Progress was slow, and he was very glad he'd mandated not using the sleeping bags. They'd have had to abandon them to be prizes to some Roman.

In the monochrome, he sought the game paths, actually saw deer and elk sleeping and stirring as they hiked past, jumped as a rabbit darted across in front of him. The shadows were a stirred, mixed mess of dark, and using the IR illuminator on his light didn't help much. That showed one clear area with stark shadows, and blacked everything else out in contrast. Fifteen minutes later, he had to piss again before he started dribbling in fear.

He was glad to see flashes of false dawn to the east, the trees slowly turning gray and ghostlike through fog, which were just as horroresque, but at least hinted at daylight.

He was still a city boy, even if that city was ten people in a couple of tents.

They passed the former Urushu village well after sunrise, circling uphill and around past the animal pens. They waved at a couple of distant parties, and kept humping.

He slowed once they were clear of the village, and paused for a moment, behind an outcropping with scrub.

"Ortiz, can you grab some of the jerky out of my ruck? Left pocket."

"Got it."

It was bland jerky, unseasoned except for salt and mustard, but it was meat and it gave him something to chew on rather than his lip. Then they moved on. There was clear sign of some predator in the brush, wolf or possibly hyena. They'd never seen a hyena here, and he wasn't sure if they had been, but there'd been some ugly looking canines that might be.

About midmorning they sighted home, its wooden walls a comfort.

Sean Elliott was not happy. A firefight with the Romans was not going to help. He agreed with Spencer it was likely unavoidable.

Regardless of what philosophers thought about the utopian lives of primitive people, they were so far craven, superstitious, short-sighted and dull. They were very clever at tools and adaptation. They had little grasp of social interaction.

The Paleo people had only immediate needs and enough resources to meet them. The Neolithics understood property and wanted control of it, which he understood. It would be nice to get along with them, but they just hadn't been interested, and now the Romans had them, too. And the Romans wanted to be in charge. The East Indians were too few to matter, though would have made better allies. Except they'd likely be able to figure out how a rifle worked if they got hold of one.

If they could all just be rational and cooperate, they'd do a lot better. But everyone wanted to be in charge.

"So it's us and the Urushu village against the rest of them?" he asked Spencer. The two sat in the cab of Number Nine for privacy. It felt odd to sit in a vehicle seat after all these months.

Alexander could hear them, from the back, but she'd proven very discreet.

Spencer said, "Yes, sir. About a hundred Romans, about half that many Neolithic levees with spears and presumably Roman discipline, and a few Urushu women they snagged as comfort women and household servants for the leaders."

The man spoke in a rush, and sipped bark tea fast, followed by devouring some soup. He still shook. He placed his canteen cup and wooden bowl down in the footwell.

Sean added, "Plus the Indians."

"Yes, sir, but they don't seem to have much say in the matter. The Romans had their muskets. We only saw them at a distance, as here."

"You think they want to do the same with us."

"I'm pretty sure that's exactly what they want, sir. Control of the weapons and exotic pussy. Pardon me, Alexander."

From the back, she said, "I understood just fine. You know why I always have a knife."

Sean said, "Yeah, if I had a company, or even a solid platoon, they'd know the score. As it is, they aren't scared enough." He kept running into shortage of manpower.

"The new leader is. The pilus prior apparently didn't think our rifles were that much different from the muskets, and had no idea we could see in the dark. He was clumsy."

"You think the other one is more stable?"

Spencer unzipped his jacket, and shrugged it off.

Sean decided it was warm, too, and they could continue this in the public area. It wasn't that busy, and the rest needed to know the score. He opened the door and climbed out.

As they walked the whole twenty feet to the kitchen area, Spencer answered his question.

"He may be, but I have no idea what the other NCOs will want. I don't remember if they took votes on these things, or if they'll do so regardless of custom."

Crap. This was bad.

"Should we leave? Or have the Urushu move here so we have more bodies?"

"Sir, if they come here, the Urushu would either be slaughtered, run off or get in the way. The Romans wouldn't be impressed. What bothers me is we can stop the Romans."

"You think so?"

"If they come in formation, even a turtle, they'll stomp in, expecting a few casualties. We need twenty good shots each to exterminate them, five shots each to break even their discipline, and there's a good chance we'd take out more than one with each burst from the Two-Forty or a Two oh Three shot. The Fifty would demolish them. But what then? Do we want to wipe them out? They have experience exploiting land like this for food and other resources. We need to ally and learn from all these groups. We could do a charcoal burn with the Romans, and work on reducing more iron."

Dalton muttered, "Always with the iron."

"Hey, fuck you, Corporal!"

"Enough."

Sean did believe Spencer could produce iron, but it wasn't going to be soon, and they had other, pressing needs.

He said, "I agree we want alliance if we can. For now, we stay here, they stay there, and we finish reinforcing. I wonder if it's even worth the goat pens, though. They're going to be wiped out in every raid or encounter."

"We still should, sir," Ortiz said. "In between, it's easier than hunting."

That was logical. But damn. "Okay. But we'll just stay here and keep an eye out. Hopefully, that little fight convinced them to not be stupid."

"I hope so, sir. I don't know. At least they've had a direct demonstration. I think our new policy needs to be to make sure they see our God Tools. Lights, screen images, knives that don't need sharpening, all of it."

Spencer said, "I think you're right. They'll have to wonder how it works and why it never runs out of charge, and what we can do."

He thought for a moment, to let it all sink in, and ran it through his mind again.

"I'll look at it more later. Write it up for Alexander's log, summaries from each of you, give her the photos."

"Yes, sir."

Next item. "I want to reinstitute PT. A run around the compound once a week, and some kind of team activity."

Spencer nodded. "Makes sense, sir. Cohesion."

He asked, "Do we have a ball to go with the bats in the back of Number Eight?"

"We do, and we looked at that, but were afraid of losing it in the rough. I was thinking of stitching something up, or a football type thing instead, to throw."

"Yeah. Crap." His brain was really lagging today.

Moving on, he said, "We managed to dig the latrine a bit deeper, so there's an actual pool. Right now, turds seem to float for a while, but they don't stick on the rocks and stink. That wasn't a fun job. Luckily, the Urushu were happy to help."

"That's a nice plus, sir."

"We reinforced the walls and roofs with more weavers. It should block wind better. We started digging a hole for a bathtub, and you can see we got another cabin roughed out. That's for you and me."

Spencer glanced over. "Sir, I recommend we be in different hooches with different roommates. We don't want an attack to take us both out at once. With Barker in his tent and each of us somewhere else, our chain is more secure."

That . . . was obvious. He blushed.

"Yeah, that makes sense. Good. In any case, we have some progress."

"Great to hear, sir. We have all summer to get ready for winter again. And I'm looking forward to a hot bath. The Romans had already built that, but it wasn't safe to partake."

"That alone would be worth teaming up if we could."

"If we could, yes."

He wanted to be reassuring. So he said, "Well, the mission was a success for intel and planning. I still hope we can work something out with them, but it's going to take a while for them to get used to the idea."

"Or to get as comfortable as Roman units ever got at the end of the Empire, and see no advantage in fighting us."

"Or that. I hope to avoid killing more if we can. We need to save the ammo." A dozen firefights like that, they'd be out of ammo.

"Roger that, sir."

He also didn't want slice the throats of any more casualties. He wasn't going to mention that, though. Their faces would haunt him forever.

CHAPTER 28

Jenny Caswell did the best she could to produce an herb and vegetable garden. The rooty things were definitely carrot family, but the carrot was an odd mutation, cultivated for only about 4000 years. These roots were edible when small, before turning woody and tough.

There were dandelions, plantains, mint, and some spring fruit coming in, but it would be a while before those developed. Still, they could have some starch from the tubers and blanched acorns they had on hand.

"What do you think about rice?" Ortiz called down from the goat pen.

"Got any?"

"No, but Bob thinks he can harvest it off the river like the Urushu. Can we build a rice paddy?"

"It's possible, but we'd need to dig out a field up here and it wouldn't be much."

"I like rice. I never got into potatoes that much."

That was not uncommon for Central Americans and Asians. They'd be happier than she would. She loved rice, but potatoes were tasty things with scallions and sour cream, and she could do that here, if she had potatoes. Rice wouldn't work as well.

Her rake was hand lashed from a sapling root. Her hoe was an E-tool, and that hurt to bend so much. It was good exercise, but Lord, her back ached as she split and carved heavy clods. The blade bounced off a rock, and the handle bit into her flesh.

"Ow."

"Yo!" Barker called from below. She turned to see him coming upslope with four Urushu, and wiped hair from her eyes before sucking on her dinged knuckle. She should probably have Alexander trim her bangs again. She'd done an okay job last time.

"Hi."

"Fish trap is complete," he said. He held a bundled hide.

"Cool. How well do you think it will work?"

"This well," he said, holding up the bundle and opening it. There were a dozen large trout in it.

"Damn."

"They swam right in. It'll need periodic maintenance, and has to be cleaned out or they'll starve and scare the others."

"It went together fast, though," she said.

"We have a silty bottom and I have a hammer," he said, pointing to the sledge held by one of the Urushu. "Then we used the anti-RPG mesh off Number Eight to reinforce and net it up. So it will need regular cleaning, but it will definitely catch fish."

Some of the Urushu had fish, too. She recognized one named Tyuga, and he grinned as he showed her two really fat ones. It was a friendly grin.

"Great," she said. Fish would be better than mammal, both in taste and in ethics. She hated killing anything with a face. Fish had less of that.

"I'll cook it in goat butter, if we can churn some," he said. Churning meant clabbering it in a bottle, then shaking it thick, and pulling it out with a spreading stick. He nodded and headed through the gate.

She went back to digging, but it was a lighter task.

That evening, they ate fresh fish fried on hot rocks with salted goat butter and wild garlic. It was fantastic. They even showed the Urushu how to do it, and since butter was beyond their experience, they were amazed.

"Om nom," Tyuga said. A pidgin was developing, and that one was an obvious onomatopoeia.

"Yes," she nodded agreement, while plucking a chunk of flesh off the skin. It was fabulous, and less guilty, and delicious.

She hoped the butter wouldn't affect their guts. It was processed from milk, but even with the cooking and chemistry change, it might still cause a lactose reaction. Hopefully not.

Alexander had sweetbreads fried in butter, and said, "These are almost palatable."

"Are they helping?" Doc asked.

"I really don't know. I needed adjustments to the dosage every six months anyway. So I know I'm off, but not how far, or in what way."

Jenny felt sorry for her. That had to suck even worse.

After dinner, she said, "It's Equinox in two days. I hadn't really thought about it, but I was thinking of something instead of a ritual."

"Oh?"

"Party. Tunes, food, wine, dancing in the compound."

She was sure Elliott would refuse, but he leaned over and conferred with Spencer.

"Sounds good," he said with a smile. "We can invite the Urushu. A shame we can't invite the others. I'd like them to see it."

"Ah, a PR thing, sir?" Alexander asked.

"Yeah, proof of technology."

Jenny asked, "How many are we inviting? Security issues and space come to mind."

"Whoever is here. It can be their secret."

So a party it was, on Thursday night.

Oglesby told the Urushu to join them for a spring ritual. There were seven in camp, three of them women. One was a hunter, one along to help cook, and one seemed to be the lover or partner of the injured man, who'd gotten a nasty foot infection. They understood drainage and cleaning, but not sterile procedure, debridement and suturing. Doc had taken care of him, but the man could only sit and watch.

Dinner was more fish, smoked this time, and bacon and ham, with cheese. She had gotten goat cheese to work. It was mild, like a salty cottage cheese but a bit firmer. It was still good. They'd find variations, she was sure. Barker planned to smoke some.

"We need to watch their lactose intake, Doc," she warned. If they got sick it would be nasty, as well as potentially bad.

"Yeah, she's right. A taste each only."

Spencer said, "Oh, God, yes. Don't want a re-match of the Vikings and proto-Micmac."

"I take it it was bad," Elliott said.

She said, "Lactose tolerance comes along after animal husbandry. The Neoliths are probably safe. The Romans are. Not the Urushu."

Doc said, "Goat should be easier, and cheese and butter are processed."

"Right."

Oglesby said, "I told them we need permission from our spirits to serve them the goat milk food."

"Aw, dammit," Spencer said, and high-stepped into the middle again. He did that well, took it seriously, and was respectful to the Urushu in context. He wasn't all bad, just prejudiced by his upbringing.

He pointed west. "The setting sun says we can serve them, as soon as it touches that pole. A taste only, I must warn, sir." He indicated with thumb and finger. "It will please the spirits."

Bob said, "Everyone should be discreet and go with small bites. I don't want them feeling slighted either, even if I could explain the biology."

"I can," Doc said. "They wouldn't get it."

They waited a few minutes for the sun to touch the fence, then distributed the cheese and bacon.

The Urushu had heard of the bacon, and a couple had tried it before. They seemed ready to change religion or start an orgy on the spot, once they tasted it and the cheese.

Then Spencer brought out wine.

Alexander said, "Let's make this a toast, each as we wish, to springtime and renewal."

They drank deeply, and the stuff was sour, bitter and nasty, but alcoholic. The burn started and she forgot how bad it tasted.

One of the laptops had been faced out the back of Number Nine, and Alexander had reluctantly let Trinidad plug in his iPod, which had a lot of music.

A slow, steady beat with lots of percussion started, and turned into something sonorous and trance-y. The Urushu stared in fascination at this magic thing.

"It's dance music," Alexander said. "Sort of. Come on. Dance."

She started moving back and forth, and Caswell saw what no one else did.

Twelve males gave Alexander their undivided attention.

Particularly to her swaying hips. She limped a bit on her scarred foot, but she still had that roll that women could do and men couldn't.

Yeah, she was going to sit this one out.

She loved dancing, and this would be great, but, no. Worse, Spencer was the one up top on watch.

She sighed and scrambled up.

"Not dancing?" he asked.

"Not right now. Too much to eat, maybe."

"I've never been a fan of butter for frying fish."

"That could be it," she said. Whatever. She didn't want to talk.

The Urushu were confused and disturbed by the music, staring around, pointing at the box. They chattered to Oglesby, he sounded reassuring. Ortiz and Trinidad started dancing with Alexander, if you could call rhythmic shifting of weight "dancing." Then Trinidad started doing some sort of movement probably derived from Kali or Arnis.

Once reassured, the Urushu started stomping feet and getting into it.

She took a scan around the horizon, as the sun dropped. The long shadows showed some herds of sheep and goats, a family group of cattle, and falcons dropping into the grass for crepuscular snacks. The crickets started up, and a couple of them were inside the truck cab. It echoed.

In short order, Doc was dancing with the Urushu huntress. He did have a fantastic figure, and he'd been popular with them all along.

Ramon had programmed some good beats. The trance got louder and segued into techno. By then, the Urushu were perfectly cool with the magic music, as long as it had beat. A cup of wine made its way around, and the dancing got more energetic and less coordinated. It was cool, and she shivered while they sweated.

Alexander was back to back with Dalton, not quite grinding. Oglesby and Doc were in a circle with the Urushu and their women.

The volume was enough to cause vibrations in something that rattled.

She took another scan of the horizon, as did Spencer. The music might be keeping wildlife away. There was nothing past the goat pen, except a distant huddle of wild sheep.

Spencer asked, "What the hell is that whomp whomp sound?"

"Probably Skrillex," she said.

"Is that a band or a style?"

"That's the band. The genre is dubstep."

"Oh, *that's* dubstep," he said. "I'd occasionally heard it, but never known the name."

"Seriously?"

"Really."

"What do you think of it?"

"It sounds like Optimus Prime fucking a dishwasher."

She fell flat on her back in hysterics. Oh, goddamn, that was hilarious, and yet she could see it.

Then she realized he was staring down at her, and that look, and she sat up again, fast.

"I may try to dance a bit," she said, and headed for the ladder.

She slid down the ladder, landed hard and staggered back, then joined the circle of Urushu. She felt safer between their hulking heights than with the soldiers.

A colored flash started. It was Spencer with one of his lights, switching from blue to red to green to white LEDs.

The Urushu cheered. They'd never seen colored lights before, and green and LED blue were unlike anything nature would offer in a sunset. They stood and stared.

Elliott bowed out and went to the tent, followed by Barker. The younger troops kept at it. Then Ortiz went up top to relieve Spencer, who went to bed also.

She knew her judgment was suffering from that awful wine, and if hers was, everyone else must be plowed. It was near midnight, the drumbeats and bass making her dizzy and euphoric, when she grabbed Alexander and said, "I'm going to crash."

"Okay!" The woman looked drunk, and Jenny hoped she was careful. There were two other females, though, so she should be fine for now.

She brushed her teeth behind the trucks, took another look at the capering figures in the firelight, and crawled into the hooch.

She kept her rifle off safe on the shelf next to her pallet, and made sure she had a knife in reach, too.

Unlike Doc, she wasn't thrilled with the idea of attention.

She missed her mother and brother, but being so isolated here brought her to lonely tears.

⁘ ⁘ ⁘

Martin Spencer looked around the camp. It was a beautiful clear day, like he'd never see anywhere in the modern world.

The spring was quite productive. With Urushu help and a better grasp of the resources, plus all the exercise they'd been getting, things moved well enough. By the end of April they had four log cabins and the tent, with two residents each. The Urushu lodge was a cabin with a wickiup at each end, on the far side of the stream but inside the camp. The smoke hut was dedicated, and Barker and Caswell took meat and vegetables through steadily. Next to it, a new, bigger sweat lodge started taking shape, with plans for a tub.

Spencer moved into a cabin with Doc, downslope of the center. They spent a day trenching around it to ensure it stayed dry in the rain, and poking additional clay mortar in the gaps. The hearth was a bed of slate at the bottom, with a slightly off-set smokehole with a sump under it against rain, and a wooden shingle over it to reduce drips. He didn't expect they'd use it much, since they still cooked everything communally, and would be in the tepee during the winter freezes. For now they were on beds of greenery, until they could lash or peg some cots together.

However, it meant a couple of hours of complete alone time every couple of days while Doc was on watch, and he was sure Doc appreciated it, too. The man's phone was mostly full of porn videos. He was a reasonably devout Catholic, a very nice young man, but had an obsession with huge tits. He probably liked private time to consider that.

Just getting away from everyone, though, while being near enough for emotional support, was a good thing. That first night, tension just melted out of him. He stared at the almost complete black of the ceiling, heard the occasional shuffle of people in the compound, and zoned to sleep, the most relaxed he'd been since they got here.

He had morning watch as the sun came up, and let the light soak into him. It was still cool and damp at night, and sunlight was welcome. Ortiz replaced Trinidad, and they watched the Urushu wake up, clean up, and help with the cooking fire and breakfast. It did go faster with more hands, to a point. They had to be reminded of the soldiers' "ritual" of hand washing, too.

There was always movement—the flocks of goats, occasional family groups of deer, wandering herds of aurochs, wild horses and the occasional rhinos. As far as one could see, there were food animals. Birds circled and landed or took off. Occasional predators padded through to the water, mostly silent but with occasional growls or howls. It was a full-time task to keep an eye out. Every shift was a nature documentary.

But he saw something to the south, up beyond the ditch. Movement, and he recognized upright human movement from its pattern.

"Sighting movement," he said.

"I see it," Ortiz agreed. "Small group."

Elliott was brushing his teeth behind Number Eight. He spat and asked, "What do we have?"

"Small number, under ten, not Romans. Should I page them?"

Elliott said, "If you think it's safe, yes."

He called, "Hello!"

There was some shuffling in the treeline, and he waved.

Slowly, one man stood up. He wore leggings and a tunic.

"Neolithics," he said. "Whatever they're called."

"Gadorth," Oglesby said.

"Well, there appear to be four of them."

"That's all?" Elliott asked.

"That's all I see. Ortiz?"

"Four," the man confirmed with binox.

"Okay, call them in."

Oglesby climbed up the back, cupped his hands, and carefully shouted some words. He pointed at the front gate.

The men waved back and started walking. He followed them, as they slipped in and out of sight through the brush and behind the wall.

Shortly, they were inside, and by the fire.

"Offer them some food," he said. "Protected guests."

Caswell said, "I believe I said that a long time ago."

Oglesby and the LT sat down to talk to them.

Elliott called, "Spencer, it's daytime, come on down, please."

"Roger that." It was light enough to go to a single watch. Well past light enough.

He slid and contorted down out of the turret, and ducked out the back. He could still bend like that, but it wasn't fun, the way it would have been at age twenty.

He joined the fire circle and asked, "Caswell, can we get ham here, please?"

She brought some over, and seemed pleased he'd asked. Minor power play. There was a lot of that going on.

He chewed the meat and wished for oatmeal. He wasn't a huge oatmeal fan, but . . . goddamnit, he'd never been big on carbs, until they were gone.

Stupid shit like that shouldn't cause stress reactions. But he remembered having cinnamon cereal or toast for breakfast. And he'd love some eggs without bird shreds.

The ham was good. He no longer noticed the gristle or other bits. He chewed, he spat, he moved on. Cal would come in tonight and clean out all the scraps in the area, plus whatever bits of liver Barker cooked for him.

The Gadorth were wiry, short, and had interesting blueish eyes with Mediterranean skin tones and brown hair. They smelled of buckskin and sweat. They had stained and large but healthy teeth. Their clothing was simple, unadorned for the most part, with a small square and line marked on the front. It seemed to be a tribal mark.

They showed great appreciation for the ham, and relaxed in their status as guests.

Martin hoped they could come to terms with them as well.

Dan Oglesby didn't know much of the Gadorth language. It was still fairly simple in construction. Tenses and cases were apparently a later invention. It had basic SOV grammar. Some of the words were almost recognizable, which supported the theories about PIE. It was a shame he'd never be able to share this information.

Rohss, the leader of this element, was balding, shaggy elsewhere, with gray shooting through the brown. He was well-wrinkled and tanned with age.

"*We Shiny Spirit settlement depart. Hunting tell of. Here arrive.*"

He translated, "Yeah, they ran from the Romans."

Elliott asked, "Okay, but why? I don't want to guess."

"*Magic thunderspear Shiny Spirit Kill.*"

"Past or here?"

"*Here*-guch."

"*Guch* means not-past?" He pointed at the rising Sun, then to the west. "*Guch*?"

Assent. *Guch* meant "now."

"Sir, they want us to kill the Romans."

"Right, I figured. Tell them our spirits don't allow that, but if they want to move to the east here, or even onto the river bank, they can associate with us and we'll try to keep the Romans away."

"I'll try. I haven't learned much of this language." He looked at his notes, and said, "You move there," and pointed over the wall, "or by water. Help-help us you. Shiny Spirits stay there," he pointed again.

After some back and forth, that deal seemed acceptable. But there was more.

"Sir, they want us to help them go get the women."

"Urushu women, yes?"

"Correct."

"If we do, they're free as soon as they leave. They don't get to keep them without permission."

He figured they wouldn't like that, and he was right. From their perspective, they'd conquered a weaker group and owned whatever they had. The Romans were a problem, and since the soldiers didn't seem aggressive, they were useful. The inherent illogicality didn't bother them. They hadn't grasped the hierarchy, only their own decline.

He explained the exchange.

Spencer said, "I don't want them too close. They'll either scare off the Urushu, or try to take the other village. I'd say they go down by the water."

Elliott said, "I agree. I also don't want to send anyone to help them bail out. That's between them and the Romans. If they can create a place, they can keep it, and we'll interdict as we can. Take it or leave it. They can camp a hundred yards downhill for the time being. Be as diplomatic as you see fit."

"Hooah, sir."

"*To water Gadorth move. Selves move. Thunder Spirits Shiny Spirits send away.*"

After some back and forth, they accepted it was the best deal they'd get, shrugged and agreed.

"Now ask the Urushu where they should go. They have a say in this."

Caswell said, "Sir, if we're fishing down there, I don't want them in the area."

"A mile upstream?"

She said, "What about they cross the river and set up there? It'll be harder for the Romans to get them there, too."

Spencer said, "Shit, why didn't I think of that?"

Ortiz said, "Because we're thinking of it as an obstacle, because we're thinking about herding. They likely are, too."

"I like that better," Elliott agreed. "They can set up rafts or such to arrange a crossing."

He relayed it, then translated back.

"Sir, they want to be sure you can stop the Romans from here."

Elliott said, "Tell them our big guns can reach the river easily."

He pointed up at the M240B on Number Nine. At least one of them looked familiar from the previous battle, and that man spoke intensely to the others.

They all agreed, and rose slowly, with open-armed gestures.

"Sir, do we want to bow or shake hands? Or just do as they do?"

"Hell if I'm bowing to anyone here." He opened his arms the same way and nodded his head.

That done, Barker escorted them toward the gate. The Gadorth understood they were being evicted fast, and their status in kind.

"I'm going to update my notes now," he said. "Alexander, can I upload it when done?"

"Just bring it to me."

"Hooah. And, sir, one point."

"Go ahead?"

"Other people either need to start learning their languages, or they need to start learning rudimentary English. I recommend the former for security. I like being the lead on the project, but if I'm the only one I'm a risk. I've been in two firefights already."

"Yeah. Make time here and there, talk to people, get it done. Everyone understand?"

There were hooahs and yeses.

Caswell asked, "Is there a risk of them learning our language?"

"Not as much," he said. "It's very complicated by comparison. They tend to single nouns and adjectives with emphatic gestures or repetition for emphasis." English was a hard language even in the modern era, if you didn't grow up with it.

Elliott said, "Still, I'd rather we could communicate with them, and not the reverse. We'll work on learning their words. As to the rest, figure on putting them to work when they're here. Don't be shy. Anything grunt labor, they can do. If they start getting disgruntled . . . okay, that wasn't intentional—let me know and we'll see about contracting it."

Dalton said, "Hey, who's gonna wind up on TCN escort?"

They all laughed, even Caswell.

Two weeks later, Jenny Caswell was nervous about the Neolithics being even that close. The scents of their campfires rolled across the river through the trees, and she could hear faint sounds now and then. It was useful for trade, though. They'd even helped improve the fish traps the Americans used now.

The trap was made of stakes pounded into the water about an inch apart, with an angled entrance to funnel the fish in. The tops were lashed with cord from the anti-RPG mesh from Number Eight to keep them in place. Small fry got out. Large fish got stuck and rarely found the escape. All one had to do was wade into chilled glacial runoff and scoop them up. She was thigh deep and fighting muscle cramps as her feet tried to curl into balls. She caught a large one, probably five pounds, and reached over her shoulder to her ruck.

Worse was the smell of fish in her ruck. She'd have to soap and rinse it again soon. However, it seemed some of the Stone Age people of both groups knew what plants to render for oil, so they'd be able to make more soap, with refined lye, not just ash.

She understood, and agreed, with Elliott's caution. It would be too easy to join one of these groups, but then get subsumed, and in the process, they might wind up destroying that culture as well.

Oglesby was twenty feet farther out, pulling out fish. There were two ways to kill them. Either crush their skulls with a hammer, or let them suffocate. She tried not to think about that as she stuffed another in back, and waved off some bugs. They were tiny little gnatlike things. They didn't bite, but swarmed in clouds and were annoying. One brushed an eyelid and she flailed to chase them away.

The fish were some form of trout, and tasty. They had enough between them for a good meal and some smoked leftovers. They needed more of this. Fish was a great source of protein, readily available, and less ethically troublesome to her than a mammal.

As she thought about that, the gnats returned.

The Neolithics seemed to be behaving themselves and weren't disposed to trouble. They had their own trap across the river, which was almost a quarter mile wide at this point. Apparently, fear of the Romans was also keeping them in line. They rafted over once a week or so and engaged in light interaction with whoever was gathering fish.

She hopped out, feet almost completely numb, then burning cold, and rubbed her legs down. You dried off for warmth, to keep the clothes dry, and to avoid getting grit into the boots, which would cause blisters and wear out socks. She was down to five pairs now, though Alexander promised to darn a couple of the least damaged.

She sat on a down log near the pebbly bank, cautious of damaging her underwear, and worked on drying her feet. They'd all be wearing leather in a few years.

Oglesby plunked down next to her, doing the same thing.

"Ow," she said as a muscle started spasming.

"Did you step on something?"

"No. Cramp. Calf." She started massaging it and flexing her foot. He reached over and pulled her leg over his.

"I can help," he said.

She picked up a tremor in his voice, and really didn't want "help."

"I'll be okay in a moment," she said.

"I don't mind," he replied. "I learned how while swimming. My calves took a beating."

Oglesby had never seemed like the type. She expected Dalton, with his "traditional" values, or Spencer, who was tough, mean and gave her those looks. Possibly the LT, playing the power card as leader. Oglesby was a kid.

His flesh was cold against hers, but his breath quickened and she knew that tension in his leg meant a pending erection.

"I'll be fine," she said, coldly. She drew her leg back, but he resisted.

She wished Alexander was around. They weren't friends, but at least another woman would catch the signals, and might offer backup. But they were alone down here.

"Okay. At least let me warm it up," he offered, pulling his coat over her leg. "And lie back to take the tension off." His hand was on her shoulder, and he probably thought it was friendly, and it was so much less than that.

She'd rehearsed a lot of strategies. If she fought him, at least one of them got hurt. He'd be resentful. If she ran screaming, he was going to deny everything, and she'd be the crazy feminist bitch.

She couldn't cry wolf.

This was going to get violent.

He'd slipped his arm around her, so it was going to be jiu jitsu. She shifted her weight slightly, and—

"I think she's fine, Oglesby," Spencer said, behind her.

OhShitOhShitOhShit.

"Ah, yeah. Sorry."

She heard him say, "I figured you might need a hand hauling fish. I'm at a stopping point on the clay, so I came down."

Oglesby said, "Nah, the trap wasn't that full." And didn't he sound casual now?

"Well, they're going to be tasty, but we'll need to smoke and dry the hell out of them to keep them, and we're going to be sick of the damned things come next spring."

"Yeah."

Spencer gave her one quick glance that seemed wistful and sad, and said, "Get dressed before you chill. I'll head back up."

Oglesby was shaken, and dressed in a hurry, not saying anything. She pulled on pants and decided she could dust them out later. A quick flick with a towel cleared her feet, and she pulled on socks and boots.

Oglesby looked at her general area as they returned, but never actually made eye contact. She'd become a thing.

At the camp, she let him stay ahead into the gate, then split around to the left and went in the back. She stepped across the creek on the stones, and went in the back gate, then across the bridge to the kitchen area. She handed the ruck to Barker.

"Here. I need a few minutes."

"Thanks," he said. "Are you okay?"

"Homesick. Give me a few minutes."

"Yes, take as long as you need," he said.

She headed toward the hooch and the CP, and tried to reengage her brain. She wanted to be alone. She wanted to wash off. She needed to tell Alexander and the LT, but she didn't trust any of the men, and Alexander was increasingly spacy since her drugs ran out.

She'd better.

She climbed in the back of Number Nine, said, "Gina, I need to talk for a moment," and tried to make it professional and nonchalant.

"Sure, go ahead."

"I'd rather be in private," she said, since she could see Ortiz's legs on the gun turret platform.

Alexander flared her eyes and looked quizzical, but followed her out in a crouch.

Once under the roof of their cabin, in the dim light, she felt slightly better.

And she hated herself for wrapping her arms around Alexander and sobbing.

The older woman hugged her back, warm and human. She didn't say anything.

It took several minutes, with her face on Alexander's worn uniform, before she could talk.

"Oglesby just tried to molest me."

"What? How?"

"We were gathering fish. I got a cramp. He tried to 'help' with his fingers and a warm coat, and wouldn't I like to lie down?"

Alexander turned her head slightly and said, "That isn't necessarily threatening."

"When we're both without pants, and he spoke in those hushed tones."

"Okay, so it was a come on. That doesn't mean it was ill-intended."

"Gina, you don't get it. Sooner or later, they're going to rape us. Possibly as a gang."

Alexander sat down on her bed and said, "Well, if they do, there's not much we can do. We might also be eaten by wolves, or die of cold or disease, or live long lives without seeing home again. I'm not going to burn myself up over every risk we face. But he stopped?"

"Spencer came down, and that old fuck was staring at my legs the whole time."

"That 'old fuck' is four years younger than me."

It frightened her that Alexander didn't see it.

"They watch us every moment, especially in the tent or the latrine. They're getting grabby, and trying grooming behavior. Soon one of them's going to get violent."

Gina said, "They're looking at the native chicks, too. Just encourage that."

"It won't be enough. How can you be so relaxed about it?"

"Because there's nothing I can do about it. I can stay here a bit more if you like. Do you want me to talk to anyone?"

"No, they'll just call me a crazy feminist chick. Or worse."

"Okay. If you want to, I'll back you up."

She meant it, and didn't realize her complete mushiness was worthless.

"Thanks."

"Do you need to sit here some more?"

"No, let's get back out. They already think we're lesbians."

"No they don't."

She really was clueless.

Jenny stepped back through the leather flap into sunlight. Oglesby and Spencer were gathered near the kitchen. Spencer gave a slight wave of his fingers, and she walked over, really not wanting to have whatever conversation they had planned.

No one else was around, they were all at tasks, including Barker.

She stepped up.

"Yes, si . . . Sergeant?"

Both men looked at Oglesby; he finally met her eyes.

"Sergeant Caswell, I'm sorry. My brain stopped thinking. It won't happen again."

Until next time, she thought.

"Make sure it doesn't," she said.

He looked genuinely embarrassed, turned and walked off.

Spencer said, "Can you think of anyone else who's a potential threat?"

"Every male here, Sergeant." She didn't say, *especially you.*

He nodded slightly and frowned. "Well, I'll be having some one-on-one talks. I can't stop them looking. But I expect them to be disciplined. I don't know what the answer is long term. But I figured that was going to come up sooner or later, and he was very eager to go with you. It was in his body language."

"I didn't see it," she admitted.

"Yeah, obvious to me. There's lust, and then there's hunger. He was hungry."

"Thank you," she said, seriously.

"Let me or the LT know, or Alexander if she can help."

"I will. Thanks."

He left.

Either she'd really misjudged him, or he was playing the friendly protector game for later, or possibly he'd even set Oglesby up to fail so the first scenario would be stronger.

Or was she being paranoid?

She'd avoid them both and see if she could team more with Alexander. They'd probably end up hating each other, and she'd want to kill the sarcastic bitch, but at least they wouldn't sexually assault each other.

She still felt cold, and it wasn't from the river.

Dan Oglesby burned. He wanted to get away from people for a while, so he stopped by the office and told Alexander, "I'll be chopping wood."

One of the Urushu, Og!sa, asked about helping. He declined. "Ni, Og!sa, Mah se they." *I find it.* I'll do it. "Find" was everything from find to make to perform to produce.

Yes, he'd been trying to be nice to Caswell. He figured she could use some help with the cramp, and a little friendly human contact wouldn't hurt. No, he wasn't ready to attack her, with that explosion of hairy bush around stained panties, on the muddy banks of a river reeking of fish. She really needed to lighten up.

He felt guilty about those pictures he had of her for "reference," as he called it. But dammit, a man had to do something, and until Elliott cleared them to date the locals, some human contact and interaction with anyone would still be nice. He'd made sure to behave since that one early encounter, though he suspected Doc had managed to nail one of the visiting female guards.

He wondered about Caswell. It was a bad cliché about feminists being lesbians, but she ran straight for Alexander every time she had a problem, even if Doc or Spencer would be a better choice for resolving it. Alexander didn't seem to be interested in anyone, but she had a pile of medical problems and was old. Caswell seemed to love hanging out with her, though. It wasn't companionship; there was no reciprocation.

Eventually they'd have to court local women, teach them some modern sanitation like toothbrushing, and form partnerships with them. In the meantime, they could at least be sociable with each other, and that's all it was—being sociable.

He had been excoriated for trying to be friendly. He hadn't been trying to rape her.

Right?

And was she, or Alexander, going to match up with local men? Or become old hags?

Either way, he'd just avoid her from now on.

CHAPTER 29

Martin Spencer had issues. They came out at night.

Late night watch with Ortiz came around about once a week. Ortiz was a good man, and probably the least bothersome.

Alexander was showing health problems, as expected. But hell, so was he. That dull ache in his gut was never going to go away. Eating bone meal for the calcium helped a little. But he was dying, slowly and painfully. And of course, the black magic drink didn't help. It was raw on his guts, but it did keep him awake. The others had tried it and didn't care for it at all, so it was all his.

Elliott would be stressed for life, unless they dissolved this command and all went native, which was still a possibility.

Barker was smoking more of the local weed. On the one hand, that was weak. On the other hand, Martin wanted real coffee and sat here in the dark trembling in fear. He hated being out in this unforgiving dark, he hated separating any distance from the group, because he dreaded some reversal.

He had no idea what was up with Caswell. She walked around as if every man was ready to drag her off and rape her. He wondered if she had been, and needed help, but there was no way to ask that question, no help he could give, and he didn't think anyone had had opportunity.

Oglesby probably had been trying seduction, not rape, and clumsy about it, but that shit couldn't be allowed. The kid had lucked out with that local chick in the field, and that was it unless and until they organized something with the Urushu, who were starting to look acceptable. This was still effectively a combat deployment, and that meant no fraternization. Hell, they'd been in combat here, with the Romans, the Neolithics, wolves and a bear.

Doc stayed busy, but was definitely sexually frustrated from handling all these naked women and having no way to socialize. Though he wasn't a social type either.

At least he wasn't a social type here. Coming here had fucked them all up.

Trinidad obviously felt left behind. There was no intel work, he was backup for the goat herding, and grunt labor otherwise, which was unfortunate, because he was pretty good at the grass and stick hut lifestyle. Possibly that was part of it. It was like being back in the rural PI for him, which Martin got the impression was somewhere he'd never planned to go again.

Dalton prayed a lot, and Martin wasn't sure if that was normal for him or not. He didn't get religion, at all. Dalton roomed with Oglesby, and they didn't seem to interact much, just crawl in, sleep, come out, go to work.

Probably the winter had stressed them all on personal interaction. He really was getting burned out on the idea, and Elliott kept trying for conversations so they could bond. He didn't want to bond with these people. He wanted to keep them alive as well as possible, have them near enough for reassurance, and try to come up with a working forge.

As far as those candid shots he'd snuck of Caswell, he was going to delete those in the morning. They were very pleasant, but it wasn't fair to her, and he couldn't choke the young bucks down if he was violating the same rule himself. It was wrong and he knew it.

Ortiz took a scan with NVG and said, "Movement."

He whispered back, "Animal or people?"

"People. They snuck up the creek and just came out of the trees."

"That's interesting." He grabbed his own goggles.

"Romans. Scale armor, cloaks, shaved faces, short hair."

"How many?"

"Eight or so. I think it's definitely some sort of infiltration. Do we want to sound alert?"

"Not yet. They obviously have no idea we can see them. Just keep your voice quiet. The gun is live, yes?"

Ortiz carefully popped the top cover.

"Yes. Are we going to shoot?"

"That depends on them. On the one hand, we want to avoid violence. On the other hand, it looks like they may want to start some."

"Shouldn't you wake Elliott?"

"Depends. If they're just lurking, then yes. But if they actually act hostile, we won't have much time. I want to actively discourage them from skulking around. If they keep sneaking back, we keep having trouble."

"Warning shot?"

Ortiz was so civilized.

"No, Ramon, if they do something stupid, you shoot to kill. Are you okay with that?"

"If they're hostile and you say so, yes, Sergeant." The man raised his eyebrows and looked serious.

"What do you see?"

"They're squatted down. All I can get is faint lines, of course. They're . . . striking flint."

That wasn't to see by. That would be an incendiary.

He flipped on the image intensifier on his carbine and squinted. Through literal slits in the piles, he could see almost nothing. "I can't see from this angle. I do see things that look like helmets and weapons. Definitely pilum. They're donning the rest of it." He caught a little flash. "Yeah, I see sparks. If they get flame, shoot them."

"Through the timbers?"

"Absolutely through the timbers." A flame flickered and wavered as the Roman blew it bright. "And there we go. *Fire!*"

Ortiz leaned forward, squeezed the trigger, and rattled off a burst about two seconds long.

Shouts came all around, and screams from the Romans.

Spencer shouted, "Hostiles contained! Threat contained. With caution, folks."

"What the hell did you shoot at?" Elliott demanded as he tumbled out of his hooch, barefoot in PTs waving a 9mm.

"Sir, eight Romans lighting an incendiary."

"And you didn't challenge them verbally?"

"No, sir, I did not. I decided they needed active dissuasion, so they don't try this every week."

The LT looked furious. All he said was, "Devereaux, take Barker. Administer treatment. Oglesby, go talk to the Urushu."

The Urushu were out of their hut and jabbering, dancing around with spears, looking frightened.

Elliott wasn't happy, and Martin didn't care. These fuckers all needed an object lesson to stop them from attacking the U.S. Army. Since they believed in gods, let them believe the Soldiers were gods, or at least had technology and powers from the gods.

Armand Devereaux wished he'd swapped for a pistol, because the carbine was bulky and in the way for this. Barker pulled open the back gate; he cleared it first and downslope, Barker had upslope. The goats were fussing around at what they thought was thunder.

Barker followed. Inside, Ortiz said, "Following," and ran to join them. They splashed their weapon lights ahead of them, along the weed- and gravel-strewn base of the palisade. It looked pretty imposing up close, and the ditch was damp and squishy.

The upright Romans shielded their eyes and looked awed and confused at the artificial lights, brighter than anything they'd have had in their time.

Three were down, another three had stayed with their buddies. He had to give them points for balls and discipline. The other two had split.

He used his phone.

"I've got three casualties, three buddies in proximity. If there were two more, they left, possibly for backup. I only saw two."

"Roger. Keep reporting."

"One dead, one through the thigh. Major muscle trauma, but he'll likely recover a lot of motion. The other has a cracked hip and an ugly crease across his chest. He must have turned to run."

The dead one had been hit low in the guts, spilled out the back, and taken a second round high in the upper right thorax. A puddle of bloodsoaked grass and dirt lay under him.

The thigh wound was ugly. The 7.62mm bullet had probably tumbled on its way through the log. A sizeable chunk of tissue was missing. The man made no noise, but he was sweating and taut-faced.

"Ortiz, can you TK him for now? I'll have to try to suture the artery and line up the muscles as best I can."

"Hooah."

The hip wound was potentially a killer. The man would have to be immobilized while the bone knit, and hopefully it hadn't cracked down into the femoral ball. The hole was far enough out he might recover. The crease had ripped iron from his armor and torn skin, muscle and a few chips of fibrous bone.

Ortiz spilled out water from a Camelbak; he soaped his hands, counted thirty, and then rinsed. The guy with the hip seemed to grasp cleanliness, and nodded faintly.

"*Medicus,*" he said. He turned to Ortiz. "How do you say 'pain'?"

"*Dolor,*" Ortiz said.

"I can't spare anesthetic, so let that tourniquet numb things for a bit. Bleeding contained?"

"Yes."

"I need to scrub that chest wound and make sure that hip is clean." He held up a cloth made from an old T shirt. The man nodded again.

"How do we get the armor off?"

From the phone, Spencer said, "It's called lorica segmentata, or at least we call it that. He should understand that word. It fastens down the middle."

"I see it." He unfastened it, loosened the sword belt across it, and they eased it over his head. He grunted considerably, cringing and sweating, teeth bared.

The other three sat back and let him work, offering invocations to some Roman gods or other. Did he hear Mars and Pluto in there? Maybe. Aesculapius. That one he knew.

The man whined and whimpered and shook as Armand debrided the wound channel. It would heal, it would just leave an impressive scar. He shifted his headlight in several directions to get a clear view of it. Shadows emphasized it more than it was.

Then it was back to the hip. He said, "Cautious? Circumspect? *Dolor.*" He wanted the man to expect it to hurt.

"*Intelligo,*" the man replied, and clutched at the stick Barker held for him. His previous whine turned to a high keen as Armand probed the wound with a cloth-wrapped finger.

"We'll cauterize if it looks infected. Could we use that damaged screwdriver as an iron?"

"Yeah. You're not going to now?"

"If it's clean and oozing, I'd rather leave it. Poking anything in might make it worse. We might also try maggots, but they might be nasty and might get loose in the cavity."

"Roger."

Then it was on to the bad one. He wasn't sure he could do anything for a flesh wound that severe.

"Ortiz, I need more light. I'm going to have to figure out how to suture that arteriole." The wound was an ugly pit of ground meat, trickling fresh, bright blood. The femoral artery was probably bruised to hell, but seemed to be intact or he'd be dead.

Ortiz said, "I've done those on calves. Baby cows, I mean."

"Can you do it?"

With a nod, the man said, "Yeah. They're going to have to hold him down. I want to carefully turn him feet downhill, then elevate the good one."

"Do you need to turn him?"

"If he hasn't already, the pain is going to make him piss and shit himself."

"Yeah, okay. I'll support the leg."

Ortiz said, "*Rotare? Girare? Circum?*" and indicated.

The three came over carefully, shying away from the helmet lights. Barker moved back to keep them covered.

Gingerly they turned the man about, and used the empty armor and a blanket one of them had to prop his legs in position.

"How are we going to remove the sutures later?" Armand asked.

"Yeah, that's a good question. I don't know."

He got on the phone. "This is a serious question. Does one of the females have a pair of silk panties? We need thread for sutures."

He heard it relayed, and the response was, "Sorry, no."

"Roger." He thought for a moment. "Okay, we're going to get it closely inline and arteriogenesis will restore perfusion over time. Not as effective, but easier. Can you get the vessels probed into place, and I'll see what I can do with the muscle? And I want to go ahead and flush it out with boiled water from the Camelbak. I'm trying to decide between some of our alcohol, or vehicle antifreeze."

He looked up at a flashlight from the wall, blinking past them.

The phone sounded again, "Also, some Gadorth are coming. We're signaling them with a light."

Ah, that's what that was. Barker acknowledged for them, and said, "I'll keep an eye out while you work."

"Thanks."

The Romans had some grasp of surgery. One stuck a leather thong in the patient's mouth, though he was barely conscious. The other two each sat on an arm. That left Armand to wrap himself around the good leg, as Ortiz took a gentle but solid grip on the right leg below the injury, and lean in.

The man grunted and hissed through his teeth, and his legs trembled as Ortiz poked and probed with a dental pick. The man flushed and sweated, and heat emanated from him in waves. Two of them spoke to him in reassuring tones. "Aesculapius" and "*medice*" were in there again.

Ortiz said, "Okay, that's done, but this muscle is a mess."

"Yeah, I can do that."

"Okay, you're up."

"This is going to hurt more."

"*Mucho dolor. Multe? Multo?*"

"*Intelligo,*" one of them replied, and spoke to his comrade.

Armand flushed the wound clean with water, keeping the pressure low so as not to dislodge the arteriole, the two veins and the mass of hemorrhaged capillaries. The tissue was terribly bruised from the supersonic bullet ripping through.

"Did this go straight through?" he asked Barker.

From downhill, Barker said, "Given six inches of wood, it probably tumbled sideways. I'm going to track the Gadorth in, so I'm busy."

"Got it. And that's what I thought on the bullet. But still hellaciously fast."

He turned to Ortiz.

"Hand me the alcohol. I'm going to use a little. It won't last forever anyway."

"Roger. This bottle?"

He looked up. "Yeah, that's it. Tremendous dolor now. Extreme. Maximus. Formidable?"

"*Intelligo, Medice,*" one of them agreed. They clutched their buddy as he turned the leg slightly and poured a precious dollop of ethyl into the wound.

The man screamed around the gag, his other leg drummed against the ground, and this one twitched in spasms. Watching the damaged muscle flail was fascinating and creepy.

He spent several minutes teasing strands of tissue into line. There was no way it would heal fully, but it should at least minimize knots and be straight and usable. He'd limp, but be mobile.

"Okay, I'm going to suture it where I can, then we bandage. Do they have any bandages?"

One of them replied, "*Fascea? Ligamentum?*"

"Yes, that."

One of them produced some gauzy linen.

"That will do." Good, they had some idea. That would help a lot on recovery. He sutured around the exit where the flesh had torn in a four-pointed, irregular star, then forced the edges of the round hole in front together and poked a knot through that. He wrapped it carefully with the bandage, which was neutral colored but seemed clean enough, and sat back.

It was morning with a hint of pending sunrise. They turned off lights and blinked as their eyes adapted.

The phone said, "We've got more incoming. Seems to be the Roman leadership."

Barker said, "Understood. We have it." Armand hadn't heard him return.

They rose, stretched, and stood back with their weapons.

Spencer's voice said, "Yeah, if you're done treating them, I want the dead guy's gear. It's useful for study, and it's more metal we can use."

"Hooah." That made sense, but the concern now was the squad of Romans striding over the rolling ground.

It appeared to be the same NCO who'd met them the first time.

"*Ave,*" he said.

"*Ave,*" Ortiz agreed. "*Medicus sanar,*" he said, and pointed at the two wounded, barely conscious men.

The centurion came forward alone, slowly, and they gave him room to look at his men. He jumped and cursed in surprise when Barker shone a weapon light on the thigh wound. He shielded his eyes, stared at the light, at the rifle, and then turned slowly to look at the injury.

He seemed quite impressed by the repairs, or perhaps at the nature of the wounds. He leaned back and looked upslope, trying to be discreet.

He was obviously examining the shattered logs. His gaze was carefully neutral, but lingered on the holes. He clearly understood that

American guns could shoot through logs and kill whoever was beyond them. They could shoot right through his walls, or out their own.

Armand didn't think any of them would cause any more problems.

He and Ortiz walked toward Barker, as Barker covered them with his rifle. Then they all strode slowly around to the front gate in rising sun, as Spencer covered them with the M240B.

Sean Elliott had wanted to be down up close, but he was needed in camp. When the second party had shown up, he knew he was in the right place.

Now he looked down from a palisade platform at the Romans. They were stoic, but sober. He wondered if they'd have to escalate to grenades or the .50 to convince someone.

The Urushu had never been disposed to violence. They'd been looking at the bullet holes and the M240B, and then realized the soldiers had magic lights that shone like the full moon.

He didn't think they'd ever be a problem. The Neolithic Gadorths had accepted the superiority of the U.S. Army, but those damned Romans were stubborn.

The Roman centurion talked to the three effectives and then the two casualties. His gestures were firm, with the classic knife hand and a stomp of a foot.

Then he drew out his sword, leaned over and hacked open the throat of the poor bastard with the butchered leg. With that wound added to the others, he gurgled, thrashed and died.

Spencer muttered through his phone, "Expected."

"Can you elaborate?"

Ortiz did. "That was the instigator, and that word is the same. The gist of it is he's saying that they're never to mess with us again. They have disgraced Rome. I think it's partly from losing, and partly from disobeying orders. But I don't think they'll do it again."

"I hope not. Spencer . . . well done. I hate wasting resources and fighting our neighbors, but well done. I think that's all you could do."

"Thank you, sir."

He felt sorry for Doc and Ortiz, having done all that work for nothing.

The Romans turned two shields into a stretcher for the remaining survivor, and six of them lifted him and started tromping away. The centurion faced up and held his hands out.

"He wants to parlay."

"Yeah. Do we bring him in?"

"I say no. He'll recognize vehicles and wonder why we're not using them. We don't want anything to suggest we have any weaknesses at all."

"Okay, I guess I go out."

He went out as Doc and Barker came in. As he rounded the corner, the Centurion removed his helmet, so he did the same. Ortiz was waiting as well.

"*Ave*, Tribune."

"*Ave* to you, Centurion."

He followed that the Romans apologized for the breach of discipline, and would return home. Would they dispose of the two dead?

Ortiz said. "I think those small pouches are personal belongings. You should return those, sir."

Elliott pointed, and Ortiz untangled them from the bodies, then brought them forward. The centurion accepted them with a nod.

"We will inter them with respect and honor," he said. "*Funerari?*"

The centurion shrugged and said, "*Sepelite.*" He placed his helmet back on, and extended a hand.

Elliott took it, shook, and stepped back. The Roman about-faced perfectly, and marched back to his men, secured his shield and spear, and kept walking.

Spencer said, "Strip those bodies. I want everything. We bury them naked just in case of discovery. We'll use everything else."

Elliott was getting tired of dead people. These poor bastards were even more outclassed than Afghans. There were no bragging rights to it, it was complete domination and extermination, every time they fought.

He hoped this was the last, but feared it wasn't.

CHAPTER 30

By May it was getting hot during the day. Rich Dalton found more chores in camp, so there was variety. He was still primary hunter, and would be for several years until they had proper ranching set up. That was his task this morning. He led his two partners out the east gate and onto the slope. The bow he carried was one of Barker's, and it actually seemed to have gotten heavier with use. That was apparently a function of wood fibers being compressed and strained.

It was a very simple bow, not like the compounds he'd grown up with. It was a D section of fibrous hardwood, rubbed with oil and with a leather wrap as grip and arrow rest. It did, though, shoot arrows consistently. That was the important thing.

As they walked, he took a glance behind them. Their village actually looked like one, now. They had the goats, with troughs for feeding and watering, that the Gadorth had burned and chiseled out from logs for them. The animals also had a better shelter against weather.

The kitchen was an open log cabin now, too, with a stone hearth and an oven of piled slate. They could fry, roast and bake. Boiling was still done in the ammo cans, now looking rough and distorted. They wouldn't last forever.

Caswell had lashed everyone a chair, and the firewood piles doubled as resource piles for shingles, poles, binding bark, anything timber related.

Rich was taken a bit aback. Alexander had taken a bunch of

rawhide thong and started crocheting what he thought was a fishing net. Then one morning she stretched it between the truck and her cabin and it was a hammock. She gave it to Barker, who slung it between two poles in his tent and seemed delighted with the comfort.

He felt blessed. Regardless of what or why they were here, God was soothing his spirit. He appreciated each moment more than he ever had back home. Even the cold and wet were experiences to be enjoyed.

Ortiz went hunting with him carrying an M4 for backup. Also along was O!ofa, who was a heck of a sneak and had a fine cast with a fletched javelin. He wore a minimal breech cloth and carried a smoked skin as a shoulder wrap under one of the Army rucks. It was no longer odd to see people almost entirely naked. It would never be Paradise, but that was another trapping of artifice gone.

He still wore his eyepro, though. There was the UV, and there was the dust. That was a mix of sand, dried grass fragments, bugs and God only knew what else.

It was necessary to walk longer for hunting, especially the plains beasts. They were getting cagier. At least the wolves and lions had learned to avoid the Americans. They didn't come nearly as close as they had, or to others.

They were a good two miles out when O!ofa pointed at movement.

"Well, we have that antelope there. Is that saiga?" It was about fifty yards away.

Ortiz said, "Or something very like it, yes."

"I wonder where the . . . ah, I see the herd. That's actually a pretty fit one."

"Stringy, but we can stew it."

"Okay. I can hit it this range. I'm going to try to cripple it, since I can't pierce the skull."

"Yup."

He eased out of his ruck, nocked an arrow, rose slowly, sighted carefully, breathed and steadied, and rolled the arrow off his fingers.

The shaft whistled as the string thrummed. A few seconds later, the antelope staggered with its thigh run through, and started screaming. It staggered and tried to run.

"Okay, out of its misery."

O!ofa knew his cue, and already had his javelin in the air. It was weighted with a small stone, but had the bone bleeder point the

Urushu liked. It sank into the beast's neck. The antelope staggered twice and fell over.

Ortiz was still the man at gutting animals. He had a steaming pile of entrails in minutes, two slabs of rib, the liver and heart, all four haunches and meat off the back.

Rich eyeballed the stack. "That's a week's worth for us, five days with guests."

"And it's just past lunch. Let's get back."

"Yeah, the cats and vultures are ready for lunch." It never took long for the cleanup crew to arrive. There were several types of raptor in the air. He didn't see any cats, but knew they were there. Then there might be hyenas later. They were scarce here, but did exist. And the wolves.

Ortiz said, "They're welcome to it." He'd even cracked the skull and the other thigh so the scavengers could get to brain and marrow.

The meat stank, but it was something they were all used to, now. He'd rinse off the blood and goop after they delivered it to the kitchen slab for processing. O!ofa carried his share wrapped in a loop of hide he'd had under his shoulder wrap. The Americans had their rucks.

Ortiz suddenly twitched and said, "Dude, nock an arrow fast." He whipped his carbine around and unsafed it fast. O!ofa muttered something and held up a javelin.

On their line between here and home was a lioness.

They took an orbit around to the south, uphill and keeping a good two hundred yards from her. She sniffed, noticed them, but turned her head toward the remains of the kill and padded that way.

"Close," he said. That could have been bad.

"Yeah," Ortiz agreed.

They kept eyes open and scanned the horizon all the way back, in case more of the pride was around.

The COB did feel like home, and give structure. Through the gate, the bridge and cabins were signs of real progress. They'd get there.

Barker and Spencer had been messing around with some sawhorse-table thing all day. He figured it was some kind of rack for drawing hides or something. They chiseled and tapped, pushed stuff around and back.

"Here's antelope," he said.

Caswell called, "I'll get it as soon as I tie this off." She was working on another chair, probably for trade goods.

Nothing would happen to the meat on the planks, so he left it there and rinsed off in the stream. Christ, it was cold. Refreshing, but cold. He reminded himself to be thankful. It was clean, fresh water. Though the rocks were protruding more.

"The water level's dropping," he said to Ortiz.

"I noticed. I wonder if it's seasonal or more than that."

O!ofa said, "A!ka, sun," and spread his hands in almost a poofing gesture.

Rich said, "Sounds like seasonal drought. I wish we'd asked earlier."

"We may need a well."

"Yeah. Hey, sir, have you been tracking the water level?"

Elliott said, "Yes, I noticed. I'm figuring we need a well."

That was good. The man really was smart.

"Where?"

"Up in what used to be that ditch. If I remember my geology, there's likely some seep there."

"If not, we can haul water every morning, but it will suck."

He flicked off drops and went to see what Spencer and Barker were doing.

They were bending a sapling over, with thong tied to it.

"That's a lathe," he said.

Spencer said, "Yes, a springpole lathe. For now, it'll work with files, stones and knives. Eventually I'll forge some chisels."

Spencer demonstrated.

"You rough the material with a hatchet, peg it to this axle, and boring that hole took half a day. There's a dead center here if needed for longer pieces. I hope to make a pin base for turning longer stock. Then you step on the pedal," he demonstrated. "And hold the tool against the work. Release the pedal and the spring takes it back."

"Nice." That was functional. "How did you come up with this?"

"This was standard in most villages from Biblical times to the sixteen hundreds. If they didn't have industry and water wheels, or slaves, they used this."

"Damn."

Barker said, "I found some nice walnut. We're going to start on some proper eating bowls."

"Oh, hell yes!"

"They won't last more than a few months, even if we smoke the wood to preserve it. But they're easy to make."

"You guys rock," he said, and meant it. They actually were pulling stuff off here.

Maybe Spencer could build that forge, given time.

By June it was hot, dry, and obvious they'd need a well. They also had to relocate latrine functions outside the wall.

Sean felt needed technically. That was better than just being the commander. Certainly that was important, but it felt different from this.

The well didn't need to be that deep. They dug about six feet into the loam and slate in the ditch, using the pick then detaching the head to use it in close quarters, and a folding saw of Barker's and an axe to chop roots left from the downed trees. It took two days of heavy, sweating work and he did his share. It felt good to work real muscles. It was much more than morning PT.

At that depth they had a muddy little puddle. That was a good sign.

"Okay, we need a good three feet so we don't churn up dirt when we draw water out. Work the slate down in a circle and keep dredging the muck out."

They lined the sides and bottom with courses of flat slate, then carefully started filling dirt in around it, placing more rocks and straight limbs as vertical reinforcements.

Trinidad spent most of the time down in the hole, seemingly comfortable in the tight confines, and letting Dalton and Spencer haul him up for breaks. He was three feet below the ground and comfortable. Sean couldn't imagine that. There were fewer roots at this depth, because he'd picked a spot with smaller trunks, juggling water table with ease of digging.

"Easier than in the PI," Trinidad said. "We dug wells because they were safer than river water. But we usually had some power tools."

In three days, it was done, complete to a sweep atop and a shingled roof to keep rain and bird crap out.

Barker said, "We'll need a cover, hide over a frame, to keep animals from drowning. It'll also limit bugs."

"Got it. Can Ortiz or Alexander do that?"

"I'll ask."

The remaining dirt was tamped back around, with another load of stream slate to make a dry standing area and walkway.

"Now this is important," he said. "Oglesby, explain as thoroughly as you can to our guests that a well is taboo. No one is to eliminate on this side of the COB. Downstream is the only acceptable location. The spirits will blight us all with sickness in the guts if they do so."

"Hooah, sir. They're actually pretty good about it anyway."

"Yeah, except I've seen them pissing in the dry streambed. Below the bottom wall is the only allowable location. That's part of why we have guards at night."

"Got it."

They had cabins, a well, a lathe, a smoke hut and a wall. They really were doing it, bit by bit. At some point, if Spencer really could forge something, or turn it on the lathe, he wanted a proper hand pump. He remembered flap valves could be made with leather.

As they returned to the COB, though it was really more of a village at this point, he smelled dinner.

"Oh, man," he said. "We've got steak?"

Once inside, he saw the circle was packed. All the troops, save Ortiz on watch, along with three visiting Gadorths, and four Urushu guards plus two patients sporting leather bandages. Doc had been busy.

"We have steak," Caswell said. "Along with salted, fatted and roasted roots, a dandelion and burdock salad. The dressing is wine, cheese, salt and mulberry juice."

"Holy shit." She and Barker were amazing in what they managed to turn out.

"I'm going to say it again," he said. "Your knowledge of edible plants, even with what we've learned locally, is a godsend. Thank you."

"You're welcome, sir. I tried my hand at the lathe, too."

His salad came in a wooden bowl, followed by steak and roots in another one. The bowls were mostly symmetrical, rough to the touch and heavy, but it was better than trying to use flat chunks of split wood full of splinters and bugs.

"So we've got water again," he said. "Goddamn, this salad isn't bad. I guess I missed greens more than I thought I did. Anyway, one-hundred-fifty-yard safe zone around the well. Latrine is in the stream when we have water, and outside downstream when we don't. We'll probably have to maintain it every year, too, between frost and floods. But we're getting there."

He wondered why all the guests were present, too? Usually they fed themselves. All the Stone Age people were delighted with the salad, wiping up the dressing with their fingers and sucking them clean. He shrugged and did the same.

"Save some room for dessert, sir," she said.

". . . Dessert?"

She handed him another bowl, this one full of berries, what looked like cream, and something else.

"Mulberries with clotted goat cream and honey."

"Caswell, if I wasn't the commander, I'd propose marriage to you."

There were cheers all around, then he looked up and saw her body language. Apparently, that was not something she was comfortable with.

"This is great stuff," he said. "Are you archiving the recipes?"

Alexander said, "I have them all, sir. Photos of every edible plant they bring in, butchering processes, write-ups on preparation and seasonings."

"Oh, good." Yes, having an admin type and combat photographer was working out to their advantage. He worried about her fatigue and memory issues, though.

They finished as it got dark, and he realized it had been hard physical labor for him as well as the others. He'd enjoyed it, felt he'd accomplished something, but was tired and ready to crash.

Spencer said, "Okay, this next part is going to be a bit irregular, since we're short on the personnel we need, but, Platoon, attenSHUN."

Everyone rose, and it seemed they'd been ready. The guests followed the lead and stood as well, except the injured. Having no idea what was going on, Sean rose, too.

"First Lieutenant Sean Elliott, front and center."

He walked over to Spencer, who saluted and said, "Well, sir, this should be done by at least a major, but we don't have one. But, it's your anniversary date back home, which makes you a captain. We don't have any bars, so Ortiz donated a spare insigne. Alexander plucked it and hand embroidered it with thread from one of Dalton's old socks, so you may want to sterilize it." He held up a velcro tab with two respectably stitched bars on it.

There were chuckles, as Spencer reached forward, ripped off the Velcro 1LT tab and stuck on the bars.

"I . . . thank you," he said. He really had no response. Yeah, it was, and he'd have promoted on schedule assuming nothing went wrong, and it didn't really matter here.

"Really, thank you all," he said. "Your support is everything I have."

He stopped, because his heart was pounding and he was tearing up.

Spencer saluted him, he returned it, and stepped back out into the dark.

Oglesby chattered away, and he was curious as to the translation. For now, he wanted to be alone somewhere he could stop being the commander for an hour or two, but his fingers kept brushing the tracks on his chest.

These were the finest soldiers he could have ever hoped to serve with.

CHAPTER 31

The Romans sent another delegation, peaceful, and after some outside discussion, it was agreed they'd cooperate on some ventures, such as a charcoal burn down by the river. The Romans wanted more access to the salt up in the hills, and knew where iron ore could be found. Martin Spencer was excited at that prospect. The lathe had restored some of his faith in his abilities. It was one thing to know how to do something, another entirely to actually do it. They needed a forge. He was starting with the advantage of some hammers, and it was still a daunting idea.

Relations remained cool. The Romans kept their distance out of respect for the guns, and pitched leather wall tents down by the river woods. The Gadorth wanted to avoid the Romans, and had seen what rifles could do. They paddled across from their settlement on rafts. The Urushu were very cheerful with the Americans, but that wasn't returned. Ten people with finite resources couldn't be too gregarious or generous.

He still had the gladius from the dead Roman, those weeks back. As swords went, it was very functional, but not pretty. He'd seen much nicer reproductions. It had character, though. He could trace the wrought iron grain of it. As modern edged tools went, it was a piece of shit, but with enough of these and discipline to match, Rome had conquered the known world, and had been so influential he could talk to them without much difficulty.

Back home, it would be worth a fortune in any condition. Here, it was still priceless, until he could produce better steel.

The decorative work on the sheath wasn't that great, either. He'd seen Pakistani-made knives with better stamping and fitting.

Still, it was a war trophy he appreciated.

He avoided, mostly, thinking about home by throwing himself into work. He was XO, NCOIC, assistant heavy lifter, cultural attaché and hoped to add "village blacksmith" to that.

The charcoal burn was something he knew of but had never done. With Urushu and Gadorth help, the Romans scoured the woods for downed timber from inch thick on up. With their mattocks and spades, and him, Barker and two shovels, they cleared a patch of ground, and turfed it down a foot to remove rocks.

"*Petrae* boom!" one of the Romans explained, in obvious onomatopoeia and gestures. He nodded. A big fire was to follow, and moisture-laden rocks would be entertaining but unhelpful.

The wood they broke and cut, with help from Martin, Dalton, Barker and Trinidad, into foot-long pieces that they stacked upright four high in a circle, with an outside perimeter to brace it, about ten feet across. There was a central log to support it, which they used as a depth marker for the mound. The mound was covered in a foot of earth from the center almost to the ground at the edge, with a small gap.

Barker impressed all parties by lighting a fire with a propane torch. Once there was a nice mound of coals, one of the smallest Romans shoveled them all up, carried them over the dirt cover, and dropped them into the central chimney where the center log had been removed.

It was nightfall, and they'd been eating cheese and dried fish all day. Martin's guts were in a constant state of irritation now, and he munched some rice cake with bone meal in it. It tasted like chalk. It helped the burn.

From there it turned into a drinking contest, with raw but drinkable Roman wine out of actual animal skins. He shrugged and took a gulp from the neck of something furry.

The wine was awful. Sour wasn't enough of a descriptor. It was bitter, slimy and tasted of leather.

Between drinks they had to seal cracks in the crust, to keep air out.

"The charcoal is supposed to cook," he explained to Dalton. "You're cooking out all the impurities and leaving just carbon."

"That's why the small air gap at the bottom only?"

"Right. And notice where they're standing and holding hides? That's to limit wind. Once it's all carburized, we'll douse the whole thing, first in dirt, then water."

The night was a haze of carousing and work, interspersed with naps. As the pile slumped, a hole would open in the crust, and flame would jet out into the greedy oxygen. Someone would shout, and the nearest men would pile dirt onto the crack to seal it. Sometimes that would dislodge another crack and start the process again.

In between guzzles of bad wine, they managed to swap dirty jokes with the Romans.

He managed to get one to provide him the essential phrase, and he waited until the crew boss shouted, "Imple foramen!" *Fill that hole!*

"Ipsa dixit!" *That's what she said!*

There were laughs. He followed up with, "What do you call that useless piece of skin above the vagina?"

Once the riddle was translated, he said, "*Matrona!*" and that got laughs, too. Then one of the Romans said something about the difference between a local woman and a latrine being that the latrine had a smaller hole and smelled better. Wow, that one dated back that far?

"I understand only half of legionary parents are married. Your fathers were married, but your mothers were not."

That got howls of mock outrage, and someone asked if the Americans ever fucked their women in the other hole, or were they afraid of getting them pregnant?

About 0400 he realized Caswell and Ortiz were standing back but in sight, holding weapons. Yeah, he wasn't up for anything himself, being fatigued and drunk, and no one trusted those Roman bastards.

Then someone called out and it was a frantic scramble with shovels and hands to close the bottom of the pile, and start splashing water into any burn-throughs before sealing them with more dirt.

Just about sunrise, the Roman in charge pronounced himself happy with the burn and dismissed his element back to their tents. Martin took that as leave to stagger back up the hill, through the gate, over the footbridge to grandmother's house, or rather, his hooch, and pass out on top of his sleeping bag, fully dressed.

His last thought as he faded was that they should name the cabin "Grandmother's House."

✤ ✤ ✤

Jenny Caswell barely made it through dinner and was ready to collapse. Alexander followed her to the cabin.

She asked, "You're crashing, too?"

Alexander said, "Yes, I'm on watch at midnight. It's getting harder for me."

"I wish there was more I could do." Alexander's thyroid issues required more sleep than before. She felt sorry for the poor woman. They ducked in the real door and inside. The door even had a cat flap for Cal. They shifted around and got onto their respective pallets, and started pulling off boots.

Alexander said, "The sweetbreads seem to be helping a little. I don't see how they're a delicacy, though. They were nasty at first, now bland."

"Good. It's interesting how much effect certain foods have."

Alexander shrugged in the dim. "Well, cutting down on starch has helped my weight."

"That's more likely the exercise."

The older woman shrugged again. "That, too."

"Did you notice how hungover Spencer is?" she asked.

"Yes, his eyes are as red as Oglesby's skin."

"He deserved it." Yes, she felt schadenfreude.

"Oh? Did he drink that much?"

"Yes, but he was swapping alleged humor with the Romans. All demeaning jokes about women. Get a man drunk and you find out what he really thinks about other people."

"I don't take jokes like that personally."

"To joke about it they have to be thinking it."

"I've made jokes about men before. What's eight inches and white? Nothing. Why is it hard to parallel park? When you've been told since you were sixteen that this is eight inches." She held a thumb and finger apart as she shuffled down into her bag.

"It's not the same. He's in a position of authority and privilege. Humor works against the dominant class; from it, it only reinforces inequality."

"I don't think I follow."

"Think about medieval jesters. They could mock the ruling class."

"I still don't follow."

It was hard to explain to someone who didn't want to get it, who was sick.

She moved on. "Well, let's change subjects. We're coming up on a year."

"Yeah. I guess we're definitely not going home." Alexander sounded cold, emotionless. She really loved her family, Jenny could tell, and they were gone.

"So now we have the rest of our lives."

"It sounds more like a sentence."

A life sentence, she thought. "In some ways, I guess it is. What do we do?"

"I guess we need to decide if we're going to be some sexless military unit, or get involved with families."

"You mean relationships, right?"

"Yes, since I'm sterile. It would still be nice to have someone to sleep and cuddle with."

"I don't have much experience with that."

Alexander said, "Yeah, I figured."

She probably didn't mean that the way it sounded.

"I mean, I've had lovers, but no one I lived with."

"I understood. We're all sort of living together now. Just without the sex and warmth. All the bad parts of barracks and roommates, and none of the good parts of family."

Jenny said, "I don't know what I'll do. The Urushu are aesthetically handsome enough, but they don't understand sanitation the way we do. The Romans . . . I really don't like them."

"And the men here?"

She shrugged in the dark. "Well, Oglesby creeps me out. Spencer's old and creepy. Doc is Doc, he always seems embarrassed if it's not professional. Barker's a decent guy, but really not my type. Dalton . . . that wouldn't work. Ortiz is possible, but he's still got some of that Latin machismo I don't care much for. Trinidad . . . also a good guy who's not my type. I'm afraid if I showed interest in the LT, it would be taken the wrong way, and he's not a good personality type."

"He's entitled to a family, too."

"Sure. But I don't think it can be me. I really never thought any male in the military was going to work for me. You?"

Alexander stretched back on her rack. "Elliott? Decent looking, but I think he thinks of me as this old lady. You said it about Doc. And he's physically lean and handsome, but his features really don't attract me. He's got very pronounced lips. They just . . . no. Dalton's an annoying younger brother, and so is Oglesby. Trinidad . . . I just don't feel anything there. Ortiz maybe. Barker's almost an older brother, even though I'm older."

"Spencer?"

"Yeah, I think that's where I've assumed it's going. But I want to see my kids, and my cats, and my husband. I don't want to settle down here."

As if on cue, Cal ducked his head under the door and chirruped. He padded onto Alexander's bedding and settled down to purr. She reached down and skritched him.

Jenny said, "I'm still concerned that if we don't have someone, we'll be seen as fair game."

"If they haven't raped us yet, I don't think they're going to. They might fight each other if we start showing interest, though. And we'd make a terrible couple."

"Yes, and even if it wasn't a cliché about feminists being dykes, I'd avoid that suggestion. And I don't swing that way."

Alexander said, "I wasn't suggesting it. It was just the remaining local option. So either we become bitter old hags, or find some trainable cabana boys among the Urushu and raise them right."

"I guess. It just doesn't interest me."

"We have Cal," she said, and suddenly was sobbing.

"We do. So we're crazy cat ladies who are so poor we can only afford one cat to share."

"Oh, gods, that sounds bad. He's letting me pet him."

Jenny leaned over slowly to look and said, "Oh . . . yes he is! Awesome." Alexander was skritching his ears. He seemed a bit unsure, but half brain-melted from the attention. He was a huge cat compared to domestics, probably thirty pounds.

Alexander "I have a pet. That's more than I could have hoped for."

"Don't tell the others. They'll get jealous."

"Yeah, I know."

Jenny asked, "Why didn't you sleep last night?"

Sighing, Alexander explained, "I get overly fatigued, and it's thyroid related as well, affects my L-Tyrosine and melatonin levels among others. Gods, I still remember those terms. And extreme frustration."

Frustration. She understood that.

Delicately she asked, "Do you need some alone time, hon?"

"It won't help."

"You could at least take the edge off."

Alexander sounded like she was reading from a script. "Thyroid issues screw with cortisol levels. I can't get any kind of endorphin rush. Nothing happens."

"I'm . . . sorry."

"Yeah, so am I. Eventually it kills me. I may make it to sixty, lethargic and fat."

Jenny didn't know if that was better than the alternative of another fifty years or more. With her family history, she'd probably live a long time, eventually becoming some wise, weird elder for the Urushu to venerate. If the Romans didn't decide to make her a trophy by force before that.

There wasn't much else she could offer. They all had problems, collectively and individually.

Patriarchal society seemed to follow from organization. Once there was a unified leadership structure, men moved into it.

She'd never liked Libertarianism, but it seemed that might be the system with the best potential for equality. If it could be socially moderated away from privileged white males, it might work. But of course, that couldn't happen, and it would never be popular.

She carefully reached over and petted the cat, too. He was good company in the dark.

Felix Trinidad was a trained intel specialist. He had little to do here, but he couldn't help but keep track of happenings.

The last couple of weeks, the number of Urushu women visiting the camp had increased. It had gone from an average of two every week to six. Their medical issues were usually quite simple, and some were unhurt. They excused their presence as cooks and support, as near as Oglesby could translate for him.

Interesting.

The next week eight of them rotated through.

He sought out the LT. Elliott was looking over a tablet and frowning. Felix noted a mention of Romans, then made a point of not looking at it while addressing him.

"Sir, did you notice the increase in women visitors?"

"A bit. They're here for cooking and such, as I understand it. I think we've reached another level of trust."

"That's one way to put it. I think they're looking for mates."

"I guess that's possible." The man's expression said he knew that was exactly it and trying to be reticent.

"Did you notice they're mostly young? Fifteen to twenty, at a guess."

"I actually hadn't. I try not to pay too much attention to them individually, just to their numbers and movement. Thanks for the information, though."

"Any specifics you want me to look for or inquire about?"

"Please. Anything. If you can discreetly ask, do so. If not, I'm sure it'll come out in time."

That wasn't very specific, but it seemed he was worried about threats, not mates. That was reasonable.

"Hooah, sir."

Today he was helping Spencer work on that forge of his, and it was past being a joke. The man was a decent mechanic, from all stories, but the forge seemed like something that would never happen.

He wanted to be fair, because reverse engineering primitive stuff was hard, but it was an obsession that wasn't yielding anything so far. Felix had seen various forges in Bataan. He didn't know much beyond bellows, fire and hit metal.

"Okay, it's really not that complicated," Spencer said. "We use the lathe to turn rods for a form, wrap it in clay and then fire it hard so it burns out and we have a pipe. That goes into a trench under where the fire will be. We make a bellows to fit it. We hammer some rocks to make a hearth. We use one of the large river rocks we dug out as an anvil. Once we have reliable water in the stream again, we'll work on reducing iron."

"You need water for it?"

"You cook the ore, then shovel it out into the water, which shatters it and blows some of the slag off. Then you forge."

While Spencer turned the sticks on the lathe, he talked to the Urushu about clay. They were all hanging about their hooch, lazing on hides and whittling crafts or doing other minor tasks while chatting with each other.

"Greeting, Nus!opfa."

"Greeting, Watcher Felicsh."

"We need to find clay you talked of, and make a . . . hollow bone."

"Need you a hollow bone?"

In Tagalog he thought, "That's a damned good question." "I ask."

He jogged down and called, "Hey, Sergeant Spencer, would a large bone work?"

Spencer stopped, stood covered in wood chips for a second and said, "Ah, shit. Way to overanalyze it."

"Is that a yes?"

"That's a 'it should to get started at least.' Faaahk." He dusted off a few shavings and stepped back from the lathe.

"I have no idea what to do with that, now."

It was almost amusing.

Felix ran back and exchanged with the Urushu, who promised to bring a bison leg in a few days.

"Eat meat and marrow first, many nom." The word "nom" had come into creole use between them.

"Sounds great."

The bellows he was able to help with, and happy to do so. He took a chunk of a straight limb, bored a hole, shaved and scraped and whittled until he had a proper mouthpiece.

Spencer was actually a decent basket weaver. He took some soaked reeds and withes, and twisted three paddle-shaped frames.

"So this is a two-stage bellows?"

"Yes, you get more consistent airflow."

Maybe the man did know what he was doing. Felix thought he'd seen one of those back home once or twice.

"Nice muzzle," Spencer said. "That's almost exactly what we need."

"I'm glad."

"Okay, I'll stitch the hide while you dig a trough to hold this bone. Are we talking aurochs, elk, bison, something like that?"

"Bison, with meat and marrow."

"Nom."

Spencer had no idea why he laughed.

It took a while with a pick to chip the hard earth down a foot, but he had it by lunchtime. It would need roughed out again once the bone arrived, but should work for now.

Lunch was dried fish with some berries and greens. It was okay, but he wasn't thrilled.

Spencer took a while to do the complicated stitching of thick hide to the frames, and expansion joints between them. The whole thing was stitched with sinew. Spencer kept it in his mouth to soften it, pulling bits out, threading them onto a bone needle, and using the awl on his multitool to bore holes.

Felix watched it bit by bit as he brought rocks from the dry bed for the forge construction.

"Not those," Spencer said. "Nothing that might soak up water. Then we need to either stack them roughly flat, or hammer and grind them into rough squares."

Three days later, he did have increased respect for Spencer. They'd slaked lime in a small, hot fire, added fine sand, hammered rocks into blocks, stacked them in the hearth, mortared them, lit a small fire to cure the whole mess, and started on another lean-to to cover it.

Felix said, "I expect the Romans could have helped with this. But of course, we don't want them inside."

"That, and they might wonder about our lack of experience in that area. I was able to fake it through the charcoal burn."

"How do we drag that fuel up here, by the way?"

"In a hide, and drag or carry."

"What if it gets wet?"

"That won't hurt it. It dries as it goes into the fire."

The Urushu showed up with the promised leg of bison, along with eight women. He recognized the number and came to an immediate conclusion.

Damn, he wanted a woman. They were tall, lean, dusky and so very, very exotic. They hadn't fulfilled the year yet, though, and he knew what Elliott would say if the suggestion was made.

"Tell them we must wait a full turn of the sun, which isn't yet. Then we can talk about it."

Elliott looked very tense and sad about that decision every time he had to remind someone.

They knew they weren't going home, he'd already made the separation between then and now, and he wanted to move on with life.

Regulations were regulations, though, until they were released.

Richard Dalton had an odd relationship with Spencer. They'd never agree on the existence of God, Christ and all it entailed, but he did find their discussions productive. He was beginning to accept there was no way he'd ever bring the man to Christ, but he prayed for him anyway. The arguments also caused him to reassess his relationship with God, and that was a good thing.

Rather than hunting, he was assigned to "Help Sergeant Spencer." He ate cold sidemeat and sought the man out. He was over by the stream.

"So what are we doing today, Sergeant?"

"I think we're going to cook some iron today. Bring gloves and eyepro."

"Really?"

It had been a snide joke for so long. Were they really going to do it?

Spencer held up a hide bucket full of cracked red rock. "This ugly red ochre is iron ore. It's a pretty good grade, too. And it comes premixed with limestone."

"That's good?"

"That'll work as a flux."

"Okay, so what's next?"

"We're doing this the crude way for now, as proof of concept. We're going to dig a hole, layer in the charge, fill the hole, light it and crank. We're going to need three people for that."

"Okay, where do we dig?" It wasn't that he liked digging, per se, but it was good exercise and let him meditate.

In an hour, they had a steep cut into the bank of the creek.

The order for gloves and eyepro wasn't really necessary. They always had them with them. These were getting scratched, though, and he'd have to use his spare pair soon. Maybe they could devise some fine polish to restore them with?

"I wish we could do this farther up," he said. "It still smells like latrine." They were about twenty feet upstream of the outhouse.

"Yeah, tell me about it. Okay, flatten out the bottom and fill it with large stones, three inches or so, for about a foot."

"Got it."

Spencer explained as he went. "Bone pipe, which the Urushu suggested instead of trying to do pottery. I wrapped it in clay anyway, in case it helps. Then we're going to layer charcoal and ore in about four-inch layers all the way to the top. As it slumps down, we'll add more up top. We fill in packed dirt around it as we go."

"Okay."

In another hour, they had a tall tube of the charge, with the pipe and bellows in place, more materials at hand, and both shovels.

"Grab a good coal from the fire."

He ran up with a shovel, scooped a chunk from Barker's cooking fire, and carried it out and around, watching the heat waves roll off it even in the bright sun.

"Okay, ladle it in there above the bone . . . and now pack dirt on it." He did so.

Spencer started pumping the bellows, slowly and evenly.

In five minutes, smoke and haze rose from the top of the chimney.

"I think you have it."

"Yeah, well get Oglesby, we'll be swapping off every fifteen minutes or so."

He spent the day pumping and zoning. He took over, squeezing the bellows rhythmically, feeling his arms burn, mesmerized by the movement and the smoke. He prayed for success once, then twice, then realized that was silly.

Oglesby took over, and was surprisingly strong. He looked skinny, but had lots of wiry muscle.

Spencer resumed, and said, "Okay, toss another shovelful of coal in the top, then more ore."

Oglesby asked, "Ah, how long does this take, Sergeant?"

"All day, most likely."

They squeezed. It got hotter, sweatier, and he found himself running upstream for water. They'd drained their Camelbaks already.

Still another shovelful of each, and one of the Urushu women brought them lunch of berries and dried bison. That was good stuff.

"Thank you," he said.

"Wilcahm," she agreed with a smile.

He knew he'd been here a long time when they started looking good, despite never having seen a razor, toothpaste or soap.

At Spencer's nod, he squatted down, and stepped in as Spencer stepped out, not missing a single pump on the bellows. They were getting pretty good at this.

A few minutes later, he realized the pumping was getting harder and less effective.

"I think we have a blockage," he said.

"Crap. Pull it out."

He did, and Spencer poked a long stick into the deep tube.

Sparks dropped out, followed by a stream of something hot.

"Shit!" Spencer shouted, jumping back. He rolled aside.

"You okay?" he asked.

"I will be. Keep pumping."

He stuck the bellows back as Spencer plunged his scorched hands into the creek.

"Goddamn, that hurts."

"What was that?"

"Slag buildup, and then a bunch of hot debris falling out."

"Are you okay?"

Spencer examined his wrist. "A couple of blisters."

"There goes your sex life."

"Nah, it's the other hand."

"Oh, well good." Were they really discussing this matter-of-factly, or just making obvious jokes about an obvious subject?

Spencer said, "You realize we completely neglected July Fourth, right?"

"I think it was a silent mutual agreement. What the hell does it matter here? And we have fire every night, and no fireworks."

"Yup. I could make and waste some gunpowder, or we could burn off some tracer or a flare or grenade, but why?"

Why, indeed. They were fitting in here, and God would guide them to new festivals, he was sure.

Oglesby took over the bellows. In a few minutes he said, "I think it's clogged again."

"Crap, well, we're done for the day. Carefully, we're going to break it open and shovel everything straight into the creek. Oglesby, you're left handed, so you take this side."

"Hooah."

He stuck the shovel into the bank, and as he opened up the tube, a huge wave of heat washed back over him. He tried not to breathe the fumes, took the shovelful, and tossed it into the trickle of stream.

"Careful, not spread out, just right here."

He turned his head to breathe, said, "Hooah," and went back to it.

The next shovelful hissed and steamed, sending bubbles through the water. Then again.

"Keep digging," Spence urged. "Get it all out, work down."

In a half hour, they had a pile of muck in the stream that didn't look like much.

Spencer said, "Okay, that dirt will be hot for hours, so don't lean on it."

He reached down into the water, pulled something, and shook it. He held it up.

It was an ugly chunk that looked like a muddy bird's nest.

"What's that?"

"Bloomery iron."

"That's it?" It wasn't impressive.

Spencer said, "At this stage, yes. At a guess, we got about fifty percent conversion before it clogged. We started with maybe a hundred pounds of ore, about twenty percent iron. So we got ten pounds of bloom."

"Crap. Is that all?"

"That's pretty damned good. We'll get about two pounds of finished iron out of this."

"Sheeit. That's a lot of work." Two pounds? Fucking seriously?

"There's a reason it was worth its weight in silver or gold early on. Help me find the rest. Anything that looks like that."

It took until dinner to comb through the dirt, crud, stone, unburnt chunks of ore, to find the spongy and sharp bits of processed ore. They were filthy despite the water running past.

"After this, we'll build a proper bloomery furnace, and if we can find coal, we can get a hotter fire."

Rich decided he'd stop with the jokes. It had been a hell of a lot of work, and had yielded results. Spencer had delivered. It wasn't much, but that just proved how tough a task it was. No wonder civilization had taken a long time with labor like this.

By the sweat of your brow, God had said. It was true.

He hoped there was a lot of something for dinner. He was starving and sore.

CHAPTER 32

Gina Alexander sat atop Number Nine, next to the turret, spinning yarn. The ten feet of height helped a lot with speed. Ortiz was on watch. She hadn't been in weeks, and Elliott had confided with her it was due to her slipping attention. It was frustrating, but she knew it was true. The old lady was broken, and starting to look her age. The scar tissue in her foot didn't help, either. It was painful to walk long distances.

She was taking a break from admin work, which seemed to take longer than it had, and she had trouble finding some of the less common functions. Brain fuzz, and fatigue. Breaks stopped her from falling asleep during the day.

She didn't like heights, but she did like the view. It was a lovely day, clear and bright, puffy clouds here and there, and a wafting breeze.

And she could watch Martin pound away on the iron.

He wore an apron of goat hide over bare skin, and his taut, lean biceps rolled with every swing of the hammer. His left hand was wrapped in leather to protect it from the heat, holding vice grips. His right hand held a ball-peen hammer from the tool kit. He pumped the bellows, grabbed the tools, pulled out the iron, placed it on the boulder, and started beating. After about twenty seconds, he'd stick it back into the fire and work the bellows again.

"Tiring?" she called down.

"Yes," he said. "It's the only way to get more iron, though."

"What are you making?"

"Well, first, I have to make this into a long bar, upset the ends—widen them—punch holes in those, cut a piece off as a rivet, and make them into a pair of tongs, so I can hold the rest of the metal more easily. I'll need to learn how to use those. I mostly used long handled vise-grips."

"What after that?"

"Shovels, hoes, plow bits, axes. Flat metal is easy. I know how to make an axe, but never have."

Would she consider being married to the village blacksmith? Maybe. That was a skilled trade.

Why was she thinking in that context?

Oh, yes. She was spinning yarn from goat wool, and remembering a Viking era event. Or was it Civil War? No, the drop spindle was Viking era, though the smiths were mostly the same.

He broke for lunch, as the Urushu hunting party returned with a young antelope and took it to the kitchen area.

"Tasty," she called down.

"Nom," they replied.

She giggled. That was still hilarious. And thank gods no one had taught them obscenities as fake useful phrases. That always pissed her off when she encountered it.

Caswell and Barker came back from upstream. No matter what Caswell claimed, Gina thought she was hitting it off with Barker and would pair with him. The young men would just have to take native wives.

"Good news and possibly more good news," Caswell announced.

"Yes?"

"We found nuts. More butternut type things, almonds and walnuts."

"I have trouble with almonds," she said.

"You don't want to eat these anyway. They'll be toxic in more than tiny servings. But they do have oil."

"For cooking?"

Spencer said, "No, for the engines!"

Barker said, "Yes, if we can grind enough, we can add some fuel. You said nut oil would work."

"Fantastic," he said. "It'll mean a lot of grinding, but yes."

"We can cook in the walnut and butternut oil," she said. "They'll also go in salads, and we can do more bacon. There are a lot of trees up there." She pointed farther uphill to a wooded meadow that was just visible over the terrain, below a slope in the hill.

Barker said, "The bee colony is coming along. It'll be nice to not have to]crack hives for honey.."

"I wish I'd studied more of these things," she said. "All I know is textiles."

"Gina, I am delighted at my repaired socks, and the new pair," he said.

"Sure, but I need a loom eventually. That's a lot of work." She'd knitted them with needles homemade from twigs.

"We'll do it."

Caswell said, "Oh, I must remember to ask the Urushu to find us flax. Linen would be nice to go under the wool."

Indeed. Linen was also good for bandages, bedsheets, filtering wine and oils, and for bandages and sanitary necessities. Those improvised pads Caswell had to use wouldn't last forever.

She twitched awake from a micronap and rubbed her eyes. She really did need to rest. She was even medically authorized one, by Doc and the LT. But if everyone else ran all day, then she would, too. Then she'd sleep badly at night.

Growling in frustration, she pulled up the spindle. It had dropped all the way down and the yarn had snarled. She knelt carefully, and started stretching it around the turret, as Ortiz watched, so she could fix that section.

"Dozed off?" he asked.

"Yeah."

"Caffeine help?" he offered some of the native leaf drink.

"Not if it tastes like that. It's bad enough to gag a maggot."

"Didn't you eat maggots in SERE school?"

"No, but I did eat other bugs, and they're much tastier than that crap. I'll be fine," she insisted.

Once the fiber was untangled, she decided she'd be safer on the ground, even if it meant shorter spins. She wrapped it carefully, climbed down the back and resumed her seat in her office.

Sean Elliott noted the date in the log. September 17, local time, August 9 home time. The anniversary of their loss and arrival.

Everyone knew the date was coming, but no one really wanted to make any preparations for it.

They were all silent at breakfast, and Sean didn't offer anything.

The existing task list would do fine, and he'd offer counsel or duty to anyone who needed support, depending on what would motivate them better. Spencer had orders for the same thing. They ate warmed up dry goat and some mixed berries with goat milk.

It was a beautiful partly-cloudy morning. Doc was all excited because the full moon had been followed by Jupiter, Mars and Spica rising in close proximity to the east before dawn.

"There's software that could tell us what date it was, if I had time to place star positions," he said.

"Is it on your phone?"

"No, on my laptop back on base, which is probably sent home now, or will be, fuck if I know. It's a great view, and I know I could back-calc, given time."

Sean wasn't sure. That wouldn't make it any easier. Whether it was thirteen thousand BC or thirteen million, they weren't going home.

A year. In some ways, it didn't feel like it. In others, it felt like an eternity

It was a significant day, a milestone. None of them knew how much longer they might have, but it would all be here.

Oglesby was the first to speak.

"It just occurred to me. I wonder how much of English and Latin is feeding into the Urushu language to become Proto-Indo-European?"

Spencer said, "That depends on whether or not it has any effect. But if it does . . . yeah, we might be causing something here."

Sean asked, "Might? Why wouldn't we be?"

Spencer said, "Well, bronze working is still ten thousand years in the future, iron another thousand or more after that. Textiles are about the same time frame, aren't they?"

"No," Alexander said. "There's textiles as far back as a hundred thousand years, flax and cotton. They're not as sophisticated, but the Urushu have nets, so they can weave or knot fabrics."

"Ah. I stand corrected. But the metal would be very useful. Knowing you can burn ochre to get metal is easy to remember."

Oglesby said, "Given the length of time, I doubt there's much continuity of any language, especially without writing. 'Ma,' 'dadad,' 'a!ka,' and 'mmm,' seem to be about it so far, with some very vague syllables in Gadorth. But stuff could feed in, decay, evolve and become something else, if either group lasts that long and passes any terms onto others. Which is unlikely."

Sean pointed out what they all knew and said, "And where do those vehicles go? I doubt we can find a way to cut them up. It would take a huge fire to melt them. They'd almost certainly have shown up in some excavation or other."

"Unless there's some secret government office hiding their existence."

"Do you believe that?"

"No, but given time travel exists, I can't say it's impossible."

There wasn't much to say past that. They really had no way to tell.

"So we'll do the best we can," Elliott said.

Dalton said, "I have a small service I've put together, if anyone's interested. A closure of the past."

"That's the future," Doc said. "I'd like to see it again."

Dalton said, "I'm fairly well adapted to here. It's tough in some ways, but invigorating."

Spencer said, "Let's keep it low key, guys. Everyone's got their own thoughts. Thanks for the offer, Dalton. I'd encourage anyone to talk about it if they want to. But find privacy for any talks, don't let them spill into a general activity."

"I'm available to talk if anyone needs to," Sean said. "On with tasks."

It didn't seem like a day to celebrate.

Before everyone got to tasks, he pulled Oglesby aside.

"Can you tell the guests we're having a meditation day and not talking much?"

"Yes, sir."

The next day, Martin Spencer took a break from sorting iron and watched Barker turn another bowl. Typically, one cracked each week. As they got better seasoned wood, and now that they had nut oil for treating them, they'd last longer. Once he could forge a couple of turning chisels, it would go much faster, though Bob did a decent job using the tip of his machete to cut the inside, and the straight edge to turn the outside.

He watched two shavings float down and land atop each other.

"Ah, hell, we were stupid again," he said.

"Eh?"

"That hot tub you want. We've been trying to figure out how to sluice cut or coop lumber into tight fits."

Barker looked up for a moment, then talked while he turned. "I figured we were going to do a lot of splitting and filing, until we can build a planer table of some kind."

"Or, we can split, shave and strake them together like planks on a Viking ship, and caulk them with pine pitch."

Barker stepped back from his work and lowered his machete.

"Goddam, are we stupid or what?"

"Well, it'll still be a lot of work," he admitted.

"Sure. But it's work we can do with what we have."

He said, "That just leaves a drain trough and petcock, which I'm pretty sure I can turn and carve."

"Good. A hot bath in winter will do a lot for morale, and smell."

Martin said, "I wonder how the Romans did theirs, and of course, we're not going to go look."

"Still don't trust them, eh?"

"Why should we?"

"I wasn't disagreeing."

"Well, that gets us much closer. Let me check with Alexander on caulking."

The place was starting to look like an Iron Age village. It did remind him of re-enactments, and that was somewhat comforting. He liked those on weekends. The Regia Anglorum site in the UK was neat. This was even better, except for the fact he could never leave it. Be careful what you wish for. Except he'd never wished for anything like this. He knew better.

His guts were steady with mild irritation, but he knew ultimately it would kill him. There were several ways it could catch up to him. It was just a case of which one was first.

If it got painful enough, or his esophagus distressed itself closed, did he have the nerve to just end it with a bullet?

It was a decision he might have to make sometime in the next decade.

Life would be nasty, brutish and short.

He walked over to Number Nine and leaned around the steps.

"Yes?" she said, looking up from spinning and tapping keys in between spins. She looked baggy-eyed and tired.

He asked, "Can you spin or twist thicker thread, almost rope, to use for caulking?"

"We can twist several strands together. There's a basic machine which I've seen. Otherwise, we can ask the Urushu for hair. Didn't the Vikings do that?"

"We could. I'd rather not impose if we don't have to." Besides, her hair wasn't that long.

"Are you building a boat?"

"Caulking the hot tub."

"Oh," she said. "That does make sense. But I better be high on the list."

"You will be."

"Let me know when. I'm still turning out blankets and hammocks."

Her crocheted blankets were much in demand as trade goods. She was basically off labor details, between managing information and turning out textiles.

And with her health obviously failing first. She was perpetually exhausted, prone to sleep, forgetful, and losing muscle tone. He thought her hair might be thinning, too.

Once they'd worked out the details on trade, they were advancing quickly, with lots of labor in exchange for goods. Without TV or other time sinks, the older cultures didn't value labor time very much, and were quite willing to work long hours for luxury goods. He wondered how much that had to do with the development of slavery.

Then there was the other item.

"I don't really know how to say this. I didn't need to last time, but . . . would you consider marrying me?"

She clenched her face and went tense all over. Crap. That wasn't good.

"As much as I'd like to, I have to refuse."

"I understand." Damn. Well, there were always two possible answers . . .

"I keep some faint hope we'll someday get home. It wouldn't be fair to give of myself to you, and have to snatch it back. It wouldn't be fair to my husband, and it wouldn't be fair to me."

"Yeah, I understood it from body language and context. I guess that comes from being so close for so long."

She said, "I am flattered. I guess I'll inevitably change my mind, and if you're still free, you'd be my choice. But please don't wait for me."

That just made her that much more interesting.

Crap.

"No pressure. Thanks for being honest."

He left before it got awkward.

He went to check on the embassies.

The Urushu had two minor casualties, one with some sort of female problem, and one with a nasty, infected boil. Doc had fixed that, was working on the first one, and the escorts were helping haul firewood in between watching their charge.

The Gadorth were waiting for blankets, and moving rock in the meantime. The outside bottom of the palisade was being faced with stone, and some maintenance was being done to the grounds. With slate sickles, they cut down the grass.

That left technical work to the Americans.

Elliott came over, with a tablet in hand. The ancients had gotten used to the Americans having strange devices, lights at night, and knives that seemed to never go dull. They accepted that these were magical devices that involved complicated wizardry and spirit intervention, which was about as readily as the processes could be explained to savages who didn't really keep calendars, much less precise measurements of anything, and didn't know what metal was other than occasional shiny bits of pyrite and gold.

"I'm thinking ahead," Elliott said.

"Yes, sir?"

"Is there a way to dismount the AC from one of the vehicles to make a fridge, and could it be powered by a waterwheel?"

He thought for a moment only. "I would say not, sir. The gas would leak out, and we'd need circulating fans. It would be some steampunk, or I guess stonepunk, bastard, and I'd love to see it, but I don't see any point in trying to do it."

"I thought so. I was hoping you had some brilliant insight."

"Short term, enough nut oil and hemp oil means we can run the engines now and then."

"I was thinking of food preservation. Refrigeration. Any ideas?"

Oh, of course.

"That I do have. Pile up a bunch of snow in winter, pack it down, cover it in a tepee or even two. It will probably last all summer."

"That's brute force and a lot of labor, but I guess that's what we'll have. Can we put drain tiles underneath?"

"We'll have to. Mortar as well. I don't think we can do it before winter."

"I'll add it to my project list anyway."

"Yeah, next year if not this year. It's not like we're going anywhere."

Nor was he getting a wife any time soon.

Armand didn't pull watch very often. He noticed the shortage and asked, and Elliott had had Alexander put him on a three-quarter schedule, since he often stayed up with patients. Even then, someone often took his watch so he could keep with his charges.

He hated being here, though was gradually getting used to it, and having good people helped. But the influx of Urushu women reminded him that he needed to get laid. Then he needed someone to live and cuddle with. This Army community thing was okay, but it would be nice to ask for a meal of choice and not be stuck with whatever they turned out. Not that it would be better, just different.

The dawn shift was always the chilliest and dampest. That wasn't bad in July, except it then got hot and nasty. In October, though, it was shivery.

He hoped they'd gotten the message through that pregnant women really shouldn't be hauling water and rocks after the fifth month. The spirits didn't like it, which was why those fistula formed. He hoped they wouldn't just shrug and continue, or figure some native ritual would fix it.

He was getting pretty good at minor GYN surgery, though. Professionally, he knew his way around a vagina.

Socially . . .

Dammit.

Next to him, Ortiz said, "Okay, I'm down. You've got it until breakfast?"

"Hooah." It was light enough they didn't need two. It was also misty and foggy as hell. He couldn't see anything outside the wall anyway. NVG showed little, either.

He was bored with his entertainment. He'd seen every movie everyone had, burned out on the ones he cared about, listened to all the music. He was losing connection with his own time, and sliding into the daily tedium of this place. The work was productive. He was glad to keep others alive and improve their well being. He wished he had more knowledge and a lot more tools. He was pretty sure that guy two weeks ago had an aneurysm, and there was nothing he could do. As far as the stroke victim, they already understood most of the basic field therapy. They weren't stupid by any stretch.

He needed something for him.

A deep animal noise sounded to the northeast.

It wasn't a bison, nor a rhino. Whatever it was, it was nothing they'd heard before. It was deep, but shrill.

"That almost reminds me of . . ." he muttered to himself, as Ortiz stopped at the door of his hooch and came running back.

Through the rising mist he saw them.

"Fucking mammoths." He stared in shock.

Ortiz said, "How? They don't come this far south. They're supposed to be almost extinct. We've never seen any, the Urushu have never seen any . . ."

He wondered, "Did they get pulled through time, too?"

"No way to know. They can't tell us."

Elliott came up, then Barker, and shortly everyone was outside. He realized Caswell was wearing only panties and T-shirt, and that he was less interested in that than the pachyderms.

Everyone clambered up the vehicles or the corner towers to stare at the huge beasts.

"They move pretty lightly for big critters."

"They do."

The Romans would probably recognize elephants at least by reputation. Did the Ancients?

They chattered amongst themselves. Oglesby talked to both the Urushu and the Gadorth at length, while pointing. Alexander came sprinting out again, her gear bouncing, and swung her camera into action.

There were twenty-three of the huge beasts, though five were juveniles no larger than a compact car. Their tusks were long, curving, magnificent things.

"Are they bigger than elephants?"

"A bit, yes."

There was a thick, musty smell from them, not unpleasant, but notable, drifting across the landscape.

They ambled downhill, and flowed to the north of the palisade, three of them feeling along it with their trunks, the rest footloose. Two others stopped to stare at the goat pen, then walked around it, as the goats baaed and muttered, hopping about and into their weather lean-to.

"They're heading north," Ortiz said. "And they look skinny. They can't eat down here, right?"

Spencer said, "Not as well as up on the muskeg, no. This growth is too coarse and lean for them, I think. They need moss, lichen, shrubby subarctic stuff that's nutrient dense."

"Poor things," Caswell said. "I don't think they can make it."

"They're heading north. There's water there and growth in the mountains that might work."

"I hope so," she said.

Armand only said, "Yeah." They were awe-inspiring beasts, and glowed with intelligence. They'd understood the fences and human settlement.

"How far back and forward do these ripples go?" Ortiz asked.

Alexander said, "I still want to know if they'll ever settle down and send us home."

Armand replied, "I wouldn't think so, any more than a ripple dislodging a pebble in a stream. It never goes back."

She sighed. "You'd think we'd be used to it by now."

"Part of me hopes I never am. I never want to give up hope."

Dalton said, "I'm adapted. Here we are, because God wills it. So we accept it and learn from it."

Spencer shook his head. "There are times I wish I had your faith."

"You can."

"No, it's not for me." He sounded insistent.

"You'll be at peace."

Spencer was definitely getting annoyed as he said, "That's not for me, either. I enjoy my anger and rage."

"Hmm. I don't know, have you—"

"Rich, drop it, seriously."

"Sorry. Dropped." Dalton was a good guy, but he was too earnest in his faith sometimes.

Armand said, "They may be farther away from home than we are."

Caswell said, "That doesn't really reassure me." She clutched herself in the cool air.]

CHAPTER 33

It was definitely becoming winter again. Felix Trinidad hated it. His background didn't include months of snow. It almost included Stone Age people in some of the remote villages, though. This was a confusing place.

He talked to Oglesby and Doc. "Notice the hair dressing and the presentation. They're looking for mates." He was entirely sure by now. The soldiers had status and the chicks wanted them.

Doc said, "Well, once the hot tub is done, we can bathe a few and get it on at the same time." He grinned broadly and snapped his fingers.

"It's funny because you think you're joking."

"It's hilarious because you think I'm not."

Doc added, "Or that I am. Anyway, I'm serious. I want some flesh as much as the next man, but we need to keep in mind all that social stuff Dan and Spencer talk about, and we have no idea what diseases they might have."

"You haven't seen any symptoms on them, right?"

"No lesions, no noxious odors other than sweat. But there's strong evidence, for example, that one form of syphilis was a mild skin ailment among the Native Americans. It turned virulent when it had to deal with clothing. You don't want to die with your dick and your bones rotting."

Felix said, "Americans tell jokes about 'Black Syph' in the PI and Korea. You're being serious."

The medic looked very serious as he said, "I'm serious that we have no idea what diseases there might be. We have to be cautious. I recommend not getting into any wild orgies."

"Hell, I only need one. They're eager, willing to please and want to make us happy. As long as she's warm I'm good. They're almost all very hot, and your height." That put them about six inches taller than Felix.

"And are you planning on having lots of kids? The only birth control is pulling out, or the two dozen condoms I have in the kit. I guess you can turn it inside out afterward, shake the fuck out of it, and reroll it for reuse."

"Wait, wasn't that a Scottish joke? 'The Regiment has voted to replace'?"

Doc nodded and smiled. "That's the one. But those are our options. Otherwise, we can make condoms out of goat guts."

Oglesby said, "Just remove them from the goat first."

Doc grinned. "Sure, we're not Afghans. But there will be diseases here in addition to that virus we all got; some are likely to be venereal. We have no background for them, or them for us, and pregnancy is a guarantee if you go at it."

"So what you're saying is it's a one way-trip to settle down and a home in the suburbs?"

Felix had figured most of this out before, though the potential virulence of infection was disturbing.

"The women will want families, too," he said. "They lose a lot in birth and growth, accidents."

He would really enjoy a woman, but he didn't want a family just yet.

But porn and the spank tank was getting really old.

Martin Spencer felt old. Between his guts burning, and the agony of creaking joints when he woke up in the morning, he had long bouts of misery. He hadn't done any smithing in two days, because his right arm ached too much.

Midshift was never good for him. He always had trouble getting back to sleep afterward. He huddled inside his gore-tex and layers, and tried to keep his focus.

Dalton was next to him, sitting next to the turret.

"What are you thinking about?" he asked.

"Settling down," Dalton said. "I guess we have our word from God. So I need to find a woman who suits me, and see about becoming a husband and father."

"Good that you're considering it seriously. I guess Doc had a talk with some of the guys."

"Yeah, I overheard some of it. No free sex here."

Martin replied, "Heh, it's never free. Just the way you pay for it changes. But I do agree it's a serious matter. Some of these kids, back home I mean, I know one chick, sergeant now, who pulled a train with a squad of Marines. We had one boy in the shop got three women pregnant in a year, and that's with modern birth control and knowledge."

"Oglesby's the one I worry about."

"Yeah, Trinidad and Ortiz are more rural, take things more seriously. I think some of that's cultural in other ways, too. Doc's just incredibly shy and uncomfortable around women."

"He does like women though, right?"

"According to his phone he does, yes." Martin thought you could have enough boob. Armand did not.

"Then he'll get over it."

"Probably."

"You and the captain?"

Martin said, "He's not my type."

"Yeah, you know what I mean. Our women and you guys?"

"They don't seem very keen on the idea so far. I hope Gina comes around."

"Someone you can settle down quietly with?"

He thought for a few moments in silence before he said, "We've talked. I don't know what you think 'old' people do, but I'm pretty sure she's not quiet, and probably ten times as versatile as the local women."

"Oh."

That had shocked the kid.

"Just because I agree monogamy is a good idea doesn't mean I'm a prude, Rich. I've probably done a lot of things you've only read about. And we're not old."

Dalton looked suitably embarrassed and Martin let him change the conversation.

"I'll take a while to see which Urushu have compatible personalities.

They're all decent looking. Trying to develop communication is going to be a task."

"Then trying to convert her to Christianity?"

Dalton looked stubborn.

"I have to try, at least. I even think that may be why I'm here."

The man was solid.

"I'm not criticizing you. I respect determination and faith. You've held onto yours a lot better than some others."

"Thank you," he said as he picked up the NVG.

"You're welcome."

Dalton stopped in mid scan to the west.

"That's . . ."

"What?"

"Did a herd come through earlier?"

Martin said, "I don't think so."

"Flat grass. Very flat."

"Romans?" he asked.

"I don't see anything. But I get the impression it may have been a cart."

That was disturbing. "Okay, then we keep a steady watch and tell relief. I've got the gun, if we decide we need it." He patted the beast and gave the belt a visual check.

"Hooah."

"Let me see." He raised his carbine and looked through the image intensifier. Yes, that was a swath. The hair on his neck bristled.

Very softly, Martin said, "That bothers me."

"I didn't hear anything." Dalton said.

He asked, "When did you last check?"

Dalton said, "I didn't see it a half hour ago, but I wasn't really looking. I go mostly by ear, you know?"

"Yes, it's easy to follow most animals and the wind, now that we know what to listen for."

"When Caswell comes on, do we want to go take a look?"

"I say we wait until daylight."

"Scared?"

"Yes. I am," he admitted. He'd been scared since they arrived, more than a year.

"Okay. I won't joke about it," Dalton said, sounding sympathetic.

"Thank you."

"But a look would be useful."

"It's a swath in the grass. Remember my theory about two outcomes to everything?"

"Yeah?"

"If whatever it was isn't there, no problem. If it is there are still two possibilities. If it can't get through the wall, no problem. But if it can . . ."

"So you want to be up top looking down with guns."

"Yes."

"Hooah."

They both had to remind themselves to look at the rest of the perimeter. This one was fascinating, and creepy.

Caswell relieved Dalton. She was not a good match for him, emotionally. They could be professional, though.

"So you think it might be a Roman incursion?" she said, when shown. Her voice was slightly muffled by hood, and it rustled as she moved.

"It might be. I don't think it's wild, but it could be." He hoped it was. With the damp, cold, foggy air, silence and location, he was shivering from fear. It was like a horror movie. Add in four log cabins, a tent and the outbuildings . . .

"Could something have rolled downslope?"

"Possibly, but it's not that much of a slope."

She asked, "Do you want to check it out while I cover you?"

"Thanks, but no. We'll watch until daytime."

"Okay."

"Anything planned for dinner tomorrow?" he asked Caswell.

"Bob said something about garlic buttered crayfish."

"I'll try it." New food was usually welcome, though some things didn't quite work out. "Any luck with the sprouting?"

"It's going to take a few years," she said. "I thought we discussed that."

"Yeah, but talking keeps me alert, and that crop circle imitation is bothering me."

"I'm not going to hold your hand."

"I've got Doc for that," he blurted out, then realized she wasn't one for wisecracks.

She replied, "Do you know where that hand of his has been?"

Was that actual humor?

"On duty or off?" he asked.

"Yeah, I think I'd rather not know." Humor, but she was very reserved about it.

"You have that luxury."

She actually snickered, bit down and tried not to laugh aloud.

"I'd rather not know what you know," she said.

"Good. Friends?"

"No. But we do have to live together."

"Okay. I'll erase your number from the outhouse wall."

"I thought Alexander put that up there."

"Is she trying to get rid of you?"

"Not as such, but we're only roomies because we're both female. We're not particularly friendly."

"I won't tell the younger ones that. Let them keep their fantasies."

"Yeah. That was predictable."

"What, my comment, or their thoughts?"

"Both."

"Yeah, it's one of those things."

"And it shouldn't be. Does anyone assume Ortiz and Trinidad are going at it?"

"It has been joked about."

"Sure. But who'd want to see it? Who secretly thinks it might be true?"

"I'm not disagreeing with your position," he said. "I've told a couple of them to cut the comments, when they got out of hand."

"It's not just the comments," she said.

"I know."

"I've seen you stare at me."

"Yeah. And Gina. And a couple of the Urushu. Aik!e, I think"

"Ai!ke."

"Yeah, her."

"And you don't understand why that makes me feel vulnerable?"

"I do. I don't know how to stop them looking. I realized Oglesby was going to try to seduce you at least. So I followed him."

"Partly because you're interested and don't want him cutting you out."

"Jenny, you're pretty good at half of it."

"What's that?"

"Yes, part of me is interested, because you're physically attractive." He chose his words carefully. "We're alone without company. Males are visually oriented. You must know this."

"Yes."

"Okay, you want me to be honest about it? Yes, you've featured in a few of my late night pity parties. My brain goes where it goes. We don't do thoughtcrime. What I think and what I do are different."

"So I've been fantasy raped. Nice to know." She was cold and distant again.

"Apart from your looks, you're not at all my type. You're too young, different emotionally, and aggravating. There's an image of you I like. Personally? I don't like you as much as you don't like me."

"Because I'm female."

"No, because you draw attention to the fact you're female. Gina is just one of the troops. She happens to be shaped funny under her uniform. You draw attention to yourself."

"I draw attention to behavior I find objectionable."

"Part and parcel." He wanted to be diplomatic so it would have some effect, but damn, she was irritating.

"So I should shut up and take, it, is that what you're saying?"

"No. You should acknowledge it exists, and ignore it unless it becomes a threat."

"It will always escalate to a threat."

"Has it? Oglesby was trying to be comforting. It was more than y wanted, but he was looking for validation, not conquest. Has any else laid a hand on you?"

"No. I'm sure a couple of them would if there was a chance."

He admitted, "If there was no one else? Maybe that's why th buddy teams are the way they are."

"Your doing?" she asked.

"Elliott's and Alexander's."

She faced away as she said, "I know some these creeps photos of me naked, too."

He remembered some images he'd deleted, hoped she co see his ears burning.

"Probably. Luckily there's no internet."

"That is a thing back home, you realize. Getting photos or video without consent, and uploading."

"Yup. Seen the sites. I avoid them."

"I'd like to stop this conversation now," she said, her voice flat.

"Sure. Anything else? Or stop entirely?"

"Please leave me alone," she said.

"Understood. Duty only. We need to make a sweep."

He used his rifle optic one way, she used NVG the other. The goats were mostly sleeping. Some distant leaves rustled slightly.

He came back around to the cut in the grass. It didn't seem to have changed. He stared at each stalk he could see.

He wasn't going to sleep until he'd examined it.

CHAPTER 34

Sean Elliott was tired.

He'd slept well enough, but once again, problems cascaded up to him. He hadn't planned on spending his life as an officer. In fact, he'd considered at some point releasing everyone and letting them vote on a mayor. He'd since realized that wouldn't work. They were a unit, and needed to remain a unit.

Dalton and Spencer took him out to the incident site they'd noted overnight. It was visible once they were about a hundred meters out, in the scrub and grass. The three were buttoned up and armed, his Bluetooth was live, and Alexander had them on speaker.

The growth was always chaotic, windblown in waves, flat from rain, crushed under beasts from goat to rhino sized. This, though, was a straight line.

Dalton said, "Something came through here. It was large, quiet, and I didn't see anything on night vision."

Sean insisted, "It must have been there somewhere."

"You'd think so. But neither of us saw it."

Whatever it was had lumbered across the landscape, but didn't seem to have left distinct footprints. He could well believe it had been some kind of sled.

"Well, keep an eye out. Whatever it is, it's respectably large. I wonder if it's the Romans again, or some culture with horse-drawn drags."

"We'd have seen horses, or heard or smelled them."

"Probably. Dogs or people then?"

Spencer said, "It could be more mammoths. If they have wide enough feet and long enough hair. They were pretty shaggy."

"I'm hoping it's not a dinosaur," Dalton said.

"It can't be. They're thousands of times farther back."

"There's Scripture that might contradict that."

Spencer said, "The Behemoth bit? No, there are too many reasons that's not supportable, and we can't debate it now. Where does the track go?"

Dalton said, "It seems to disappear over the west ridge. Toward the Roman settlement."

Sean looked behind them to the reassurance of a picket wall with a gatehouse, standing up from the weeds. Looking again at the drag marks, he said, "Yeah, I see it. I don't think it was them dragging something, but that's not impossible.

Dalton said, "Dunno. Let's just keep watching. But it's creepy as fuck."

"Yes it is."

He went back inside and out the east to supervise the tiling for the deep freezer. The tile would run into a secondary trough for the goats, so they'd have additional water. He was trying to decide how much fence to put around it after that, to keep predators from raiding the fridge.

The tiles were split timbers, and that had gotten much easier with the froe. Spencer said it was the ugliest tool he'd ever made, but it worked, mostly.

The man had made a tool from dirt. There was no shame in that.

It was heavy, dulled easily even after carburizing. He'd likely have to do it again. But hafted with a cut-down baseball bat from the Hajji-Be-Good box, it split shingles and planks.

The planks were laid out in step from the bottom up, and some notched ones at the bottom led into a scraped out log. He was sure they'd have to oil-soak some wood within a year or two as these ones rotted, but one step at a time.

"Good," he said and gave a thumb up. It was decent looking. "Now split some more, and we'll take them over there." He used more gestures and pointed at the new sweat lodge, which had almost enough wood for a hot tub, and he wanted that done by Thanksgiving.

The place was starting to feel like a village. Add some actual fields if they could, and some other herds and birds, and it would be like something out of history.

He hoped they could grow some kind of grain. A walnut butter sandwich would make him feel a lot better. Or ham and cheese.

He looked around and let data soak in. He was wondering if the timbered palisade was enough for the duration, or if they should work on stone walls. If so, here, or elsewhere? Realistically, the ten of them were not going to create an empire. That would be a nice story, but wasn't feasible. They could make themselves as comfortable as possible, and expect any children to grow up native. Oglesby and Trinidad were already flirting heavily with the women. He also needed to figure out if that would mean moving their wives in, or building a village outside, allowing them to shelter if attacked. That village would need another wall. That could be lower, of piled stone.

They really would have to follow up with the Romans again. The Gadorth across the river now had stopped being a problem. They seemed to have settled in and were trading for wives. Well, treating. Diplomacy rather than property. Either way, it wasn't an American problem anymore.

If he had a company, or at least a platoon, they'd have built as fast as the Romans, with much better knowledge. They had no lack of education and training, just not enough hands and backs, even with native help.

More fences were going in. Ortiz wanted a horse corral and a field for cows.

A very nonnatural noise made him recoil, and everyone else as well.

"MERGHAN PAHRRY, US NTEN PROACH YU."

It came from a bullhorn or loudspeaker, very clearly, and was quite close. He took a deep breath as shock rippled through him.

Then he replied in a loud, clear voice, "Contacting unit, say again. Your message not understood."

"Umerkhan parrdy, us ntenth uproach you."

It sounded like English, but very fuzzy and soft. Uninflected? Almost as if someone was slurring drunk.

"Do I understand you intend to approach us?"

"Crec." *Correct.*

"Please approach slowly."

The voice said, "Fru ees."

He shouted orders, and let the bluetooth relay them inside.

"Arm up. Alexander and Barker watch south, Dalton and Oglesby get up top with Doc. Everyone else watch the arc north and west. Assume we can be heard."

Out past where the corral was to be, a humming noise rose, and there was a faint trail of disturbed growth. Whatever it was shimmered like heat waves, then darkened, and finally turned into a bumpy ovoid, pale gray in color. It appeared to be some kind of hovercraft, and it slowed as it approached, from possibly 10 mph to a slow walk. It stopped a good twenty meters away from the palisade and sat for a moment.

He shivered. So the rift in time had affected all eras. How far back? How far forward?

The voice said, "Us pear." He caught the bare schwa sound in there, almost inaudible. "Us appear," is what had been said.

"I understand," he said. "Alexander, Barker, how do we look?"

"Clear this way, sir," Alexander replied in his ear.

A faint popping sound came from the vehicle, two doors appeared somehow, and two figures stepped out, legs first, no obvious weapons or threatening intent.

They were tall. Goddammit, how often was this going to happen? And they were either wearing heavy clothing, or were ripped with muscle. Jesus. They wore soft caps and wraparound visor shades, too.

"So you're from our future," he said.

"Crec." The nod was familiar. "Oy Torand Cryder n Rusen Arnet. Compren muy anlsh?"

"Comprehend your English? Yes, just barely. It sounds very soft and . . . unemphasized."

"Zis bedr?"

"A little. If you're adding emphasis electronically, it's helping."

"Norilly lecthronic, djustn. Udjustng. Uhdjustin."

"Those last two are close. Adjusting."

"Djusting."

"That will work, if you can speak slowly."

"Will do. Intro yosel? Yoself?"

"'Yourself' is our word. Yes, I will introduce myself." He was surprised he wasn't more shocked, but by now . . . "I'm Captain Sean Elliott, United States Army. We're from the year two thousand twelve by our dating."

"Norilly fr us. No'v Yebram Langn?"

"Abraham Lincoln. He died in eighteen sixty-five by our calendar. We are . . . one hundred, forty-seven years after that."

"Gorrit, wooz. Neressn time."

"When are you from?"

"Won't say. Dunno maddr."

Spencer was behind him and asked, "Do you know how we got here?"

"Mebe. All fuct."

That got a laugh that spread.

He said, "Yes, sir, it certainly is fucked. But if you might have any insight that helps, we're quite willing to be of assistance."

"Wooz. No hostl? Coloprate?"

"No hostile intent? Not between us. And yes, cooperate, collaborate, whatever you want to call it, we'll do what we can if . . . well, toward getting home. Or building one."

Was it possible? Or were they all stuck here? Even if so, someone with better tools and a rational mind was welcome.

Assuming, of course, they proved trustworthy. He did make note that the palisade had once again degraded in quality relative to the threat.

"Could you park your vehicle there and come inside with us? And if you don't mind, we'd like to identify your weapons."

Torand Cryder, if that was the proper way to say his name, held up a device. "Zis cn be wepn if nessary."

"You don't have dedicated weapons, then?"

"Yeah. Zis. Wepn, tool, varies."

"It can be several things?"

"Right."

"Understood. Do you recognize ours?"

"Rifle ting. Knife. Pistola. Roj."

"Fair enough. Please understand I'm cautious of any group here."

"Make sens. We culd use co-op. Nummers help."

"Yes, they do."

The two men walked forward. Cryder locked the vehicle with a perfectly normal looking remote, as found on any twenty-first century key fob.

"Torand and Rusen?" he asked as they approached. Both were very handsome, Arnet with softer features, and those appeared to be muscles. These guys were ripped like the Rock.

"Cryder nd Arnet," Cryder said with a nod and a faint bow.

Sean returned the gesture. "Understood. How did you get here?"

"Some kine temprol disrupshn."

"Yeah, I was hoping you had more details than that."

"Sorry."

There were two of them. They had higher technology. They didn't seem disposed to violence, and had made the same assessment of the other groups that he had.

Before crossing the stream, he gestured for Spencer to come over.

"Martin, advise me, please." He turned to huddle with the NCO.

Spencer spoke quietly and close. "Sir, I say we let them in. We'll want to keep someone on watch to make sure, though I don't think we can do much to them if it comes to it. They have a vehicle that still works, so they have shelter. We give better shelter. There's nothing they really need from us that they can take since we don't have much. We couldn't stop them if they did. We can't get anything from them by force if we don't know how their stuff works, like the Romans with a rifle. They seem willing to share some resources. I think it's all positive. For once."

"That's enough." Spencer could talk a lot once he started. He likely did well at parties, but he got annoying here, fast.

Elliott turned back and said, "Cryder, Arnet, welcome to COB Bedrock."

"Wooz. Where'd I park?"

"If you can, that corner by the creek." It was about the only place it would fit, if they could even get there.

"Roj."

Arnet trotted over and hopped into their egg-car.

The vehicle left wipes as if on tires, but none were visible. It didn't blow air like a hovercraft. It was also quite quiet. It could turn sharply enough to suggest four-wheel steering. Arnet drove it across the field, down into the stream. The power source hummed and howled as it rose back up the near bank and bounded across the slope, then up to the main gate. Barker had that open.

Once inside, Arnet drove slowly, managed to turn between the hooches and kitchen without brushing anything, past the gawking Urushu and smoke hut, to the creek and parked it.

Apparently the subordinate, Arnet, pulled on some levers that hadn't been there, and a tentlike compartment popped out from the side, sort of like the crank-out living room on some motor homes.

"We found a trail to the west last night," Sean said.

"Yeh, us. Reconznce. Okay?"

"It is now, yes. Thank you."

Spencer was eager for information, and had a duty to find out their background. He walked directly up to their site, across from the Urushu.

"Martin Spencer. Acting First Sergeant. How long have you guys been here?"

Cryder said, "One thiddy fi days." Damn, they were tall, muscular, perfect specimens. Obviously better fed and exercised.

"In the area? Or did you just pass through now?"

"Yeh, area. Kep low for recon. Finly brainfuct all lone."

He sympathized.

"I know how that is. Are we going to share food, or do you need something special?"

"We share. Got some flavings."

"Oh?"

"Sure. Prosser genrate multi flaves."

Oh, goddamn, that could be awesome. Pepper? Jalapeño? Something?

"That alone is probably worth the linkup. Glad to have you." He offered a hand.

Cryder nodded and smiled as he shook it. "No prob. You need labor? We do some."

"Absolutely. Whatever you're willing to do will help."

He realized they were clean shaven, too.

Two. The size fit the algorithm they thought they saw. So these guys should be relatively near future and from not far away. Could that explain the garbled English?

But, they had sci-fi gadgets, and hopefully some tools, so perhaps he wouldn't have to hammer out some more substandard lumps.

"Do you need some kind of lodging? We might have to build another cabin." They were quickly running out of room and would have to expand the palisade like this.

"We rest in vicle. Noprob." Cryder extended a hand again, and he shook it. That seemed like a dismissal. Except . . .

It turned into back-patting and borderline hugging. Yeah, he could guess they were short-changed on contact. God knows he was. It got uncomfortable fast, though. Not because it was unwelcome, but because it was unfamiliar.

"That's enough, please," he said, and the embrace broke.

"Sorry. Good tsee pipl gain."

"I know. It is. We've gotten unused to touching, though."

"Nerstand."

Arnet was more reserved, offering just a hand.

"Do you have any specific food needs?"

Arnet said, "Back home, yeh. Here, nah."

"Meat, roots, rice and edible leaves are okay?"

"Yeh, yeh, and we add flavr."

"Sergeants Barker and Caswell handle most of our food." They had approached, so he introduced them. He noticed Dalton and Ortiz were well back with the M240 and a grenade launcher.

"Wooz. Hi."

Cryder was a bit less clutchy with Bob, and when he got to Caswell, she raised her hands and said, "I don't touch." Her eyes were wide and nervous.

Cryder nodded. "Nerstood. Greeting."

Good. Caswell looked bothered by more attention, probably because both were male. He did understand her caution. He just thought she dwelled on it overmuch.

"Can we look at your vehicle?" he asked.

"Sure, lemme scure."

It locked with a keyfob that also dropped the screen that made it invisible.

Uncamouflaged, it was a dull tan-gray that could easily be mistaken for a rock at a distance. It seemed to have a rolling undercarriage, almost like treads but full width of the vehicle, or perhaps that was an air curtain, though it hadn't blown that much air when moving. It had two seats with space behind for them to recline into couches, which in addition to the tent annex was apparently where they had been, and intended sleeping. Otherwise it was a relatively smooth, approximate ovoid with flattened sides and soft corners. There was space farther back for the apparent power plant and possible cargo. He rapped the shell. It was some form of plastic.

"It's meant for two people only, then," he said.

Cryder said, "Yeh. Per pair ishu."

"Are you military?" They seemed to be in uniform, but he wasn't sure.

"Simlar. Orders, equip, fighd az need."

He noted, "You still have motive power."

"Yeh, seval years."

"Well, we'll share if you can. I'm not sure if there's a compatible trade, though."

"Haul stuff, mayb."

"Oh, we could use a salt run to the hills, yes. Possibly rocks for reinforcement."

"Wooz. Can do."

"Okay. Is there anything else you need right now?" They seemed to be entirely set, and he wondered why they needed anyone else. It could just be a need for human company, since they were only two and had been here alone five months.

"Designated dumper?"

"Trash or human waste?"

"Human."

"That building there, or the stream below it, not above. We get cooking and drinking water right here, actually."

"Wooz." He nodded. "Wooz" seemed to be their "hooah."

"Do you need food? We'll do dinner, evening meal, around eighteen hours, of twenty-four. Clock starts at the middle of the night, approximately."

"Will join. Wash place?"

"Washing or bathing?"

"Bathing."

"We're still working on that. We use the stream here when it's warm enough, boil water when it's cold. That hut will eventually have a tub with heated water." He pointed.

"We can heat some."

"That's welcome if it won't strain your fuel supplies."

"Run wahder fr long time. No prob."

Gina was curious about the newcomers and setup, and what they'd have for communication equipment and supplies. That, and she wanted photos.

"Did you say you have running water? Hot water?"

The taller male said, "Hot wa'r? Easy."

He turned to the vehicle, opened a seamless hatch, pulled out what was obviously a siphon hose, and dropped into the water with a soft splash. The other side of the hatch extruded a nozzle.

"Cold," he said.

Then another extruded at the rear.

"Hot," he said as he pointed.

She held her hand underneath and it started flowing automatically. At once she snatched her hand back, scalded. But . . . no, not scalded. It was regular hot water, the kind she hadn't felt in almost a year.

"I'm tempted to strip naked and shower right now," she said.

"Go head," he agreed.

"Uh, I can't right now, and I'd prefer some privacy."

"Ah, yeh, yr cultr need priv."

He touched a panel and a bar extruded. He dragged it out and around in a semicircle and reattached it to the rear. Then he pulled on it somehow and a curtain fell from it.

"Holy shit." They had a field shower in their vehicle.

She reached in and felt it on her hand again. It was hot, clean water.

"How much is there?" she asked. "Is it an onboard fuel supply? And how long does the power last?"

"No wor," he said. "Go do."

That settled it. She reached down and unlaced her boots, stripped out of everything. She stepped through the curtain into a small tract of paradise.

She turned under the water, letting it run all over, relax her muscles and make her feel the cleanest she'd felt since they got here, even without soap. Her feet were in a puddle of mud, and what did it matter? But even that changed texture and became a plastic floor with a bowl, and her feet rinsed clean. That was an amazing feeling.

Reluctantly, she stepped out, shy again. Everyone had gathered.

Caswell tossed her a towel, then said, "Is that all you're going to take?"

"I thought I was in there for an hour."

"No, about five minutes."

"Well, I can always get back in line," she said, wrapping the towel and tying it at her breasts. She chilled off fast in the fall air, but so what? The shivers added to the sensation of being clean.

It was tragic and amusing how fast everyone else got in line. They didn't even pay attention to her naked, washed body.

Spencer almost had to shout.

"We're taking numbers," he said. "We'll go from lowest rank up. Everyone else back to work, you won't be waiting long. Oglesby, get clean."

Her feet were muddy, but she was clean, really clean, for the first time in two years. How good was the future people's power supply? Could they manage a shower a month until they had something of their own set up?

With winter coming, that was a distracting idea.

CHAPTER 35

Ramon Ortiz was ready for a hunt. Barker was managing it today, with his bow. The man had gotten pretty damned good with that thing, and he had to admit Barker and Spencer had done a respectable job of making them. It had a heavier draw than he'd ever use, but that did mean an occasional antelope without wasting ammo.

Barker came up, his sleeve wrapped down with leather, quiver on his back with his Camelbak, and bow in hand. The quiver was made from a tube of wolf fur with the head still attached, arrows inserted through the mouth. That was still funny and sick at the same time, even six months later.

One of the future people, Arnet, walked over, as calm as if he did this every day. Certainly more comfortably than Americans did around the others.

"Huntin?"

"Yes."

"I join?"

Ramon looked at Barker, who said, "Sure, if you wish."

"What game?"

"Depends on what we see."

"Fair. Please lead."

They headed over the bridge and out. Caswell was in the kitchen, and he said, "Caswell, Arnet is coming with us."

"Roger that," she agreed, eying the three of them.

He didn't think Arnet planned to shoot them in the back, but it

487

wasn't impossible. He deliberately lagged back and took the rear. He had his rifle ready and a knife.

It was interesting how game came and went. Periodically, the herds would get the idea that the soldiers were a threat, and give distance. When that happened, they switched to hunting with rifle. The animals had a threat radius, and rifle was outside that. After a while, they'd get bored or lazy and move back in to bow range. For now, they were moving back out.

Barker said, "Well, we have those saiga over there, or there's probably deer in the woods down by the river."

Arnet said, "Warabout aurx?"

"Aurochs? It would take more than one bow. Occasionally the Urushu bring us one they hunted as a group. They took to the fletched javelins I made for them real quick."

"Want that one?" Arnet asked. He pointed at a young bull a few hundred yards away.

"If your gun can take it, sure. We'll need help hauling it back."

"Wooz."

Arnet raised his . . . thing. It shaped into something like one of the high tech European rifles, and then let out a bang with a hollow hiss, like a silencer. It didn't seem to recoil much.

The aurochs in question shuddered once, staggered, dropped and twitched.

Barker said, "Headshot."

He started walking that way.

Arnet said, "Creed, Ani, banged aurx, need lifts, wooz?"

It took a moment to realize he was talking on a radio.

"Arup. Pend. Goo." Arnet turned and said, "Urushu send lifts."

Barker asked, "Lifters? Haulers?"

"Yeh, same."

"Goddam, dude, thanks. Steak for dinner. For several days. Next time we should get a pig."

"Bacon?"

Ramon said, "Bacon, hell yes, my man. I am so glad you still have it in the future. They've learned to like it here."

The tall man smiled and said, "Real bacon is wooz. Do us. Soon?"

That was something neat to have in common. Bacon. And yes, that helped a lot.

Once at the carcass, he sliced the throat and let the blood go. They got enough from the goats anyway. This thing was huge. He started at the loins and hooked the guts. The hide was thick enough it was a fight. He had to pull and stretch to get a knife under it and rip the belly open.

He was halfway through pulling out ropes of entrails when a half dozen Urushu arrived. He let them take over the dirty work, since they seemed to enjoy it, shouting, singing, hooting and splashing each other with blood. In an hour, it was skinned, sectioned and en route back to the COB.

Trying to keep relations good, he said, "Nice shot, Arnet. Impressive weapon."

"Tang. Works. Be'r stuff at home. Gah."

"Gah, indeed."

They all missed home.

Felix Trinidad took it upon himself to study the newcomers. It wasn't that he didn't trust them. If they'd had designs on enslaving people, and the means to do so, they could have done it. And, there were only two of them. Worst case, a large fire should cook them inside their vehicle, even if they closed up inside it. They'd need oxygen at some point.

It was interesting to watch them, though. They didn't socialize much, even after the five months they said they'd been here. They showed up for dinner. They helped with occasional chores regarding food or building, but few of the heavy lifting jobs. Of course, they were providing hot water and clean drinking water, filtered through their vehicle. It was hard to demand more of them.

It had only been a week, too. They might acclimate more. But he got the distinct impression they thought of him and the Americans as primitives, the same way he considered the earlier people.

They'd offered more help. They had references on their devices, and the number of edible plants suddenly increased.

Still, he wanted to discuss his findings with the captain.

Elliott was already talking to them, and he approached visibly, in case he wasn't welcome. The captain waved him over.

"This is Felix Trinidad," he said.

"Hi, Felix," Arnet said in reasonably accented English. He was tall but not as broad as Cryder. He wore the same fitted coverall, or one just like the one he'd arrived in, but didn't act cold in the fall air.

"Hello." He turned to Elliott. "Sir, I have some numbers to go over when you have time."

"Sure, in a few. We're trying to compare some here, actually."

He paused and waited, and Cryder spoke again.

"It's hard to spesfy. Power cell inten'ed life is two years stanard use. Replacemen ad one point six, nomnal. When we arrived, fairly fresh ad point four years use. Expec one point six, but safedy marjn of twenny pecent. So two years. Assumes reglar road use. Off road is harder. We've driven less. Used power for some heat last winner when we arrived. Solar gives extension, like yours. If it's only wa'er and some tool use, indefnite."

"But I assume that's subject to equipment wearing out?"

"Inevtable, evenchly."

"Well, we're very grateful for what you do offer. Your knowledge is even more valuable."

"Wooz. Keeping scan for tempral effec. Still hope to go back."

"What do you know about that?"

He shrugged. "Messing about our time. Obvious something fuct. Happens once, can happen again."

"So you know of a cause?"

"Possible cause. Def involvement and research."

Felix felt a ripple at that. A good one. Just the fact that someone knew of a possible cause was a relief. And the logic was sound. If it could be done once, it could be done again, assuming they knew what they'd done. Though analyzing the effects would aid that, even if they weren't sure.

Of course, they'd have to know who went missing, where and when. It was all a tease unless someone actually showed up.

Elliott said, "I'll let you get on with your tasks, then. If you need help, let us know, and I will schedule that run for salt and other supplies. Thanks."

"No worries. Wooz, Captain."

Elliott looked at Felix and inclined his head toward the tepee. They walked over that way, through weeds and across gravel.

"What's up, Felix?"

"Some observations is all." He waited until they were behind the tent. "I don't know if they can hear us here, but they can't see us at least."

"Noted. Specific concerns?"

"Not really. They're remote and almost seem lazy. I'm wondering about their culture, or psychology after five months alone."

Elliott tilted his head and said, "Well, five months alone with any one of you would drive me bugfuck insane. So that's possible. I guess it depends on how much interaction they need, though obviously some."

He said, "They keep looking at their glasses, like they're playing a game or surfing the net or something. But I think they also have cameras and such in there."

Elliott nodded. "That makes sense, and they watch us a lot."

"We watch them a lot. They seem to be as cautious of us as we are of the Romans."

Elliott replied, "I can see that. Their technology is more sophisticated, and they apparently aren't quite military. I don't know how they view the notion of war."

"They spend most of their time near the vehicle, like we did when we arrived. They seem more dependent on it than we are on ours. They use it for power, water, shelter, entertainment. Other than food, they seem self-contained."

"You're right," Elliott agreed with a squint in that direction, even though the tent was in the way. "I'd seen that but not noticed it. It makes sense they have better tools. The Neoliths weren't really inconvenienced. The Romans were up to speed in a couple of months. The Indians were too few to really matter. We barely know they exist. We've taken over a year and are still building up to what we consider field conditions. They're only two, and have more tech but no way to exercise enough manpower. I gather they needed someone for companionship and work, just like we have the visiting Urushu. We don't interact with them as much as they do with each other."

"Exactly."

"Okay, then that helps me understand how they think."

"How we think they think, sir."

"Hooah." Elliott grinned and shrugged.

✧ ✧ ✧

Richard Dalton worked hard. It was cool and brisk and cloudy gray, but he was in a T-shirt anyway. He was digging a substantial hole.

Cryder, whom he guessed was the NCO of the future pair, dug across from him. The man was tireless, but not very skilled with a shovel. Rich had had months here and years before to get very good at throwing dirt.

Trinidad worked between them, scraping and smoothing the sides of the hole. They were aiming for three feet deep and eight feet across.

It actually went fairly fast. In the meantime, Barker, Spencer and Arnet split planks with axes and the froe, and ran them over some tool on the future vehicle to smooth them. Then three of the Urushu burnished the surfaces with limestone, sanding back and forth. Barker called it "Holystoning." It was a reference to scrubbing deck timbers with stones the size of Bibles.

Three of the Neoliths, supervised by a Roman—Caius, he thought—stirred a pot of pine pitch over the fire. The pot had been made by the Roman smiths. If all went well, they'd have a tub together this evening.

There were already steam-bent planks for the inside, and rope from braided goat hair for the outside.

"This ll be bedr," Arnet said.

"Than the original plan? Yes."

That had called for a tub, heated rocks, and then bailing to drain. This should actually have a drainpipe, and hot water provided from the future people's vehicle.

He wondered about that. No one had asked yet, that he knew of.

"Arnet, what should we call your people? We have the Urushu, Gadorth, Romans and Indians. We're Americans or soldiers. So what are you?"

Arnet shrugged. "'Minders' works."

"That's a bit awkward with our usage."

"P'trollers? Wozzies?"

"What is your country called?"

He shrugged again. "Norilly countries anymore. Alleges, Tribs. Unities. Polities."

"We have to call you something."

The man shrugged again and said, "Cogi works."

"Cogi?"

"Yup."

"Ok. Cogi it is. How are we on digging?"

He'd give them this. They might not work often, but when they did, they worked hard. The man had done a third again the digging he had.

Trinidad said, "We're round to the line. How's depth?" He handed over a measuring stick. Rich moved it around the perimeter a few inches at a time. It was quite even. Then Captain Elliott handed him a longer stick with a plumb line.

"It should have the same perimeter mark and distance all around."

"Got it." It was fascinating how simple tools could be so accurate. He moved it around, but they'd laid things out well to start with.

"We're good," he said.

Spencer said, "Take a break, then get ready to be sticky."

As the Urushu finished polishing, Spencer and Barker brought the planks over and laid them in a broad sunflower around the hole. Doc brought a platter of round somethings up from the kitchen. Rich drank some water and had one of the round things. It was a treat made of a rice ball stuck together with honey. Damn, that was good. It was sticky and filling and he drank more water, then sucked his fingers clean.

Spencer said, "Okay, I'm going to be in the hole with Ortiz. Trinidad hands the boards down. We lay everything out and then caulk in between with rope soaked in pitch, and assemble fast before it cools. We have extra pieces, because if we screw up, it's hammer and prybar time. The reinforcing planks go in the middle, the rope goes around the outside. I nail the planks in place. We caulk the bottom." He pointed at a limb with a hole bored through it. "Drain pipe goes under here, we fill around it with cement, drill a hole, then caulk the joint."

Elliott, looking on, said, "Simple, right?"

"On PowerPoint, yes. Any final suggestions, sir?"

Elliott said, "Go ahead."

It got messy.

Barker and Spencer rolled the large floor next to the hole. It looked like a giant round shield, reinforced with crosspieces that fit into a tamped and shaped hollow.

Then came the first rope, and skins around the outside. They started standing the shaped planks inside it, braced against the floor. Rich held four of them in place, as others were set at cardinal points and the base rope tied. Then the top rope followed, and other vertical planks.

Some slipped sideways, some out of alignment, and Spencer let out with a stream of profanity that Rich had never heard from him. The man didn't swear much, but apparently knew how. Some of that was impressive.

With much shifting, cursing and beating, it took on at least an oval. Then the inside boards were forced into place, though they weren't quite round. They stretched the shape until gaps appeared.

"Good, it's tight."

"I see huge holes."

"Yes, but it's tight against the ropes. Brief break."

But although he said "break," Spencer walked around with the hammer, tapping stuff into alignment. He muttered and squinted as he went.

"Okay, next. Doc, you're up."

Doc stuck a stick into the rope, much like a tourniquet, and started twisting.

"Easy!" Spencer said. "The rope won't take that much force. Just keep tension on it."

He and Barker walked around tapping with hammers. Some in, some sideways, some down. It seemed to be much like when they did metalwork. Fraction by fraction, the tub came together like a broad half barrel. Doc kept taking up tension, and the gaps disappeared. The inside supports creaked and shifted into an almost perfect circle, with more tapping.

"Okay . . . let's wrap it up. How's that glue coming?"

Barker took a look and consulted with the cookers.

"Better be soon. It's getting thick."

"Okay, let's do it." He grabbed one end of a rope as Alexander took the coil and started winding it around the upper band. Three windings left them with a few feet left over, that Spencer tied into a knot and drew tight.

"Paint it!" he said.

The iron pot of bubbling pitch was carried over between lift sticks, and the crew started painting the cracks and ropes. Their brushes were made of willow, hammered with rocks until it split into fibrous ends.

Hot sap splashed around, sticking to everyone and everything. The ropes soaked it up when hot, then were coated with more. Each joint got a layer, reinforced by stuffing fleece into the gap. Then the whole assembly was tilted over, with much straining of muscles, so the floor and the edge could be covered.

Then it was time to roll it into the hole. That took Spencer, Barker, Arnet, Cryder, Rich, Caswell almost underneath, Caius and two of the Urushu. It slipped as it reached the edge at a tangent.

Caswell shouted, "Woah! Woah!" and backed up the side fast, dislodging dirt as she went.

It slid down into place, and Rich avoided splinters from the well-fitted wood, but his hands were sticky and cracking with hardened pitch. He wasn't sure how that would come off, except through wear.

"Okay, we've got it in. It should be ready for our first hot tubbing tomorrow."

It was already almost dark.

Spencer said, "Much as I hate to, I'm going to drain a cup of diesel for people to use to clean the tar off. Use it sparingly. Then you'll have to clean with soap to get rid of that. Oglesby, explain to the ancients this is a magic potion that can clean or burn. They must use it in small amounts only by direction. The Romans are probably familiar with naphtha."

"Hooah."

They had a hot tub. They had a fucking *hot tub*! Rich felt for a moment they could do anything, then reined in the pride. God hadn't sent them here to show off. This was a good thing to have, and they'd earned it, but they were subservient to God and the world, not any kind of masters.

Ramon was ready for the hot tub. He'd had a cup of Spencer's wine, steak, and berries with cream. It was a bit chill, and perfect for a hot soak.

The dome was lit by a hanging lamp that Arnet brought along. It was a glowing globe, better than the flashlights they'd had to use for so long. A hose ran under the scraped skin lodge cover and into the tub, and wisps of vapor hinted at heat. Another hose ran back out to the future vehicle, which had more and more useful gadgets aboard every time they needed something. It was fascinating how tools changed the productivity, for a tiny society.

There was a small arc of tent to crouch and squat in, and protruding sticks from the frame were used as clothes hooks.

"Speech!" Dalton said.

Spencer shrugged. "This was sort of my idea, sort of Bob's, and everyone worked on it. It will have medical uses, hygiene uses, and social uses. Let's plunge our bodies in the water of decadence."

He started peeling off his clothes. He bumped into Dalton and the LT next to him.

They'd all seen each other in various stages of nakedness, but this was a little more. They caught on limbs and giggled as they tried to make it work. Ramon stripped to underwear, then as Spencer and Barker plunged feetfirst into the tub there was suddenly a bit more room, he dropped his shorts and slid in.

Hot water. He was sitting in hot water. It had that tingly burn under his balls. Even the shower hadn't come close to this. It was amazing, almost too hot, and stung his skin, then evened out. He gasped, and his face started sweating.

Caswell looked quite nervous and small as she climbed down in. That was some serious bush, and it matched her hair. The Urushu had a lot less body hair. He wondered what genetics were behind that. That kept him from noticing her lean build and hips too much.

Cryder was powerfully built and very male. Arnet . . . he wasn't hermaphroditic, but was very androgynous. Ramon had never seen a build like that. Slim, soft, but obviously muscular. It was creepy.

Then Alexander slipped out of her pants and stepped over. She didn't seem bothered at all.

She was obviously a mother, with some stretch marks and a little belly fat, but in pretty toned shape on the whole, better than he'd thought she was, when she'd bulged through her PTs. Did she shave? Or electrolysis? Because she was still very smooth. And those tetas . . . she couldn't be forty-five, because those looked very natural, and spectacular.

He was very glad to be sitting under water.

"Oh, even having hot showers, this is fantastic," she said, and dunked her head for a moment, before running her hands over her hair.

It was fantastic, even without naked chicas to look at.

All the American men and Trinidad were very carefully not looking at each other, and not looking at the women. They looked at the curving roof, the struts, the water surface.

Cryder said, "Feels great. Tanks."

"Thanks for the help with the pump and tools. That made all the difference."

"Wooz. Why staring?"

Yes, they were all looking at him, rather than make eye contact with each other.

Alexander said, "Look, tits!" and rose up enough to bring them out of the water, then shimmied her torso. "I have tits! Look at them!"

Ramon broke into hysterical laughter with everyone else.

"And some of you are hung like stud horses, and some like stud gophers," she said. "Deal with it."

Spencer said, "Nice tits. Pass the wine."

And just like that, they were friends again. Though Caswell still looked a little shy, but she was smiling.

Maybe she'd relax some day. She was cute, and very useful. Alexander was lush and smooth, if older. She had some skills, too. Though he'd probably have to marry a local girl.

Dalton said, "Everyone please remember, there is no farting and no coming in the hot tub."

Spencer said, "If this was San Francisco, a young man like you could do both at once."

Everyone howled. Man, that was rough.

The water was hot. It swirled around him, and he tried to ignore all the other feet and hands. Realistically, this would fit six people, not eleven. Everyone wanted to try it, though.

Elliott said, "So, hot tub and shower. We have some tools. Next year we might have wind-powered electricity, too, and maybe engine fuel."

"No business talk in the hot tub, either," Caswell said.

Oglesby said, "She's afraid we'll want her to turn it into a giant stew pot."

"I'd be cooking you," she snapped, pointing her finger but grinning. "Boiled asshole stew!"

The Cogi seemed a bit put off, but didn't flinch. They sat touching and didn't seem bothered by it. Ramon was bothered by Dalton against one side of him and Trinidad on the other.

"I'm good for now," he said. "It's been tested. I'll wait for more room to stretch out."

He pushed himself up, then realized everyone could see him hanging there when they turned to pay attention to him.

It was cold all over as he climbed out. Even with the bodies and the dome there wasn't enough heat to compensate. He watched steam roll off his skin, and then his breath fogged up.

It was no worse than an Army shower point. He just hadn't had even that luxury in a year.

The gravel kept his feet as clean as could be expected. He toweled fast and pulled on undies, then wrapped the towel over his shoulder and worked on pants, squatting under the dank goathide roof.

"I'll relieve Doc so he can come down."

And despite the chill, he felt clean, really clean, for the first time in a year and a half.

"Sergeant Spencer, Sergeant Barker, your hot tub is fucking awesome."

"Thank you!" they both said, with raised wine mugs.

He stepped out into the air.

"Hey, Doc, let me grab a jacket and you can go tubbing."

"Awesome, man."

"How's it look?"

"Quiet and clear."

Behind him, Caswell said, "I'll join you. I'm good for now." She had dressed fast and was tying her hair back with a leather cord.

"Warm enough?"

She said, "The water was great. The air is cold. You're all silly."

He said, "We can take turns from now on, unless a couple wants to use it together."

She cocked her head and replied, "I can't see Dalton coming out of the closet."

"No, but Oglesby might."

Was she actually cracking jokes? The serious feminist and political correctness girl?

"Are we going to let the others use it?" he asked.

"I expect they can, after we do, or if it filters clean enough through the Cogi's vehicle."

"I wonder what they'll trade for that."

They continued the discussion up in the turret and on the roof, while Doc went shyly to the tub.

Caswell replied, "I'm worried about social effects more than technical. They may have a hot spring they travel to for rituals, and we'd be taking that. Any number of things we do could damage their culture without thinking."

"Sort of like ruining migratory patterns for birds by feeding them, or how a few predators can change an area's dynamics."

"Exactly," she said. "I know we have to do right by ourselves, but when we can, we need to consider this environment and their culture, too."

"I don't think the Romans will," he hinted. There was no way not to change things.

"They're not the way I imagined them," she said. "I expected more civilization. They invented the word. They're more barbaric than most of the others."

"Yes, it's not our type of culture."

"It may have to be," she said.

"I don't want to adopt too much of it. I'd rather convert them to ours. Soap at least."

"We aren't enough," she said. "And neither Gina nor I is going to settle down with anyone here."

"No?" he asked, tense and curious.

"If we pick any of you, the rest will be unhappy and resentful. Gina can't get pregnant, but I can and don't want to yet."

"What's the alternative, then?"

"Fingers, just like you."

Yes, they all understood that, but no one wanted to discuss it with each other. Well, not with other guys. If she wanted to tell he'd be glad to listen.

"We need families," he said.

"We do. It's not going to be fast or easy, though."

She was probably right about that.

CHAPTER 36

The tub was a useful trade tool, especially in winter. The Romans wouldn't share theirs with lesser barbarians. The next day, with Sean Elliott's consent, the Urushu took a turn. They were familiar enough with pools of water, and Caswell reported they dammed sections of the river to create plunges for summer. To have that water inside and hot, however, raised relations to an entirely new level. They soaked and sang and shouted.

"I assume that's positive," Sean said.

Oglesby said, "Yes, they love it. They're thanking us, and the future people, and the spirits."

It certainly sounded joyous.

"While part of me wants to exploit it for all the labor we can get, another part wants to be charitable, and of course, we're using Cryder's vehicle."

Doc said, "Yeah, but they're using a lot of our resources, too. I offered it free to people with sore joints. I also warned that it would hurt pregnant women."

That was decent. And pragmatically speaking, he said, "Well, if they choose to gift us, we'll make sure our future friends get a share. Either way it helps us be a focal center, which means this will be a town, given time."

"It pretty much is now," Oglesby said. "There's another group of pilgrims supposed to arrive today."

That was interesting. He couldn't keep track of everyone anymore.

He made a note to talk to Spencer and Alexander about that. It was important not to have strays in the COB.

"Thank them for visiting. Show them the way out."

"As before, hooah, sir."

Having friends was becoming necessary. Spencer was project manager and first sergeant. Barker was senior craftsman. Alexander ran increasing amounts of admin, with all the visitors. Caswell supervised three kitchen help. Ortiz was in charge of animals and veterinary work. Doc worked full time on everyone's ailments. Oglesby had to run around translating. Trinidad watched everyone and drew up threat warnings, cultural analyses, resource needs and interactions, which Alexander compiled for him, with an index. That left Dalton to be full-time security, hunter in chief, roving badass and general backup. They'd become management by default.

The Urushu were firm allies, appreciating all the knowledge and technology, and happy to share their own wisdom of plants, animals, minerals and utilities. They kept salted and smoked hides coming for tent covers, hut linings and bedding. The Gadorth provided semi-skilled labor in fence construction, weeding and hoeing, and could make clay artifacts that were of limited use without a nonporous glaze. Still it helped to have jars to hold dry goods. The Romans offered some useful skills that were tweaks of the basics, but much improved.

With hot water and additional recharging power from the Cogi, they were advancing quickly.

"Sergeant Spencer, what do you place our tech level at now?"

"That depends. We don't have a powered forge hammer or powered lathe. We're still working on textiles. Lodging and water supply is around thirteen hundred or so. The tools are about the same era, for a remote area, not a city."

"That's a long way from the Old Stone Age. That's what I wanted. Thanks."

"You're welcome, sir. We're doing it, but I wish it were further along."

"We'll get there."

This winter they'd build that ice storage, and just maybe the Cogi could provide cooling power for the mass. That would improve food storage either way. Next year, it was probably time to build a satellite compound the other groups could use. That would provide secondary defense for them, but keep their increasing numbers separate from here.

When time and circumstances permitted, he needed to find out if the Cogi would support that effort with more energy. They were cagey about their supplies, and he didn't blame them, since he was too with earlier groups. They might have resources if asked, though, that they wouldn't blanket offer. It was also possible they had stuff the soldiers hadn't thought about yet.

Eventually there would be another generation here, and then they'd need a political process. He wasn' t sure that was something he liked. It did simplify things to have everyone under military discipline, but he couldn't maintain that indefinitely, and some of them were already looking for local wives. Oglesby, especially, got to meet a lot of them, as did Doc. Both were obviously attracted to the younger Urushu women, and flirting heavily.

If he was correct, Caswell was keeping an eye on Arnet. He being an outsider, but with modern sanitation, might clinch that deal.

The captain was dealing with long-term thoughts, as he should. It was Martin Spencer's job to run what was here. That included more resources for current needs.

He walked over to the Cogi vehicle. It was interesting how they hung around it, like teenagers with a TV. Although, given how it worked as tent, power supply, and resource center, it wasn't really more remarkable than Gina hanging out at Number Nine. It was just that they both did, and didn't seem to have a lot of involvement in much else. Now that they had better sources of food and a hot tub, they seemed content to chill and let others work. They were both reclined in chairs in the shade, visors on, but obviously awake. As he approached, they raised the darkened lenses and looked at him.

"Cryder, you said we could possibly use your vehicle for a salt run into the hills?"

"Wooz."

"When can we do that?"

He shrugged. "Never."

"'Never'?"

"Sorry. When ever. Langage drft."

Yes, there had been a slight emphasis before the N. Damn, their

English had gotten sloppy by comparison. He supposed the Americans' was overly formal and wordy.

"Gotcha."

"Wanna do now? Weather nice, plenny time."

"Let me confirm with the captain."

Elliott was outside the fence. Rather than shout, he pulled out his phone.

"Sir, it's Spencer. Cryder says we can make a salt run today. I'm free. I'd want a couple of the help. Urushu or Neolith."

"Sure, if we can get that done, great. Do you need shovels?"

"Cryder, do we?" He looked over.

"Got tools. Should be good. Can sit four inclusive."

"We're good, sir."

"Do it, then. I'll have Gina arrange to cover your shift."

"Roger."

He turned to Cryder. "Let me grab two people to help and we can go."

"Wooz."

He didn't recognize the Neolith volunteer, but the Urushu was Ki!cla. He was short by their standards, barely six foot two. He was probably seventeen and and very eager to help the "Ahmerkin."

"We will ride spirit beast," he said, indicating the future vehicle. His Urushu was limited, but he could make himself understood.

Ki!cla jumped and clapped hands in glee.

He thumbed his phone for the Gadorth translation and said, "Atop hut-horse." His pronunciation probably sucked, but Zikom, which was as close as he could get to the name, seemed rather sobered in comparison. He nodded, though, and followed.

Cryder pressed a button that folded up the shower stall and disconnected the tub hoses. The vehicle hummed steadily and softly, and they walked alongside as he maneuvered along the south track, between the bathhouse, smoker, Urushu lodge on one side and the kitchen, work area and Oglesby and Dalton's lodge. Arnet remained in a chair in their area, wearing his coverall and goggles. He seemed aware, but didn't react much.

Once outside the gate, Cryder did something that opened it up like a Jeep, with four seats. Given the puffy clouds and light breeze, that was just fine with him.

It took some coaxing to get them into the passenger side, and he climbed in behind Cryder, so they each could keep control if the Stone Agers freaked out.

The Stone Agers twitched and clutched at the sides as it started off, but settled down as they rolled. At least it felt like rolling. They were about as high off the ground as a HMMWV, but smoother over the terrain.

"Where?" Cryder asked without looking over.

"South and east, toward that ridge." He pointed to where it was supposed to be, and hoped they could either use some kind of sensor or eyeball it as they got closer.

"Roj. What range on your phone?"

"A hundred meters or so, here."

"Zatall?"

"We don't have an actual cell tower, we're using a network through one of the computers."

"Shit. Ll fix that. Wooz." He spoke into his own mic. "Arnet . . . warra setup tower recep commo call check band w Elyot."

"Wooz, do."

"Okay, we set you on ours, LOS range unless aerial fly."

"You have a drone antenna?"

"Yeh."

"Cool. Duration?"

"Balloon. Several weeks."

"Damn. After that?"

"Bip antenna."

"Bip?"

"Build in place."

"From sections?"

"Carbon in, nanotube out."

"Oh, printed."

"Solid, but yes."

The two primitives wouldn't have understood the discussion even if they knew the language. They watched the conversation and watched the terrain, but took no part. They did smile when he made eye contact. They hung on tightly.

"Did you say LOS?"

"Yeh. Drone approx two fifty kilmtr. Base antenna approx fifty."

"Goddamn, that's great, if you can carry our bandwidth." Just how much tactical footprint did these two guys have?

Cryder snorted. "Course."

"Well, I assume you can, but I don't know what frequency it is or how it's transmitted. Not my field."

"Nod."

He'd actually said "Nod" rather than doing it. He still didn't make eye contact. Very aloof.

They were moving at a good ten miles per hour, he figured. It would only take about an hour to get there this time, unlike walking. They rolled smoothly up and down the ridges and dips, displacing growth with a faint crunch under the track.

Martin asked, "How much can we load aboard?"

"Gorra empty tub, holds two unnerd liter."

"That should last a while. Great."

"Nod, we use some for wa'er and food."

"Yes, I can understand water treatment. We use it for food, preservation of food and hides, might use some to develop ceramic glazes, but we don't know quite how."

"Can show."

"You know how to do ceramics?"

"No, got files."

"Information?"

"Yeh, for field critcalties."

"Damn. We're going off our own knowledge."

"Wooz. Done well. No files?"

"Oh, we have lots of files and books on all these subjects, but not with us."

"Ah."

Yeah. What he wouldn't give for thirty minutes on Wikipedia, copy/paste and Gina's laptops.

He spotted one of the outcroppings, pale under an overhang.

"Over there," he said. "See the salt lines?" They were white with tinges of pink and gray. Actual rock salt, and the ground below it was bereft of green from salt poisoning.

"Yeh, good stuff. We can process, too."

"Refine it?"

"Yup."

"That would be fantastic." They could have sodium chloride, calcium salts, potassium . . . he could probably work up a reasonable chemical industry.

"Reglar trips then, have primtives mine fr us."

"If they're willing, yes. We'd have plenty to trade."

"Them or you. We do tech end."

Yes, that was a negotiating point he held. Spencer decided to drop that line for now.

"We're here."

"Yup. Shovel things here." Cryder reached back, grabbed two tool things with protrusions, twisted and pulled until they turned into very efficient looking shovels.

Zikom and Ki!cla had enough practice with shovels to go straight at it, digging away at the dirt over the vein, scraping at it, piling it up.

Cryder twisted another tool into something like a coal shovel.

"Yours," he said.

Spencer was rather irritated. The man intended to sit there while they did the work. On the other hand, he was trading transport and technology, and he had to protect his own vehicle.

He wondered if the Gadorth and Urushu felt this way about him and the other Americans.

Cryder sat back with his goggles and some kind of control glove and played whatever game he had cued up.

The Stone Agers dug, he shoveled, the bin was easy to reach and had an agitator built in so everything settled down as he loaded. He'd toss in a shovel load, the bin would shake for a few moments, and it seemed to detect gaps and continue until they compacted. It only took an hour to get a full load of coarse salt, white with hints of gray and pink.

Cryder tracked their progress, and as they reached the top, said, "Wooz. Back now."

As they rolled downhill, he could see the COB when they crested ridgelines. It was a neat little place. They'd need to expand shortly. They'd likely expand forever.

"Cryder, is our presence going to interfere with the time line? Do you have any information?"

"No info. Various possibles."

"We figured either it has no effect, things correct around us. It has some effect and things adapt to it. Or it splits off a new time line."

"Prolly not last."

"Oh?"

Cryder shrugged. "Just prolly not."

"Okay."

Well, the future people seemed a bit less worried about some aspects. Was that good?

He was hesitant to ask the next question, but did anyway.

"How did you find us?"

"Metal mass. Magnetmetr."

"Yeah, I guess it would be pretty distinctive."

"Wooz."

"We have that, but not small enough for trucks."

"Nesry on field."

"If we had it, we'd use it, for sure." He was still a bit irked about Cryder treating him as common labor. He was quite happy to take a turn digging, but Cryder had been gaming. On the other hand, he had helped with the hot tub.

The hierarchy was established. He was near the top at least. Nor was he above manual labor, far from it. It was just a bit depressing to see how fast it adapted.

His phone rang. He pulled it from his pocket and stared at it in shock.

"Hello?" he answered.

Gina's voice said, "Spencer, we have cell net!"

"Yes, Cryder said they were going to do that."

"Isn't it great?"

"I don't know yet, but I like it, and I can see uses for it."

He wondered if there was some way to build a map of the area and locate themselves. That would be a great addition for traveling.

Back at Bedrock, Cryder put the vehicle within an inch or two of starting point. In only a couple of minutes, the water was connected again, and the shower stall erected.

Zikom and Ki!cla bowed out with profuse thanks. Cryder waved, and adjusted something on the control stem.

"Chloride salt in here. Magnesium here, potassium here." He pointed at three different compartments the bin had apparently separated itself into.

"Awesome. How long?"

"Hourso."

"Can you refine any from the stream water?"

"Does. Slow, though."

"I imagine. But good, that helps."

Gina found Arnet easier to talk to than Cryder. He was more verbal and used his hands for emphasis. He was lean, taut, with a twinkle to his eyes. He had healthy looking light skin with a nice olive cast under it, not just pasty white. His hair was gorgeous, even in the wild.

She looked at the frame showing connectivity. "Okay, it's a network, and now we have better commo. Thanks very much."

"Noprob. Wooz."

"Do you have a way to create grid coordinates either based on Earth proper, or zeroed on this area?"

"Either, both. Should I?"

"Please. And a map would be useful."

"You had aerial maps of ground?"

"Yes, fairly good ones, depending on the area." She thought about scale. "Three meters shown in a two-centimeter square on some civilian systems."

"We have maps, general area, simlar rez."

"Great. How do we transfer those?"

"Waita, gorra check with Cryder."

She shouldn't have assumed they'd share that intel, but at the same time, they'd mentioned it. She held off on calling Trinidad, because he would want to see this, too.

"Cryder says okay. Want me to file it?"

"Uh, I prefer to be the interface. Can we make the formats compatible?"

"Show where you want to file," he said.

She opened up a new folder for now. She'd put it in the intel folder later. There probably wasn't anything there the Cogi didn't have already, but it was encrypted and she took security seriously.

"There," she said.

He nodded, pointed at the screen, thumbed his device, and said, "Okay."

She looked, and there was a file there, in .jpg.

"How did you do that?"

"Jus told grip to find format and send."

There was a wireless connection, but how had he accessed it that fast, into the laptop, and in the right format? In seconds?

"How much access and bandwidth do you have with that?"

He shrugged. "Hard to define. More than yours."

"I gathered. Can I ask you not to try to look at our files without asking? As a courtesy?"

"Yeah, we respect that priv in our culture. Image takers all over." He tapped his glasses.

"We're starting to get that in ours. Were," she said, holding up her phone. He nodded.

"I won't go in wout asking."

"Thank you," she said. She was still going to disconnect power when away, and bury personal info behind more encryption. It might not help, but she had to try.

She opened the file and let out a gasp.

"That's one hell of a map," she said.

It showed both Roman settlements, the Gadorth village across the river, the Urushu upriver and another one beyond that. South it showed the hills. North it showed the river and the wooded plain. It was a good forty mile view.

"Thank you," she said.

"Wooz. I let you work."

He rose and slipped back out.

She clutched Cal with one hand as she zoomed in with the other. South . . . ridge . . . no. Not there. It would have been . . . Urushu village, now Roman camp, and south, then . . .

That was it. That dirty little round spot was where they'd come through.

It almost seemed like it should have some kind of shrine marker.

She panned away, not wanting to be reminded of it. She had trouble remembering anyway. They'd come through . . . and a week or so later they'd reached the Urushu village. There was something about a tribal dance.

Her memory would get increasingly fuzzy as she got more lethargic. Eventually depression would reach critical stage. She already wanted a nap.

She wondered if the sweetbreads were doing any good at all. They weren't terrible, but weren't particularly tasty, and she had no idea how far off kilter she was.

Still, they now had modern telecommunications. It was actually possible they'd achieve twentieth century technology here. Spencer knew how to make radio coils. They had limited electricity, and if they could draw wire, might manage a windmill and a bank of lead-acid batteries. They could build windmills or waterwheels. They might actually manage it. They had knowledge, they now had labor, and the Cogi had references.

They would never have chocolate, though.

Nor Synthroid.

CHAPTER 37

Martin woke when his phone beeped. It was a message.

Message?

He picked it up, clicked it open. Text message.

Silence your phone.

What the hell was this? He silenced it, and texted back, *Who is this?*

The next text was an image file. He opened it.

That was a photo of Gina, from neck to thigh, naked. He slowly enlarged it and panned across it.

Damn. Thank you.

You're welcome. You can save this. It's better than trying to sneak peeks.

You caught me.

My friend, everyone is trying to sneak peeks. ;)

Yes.

Doc is on watch, so you have an hour. Any ideas?

He took a long, deep breath. He wanted human contact. He wanted a partner. But interaction was still very high on his list, and this was interaction and feedback.

Quite a few, he typed. *Dumb phone. Slow msg.*

Then you read and I'll tell you a story. I'm here alone, and I'm going to do some things . . .

He missed an hour's sleep and loved every moment of it. He was on after Doc, and was cleaned up and ready to go on shift.

Doc had been on with Caswell. He nodded. Those interactions weren't going to be common, but might be workable when they were both alone.

Apparently, Gina's "still married" wall was developing cracks. His was gone. He wasn't sure what adjustment he'd made—his family wasn't even alive yet, and wasn't dead, but he accepted they were lost to him. He could only wish them well.

Sexual interaction with a woman he was very interested in should not trigger PTSD.

Especially one with such a vivid imagination. If she was serious about some of those comments, she was more flexible than some porn stars. Whew.

"How does it look?" he asked Doc.

"Quiet. Creepy cracking noises from the trees again."

"Well, we won't have that problem next year."

"Yeah. Less trees."

"It's ecologically sound."

Caswell said, "I know you're joking, and I know it's unavoidable. I just . . ."

"I know," he said. "I like trees, too. Shade, climbing. I wish we had some close, but security issues, ease of resources."

"I know," she said. "I don't have to like it."

Doc slid down and away.

Martin said, "In A-stan and Iraq, I hated seeing piles of usable stuff left in the desert. I know it'll get reused by locals, but so much was stuff we could have taken. And I'd give a testicle for a hundred pounds of loose scrap tools here, that I could forge into stuff."

"Well, I just pinged Ortiz," she said. "Having phones again is another odd thing. I'd gotten used to not having so much communication. It's useful, but I almost wish we didn't have it."

"Eh, I've only got a dumb phone, and I'm glad we do have it. It's going to help scouting missions a lot."

"There is that," she said. "And photos."

"Yes, those could be important."

"Or just artistic," she said. "I'm not as good as Gina, but I'm a fair photographer."

"True. We can build our own gallery of stuff. Having that scroll in the tepee in winter could make a big psychological difference."

"I'm not sure you'd want all of my photos scrolling," she said. "Here's Ortiz. Take care."

He wasn't quite sure what she'd just said or implied. It didn't fit her public persona, but he'd rarely seen her private one.

He was glad it was dark, because he was sure he was blushing.

Caius studied the Americani camp openly, standing two hundred yards downhill. It was impressively built. There were details he might have done differently, but it was certainly proof against anything short of a major assault or a siege. The small gate was protected by rampart and ditch. The main gate might be charged by a ram, but those banduka would chop to bits anyone who tried.

The evening sun illuminated it well, and he could see the man on watch atop their central redoubt. He was reachable with arrows, but his weapon outranged any bow. They could see in the dark, or turn on directional lanterns that outshone the moon. They were disciplined and took their task seriously. Their armor could stop spears, and they had those strange glass eye covers that cut the sun and protected against debris, and the others that could see in the dark.

The pilus prior had been an idiot not to believe him about their strength. If one banduka existed, and they obviously did, since the Indians had them, then better ones could. He had not lied when he stated the female had fired eleven shots in a few seconds, eight of them at once. Why the man chose to ignore that advice when three Americani arrived in camp with weapons was simply boggling. The man had deserved to die. As had the fool who'd tried to instigate a fight here.

Now the Romans had an embassy of sorts, downhill from the camp, but uphill from the other savages. The Americani had offered a bucket of salt as incentive.

He was impressed with their tribune's patience. The man could have wiped them all out. On the other hand, he was busy governing his own village here.

Caius didn't perceive a military threat. He did think it was entirely possible Tribune Elliott would attempt, intentionally or not, to draw more people, including Romans, into a town around his fort. An alliance between the two was possible, but Rome and her soldiers would not serve another, even if he claimed to be from some future Rome.

Nor was Caius sure of that claim. The Americani language had lots of Latin vocabulary, but the grammar was wrong and there was lots of Germani, too.

Whatever they were, they weren't really Roman. They'd displaced Rome. That irritated him deeply, and also frightened him. If they could do that to the Empire, what else could they do? What was the future?

They wouldn't tell him. But it obviously didn't include Rome.

They wanted help with several mundane tasks, from leather and pottery to ironworking. These were things every unit should have a craftsman in, and know the basics of. If they didn't, it meant they'd lost those skills.

That was another item of note and concern. They had banduka that fired a lot of bullets. How were those made if not on a forge?

He would treat with them, but he'd choose his ambassadors carefully, and counsel them to keep tight tongues.

Winter was inbound. Sean Elliott looked around his small command in satisfaction. This time, they had baskets and boxes of fruit, dried and ready. They had smoked meat, dried vegetables ready to add to thick stews, salt, fat. They had a huge rick of firewood in useful lengths, both solid sections and split. The Urushu had a lodge with a hearth. The Gadorth had a longhouse. The Romans had a small roundhouse. Those were both outside the wall, visible from the turrets.

Cryder and Arnet mostly stayed in their vehicle. Occasionally they'd offer an insight, or run some kind of scan to help find materials. Their library was very useful, at least the parts they shared. He noticed they were very protective of it, either because of technology or history they didn't want to share. They did share their transforming tools.

But for labor itself, they'd do about ten minutes each, then disappear for half the day. They had some kind of game software with them, as well as all the vast memory of their library, and didn't really have much interest in anyone except to study the primitives. They were always there for meals, of course.

Those meals were flavored with their refined salt, so he decided it was still fair, all in all.

This would be a lot more comfortable than the previous winter, now that there were timber or gravel walks between most buildings, a second windbreak around the latrine, and a sweat lodge with a hot tub. A weekly bath and soak in the heat would do wonders for all of them.

He already had plans drawn for next year. An annex downslope, which might affect waste matters, though if they could pipe water from upstream, that went away. Cryder said the Cogi vehicle could shape wood troughs for an aqueduct, and the Romans would certainly know how to build one and understand why. They would build another corral with a higher fence and see about some aurochs. They might manage to clip and domesticate some fowl. That gave them a full range of meat, a reasonable number of tubers for starch, some greens, rice, nuts, berries and occasional honey. Oh, yes, Caswell wanted to build another hive, and they had split timbers to do it with.

At this point, he figured their past, now future, was gone. They would have to do the best they could here, and if their developments caught on and fucked up the timestream or whatever? Well, the timestream should have thought about that before it sent them here.

He was going to need a wife. He also needed to pursue the idea of a mayor for the town, and letting people's terms of service expire. The Army discipline had been useful, but they were working more as a community now, and eventually the Army would be more prison than home. Especially as two of them weren't even Army.

He could probably hold off that discussion until spring, but he needed to have answers ready when people started asking.

For now, the standing order of "No fraternizing in the COB" had somewhat limited interaction. Oglesby and Doc had regular, or at least repeat, girlfriends they met with every couple of weeks. There weren't any disease outbreaks and no one was pregnant yet. He wasn't sure what the rest were doing, and while he needed information for decision making, those weren't the kind of questions he was prepared to ask, especially of the females.

Though he did get the impression Caswell was interested in Arnet. He wondered how that would work out.

Except for the cold, Felix Trinidad felt almost at home. He had a small but sealed cabin with a slate floor. It had a fireplace and chimney that drafted well. His pallet was a sleeping bag set on his foam pad atop quilted hides set on a frame of pegged timbers and rawhide. It actually wasn't bad, and more comfortable than many Army beds. Caswell had done a good job with them. He had a battery powered light and phone. His clothes were hung on a line to give some privacy between his bunk and Ortiz's. On the whole, it was better than quite a few field deployments, and on par with parts of the PI, including the village he'd lived in until he was ten.

His phone chimed then, and he raised it to look at the message. A frigid draft blew into the bag as he did so.

ALL: Extreme cold inbound. Advise tepee.—Gina.

He replied with "ok" and lay back. It would take a few minutes to warm his shoulders up again, and that was with two logs glowing on the hearth.

The cold still sucked, and that was like nothing he'd grown up with, but he'd learned to deal with it. These extreme spells, though, were miserable.

Spencer had mentioned the possibility of sheet metal for stoves that would radiate heat better, if the Cogi could help. Eventually, maybe. They had made a lot of progress.

He sighed. The tepee was open, and it wasn't going to get any warmer tonight. He might as well move now.

First was to reach, stretch and grab his coat down from the hook. He shimmied in, waited for it to warm up, then unzipped the bag and got vertical fast, stepping into his athletic shoes from long practice.

He backed out the door with the rolled bag, and jogged through the maze to the tepee. Then he had to hike it all under one hand to open the tent flap and wiggle in.

"I got it," Oglesby said, and held the hide aside for him.

"Thanks."

"No problem."

Spencer was dressed, and rushed out with him to get the foam pad and roll of hides. That got the essentials over, and he left it all in a pile in his arc of the tent while standing almost in the fire to warm up. He shivered and let himself smoke like a haunch of meat.

Then it was time to lay out his hides on the bed of fleece and leaves that Gina and Barker had built for everyone, lay out his bag, and decide if he really needed to piss or not. He did, so he ran back outside and to the streambank.

There was nothing quite like draining your bladder while standing in snow with cold wind blowing over your dick. He felt his jaw ache from clenching teeth, forced it to relax and then felt his teeth chatter, and pulled his PTs up fast as he turned back toward the tent.

Up at the Cogi corner, that looked like Caswell stepping into their tent.

Very interesting.

There was a rationale to it. She didn't want anything to do with her own unit, which he understood, and the ancients were exotic in all definitions, and less than glamorous. The future men, though, were built like gods and not attached.

Her presence there wasn't information he'd share with anyone except possibly Elliott. Anyway, she might have some mundane reason for being there.

Maybe.

CHAPTER 38

Winter was a lot easier the second time, though having better lodging and more firewood helped a lot.

Bob Barker admired the second tepee, or what would be one. It had two covers and overlaid poles. After every snowfall, they untoggled the front, and shoveled in as much as possible. The pile was four feet deep now, and a good fifteen feet across.

The Cogi's shovels changed shape into scoops. Otherwise, panels of bark, two regular shovels, and a cooler had to suffice.

He had a scoop, as did Dalton. They threw snow into the tent and two of the Urushu stomped it down with improvised snowshoes.

"Harder," he said. "Pack it to ice." He pantomimed and they nodded.

Behind him, Negrus, a Roman, and Ikaya, one of the Urushu, piled up snow for him to shovel in, then retreated for more. Beyond them were five others. This wasn't efficient, but it would hopefully last all winter.

From the side, watching, and occasionally throwing a shovelful, was Arnet.

"We got fridge."

"How big?"

"Half cubemeter."

"Better save that."

"Nod. Tryng to ask device how to connec to zis pile n chill."

"If you can find a way to do that, that would be great. It would last all year for sure." He had no idea how such a device would work, but if they had it, great.

"Should anyway. I work math."

"Glad to hear it. We'll see how right you are in fall."

Arnet almost snorted in disdain.

"I'm right. Easy math."

He didn't have to answer because a snowball hit him. He turned to see Ortiz shaping another one.

"Thirty seconds," the man said, "then back on the job, motherfucker. Better throw fast."

Next to him, Dalton grunted and pivoted the shovel so it catapulted a bucket of snow in a high arc.

Ortiz said "*mierda*" and backed up fast, but kept watching the incoming fall. Bob took that moment to scoop up snow, crunch it into a ball, and heave.

It was a great shot, until Ortiz ducked from the falling snow and took the ball straight to the cheek.

"Oh, shit." He ran forward, waddling in thick clothes, snow and undergrowth. Ortiz was on all fours, shaking his head.

"Serves me goddamn right," the man said, and stood slowly. He had a hell of a welt, with scratches, on his left cheek, just above his beard.

"You okay, man?"

"Yeah. Let's get back to it."

"We'll have a real game later. We can build a snow fort."

The snow cone was six feet and packed when done for the day.

He enjoyed his hammock in his tepee. He didn't mind the tent being used as a clinic space, inclement weather chapel or dining room. He didn't really mind everyone piling in for comfort in the cold. It did get frustrating in a hurry, though. Tent fever, like cabin fever.

It was easier this winter than last. On all but the coldest nights, everyone's log hooches were plenty warm. So when they did have these extreme arctic blasts—this was the third one this winter—there was a scramble to move in, shift around, get comfortable, then a few days later they'd move back out. That meant using a floor bed so he wasn't dangling above people, and he rolled it up so they could throw up ponchos for privacy. You could imagine you were alone, despite the shifting and snoring.

At least those events kept the bedding fresh.

The cabins would be warmer once they built proper doors from split wood, with hinges, and sealed them with leather.

Gina had managed to train the cat to excrete around the perimeter of the camp, so he stopped spraying the tent poles. That had been pungent. There was still a hint of it, but under the hides, the sweat, the smoke, it was barely noticeable. Cal patrolled around, letting everyone have a skritch, before he retreated to sleep curled against her legs. Lucky cat. Cal had slept on his pallet one night last week, and it had been very comforting. The little fella was cute, and brought dead things to them every couple of days. He understood dead game meant salted liver, and obviously thought that a very fair exchange.

A week later, he had people piling in again, letting in cold, thumping around. He helped Caswell drag in her bag, last of all. She did like privacy, but she was hours behind the others. She was out of breath, too, and her hair . . . hmmm.

Well, he wouldn't mention that. She might have been alone, or perhaps she'd found someone local.

"Impending Christmas and New Year's again," he said.

"Don't remind me. It's still not something I look forward to."

"Yeah."

This year, holidays had been much more notional. Each one reminded them of their old homes. What did July 4th matter here? And Christ hadn't been born on 25 December anyway, and to celebrate it 11,000 years before he was born was just silly. Thanksgiving sort of remained. New Year's was mostly a calendar function.

He realized he didn't know when anyone's birthday was, other than his own, and he'd never shared his. It just really didn't matter.

"We're going native," he said.

"I don't understand?" she said, as he helped her adjust the bag and her thick fleece blanket. The people who didn't have those were very jealous. Spencer's featured the *Cars* movie characters, borrowed from his son, and he caressed it often, but it sure was warm.

He said, "Most holidays, our birthdays, forgotten. Old foods. We're more and more part of this time."

"But never will be completely." She rolled out her bag on the pile of furs and boughs.

"Any kids will be. We're going to be those strange old people with the knowledge and the magic devices."

She said, "Better a tribal elder than a ragged hermit."

"Aye. Still, I'm less depressed about being here, and that's sort of depressing."

She shrugged. "It is. Except I can't get up the energy to care that much anymore."

"And that," he agreed.

Three days later everyone moved out again. He kept stew cooking inside for people passing by, or coming off watch, or Doc's patients. His lodge was sort of the local inn, and it was the winter kitchen. It was light enough in daytime even with the smokehole reduced, and at night he had four little LED lights, the batteries constantly charged by Arnet and Gina. Except one had failed entirely two months back. Eventually they'd all burn out.

He shrugged. It was what it was.

Despite the cold he went to the lathe and turned another bowl, kicking the pedal, scraping the wood, and letting the pole unwind the spindle. Spencer had laboriously hammered and ground him three steel chisels from socket extensions from the tool box: a gouge, an inside scraper, and a parting tool. Others would have to wait on more iron and more charcoal.

Every morning they did PT. They filled their Camelbaks from the Cogi's filter and refilled the boiling pot. Once a week they did laundry, more essential than ever now that all the deodorant and soap had run out. They were using wood ash and gazelle fat for soap, though Caswell thought she could make something from vegetable oil, eventually.

Stand watch, cook meals, carve wood, make arrows to replace the lost ones, with sharpened bone points. He brushed his teeth religiously, held workshops with the Urushu and Gadorth to swap skills, and slept. It was a living. It was even occasionally fun.

It was becoming routine.

Martin Spencer hated Excel, but they couldn't spare paper. He'd reluctantly learned how to create slides.

It wasn't hard, just annoying. He was in the fucking Stone Age, using Excel. That was so Army it was . . . something.

Spring this year led to a frenzy of planting seed they hoped would sprout. Rice went into an excavated swamp upstream. Dandelions had been moved into a plot last year, and came up. The wild onion did well, and they spent hours cleaning bulbs and sorting them. The pine shoots were back, and some mulberry type berries. Martin planned to use some of those for wine again.

He was glad to provide that service, and wished he could find sweeter stuff. Though he also needed to get that still going this year. He didn't want to loot the truck, though.

Possibly he could freeze distill again this winter. Or even process something with specific gravity in the cold, since they had a ten-foot-high chunk of ice in the ice tent. A year-round still would be nice.

His guts were hanging in there. The Cogi's processor was able to refine a calcium tablet from bone that helped keep the acid under control. It was palliative, rather than preventative, but it beat dreading eating and dreading not eating for the agony each brought. He was still in pain, but it was an easier medication to take and worked better than just bone meal. It was like chewing Tums, nonstop.

Each page was a note to himself, about firewood, charcoal burns, food levels, water supplies, new projects. He spent an hour or so every couple of days talking to the LT and Gina, offering advice on projects, estimates on needed resources, and letting Elliott decide what to pursue, while Gina logged it into a schedule.

To make it worse, his eyes, near perfect, were starting to lose their close focus. He could see the screen fine, could beat metal fine, but he couldn't closely eyeball projects under a couple of feet away. There weren't likely to be any glasses here in his lifetime.

He was only too glad to go to the forge.

There was good news there. The Cogi had furnished him with a sealable pipe. It wasn't quite ceramic, and wasn't quite plastic, but it threaded airtight. Iron ore plus some lime and charcoal in the pipe, pumped for several hours at heat, carburized into steel. With better quality material, he was hammering out much better artifacts. They had two more axes, and he hoped to finish a proper adze in a few days, to help with shaping logs.

He had an appointment for the next day, to talk to a Roman smith. The idea was fascinating from an historical perspective, and humbling from a professional one. He needed to talk to a man from two thousand years prior to get straight on the task, a man who had no idea what martensite, body-centered cubic structure, or molybdenum were. At that, Martin had no idea how to refine molybdenum.

It was still chilly, and even though he'd adapted to being outdoors, he enjoyed the heat emanating from the glowing mouth of the fire. That and his leather apron kept him comfortable enough, though his feet were chilled. Also, his boots were starting to split. He knew how to make heavy welted-soled shoes, and would need to do that, too. Perhaps he should try to forge some needles.

Then he needed chisels, a real anvil, real tongs . . .

There was nothing romantic about the Dark Ages. Or about getting old.

"Dinner and formation," Barker called.

Dinner was planked fresh trout with salt, and enjoyable, if a bit dry, but they had lots of it. It didn't feel as filling as steak and potatoes, but it was still good. The Cogi sat back away from the others, out under a portable umbrella. After those initial greeting hugs, they'd kept their distance.

Elliott said, "Okay, Sergeant Spencer is having a Roman guest tomorrow, to talk about forging. So let's try to impress him. Part of this diplomacy is slipping hints about how awesome we are, and of course we can wipe out entire cities from miles away."

It was Trinidad who said, "I'm concerned they'll know it's an act, and also realize we don't have the tools we need for our high-tech stuff."

"Yeah. Don't overdo it, but do hint a bit. Let's talk while we eat."

Spencer decided to eat first. They'd talk about this for hours, just to kill time, and he'd hint to Elliott as to what to say.

Ortiz said, "If you run out of Latin, use Spanish. Not that degenerate German you English speakers like."

And off they went.

Oglesby asked, "Aren't there Germans in Mexico?"

"Yeah, we don't let them speak that crap. It stops them from taking over."

Martin had expected Nazi jokes within five minutes. He was wrong. It had taken ten seconds.

He didn't have popcorn, but he did have rice cake. This was going to be entertaining, and hopefully not any more of a disaster than any other Army function.

Publius Horatius Naevius, tesserarius and blacksmith, arrived at the Americani camp with his two escorts, Aelius and Camillus. He was rather nervous, since the banduka the Americani had could rip holes through logs and armor, but passage had been guaranteed and they met him with an open gate.

He was impressed with the Americani. Their camp palisade was taller and stronger than the Roman one, and they had only the ten people. The Americani were respectable. The barbarians in camp weren't worth much even with proper tools. They were doing odd chores, as they did for the Romans.

He was cautious of those two others, the "Cogi." He didn't like that name. What exactly did they know? He'd seen them only at a distance, and their gear was even more bewitched, almost godlike.

He was met at the gate by the one who looked almost Latin, who said, "*Toma tus armas a Optio Regina Alexander ahi dentro.*"

He parsed that, and carried his arms to the command hut, which appeared very much to be some sort of wagon with a lot of doubled wheels.

The Roman influence on this future culture was obvious. But was the optio tribuni really named Regina Alexander? That was a rather arrogant name for a woman, nevermind the ridiculous concept of women in the Army.

"Here are my arms, Optio," he said slowly. Their language was bastardized with Germani and some other stuff, but they could communicate well enough slowly. But by the gods, they were terrible with cases. Imperative could be deduced, and sometimes Accusative, but that was about it. Nominative and Genitive might as well not exist. It was an awful language.

"*Gratias,*" she said, and pointed. "Put *hic.*"

She sat at a stool with three illuminated tablets in front of her. They glowed from within, due to some magic from the gods they'd learned to control, like fire only smaller and cooler.

On the leftmost, she touched an image and moved it. It just followed her finger. On it were letters. Latin letters.

Of course an optio was literate. He just had trouble imagining a woman optio.

"Your army also requires staff to be literate, I see."

"*Omni est,*" she said. Gods, it was comprehensible, but savage. But all of them?

"All of you? If you are from a headquarters that is a useful thing." They were all tesserarii or optii, none of them pedes.

She obviously thought over her response, before she carefully said, "*Integer pedes literate. Nos mandate it to scribo.*"

"Impossible!" She must be joking with him.

"Very possible. We commence educating it at *ano quarto.*"

She tapped small stones in front of the tablets, and more words appeared, very fast, so much faster than scribing them or cutting them. He watched for a moment. She dragged another stone and a section lit in blue, disappeared, and appeared on the rightmost screen.

"What are you inscribing?" he asked.

"I am recording our levels of commisaria and loges."

She had a fine arse, excellent teats, and that striking straw-colored hair with blue eyes. A northerner for certain. A barbarian woman. Yet she was optio to the tribune, literate, and apparently a soldier.

Their banduka were faster shooting, tremendously more powerful and better crafted than those the Mughal barbarians had. They could see in the dark, light the dark, and their Optio Valetudinarii Arminius, the African, was very good with surgery. Truly the gods blessed these men and women, but here they were, consigned to the savage world of stone-chipping barbarians.

The other female arrived to take him to the forge, where he was to work with Centurio Martin. She carried one of the banduka and a knife almost as big as a gladius, but single edged.

"I am Optio Statorum Jennifer Caswell," she said slowly.

"Why is your uniform blue, Optio?" he asked. She was wearing the shapeless silky covering they wore for exercise and casual work. The others he'd seen were gray.

"I am from a different . . . separate . . . legio," she said.

"Oh? What is your legio?"

"Aeronauticus."

"Air and sea?"

"Solo air. Felix is a mares. Barker used to be."

"Nauta," he offered.

"Gratias. Nauta. Felix is an inquisitor. Our navis are a tertia of a mile long, travel thirty miles in an hour, and have great guns that can demolish cities." She used her hands for emphasis and counting as she walked.

He did not think she was joking.

"What is aeronauticus? To navigate with air?"

"*Aer perum et caelo*," she said. "We fly."

"With Apollo's help?"

She grinned. "We have an aerovehicle named Apollo, actually. You're aware straw rises in flame from the calor. Suffice calor, ventus impetus, can levitate a vehicle into the air. We fly across continents. That's how we came to Asia from the occidens."

It was hard to translate, and sounded ridiculous. Was that true?

"How fast do you go?"

"Say that again, please."

"What velocity is achieved?"

"Ah. Inter duo cento miles in an hour to tri milles, depending on what type of craft."

Not even the gods could travel that fast. But they must. Unless she was lying. He didn't think she was lying. "That would span the Empire in a hour."

"Yes, easily. Our . . . well, I suppose it is an empire, stretches tri milles miles across a continent, and we travel to other continents to fight, trade and visit. The Nauta has craft that fly from ships, too."

She delivered him to Centurio Martin and Tesserarius Robertus, who had a brisk fire in their forge. It was a bit odd-shaped of a forge, but certainly hot enough.

He realized he'd been completely distracted from Jenfer's striking green eyes and pale skin. Oh, to sire sons on her.

"Gratus, Publius," Martin welcomed him.

"Greetings. Your women tell fanciful tales of flying through the air and of all your troops being literate."

Martin smiled oddly and said, "I'm literate in our language, somewhat in Latin, in Germanic and in Gaulish."

"I see," he said, not entirely believing. It was almost as if they were trying to impress him. Trying hard. On the other hand, that was how diplomacy worked. But he was only a smith, not a centurion.

"Well, we nullus cognosci a multitude. Multum ferro work is by carborundum magnum segmentum cum tools. Forging is limited. So we request assistance. Especially as we mostly work with optimum ferrum, hard and clean."

"I see your wagons are made of iron," he said.

"Yes, milles of libre of it. We have no way to separate one, though."

Thousands of pounds of iron? He looked at the wagons. Yes, thinking about it, they had to be. That was a Vulcan-blessed lot of metal. He had trouble with the last part, but it was about making pieces from it, he thought.

"Grind it," he said.

Robertus said, "It would take forever."

"If you have a century of men with hard lime, you could create a powder of good ore."

The two looked at each other.

"That's not impossible," Martin said. "It's not for now, though."

"Well, what can I show such masters as yourselves?" he asked, not entirely joking. Their Latin was laughable, but he could puzzle it out with pantomime. They knew a lot of bases, but had no grasp of grammar. They had a lot of Germani in there.

Martin handed him a hammer, and it was the nicest hammer he'd ever held. The grip was shaped to swing in the hand, of some very strong wood. The head had a flat face and a peen, and its balance was very sweet. He let it drop in his hand, and it fell right where he wanted.

Martin showed him several tools.

"I can manage tangs and sockets, after a fashion. I need to fabricate improved sockets. I'm no bueno cum cavum shapes, either."

"Show me what you are doing."

Publius watched the two of them work, and tried not to smile. They worked hard, pumping, heating, beating. For basic drawing and upsetting, Martin wasn't bad. However, he was charitably at the level of apprentice.

To be fair, his anvil was rock, and without a good large furnace, making a proper iron one would be difficult.

"It's easier to raise bowls over a form than dish them," he said. "Can you find a domed stone and set it in a wooden block?"

"I can. Sic dishing plates—cavum fasciendum? for making hollows, though. I just don't possess unum."

"Those are for shallow items only."

"Ah."

"You are welding too hot."

"I know. I'm experience cum materia that require extreme calor."

"What flux is that?"

"Straw ash." He had to examine it to determine the words. Yes, that was marginal.

"You have salt, yes? Salt and clean sand with some iron filings will work much better." He had to demonstrate with latter with their sharp file on a scrap piece, and point at the streambank for sand.

"Huh. That makes sense. It's not what we used at home." Martin might be a good centurio, but he was not much of a smith.

He talked and showed how to dome metal and planish it evenly. The granite anvil wasn't flat, but did give enough resistance. It was hard, sweaty work.

Their hammers were amazing, though. He'd never held anything like them. They were heavy, but very balanced and effective.

He became aware that Optio Regina was pointing something at them, and the two "Cogi" were staring from a short distance. He raised his head to look at them.

"I am making engravings," she said.

"Engravings?"

"Using a similar method to my screens. We call them photo graphs."

"Screens?"

She sketched a rectangle in the air.

"Ah, your tablets."

"Yes, gratias."

He stepped back, panting, and Martin took over while Robertus pumped the bellows for him.

Optio Regina turned her device around, and there was a tablet on it, with a miniature picture of him working, as if seen by eyeball. It was not engraved or painted. It was flat, and it was completely perfect. It was a light-picture. It was so perfect it scared him. Then he thought how well it could relay information.

"How does that work?" he asked.

"The light is gathered and stimulates small cells like a fly's oculus. Each cell, called a 'pixel,' appears on the tablet. They are identified by location on the tablet and color for reconstruction later."

"But there must be thousands of them," he said. It was a picture as vivid as the eye showed.

"Decem millions," she said. "The camera has a modus to sort them."

He could well believe the ten of them could easily fight the entire

Roman century, given their devices and knowledge. Yet they were ignorant of charcoal making and basic smithing.

Martin stepped back from the rock anvil and held up the piece he was working on. It now looked like a deep ladle with a long handle welded on. Martin seemed pleased with himself.

Publius decided not to mention that he'd done better ones by age twelve.

"That is the way," he said. "But you will need more practice."

"I'll be getting it," Martin said. "Would you like to examine our baths? I wonder how they compare to yours."

Publius understood they were using hospitality to gain information. The centurio had warned of that, but they hadn't asked about anything the Romans had in the way of weapons or tactics. They didn't seem to care about those things at all.

But atop the wagon, the one called Felix sat with that large banduka that could fire dozens of projectiles in a moment, through solid logs. It would destroy the century in seconds if turned on them.

They understood Latin adequately, but there were obvious Germani words in their speech. He recognized them from his first campaign. Had future Rome become so corrupted by barbarians?

He would not want to fight them, however.

At lunch, they served a salted fish and salted pork, with nuts. He sat under the awning for the purpose, and continued talking to Martin and Robertus.

"Your double bellows is impressive."

"Thank you. I wish I had more practice. We appreciate the trade."

Publius wasn't sure exactly what was being traded. Just that he was helping them with smithing, and something in return was coming to the Romans.

Another sat down next to him, with light hair, bronze skin and solid muscles. A definite warrior.

"I am Richard Dalton. Tesserarius in line."

"Publius Horatius Naevius."

"I am pleased to meet you. May I offer you wine?"

"Of course you may, and thank you." He accepted a kidney-shaped metal cup with wine in the bottom third. It was full of sediment and a bit sour, but strong and clean enough. It washed down the salted meat just fine.

"What year are you from in Rome?" Tesserarius Richard asked him.

"The ninth year of Claudius Imperator."

Richard grinned and clapped. "Perfect. You've heard of Jesus Christ?"

"I don't know that name." The fish was some form of river trout. Quite good. There were herbs with the salt. There were no crops here, but there were wild herbs and the Americani knew of them, it seemed. He might ask for those, too. The gods knew the food in camp was mostly rice and boiled goat.

Tesserarius Richard said, "A Nazarene . . . priest, I guess. In Judea."

"I have not served in Judea." This was an odd query.

"He performed miracles, and was executed by Pontius Pilate. He ambulated on water, fed five milles people with only a minuscule basket of food. And after being crucified, he vivified on the third day." It took Publius a bit to determine what all that meant. It sounded like any number of stories.

He asked, "Which gods did he invoke?"

"The one true God of the Jews, and now the Christians, named after him."

"I haven't heard of this. There are a lot of priests all over Judea, though." One god? That was the Jews. This man claimed to worship the Jewish god?

The man was insistent. "He would have mortare only a few anno ago."

"I have not heard of this priest you revere."

The answer obviously frustrated Richard, who said, "Very well. Gratias for assisting with your responses."

"Thank you for the fish," he said. "It is delicious."

He saw Centurio Martin smile, and wondered what the joke was.

Their bath wasn't very good, either, but it was quite warm and clean.

CHAPTER 39

Sean Elliott was satisfied with progress. It was May and humid and warm, and the creek was drying up again, but the well was clean and produced water. He'd devised a sand and gravel filter with a leather catch basin. He planned to replace that with concrete, hopefully this year because he didn't want to depend exclusively on the Cogi's filter. Roman concrete wasn't great, but wasn't bad, and the local Romans had knowledge of it.

Their periodic visits had been carefully orchestrated to get technical knowledge from them, while imparting as much awesome as possible through real but impressive claims of American military might. It seemed to be working.

As for his element, he couldn't ask for better people. Their personalities clashed as much as anyone's, but their breadth of knowledge was amazing and their determination shone through. They'd survive. The only questions were how far they could advance, and how much information could they leave for the next generation of theirs, or of the Urushu.

He saw Oglesby walking his way with one of the Gadorth. It was interesting how most of the soldiers had turned into managers and liaison, now that they had trustworthy local labor.

"What's up?" he greeted.

"Hey, sir, Sadi'a is a junior chief for the village." He indicated the local.

Sean nodded acknowledgment and said, "Relay my greetings. What's up?"

"He says we have to plan a hunt for midsummer."

"Okay. A ceremonial thing?"

"Yes."

"We're in. Traditional or guns?"

"Traditional. Spear throwers and hand-thrown spears."

"Okay. Can we wear body armor? It's our traditional dress, after all."

Oglesby spoke clearly overall, with some pauses and hesitations, and pantomimed armor.

"Sir, they say if that's our traditional clothing for hunting, we should of course wear it. They'd like us to use their traditional weapons."

"Seems fair. Is this a cow? A bear? Something cool?"

"Yes, sir. A rhino."

"A . . . rhino." That sounded dangerous, and horribly unPC.

"With spears. They specifically want Doc along, too."

"Well, good. I guess." Rhinos, with spears. "Do we really need to do this?"

"It's important to them, sir. They do it every midsummer. They ask for our two best hunters."

That was complicated. The best hunters would be Barker and Dalton. However, as commander, he should lead by example. Except if he did get badly hurt, then leadership could be damaged.

"I'll send two hunters and Doc," he said. "After we consult with the spirits on who is best suited."

Jenny Caswell had mixed feelings. Being selected as a hunter was good, if it was to show equality, bad if she was a token.

Then, there was killing a rhino. She didn't like killing animals anyway, and this was a magnificent beast whose entire genus was near extinct in their era. This species was already gone.

It felt a lot as if she'd been railroaded into it, and couldn't gracefully bow out.

Stupid male egos were part of the culture here. If only that could be directed somewhere else. It was much easier to do that with a modern, technological society.

She had three javelins, with hardened steel tips Spencer had forged for her, and fletched by Bob. Then she had a heavier stabbing spear, with a tubular iron point to cause hemorrhaging, cut from a pipe section from Number Eight.

Other than that, she had helmet, armor with plate, and a Camelbak Hawg with a handful of useful things in the outer pocket.

Elliott, Doc and she, three Urushu in rawhide, three Gadorth in armor of hardened hides, and two Romans in their armor plodded uphill to find a rhino. They were following a watercourse smaller than their own.

One of the Urushu, Zhu!yi, pointed, cupped his hands, and said, "Ak!a."

She raised cupped hands to her lips. "Ak!a?" she asked. "Drink?"

"No. Ak!a." Zhu!yi moved his hands around in a circle.

"Pond or lake, I think. Mare."

One of the Romans, Fulvius, grinned. "Lacus."

"Okay, good. We're looking for rhino at a lake." She pantomimed a horn and drinking.

"Yes." Zhu!yi nodded.

It was amazing how a few words and signs could be used so well.

On they trod. It wasn't a long trip, but it was all uphill and cross country. It was hot, sticky and dusty, and she wasn't as tall as the Urushu or Doc or Elliott. The Romans clustered back with her. She could tell they were watching her, and was glad for weapons and the male soldiers.

There weren't any Latin comments she wasn't supposed to hear, so that was good. She was not going to drop farther back, though. She lengthened her pace and moved forward, almost trotting to keep up with Elliott. He looked over at her, she looked back, he nodded and said nothing. He didn't slow down either.

Good. He understood.

A half hour later, they were up on the higher plain. It was rolling, scrubby ground with short, twisted trees, as she remembered. There were occasional bursts of green and taller brush in low areas, but no actual watercourses. There was a depression with muddy water in it, either from dew and rain, or from a water table in the bedrock. Far to the south were the long, low lines of the Hindu Kush.

Here there were saiga and some of the prettier antelope in family groups. The grass shifted now and then as burrowers ran underneath. A herd of aurochs grazed far to the east, and ahead, rhino.

Zhu!yi pointed at each of them, and a direction, and gestured envelopment. He indicated a horn and said, "Sita," meaning "Small."

"Minisculus," said Elliott.

She added, "Stihb," for the Gadorth. She'd been picking up some vocabulary.

Zhu!yi indicated a smaller beast at edge of the group, probably a yearling.

Then she was trudging through waist-high scrub with Elliott, plodding through the heat, approaching the rear of the herd, where they hoped to surround and kill a baby rhino.

It seemed like a hell of a challenge, and that made it even more offensive. In a few thousand years, these animals would be on the verge of extinction. Even here, they were a trophy. The Woolly Rhino had been almost extinct in Gadorth territory, as far as anyone could tell. It was a magical beast to them, and they needed to kill one for some fucked up reason of chest-thumping.

She had to do it, though.

In another twenty minutes they had it surrounded, along with several of its peers. Slowly they moved in, tightening the circle. She fumbled with the javelins, and hoped her throws would match her rifle skill. She'd had little practice. Helmet and armor made her even clunkier.

They were about a hundred meters out, when the Gadorth, whose names she'd not bothered with, stood and hurled, with a yell. In a moment, the Romans stood, cocked back and threw in perfect unison. Elliott raised his hand back and down behind him, and heaved. Doc threw his flat and fast. The three Urushu chucked their lighter darts from long practice, and she brought up the rear. Her first one was short. Most of the others hit and the beast made an almost trump sound in pain. The second volley hissed through the air as the other animals panicked and ran. She was late on that, too, but thought she hit.

One of the rhinos thundered toward her, bent on goring or running her down. She dropped into a high crouch, ready to spring from its path and try curling into a ball. She felt the ground shake, saw others mill about and more javelins fly at the target, then the beast lowered its head and she bounded to the left and rolled, clutching the weapons in an outreached arm, then pulling them in.

Nothing happened, so she glanced up and saw she'd evaded the charge. The target animal, though, was now staggering toward her, sharp sticks protruding from back, flanks and rear legs.

She wasn't sure why, but she found herself setting the spear butt into the ground and leaning into it. She'd have to dive again if it kept going.

Then it lowered its head, presented its horn, and dug in its feet. She stretched out, and when it seemed to rise over her, she dropped the spear and rolled again.

This time she wasn't fast enough. A leg kicked her hip painfully, and she bounced off a rough, leathery knee, then landed flailing and flat, the helmet wrenching her neck. The air whuffed out of her.

Above that she heard the rhino utter a sound like a bellow, moo and trumpet all at once. It had collided with her spear. The shaft snapped off, but only after momentum drove it clear into the shoulder joint. The creature was on three legs now, limping in a circle.

Elliott ran in and rammed his spear into one flank. It screamed in response, thrashed, and staggered back up.

Then it charged.

One of the Gadorth didn't shift in time, and got thrown under the beast. After it passed, he crawled away, apparently intact.

She rose painfully to her feet, limping as fire shot through her hip, and looked at her hand to make sure she still held the stabbing spear. She didn't. She had a javelin. She'd used the stabbing spear. Right.

Shaking her head of fuzz, she hung back.

Two more stabs in the hamstrings forced the poor animal to remain on the ground, dragging those legs behind. It still had a front leg to crawl with, one injured one to swing at humans, and the horn and teeth.

She felt ill, and it wasn't just nausea from the impact. This was vile. They were killing it because they could, not because they needed to. It fulfilled some cultural demand to prove machismo.

One of the Romans stabbed it in the neck, causing enough damage its head drooped. It bellowed, the sound tapering to a howl of agony.

Sobbing in pain and loathing, she moved in, wanting to put it out of its misery. She limp-jogged toward it, chose a spot behind the ear and inboard, took the javelin, and threw her weight into it.

The shaft bent, then straightened, as the steel cut through the hide. She'd picked the right spot, directly along the spine, and the tip slid deep into the rhino's skull. She stirred the shaft in a circle.

In response, the animal's eyes fluttered and rolled, it gargled out what was almost a laugh, and its entire body twitched, then went limp.

She turned away and vomited.

She saw Elliott's boots in front of the greasy puddle of puke.

"Should I leave you alone?" he said, barely above a whisper.

She nodded.

His boots stepped back and he started exclaiming loudly to the group. Doc's boots came into view, then moved away, too.

She wouldn't join this hunt next summer.

The Gadorth scattered about the area, bringing back gnarled sticks, dried dung, and dried grass of two kinds. One unwrapped a bundle of leaves to reveal a coal, which he applied to tinder. Momentarily, a fire flared up, hot and with dirty yellow smoke. He fed it with twigs, dung balls and heavier sticks.

She watched as a scarab wiggled out of a smoldering dung ball. One of the Urushu snatched it, peeled open the shell, and sucked the guts out as if it were a tiny crayfish.

She couldn't throw up again. The first one was excusable as a battle reflex. Not now.

She focused on analyzing the ritual as her guts roiled.

However they'd developed it, or it evolved, the pungent smoke kept other animals at bay. Meanwhile, the others caressed the carcass almost as if it were a departed pet, then used heavy flint knives to hack through the hide, sectioning it. Parts of the muscle underneath still twitched, dead but with remaining lactic acid and nerve impulses.

She actually couldn't throw up. There was nothing left. She choked back bile.

Men pulled out chunks of flesh, and nibbled some, even raw. More was jabbed on javelin tips then held over the fire for a quick roast. The eater would hold the speared meat to his mouth, bite it, slice off next to his lips with a flint cutter, then stick the rest back into the fire for more cooking while he chewed the fresh meat thoughtfully.

Their reverence while chewing, and the creepy caressing of the corpse, plus the additional fires being built at cardinal points—the first had been due west—showed how important this was to them.

Two men sawed off the two-foot-long front horn. Their task was complicated by the presence of two others bashing in the skull with a hammerstone.

Doc joined them with a hatchet, and several brisk swings threw gobbets of bloody bone and flesh around. Then the bone split.

She couldn't decide if that were some kind of spirit release, or . . .

Zhu!yi dug his hands in, pulled out a jellylike mound of pinkish gray brains, and took a bite. He offered some to each of the crew gathered around the head, including Doc, then came back.

He offered them to her, and she gravely nodded and scooped up a spoonful's worth on her fingers. The texture was revolting, and she forced herself not to cringe and scream.

Someone else had a door cut in the side of the carcass and was pulling out liver.

This was worse than the hunt. She decided her hip was injured enough for Doc's attention.

"Doc, can you look at my hip?" she asked, sitting down. Lowering her voice, she said, "And help me make this disgusting goo disappear."

With her pants at half mast, he probed gently and said, "Bruised, possibly deep bone bruising, but I don't find any signs of fracture. It's going to hurt like a son of a bitch, though."

"Yeah. I can live through it." In fact, it felt slightly better sitting, and the pain helped her ignore the butchery and carnism going on a few yards away, with guts being drawn out for divining, and bones being sawn for dice or some other purpose. The Romans laughed loudly at something.

She'd visit Arnet later for whatever medication he could provide, and perhaps spend thirty minutes with his neural stimulator. He liked to look and didn't touch. She was sure the not touching had to do with her being more primitive than they, and she'd be offended if she didn't understand it.

And his neural stimulator was very good. It wouldn't stop the pain, but she wouldn't care.

Suddenly woozy with fatigue, she let Doc help her fasten her pants and lie back with her ruck as a pillow. She felt herself pass out.

Armand Devereaux knew Caswell had a battle with herself over the hunt. She was a vegetarian, killing and eating from necessity, and a woman who needed to prove her status. She'd done that. It had to be tough, though.

After all that, she shook off his attention, too.

"I can walk," she said. "I'm bruised, in pain, but not injured."

"I hope you're correct," he said. If she had any serious trauma, it wasn't going to get better.

After all that, they had a backpack full of rhino filet, the tail, a large marrow bone and a souvenir section of hide to paint on. Most of the huge carcass had been left there. Each group took a few chunks, and the rest had been left for the wolves, after an appropriate Gadorth ceremony, which was pretty damned boring. He had a few photos on his phone for Trinidad to scope over.

They'd not recovered most of the spears, nor tried to. The Romans did take their iron points back, cutting them out with daggers as needed. He didn't blame them. Iron here was more precious than gold. If only they could dismantle an MRAP they'd have steel for a century. But the big chunks weren't salvageable.

After that, each spear haft had been anointed with blood, and each of the hunters had a stained right hand. He wasn't sure what it was supposed to represent, but it was sticky and he wanted to wash as soon as they were home.

The captain said, "I've invited them to sauna and tub with us."

"Makes sense. That'll also take off some of the aches and pains. We can alternate with some ice."

"Yeah, we'll give them our ritual, complete to wine. How are you doing, Caswell?"

She looked rather stern as she said, "Sir, Doc, I'm fit enough to make it back. Please stop being solicitous. I'll let you know if I need help."

"Roger, sorry."

His Camelbak was dry. It was near dark. It had been a long, long day, and his nose was filled with the scent of rhino meat rapidly assuming ambient temperature. That stank bad. He wasn't at all sure about eating any. His feet ached, and his knees, and his shoulders were tender even from light carrying, after tossing spears around. He'd thrown hard, and possibly overextended his right shoulder.

The wolves started baying.

Elliott said, "I want custodes on duo lateral. Oculare con lupus." He pointed where he meant, and at his eyes.

It wasn't great Latin, but it was passable. He was understood. The irony was that Armand's medical Latin covered terms the Romans didn't really know about.

They were met outside the gates by shouts and hails, and he gratefully left his ruck with Barker.

"I'll need to wash it," he said.

Barker took a whiff and said, "I got it. Goddamn, this stuff stinks."

"Yeah. Probably tough as fuck from adrenaline, too. I expect it tastes nasty. It did at lunch."

"Marrow bone and tail? We can definitely do soup out of that. I wish we had tomatoes."

Twenty minutes later, he entered the sweat lodge. Two Urushu women were in attendance with a tray of towels, real soap, and some kind of sweetened tea. He undressed and lowered his aching body into a warm tub that got warmer as the Cogi's heater cycled the water through.

"Oh, that feels good," he said.

Caswell was naked across from him, and she looked good even bruised up. That hip was going to be pretty colors of contusion for a couple of weeks. There was definitely a bone bruise.

"I'm going to check range of motion," he said. "This is professional."

"Go ahead," she agreed, as he took her leg and moved it carefully in several directions.

"Any popping or binding?" he asked.

"Only muscles," she said. "I'll be sleeping on my side for a while."

It was a nice leg, and he was done with medicine, so he let it go and moved back.

The Romans came in, and undressed quite casually. Everyone was more relaxed about it than the soldiers, even after two years.

The Romans climbed right in, plunged their heads under, sat up and spat. One was on either side of Caswell.

A few moments later, Caswell slid around and sat touching him. She obviously wasn't comfortable between them.

Elliott came in, and she said, "We saved you a spot next to me, sir."

"Thanks. I'll be right in." Elliott slipped off his uniform, which was caked with dust, sweat and dirt. He had a bundle of clean PTs to don afterward.

Armand wasn't sure if they'd groped her or if it was just presence. Either way, she was welcome next to him, and he'd be a gentleman, as much as he wanted some contact himself.

"I'll get out," she said. "I'm clean, it'll make room for someone else."

She stood, and her hand swept over him, brushing the throbbing erection he had. He forced himself not to twitch, she said nothing, and in a moment she was up on the floor wrapping a towel around herself.

It had been an accident, and neither was going to mention it, and goddamn he wanted more of that. He might have to arrange another sly meeting with one of the Urushu, who were quite willing, if a little confused by the attention.

He needed a permanent housemate, and Spencer wasn't it.

Once he felt clean and calm, he dressed and stepped outside.

He had to be careful to be discreet. Anyone with NVG would be able to see him easily. He walked west, then slipped around behind the smoke hut and back past the lodge. Through the hide, he could hear the others still splashing, and the faint hum of the Cogi pump.

He went past their vehicle carefully, though they typically buttoned it up to sleep and didn't react to anyone who didn't actually knock. They might see him, but they wouldn't say anything.

The Urushu had set more stepping stones across to their lodge.

Despite his own warnings, he'd been involved with three women. They seemed delighted with his dark skin, and that was flattering, but also a bit off-putting. They saw him as an exotic plaything and potential genes. Of course, they also appreciated the medical care. But race very much entered into it.

He was in luck. Olshi was here, and she smiled as soon as she saw him.

CHAPTER 40

Sean Elliott sat sipping wine in front of the kitchen, waiting for dinner. They actually had a little down time most days now.

The Romans traded wine for Spencer's steeled iron and Barker's bacon. Their stuff was dry, but he'd gotten used to it.

The well upgrades were working . . . well, well. Sean shook his head. English was a fucked up language. Additional digging and lining put it deeper into the water table and let them draw clearer water. Those digging tools the Cogi had were amazing.

They still had ice, and it was lasting well enough they could have the luxury of a cold drink. Barker came up with a mix of wild fruit wine, fruit brandy, more fruit, water, honey and a sprinkle of salt and herbs that was very refreshing. It wasn't sweet tea, and it wasn't Coke, but it was what they had, and no one back home would ever taste this, either.

Spencer said, "You know, Captain, we can work on a still with some tubing from the trucks. With a fire and the ice house, we should be able to turn out better brandy. We just need to get the Romans to make some amphorae."

"I like the idea, but I still hope to keep the trucks functional."

"One as a parts source for the other. Actually, I wonder if the Cogi can make glass here. Arnet? Hey, Arnet!"

The tall man came over in a long, lanky stride.

"Yeah?"

"Can you guys make glass bottles with your fabrication gear?"

"No prisely glass. Sorra polycermic."

"It would work as a sealed container for liquor, though, yes?"

"Sure. You need liquor? We've vodk."

". . . you have vodka?"

"Yeah."

"And you haven't been sharing?"

Arnet shrugged. "Production limited, need for med use, too. Warn't sure you cared."

"Sir, if you can spare some, we will certainly be grateful."

"Okay. Ll tell Cryder."

Barker stuck his head out of the kitchen.

"Did he say 'vodka'?"

"Yes."

"Well, I prefer bourbon, but I ain't picky."

Sean was eager, too. He had to keep sober, but a stiff shot of something would take so many stress edges off it would be legitimate medicine.

Five minutes later, Arnet came back with a flask similar to a water bottle.

"Here," he said, and flipped the top with his thumb.

The iced juice was mostly gone. Sean held up his canteen cup and Arnet poured two heavy glugs into it.

"Thank you very much."

He took a whiff, then a sip, and felt the burn. It was vodka, and it was clean, but he hadn't had anything high proof in over two years. It stung his throat and seared his sinuses.

"Goddamn, that's strong. What proof?"

"Dunno proof."

"What percentage?"

"Sixy-eight."

Almost 140 proof. No wonder it packed a wallop.

"Yeah, everyone can have a solid two ounces of it if they wish, and if you can spare it."

"Sure. Zis bottle yours." He handed it over.

Spencer had his cup out already, Barker was right behind.

Caswell said, "Sir, I request a medicinal dose."

Yeah, she'd had a rough time on the hunt. He poured a triple for her, doubles for the others. They all seemed to have heard the rumor transmission, even Ortiz and Dalton, who were outside the wall at the time.

"Damn, sir. Well scored!"

"You're all welcome. I wish we'd asked sooner. Save some for Alexander." She had watch.

He took another sip, and felt his brain start to soften as he got warm and fuzzy inside. He added a splash more wine and a scoop of ice, and it was a decent cocktail.

Barker said, "That's everyone, sir. Do we want to serve any guests?"

"Boy, I'd like to, but it was gifted to us and I don't know how much they can spare. Oh, fuck, it, sure. Start with the Romans and work back. Junius!" he called. "Potio!"

The Roman came over at once, sweaty and worn looking. He sniffed at the offered cup, jerked back, sniffed again, raised his eyebrows and locked eyes as he sipped.

"*Zeus pater!*" he exclaimed. "*Potens!*"

"*Sic est.*"

Junius mimed permission to share with Vitius and Ponti.

"*Procedo.*"

"*Gratias.*"

Doc had his music turned up, playing something house or techno. It was pretty good.

"What is that?" he asked.

"Psykosonik. Early nineties techno. Want some rock?"

"Got Coldplay?"

"I think so. After this."

It was as spontaneous party, and goddamn did they need it. Even Caswell was cheerful again, though still favoring that hip.

Dalton said, "Sir, the Gadorth and Urushu have to be initiated into the order of the booze. If I may." He reached for the bottle.

"Go for it."

Dalton charged his glass, added a little ice, a mint leaf and some fruit juice, then faced one of the Gadorths.

"Oglesby, help me out here. Klar, this is a ceremonial drink of our people. It is powerful, so you should sip it. I offer you vodka."

Klar sniffed it, looked around to see how the others were doing, then took a sip.

He almost dropped the cup and started rubbing his lips and making spitting noises.

Then he came back for more.

With a big grin, he said something to his buddy, who nodded, took a swig and almost choked. Then he stuck his nose in the cup and just snorted fumes.

Sean lost it, laughing. Then he tried it, and damned if it didn't work. Logically, enough fumes could get you high.

Barker got out the evening roast, unwrapped it from leaves, and started slicing off chunks of meat for anyone who was nearby. They didn't bother with plates, they just took the slices and tore into them. It was salted and smoked aurochs haunch, a bit tough, but very tasty.

They had music, meat, liquor, it was warm but not sweltering, and they had a protective wall. It was a good night.

Klar's friend still had his nose in the cup.

The drinking continued after dinner.

Martin Spencer had gotten pretty good at reducing iron. He now had a semi-permanent reduction furnace, built of rock and lined with fired clay and lime. Every few days they built a charge of layered limestone, charcoal and iron. Instead of bellows, they had a heater blower from Number Eight running into a clay pipe, powered from a line run from the Cogi's vehicle. Charge the furnace, turn on the blower, shovel in more contents depending on flame color, and wait for molten steel to puddle in the bottom. That was raked out into the water, giving a reasonably pure carbon steel.

At that point, he'd have had the fun job of beating it into some artifact or other, if the Cogi hadn't had a 3D metal printer and fabricator of some sort that could be programmed to turn out an axe head, a hammer, almost anything. He wanted to produce enough steel they could make him an anvil, but first, they needed hand tools for construction.

So he got to do the dirty, sweaty production of material, not the fun part of making tools.

It was fine. He could stare at the flames jetting from the furnace and meditate that way, periodically shoveling in limestone or charcoal or thick red clay. Occasionally he had some bituminous coal to feed it, scavenged from an outcropping up to the east.

He still planned to keep smithing. None of the modern or future tools would last forever. Eventually, they'd wear out. Barker's phone had died the week before, and nothing would revive it. Gina had it stored in Number Nine just in case.

The coal and various oily plants, including hemp, were also fed into the Cogi's machine, to be converted into a passable grade of diesel fuel. The two of them, and their vehicle, were a boon to progress. As long as their machine held out, they could produce fuel, tools, and possibly even replacement parts for the existing gear.

Arnet was the more social of the pair, Cryder generally spending most of his time vegging out in their tent, and occasionally doing hard calisthenics and running. Arnet actually helped here and there, moving around between work parties. Today he was at the furnace.

"Is fascinating," he said.

"It is. I've learned to tell the metal state by color and flame height. And to think our illiterate ancestors did it by hand, having to use manual bellows."

"Until waterwheel."

"Yes, that's about the time industry really started to develop. There's a huge jump in production about then."

"Frustrating being here. Glad we have the tools we do."

"I'm glad as hell you guys wound up with us and not elsewhere. I really appreciate the support, Arnet. I wish we had more to share from our end."

"No ish. Good food, good people."

"Thanks. We do try."

They stood watching the roaring flames. The flames were a deep orange, but gradually faded to a more normal fire color. That meant it was time to add more lime. As they burned lower, more fuel was needed. When the sparkles stopped, more iron.

Arnet raised his morphable shovel and poured in another load of charcoal lumps. They resumed watching.

Martin said, "The fuel's going to be useful. I'm wondering if we can eventually make more vehicles. Smaller ones."

"Possibly," Arnet said. "Start with wheeled carts."

"Yeah, Cryder mentioned that. Good idea."

"Will get there. Build up slowly."

"How long will the medical dispensary last?"

"Depends on chemicals," Arnet said. "Your stomach meds pretty straight."

"Good," he said with relief. Their stomach med was a field expedient, but worked well enough. He had occasional indigestion, but it was much more comfortable than the constant low-grade burn he'd had for months. They now knew to ask for anything they might need, in case the Cogi had it. Just as the Romans and Gadorth asked the Americans for regular tools. There was a tech hierarchy. Though even the Cogi's resources were meant for short-term battlefield use. They couldn't supply him long, and not with more complicated drugs, like those Gina needed. Still, it helped.

He wanted to ask about Caswell's regular visits to their camp, but there really wasn't a way to. On the one hand, it wasn't his business personally. On the other, he did need to know the involvements of people he was responsible for. He was pretty sure Doc had hooked up with that one chick who was here every week, and Oglesby obviously had a thing going.

He had phone texts with Gina, which was better than not having Gina, and he didn't want to admit he loved her, because that would mean further separation from home, which he didn't want to think about.

"More lime," he said aloud, and shoveled some in.

"Ready soon?" Arnet asked.

"Maybe another hour."

"Get lunch?"

"We should. You first."

Barker came back with Arnet and brought him meat rolled up in a grape leaf, with some river rice and wine.

He took a huge bite, and said, "Goddamn, that's good."

"Thanks. It'll keep getting better."

"I will create a religion after you if you can get rye bread."

"It won't be soon," Barker said with a twist of his head. "But I do intend to try, if Caswell and Ortiz can get a grain cultivated. They say they can get something next year, possibly, but it would only be enough for holidays."

"Even that would be great. And we need new holidays."

"We do. I'm kinda liking Gina's pagan ones based around solstices and full moons."

Martin said, "As far as holidays go, yes. Since I'm not religious, and our traditional American holidays don't matter a damn here."

It was common during deployment to not worry much about holidays, other than possible down time. Here . . . he really wanted to forget the future.

CHAPTER 41

Elliott's phone beeped. He answered it.

"Elliott."

"Elyot, Arnet here."

"Yes, Arnet, what is it?"

"Wanna show you. Come over?"

"I'll be right there."

He was only too happy to get away from PowerPoint and AutoCAD. He was trying to design expansions that would give them more protected area, as secondary outlots.

It was sunny, breezy and tall white clouds swept the sky. It was pretty much never not beautiful here, and largely safe, now that detente had been reached all around.

Over at their vehicle, Arnet had his device out, and a screen up on the dash, too.

"What is it?" he asked.

Arnet pointed at a graph that had intermittent spikes on it.

"Zat's probly tempral warbles."

"Temporal? Time?" Is that what it sounded like?

Arnet said, "Yeh, some dribble of senso."

"Regarding time?" he repeated urgently.

"Zact. Flutter in instro. Same as grav tingles show erdquake, wooz?"

He took a moment to process that.

"Uh, we haven't successfully predicted earthquakes, but I get your meaning. So there is something going on in the time continuum? Not just aftershocks of our transit?"

"Right. Fresh. Warbles. Means zey seek."

Ripples ran through his body, his brain flipped, and he took a deep breath and gripped the edge of the vehicle to avoid shaking. It felt like a panic attack, like the day they arrived.

"How will they find us?"

"Oh, fine dis," he said, slapping their vehicle. "No worry, easy sense. Posbl fine yours, too."

"That would be even better. How will we know?"

"Sig pop enough, we'll know."

"But does that mean we can go home?"

Arnet shrugged. "I sume so. Warbles mean senso. No reason for senso wout intent to pull back."

"Yeah. You realize I'm pretty excited about this, right?" Excited? He was shaking in response. His fingers tingled.

"Wooz. We too. Home, man."

"How sure are you?"

Arnet shrugged again. "Sure zey doing summa. Proble zey look. Likey zey trying."

"What do we need to do?"

Cryder came around.

"Needa contac all groups, plan for meet at transit locus."

"Only one? Not each of us back where we started?"

"Dunno," he said. "Try cent point first. If sig clarifies."

"Shit. First we have to make sure they all get it."

That gave him another mission.

He turned and forced himself to walk. He wanted to sprint and skip. He started to shout at Alexander, then realized he should keep it quiet.

He didn't dare get his hopes up. He had no idea what those sensors were, what the Cogi's motivation was, or what technology the Cogi had. Actually, they'd never even said if it was their fault, just that they had an idea what was involved.

He forced his panicked walk slower, took another breath, and stepped onto the back of Number Nine.

"Gina," he said. She had several windows overlapped and the cat on her lap. Wow. He was almost domesticated.

"Yes, sir?" she replied.

"I need a written message to send to the Romans, assuming they're literate, and a verbal one to go to the Gadorth. You've held a high clearance?"

"Quite high, yes, sir."

"This is diplomatic stuff."

"No problem, sir. How do I draft this letter?"

"I'll tell you what it should say. Can you work with one of the Romans on wording?"

"I can. Why me and not Sergeant Spencer?"

"I'll cover that later," he said. Crap. He wasn't sure. He wanted to tell everyone. He needed support. She was effectively the CQ, personnel, logistics and commo sections. She seemed logical.

"Understood."

"I need to meet with representatives of both groups regarding future development. Day after tomorrow. Their safety is guaranteed. They will be treated as guests."

"Got it."

It was hard to hide anything from Felix Trinidad. He was good at intel. He respected Alexander's ability to disappear in a crowd of two. He had that, too.

He also knew what to look for.

Elliott had had several frantic conversations with the Cogi. He'd sent invites to the other displacees to come here. The Cogi were excited about something, chattering to each other and in much better spirits than they had been. In fact, they were actually in spirits, not in their previous calm state, which he now deduced was an emotional holding pattern, like the soldiers had had the first few weeks, just longer.

Someone thought there was a possibility of going home. They weren't talking about it publicly, so it wasn't definite.

It was possible, though.

As much as they'd done here, as neat as it was, he didn't think anyone would be unhappy to go, if they could.

Probably none would be as glad as he, though, except possibly Doc. He was the only Filipino in the world. That remained a very lonely thing.

For now, he'd be hopeful, but cautious, and not tell anyone else.

He'd pray, though.

✤ ✤ ✤

To the commander of the Roman garrison, greetings, from Tribune Sean Elliott, Army of the United States, Castrum Sub Petrum. I request an envoy of your garrison, with the appropriate authority, to discuss matters urgent to us all. The Gadorth people will also be present, and the Indian banduka contingent may wish an observer. Your envoy's safety is guaranteed, and all lodging and food will be provided as a courtesy for this favor. This meeting is to take place the day after tomorrow.

Caius read the missive again.

"That is interesting," he said, and took a sip of wine. Not bad. It was getting better.

"Is it a trap?" Centurion Vinicius Petronius Niger asked.

"I see no reason it should be. Their banduka are substantially more powerful than those," he waved at the Indians' fire tubes racked behind him. "They can shoot through trees a hundred times a minute. Their armor is reportedly stronger than our iron. If they wanted to attack, I have no doubt they could."

"Who are you sending, sir?"

"I would like to go myself, but this place doesn't do well without a firm hand. You will go on my behalf. Take a maniple. If it's an outside threat, we will support the local communities, but the numbers involved will be my decision. If it's about trade, use your best judgment. We want resources to come to us."

"I understand, sir."

"I suppose two of the Indians can go along. They can take pilum. The banduka remain here."

"I'll gather materials and leave at first light. We'll be there a day early."

"Well done." He'd made a good choice with Petronius. He was a very solid individual. He'd handle it.

Rich Dalton was up top. He was looking forward to his shift ending. Whatever was going on, it was a war council. Six Romans had arrived with two Indians, and were in that lodge.

"Cryder, this is Tower, do you have range on the Romans?"

"Tower, we have range. Senso guns watching."

Rich wasn't sure how their weapons' controls worked. He knew they had some sort of computer tracking, and a certain amount of autonomous action. They were oriented across the compound in front of the huts the visitors were using, so any attempt at nighttime violence would be caught in a devastating crossfire. The Cogi had been trustworthy so far. Interesting how the more advanced groups with better weapons were less interested in proving it.

He wondered what religion they followed. They didn't seem to care about any particular food, but then, Caswell had abandoned vegetarianism for the duration. He'd like to ask, but they weren't very social.

Shift end approached, and Trinidad climbed up to relieve him. He made a final view of the perimeter in the falling dusk, and saw movement.

"Sir, the Gadorth contingent is coming uphill. I count six."

"Roger," Elliott responded. "Alexander, how many are on site now?"

"Four, sir."

"Yeah, keep a good eye on them, too. That's a notable force."

Trinidad said, "I heard, sir. Got it."

He understood why the captain was nervous. The Urushu seemed totally peaceful, but both the Romans and the Gadorth had staged attacks before. They had potential elements inside the COB now, so it was necessary to watch them, and look for any staged forces outside.

"What do you think is up, Trinidad?" he asked as the Filipino settled in behind the M240B.

"I don't have enough information to speculate."

"Think we're going home?" If God had arranged for them here, God could arrange to send them home.

"I dunno."

Trinidad was so cool when being evasive. But after two years, Rich knew how he presented.

"Hah. You think we are. I know there's been rumors."

"In A-stan, I remember rumors of golden conex boxes full of exotic food and supplies," the Filipino replied. "Back in the PI, there are stories around base of America, the big PX."

"True. And rumors are only rumors. But you're being evasive."

Trinidad shrugged. "Because I don't know. I hear rumors, too. I don't have data to analyze, and I'd be talking to the commander if I did, dude."

"I understand." He did. It was all rumor, and it would be bad to get hopes up over rumors. It could more easily be something like forming a federation like the Iroquois, or planning some large scale agriculture.

Either way, even off watch, he was going to stay armed and keep an ear out. Even if the other groups didn't attack, they might just start fighting each other.

Sean Elliott paced nervously. He had to explain to two primitive groups, three including the Indians, that they might be able to go home. He had no mechanism ready. It was only a possibility.

Arnet and Cryder sat on their vehicle, on extruded seats. He stood. It was a beautiful afternoon, and across the trickle of creek the Urushu at their embassy lolled about on logs, using flint and bone to scrap sticks into something or other and watching the later people curiously.

The Gadorth, Romans and Indians had logs to sit on. He nodded as they arrived, and they sat in groups, wary of each other.

Sean said to Cryder, "I think we need to demonstrate some of your tools to them, to reiterate your knowledge."

Cryder said, "I will try to be very clear to them."

That was interesting. He could speak, or had learned to speak, contemporary English. He just chose not to.

"What then?"

The two looked at each other. Arnet said, "Sig increasing. Fig we build secondry arceiver and trangulate it. Find zero point, camp and wait."

"And we need them to camp and wait with us, without any violence. We'll also need enough food for days? Weeks?"

"Weeks possible."

"What happens if the transfer happens when someone is away hunting?"

Cryder shrugged. "Proble a second transfer is arranged."

"Yeah, but 'probably' isn't good enough, and those poor bastards will be bugfuck gibbering insane."

He shrugged again. "All is unknown at this point." The man seemed quite calm outside, but was he a little jittery with his gestures?

"Fair enough. I haven't told my people yet, other than our administrator." He shifted his feet and continued, "But I think I need to. We'll need extra security. I value their input. I'm hesitant to do so until we know it's a likely thing. I'd hate to get everyone's hopes up then smash them."

"Nod. Can't say how likely. I hope. Good sig. I don't know the tech, can't say how well they can read us, what they can do as far as—"

Bang.

The report startled them. It sounded about like an arty simulator.

The goats started howling and screaming.

He shouted as he grabbed his phone and started walking. Arnet and Cryder followed.

He pointed at one of the Romans, made a circling gesture and pointed at the ground. "*Remaneo,*" he said.

Into the air he snapped, "Report!"

From the northeast corner post, Barker replied, "Sir, unknown. It's east of us, near the goat pen. I don't see any threats. Animals all got agitated, but seem fine now."

He got his phone up and punched for Dalton. "With me," he said. He did the same with Spencer. By then, he was at the east gate.

Spencer came running up, handed him a carbine, and checked his own load. He drew the charging handle back, checked for brass in chamber, and nodded as Dalton ran up.

"I just got back from hunting," Dalton said. "I didn't see anything that way."

He put the phone on speaker and slung it in the pouch around his neck.

"Barker, are you receiving?"

"Yes, sir." It was a bit muffled, but audible.

"Keep us covered and observed. We're going out. Dalton lead, Spencer, rear."

"Hooah."

The gate was generally open daytime, to allow access to the animals and the ice tent. It was in clear view of the watch turret.

Barker said, "Sir, Ortiz called Alexander. He says something exploded in the goat pen."

"Understood. Break. Dalton, lead us carefully, go."

They trotted out, crouched and with weapons at low ready. Dalton went right, he went left. He hoped to God Cryder and Arnet knew how to do this. There was nothing ahead of him, so he risked a quick glance. They were fine, moving forward, covering arcs. He pulled back into the movement.

Christ, it had been two years here and then time back home since he'd last rehearsed this, and he'd never done it in combat. His heart thumped.

Ortiz stood on this side of the ice tent, looking around it. He was armed, as he always was out here. He waved.

Dalton moved back in front as they reached the goat pen. There was something there.

"Talk to me," he said.

"I don't see anything in the area, sir. I'm looking out and east."

Barker said, "You're still alone. I got nothing."

Spencer said, "South is clear."

Arnet said, "North."

Cryder shouted, "Contact!"

Sean turned that way as everyone else did, too, weapon up and ready.

Then he realized Cryder was referring to the object in the field.

"What is it?"

"Message drop. I need to get it."

Shit. Message drop. Actual contact.

Well, everyone knew now.

"Help me get to it," Cryder said.

"Climb over the fence."

Cryder hesitated.

Ortiz hand vaulted the fence, and Cryder easily followed. Interesting. He wasn't comfortable around domestic animals up close. That wasn't ridiculous, but Sean could see how it wasn't something that had come up, and could be a bit embarrassing.

The tall man bent down and lifted the box. It was about the size of a 7.62mm ammo can, in an orange so neon bright it could be used for a rave. It hurt to look at.

With a twist and pull he opened it.

Then he started howling into the air and leaping around like ballerina on crack. He twirled, rolled his leg overhead, jumped into splits and came back over the fence.

"Zey found us!" he shouted.

⁜ ⁜ ⁜

Martin Spencer had figured something was up when the LT had called for a powwow and consulted with the Cogi. It had been easy to guess it was temporal related, but he'd not dared hope it was this.

It was. Contact with the future.

The fire was up, and the Cogi hung a lantern that flooded the area with a warm light. Martin felt much lighter, less tense, but nervous.

Things were never that simple, he thought.

There were two Moghuls, five Romans, the soldiers, three Gadorth, and four Urushu present. All the earlier people stared at the lantern trying to figure out its mechanism. The soldiers and Arnet looked at Cryder.

Cryder apparently spoke passable Latin. He used that, then switched to English as Oglesby translated for the Gadorth. Arnet used Hindi for the two Moghuls present. He said they were from even further forward in time than the Americans, and had even better tools. He demonstrated his folding tool as shovel, pick, prybar, axe and hammer. That was fascinating. The mass could shift around.

Then Arnet morphed his handheld into what looked like a bullpup carbine and blew a section of log in two. That got everyone's attention. There wasn't much noise. The log cracked and split, and that was it.

Cryder resumed, and the English part was, "We got messages through the air and light from our people, then they sent a box through the thunder that had this message." He held both up.

"They have marked a spot for us to meet, where we will go to them. Then they will send each of us back home."

There was much chattering in Latin and in proto-European. But the official announcement had the soldiers elated, too. They'd all known what the story was, but having it said gave it credibility.

A pair of arms wrapped around him from behind, and he jerked, then realized it was Gina.

He patted her arm. "I hope so," he said.

Barker high-fived, and he returned that, as Trinidad punched him in the arm. Everyone else was too far away, and Dalton and Ortiz were up top with guns live.

The Roman spoke slowly, asking what was involved. Oglesby translated for the Gadorth.

"'When can your gods send us back?' they ask. Yes, I explained the gods aren't involved. They don't get it."

Cryder said, "Today's message gives us a wick over two weeks to reach a location on a bluff downriver. I make guess that was chosen as a distinct landmark. Have grid from here and from our home measure. I can find it."

The Romans had cracked open some mead and were passing it around. Martin accepted the pottery jug and took a swig. Not bad. A little dry for his taste, and a tad bitter, but very drinkable. Better than their previous efforts by far.

"Sir, with your permission, I want to get out the wine and hooch."

"Do so."

Barker said, "Way ahead of you," and thumbed over his shoulder. Under the kitchen awning was the wine tub.

There were plenty of volunteers to help open it. The Roman privates appointed themselves guardians of the booze, by holding up hands in the universal "Stop!" gesture, then popping the lid open and dipping out liquid. They tasted it first, of course, and made faces.

"Whew. Acutus! Fortis! *Bonum effercio!*"

"Thanks. Yours was bonum, too."

The stuff got passed around, and Oglesby explained to the Gadorth to wait a moment. They held their cups, expectant and confused. The Romans understood.

With everyone ready to fortify themselves, Elliott said, "Ladies, gentlemen, Romans, Gadorth, Warriors, Soldiers, to a hopeful trip home. Toast!"

"*Hooah!*"

The two Moghuls sipped, chattered to each other. They were almost certainly Muslim and forbidden from drinking.

Doc apparently anticipated that, and told Oglesby, "Tell them it is a tonic and a health potion to aid in calming the nerves." Which, he reflected, was true. "As a doctor, I prescribe it."

Thus reassured, they drank, too.

He hoped it worked. He really, really hoped it worked. He hoped the "nerve tonic" worked, and he hoped the return trip worked.

This place had become home, and he was sick of it.

CHAPTER 42

Sean Elliott watched their labors disappear in wreckage.

"Ready, and push!"

Two engines roared, twenty-odd people shoved, and a third of the north palisade collapsed.

They were back down to the tepee and vehicles for sleeping, all the other cabins and hooches having been destroyed and tossed into the stream. The smokehouse remained, and the steady crack of rifle fire in the background was Dalton head-shooting goats so the meat could be smoked. Arnet was out killing a couple of aurochs. They already had salt, onions and some rice loaded.

Sean reflected that he felt most useful now, destroying their former home in a hurry. They had twelve days to reach a point thirty kilometers downriver, and the MRAPs wouldn't get through the forest, so they'd have to go uphill and around.

"This will be enough?" he asked Cryder again.

"Yeh, river'll change course sevral times, all ziss floodplain, during next short-freeze and melt."

"Is that the Younger Dryas Sergeant Spencer mentioned?"

"Yeh, that."

He'd accept that. Of course, there was no reason someone couldn't prop the timber back up. On the other hand, it would all rot eventually, and the Urushu had shown no interest in changing their architecture style.

Barker and Spencer backed and filled their vehicles cautiously, lined up with the next section, and waited for the signal. They nodded to him, he gave a thumb up, and made sure all the local help were in place.

"Ready, and push!"

The timbers creaked, leaned, cracked and crashed.

Caswell had two people assisting her in gutting, skinning and butchering goats into what was almost jerky strips. Those were dredged in salt and herbs, then taken to the smokehouse, which leaked roiling brown smoke from an almost too-hot fire. By tomorrow, they'd be ready for a couple of weeks of dry transport.

His phone beeped. It was Ortiz. "Goats are done. We took care of a few pheasants and ducks. Kicking the fence over now."

"Hooah."

It took far less time to dismantle than it had to build. By dinner time, all they had was a kitchen area, latrine, smokehouse and tepee. Spencer's forge had been shoveled into the creek, and the lathe and other tools were in the miscellaneous junk pile. The icehouse tepee had been dragged to the stream, where it caused the water to swirl and slosh over it. The ice pile would melt faster in the sun, and with some dirt scattered on it to reduce albedo, it would be gone in a couple of weeks, he figured.

It was impressive. All the hooches, the cabins, the hot tub, the kitchen ramada, were a pile of broken timbers about eight feet high and twenty across.

The ragged flag was back in a bag and behind the passenger seat of Charlie Eight again.

"Everyone police for plastic and metal. Bring it all with us. Doublecheck the kitchen area and tepee."

He didn't sleep well that night, being restless and excited. He woke, checked his phone again, realized it was 0300 and only a half hour since he'd last checked it. Around him, people shifted, snored, rustled.

It didn't matter. They were done here, and he could rest in combat naps en route, or wait for fatigue to catch him. They were in vehicles, there was no enemy, and they had support.

He hoped the trip home was real.

He rolled out exhausted around 0500, decided he was done for the night, and found the Roman Caius and Oglesby on watch. Once it was understood they were going home, most of the hostilities had vanished.

"Morning."

"*Mani.*"

Oglesby said, "The goat is ready, sir. I hope to be completely sick of it within two weeks."

"Same here, brother. And beef jerky."

Oglesby tossed a long rope of meat down from up top. He took it and chewed. Not bad. Though yes, it would get boring fast.

"When are we rolling, sir?" Oglesby asked.

"I figure to let people wake up naturally. Then we go. Not much left, is there?"

The wall had been a comfort for a long time. Now, it was a tangled mess. Nothing was nearby, though. The smell of upturned earth, rot and splintered wood didn't attract interest from wildlife.

Dan Oglesby was outside around 0700, as was everyone else, gathered around, eating some leftover stew with rice. The Urushu gathered nearby their still-standing lodge, obviously sad at the parting. They wore red ochre face paint and black mud of some kind. They had capes over their shoulders, breechcloths and footwraps.

As the Americans finished eating, they rose and approached across the stepping stones, carrying bundles.

Dan stepped out to talk. This was formal.

"Greeting, Uhk!i and Ghitra and Ytuvo."

Uhk!i said, "Greeting, Dan Knows Speaking. This day you leave?"

The others laid the bundles down as Uhk!i spoke.

"We must. The spirits say we may be-go home."

"That is fine for you. If the spirits say not, you always our camp wilkahm." He used the English word, and gestured upstream with both hands.

Dan said, "We are very pleased at that greeting." He did want to be polite, as much as he wanted to GTFO.

Ghitra asked, "Shiny spirits will go with you?"

"Yes, all us from elsewhere. Americans, Romans, Mughals, Cogi, Gadorth. We all go."

"Have your spirits said you come again?"

"They have not."

Ytuvo said, "We hope so."

"So we," he lied. They were wonderful people, but he wanted out of here.

Pointing at the pile behind himself, Ghitra asked, "Can share gifts before you go?"

"We can. We have more woven cloth for you, and the rest of the fine salt." He pointed at the leather buckets and rolled fabric near the tepee. "Those are for Urushu to use and enjoy."

"That is very good. You leave the magic axes you made?"

"Those we must take. The Urushu will learn that, too. Not your children, but eventually your children's children's children will be known as some of the finest makers. This area of the world is where many things were first discovered and created." Actually, India, but close enough. And this area did have some firsts.

"You know this? Your shaman say so?" Ghitra pointed at Spencer and Caswell.

"Our speakers tell of it, with the magic markings. We are so many generations ahead."

"You said that before and it makes no sense."

Dan said, "The spirits say you will know it in time."

"We very glad your spirits take you back."

"They did not send us here anger. They Cogi's spirits said we should learn things."

"Spirits can do great things."

"They can."

"I wish you may stay, Dan Knows Speaking." Uhk!i's eyes were wet.

"I wish I may stay, too," he lied again. They were a very hospitable people.

"We crafted sleeping hide for each you."

Uhk!i took one from the pile and unrolled it. It was quilted, thick, and very soft.

Dan ran his hands over it. The leather was buttery, the fur thick, and turned in on itself almost into a bag, but loosely stitched to make a quilt. The other two took one to each of them.

Elliott said, "Admire them quick and roll them up. We'll need to stow them."

"That is fine work, Uhk!i. Please thank your mates."

"We will. You are gracious with salt and the cord-net."

"I hope you will be comfortable. We must leave now."

"Of course."

Then they were hugging. Each of the Urushu had to hug the Americans, pat the women's bellies, and rub shoulders.

Uhk!i stepped forward again, jumped in the air, and clapped his hands over Dan's head.

"Travel of safe. I will miss you, friend."

"And I you." He really would. He wanted to go home, but he would miss them.

"We're done, sir," he said. His voice cracked.

Elliott nodded. "Saddle up!"

Gina Alexander was scared, watching the Cogi depart in their vehicle. They were heading to the Roman camps to spread the news and get them moving in a hurry. From what she knew of Roman military ops, that wouldn't take long. The Cogi armor should be proof against anything the Romans had. One good demo of weapons and instructions should do it, especially with Cryder speaking Latin.

It was just that with them gone, the soldiers had only a map. It wasn't that the Cogi's presence made the recovery more likely, but what if something went wrong? They were the only ones who had a way to communicate. There were myths or theories about burying messages for the future, but those didn't seem likely.

Gods, she was dragging this morning. Every night was half sleepless. Every day lethargic.

She remembered when they arrived here . . .

No, she didn't. It was two years ago. They'd . . .

She remembered the Urushu village, vaguely. A long lodge. The Romans had it now. Did the Gadorth have it in between? It must be in the logs, but she couldn't remember.

Her memory holes were increasing. She could recall when prompted, but access to the information didn't work.

Caswell asked her, "How are you doing?"

"Scared. Exhausted. I can't remember things I should. I hope this works."

"Something came back, and they say we can go forward."

"Yeah, I can remember last week just fine. It's last year I have trouble with." She tried not to be sarcastic about it, especially under the circumstances, but it came out that way.

Up top, Ortiz called, "Sir, I see the Gadorth element approaching."

"Good, Oglesby, confer with them."

"Hooah, sir." He trudged off quickly.

The Gadorth slogged through the grass, and accompanied Oglesby back. He said, "The rest are following, sir. They're bringing their wives."

Elliott said, "I was worried about that. That's the Cogi's problem to explain. We'll use force if needed, but it's their call."

Dalton asked, "Worried about disrupting the timeline?"

Spencer said, "That, or there being limits on how many people or how much mass can go through."

"Point."

"So they can walk behind. Well behind. We'll take our envoys with us. Gina, stow their weapons."

"Yes, sir." She pointed at the Romans' spears and swords, and they reluctantly handed them over. She slid them under seats in the back of Number Nine and directed them to Number Eight. It was going to be crowded back there, and no one was going to be armed.

She was going to miss Cal. He'd scampered off early to hunt. They wouldn't be here when he returned, and he'd have no idea where they'd gone. It seemed cruel.

Bob Barker teased the throttle periodically. The engine was warm, and he wanted to roll. The tanks had been topped up with a mix of nut oil, animal drippings and a precious little vegetable oil, plus some the Cogi had manufactured aboard their vehicle.

He just hoped the info was correct, because coming back and rebuilding this shattered village would be a bitch.

The Romans handed their weapons to Gina, and stood in a cluster, waiting to board. The vehicle was much more intimidating with the big diesel running. They didn't look scared, but they did look cautious. Hell, it was unfamiliar to him after all this time. Even the seat felt odd.

Caius, though, appeared rather excited.

His expression was obvious. "Request permission to come aboard, sir?"

Bob looked at Elliott, who shrugged. He turned back to Caius, grinned and waved. Caius ran around back, trotted fast up the ramp, clambered up into the turret, and took the view as he would from above a horse or stockade.

The others followed and took seats, the Indians sprawled on the floor. The Gadorth were on foot, except two who were injured and riding in Number Nine. They were a huge mass of movement, and would have to hunt for food as they went. That would slow things down. Though the vehicles were pretty much limited to walking speed anyway.

Elliott shouted, "We're rolling!"

He engaged gear and revved up.

Slowly, slowly, as they had two years before, they crawled across the terrain, guides on foot ahead, at a slow walking pace. Crossing the slope like this, he found himself frequently adjusting course up or downhill to avoid reaching too steep an angle and rolling. It wouldn't do to bust everyone up now. Dalton walked ahead, covered by Caswell, and did a decent job of finding what passed for a smooth route.

They were about five hundred meters out when Alexander's voice came through the phones. "Fire in the hole!"

The Cogi vehicle spat something in a shallow trajectory, that arced back behind them. He looked in the side mirror to see it slam into the pile of timber. Dark smoke erupted, and in moments there were flames as well.

"Was that planned, sir?" he asked Elliott.

"Not by me." The man shook his head. "I don't have reason to object, but I wish they'd asked."

"I guess that's why they said there was no need to spread the debris out."

"Yeah, but I would have liked to have been informed, if not consulted." Elliott gripped the window handle, pushed on the dash, then said, "Fuck it. Drive on."

"Aye aye, sir."

He drove. Over the furrows and gullies, up and along them where the terrain dictated. Since they had to go high enough to clear the forest anyway, that wasn't a problem so far.

"How's Caius doing back there, sir?"

Elliott looked over his shoulder. The Roman rode the turret like a pro. It would make a great WTF photo, with the American flag billowing behind him.

"Having a blast."

"Well, it is a nice day, and we're moving again."

"Hooah."

They paused after two hours, and swapped ground guides. Marius insisted on swapping with Caius, who argued, but not too hard, and changed places.

"Are you up to driving more?" Elliott asked.

"I'm good all day, sir."

Actually, he was half wired already, but he figured he'd get into it, and he didn't trust most people to drive these unstable beasts. He rubbed his eyes, took a deep breath, and gripped the wheel again.

Cal came back after the noise and shaking stopped. He sniffed around the area. All the musty logs had been shoved down. Some had been burned and the ground was rough. The humans were gone. He didn't smell any death. There was a very strong smell of their big rock things. Those were gone, too.

They were probably all hunting. He hoped they'd bring the salty liver.

In the meantime he should probably hunt for himself, and have some meat ready for them. They liked pheasant, and there were some not far from here.

He went east, burrowed into the weeds, waited. Shortly, he smelled a bird, stalked low under the grass, sprang and felt its neck snap. He carried it jauntily across the stream and placed it near the females' fallen cover tree. Then he took a nap.

He awoke, but the humans weren't there yet. So he ate some of the pheasant. It would be better with more salt, but it was okay.

They would probably be back later.

The tall shelter was gone, and the females had taken their beds. He sniffed around further.

They'd gone that way. That nasty smell was the big rock things. Perhaps he should follow.

He didn't even need his nose. The rock things had flattened the grass like a large beast. He trotted along easily, watching for large animals that might crush him or other predators that might eat him. He missed the logs that blocked things. Those were a fine thing the humans did. It made rodents much easier to catch.

Ramon Ortiz was twitchy. It had been two years since they'd moved these beasts. The drivers were rusty, the terrain terrible. They were nervous, irritable, excited, and he expected someone to roll one from being overeager and under practiced.

This was going to be the longest convoy op he'd ever done, timewise. The planned route was ten days, all of it very rough field.

Walking out in front, he at least had his phone for some quiet music, and contact with the vehicles. Modern commo was a lifesaver.

The terrain was convoluted, and he took the task very seriously. Rushing now could fuck them all up right before they got home.

"I don't like this ridge," he reported. "I think we should go straight uphill."

"Do it," Elliott agreed. "We need to go that way anyway."

An hour later, Dalton replaced him. Two Gadorth with dogs took each flank to keep threats away. He climbed in the back of Number Nine and stretched out to rest.

"Shit, everyone out," he heard from Spencer at the wheel. He stood, and waited while Oglesby dropped the tail.

"What's up?" he asked.

"Steep grade. Need to be as bottom heavy as possible."

"Hooah."

The ramp lowered. They all climbed out and spread to a safe distance. From the outside box, Oglesby cranked the ramp far enough from the ground not to drag, low enough to help center of mass.

Spencer started rolling up the slope and the MRAP leaned drunkenly.

"Goddam, these beasts are top heavy," Oglesby said.

Ramon replied, "Yeah. Great on paved roads. Who could ever have predicted the Army would wind up in places without them?"

Ahead of the vehicle was a steep, chaotic landscape heading up onto the hills. MRAPs could handle a twenty degree lateral incline . . . usually.

Ramon's phone said, "Okay, Ortiz rear, Trinidad front right, Caswell front left. Guide me."

Spencer eased into the throttle, running up the slope and turning into the incline. The vehicle swayed, then the tires slipped.

Spencer let it ease back down, revved up a little faster, and rolled again.

The tires caught, the truck bounded over a bump, then slid while teetering sideways. Ramon clenched up. If they lost it here . . .

Spencer slammed the transmission and revved, and the vehicle crashed back to the ground, bottoming out and sending sparks off a boulder.

"Okay, that's not going to work. What about if we use the available labor to fill in the slope?"

Elliott said, "Okay, that sounds safer. Oglesby, get them digging."

Oglesby talked, and the Gadorth looked at the terrain, but without real interest. He said something else, and most of them shrugged or waved their noses.

Then he said something else, and they fell to digging as if there were diamonds in the ground.

"What did you tell them?" Ramon asked.

"They weren't interested in helping much. They said we can walk easily, what do we need the noisy thing for? I suggested they weren't fit enough to dig. So they're proving me wrong. But I don't know how often I can do that and make it work."

In only ten minutes, the slope looked flattened enough, from shovels and sticks, to let the truck pass.

Spencer said, "Okay, trying again."

This time, the tires threw dirt and rock, but climbed jolting over the hump and onto the ridge above it.

After some minor refreshing of the slope, Number Nine followed. Barker clashed gears and twisted the wheel to keep traction, and bounded up the obstacle.

Elliott said, "It's getting toward sunset. I want to laager here. Our guests are welcome to stay in the area, but I want to dissuade them from approaching. Suggestions?"

Ramon said, "Use the M Two Forty to kill dinner. Is that a herd of aurochs I see? Food for everyone in a few seconds of thunder. That should do it."

"I like it. Dalton, do you want to do the honors?"

"I'd love to, but Ortiz suggested it. He should do it if he wants."

Did he want to machine gun a few cows? No, not really. But he would make sure it was done cleanly, and it would be nice to shoot something to let off tension.

"Sure," he said.

He climbed in the back, up into the turret, checked the feed tray, and leaned back. There were three close together there. He could sweep from there to there, and . . .

He squeezed the trigger, the gun hammered, and brass clattered. Through the muzzle flash he saw hide and blood splash, and three cattle convulsed, staggered and fell down.

The Gadorth shouted and howled, some of them lying prone, then cautiously getting up. They looked around in fear and confusion. The Roman contingent had freaked out, too.

Oglesby pointed and said something that included "os," which seemed to be their word, almost recognizable. They nodded and trotted over, looking cautiously around and back at the turret and Ortiz. They reached the carcasses and started butchering.

Goddamn they were fast. It took minutes only for the men to completely skin, gut and section the animals, and bring the chunks back. Barker used his torch to get a fire lit, a good hundred meters from the vehicles, and the Gadorth took the hint and gathered around it. They plucked sticks from the scrub, skewered fresh meat, and started roasting.

God, he was tense. Those scrambles up the bluffs had been terrifying. It wouldn't do to lose a vehicle or take any casualties now, that they were so close. Hopefully. He wished there was wine left. He didn't like smoking and no one wanted to risk it now.

He threw his poncho over his bag as he had two years ago, and hoped this was it. He listened to the crackling of their fire, the calls of the Gadorth, animals making noises and the Roman contingent joking, and felt very, very alone. He was a long time getting to sleep.

CHAPTER 43

Gina Alexander was wiped after a week of trekking. Jerky was too boring to eat, but the drain on reserves required it. She tried to drink extra water, but was still shitting out what felt like rocks. Add in being one of two females, apart from a small handful with the Gadorth who were not disposed to friendship, and she felt exposed and uncomfortable. Even riding in the back was tough on the knees.

"Break!" Elliott called. She sighed. Next rotation would have her out as ground guide again. Her knees and ankles couldn't take much more.

Martin clomped up the back and sat down across from her.

"Still tired?" he asked.

"Exhausted, but my knees and ankles are giving out."

"Stay here. I'll have Caswell cover for you."

"I need to do my share," she protested, without really feeling it.

"You've done it and then some. You're injured. Stay in the vehicle. Should I make it an order?"

She was grateful, but embarrassed. She really wanted to pull her shifts, but she was in rough shape. Ortiz started rolling again, jarring her knee and sending spikes through it.

Yes, she'd stay here.

Above her, Doc shouted, "Contact right!" and she perked up. Was it?

"It's the Cogi!" he added.

That was a huge relief.

"I have them on phone," Elliott said. "Wish they'd done that earlier."

Yes, why hadn't they called ahead? Or kept in touch? They were so distant, unless approached. Though Caswell got along well enough with Arnet. Very well enough.

At once, they stopped and debriefed. She observed from the back.

Arnet was the intermediary, as before.

"Three more days," he said from the open passenger side. They had the panels off like a HMMWV.

"Good to know," Elliott replied. "We can't go faster on this terrain with these vehicles."

"Yah, grubby," Arnet said with a sweep of his hand.

"If you mean something like crappy or crummy, yes. They're for roads."

"Wooz." He shrugged. "Well, follow us. Terrain map in roller should help."

"That's much appreciated. Thanks. How are the others doing?"

"Romans marching. Cautioned to minimize footprint."

His English was getting pretty good. Of course, he basically spoke English.

Elliott sighed and looked disgusted as he leaned against the fender. "I'm sure they'll listen to that instruction."

Arnet shrugged. "Mebbe. Is what. They know where to go and look for sig."

"Can they navigate that well without at least a compass?"

"Good map. Vis point. We left marker."

"Ah, you've already been there?"

"Send drone, obv."

A drone. Of course. Elliott said, "Oh, right. Thanks all around. We'll follow."

She hoped it all went smoothly. She was running out of energy.

"Up there," Cryder said and pointed. Bob Barker followed his finger.

Yes, that was a very distinctive outcropping, and was even on the Army terrain map. It hadn't changed, wouldn't change, much. It was a little larger and craggier, but definitely the same feature.

The pillar of smoke made it easier to spot.

"Someone there?" he asked.

"Drone left marker."

"Ah."

"Up the back," Elliott said. That was obvious, but Bob didn't mind. It was good to communicate.

Four sweaty, breath-wearing hours later they crept up on top. Romans and their Gadorth serfs appeared, already set in a camp supervised by Romans, of course. He was relieved to have Arnet and Cryder along. The Romans were perpetually stubborn. On the other hand, they were some building motherfuckers. They had a basic picket set already.

Dalton led the way into the laager, hand raised. He stopped, clenched his fist in both signal and triumph, and pointed. Bob rolled up to the spot, and at a nod from both Elliott and Dalton, he killed the engine. Spencer pulled up and angled in behind. That gave them two sides of cover.

Cryder seemed to anticipate, and the Cogi vehicle rolled through the scrub and past bystanders who hopped aside, until it filled in another side, giving the modern and future people a three-sided camp within a camp. And they still had concertina wire and whatever the Cogi brought.

There wasn't a lot of trust for the earlier peoples.

Elliott said, "Bob, we're expecting to go home, so use whatever tools you need to get comfy. Impress the yokels."

"Hooah, sir," he said. Hey, he'd gotten it right, though "Aye aye" still sounded better.

He took the propane torch and got ready to do more fire magic.

Gina Alexander really hoped they were going home. She hurt, had no energy, and needed a nap. Every joint ached and creaked, her ankles stabbed. Her foot cramped around the damage that spear had caused.

"Fire," Bob said, and indicated a dead, scrubby tree. She limped over and broke off a few small limbs.

Spencer said, "It's bivvy bags and ponchos, but should be just a couple of days. Oglesby, dig us a hasty latrine over toward the edge, and feel free to piss over if the height doesn't scare you. We'll use the front of Number Nine as one side, and cord up a poncho as a privacy screen from the other groups."

"Hooah."

Arnet came over.

"I have input."

Spencer said, "Speak, freak."

It took the Cogi a moment to track that.

"We marked primter. Vital to stay inside. Best guess as to radius."

"Roger that." Spencer turned and shouted. "Did everyone hear that? Radius is marked. Stay inside on penalty of abandonment."

She would have no problem at all with that order. Bivvy bag, poncho, latrine and the jerky. She'd sit right there if need be.

"How long?" she asked.

Cryder turned and said, "One point nine days."

Yes, she could starve for that long if necessary.

Bob came out and clicked his blowtorch. The fire lay flared up in seconds.

Arnet said, "Got tub of wood in truck," and waved his hand. Dalton and Ortiz ran over to unload it. That was gracious of the Cogi, she thought.

By evening, they had a watch atop Number Nine, a firepit, coolers to sit on and shade and windbreaks to bivvy in. It was good enough. Though she knew she'd wake in pain even after sleeping on the litter, even with a geek pad. The sun sank into the west, down past the forest below as the east turned indigo then black.

She stared at the bright and gleaming stars and drifted off.

She woke late in the night, stared up, and noted how beautiful the stars were. With luck, she'd never see them like that again.

Something shifted against her. She reached out and felt Cal's fur, then realized: Cal was here.

"Cal!" she exclaimed, and hugged him close.

From a few feet away, Dalton said, "He crawled under the MRAP about an hour ago."

"Good cat, Cal." Could she take him along? He was as much family as the other soldiers at this point.

"Yeah, I hope he doesn't decide to go hunting just before we head for home."

She had an idea.

"Can you hold him? I'll crochet another harness and we'll keep him at hand."

"Sure. How long does that take you? Three minutes?" In the bare glow from the embers, he was smiling.

"Hah. Closer to ten." She still had her bone net needles, dug out the #8, and searched for a hank of 550 cord.

Dalton sat up and held Cal firmly. The cat didn't seem to mind so far.

"Damn, he's big."

"Yes, about three times the size of a housecat." She started looping and pulling. She would have to actually tie him into it.

He looked concerned as she fastened it around his neck, probably remembering the surgery last time he was restrained. She tied the second strap around his chest, then ran out a length of cord and tied it to a log.

Cal wasn't convinced. He tugged at the cord and darted around, snarling, though in frustration more than anger.

"No, that won't work, he might drag it through the fire. I guess I need to move to that side—"

"I'll swap with you."

"Thanks. Then I'll make sure he can't reach the edge of the circle."

It was dusky in the east by the time she moved her stuff, sat down, caught the cat, calmed him, and fed him a sliver of jerky. He seemed to accept the humans knew what they were doing, and mostly settled down.

Spencer staggered over, wincing himself from sleeping on the ground. Yes, being Army-old sucked.

"Well, I'm up," she said. "Are we going to have any assigned chores?"

Spencer said, "If not, I'll find some. I don't want anyone getting bored and starting fights with the Romans or Gadorth."

Dalton asked, "What about an actual wrestling tournament?"

"And lose their respect?"

"The LT and Caswell clobbered those Gadorth. The Romans are even smaller. I'm not worried."

"Hmm . . . if we do brackets, we can set them up with each other first, and not have to worry about us until the end."

She said, "I would rather watch them clobber each other than any of us. That would be more satisfying."

"I like that better," Spencer said.

⁜ ⁜ ⁜

Richard Dalton stuck to his routine. He prayed, brushed his teeth, ate some jerky, checked with Spencer for chores, and made sure his gear was good to go.

The day passed with wrestling. The Romans had brought the rest of their wine, and were well-lubricated by midday. The centurion kept them mostly in line, and everyone else gathered to watch.

The Romans had left all their camp followers behind. They were practical people, if nothing else. He also suspected some of them had families back home who wouldn't approve of savage barbarian wives. Though some were probably pissed off, but he figured they were used to disappointment.

They also had some kind of sacrifice going, were divining a goat's guts, and rattling their banners and such. Whatever they did for worship, they were doing it.

They were after Christ's time, but the Word had not yet reached them, not even as secondhand news. Well, it could take a while. John had written decades later. The message was still spreading even in their time in America.

Cryder and Arnet walked among the Gadorth with Oglesby, apparently constantly reassuring them that the gods had assured them this was the thing to do. The Gadorth really didn't want to get rid of their native wives, but Cryder insisted, with Oglesby's help, that the spirits would kill and banish anyone who was out of their time. With much arguing, the group split. It didn't look as if most of the Urushu women were that unhappy about staying here and not going with the Gadorth.

He hoped it was right. Mercy, but he was tense. He couldn't eat, didn't want to go to the latrine even though it was inside the marked zone, and it wasn't just the smell. What if the chosen radius was wrong? What if it cut someone in half?

What if nothing happened? They'd already destroyed their camp, they'd have to start all over again.

Dear God, we accept Your judgment in this matter. We have learned much, become close, and my faith in You is stronger than ever. If it fits your plan, please let us go home. In Your Son's name, Amen.

That was all he could do.

The day was long, with a cool wind turning brisk toward evening. If this didn't work, they'd have to rebuild fast for the winter. On the one hand, they knew how, and had help from the Cogi, and basic labor from the Urushu. On the other, it would mean starting over.

No one talked much. No "When we go home" chatter. Not even "if." They were all afraid of jinxing it.

The Romans got onto singing something that sounded like a campaign song. Meanwhile, the Gadorth were beating some kind of drum and sticks and doing something that could be an American Indian dance.

By midafternoon, everyone was in the trucks, sitting on the benches, messing around with their phones for music or movies or games. That hadn't really been a thing for a year now, but here they were, already reverting. That was something to note, that dependence on gadgets. He caught himself watching *The Incredibles*, halfway through and not sure where the first half had gone. He had his back to a tire and his shoulders itched.

He thought back to COB Bedrock. It was a fence and some huts, really. They'd just managed to reach the technology of the Middle Ages, though some of that they'd not known and couldn't duplicate. With all their training and knowledge.

He muttered to himself, "We've done so little. All our knowledge, once we got here, didn't make that much difference."

Elliott overheard him.

"We didn't have enough people. Given an entire engineer company, we might have pulled it off."

"Yeah. You have to have family and community."

Something else bothered him.

"What if we need the mammoths?"

"Mammoths?"

"We have all the groups here, all the survivors. What if we need the mammoths?"

"Cryder assured me the dead and missing weren't necessary. He did try to make sure everyone was accounted for. He came by this morning to double check my count."

"Good." Yeah. The thought of someone left here alone was a nightmare.

He decided he'd walk inside the perimeter, and make sure everyone was accounted for, from all groups. Leaving someone would be almost as bad as being left behind.

✣ ✣ ✣

Sean Elliott didn't sleep to speak of. He knew he zoned out and catnapped, but that was it.

This morning they would go home. Hopefully. So they were told. The rising sun cast long shadows over the other groups. It was warm, and the field was full of bugs. It was amazing how pruning and gravel made a lot of them go away. This was a raw field. He slapped and waved at annoying little things.

He was almost as tense as when they arrived. He really needed to see about some anxiety medications or something.

Oh, fuck that, he had every right to be a jittery bundle of nerves.

Arnet ambled over, wearing his uniform in basic gray.

"Do you have all your artifacts?" the man asked. He was still clean shaven with neat hair. It was as if he'd been in the field a week, not a year.

"Everything we didn't consume or destroy," he confirmed.

The Cogi turned to the musketeers and asked the same thing, then the Romans and the Gadorth.

Arnet advised him, "It may happen at any time. Stay well widin the marked area, just in case."

"Understood. I'll keep four people on watch at a time."

"Thank you. We unnerstand each other. The difrence between you and the other groups is signif."

Dalton, in full battle rattle, was up behind the M240B. All the other-time refugees knew what it could do, and they moved nervously, interacting only within their groups.

They had water, some jerky and time. He wasn't sure if it was going to happen or not. All they could do was be patient.

"Hurry up and wait," Trinidad said.

"And watch the savages for any signs of betrayal." He wasn't joking.

"I wonder if the Cogi think we're savages."

He shrugged. "Probably, but we kept them alive and they hang out with us, so we're better than average." He didn't care what the Cogi thought of them if they got home.

"Or just better than the worst."

"Dunno."

Twenty minutes later, Cryder shouted.

"Elyot. Got sig."

"Signal? Temporal?"

"Yu. Summa spike. Postive devpment, wooz?"

"Very. What now?" He fought down excitement. He didn't want to get any hopes up.

"Hang. Will track." He jumped into the vehicle, slapped down the door and started rolling for the perimeter.

Elliott was half in a panic. On the one hand, Arnet was still here, and he didn't think Cryder would leave him behind. On the other, what if he got snatched back in the vehicle?

But he said someone had located them.

Gina tried to keep Cal calm. He wanted to prowl, to hunt, and the humans weren't letting him. He wasn't up to scratching yet, but he growled, had his ears back flat, and definitely didn't like being in the vehicle.

"Easy, boy," she said.

Barker was rummaging through the coolers.

He said, "Hah. I knew I scorched a bit of liver. Feed him this." He dropped it on the scuffed and dusty metal floor.

The cat sniffed the morsel and disdained it for several seconds to show his disapproval, but then scarfed it down.

"When will we know?" she asked.

"About oh nine twenty-five. It hasn't changed."

"I didn't know the exact time," she said.

"We talked about it this morning. And last night. And two weeks ago."

"We did?"

"Yes."

That scared her. Small but important details that everyone knew were not in her brain.

The BANG caught them by surprise, as it had the first time. That was followed by a bone-jarring thump. They'd fallen about four feet. Cal yowled almost like a housecat and scampered behind her legs.

She looked out the back while fumbling for her weapon. They were no longer on the promontory. They were under a huge semi-translucent dome, bigger than any football stadium.

People in what were obviously lab clothes ran back and forth. The outfits were white coveralls and hoods. The people were all over six foot, lean and perfect. Most were blond, all had clear skin and were very European.

Cryder appeared behind the vehicle, said said something that was almost English, and five lab people ran over.

One of them was at the rear of the truck facing Gina in a second, and he or she said, "For safety, I must have your weapons."

"Ah, sir?" she asked, looking over at the captain, who had sprawled on the ground when they dropped. She wasn't about to hand over anything without his say so, no matter how amazing this place might be.

He stood and dusted himself. "Yes," he said. "I don't think we have a choice. Rules for POWs are in effect, just in case."

She locked the bolt back, dropped the magazine, checked the chamber and handed the rifle and magazine over. Her respondent, who Alexander felt was female based on body language, took it and stuck it against her back. It remained there.

The woman then pointed at her RAT-7.

She didn't think of that as a weapon. It was her friend, her companion, that had kept her alive. Reluctantly, she unsnapped the mounts and pulled it off her belt. She offered her tanto, but didn't mention her neck knife, her folder or her Gerber plier.

Then the woman wanted her camera.

Without it she was naked. She understood they wanted security, and might be concerned about either contaminating images, intel leaks, or even think it was a weapon. It was their country, she'd abide by their rules, but that was her other friend. She felt helpless. Her smaller knives were not discovered, and she wasn't going to offer them.

"Please come all with us."

She grabbed Cal's harness and pulled as he snarled and hissed. Once he was out from under the seat, she grabbed his forepaws, tossed him under her arm and gripped.

Bereft of weapons and large gear, but still with pocket knives and accessories, they followed the lead, as other future people surrounded them. Yes, they all looked like beautiful Norse gods. They varied from feminine to masculine, with other androgynes in between.

She yelped for a moment as the floor shifted. It was like a sliding walkway, but she didn't see any obvious signs of it, and the floor alongside wasn't moving. Gravity control? Matter manipulation? The colors here were dizzyingly geometric, obviously art, almost Southwestern but tremendously more sophisticated. She raised her phone and hoped it might get an image. Likely, they had the device blocked or would take it. In the meantime, she meant to try. They rode around half the dome, as dozens of people in coverall suits approached the other groups and made them pile up spears and swords.

Then they were through a door and in a smaller room, barely fifty feet across with a vaulted ceiling. As large as it was, it felt enclosed after being outside for months. There were chairs, amorphous looking and smooth gray.

"You will be safe and comfortable here while we study."

The captain said, "We may as well get comfortable. Likely there's more paperwork to be done here."

"So we're in the future now."

"Yes, so it seems they can move stuff back and forth. We may get home."

Gina said nothing. She wasn't going to stress over it unless and until they were home. But the hope was there.

She leaned back in the chair with a bit of stretch and it reclined.

"Wooaaah!" she yelped. She threw her arms out, and the chair extruded rests under them. Cal jumped away and under the chair. She hung onto the harness end like a leash.

"Oookay, that's a bit disturbing," she said.

There were noises around her as the others discovered the same thing.

"But I am comfortable." Very comfortable. She felt as if she were hanging in air, completely free of the ground. She raised an arm, let it fall back, and couldn't feel much change. The material was springy, but that light.

"Oh, yeahhhh," Dalton sighed from her left. "That is so much better."

The female said, "This place is for you. Ask any questions. I depart." She turned and walked out. And somewhere along the way, all the weapons she'd accumulated had vanished.

Caswell said, "Well, it seems comfortable enough physically."

"But not otherwise?"

"All the ones giving orders present as male. And they're all very Caucasian."

"I noticed that," Devereaux agreed.

"What does it mean?" she asked.

"Dunno."

"And who do we ask questions of, if we're alone?"

He twitched suddenly.

"Did everyone else hear that?" he asked.

"No?"

"Can you speak so everyone can hear?" he spoke while looking up.

"Yup. I'm th facilty tendant. I cn ans ques und pervide service." The voice was a well-modulated baritone, speaking Cogi English.

Elliott asked, "What year is this by our calendar? We are from one hundred forty-seven years after the death of Abraham Lincoln."

"Uh dun have pmission t rlis th info."

Ever practical, Spencer asked, "Where are the latrine facilities?"

"F you walk to'ard th sexion of wall now lit, the relief and sanitary facilities ll 'pear."

Caswell asked, "Is there anything to eat or drink?"

"Food and bevage 'll 'rrive shorly. How do y' dvide the day cycle?"

"Twenty-four hours, each of sixty minutes, each of sixty seconds."

"Bevrage will be pervided at once, in under three minutes. Food will be provided within twenty-six minutes."

Spencer muttered, "Damn. Future shower first, or food first?" And damn, it had corrected to their idiom and pronunciation within three sentences. That was one hell of an AI, or one hell of a translation algorithm.

"I am not programmed to make subjective choices for you, and as yet lack sufficient knowledge to advise."

"It's common in our era to ask rhetorical questions that do not require an answer. That was an example."

"I understand. Be advised I will always respond to a question. Here is your selection of beverages."

They came in through the floor, on a table that seemed to materialize. It was a cool blue color. The containers were open pitchers of some transparent plastic, as were the glasses. They looked high tech, but were clearly recognizable and plain enough.

"What are the beverages?"

"Chilled water, juices of fruits and vegetables, bovine blood, bovine milk, sweetened effusions of herbs, blended sweetened cocktails, extractions of coffee and cacao, mild fermented fruits and grains with alcohol."

No one moved for a moment.

The captain said, "We do not need the blood, and we do not want anything extracted from any mind-altering substance other than alcohol or caffeine."

"I accept the input. You may blend to choice and I can then repeat the selection automatically."

"Oh, thank you." She looked forward to orange juice. And did they have chocolate?

"You are welcome."

CHAPTER 44

At once they were at the table, grabbing pitchers and sniffing.

Martin Spencer went for hot, sweet coffee. He grabbed the carafe, poured it into a cup, sipped to check the temperature, then guzzled it down. Oh, fucking God, that was good, he thought, as it suffused his tastebuds. It was sweet, savory, spicy, unlike any coffee he'd ever had, but it was coffee, it was wonderful, and it was hot. Oh, Jesus, that was better than sex. Probably.

He tried to sip, but realized he was gulping. He'd finished a pint-sized cup that fast. And he was already getting a buzz. Shit.

"The food is ready."

The table slumped and reformed, and a line of platters appeared.

"RYE BREAD!" he shouted. There was a plate of cookies, steak, chicken, pork, fish of some kind, sweets . . .

He grabbed a plum of some kind, took a bite, and it was so sweet. And not a plum. It was a seedless grape, a good two inches in diameter.

He grabbed a warm miniloaf of rye about four inches across, used a paddlelike spreader to coat it thickly in butter, and took a huge bite.

Oh, God, that was even better. He munched, swallowed, finished it. He grabbed a plate and put sautéed mushrooms on it, with some salmon. That disappeared and he followed it with a classic bottle of Coke, until he was belching. Then he went for the cookies.

They had beer. One was a red ale.

He looked over to see Gina eating chocolate, her expression blissful but with tears streaming. Under her chair, the cat dug into a bowl of something shredded and pink, gulping bites, then looking around to make sure no one was challenging him for it. He didn't look domestic at all.

All Martin remembered afterward was that he'd never eaten so well in any restaurant. He was stuffed, in mild pain, and almost ill from the sudden influx of sugar, starch and caffeine. He slumped back in the chair and wondered if there were some ulterior motive, with this to soften them up. Because at this point, he'd say or do anything to avoid the Stone Age.

Then the pain started increasing, along with nausea. The food was too much, too rich, too fast, and he was going to be painfully, violently sick, he hoped. It would be worse if he didn't.

He slid out of the chair onto the ground, because it was cooler and evened out his blood flow slightly. He noted the floor was perfectly smooth, no seams.

The attendant asked, "Are you not well?"

"Ate too much. Nausea." He hoped that was enough info.

"I have summoned a physician."

A moment later, he heard running footsteps. A figure appeared, this one androgynous.

She? said, "You are suffering from dietary shock?"

"That's probably it, yes." He tried not to double up. It felt better momentarily, but then he'd have to stretch out again. There was no way to get comfortable, and he hoped they could induce vomiting. He'd feel better for getting rid of it.

"You must drink this," she said and passed over a vial. He took it and chugged it.

"Grape juice?" he asked. It was cold, fresh and almost too sweet.

"Grape juice is the carrier. You must all drink. I will advise the attendant to moderate your diets." She handed a vial to each of them.

He crawled to his knees, awaiting the vomit, and hoping she had a basin, or maybe they had robot floor mops. Then he realized he felt a bit better.

Then he felt a lot better. Then he felt normal.

"Thank you very much," he said. "What did that do?"

"It has inhibited your enzymic digestive process, and is deconstructing the food into component materials."

"It's digesting for me?"

"It is not an exact process. Your elimination will be abnormal."

That was probably better than throwing up. Probably.

He wasn't aware the doctor had left, but he was aware he was in his chair again, and completely vegged out. The gray background was so neutral it was invisible.

Everyone seemed to be pretty stunned and lethargic. And he realized it was a potential problem, because their control would be lacking.

"Attendant, I need to adjust a setting," he said.

"Ready," the computer, if it was a computer, replied.

"Can you please limit the alcohol to . . . I'm not sure of servings, hold on."

"I wait."

Martin said, "Alcohol content should not elevate our blood ratio beyond approximately one tenth of one percent. This level should not be reached more than once a day."

"I accept the input."

"This is a collective decision and only the captain may authorize variations."

"I accept the input."

"Are you a person or machine?"

"The inquired choices do not permit a comprehensible answer. I am more constructed than birthed. My status is acceptable to me and undefinable by your terms. If I am unable to assist, an individual will respond, as the physician did."

"What is our location?"

"You are in a quarantine facility."

"Where is it located?"

"I cannot share that information."

"Are we allowed to tour the facility?"

"You may examine anything in this room. The staff will have to decide if visits to other areas are permissible."

"Can we see outside the facility?"

"Please define if you wish a viewing window of scenery, or to leave the facility."

"Please answer both."

"I can provide a viewing window of any natural habitat. I do not have permissions for you to leave this room."

"Okay," he said. "I'm going to check out this bathroom and shower. How many facilities are there?"

"The relief and sanitary facilities are sufficient for any or all of you."

"Thanks."

It wasn't the first time he felt nervous about checking out a bathroom, but previously it was either under fire or because some primitive tribalists had been there. This time he was afraid of both observation, and being technically overwhelmed, but damn, to not have to shit in a hole in the ground or over a stream would be so nice.

He approached the wall, where he thought it had been lit earlier, and it melted away. He looked behind him and saw the rest of the room.

"How do I close the door or otherwise make a privacy screen?" he asked.

"The view is one way only, but I can set your preferences to opacity."

"Please. Am I observed here?"

"I do not have that information. Any observation would be by research personnel. As you are sentient, your consent would be needed for any publication of the record. Any record would most likely be short term for medical and scientific reference only."

"Thank you."

Well, that thing looked like a toilet, of a science fictiony, hotrodded, drugged-out fashion. It was certainly very comfortable to sit on, and it took care of the job nicely. There was nothing like exile to the Stone Age to make you appreciate the simple pleasures, like taking a dump in a warm, heated room with a padded seat.

"Is there toilet paper?"

"Referencing. No. If you are done, the system will cleanse you."

"Okay, I'm done," he said, trying not to clench up. But it was relatively anticlimactic. Warm water and warm air sprayed, and he felt clean. Trust the future to have a computerized bidet. And it still felt odd talking to one's computer while doing it.

"What about a shower?"

"The area adjoining is the wash area. Would you prefer a shower to a bath?"

"Wow. For right now, yes, but I certainly would enjoy a soak later."

"Step in to the shower. The activator is to your left. Think of what you enjoy and the settings will adjust accordingly."

He was afraid he'd spend hours in the shower, but the hot water the Cogi had provided had given some transition.

"Can I shave?"

"Please describe the grooming style you wish."

"Really?" He thought about his standard buzz. "Okay. No beard or moustache. Sideburns stop at the forward ear protrusion. Hair one centimeter long all over, blended to three centimeters in front. Tapered and block cut in back."

"Understood." He felt something foamy on his face, and then tingly skin. He reached up. Yes, he was missing the lip caterpillar, and it felt funny.

In twenty minutes he was more refreshed than he'd been in years. More so. Apparently, the shower picked up his sexual tension, and a rush of water, air and whatever else had him sagging against the wall in a flush. Really? They'd automated their showers for that?

"Would you like to continue the shower with your partner?"

"Partner?"

"The one you call Gina."

"She's not my partner, unfortunately."

"Interesting. Both your thoughts suggest otherwise."

"She's thinking about me right now?"

"I cannot furnish details without permission. Should I ask her?"

"No, not at this point. You can read our thoughts?" That wasn't unexpected, but was disturbing. He also realized his question had been answered. Damn, he wanted to nail her, and touch her, hold her, feel reassured.

"I cannot read thoughts. I can infer connections from expression and body language, and you did say her name a few moments ago."

"I did? I better watch that. I'll admit we've shared some thoughts and ideas, but no contact." He blushed.

"Contact is not necessary for partnering."

"It mostly is in our time. I guess you're getting away from that."

"Relationships are a matter of perception and agreement."

"Got it. Well, I'd like to finish, I guess."

"Are you finished showering? Or would you like to continue the stimulation?"

Dear sentient computer. Please jack me off with jets of warm water.

Blushing more, he said, "Please continue. It's something we're not that open about."

"I do not fully comprehend but accept."

He didn't think he could continue, with the computer present. But he did have some thoughts, and knowing Gina was interested . . . and the warm water . . .

He leaned against the wall and shook, gasping. Holy crap, that was . . . wow.

It even blew him dry, and seemed to use humidity control as well.

When he stepped out, what looked like a brand new uniform and underwear was hanging on a rack.

The underwear was his brand, but new, without label. It couldn't be his uniform, either. It felt more comfortable than anything he'd ever worn. The fabric was as smooth as the finest cotton. He dressed and walked back through the wall, which melted around him and he was back in the main room.

From the relaxed but guarded looks he saw, everyone else had made the same discovery. The shower had a setting for sexual release. And it reacted to either thoughts or body language. There was nothing wrong with getting that clean and comfortable, but no one wanted to admit it, and after two years they could read each other very well.

"I may have to shower four times a day for a while," he said.

Embarrassed giggles turned to relieved laughter. Good. That did it.

"New uniforms," Trinidad said, holding out an arm.

The captain said, "Yes, duplicated. We have a stack over there."

"What next?"

Elliott said, "System, do you have a name?"

"My default setting is to be called 'Attendant' or 'House.' You can set any name you wish and I will respond to it."

Caswell said, "We could call him 'Dobby.'"

"No!" Elliott said. "And 'him'? The voice I hear is female."

"My voice is optimized for your language and comfort perceptions. While your English is very rich and complex, it is root to one of our dominant languages, as you are aware. The Neolithic language is more awkward, as it lacks terms for many technological developments. I had to create the terms 'shit pot' and 'washing place,' for example."

"And how are the Romans taking it?" he asked. He kept looking at the ceiling as he spoke to the Attendant, even if he didn't really have to.

"They find the facilities impressive but un-intimidating."

Elliott asked, "But we won't be able to meet with any of them?"

"I have no control of that matter. I do know status, presence and response of all past-history groups is being discussed by relevant parties who will meet with you when they have concluded."

"Well, I guess we stick with 'House,' though it seems unfriendly."

Caswell said, "I'm going to use 'Dobby' anyway." She seemed more relaxed than she'd been the entire time they'd been gone. Well, he probably was, too. She was positively giddy, though. Was she drunk?

House said, "I can respond to any number of referents. Can you explain 'Dobby'?"

Barker said, "She can. In the meantime, what else is there to do? Entertainment?"

He noticed the wall now showed a broad forest panning past, as if from a slow aircraft at low altitude. It was rather pretty, but not as raw or wild as he remembered, and certainly not to where they'd just been.

"There are limited numbers of video and sound performances from your era. Movies, I believe you called them. No direct access to information sources is allowed."

Gina asked, "Can you make sure we don't overeat? There is a lot of food here, and you keep bringing more."

"The system now optimizes your intake based on activity level and metabolism."

Gina said, "My metabolism has problems. I was taking medication for it until I ran out. Can you account for that?"

"I have the scans Cryder took. You will momentarily be provided with a cocktail to raise your levels to optimal. It will take several days to achieve full effect."

"Oh. Thank you." She had that sad-relieved look again. He felt really sorry for her, with her entire system breaking down. His stomach hurt like hell, but her brain didn't work.

Caswell said, "I'm a vegetarian by ethical choice. What meal choices do I have?"

"I can provide almost anything. Is your ethical concern about the death of animals?"

"That, and resources consumed to produce it."

God, he thought she was over that. She'd had to kill enough rodents and birds to protect her vegetable patch. Dead was dead.

House said, "The meat is grown in tanks. The bodies do not have central nervous systems and are never technically alive by our standards."

"Oh," she said again. "Very well, then."

Trinidad asked, "How long are we staying here?"

"I do not have that information. Hypothetically, you may be here for the rest of your lives, if there is no way to send you home. In such case, you will have more access to our society, and we hope you will find it more comfortable than the distant past. It is possible the scientists will be able to send you home to your own time, or . . ." House's voice suddenly changed tone, becoming less friendly and more automated. "I am not authorized to speculate on other outcomes."

Dalton said, "We want to go home. No matter how cool it is here, we want to go home." His eyes were damp and his ragged voice held back a sob.

"I perceive you may wish to rest or meditate in private. Your couches can move anywhere in the room you wish, and privacy screens can be raised on request. If you speak, I will hear you and respond if I believe you are addressing me, or if your cognitive function indicates so. Otherwise, I will be unaware of you except in an emergency. I understand privacy is important in your society."

And what did that say about their society? Did every building have one of these? Were they networked? Did the entire planet have access to everyone else's thoughts, not just words?

Elliott asked, "Given our arrival time here and the day cycle when we left the past, what is the approximate local time for us?"

"It is approximately oh three thirty-seven your subjective time."

Fuck, had they been here that long? It had been noonish when they popped through. But yes, they'd eaten, jawed, eaten some more . . .

Elliott winced. "Crap. Would it help to be on the local cycle?"

"It is not necessary."

"Can you wake us all at oh eight hundred?"

"I can and will."

Barker asked, "Can you provide anything to help us sleep?" He'd been hitting the coffee, too.

"I can provide a nontoxic somnatic gas into your private areas. It will have a scent you find pleasant, and has none of the side effects you call a hangover."

Elliott said, "Then we'll do that."

"I comply. Will you please explain your hierarchy? I recognize your rank structure but understand it may have changed during your displacement."

Martin said, "It's looser than it should be. The captain is in charge of plans. I am the senior NCO and in charge of implementation. I had more experience in the areas of history and disasters, but now we're all pretty well versed in it."

"You are the acting top sergeant, I deduce."

"Acting first sergeant, yes."

"I understand. If you will take your couches and find a comfortable location each, I will help you sleep and wake you in four hours, twenty-three minutes. You should find yourselves fully rested."

Gina Alexander closed her eyes, then opened them. She didn't feel sleepy at all.

House said, "Are you awake?"

"Yes." She was, quite comfortably, with no aches, no fatigue. Whatever they'd dosed her with had worked.

"I will have breakfast ready shortly."

"What time is it?"

"Oh eight oh-two, by your clock."

"I was asleep?"

"You were asleep, and had three full REM cycles. Do you feel poorly?"

"No, I feel fantastic. It's the best sleep I've had in years." Oh, yes, that had been good. She felt wonderful . . . healthy.

She started weeping.

"May I help?"

She rattled off, as she had so many times in the last decade, "I don't sleep well. It's my thyroid, my brain chemistry, and various feedback loops. I never sleep a full night. I'm always tired, cranky, have trouble tracking." She paused for a deep breath. "This is the first time in a decade or more. And I know it can't last after I leave."

"I will relay the information to our medical staff. I cannot speak for them, but I will inform them."

"Thanks. Can you open the door so I can get breakfast?"

"Yes. I have cleaned and duplicated your PT uniforms, if you'd like to change. The others have done so."

"Yes, thank you."

She always felt self conscious in PTs, because she wasn't nearly as lean and buff as the others. Some of that was age, some thyroid, some joints. But her face was youthful and she was constantly mistaken for a thirty-year-old, only her body was clearly a damaged forty-four. She stood out and was shy about it.

But, PTs were a lot more comfortable than ACUs, and she wanted food.

The walls shimmered and disappeared, and she saw the table, piled with bacon, pancakes, fruit and breads. The smell was amazing. And she wanted pancakes so much, but even without the months of an enforced paleo diet, she knew she shouldn't. Watching Martin near puke had been scary.

One pancake. And definitely scrambled eggs.

"Morning, Alexander," Spencer said.

"Good morning, Sergeant. Sorry I'm last."

"By a whole two minutes. No problem."

"Any news?"

Elliott said, "Nothing from our hosts, but we're going to do some exercise in a while, and they say they want to debrief us. I've already told them we will only discuss incidents in the past, not our own time. I figure you understand protocols on how to talk."

"I've done public affairs and intel, so yes, I know what I shouldn't say." And she was still hanging onto the phone and memory sticks, in her clothes. Could she get those home intact? Were they going home?

Bacon first, ask questions later. And a pancake with maple syrup that tasted real.

The future was tragic in its utopia.

Of course, Cryder and Arnet were soldiers too, so there was a military in the future, which implied other militaries or lots of unrest. So it wasn't utopia.

Though anyone from the Paleolithic would gladly have moved to Rome, Viking Scandinavia, or twenty-first century America and had no complaints.

The pancake was delicious. She felt a buzz from it and the real maple syrup. She craved more, a whole stack, because she hadn't had any wheat at all in two years. She also knew it would make her horribly sick, with Martin's example of yesterday, and that it would wreck her metabolism and her weight.

She stuck to bacon, ham, and fluffy scrambled eggs, with a large mug of dark, bittersweet, very rich and savory chocolate.

"Alexander, are you with us?" she heard, and snapped to.

"Uh, yes, sir," she said. "I zoned for a moment."

She blushed and realized it had been several minutes, staring into the mug, eating her food, while the others had been talking. She recalled voices, but not what was said.

"I'm sorry," she said. "I missed it."

Elliott said, "I said we should stay together, not get out of sight of each other for any debriefing or interrogation and not discuss anything we're unsure of. Check with me first."

"Of course, sir."

"Please paraphrase it back."

She blushed again. "Stay in sight of each other, don't discuss anything questionable without asking you."

"Correct."

He continued without comment.

"Okay, so until we know what else is going on, we stay here, together. Prepare to be bored if necessary."

Martin said, "What about House? He may have entertainment options."

House said, "I can show you any surviving entertainment from before your era, or landscapes. There are also reconstructed board games available."

Before anyone could respond, House spoke again.

"There are visitors outside. Are you amenable to receiving guests?"

They looked around at each other.

"Yes."

"Very well, please stand by."

Sean Elliott looked around. There was no sign of a door, but three people appeared within the wall and walked toward them.

Alexander said, "Oh, that's fantastic."

He assumed she meant the androgynous . . . woman? wearing feathers, because he was looking at the naked chick.

She was easily 6'4", and allowing for hips to match the height, she was absolutely stunning. She had dark, lustrous green hair, in a comb held up by static, perhaps. She had eyebrows but not a single other hair below them. High cheeks, green eyes, fantastic muscle tone, and no, nothing resembling a bra, unless it was invisible. Her tits were defying gravity. And the rest of her . . .

Okay, she wasn't totally naked. She was wearing shoes, if you could call those pads under her feet shoes. They were like bootliners, in a green to match her eyes and hair. And she had geometric paint on her belly, around her nipples, around her throat, also in shades of blue, green and yellow.

He looked away, throat tight, and realized Alexander was looking at the feathers. Yes, they looked real, and to be skin mounted, but at least they covered most of the person's figure. And did they have a gender? It was impossible to tell. Either a slender man or a fairly buff woman.

Alexander asked, "Are the feathers real?"

Everyone had gathered around now, a polite, respectful distance away. And now he noticed the man. He wore shorts, and had muscles like an Olympic swimmer. He was hairless except for eyebrows and a bizarre haircut that made him look like he was wearing a cap.

The person in feathers said, "They are real, but they are not grown from me. They are grown on flesh in a lab and are held on with a mucilage."

"Does a device do the dressing?"

The person paused. Hell, he was going with "her."

"Yes, my servant mod assembled them for me. It doesn't take long."

Then the naked woman said, "I apologize. It is clear my presentation is surprising. Stand by."

A moment later she shimmered and turned blue to the neck, appearing to wear a skintight suit that then softened slightly around her groin and nipples. She was almost as dressed as a stripper now.

She said, "Should we take seats?"

The house produced three more seats, and everyone chose a place and sat. Chairs materialized under them again. It was disturbing how fast they'd gotten used to that. If they did go home, he half expected to sit and fall because he'd forget to grab a chair physically.

"I am Researcher Twine. This is Researcher Ruj and Assistant Zep," she said, pointing at the man and the woman in feathers. "I have all your names, and I am glad to make your acquaintance."

"Do we call you Researcher, or Ms, or something else?"

She said, "My chosen name is Alexian. Lex or Twine is fine." Her expression . . . yes, she was a scientist, and they were her subjects. She was placid and aloof.

Mr. Ruj said, "Please call me Ed."

The last said, "I am Larilee. Lar informally. Glad to meet."

He wanted to clear the rules up front.

"Can we ask you questions?" he asked Twine.

"You can certainly ask, but we are limited in what we can answer."

"I assume little about this time? That we can ask?"

"Yes," she said. "It's a policy, it doesn't have to make sense."

"I would assume you're worried about changing the time stream."

She shrugged, shoulders rolling and breasts shifting. "That would make sense, except your recent excursion doesn't seem to have affected anything. And the speculative literature of your era explored most of the things we have now. So without detailed knowledge, it won't matter. Can those Romans duplicate your vehicle's ignition? Or even its engine?"

Ed Ruj said, "We don't believe any temporal matrix is at risk."

"Can you tell us what year this is?" He hid behind a glass of juice for a moment. Strawberry juice. It was sweet and delicious.

Lar Zep said, "It is not terribly far. We are all from within a general timeframe in history."

"Within a thousand years or so, then?" He realy wanted to know.

"That will suffice for comfort, and we cannot confirm."

Moving on, he asked, "What do you research?"

Ed Ruj said, "In this context, yourselves. The opportunity to talk first hand to people from before . . . from the past is thrilling."

"Before what?"

"Many things, that we can't discuss." He shifted nervously.

Trindidad asked, "Is everyone in your society Caucasian?"

They looked at each other for a moment, and their expressions suggested they were reading screens in front of their eyes.

"No. However, we do not consider skin color a differentiator, and in fact, people often choose any number of . . . natural or artificial shades."

"Well, what can we answer for you?" he prompted.

"We desire, and need, information about yourselves. This will aid in returning you properly to your time."

"What specifically?"

"We would like to start with your full identities, including names, any culturally relevant identification codes, your dates of . . . birth, and family histories."

That was a lot of information. He didn't like it.

"That's more than we are comfortable sharing."

Spencer said, "Yeah, I'd rather not. If you've read our speculative fiction, you know information like that can determine how important it is to keep someone alive. We'd prefer to assume we're all essential."

Twine said, "I understand. Our culture is different from yours in terms of what is considered private. Much from your era is archived, but there are of course gaps."

Should they continue to consider themselves POWs? He swapped glances with Spencer, and wondered about a conference to discuss it. But he had to make the call, and he assumed anything they muttered or wrote would be noted anyway.

"Is giving this information a condition of our return?" he asked.

Twine shook her head.

"I don't want to phrase it like that. You are under no compulsion to offer anything, and may stay as long as you wish. We will attempt to return you home if you wish, and encourage it. The more information we have, the easier that will be. Certain human elements of the discussion would like background information toward that. We are strictly researchers, we don't set policy but can advise."

If he was drawing the lines, the scientists were fine with it, and the military wanted to make sure they weren't ancestors to any assassins. Or perhaps that they were, so as not to disrupt things.

He looked around.

"Soldiers, I can't order you to reveal personal information. I think it might be best to offer what you can."

He turned back to Lar, who was closest. "Is our return all at once? Or can some choose to travel later?"

She leaned forward on the couch. Her feathered brow wrinkled as she said, "We don't know. It would be best to send you all at once. Additional trips may not be possible for technical or policy reasons."

"Thanks." If anyone wanted to remain, he'd have to remain with them and send Spencer as NCOIC. He couldn't, as commander, leave anyone behind.

He wanted to discuss it in private, but it seemed impossible they wouldn't spy on anything he said. He would, if he were them.

He looked around and reiterated, "So, we're displaced, not POWs. I don't have any evidence these people are hostile. They're not signed allies. They seem to fit a neutral status. I'll share information if it will help. Please consult me if you're unsure."

The Cogi were obviously paying attention and studying the exchange between commander and troops, status being of note between all parties.

Lar said, "If you prefer, we can speak to you individually as well."

He asked, "Are you able to speak to us privately while we remain within view of each other?" It was a psychological matter. "We're displaced . . ."

He stopped talking. They were displaced, scared, cut off from their own people. They'd had only each other for two years. He had a serious phobia about not being in close proximity to them at a time like this.

Ed said, "Certainly we can do this thing."

"Then I'll go first. What shall we talk about?"

Suddenly he couldn't hear anything from the others. No movement, no mutters. He looked over and Spencer gave him a thumbs up. So there was an audio privacy screen, but they were still in proximity.

"Everything is of interest," Lex Twine said. "Your experiences in the past, back home, your interactions. We can analyze everything later. First, we want to know how you feel."

So he talked. He summarized his training, education, career. He spoke of his parents and brother, and Lacy, and would he see her again? They'd been dating three months when he deployed. How would all this affect his personality and what about the deployment itself?

It felt like a debrief and a psychoanalysis at the same time.

Lar was genial, and her very neutral form made her easy to talk to. She didn't appear to judge anything, nor to write nor record, though he was sure she was recording. He asked.

"The system will remember, and my memory is what you would call photogramic."

"Photographic."

"Thank you, I will remember that word. I would like to ask some other questions."

"Okay."

"This will be a collective inquiry. I'm going to have some pineapple juice. Would you like something?"

"That sounds good, thank you." The pineapple here was sweeter, tangier, but less acidic. He wondered how far agriculture had come. He wondered what year it was. Given human development, it might be a hundred years from their time, or a thousand.

He sipped juice, and felt the ongoing conflict of being physically very comfortable and emotionally wired. After the permanent bivouac of the Stone Age, this place was a sybaritic paradise. But he wanted to go home.

Lar said, "We need to talk about major events in your timeframe, to help narrow down our window. We don't want to discuss anything traumatic, but more detail helps."

"Are you familiar with the terrorist attack on the World Trade Center in New York City, September Eleventh, two thousand and one?"

She said, "Searching. May we show an image?"

"Yes."

In the air appeared a video of the plane smashing into Tower 2.

"That's it."

"Interesting. We are aware of that event."

"It was that significant?"

"We understand it was for you. Our condolences for the loss of your people."

He wondered again about their accents, and what time it was. "You sound American, but there's obviously some enhancement to your voice. Which nation are you now?"

She almost shook her head. "That distinction isn't germane. We associate ourselves differently from geography."

"Is English your primary language?"

Lar said, "Yes, but as you are aware, it has softened over time. How far after that date do you place yourself?"

"Eleven years, assuming the earth's revolution hasn't been changed."

Ed said, "That's an astute inquiry. I can inform you that it has not."

Lar said, "We will look for other major events. Our timeline may have errors. It is a paradox that the more information we have, the harder certain details are to confirm."

He suspected they were fishing, but they might be telling the truth. Certainly too many eyewitnesses complicated things.

"The geographic area we were in we called Afghanistan."

"Yes, we have a map of it at that time."

The image floated in the air, and he reached out tentatively.

"Right about there, if you can zoom." He spread his fingers, and it did zoom, just like a phone. He brought it in until he found about where the base was.

"We built military facilities in increasing number in that timeframe."

"Is this closer?" The image updated.

"Closer, but not there yet."

"This?" It rippled again.

"Just about. So we disappeared . . ." he zoomed in twice more. "Right there."

"We have the date, but need further imagery or events to localize it. You say this layout of that military field facility is appropriate?"

"It's probably a bit earlier than we were. There was an American national election. A flood on the American east coast. If you go a couple of years earlier, there was a large earthquake in Japan."

Lar said, "We have the earthquake. That was significant."

Ed looked at something in his hand and said, "And now we have the smaller events."

"Is dating them a problem?"

Lar said, "Dating them numerically is not a problem. Placing them against the temporal background we have available is largely hypothetical. You have probably deduced this is a new, little-tested field."

He noticed the two of them were talking while Twine watched. Was she senior and they research fellows? Or did she represent an intel source?

"Will it get better with practice?" he asked.

Lar said, "Theoretically, but given the fallout incidents with this use, we may have to discontinue until more advanced capabilities exist."

"But you can send us home?" he asked urgently. Please . . .

Ed said, "Physically we can. The advisability and safety are being reviewed. We have input, but no conclusive authority over that. Morally, we should send you home. What repercussions it may have for others is a counter question."

"I understand."

They weren't home yet. Though this prison would be much more comfortable, if it must be.

CHAPTER 45

Dan Oglesby was playing Halo when he heard his name.

"Yes?" he replied.

"This is Researcher Twine. I am informed you have knowledge of the Neolith language."

That sounded much more interesting. He put the controller down.

He spoke to the overhead, "I was able to compile a basic lexicon and grammar, and a workable pidgin."

"Would you be willing to assist us in communicating with them?"

"If you need me to, sure."

She said, "We could engineer the translations ourselves, but if you have them already there is no need to duplicate the effort."

"I'll be glad to help." It was nice to be needed professionally, and it would help with the boredom. He'd forgotten how to play, the controller was different, and he really didn't care about it anymore.

Her voice said, "The attendant will guide you to our location."

"This way," said House's voice. A line lit on the floor, and he walked along it.

The route was surprisingly direct, out a doorway that was almost ethereal, right, down a corridor that was decorated with more optical art, and right again through a door. There was some kind of frame for the door, but it wasn't obvious, and they had a hologram or something hiding it. He just followed the line through and it wasn't there.

The Gadorth had been equipped with hide and limb shelters,

607

though obviously for comfort, not necessity. They were all gathered around their eating table, which appeared to be slabs of wood, and there was a fire on a rock hearth near the far wall.

"Heyla, Muta," he greeted the nearest one he recognized.

"Heyla, Dan! Woosi gahn nit la." *Welcome at our new home.*

"Tat woosa, Muta." *Thank you I am welcome.* It was also "feel welcome" and "for welcoming me." Their grammar and syntax was flexible, with context mattering for most statements.

Lex Twine, he was embarrassed he couldn't remember her full name, was there with two other subordinates. She wore what was almost a casual pantsuit without a collar, in vivid blue with a black skin-hugging shirt. The others wore T-shirts, as near as he could tell, and pants that were even more covered in pockets than ACUs. One each female and male, tall, blond, beautiful.

Twine said, "Thank you, Specialist Oglesby. Or do you prefer Dan?"

"Either is fine, I guess. I enjoy being informal, but it's nice to be recognized, too." And damn, she was hot. He tried not to stare at her boobs, just below his eye level. Everyone here so far was perfectly formed and fed. They varied from elfin to curvy, but all the women were smoking. He wasn't sure about the androgynous ones. Those were a bit creepy.

He didn't know what discussions had gone on, but the Gadorth seemed to know the scientists were off limits. They didn't approach Twine or the others. They didn't seem to know about House, either.

He noticed one Cogi man near the back, who seemed to occasionally point at things for them. So they had a live host. That made sense. He gathered a voice from the sky would terrify them.

Twine asked, "Can you preface translations in English so we can build our own lexicon?"

"Of course. I also have written notes if those are of use."

"Please! Where are they?" Alexian. That was her name.

"They'll be in my bags in our vehicle."

"Can you extend permission for us to retrieve them?"

"Sure. You know which bags are which?"

"If not, a DNA sniffer will easily tell."

"Ah, right. Just bring my laptop to me and I'll take it from there. Do you have one-hundred-ten-volt electrical power?"

"We can provide any current needed, but we can also read the data remotely. If you consent, I promise all other data will remain unseen by people. An automatic system will scan for your notes."

"Oh, sure, if you can do that." He wasn't really sure about that, but it wasn't as if he could stop them, and other than his porn there really wasn't much private content.

The Gadorth seemed to be engaged in a scientific study of foodstuffs, trying a bite each of everything offered and discussing it boisterously.

Twine said, "We're trying to localize them as we localized you, but it may not be feasible."

"I know Sergeant Spencer said Doggerland. It was turning swampy and marshy but was not yet inundated. He figured they were about six thousand BC, by our counting."

Twine flipped her eyebrows, grabbed a phone, and rapidfired almost-English into it.

"Twine doc tempi third point corel Romn, 'Mehrgan backcalc split time source."

Someone said, "Yeah. Rici!"

Turning to him, she said, "We should be able to work out the time. Location is harder."

"How critical is it?"

Her gorgeous grin stabbed him. "Now you ask too many curious questions, Dan. Shall we talk to your friends?"

"Certainly." He turned and called, "Muta, ku sif ta."

Muta came over and clutched his shoulders again, and started introducing everyone by name and background. They didn't quite use chosen cognomens, nor patronymics, but almost clan references except they combined past and present into a compound word. It had taken a while to figure that one out. He explained that to Twine.

"I understand," she said. "We're picking up a lot from your interactions. Keep going."

He was there all morning, and it was fascinating to see their combination of primitive and ultramodern. Their latrine had squat holes and a cascade of water like a waterfall that was lukewarm. The food service was the same. Their huts were notional covers with bedding that was obviously supported by the same tech as the reclining seat-beds the Americans had, but disguised as quilted hide. It was a Potemkin Village illusion for comfort.

Seeing that, he wondered what the future really looked like, how much wasn't being shown them even in their own quarters. Still, he was able to sprawl when sleeping now, rather than being confined to a bag width. The beds here would open as wide as you wanted.

"How are the Romans and the Indians doing, Ms. Twine?"

"The Romans are fascinating. They are well-bonded as a unit, and are much less . . . reserved . . . than your people. They are consuming much, and while self-policing, need a lot of support. The Indians are obsequiously grateful and seem exhausted. They are resting and uninterested in much other than talking amongst themselves and a table game variant to chess."

"The Romans were using them as indentured labor."

"So we deduced. Captain Elliott has given us some summary of the interactions. You are all to be lauded on your efforts to act as intermediaries and avoid conflict."

"Thank you, ma'am." Yeah, they had tried.

"Your data and translation is most helpful. I don't know how closely we can return them, but it should be within a few decades and kilometers. Unfortunately, that is the best accuracy we are likely to get. We may be able to narrow it down."

"Decades? Is that as close as we'll get?" That was a disturbing thought. Though if they arrived in the 1950s, they could be rich choosing stocks.

She smiled and placed a hand gently on his arm. "We can be more accurate in your case, since we have specific time ticks to work with. They lack a calendar, maps, or significant records."

"I see." That was reassuring.

"Please keep in mind that is not my field, and I can only give you an overview. I have no decision-making authority on that."

So it wasn't definite they were going home.

"Well, this place isn't home, but it's more comfortable than a bug-filled cabin in proto-A-stan. I am grateful." A fuck of a lot more comfortable.

"Thank you. I will relay that. You can return now." She smiled again.

"Are you visiting later?" he asked hopefully.

"I am. Should I dress down?"

"Uh . . ." It sounded as if she were offering . . .

She said, "All the men in your element seem to appreciate my appearance. I'm flattered. If you'd like to see my natural self, I don't mind, if it won't make you uncomfortable."

Whew.

They were going to hate him, but after his previous interactions with natives, he said, "If you're asking me, why don't you dress up a bit, and use your natural appearance to display the outfit?"

"I'll consider it," she said. "There's your light."

He looked down. Yes, so it was.

"Have a good day, Ms. Twine," he said.

"And you, Specialist Oglesby."

He was glad she chose to be formal. Whew. Brains, beauty, and that voice. Amazing.

He needed a drink.

Armand wasn't nearly as comfortable as the white troops. There was no one here with any melanin at all. Well, that wasn't true. Some were tanned bronze or olive or even darker, almost black, some were sheened in green or blue. He suspected a lot of that was done with chemicals. A couple had faint Asian casts to them, Korean or Japanese in ancestry. There was no one the slightest bit African in features, though.

It didn't make sense for people to have split themselves up by race so thoroughly. Racial mixing was well underway in the twenty-first century, with air travel as common as it was. For it to not only stop, but regress, suggested some serious disaster.

He and Trinidad were away from the others. He wanted to think and didn't want TV.

"Felix, what do you think of the genetics here?"

"Red hot Swedish babes, all of them," he said. "I wonder where everyone else is?"

"Yeah, exactly that."

"They seem to have separated genetics, culture, appearance. Which I guess to mean there was a massive war and the Euros won. Or some kind of economic collapse, except that wouldn't explain clarifying gene lines."

"Yeah. It's like some Nazi master race bullshit."

It would take a long time, too. You didn't wipe out entire gene lines instantly. There were always half breeds and diluted ethnicities.

"They treat us all the same that I can tell."

"They do. But they won't explain how this happened, and it's important."

Felix said, "I see other races, but not Africans. There are several with Asian ancestry of different types, including South, East and Chinese. I don't see Filipinos or Malays. There are obvious Hispanics and what look like Siberians. The rest is or entirely are Caucasian. So I'm thinking we're in Asia somewhere, which makes sense. It's likely in A-stan."

He said, "With the Euros in charge, and no Africans."

Felix nodded. "It looks that way, and I understand your distress."

He hesitated, and asked, "Attendant, I have a technical question."

"If it concerns genotypes I cannot give you an answer."

"Are you unable or not allowed to?"

"The parameters do not permit of an answer."

Was that to the first or second question?

Felix said, "Want me to ask for you?"

Was there a discreet way to do that? Hell, Felix was intel. And he'd already asked openly, once.

"Sure, if you can."

Just then, Spencer called.

"Listen up! PT time. We're going to do calisthenic warm-ups and run around inside our oversized yurt, here."

That might help. He fell into formation.

"We'll start with pushups."

Dalton replied, "The pushup!"

"Funny. I'm informal here, but let's do it. Two minutes on the clock . . . now."

A half hour and two miles later, with situps and leg lifts as well, he was sweaty, endorphin high and flushed.

The attendant said, "Larilee Zep is approaching."

They turned as she came through the doorway.

"Good day," she said.

"Good day, ma'am," Felix said. "Why is it we see several racial influences among the staff here, but no Africans?"

Well, that was direct.

"That's a complicated question," she replied, and he was sure she was trying to cover something. "Some of it has to do with genetic diseases, and I can't share more than that. There is no direct animosity or intent to exclude anyone. In fact, most people have very mixed lineage at this point. There is almost no one with what you would consider pure genetic lines, which were questionable even in your era."

"Thanks. What is your makeup, if we can ask?"

"I am . . . part construct. Fully human, but with selected traits."

"Is everyone who looks androgynous like that?"

"No, that is a personal lifestyle choice. Forgive me. You deserve answers, as far as I can and am allowed to give them. But we don't generally ask such things of strangers here. Privacy is scarce in many ways, so we cherish what there is. However, I'll answer as much as I can as a diplomatic courtesy."

"So are there Africans, or people with African ancestry here?" Armand asked.

"Yes," she said with a nod. "Few, but present. We do not divide ourselves along those lines, and there is no reason for any animosity."

He was still sure she was hiding something.

"Thank you," he said.

After a week, they settled into a dull routine. Richard Dalton hated it. They could watch any number of movies or TV, read books, or sit and talk. There were board games, Xbox, pretty much any recreation from their time seemed to be available.

After two years in purgatory, they were novelties, but everyone was rusty at games and had to learn over again.

For himself, a lot of it just didn't seem to matter anymore. He'd rather work or talk to people. Those were what mattered.

He held service on Sunday and almost everyone attended. Even Spencer lurked in back.

They sat at the dinner table and he read from Job 38.

"Bored, Sergeant?" he asked afterward.

Spencer said, "Partly. But you can be a very motivational speaker. You should pursue it."

"You think so?"

"You kept several of our people in good spirits during this. Really. Don't underestimate yourself."

"Thanks, Sergeant."

"You're welcome. I hope it can be 'Martin' sometime."

"Time for pancakes," Barker said. "And bacon."

Wheat was so awesome when you didn't have it for two years.

"A timeless combination." He said. "I do miss the acorn pancakes."

Barker pointed at the table. "Yeah, but I ordered vanilla buckwheat with honey and peaches."

"Damn. Awesome."

The food here was always perfect, every time, and still managed to be unique every time.

"Is the food prepared by hand?" he asked.

Attendant said, "Some is. The rest is automated, but, there are algorithms to allow variation across a spectrum. You can request adjustments or select a particular variation by referencing it."

The contrast was extreme, between whatever one could hunt and find in the vagaries of nature, or whatever one chose from an infinite selection. This was easier, but he wasn't sure the other wasn't better for the soul.

Cal hovered around, waiting for the humans to toss him bits of something. He was fond of ham and bacon, and was convinced lamb was caracal candy. He brushed against Rich's legs. Rich tossed a bit of bacon down, and the cat snatched it with a protective growl.

Somehow, the facility-cleaning bots managed to take care of the cat piss and turd deposits. Rich wasn't sure where the cat went, but it was probably in spots to mark territory, and was never visible.

He thought back to the food. It was an interesting moral lesson. He'd been in the wilds of God's world for two years, living by the sweat of his brow. Now he was inside a cocoon that could provide anything without effort.

That afternoon, Researcher Alexian Twine returned. She was dressed in a coverall that had flowing legs, no sleeves and was V-necked. That was strangely hot.

"Richard," she asked, "may we discuss your faith with you?"

"Of course!" he said. Did they still have Christianity?

"Thank you. Your interpretation of Scripture will be most welcome."

"Don't you have records?"

"Yes, but few from nonscholars, and a personal interaction is always a sociological desideratum."

He retrieved his Bible, well worn and sagging as it was. He would certainly get another copy at home, but this one was special and would be with him for life. Its Word had given him so much solace in the last two years.

A bubble formed around them, with several of the morphing couches. He sat upright for this. It didn't seem respectful to Witness from a sprawl.

Twine was joined by Ed Ruj in those snug shorts, and two other people. Mas Johns was short by the standards here, only about six foot, and wiry lean in spandex or something similar atop what looked like mundane jeans. Gella Xing was more Asian than anyone he'd met so far, with a lot of Chinese ancestry. She was striking, with her height. She was at least 5'10". She wore a long, flowing skirt and a layered lace top. They all took seats and stayed upright.

Ed said, "I see you brought your Bible. It's been well used."

"It kept me alive for two years, whenever I felt depressed, frustrated, lost."

"Excellent. I'm glad it worked for you."

"Are you Christian?"

Twine said, "None of us are, but we've read and studied the major religions of your era. Christianity does still exist, if you are curious. There is much philosophy and lifestyle now, but not many people practice actual religions."

"Okay. Then what can I tell you?"

"What does it mean to you?"

He thought for a moment. Obviously Christ had not returned in their time, or they wouldn't need him.

He chose several passages, and found them in seconds from familiarity, he'd thumbed this book so often.

He decided to start with the basics, of Isaiah 53:3-7.

> He was despised and rejected by mankind,
> a man of suffering, and familiar with pain.
> Like one from whom people hide their faces
> he was despised, and we held him in low esteem.
> 4 Surely he took up our pain
> and bore our suffering,
> yet we considered him punished by God,
> stricken by him, and afflicted.

⁵ But he was pierced for our transgressions,
he was crushed for our iniquities;
the punishment that brought us peace was on him,
 and by his wounds we are healed.
⁶ We all, like sheep, have gone astray,
each of us has turned to our own way;
and the LORD has laid on him
the iniquity of us all.
⁷ He was oppressed and afflicted,
yet he did not open his mouth;
he was led like a lamb to the slaughter,
and as a sheep before its shearers is silent,
so he did not open his mouth.

He continued with John 3:16, Corinthians 1:15. They paid attention, their faces showing interest, but they weren't moved.

That was fine. Not every seed found soil.

Seed! Matthew 17:20.

He quoted it. "He replied, 'Because you have so little faith. Truly I tell you, if you have faith as small as a mustard seed, you can say to this mountain, 'Move from here to there,' and it will move. Nothing will be impossible for you.'"

Xing asked, "What does that mean to you?"

He took a deep breath.

"We had no idea what had happened, or where we were. Then we found we were lost, with no way home at all.

"The Word of God kept me calm. I knew that with faith, I would find first comfort, then the solution God wanted me to have. It might not be my solution, but it would be one I could handle. God only gives us what we can survive, as a challenge to our spirit. I embraced it and accepted it. I sang His praises, and trusted for an outcome. And it was better than I could have hoped. I learned to appreciate the plants, the animals, the weather as I never had. And then I was brought here."

Twine asked, "Did you speak to God or Christ?"

"Not directly," he said. "God moves one through clues, hints, in the dead silence. Late night on watch was a time to meditate, and I knew what was intended, and followed."

They all stared at each other for a moment.

"Interesting," Xing said. "That's different from now."

He'd gathered that.

"Can you tell me what's changed?" he asked.

"No one here is so literal," she said. "It's und—taken to be metaphor. Parables and motivation."

"Metaphor? God is real, and Christ will return."

They said nothing, only blinked.

A moment later, Twine said, "That will be fascinating when or if it happens. Certainly worth studying."

She obviously had no idea what to say and was trying to be polite, in her detached, scientific manner.

Xing said, "So you're expecting Christ to return."

"Yes."

"Do you know when?"

Sigh. These were such basic, aggravating questions, but he must have patience.

"I don't. No one does. The point is to live every day as if judgment will be upon you, to strive to be better."

"That makes sense. But do you need Christ to do that? Can't you just make the decision to be your best?"

"Of course," he said. "But Christ isn't the reason. Christ is the cause and the reward."

Ruj said, "The reward is everlasting life and peace."

"Yes!"

They sat for a moment, swapping glances and expressions, obviously communicating. He suspected the house or their glasses or both were almost telepathic.

Xing asked, "What date do you assign to the beginning of things?"

"One researcher estimated four thousand and four BC, by our calendar."

She said, "But you were thousands of years before that. The Gadorth were before that, and you were twice as far back."

"I'm told that's true, but it contradicts what I know."

"What you know . . ." she was silent.

He shrugged. "All I can do is pray for guidance. Obviously we've misinterpreted in my time. But it was created. God told us so."

"I respect your determination," she said, with a serious face. "Thank you very much for sharing your beliefs."

"You're welcome," he said, but he wasn't sure he felt it.

He was escorted to the edge of the area, almost like a prisoner, even though he was in the same room and had nowhere to go otherwise. He wanted to be alone for the walk.

Back near the table, the others greeted him.

"How was it, Rich?" Barker asked.

"Interesting?" asked Caswell.

"They were laughing at me," he blurted.

Elliott asked, "They don't have religion at all?"

"Nothing like ours. They say they have Christians, but they don't accept Genesis, or the Gospels, the Resurrection. It's some watered down philosophy."

Gina said, "Ah, like fluffy bunny pagans."

"How's that?"

"Some, a lot, of pagans pick and choose what is convenient so they never actually have to work."

He remembered her saying that before. "I don't think it's that. I think they use it as a guiding principle. But they don't believe it as real, only as philosophy."

"That must be hard on you," Caswell said. "I don't like that myself."

He shrugged, shook his head, went to the table and said, "Attendant, can I get a roast beef and cheese with horseradish?"

"Is that a sandwich?"

"Yes, on French bread, please."

"Medium rare for the beef?"

"Thanks."

The others left him alone, with sound screens set up while they gamed or watched movies. He chewed his sandwich and thought.

It was undisputable that God had created the world, made it, put them here, sent them back, and brought them forward. He'd learned much about people and himself.

It seemed that the farther one was from nature, the harder it was to accept and believe. That made sense. The Amish worked with that.

While he pondered, Spencer came over, and entered the area. He saw, then heard as the bubble was breeched.

"Hey, Rich."

"Sergeant."

"I need to give you some advice."

"Okay." He wondered what this was going to be.

"Son, you've just had a fight with your beliefs and the real world. You know I don't believe anything of what you do."

"I know. Neither do they. Are you going to tell me you told me so and to give up?"

Spencer shook his head and pointed a finger.

"No. I'm going to tell you you must not do that. That faith kept you strong. It kept you sane. It helped your friends and compatriots. No matter what you hear from me, from the Cogi, or from anyone else, I'm telling you you must hang onto that faith. It's part of what you are.

"Over time you'll probably refine and change your beliefs, but I'll be very unhappy if you abandon them. If your god is real, this is yet another test of your faith, character and strength.

"I have every confidence in you."

Ripples and chills went down his spine.

"Thank you . . . Martin."

"You're welcome. It's a privilege to serve with someone of your character."

He hoped Spencer would leave before he teared up.

"Thanks. I need to be alone to think."

"Certainly. And well done."

Spencer rose and walked back out to his couch.

Damn.

God truly did work in awesome ways.

CHAPTER 46

Sean Elliott still couldn't get away from briefings. Every day was consumed with briefings. They were the ultimate TOCroaches here, rising, exercising, showering, holding formation, taking turns talking to the researchers, eating lunch, repeating, then bullshitting around an indoor campfire at night.

The campfire helped. The two main fires at COB Bedrock had burned nonstop. It was as much a cultural icon as generator hum had been before that. It was on a hearth between the end of the table and the viewing wall. They had a large, neat pile of seasoned cut wood to feed it. The ash was whisked away by some cleaning process through the floor or once it spilled off the hearth tiles, which looked like very pretty gold-veined marble.

Every day he received a short update on status, and was thanked by the Cogi for providing yet more historical information.

They'd been here a month, and even with House's help balancing food, they'd all gained weight and softened.

"Is there an update on returning home?" he asked again. He sat on a couch, in one of the privacy bubbles, watching the troops around him.

On a couch across from him, Twine told him, "We have found the exact location and time of your disappearance. We are attempting to refine the point."

"I assume that's hard."

"Since we have done this only once on purpose, once by accident, yes. Several factors and controls come into precise play."

He visualized an old 1950s Bridgeport mill with manual feed and indexing, no digital readout, and out of calibration. Could one drill a hole in the proper location and plane?

He said, "We do hope it's soon. I know I keep asking, but we're getting antsy."

He said that every day.

"Very understandable. I am sorry it's so slow," Twine replied, her mouth twisting. And she was eternally gorgeous, even when wearing a coverall, though it was fairly form fitting. He almost wanted to ask if they had people the soldiers could socialize with. But he didn't ask. They had each other, movies, privacy as needed, and the shower.

"Additionally," she said, "We are still discussing the practicality, secondary effects, feedback effects and risk factors of doing so. Those are part scientific, part economic and part political. There is an ethicist assigned to your case."

"Can we speak to this ethicist? So we can make our needs known better?"

"You do already. One of the regular researchers here handles that. I can say no more. The intent is to keep hands off for neutrality."

"Neutrality is great, except for the fact that I really want to get back to my own world." He realized he'd raised his voice.

She nodded. "Your tension is valid and I'm very sorry I can't do more. If it were solely my choice, I'd send you home at once, and regret the loss of your presence. It's very informative, and you are complex and amazing people."

"Thanks. I do appreciate your support, but gah, it's . . . frustrating." He put his head in his hands.

"I understand and we are doing what we can."

"I appreciate the regular reassurances. They do help." He meant it, but it was also an attempt at persuasion.

"You're welcome. We do have potential good news on another matter."

"Oh?" he asked, twitching.

"No matter the outcome, we would like to improve your health."

"How so?"

"Your teeth need repair, and your previous reconstructions are crude by our standards. Three of you have innate medical problems. We offer to fix those."

That was a hell of an offer. With no strings? He was leery.

"What are the negatives of doing so?"

She said, "It may make you harder to recognize back home, on detailed examination."

"Will our DNA and fingerprints remain unchanged?"

"Yes," she said with a nod.

"Then that and fingerprints will ID us. Anything else supports our story." He hoped. Damn. He needed to think about this.

"Do you concur, then?"

"It's up to each individual, after we decide if we should proceed."

That evening he raised the issue after dinner. And wasn't it great to choose anything you wanted? He chose spaghetti, with tomato sauce and fresh bell peppers. God, he'd missed it.

"Ms. Twine says they can restore our health."

"To what?" Barker asked.

"To whatever we want. Apparently, joint, hormone and other problems."

There were nervous looks back and forth, especially between Alexander and Spencer.

"What's the catch?" Alexander asked.

"No catch. Apparently it's easy for them."

Spencer shrugged and said, "Ah, hell, I'll be the test case. My guts and shoulder aren't getting any better." They'd given him an analog to his Zantac at his request, and he'd been much better, but Sean understood that not taking pills daily was something the man desired. He didn't blame him. Getting old scared him, and Spencer really wasn't old.

Ortiz asked, "Any word on when we get home? Do we?"

"They said they've narrowed down when. They're discussing details of how, and potential problems. They don't want another cascade of groups displacing." That latter was speculation on his part, but if it happened the last time . . .

Actually, he had no idea who, how or why it had happened. They were completely obtuse about such details.

Alexander said, "The irony is that once they can work it out, they can send us anywhere. We won't have been missing. Except that we're getting older here." She had damp eyes. "I want to see my kids."

✢ ✢ ✢

Gina Alexander watched as Martin came back from the doctors with no obvious side effects. They'd chosen a distant part of the dome and sat down, talked a bit, and handed him something. She watched while petting Cal, who seemed to have adapted to this strange place by nesting in an open dog bed that House had provided. In between, he demanded food, and got both raw animal and human table scraps.

Ten minutes later Martin was back.

"How do you feel?" Gina asked anxiously. She cared about him, and she wanted to be next. She hugged Cal until he growled at the restraint.

"Well, I can't tell much that soon, but I'm not hurting anymore. That happened fast. I'm tingling all over. I do feel better overall. It could be placebo effect, though."

Nothing had happened by dinner time, so she decided to risk it. She let Cal down to the ground, and he headed under the table for safety.

"Go ahead," Elliott said. "Good luck."

Lar, the assistant, escorted her over. She recognized the doctor from their first day, when they'd overeaten. She didn't recognize the second one, a man. They wore what were probably lab coats, but slicker. They had almost normal looking hairdos, with just an odd feathering that made them look light and fluffy. One actually had brown hair, not blond.

The doctor asked, "Hello. Who are you?"

"Regina Alexander. I go by Gina."

"Good to see you, Gina. Just relax and we'll do analysis in a few moments. It won't hurt."

"I'd assumed you'd use remote telemetry," she said with a hint of snark.

The doctor smiled. "Please accept apology. Other groups are less experienced and feared probing."

She said, "They might be, but there are few medical devices that would scare me. I've been worked on by quite a few. Knees. Ankles. Wrists. Hormone meds. I've delivered two babies the natural way."

The second doctor looked at a clear HUD screen in front of him with graphs and images glowing from it.

"You mentioned hormone imbalance. In fact, your thyroid is suboptimal."

"Yes, by about two thirds."

He said, "It ranges from twenty-six percent to sixty percent functional, depending on process and input. Your approximation is close. What treatment have you had?"

Damn, they were wordy.

"I was taking Synthroid, and vitamin D and iodine supplements."

He scanned whatever he had access to, and nodded.

"We can regeneratively restore your thyroid to proper function, if you wish."

"What side effects would there be?" She now knew how the Urushu felt when presented with modern technology. For a decade she'd suffered with weight, attention, mood, memory, and lately she'd been a slug. To have it fixed . . . but what would that lead to?

"None. It should last the rest of your life."

"Please do. Oh, yes, please."

"A scan shows trauma to your reproductive system."

"Yes, my tubes were surgically plugged and I had endometrial ablation. Another pregnancy with the thyroid issues would have been very bad."

"We can restore that."

"Please don't."

"No?"

"It's fine as it is."

"Certainly. Though with the thyroid damage repaired, you would be perfectly fertile again."

Gods, no.

"No, I'm forty-four. I'm not up to more kids. Two is sufficient." And she wanted to see them.

The doctor looked troubled.

"Very well, as you wish. Is there anything else you would like addressed?"

"My knees, ankles and wrists still hurt from old injuries, and I have trauma to the sole of my right foot recently."

"Were there fractures?"

"One wrist, one ankle. The rest was lots of soft tissue and compressional damage and a puncture wound."

"What about your teeth?"

"If I have any cavities, please fix them."

Just like that. Like ordering food. *One knee job, a tooth fix, and a side of thyroid repair, please, extra large.*

"You have respectable teeth, under the circumstances, but there are old repairs. We can regeneratively restore those, too."

Uh . . . She said, "That will affect how we are identified back home."

"Your commander says fingerprints and DNA will be sufficient. If you'd like us to, we can."

She could ask him easily, but there was no reason they'd lie about it.

She asked, "Can you fix any cavities to resemble the original ones?"

"We could, but it's easier and better to regenerate them."

"If Captain Elliott approves, then I'll take it. Thank you." She was placing a lot of trust in him, and them, but he'd brought them this far.

The doctor held up a glass.

"This is your medication. Drink it." It wasn't much of a bedside manner.

"That's it?"

"Your fallibilities are easily addressed. That will cause regeneration of the tissue."

She sipped it. It tasted like strawberry juice. She drank it in two mouthfuls. She crushed the cup and it disappeared in dust.

"You should notice the tooth fillings falling loose over the next two days or so. The other problems will be less noticeable until they're gone."

"Thank you very much," she said.

"You're welcome, Gina. You can send the next person."

It was just like an Army processing line. In, out, next troop, hurry up and wait.

Some things never changed.

Sean Elliott didn't feel much different after the medical treatment, though the two fillings he'd had were crumbling out, and there was new enamel under them.

Spencer and Alexander seemed bouncy.

"I don't hurt!" she said. "My knees and ankles bend without grinding. There's no pins and needles in my wrists." She squatted, bent, shimmied upright with a nice jiggle.

"I'm alert, and I can remember things," she said.

Then she added, "Some things. I still have gaps."

"Great to hear," he said. They'd fixed the aftereffects of an aircraft crash. In minutes. How long did they live here? If Alexander was forty-four and looked thirty, how old were some of the Cogi?

Twine was dressed in a leotard over tights this morning. Her makeup and hair were blue to match. Her hair was swept up and back. Against her skin it was striking, almost like an anime character.

"Good morning, Captain," she said.

"Good morning, Ms. Twine." She was being formal, so he was. It varied day to day.

"We are to meet with what you would probably call a committee, regarding your return. Can you speak for all your soldiers?"

"That depends on the subject, but I believe I can for what's involved."

Goddamn. Could they be . . . ?

"Please come with me then."

She explained as they walked. She was tall, strode quickly, and he had a view of her amazing ass. He brought his eyes up to her shoulders and watched those muscles roll instead. Wow.

"They've seen all your briefing information," she said. "They may have a few additional questions. Be honest. 'I do not have that information' is a very good answer to give, if you don't have the information. These are as much scientists as politicians. Consulting experts."

"So they'll talk to the leadership?"

"For these matters they are the leadership. They'll take input from elsewhere as well, but they will decide."

"Got it," he said.

It was nothing like he expected.

They walked into another domelike room, a bit like a planetarium. It was half-lit, with seats around the arc but not in rows. Some were higher than others, and he saw one of them change locations.

"Welcome, Captain Elliott," someone said. "Is that pronunci correct?"

"Yes, sir, it is."

"Great. Grab some food or what have you."

"Strawberry juice will be fine, thank you very much."

"Riz."

A glass appeared, held by some kind of serving machine.

A screen in front of him showed faces and names. It slid down and to the left and poised there, easy to see, but not intrusive. There were sixteen people here, nine males, five females, two he wasn't sure about.

Someone else said, "Dokey, so translost to Paleolithic, two years subjective. Arnet and Cryder recovery brought you and displacees here, crave to go home. Substantially correct?"

That was a quick summary.

"Yes, ma'am, we'd like to go home."

"Social vs practical. Comprend."

Another said, "Era still subject to strong familial emotional ties. Fascinating, but respectable."

"Compassion for feelings, pers. Comprend vs symp."

"Wooz."

The first inquisitor said, "Appears minimal present contact. Well done. Observed tech within base for past-contemp spec. No risk. Approve."

"Approve." "Approve." "Well done, Prof Twine. Approve."

He heard her reply, "Tank, graz."

"Spec on further temporal flashout?"

"Unknowable."

"Opinion?"

"Shielding upgrade. Threat issue—"

Audio went silent. He could see them talking and addressing each other, but he heard nothing. Apparently he wasn't cleared for this part.

Audio came back with someone saying, "Risk feasible. Compassionate flashout."

"Public react?"

"Nah, do it."

"Go."

"Reasonable permit survive, simplest. No sido."

"Captain, do you have any add comment?"

He took a deep breath, and said, "Sirs, ma'ams, we're very grateful to you for recovering us, and your hospitality here has been exceptional. I know there's many other issues to consider, but if there's any way at all, even with risk involved, we'd like to return home. I don't know what specific information I can offer, but I'll answer anything you ask."

"Fair. You are welcome for your stay, and thanks and graz for your information on your era. Good stuff. Conclude?"

It was agreed, and they disbanded without any ceremony. He was alone with Twine in moments.

"That was strange, from my perspective," he said, leaning back in the chair. It was almost like stadium theater seating.

"You did well," she said, and brought her chair down near his.

He faced her and said, "Thanks. What about the other groups?"

"Those have other issues, still resolving. For one, we can't place the Gadorth to an exact time or place."

A small part of him wanted to stonewall and insist they all be returned, but he had no bargaining chips, it wasn't his problem, and he was afraid they'd call his bluff.

"There are some details of concern," she said.

"Yes?"

"We know the exact location to send you, but don't want to mix your arrival and departure."

"In case we wind up back where we were?"

"That would be ironic. They fear the coalescing waves would kill you, among other side effects."

"Yes, let's please avoid that." He had no idea what energies were involved here, but he imagined intersecting nuclear events.

"You will be nearby temporally and spatially, but probably not exactly."

"Understood."

"Let's discuss how you will present to your own people."

It was another two hours and a lunch before they were done, but it was a very productive discussion.

She led him through the insane corridor back to their dome.

She said, "Your people appreciate touch in friendship."

"Yes?"

"May I offer you a hug before you leave?"

A hug, and anything else she wanted to offer, was absolutely fine with him.

"I'm almost afraid I'd like it too much."

She grinned. "That's a normal response, too." She wrapped arms around his shoulders and neck, pressed against him knee to cheek, and he clutched her. He'd never appreciated a hug more in his life. She was a human being, warm, and firmly soft.

He realized he was weeping.

She broke the touch and stepped back.

"I will try to visit before you depart," she said. "I have other projects to monitor, but this one is special to me, you all are. Do you need help relaying the news?"

"I may. Thanks very much, for everything."

"You're welcome. I'll answer any questions then leave your group alone to discuss it."

"Thank you," he said again, and realized he wanted to say it to everyone, repeatedly.

He turned and stepped through the doorway, with Twine following.

Everyone was sitting around the table, and they looked at him, tense and eager.

"They're going to try to send us home tomorrow."

There was a collective inhale and everyone went rigid.

"They can't guarantee where or when. It will be within a few hundred miles, and within a few months. We may actually arrive before we left, in which case, we have to go to ground and stay hidden until we know we've passed our disappearance date."

"This is very important," Twine said. "We can't predict what would happen if you encountered yourselves. It might pinch off a new universe. It might cause something like the shock that sent you back, only worse. Or your past selves might just react very badly to your current selves."

Spencer asked, "What do we do about a cover story?"

Elliott said, "That depends on if we're before or after. If we're after and have been missing, there's any number of things we can say. Hijacked is easiest. But we'll have to agree on details, and I'm afraid they'll find holes, in which case we get accused of espionage or treason. If we're before, then we have to wait until after, and we're very different than we were last year."

Jenny Caswell said, "They're going to think us nuts or lying, either way."

"So we have to be able to prove we were here, without too many details."

Twine said, "I will leave you alone for now. If you need help, just call. I'll be available."

"Thank you!" everyone chorused.

Sean was nervous about one thing. He was catching on to their language. When the committee concluded, the chairperson had said, "We've decided we can let them live. That's simplest and I don't think there will be any side effects."

"Okay," he said, to get past that disturbing memory. "We'll be in Asia, sometime within a few months. Then we have to make sure we're not early. So we may have to stay hidden another several months. Everyone understands that, right?"

"Yes, sir."

"I will collect all your phones. There's no communication until I make it. You don't need them here, so you may as well hand them over now. Pull the cards or batteries if you like. I just want the bodies."

There was a little grumbling, but everyone was very sober and complied.

Trinidad said, "If we might be a while, we need some supplies."

"Yes, put a list together and we'll have them supply us."

"Toilet paper and chocolate!" Alexander said.

"Coffee and toothpaste and razors," Spencer added.

CHAPTER 47

Gina slept only because House dosed them again.

She did feel better overall. Her joints didn't ache, she was down four pounds in a week, and her mental acuity was buzzing. She had checklists memorized, and could rattle from memory everybody's gear.

"Ms. Twine, will I be able to get my camera back before we depart?"

"Of course. It was necessary to delete most of your images."

She'd expected that.

"I understand. Were they of use to you?"

"More than you can imagine, especially with our conversations. You are gifted in your field."

"Thank you very much." Good. If only they knew how gifted. She shifted slightly as the duplicate memory cards in a shielded pouch in her bra itched. Of course, it was possible those had been scrubbed remotely. If so, she had another memory stick secured somewhere else.

She'd remembered to do that before they bounced forward, even with her brain broken. She wanted to brag about that fact.

"You'll take care of Cal?" she asked.

"Absolutely. He's a very handsome animal. The species still exists, but has changed, and we'll examine him noninvasively, as we have been."

She was going to miss the stinky furball. It was possible to buy them as exotic pets. She might do that.

"Thank you," she said. Once again, they were losing a connection.

They were escorted to their vehicles, which were clean, surrounded by gear, and had crates of supplies nearby.

"Those are MREs," she said.

"Close copies. They may taste different, but are at least as nutritious and will look the same to observers, in case you must delay."

Dalton asked, "What about ammo? We're going back to a war zone."

"You have full combat loads as you described, cased and ready. You can load as soon as you board."

Spencer said, "Mags in, chambers empty until we arrive, then we'll reassess."

Details, details, and they were all eager. Were they really going home? It had been two and a half years, longer than any scheduled deployment, in places no soldier had ever thought of going.

"Are you all ready, then?" Twine asked.

Spencer said, "Yes, ma'am. We'll don armor and load up."

"One moment, then."

She stepped over and hugged him, full body.

He looked a bit stunned as Twine turned to Gina and offered the same, with the tall woman's bosom in her face. Gina didn't mind. It felt good to be touched. Would she see her kids?

Lar had a lighter touch and was more like a cat, lithe and easing into it so it was hard to tell when the hug started and ended. Ed was warm and strong and seemed a bit bothered. He hugged like a wrestler.

"Thank you," she said afterward.

"You are all welcome. Thank you for the information and your company. I'm sad we won't meet again."

"So are we."

They kept losing friends, even though few died. It was strange and bothersome.

Martin Spencer sat aboard the MRAP, and waited. This wasn't the bored wait of nothing. This was the tense wait of impending combat, or another loss in time, in which case he wasn't sure anyone would risk the effort to recover them.

How fucked up would that be, to wind up in some desolate primitive world after experiencing the limited but insane hospitality of the far future?

The vehicles had been repaired, and with reproduction twenty-first century tools, so as to minimize even that transfer of technology. He gathered the future folk were very unhappy with the dissemination of knowledge in the past. It certainly gave their very free society something to argue about.

And fuck them, too. Perhaps they'd have the iron will to live as natives. Or perhaps they'd have curled up and died, being even further removed from nature than he and his comrades.

Then he just hoped it worked.

From overhead, House said, "The system is in power, and the transfer is pending. There is no way to predict exac—"

BANG.

They fell, but not as far as the first time, only a few inches.

They'd moved. Scrubby growth, distant sheep . . .

Well, it certainly looked like Asscrackistan.

Elliott said, "Unass, perimeter, scan."

He took the rear and looked about. They were on a hillside, in what looked like spring, with little around them.

And he could smell the difference.

"I smell farming, industry and chemical crap in the air," he said.

"Yeah!" Ortiz agreed. "It definitely smells like home. And I don't care about the pollution."

Elliott said, "I have signal."

"Yes?" The tension was palpable.

"It's March third."

"What year?"

"Next year. Our next year. We've been gone six months."

Ortiz shouted, "Get the fucking radio up, we're going home!"

Spencer said, "Let me do the talking. I know what they want to hear."

He took the radio, switched to Guard frequency and clicked it. "Charlie Nine to any allied unit. Emergency, over." He gave their convoy and route number. He waited a painful thirty seconds and repeated.

"Unit identified as Charlie Nine, this is Trumpcard. If this is a joke you are in trouble, over."

"Trumpcard, no joke. This is Charlie Nine. I believe we've been out of contact about six months. It's a long story for debrief. We need rescue and recovery. Charlie Eight is with us. All personnel are fit and capable, over."

"Charlie Nine, understood. We have your grid. Identify your last four, over."

"Fower fife two tree, over."

"I will be damned. You're real. Welcome home, over."

He felt tears welling up.

"Thank you, sir. It's great to be here, over."

"We are on station, and should have you in range. Keep your line open, over."

"Roger. Charlie Nine, listening, out."

Shit, they really were home.

He turned to the rest and said, "Okay, they're going to show up. We do exactly as they say—they have to confirm we're not hostile. Expect to be treated like prisoners at first. Expect to be positively identified. Then we get to talk. It's going to be weeks or months before we're done. But we're back."

No matter what happened next, it would happen in their own world.

CHAPTER 48

Sean Elliott fidgeted. It didn't take long, but thirty minutes seemed forever. They were in a rural area, nothing nearby except some goats. But there were roads in the distance, and a contrail overhead. Then a distant roar resolved as a pair of Predators.

The JSTARS bird called again, inquiring about signal.

Spencer replied, "Negative, I do not have smoke. I can improvise panel, or remain on air, over."

Tension. It was like sex, or the first night at OCS. It was less shock inducing than having disappeared in the first place.

Another flyby, this time a pair of OA10s.

Off in the distance . . . "I hear helos."

"Yeah. Again, expect to be cuffed and manhandled. They won't know who we are, only that we're claiming to be someone long gone. Be very compliant."

He did feel almost as helpless as when they'd disappeared. Now he had to explain, and fast, and not get his people locked up as loons.

"Shit, that's a big response," Dalton said.

Spencer said, "Ten of us. They normally send four or six birds for one downed pilot. They'll want to split us up. Females, you should buddy up."

The helos circled, and they all had guns. There were two Chinooks and two Apaches. The gunners were there to protect them against possible threats, but also to hose them down if it looked like a trap. Disappearing for six months was hard to explain.

Spencer said, "Soldiers, do exactly as they tell us. It's their game now."

The Chinooks orbited again, and they watched as they settled a hundred meters north, whomping rotors whipping wind across the scrub.

Over a bullhorn, someone said, "Place your weapons down."

It was good to hear American voices, even if they weren't yet friendly.

The other birds hovered. They were Marine choppers, and it was Marines who debarked at a run, first enveloping them, then moving in in pairs. They shouted orders clearly but loudly, and he complied, feeling a wash of anger, fear, relief and more fear. They were now back in the system, with an unbelievable story.

They were separated, and that hurt, too. They'd been family for so long. But the recovery unit needed distance to do their debrief.

One of the Marines was a captain, lean and wiry and looking young. He squinted in the sun as he looked at his tablet.

"What's your name, rank and duty station?"

"Sean Elliott, Cap . . . First Lieutenant." He gave his unit number, still a reflex in his memory. He'd have to remember he was a lieutenant, though. His promotion wasn't effective here, until they approved it. Hell, he didn't actually have time in grade yet.

"Last four?"

"Four niner eight three."

"Tell me about your first pet."

Yeah, that question, off his recovery sheet.

"Bonzo was a Labrador with big feet. He'd beat on the door to get in. He broke his chain and was hit by a car when I was nine."

The Marine captain looked at his tablet and nodded. So they'd confirmed he was real.

"Okay, Lieutenant, we have to take you in for further debriefing."

"I understand. I can vouch for my people, and of course you'll check them yourself. I will not discuss our activity until we are on base. It's a sensitive matter."

"Understood, Lieutenant. I'll relay that to my chain."

He had no idea what would happen now. They'd probably accuse him of desertion, of some kind of political or financial sellout, or of gross incompetence.

If so it would still be worth it. They were home.

They were already searching his ruck.

"What's this, sir?" one asked, holding up the handled blob of a Cogi flexitool.

"That's one of the things I'll discuss with higher command. It's not dangerous."

They didn't seem entirely convinced.

En route, the Marines didn't talk much, but of course, it was loud. They'd left crews to drive the vehicles back. Sean had a ruck with important things stowed, and they'd taken that from him. The Marines did watch them pretty closely. It seemed to be part curiosity and part professional interest.

They landed at Mazar-i-Sharif and were hurried inside a hangar. There were tables, pads, medics, laptops, an entire element ready to deal with recovered MIAs who might be badly broken.

A colonel waited for them. Elliot saluted and said, "Sir, I can thankfully report that we are all alive and in good health."

The colonel, Findlay, said, "Excellent, Lieutenant. Welcome home." He extended a hand for a firm handshake, then said, "Procedures, of course." He indicated the table.

Sean went first, identifying himself to a female staff sergeant, rattling off personal information. A medic approached and looked him over. Two others asked questions. At the end was a chaplain.

"How are you feeling, Lieutenant?"

He breathed deeply. How did he feel? He was home. There was no way he could express it.

He said, "Very good, sir. I'm delighted to not need your services just yet, though do please check with my people, and I hope you'll be around while we're debriefed."

"Of course. Welcome home."

An hour later they were in a briefing room, sitting around a table, waiting. He felt less relieved, more tense.

"So we tell the truth," Ortiz said.

He said, "I can't think of anything that would work better."

Trinidad said, "Neither can I, but I'm scared."

"Yeah."

They didn't speak much past that. Sean wanted to offer something, but he wasn't sure what.

The door opened, and a staff sergeant said, "Lieutenant Elliott, sir, can you come with me please?"

He rose, put a hand on Ortiz's shoulder as he walked past.

The NCO took him across the hall and into a room with Colonel Findlay and a man in unmarked tan field uniform. He looked Italian, shorter, and fit. Almost like a Roman.

It was a basic field office. Out the window he could see tents and an occasional troop moving about.

"Sir, Lieutenant Elliott reports as ordered," he said with a salute.

Findlay returned it, and offered a hand, though he wasn't smiling.

"Welcome back, Lieutenant."

"Thank you, sir."

"You said you wanted to discuss your . . . activities in private. It's me, and Special Agent DiNote from Air Force OSI. He's the investigator at hand, so it's his job."

DiNote had an ID folder out with badge and card that identified him. There was no reason to question it, so Elliott shook his hand and said, "Good to meet you, sir."

"And you."

DiNote turned on a video recorder, and said, "Do you understand we are now recording?"

"I do, sir."

DiNote mirandized him from a card, then said, "I need to read you the following from the UCMJ. It's a formality, but necessary."

"I understand."

DiNote read it off a screen, but seemed very familiar with it.

Uniform Code of Military Justice (UCMJ)

ART. 31. COMPULSORY SELF-INCRIMINATION PROHIBITED

(a) No person subject to this chapter may compel any person to incriminate himself or to answer any questions the answer to which may tend to incriminate him.

(b) No person subject to this chapter may interrogate, or request any statement from an accused or a person suspected of an offense without first informing him of the nature of the accusation and advising him that he does not have to make any statement regarding the offense of which he is accused or suspected and that any statement made by him may be used as evidence against him in a trial by court-martial.

(c) No person subject to this chapter may compel any person to make a statement or produce evidence before any military tribunal if the statement or evidence is not material to the issue and may tend to degrade him.

(d) No statement obtained from any person in violation of this article, or through the use of coercion, unlawful influence, or unlawful inducement may be received in evidence against him in a trial by court-martial.

"Do you understand all that, Lieutenant?"

"I do. Am I being charged?" he asked.

"Not at this time. It's now standard for returning MIAs whose circumstances are not known."

He wondered why it was "now standard."

"Very well," he said. He turned to Findlay.

"Sir, before we continue, can I ask you to summarize what happened at this end, from the convoy's point of view?"

Findlay looked slightly confused, but said, "Sure, Lieutenant. It came under attack, there were at least two explosions. The convoy commander deployed his troops to counter the attack. No hostiles were found. There was a substantial area of road damaged in the attack, but no one knows how. It appeared to have been caused by a number of emplaced charges, but no residue was found. We assume your vehicles unassed the area and sought cover before you were captured or displaced."

"That helps, thank you, sir."

Findlay said, "So talk to me."

Sean took a deep breath and tried to calm his hammering pulse. They were not going to believe him.

"Well, sir, it's a complicated story, and it's going to be hard to believe. I have one piece of supporting evidence. It's in my ruck."

DiNote asked, "That gray object with the handle?"

"Yes."

"What is it?"

"I need to show you."

Findlay said, "I'd like to hear first." He looked tense. Understandably.

"I really need to show you, sir. Have EOD check it out."

"I did. They can't do anything with it. It's inert."

"Then can we please see it?"

Findlay grabbed his desk phone, called a number and said, "Bring it. Thanks."

Shortly, a sergeant wearing the EOD badge walked in with it. He seemed casual enough.

Sean took possession and waited while the obviously curious man departed.

Findlay said, "Okay, so let's see it."

Sean waved his hand and the device came to life. It flowed into a large wrench, then into a shovel. With a twist and pull, it rolled on itself until it became a grid framework, almost translucent.

DiNote grabbed a DSLR camera, twisted knobs, and snapped photos and video.

He flipped the tool and it shrank into bolt cutters.

Nervously, he passed them to the colonel, handle first.

The colonel took them, looked at them, and didn't flinch too badly when they changed into a shovel again, then flowed amorphously and resumed a ball with a handle.

"Mister DiNote, do you want to try?"

DiNote took it, and it shifted into a bat.

"Huh. I was thinking about baseball."

Sean took it back.

"So that's the supporting evidence."

Findlay stared at the device, and said, "If you say 'aliens,' I'm going to punch you."

"Time travel, sir."

Findlay twisted his head, sighed, gritted his teeth and said, "Okay, son, you're telling me this came from the future."

"Yes, sir."

"How far?"

"They wouldn't tell us. I'm guessing a hundred to a thousand years, sir."

"Then we need to get this to a lab. I'd say it's the most fucked up story I've ever heard, except there were witnesses to you disappearing."

Oh, good. Sean relaxed a fraction. "I'm relieved you believe us, sir."

"I don't know what the hell to believe. But you are who you say you are, and you don't strike me as a traitor."

Findlay stuck his head out the door and called. A moment later, the staff NCO came in.

He said, "Get a photographer here. One of ours, not allied. Then we need to get this damned thing to a lab and start figuring it out."

He'd have to tell the colonel about the lifespan of that device. But he'd wait a little bit. It was good for about twenty more transformations, then its battery would fail and an internal process would cause it to flake apart.

Turning back, Findlay asked, "So how did you wind up in the future?"

"First we wound up in the Paleolithic, about fifteen thousand years back."

Eyes wide and nodding, Findlay prompted, "Uh huh. And how did you determine the year?"

"Devereaux is studying astronomy, and Spencer knows a lot about prehistory. They were able to estimate."

Findlay gave him a suspicious look. "For that matter, how did you know where you were?"

"Not far from here, sir. We didn't move much appreciable distance. The Amu Darya was still there."

DiNote was making notes, in addition to the video.

Findlay asked, "Then how did you get to the future?"

"Sir, we weren't the only people displaced. There were some Neolithic people, ancient Romans, east Indian Mughals, and two people from the future time. Eventually, contact was made and they took us all forward."

"And then back here."

"Eventually. And only within six months. They couldn't pinpoint exactly."

"Are they here?"

At least the colonel asked intelligent questions. That was a good sign, right?

"Not that I know of. They seem afraid of what they've created."

"Yeah, that's now. Give them five years." Findlay paused a moment. "Any other U.S. or Coalition forces?"

"None that we saw, sir."

"Damn. Well, that answers that."

"Sir?"

"I was hoping we might find some other MIAs. So, why don't you tell the whole long story to Mr. DiNote. He'll ask questions as needed. I'll make sure someone brings coffee and I'll listen in."

"Very well. Ready, sir?" he asked DiNote.

"I am, Lieutenant." Through it all, DiNote had been a stoic observer. He seemed prepared to take any story down and analyze it later.

"At oh nine fifty seven, we experienced a loud noise and sharp impact to the vehicle. I assumed we were under attack, and . . ."

Armand had expected debriefing to be long, but this was beyond even that. They'd been billeted in a tent, and Elliott stayed with them. That was partly companionship, partly being a very good officer, and probably partly fear of being separated after all this time.

And partly because there were guards outside the tent.

It was 1600 the second day before they got to him, after Elliott, Spencer, Barker and Trinidad.

There was an AFOSI officer, and an interrogator in civilian clothes and a beard, proving nothing. He could be any branch, civilian or contractor.

His interrogator asked, "So you were able to tell what year it was by the position of the stars?"

"Not the year, no. I could tell it was one of several timeframes, and the weather and animals narrowed it down. That was Sergeant Spencer's work."

"Okay. Keep going."

He talked for hours, about the medical issues of the Urushu, the interactions and fights, the rhino hunt, the Cogi and their gear, and their time. He wasn't sure any of it was believed. It just went on and on.

The next question was, "You mentioned casualties in a firefight. You administered to them?"

"Yes, sir. I logged it here."

"All four men with gutshots died before you could treat them?"

"They were skinny guys and hit pretty hard. I expect psychological impact added to shock and trauma." *No, motherfucker, I will not rat my commander out for mercifully cutting their throats.*

"You provided substantial medical aid to the native population."

"Whatever I could do without using our own resources. They accepted instruction in washing and basic sanitary practices. They understood suturing and bone setting and a few other basic skills."

"What ethnicity were they?"

"It's difficult to say. They looked a bit like South Asians, only with long curly hair, not straight. Dark skin and eyes. Height from six foot to six and a half."

"Why did you build your own camp instead of remaining with them?"

"We used our tools a lot, didn't want to share and didn't want to have to explain, or risk messing up their culture and our past. The capt—lieutenant and Sergeant Spencer insisted, and it made sense. We also wanted to avoid fraternization. That was my recommendation, because we had no idea what disease vectors might exist that each group wouldn't have any natural immunity to."

"How does that work?"

"Diseases adapt to the local population, and immunity adapts back. Just as smallpox wiped out a lot of Native Americans, we didn't want to catch or spread something mundane that could be disastrous."

"Did you learn their language?"

"A pidgin form. Specialist Oglesby knows it well."

They seemed to take him seriously, but kept staring at each other.

Felix Trinidad sat in the tent, bored and worried. He wasn't sure how this would play out, but he thought there was a good chance their careers were over. They'd been gone six months and had an unbelievable story.

It might have been better to remain with the Cogi, but he understood why people with close families wanted to be home. He'd like to see his, after this much time.

The tent door rustled and opened. The major who came in wore Medical branch insignia. Caswell and Alexander were with him.

"Good evening, men." The man was barrel chested but seemed friendly, not intimidating. He seemed relaxed and was smiling.

"Evening, sir."

They all looked at him. Who was this guy?

"I'm Major Carnody. I'm here to check up on your well being."

Elliott said, "It would be better if we weren't guarded and being extensively interrogated. I know they need intel, but it is a bit of a drain."

Carnody nodded. "I imagine so, and I'm sorry that's happening. I'm told you're all in excellent health."

He was a psychiatrist or clinical psychologist. Daniel had him figured out. He was here to see if they were conspiring on a story, delusional, or otherwise.

Elliott asked, "How much background do you have and what can we talk about, sir?"

"I've been told you say you were displaced in time, distant past and far future, and came home from there. The discrepancy in return is due to targeting problems."

Elliott raised his eyebrows and said, "I don't think we should discuss it without written approval from Colonel Findlay, sir."

"I have it here," he said, opening a folder and carefully withdrawing a letter. "If you prefer to talk to him directly, I understand."

Elliott glanced at it. He nodded to Felix and the others.

"Okay, sir. Go ahead."

"So how did you stay fit? Exercise program?"

This was a group debriefing, to go with the individual ones. Felix wasn't looking forward to his, since he knew exactly what they'd ask and how.

Elliott said, "We did. We also had a very active lifestyle. Chopping wood, building a palisade and lodges, hunting and later fencing and wrestling animals. Trying to grow a few edible plants. You'll need to ask Sergeant Caswell, but part of the problem is that there's very little in the way of edible plants back then. Almost everything we eat has been domesticated for thousands of years.

"Anyway, I'm rambling. We had PT as well. We were basically in the field for two years, at our own COB. We even called it COB Bedrock."

"The Flintstones," Carnody said. He took an empty chair and turned it around backward, then sat under the light in the middle front of the tent.

"That's what it felt like. Sergeant Spencer had a forge going to produce iron."

The psychiatrist turned to Spencer.

Spencer said, "Direct reduction furnace for smelting. Forge for working. Though you can sometimes use the heat above the furnace for some quick and dirty forging, if you don't care about impurities."

"What did you use as an anvil? A truck bumper?"

Spencer shook his head. "No, sir, not massive enough. Granite works. It makes some of the detailed shaping harder, but it's doable. It worked for the Vikings."

"And you kept in top shape." The man was offering leading statements to get them to talk. He acted very cool, but it was an act. He was gauging everyone. He met Felix's eyes for a moment, and smoothly looked away.

Elliott said, "Well, the Cogi, the future people, gave us all medical treatment, including replacing our fillings with regrown teeth."

"Really? Can I see?"

Elliott stepped under the light and leaned back. Carnody looked in and raised his eyebrows.

"Do you all have restored teeth?"

"And metabolisms," Alexander said. "I haven't taken Synthroid in months, but my mental acuities are with me. Mostly."

"What other food was there?" Carnody asked.

"Lots of meat and fish. Berries seasonally. Apples, remarkably like modern apples. Lots of roots that were eh."

Jenny Caswell said, "Variations of carrot, Queen Anne's Lace, cumin, fennel, dill. All part of the parsley family. The roots are marginally edible if you get them young, before they go woody. The seeds and greens can be used in salads. Very tasty."

Dalton said, "Matter of opinion. They add a bit to meat, but they aren't really salad. Edible, but I never thought them tasty, just garnish."

Carnody was amazingly cool. "So tell me about the locals."

Oglesby said, "I can talk about language and stuff. How familiar are you with linguistics?"

The major tilted his head. "Moderately."

"Okay, well their language is tonal, with lots of fricatives and dentals. Grammar is indistinct, relying on context and gestures to differentiate subject and object . . ."

The Urushu were a subject of discussion for a half hour. At the end of it, Carnody said, "Fascinating. Well, if you're all feeling good for now, I'm satisfied. I'm sorry you're being sequestered."

Felix said, "I hope they can believe us. We can't tell them what they want to hear, especially as we don't even know what that is."

Carnody said, "I'll be sending contact information to your families, letting them know you're all still alive."

"Oh, thank you, sir!"

Felix started tearing up, even though he didn't have a lot of close family. His mother and aunt would be told, though.

CHAPTER 49

General McClare wondered what the hell he was going to report. Ten troops had disappeared, presumably captured, since it was unrealistic for ten to defect or flee at once. Now they showed up with some fucked-up story about time travel and some weird gadget.

Findlay seemed convinced, as did this OSI investigator. They seemed embarrassed at being convinced.

"What do you think, Carnody?" he asked the man across the desk. The office was very nice for a putative war zone. The desk was real mahogany.

Carnody said, "Sir, I think they believe what they're saying."

"But you don't think it's true."

"I didn't say that."

He looked at Special Agent DiNote. "So what do you think?"

"As the major said, they seem to believe what they're saying. More importantly, the stories are consistent with each other and amongst themselves. It's easy to agree on major details. It's impossible to agree on minor ones. But when asked about small details or local people, they all have roughly the same information. It's as if I asked you about your neighbors' kids. If you tell me the same thing the parents do, I have to assume you've met the kids."

"So they're all remembering the same things?"

"With enough differences it's not a memorized story, yes."

"Does that mean it's real?"

Carnody shrugged. "Now we get into metaphysical questions of

649

what real is. I don't know. They share a commonality of memory of events, but they are individuals with specific interpretations. For example, Devereaux, the medic, young black man from Queens."

"Yes, I saw him."

"He started crying when he told me how glad he was to see black Marines in the unit that recovered them. Because there were no black people in the distant past or future. He said he felt even more alone."

Findlay said, "I can see that. I'd never have thought of it."

Carnody said, "Exactly. No one would, unless they experienced it. Now, they'd experience that in most of A-stan, too. However, he'd know he was going home in A-stan, or was at least in this world. It really felt as if he was speaking as someone who'd gone to a world with no black people. But you put together a couple of hours of comments like that, and these people really believe the experiences they talk about. They're not lying, not faking and really do remember what they say."

"So there was an explosion, they were in the past, like that."

Findlay said, "So they say. We have no evidence of them driving away. They have some space age gadget that's a prototype at best, and a very sophisticated one. They have a story that does fit facts."

It was like something out of a blockbuster movie. "I don't want to believe it."

"They said they didn't, either. Took them days to come to terms with it, even while realizing there was no choice."

"So I ask again, are they telling the truth?" And how the fuck were they going to explain this if it was true?

Carnody said, "They are not lying. There's no indication of desertion, collaboration, anti-American sentiment, anything. They didn't want to be where they were, they're glad to be back, and they're honest. I can tell you that. What actually happened will have to be asked of scientists. But there's medical stuff, too."

"Yes?"

"Spencer. He has a filling with four metal pins in it. Had. He now has a perfect tooth with four pins under the enamel, in the same location. He said they got medical treatment that healed their teeth. It apparently displaced the fillings, but not the pins. Here."

Carnody pulled out two X–rays. That was definitely the same tooth, but with less shadow. The filling was gone, the pins were there. The filling in front of it was also gone. That tooth was whole.

"They all have perfect teeth, but their other teeth match records. Their DNA matches. We don't know of anyone who can regrow enamel yet. So it was done somehow."

"Definitely not plastic or ceramic crowns?"

"Nope, they're real teeth."

McClare put his face in his hands and rubbed his forehead.

"We need some kind of cover for the media. We can't say 'time travel.' We'll get accused of every conspiracy and war crime the internet has, and a few more."

DiNote, the investigator said, "Say little."

"That's my position. Captured, escaped, still have critical information we need, NDA."

"Which is effectively true, if we accept their stories."

"The truth is the best way to lie. Do we believe them?"

DiNote said, "You keep asking that, sir. They believe it. You tell me there were no signs of disappearance, and the impact area didn't match anything we've seen before. Here they are. Their story does match, and they're consistent, and they have that artifact that we've never seen before. If it's some foreign prototype, whose? And why would they have it?"

"Yeah, that's hard to fake."

"Very convincing, yes."

"I showed their pictures to people who deployed with them. They IDed them. Their personal stories in their ISOPREP files match."

McClare said, "If I accept this story, the next thing is we have to start working on threat analyses against time travelers. Terminators? People wanting to fix things preemptively?"

Carnody said, "I'm so glad that's not my field."

"It's ridiculous. But it appears to be true."

Findlay nodded. "It does."

"I've led men in combat, been in some of the worst hellholes in the world . . . this scares the fuck out of me."

Findlay said, "I'd be worried if it didn't, sir. And yes, I'm scared, too. Terrified. It's impossible, except I can't find any holes in what I see."

"We'll talk to them in person tomorrow. Or I will."

Gina woke early. She wasn't sleeping as long as she had, but it seemed to be very productive sleep. That felt so good.

After breakfast, Carnody was in the briefing room with Findlay, DiNote, and a general McClare. He was barrel-chested, shaven-headed, with gray eyebrows and big hands.

McClare said, "Seats at ease. I've heard a bugfuck insane story, but I've been shown enough bits to make me think it might be real. Major Carnody says you appear to believe the stories you tell. So convince me."

Elliott asked, "Do you have our flexitool?"

"This thing?" He held up the blob.

"Yes. It's good for about twenty more changes before it shuts down. They did that on purpose, but here. Shovel," he took it and twisted it and it morphed. "Axe. Prybar." It shifted into some other unobvious tool. "I have no idea what that is."

Gina chuckled, with some others.

Devereaux said, "All our teeth are fixed without fillings. You can compare to dental records. We have regrown enamel."

McClare said, "We did. There's no modern explanation for that."

Gina said, "Sir, can I borrow that projector?"

"Go ahead."

She plugged her laptop in, fussed with it, and then inserted a memory stick.

The images came up on the wall. She flipped through them.

"This is a herd of woolly rhinos, now extinct. This is a wandering herd of mammoths. We think they were displaced. This . . . is a lion. This is the camp we built. This is a native camp. Look at their tent art. Here's some Romans working on a charcoal burn."

She changed files.

"In case you think I somehow photoshopped in the field, here's video."

She rolled one. The strange sounds and movement were mesmerizing.

McClare asked, "What the hell was that?"

"Two Urushu women throat singing. I shot it in IR. Here's another."

This video was the Neolith village, with a pan of people moving around the huts and racks.

"What have you got from the future?" Carnody asked.

"Nothing. They didn't allow it."

"But they let you keep these files?"

"I didn't tell them about these files." She smiled slightly.

McClare said, "This is some truly fucked-up shit, but I'm forced to believe it. I have no fucking idea how you'd fake the video, the teeth, and that . . . thing."

He nodded, and Carnody grabbed a sealed electronics pouch.

McClare looked stern as he said, "Your phones are here. You can have five minutes to check in with your families. Then we need to talk some more. You can tell them you're alive and well. Don't mention any goddamned time travel. Stay in public." He indicated the room they were in.

Gina was closest, at the projector. She snagged hers before the stampede arrived.

She turned it on, menued and clicked. Then she waited, stared at it, waited, as the crappy Afghan cell net responded.

Was he there? It rang once, twice—

"Hello?"

Blake sounded tired, sad, listless, but that voice sent a rush through her.

"Love, it's me. It's Gina. I'm alive."

"God, it's good to hear you," he said, and she could hear the tears and twenty years of warmth. "They said you'd been recovered."

"I'm completely fine. We're debriefing. It's so good to hear you. I wish I could be home right now."

"Debriefing?"

"Yes."

"How long?"

"I don't know. I really don't. Weeks maybe."

"Fuck, I hate the Army." He didn't. He'd done six years. But she knew what he meant.

"It really must take that long. I'm sorry. Lots happened and I can't talk about it yet."

"As long as you're alive and well."

"I really am." She started crying. "I'm very, very well. And so much better hearing you." And the kids in the background. Her kids were still there, and still kids.

He said, "The kids are here, jumping at me."

"Yes, put them on."

"Mom!" His voice was a lot deeper.

"Dylan, is that you?"

"Yes. You're not shot?"

"No, I was not shot, or blown up. We were lost, we're back here now, and we're all fine. We've got to take care of things here, but I'll be home soon. Can you put your sister on?"

"Here, Mom!" Aislinn sounded perfectly fine.

"Hey, Sweetie!"

"I'm glad you're safe."

"So am I. I'm sorry you were so worried."

"We always knew you were alive, Mom. You're too mean to die."

"I love you too, Sweetie. Put Dad back on. I can't talk long."

"Here."

"I need to go. I have no idea when I can call again. I can't talk about much."

"I understand. It can wait until you're here."

"And then it can wait while we get reacquainted."

"I love you."

"I love you. I have to go."

There was an entire room full of teary-eyed people around her.

Even if they were believed, they were still sequestered. They each spoke to an entire squad of intel, generating whole books of data.

Rich Dalton felt a range of emotions. It was aggravating as fuck to be held like a prisoner, meals brought in boxes, no e-mails or other contact home. It was amusing to watch the head-scratching as the Army tried to figure out which box this problem fit into. It was unpleasant to discuss details of years of separation, anger, loneliness. It was boring in between to sit in the tent.

They did PT every morning, talked all day, ate, watched TV at night. TV didn't interest him anymore, and it wasn't just AFN. They had new movies, which were good. Though X-Men was far less attention-grabbing now.

The chaplain stopped by daily, and held service for them on Sunday. Even Spencer sat in the back and participated. Was it possible he'd ever accept Christ? He was a good man, a good friend, and Rich's discussions with him had been very educational.

Monday morning it was back to debriefing, in a room that looked like a box, somewhere in a building. He was taken in by a circuitous route and the van had no windows in back.

"So you hunted fairly regularly?" His interrogator appeared to be a civilian, but might be military in civilian clothes. He was identified as Mr. Ahrends. He was about forty, with shaggy hair. He wondered how many people had been confided in this secret, how reliable they were, and when the story was going to leak.

He'd been through this with two others. It was getting annoying.

"Yes. Every day to once a week, depending on the game. Goats were easy, and well within the capabilities of an M Four. Larger animals were tastier but harder to shoot. The bows we made did the job fine. We got sick of goat pretty quickly."

"But do you have numbers? How many of each?"

"Heck, I don't know. Hundreds of goats, if you include the ones we started penning and raising. Dozens of aurochs, that's the wild predecessor to the cow. Some antelope and deer and elklike things. A few pigs. Why?"

Ahrends said, "We'll have to have a tally for the EPA and the Department of the Interior."

That was bizarre. "Wait, you're telling me that the Department of the Interior, in the U.S. twenty-first century, wants to know how many goats I shot in a chunk of desolate wasteland that predates Afghanistan by several thousand years, for . . . what, exactly?"

Ahrends said, "It was a military operation and event. They have to have the information for summary."

"But isn't this already classified way beyond anything, ever?"

"Yes, but we're not going to tell them when."

Exasperated, he said, "But aurochs are extinct, so you can't even give them those numbers. Pardon me, sir, but this is the most retarded fucking thing ever I've heard."

The man just stared at him. Rich couldn't tell if he agreed about the stupidity, but had a job to do, or felt personally affronted.

The silence continued, so Rich said, "I don't know, sir. Assuming two years and two months at three goats a week, you get three hundred and thirty goats. The rest I'll have to think about."

Ahrends said, "Do so, and get me the best numbers you can. Oh, I wouldn't mention aurochs being extinct. EPA might have a shit fit. Just say feral cows."

At least the man realized how completely stupid this was. It was just a job.

"Were there any fuel spills? Please tell me no."

"We didn't use any fuel except in transit. None was available to spill."

"What about toxins or medications encountered?"

How many local plants counted as drugs? What had Doc used on them for wounds and pain and such? What berries were in Spencer's wine? What had they smoked?

"I have no idea, sir. Nothing I took or was exposed to voluntarily. I'd ask Sergeant Devereaux about medications."

"Thank you. Next question . . ."

That afternoon, he met with another scientist. He'd never paid much attention to the huge variety there were. He'd talked to archeologists, paleontologists, anthropologists, botanists, petrologists, linguists, though most of those went straight to Oglesby, epidemiologists, others he couldn't remember.

This one introduced himself as "Van Caster. I'm an engineering anthropologist."

"You study old buildings?"

"And construction methods, yes."

"Okay. Do you want to know about our buildings or theirs? And which theirs?"

"All."

"You really want to talk to the lieutenant, Sergeant Spencer, and Sergeant Alexander, since she took photos."

Caster said, "I have and will again. I just want a summary of what you thought and saw, anything that jumped out."

"They seem awfully small, dark and low at first. Then you realize in winter that's a good thing. They have larger ones for winter and for visitors. That's the Urushu, the Paleolithic people we lived near."

"I have the photos. I can't really tell much from this about the inside." He pulled up an image on his laptop. It was a shot into the dark inside, in surprisingly good detail. Alexander was one hell of a photographer.

"Oh. Raised beds on cut limbs with moss and grass as padding under animal hides. They were reasonably comfortable for camping."

"What's at the end here?"

"That was a latrine. A dug hole lined with a hide they tied up and took out every morning."

"That's interesting." The man made notes.

"They used hide for everything. Mattresses, blankets, clothes, doorways."

Caster said, "And covering the structures." He had another image up.

"Oh, yes, this was the winter lodge. They had a lining, too."

"Great. Insulation, then."

"Yes."

"How did they shape the support poles?"

"I think they were soaked and heated."

"They were set in a rock base."

"Yes, just river stones piled up. Same for the walls. They weren't actually built, just stacked."

At least it was less annoying than questions about killing food, or relations with native women.

Jenny Caswell was managing to stay calm. She felt safer back here, but it was less satisfying. She was a troop on base, one of many, not someone who could feed and educate a unit in the wilderness.

They met in the briefing room several times a week for updates on the process. That evening, she walked in with the escort she always had, took a seat, and waited.

General McClare came in with the three other officers. He'd given a standing order to not come to attention.

"Evening," he offered.

"Good evening, sir," she said, along with everyone else.

McClare said, "We're in the conclusive phase of this now."

"Meaning? Sir?"

"It means I believe you're telling the truth, the scientists believe you're telling the truth, and someone far up at the Pentagon believes it, too." He held up one of the blankets the Urushu had gifted them with. "The scientists tell me that hide is some sort of Asian camel. Extinct since just after the Ice Age. I don't fucking believe it, but I'm forced to believe it." He rolled it up and put it on the table.

"Since there's no additional data available at the present, we're going to return you to duty."

She felt a rush ripple through her spine.

"Home?" she accidentally said aloud.

"For most of you, yes, home. Most of your units have rotated CONUS."

Colonel Findlay said, "I'll be working on the arrangements. Part of the delay was in developing a cover story as to your whereabouts. I've printed a summary here," he said, holding up a binder, then handing the stack to Elliott to distribute. "It says you were hijacked and taken into the remote mountains. The natives seized your equipment and held you prisoner, but you were not mistreated. They spent several months trying to manipulate both Kabul and the Taliban into ransoming you. We knew you were alive and kept silent for your safety. We negotiated your return by securing their province. We did secure it."

Bob Barker asked, "But how did we disappear so close to the FOB?"

"Mid range IED, to damage the road but not the vehicles, and a dozen hijackers in waiting. I even have some 'captured' video to prove that, shot by some role players. They were 'reenacting' your capture based on 'your' reports. Then we had another group replay them. If anyone comments, we'll say the press got the wrong video. If they even play it. Things have changed in those months. We're pulling out steadily, and no one cares about the war after the election."

He continued, "We'll coach each of you through an affidavit mostly consistent with the video, and your recovery is deemed not for public release. If anyone asks, you don't talk about it."

Spencer said, "So we don't get to sell a book."

Findlay shook his head. "Afraid not, Sergeant. You get a POW medal, a CAB, and an MSM. You don't want to talk about your experiences, but you're glad to be home. I went to a lot of effort demanding that you all be allowed a medical retirement if you wish, or return to duty. I'd recommend not granting any interviews, and if asked, just say there isn't much to tell, you were kept in a remote village in primitive living conditions, and were recovered by a Marine contingent once we found you."

Ramon said, "That's true, as far as it goes."

"Exactly. And on the positive side, you may get called later to consult, at a healthy rate of pay. The scientists want to know more."

Trinidad said, "But I can't lie."

"Neither can I," she said. Yes, there were clever evasions, but that was still lying.

Findlay said, "You don't have to lie. Just don't talk about it." He put a foot up on a desk and leaned forward. "Let me give this to you straight: No one would believe this. Hell, we're not sure we believe it. There's not enough hard evidence for most people, and it would be a circus in the press. You'd be hounded by every conspiracy nut, new ager, sci fi geek, tabloid reporter and freak on the planet, as well as all the legitimate scientists all bent on disproving you, in addition to the ones we're bringing in who do know it's real and will treat you with respect. You really want to limit it to discussions with them. Because if you go public, we'll deny it."

"And humiliate me in public?" she asked.

"No, ignore you totally and let the public do the humiliating."

She was silent.

"It may come out, gradually, as it's studied. In the meantime, you get a decent deal. I'd take it."

Next to her, Alexander said, "We're home. I want to see my family. Please don't fight this."

She wrote what they told her to write, in her own words. It didn't say much, and was vague enough to fit the real events, or the fictionalized account.

EPILOGUE—HOMECOMING

Sean Elliott looked at his gear. It was most of the same stuff he arrived with, though his knives were worn down from heavy use. He had an authorization letter to get them through the Naval Customs Unit.

They were all flying to Kuwait, to Leipzig, to Baltimore, and from there to their home stations.

"So, everyone has contact info, right?" he asked.

"We all do," Gina said. "I'll be in touch. E-mail, probably. I don't trust FB."

Trinidad said, "Yeah, we can't put anything down as text."

"We can have a reunion," Barker said.

"Hell, we're not even home yet."

"Oh, I want a reunion!" Caswell said. "In a year. We should be settled by then."

Elliott said, "I've got names here for the therapists they mentioned."

They each had a specialist they could talk to, read into the secret. He wondered how long this secret would remain secret. Ten of them, four officers, medical and dental officers, a chaplain, several intel people and now therapists. Add all that together and it was amazing it wasn't tabloid web already.

Spencer said, "They can help us with the media whores, conspiracy nuts, and general retards we'll have to deal with."

"Here we are," Dalton said.

He looked ahead. That was a crowd of about three hundred, all

661

rotating stateside. As they entered, he tensed up. It was too many people too close.

They sat together. As with most rotations, troops clustered in cliques and tended not to talk much. Some gregarious specialist tried to engage him. He just nodded, grunted and pretended to doze off.

The whole tedious briefing and process took hours. Check weapons. Check classified material. Be informed that no war trophies were allowed, no porn, no body parts, no personal weapons without command authorization. No cuffs or batons unless MP. No Cuban cigars. No more than two copies of bootleg media.

The briefing NCO said, "Personal pleasure devices . . . these are not prohibited." There were cheers, jeers and catcalls. "Just be sure to tell your inspector so they can be discreet."

It was so ridiculous, then Spencer burst out with, "What, so I can have a blowup doll but no handcuffs? What's the point?"

Three hundred troops howled with laughter, and next to him, Jenny Caswell fell out of her chair, choking. Holy shit, that was funny.]

Tedious hours later, after a stretch in Germany, they landed in Baltimore and staggered down the jetway. Ahead was luggage, thirty days leave, and then?

They all shook hands and hugged. Spencer, Barker, Alexander, Trinidad, Ortiz, Devereaux, Caswell, Dalton, Oglesby. They were a family.

It was the first time he'd touched either of the women.

"We have to stay in touch, for our own sanity," he said. "That's an order."

"Hooah." "Yes, sir." "Aye aye."

They stood nervously, looking at phones for time, but unlike everyone else, not texting. They all took a long look at each other, then mumbled and teared up and started drifting away. It was time to break from a bond no one else on the planet could ever have, even other combat vets. He waited for the others to disperse, though none of them were going too far yet, just to get boarding passes. He and Spencer were on the same leg.

"What do you think, Martin?" he asked.

"I think I may retire, sir. I dunno. I'm taking the sixty days leave and will consider. We all did more than anyone could anticipate. I feel heroic enough to call it quits while most of me still works."

"Yeah. How are your guts?"

"Good enough. I wonder if they'll go out of whack again, but they're fine for now."

"Glad to hear it." The man had seemed old the last year in the past. Now he seemed a lot more lively.

As he grabbed his bags and headed for ticketing, he heard Caswell shout, "Sergeant Spencer!"

"Yes?"

She ran up and hugged the NCO in a tackle.

"Thank you for being a gentleman," she said. "I . . . misjudged you."

He smiled. "Not entirely. No hard feelings."

Sean wasn't entirely sure what went down there.

He realized the three of them were on camera, and pointed. There were a half dozen reporters waiting for them.

She gave a half snarl, half smile at Spencer, then at him, and said, "I got your back, gentlemen."

⁘ END ⁘